KU-326-399

Agatha Christie

POIROT
FOUR CLASSIC CASES
·
THREE-ACT TRAGEDY
·
SAD CYPRESS
·
EVIL UNDER THE SUN
·
THE HOLLOW
·

HarperCollins*Publishers*

MILTON KEYNES
COLLEGE LIBRARY

D

PO19130 £12.99 11/06

823 CHR

B020004

HarperCollins*Publishers*
77–85 Fulham Palace Road,
Hammersmith, London W6 8JB
www.harpercollins.co.uk

This edition first published 2004

2

This collection copyright © 2004 Agatha Christie Limited,
a Chorion company. All rights reserved.
www.agathachristie.com

Three-Act Tragedy © Agatha Christie Limited 1934
Sad Cypress © Agatha Christie Limited 1940
Evil Under the Sun © Agatha Christie Limited 1941
The Hollow © Agatha Christie Limited 1946

ISBN 0 00 719065 4

Typeset in Plantin Light and Gill Sans by
Palimpsest Book Production Limited,
Polmont, Stirlingshire

Printed and bound in Great Britain by
Clays Ltd, St Ives plc

All rights reserved. No part of this publication may be
reproduced, stored in a retrieval system, or transmitted,
in any form or by any means, electronic, mechanical,
photocopying, recording or otherwise, without the prior
permission of the publishers.

This book is sold subject to the condition that it shall not,
by way of trade or otherwise, be lent, re-sold, hired out or
otherwise circulated without the publisher's prior consent
in any form of binding or cover other than that in which it
is published and without a similar condition including this
condition being imposed on the subsequent purchaser.

CONTENTS

THREE-ACT TRAGEDY

Dedicated to
My Friends, Geoffrey and Violet Shipston

CONTENTS

Directed by
Sir Charles Cartwright

Assistant Directors
Mr Satterthwaite
Miss Hermione Lytton Gore

Clothes by
Ambrosine Ltd

Illumination by
Hercule Poirot

FIRST ACT • SUSPICION

CROW'S NEST

Mr Satterthwaite sat on the terrace of 'Crow's Nest' and watched his host, Sir Charles Cartwright, climbing up the path from the sea.

Crow's Nest was a modern bungalow of the better type. It had no half timbering, no gables, no excrescences dear to a third-class builder's heart. It was a plain white solid building – deceptive as to size, since it was a good deal bigger than it looked. It owed its name to its position, high up, overlooking the harbour of Loomouth. Indeed from one corner of the terrace, protected by a strong balustrade, there was a sheer drop to the sea below. By road Crow's Nest was a mile from the town. The road ran inland and then zigzagged high up above the sea. On foot it was accessible in seven minutes by the steep fisherman's path that Sir Charles Cartwright was ascending at this minute.

Sir Charles was a well-built, sunburnt man of middle age. He wore old grey flannel trousers and a white sweater. He had a slight rolling gait, and carried his hands half closed as he walked. Nine people out of ten would say, 'Retired Naval man – can't mistake the type.' The tenth, and more discerning, would have hesitated, puzzled by something indefinable that did not ring true. And then perhaps a picture would rise, unsought: the deck of a ship – but not a real ship – a ship curtailed by hanging curtains of thick rich material – a man, Charles Cartwright, standing on that deck, light that was not sunlight streaming down on him, the hands half clenched, the easy gait and a voice – the easy pleasant voice of an English sailor and gentleman, a great deal magnified in tone.

'No, sir,' Charles Cartwright was saying, 'I'm afraid I can't give you any answer to that question.'

And swish fell the heavy curtains, up sprang the lights, an orchestra plunged into the latest syncopated measure, girls with exaggerated bows in their hair said, 'Chocolates? Lemonade?' The first act of *The Call of the Sea*, with Charles Cartwright as Commander Vanstone, was over.

From his post of vantage, looking down, Mr Satterthwaite smiled.

A dried-up little pipkin of a man, Mr Satterthwaite, a patron of art and the drama, a determined but pleasant snob, always included in the more important house-parties and social functions (the words 'and Mr Satterthwaite' appeared invariably at the tail of a list of guests). Withal a man of considerable intelligence and a very shrewd observer of people and things.

He murmured now, shaking his head, 'I wouldn't have thought it. No, really, I wouldn't have thought it.'

A step sounded on the terrace and he turned his head. The big grey-haired man who drew a chair forward and sat down had his profession clearly stamped on his keen, kindly, middle-aged face. 'Doctor' and 'Harley Street'. Sir Bartholomew Strange had succeeded in his profession. He was a well-known specialist in nervous disorders, and had recently received a knighthood in the Birthday Honours list.

He drew his chair forward beside that of Mr Satterthwaite and said:

'What wouldn't you have thought? Eh? Let's have it.'

With a smile Mr Satterthwaite drew attention to the figure below rapidly ascending the path.

'I shouldn't have thought Sir Charles would have remained contented so long in – er – exile.'

'By Jove, no more should I!' The other laughed, throwing back his head. 'I've known Charles since he was a boy. We were at Oxford together. He's always been the same – a better actor in private life than on the stage! Charles is always acting. He can't help it – it's second nature to him. Charles doesn't go out of a room – he "makes an exit" – and he usually has to have a good line to make it on. All the same, he likes a change of part – none better. Two years ago he retired from the stage – said he wanted to live a simple country life, out of the world, and indulge his old fancy for the sea. He comes down here and builds this place. His idea of a simple country cottage. Three bathrooms and all the latest gadgets! I was like you, Satterthwaite, I didn't think it would last. After all, Charles is human – he needs his audience. Two or three retired captains, a bunch of old women and a parson – that's not much of a house to play to. I thought the "simple fellow, with his love of the sea," would run for six months. Then, frankly, I thought he'd tire of the part. I thought the next thing to fill the bill would be the weary man of the world at Monte Carlo, or possibly a laird in the Highlands – he's versatile, Charles is.'

The doctor stopped. It had been a long speech. His eyes were full of affection and amusement as he watched the unconscious man below. In a couple of minutes he would be with them.

'However,' Sir Bartholomew went on, 'it seems we were wrong. The attraction of the simple life holds.'

'A man who dramatises himself is sometimes misjudged,' pointed out Mr Satterthwaite. 'One does not take his sincerities seriously.'

The doctor nodded.

'Yes,' he said thoughtfully. 'That's true.'

With a cheerful halloo Charles Cartwright ran up the steps on to the terrace.

'*Mirabelle* surpassed herself,' he said. 'You ought to have come, Satterthwaite.'

Mr Satterthwaite shook his head. He had suffered too often crossing the Channel to have any illusions about the strength of his stomach afloat. He had observed the *Mirabelle* from his bedroom window that morning. There had been a stiff sailing breeze and Mr Satterthwaite had thanked heaven devoutly for dry land.

Sir Charles went to the drawing-room window and called for drinks.

'You ought to have come, Tollie,' he said to his friend. 'Don't you spend half your life sitting in Harley Street telling your pateints how good life on the ocean wave would be for them?'

'The great merit of being a doctor,' said Sir Bartholomew, 'is that you are not obliged to follow your own advice.'

Sir Charles laughed. He was still unconsciously playing his part – the bluff breezy Naval man. He was an extraordinarily good-looking man, beautifully-proportioned, with a lean humorous face, and the touch of grey at his temples gave him a kind of added distinction. He looked what he was – a gentleman first and an actor second.

'Did you go alone?' asked the doctor.

'No,' Sir Charles turned to take his drink from a smart parlourmaid who was holding a tray. 'I had a "hand". The girl Egg, to be exact.'

There was something, some faint trace of self-consciousness in his voice which made Mr Satterthwaite look up sharply.

'Miss Lytton Gore? She knows something about sailing, doesn't she?'

Sir Charles laughed rather ruefully.

'She succeeds in making me feel a complete landlubber; but I'm coming on – thanks to her.'

Thoughts slipped quickly in and out of Mr Satterthwaite's mind.

'I wonder – Egg Lytton Gore – perhaps that's why he hasn't tired – the age – a dangerous age – it's always a young girl at that time of life . . .'

Sir Charles went on: 'The sea – there's nothing like it – sun and wind and sea – and a simple shanty to come home to.'

And he looked with pleasure at the white building behind him, equipped with three bathrooms, hot and cold water in all the bedrooms, the latest system of central heating, the newest electrical fittings and a staff of parlourmaid, housemaid, chef, and kitchenmaid. Sir Charles's interpretation of simple living was, perhaps, a trifle exaggerated.

A tall and exceedingly ugly woman issued from the house and bore down upon them.

'Good morning, Miss Milray.'

'Good morning, Sir Charles. Good morning' (a slight inclination of the head towards the other two). 'This is the menu for dinner. I don't know whether you would like it altered in any way?'

Sir Charles took it and murmured:

'Let's see. Melon Cantaloupe, Bortsch Soup, Fresh Mackerel, Grouse, Soufflé Surprise, Canapé Diane . . . No, I think that will do excellently, Miss Milray. Everyone is coming by the four-thirty train.'

'I have already given Holgate his orders. By the way, Sir

Charles, if you will excuse me, it would be better if I dined with you tonight.'

Sir Charles looked startled, but said courteously:

'Delighted, I am sure, Miss Milray – but – er –'

Miss Milray proceeded calmly to explain.

'Otherwise, Sir Charles, it would make thirteen at table; and so many people are superstitious.'

From her tone it could be gathered that Miss Milray would have sat down thirteen to dinner every night of her life without the slightest qualm. She went on:

'I think everything is arranged. I have told Holgate the car is to fetch Lady Mary and the Babbingtons. Is that right?'

'Absolutely. Just what I was going to ask you to do.'

With a slightly superior smile on her rugged countenance, Miss Milray withdrew.

'That,' said Sir Charles reverently, 'is a very remarkable woman. I'm always afraid she'll come and brush my teeth for me.'

'Efficiency personified,' said Strange.

'She's been with me for six years,' said Sir Charles. 'First as my secretary in London, and here, I suppose, she's a kind of glorified housekeeper. Runs this place like clockwork. And now, if you please, she's going to leave.'

'Why?'

'She says' – Sir Charles rubbed his nose dubiously – 'she *says* she's got an invalid mother. Personally I don't believe it. That kind of woman never had a mother at all. Spontaneously generated from a dynamo. No, there's something else.'

'Quite probably,' said Sir Bartholomew, 'people have been talking.'

'Talking?' The actor stared. 'Talking – what about?'

'My dear Charles. You know what talking means.'

'You mean talking about her – and me? With that face? And at her age?'

'She's probably under fifty.'

'I suppose she is,' Sir Charles considered the matter. 'But seriously, Tollie, have you *noticed* her face? It's got two eyes, a nose and a mouth, but it's not what you would call a *face* – not a *female* face. The most scandal-loving old cat in the neighbourhood couldn't seriously connect sexual passion with a face like that.'

'You underrate the imagination of the British spinster.'

Sir Charles shook his head.

'I don't believe it. There's a kind of hideous respectability about Miss Milray that even a British spinster must recognize. She is virtue and respectability personified – and a damned useful woman. I always choose my secretaries plain as sin.'

'Wise man.'

Sir Charles remained deep in thought for some minutes. To distract him, Sir Bartholomew asked: 'Who's coming this afternoon?'

'Angie, for one.'

'Angela Sutcliffe? That's good.'

Mr Satterthwaite leaned forward interestedly, keen to know the composition of the house-party. Angela Sutcliffe was a well-known actress, no longer young, but with a strong hold on the public and celebrated for her wit and charm. She was sometimes spoken of as Ellen Terry's successor.

'Then there are the Dacres.'

Again Mr Satterthwaite nodded to himself. Mrs Dacres was Ambrosine, Ltd, that successful dressmaking establishment. You saw it on programmes – 'Miss Blank's dresses in the first act by Ambrosine Ltd, Brook Street.' Her husband, Captain Dacres, was a dark horse in his own racing parlance. He spent a lot of time on race courses – had ridden himself in the Grand National in years gone by. There had been some trouble – nobody knew exactly – though rumours had been spread about. There had been no inquiry – nothing overt, but somehow at mention of Freddie Dacres people's eyebrows went up a little.

'Then there's Anthony Astor, the playwright.'

'Of course,' said Mr Satterthwaite. 'She wrote *One-Way Traffic*. I saw it twice. It made a great hit.'

He rather enjoyed showing that he knew that Anthony Astor was a woman.

'That's right,' said Sir Charles. 'I forget what her real name is – Wills, I think. I've only met her once. I asked her to please Angela. That's the lot – of the house-party, I mean.'

'And the locals?' asked the doctor.

'Oh, the locals! Well, there are the Babbingtons – he's the parson, quite a good fellow, not too parsonical, and his wife's a really nice woman. Lectures me on gardening. They're coming – and Lady Mary and Egg. That's all. Oh, yes, there's a young fellow called Manders, he's a journalist, or something. Good-looking young fellow. That completes the party.'

Mr Satterthwaite was a man of methodical nature. He counted heads.

'Miss Sutcliffe, one, the Dacres, three, Anthony Astor, four, Lady Mary and her daughter, six, the parson and his wife, eight, the young fellow nine, ourselves twelve. Either you or Miss Milray must have counted wrong, Sir Charles.'

'It couldn't be Miss Milray,' said Sir Charles with assurance. 'That woman's never wrong. Let me see: Yes, by Jove, you're right. I *have* missed out one guest. He'd slipped my memory.'

He chuckled. 'Wouldn't be best pleased at that, either. The fellow is the most conceited little devil I ever met.'

Mr Satterthwaite's eyes twinkled. He had always been of the opinion that the vainest men in creation were actors. He did not exempt Sir Charles Cartwright. This instance of the pot calling the kettle black amused him.

'Who is the egoist?' he asked.

'Rum little beggar,' said Sir Charles. 'Rather a celebrated little beggar, though. You may have heard of him. Hercule Poirot. He's a Belgian.'

'The detective,' said Mr Satterthwaite. 'I have met him. Rather a remarkable personage.'

'He's a character,' said Sir Charles.

'I've never met him,' said Sir Bartholomew, 'but I've heard a good deal about him. He retired some time ago, though, didn't he? Probably most of what I've heard is legend. Well, Charles, I hope we shan't have a crime this weekend.'

'Why? Because we've got a detective in the house? Rather putting the cart before the horse, aren't you, Tollie?'

'Well, it's by way of being a theory of mine.'

'What is your theory, doctor?' asked Mr Satterthwaite.

'That events come to people – not people to events. Why do some people have exciting lives and other people dull ones? Because of their surroundings? Not at all. One man may travel to the ends of the earth and nothing will happen to him. There will be a massacre a week before he arrives, and an earthquake the day after he leaves, and the boat that he nearly took will be shipwrecked. And another man may live at Balham and travel to the City every day, and things will happen to him. He will be mixed up with blackmailing gangs and beautiful girls and motor bandits. There are people with a tendency to shipwrecks – even if they go on a boat on an ornamental lake something will happen to it. In the same way men like your Hercule Poirot don't have to look for crime – it comes to them.'

'In that case,' said Mr Satterthwaite, 'perhaps it is as well that Miss Milray is joining us, and that we are not sitting down thirteen to dinner.'

'Well,' said Sir Charles handsomely, 'you can have your murder, Tollie, if you're so keen on it. I make only one stipulation – that I shan't be the corpse.'

And, laughing, the three men went into the house.

CHAPTER 2

INCIDENT BEFORE DINNER

The principal interest of Mr Satterthwaite's life was people.

He was on the whole more interested in women than men. For a manly man, Mr Satterthwaite knew far too much about women. There was a womanish strain in his character which lent him insight into the feminine mind. Women all his life had confided in him, but they had never taken him seriously. Sometimes he felt a little bitter about this. He was, he felt, always in the stalls watching the play, never on the stage taking part in the drama. But in truth the rôle of onlooker suited him very well.

This evening, sitting in the large room giving on to the terrace, cleverly decorated by a modern firm to resemble a ship's cabin *de luxe*, he was principally interested in the exact shade of hair dye attained by Cynthia Dacres. It was an entirely new tone – straight from Paris, he suspected – a curious and rather pleasing effect of greenish bronze. What Mrs Dacres really looked like it was impossible to tell. She was a tall woman with a figure perfectly disciplined to the demands of the moment. Her neck and arms were her usual shade of summer tan for the country – whether naturally or artificially produced it was impossible to tell. The greenish bronze hair was set in a clever and novel style that only London's best hairdresser could achieve. Her plucked eyebrows, darkened lashes, exquisitively made-up face, and mouth lip-sticked to a curve that its naturally straight line did not possess, seemed all adjuncts to the perfection of her evening gown of a deep and unusual blue, cut very simply it seemed (though this was ludicrously far from the case) and of an unusual material – dull, but with hidden lights in it.

'That's a clever woman,' said Mr Satterthwaite, eyeing her with approval. 'I wonder what she's really like.'

But this time he meant in mind, not in body.

Her words came drawlingly, in the mode of the moment.

'My dear, it wasn't possible. I mean, things either are possible or they're not. This wasn't. It was simply penetrating.'

That was the new word just now – everything was 'penetrating'.

Sir Charles was vigorously shaking cocktails and talking to Angela Sutcliffe, a tall, grey-haired woman with a mischievous mouth and fine eyes.

Dacres was talking to Bartholomew Strange.

'Everyone knows what's wrong with old Ladisbourne. The whole stable knows.'

He spoke in a high clipped voice – a little red, foxy man with a short moustache and slightly shifty eyes.

Beside Mr Satterthwaite sat Miss Wills, whose play, *One-Way Traffic*, had been acclaimed as one of the most witty and daring seen in London for some years. Miss Wills was tall and thin, with a receding chin and very badly waved fair hair. She wore pince-nez, and was dressed in exceedingly limp green chiffon. Her voice was high and undistinguished.

'I went to the South of France,' she said. 'But, really, I didn't enjoy it very much. Not friendly at all. But of course it's useful to me in my work – to see all the goings-on, you know.'

Mr Satterthwaite thought: 'Poor soul. Cut off by success from her spiritual home – a boarding-house in Bournemouth. That's where she'd like to be.' He marvelled at the difference between written works and their authors. That cultivated 'man-of-the-world' tone that Anthony Astor imparted to his plays – what faintest spark of it could be perceived in Miss Wills? Then he noticed that the pale-blue eyes behind the pince-nez were singularly intelligent. They were turned on him now with an appraising look that slightly disconcerted him. It was as though Miss Wills were painstakingly learning him by heart.

Sir Charles was just pouring out the cocktails.

'Let me get you a cocktail,' said Mr Satterthwaite, springing up.

Miss Wills giggled.

'I don't mind if I do,' she said.

The door opened and Temple announced Lady Mary Lytton Gore and Mr and Mrs Babbington and Miss Lytton Gore.

Mr Satterthwaite supplied Miss Wills with her cocktail and then sidled into the neighbourhood of Lady Mary Lytton Gore. As has been stated before, he had a weakness for titles.

Also, apart from snobbishness, he liked a gentlewoman, and that Lady Mary most undeniably was.

Left as a widow very badly off with a child of three, she had come to Loomouth and taken a small cottage where she had lived with one devoted maid ever since. She was a tall thin woman, looking older than her fifty-five years. Her expression was sweet and rather timid. She adored her daughter, but was a little alarmed by her.

Hermione Lytton Gore, usually known for some obscure reason as Egg, bore little resemblance to her mother. She was of a more energetic type. She was not, Mr Satterthwaite decided, beautiful, but she was undeniably attractive. And the cause of that attraction, he thought, lay in her abounding vitality. She seemed twice as alive as anyone in that room. She had dark hair, and grey eyes and was of medium height. It was something in the way the hair curled crisply in her neck, in the straight glance of the grey eyes, in the curve of the cheek, in the infectious laugh that gave one that impression of riotous youth and vitality.

She stood talking to Oliver Manders, who had just arrived.

'I can't think why sailing bores you so much. You used to like it.'

'Egg – my dear. One grows up.'

He drawled the words, raising his eyebrows.

A handsome young fellow, twenty-five at a guess. Something, perhaps, a little sleek about his good looks. Something else – something – was it foreign? Something unEnglish about him.

Somebody else was watching Oliver Manders. A little man with an egg-shaped head and very foreign-looking moustaches. Mr Satterthwaite had recalled himself to M. Hercule Poirot's memory. The little man had been very affable. Mr Satterthwaite suspected him of deliberately exaggerating his foreign mannerisms. His small twinkly eyes seemed to say, 'You expect me to be the buffoon? To play the comedy for you? *Bien* – it shall be as you wish!'

But there was no twinkle now in Hercule Poirot's eyes. He looked grave and a little sad.

The Rev. Stephen Babbington, rector of Loomouth, came and joined Lady Mary and Mr Satterthwaite. He was a man of sixty odd, with kind faded eyes and a disarming diffident manner. He said to Mr Satterthwaite:

'We are very lucky to have Sir Charles living among us. He has been most kind – most generous. A very pleasant neighbour to have. Lady Mary agrees, I am sure.'

Lady Mary smiled.

'I like him very much. His success hasn't spoilt him. In many ways he is,' her smile deepened, 'a child still.'

The parlourmaid approached with the tray of cocktails as Mr Satterthwaite reflected how unendingly maternal women were. Being of the Victorian generation, he approved that trait.

'You can have a cocktail, Mums,' said Egg, flashing up to them, glass in hand. 'Just one.'

'Thank you, dear,' said Lady Mary meekly.

'I think,' said Mr Babbington, 'that my wife would allow me to have one.'

And he laughed a little gentle clerical laugh.

Mr Satterthwaite glanced over at Mrs Babbington, who was talking earnestly to Sir Charles on the subject of manure.

'She's got fine eyes,' he thought.

Mrs Babbington was a big untidy woman. She looked full of energy and likely to be free from petty mindedness. As Charles Cartwright had said – a nice woman.

'Tell me,' Lady Mary leaned forward. 'Who is the young

woman you were talking to when we came in – the one in green?'

'That's the playwright – Anthony Astor.'

'What? That – that anaemic-looking young woman? Oh!' She caught herself up. 'How dreadful of me. But it was a surprise. She doesn't look – I mean she looks exactly like an inefficient nursery governess.'

It was such an apt description of Miss Wills' appearance that Mr Satterthwaite laughed. Mr Babbington was peering across the room with amiable short-sighted eyes. He took a sip of his cocktail and choked a little. He was unused to cocktails, thought Mr Satterthwaite amusedly – probably they represented modernity to his mind – but he didn't like them. Mr Babbington took another determined mouthful with a slightly wry face and said:

'Is it the lady over there? Oh dear –'

His hand went to his throat.

Egg Lytton Gore's voice rang out:

'Oliver – you slippery Shylock –'

'Of course,' thought Mr Satterthwaite, 'that's it – not foreign – Jew!'

What a handsome pair they made. Both so young and good-looking . . . and quarrelling, too – always a healthy sign . . .

He was distracted by a sound at his side. Mr Babbington had risen to his feet and was swaying to and fro. His face was convulsed.

It was Egg's clear voice that drew the attention of the room, though Lady Mary had risen and stretched out an anxious hand.

'Look,' said Egg's voice. 'Mr Babbington is ill.'

Sir Bartholomew Strange came forward hurriedly, supporting the stricken man and half lifting him to a couch at one side of the room. The others crowded round, anxious to help, but impotent . . .

Two minutes later Strange straightened himself and shook his head. He spoke bluntly, aware that it was no use to beat about the bush.

'I'm sorry,' he said. 'He's dead . . .'

CHAPTER 3

SIR CHARLES WONDERS

'Come in here a minute, Satterthwaite, will you?'

Sir Charles poked his head out of the door.

An hour and a half had passed. To confusion had succeeded peace. Lady Mary had led the weeping Mrs Babbington out of the room and had finally gone home with her to the vicarage. Miss Milray had been efficient with the telephone. The local doctor had arrived and taken charge. A simplified dinner had been served, and by mutual consent the house-party had retired to their rooms after it. Mr Satterthwaite had been making his own retreat when Sir Charles had called to him from the door of the Ship-room where the death had taken place.

Mr Satterthwaite passed in, repressing a slight shiver as he did so. He was old enough not to like the sight of death . . . For soon, perhaps, he himself . . . But why think of that?

'I'm good for another twenty years,' said Mr Satterthwaite robustly to himself.

The only other occupant of the Ship-room was Bartholomew Strange. He nodded approval at the sight of Mr Satterthwaite.

'Good man,' he said. 'We can do with Satterthwaite. He knows life.'

A little surprised, Mr Satterthwaite sat down in an armchair near the doctor. Sir Charles was pacing up and down. He had forgotten the semi-clenching of his hands and looked definitely less naval.

'Charles doesn't like it,' said Sir Bartholomew. 'Poor old Babbington's death, I mean.'

Mr Satterthwaite thought the sentiment ill expressed. Surely nobody could be expected to 'like' what had occurred. He realized that Strange had quite another meaning from the bald one the words conveyed.

'It was very distressing,' said Mr Satterthwaite, cautiously feeling his way. 'Very distressing indeed,' he added with a reminiscent shiver.

'H'm, yes, it was rather painful,' said the physician, the professional accent creeping for a moment into his voice.

Cartwright paused in his pacing.

'Ever see anyone die quite like that before, Tollie?'

'No,' said Sir Bartholomew thoughtfully. 'I can't say that I have.

'But,' he added in a moment or two, 'I haven't really seen as many deaths as you might suppose. A nerve specialist doesn't kill off many of his patients. He keeps 'em alive and makes his income out of them. MacDougal has seen far more deceases than I have, I don't doubt.'

Dr MacDougal was the principal doctor in Loomouth, whom Miss Milray had summoned.

'MacDougal didn't see this man die. He was dead when he arrived. There was only what we could tell him, what you could tell him. He said it was some kind of seizure, said Babbington was elderly, and his health was none too good. That doesn't satisfy me.'

'Probably didn't satisfy him,' grunted the other. 'But a doctor has to say something. Seizure is a good word – means nothing at all, but satisfies the lay mind. And, after all, Babbington *was* elderly, and his health *had* been giving him trouble lately; his wife told us so. There may have been some unsuspected weakness somewhere.'

'Was that a typical fit or seizure, or whatever you call it?'

'Typical of what?'

'Of any known disease?'

'If you'd ever studied medicine,' said Sir Bartholomew, 'you'd know that there is hardly any such thing as a typical case.'

'What, precisely, are you suggesting, Sir Charles?' asked Mr Satterthwaite.

Cartwright did not answer. He made a vague gesture with his hand. Strange gave a slight chuckle.

'Charles doesn't know himself,' he said. 'It's just his mind turning naturally to the dramatic possibilities.'

Sir Charles made a reproachful gesture. His face was absorbed – thoughtful. He shook his head slightly in an abstracted manner.

An elusive resemblance teased Mr Satterthwaite – then he got it. Aristide Duval, the head of the Secret Service, unravelling the tangled plot of 'Underground Wires'. In another minute he was sure. Sir Charles was limping unconsciously as he walked. Aristide Duval had been known as The Man With a Limp.

Sir Bartholomew continued to apply ruthless common sense to Sir Charles's unformulated suspicions.

'Yes, what do you suspect, Charles? Suicide? Murder? Who wants to murder a harmless old clergyman? It's fantastic. Suicide? Well, I suppose that is a point. One might perhaps imagine a reason for Babbington wanting to make away with himself –'

'What reason?'

Sir Bartholomew shook his head gently.

'How can we tell the secrets of the human mind? Just one suggestion – suppose that Babbington had been told he suffered from an incurable disease – such as cancer. Something of that kind might supply a motive. He might wish to spare his wife the pain of watching his own long-drawn-out suffering. That's only a suggestion, of course. There's nothing on earth to make us think that Babbington did want to put an end to himself.'

'I wasn't thinking so much of suicide,' began Sir Charles.

Bartholomew Strange again gave his low chuckle.

'Exactly. You're not out for probability. You want sensation – new and untraceable poison in the cocktails.'

Sir Charles made an expressive grimace.

'I'm not so sure I do want that. Damn it all, Tollie, remember *I* mixed those cocktails.'

'Sudden attack of homicidal mania, eh? I suppose the symptoms are delayed in our case, but we'll all be dead before morning.'

'Damn it all, you joke, but –' Sir Charles broke off irritably.

'I'm not really joking,' said the physician.

His voice had altered. It was grave, and not unsympathetic.

'I'm not joking about poor old Babbington's death. I'm casting fun at your suggestions, Charles, because – well – because I don't want you, thoughtlessly, to do harm.'

'Harm?' demanded Sir Charles.

'Perhaps you understand what I'm driving at, Mr Satterthwaite?'

'I think, perhaps, I can guess,' said Mr Satterthwaite.

'Don't you see, Charles,' went on Sir Bartholomew, 'that those idle suspicions of yours might be definitely harmful? These things get about. A vague suggestion of foul play, totally unfounded, might cause serious trouble and pain to Mrs Babbington. I've known things of that kind happen once or twice. A sudden death – a few idle tongues wagging – rumours flying all round the place – rumours that go on growing – and *that no one can stop.* Damn it all, Charles, don't you see how cruel and unnecessary it would be? You're merely indulging your vivid imagination in a gallop over a wholly speculative course.'

A look of irresolution appeared on the actor's face.

'I hadn't thought of it like that,' he admitted.

'You're a thundering good chap, Charles, but you *do* let your imagination run away with you. Come now: do you seriously believe anyone, *anyone at all,* would want to murder that perfectly harmless old man?'

'I suppose not,' said Sir Charles. 'No, as you say, it's ridiculous. Sorry, Tollie, but it wasn't really a mere "stunt" on my part. I did genuinely have a "hunch" that something was wrong.'

Mr Satterthwaite gave a little cough.

'May I make a suggestion? Mr Babbington was taken ill a very few moments after entering the room and just after drinking his cocktail. Now, I did happen to notice he made a wry face when drinking. I imagined because he was unused to the taste. But supposing that Sir Bartholomew's tentative suggestion is correct – that Mr Babbington may for some reason have wished to commit suicide. That does strike me as just possible, whereas the suggestion of murder seems quite ridiculous.

'I feel that it is possible, though not probable, that Mr Babbington introduced something into that glass unseen by us.

'Now I see that nothing has yet been touched in this room. The cocktail glasses are exactly where they were. This is Mr Babbington's. I know, because I was sitting here talking to him. I suggest that Sir Bartholomew should get the glass analysed – that can be done quite quietly and without causing any "talk".'

Sir Bartholomew rose and picked up the glass.

'Right,' he said. 'I'll humour you so far, Charles, and I'll bet you ten pounds to one that there's nothing in it but honest-to-God gin and vermouth.'

'Done,' said Sir Charles.

Then he added with a rueful smile:

'You know, Tollie, *you* are partly responsible for my flights of fancy.'

'I?'

'Yes, with your talk of crime this morning. You said this man, Hercule Poirot, was a kind of stormy petrel, that where he went crimes followed. No sooner does he arrive than we have a suspiciously sudden death. Of course my thoughts fly to murder at once.'

'I wonder,' said Mr Satterthwaite, and stopped.

'Yes,' said Charles Cartwright. 'I'd thought of that. What do you think, Tollie? Could we ask him what he thinks of it all? Is it etiquette, I mean?'

'A nice point,' murmured Mr Satterthwaite.

'I know medical etiquette, but I'm hanged if I know anything about the etiquette of detection.'

'You can't ask a professional singer to sing,' murmured Mr Satterthwaite. 'Can one ask a professional detective to detect? Yes, a very nice point.'

'Just an opinion,' said Sir Charles.

There was a gentle tap on the door, and Hercule Poirot's face appeared, peering in with an apologetic expression.

'Come in, man,' cried Sir Charles, springing up. 'We were just talking of you.'

'I thought perhaps I might be intruding.'

'Not at all. Have a drink.'

'I thank you, no. I seldom drink the whisky. A glass of sirop, now –'

But sirop was not included in Sir Charles's conception of drinkable fluids. Having settled his guest in a chair, the actor went straight to the point.

'I'm not going to beat about the bush,' he said. 'We were just talking of you, M. Poirot, and – and – of what happened tonight. Look here, do you think there's anything wrong about it?'

Poirot's eyebrows rose. He said:

'Wrong? How do you mean that – wrong?'

Bartholomew Strange said, 'My friend has got an idea into his head that old Babbington was murdered.'

'And you do not think so – eh?'

'We'd like to know what you think.'

Poirot said thoughtfully:

'He was taken ill, of course, very suddenly – very suddenly indeed.'

'Just so.'

Mr Satterthwaite explained the theory of suicide and his own suggestion of having a cocktail glass analysed.

Poirot nodded approval.

'That, at any rate, can do no harm. As a judge of human nature, it seems to me unlikely in the extreme that anyone could wish to do away with a charming and harmless old gentleman. Still less does the solution of suicide appeal to me. However, the cocktail glass will tell us one way or another.'

'And the result of the analysis, you think, will be – what?'

Poirot shrugged his shoulders.

'Me? I can only guess. You ask me to guess what will be the result of the analysis?'

'Yes –?'

'Then I guess that they will find only the remains of a very excellent dry Martini.' (He bowed to Sir Charles.) 'To poison a man in a cocktail, one of many handed round on a tray – well, it would be a technique very – very – difficult. And if that charming old clergyman wanted to commit suicide, I do not think he would do it at a party. That would show a very decided lack of consideration for others, and Mr Babbington struck me as a very considerate person.' He paused. 'That, since you ask me, is my opinion.'

There was a moment's silence. Then Sir Charles gave a deep sigh. He opened one of the windows and looked out.

'Wind's gone round a point,' he said.

The sailor had come back and the Secret Service detective had disappeared.

But to the observant Mr Satterthwaite it seemed as though Sir Charles hankered slightly after the part he was not, after all, to play.

CHAPTER 4

A MODERN ELAINE

'Yes, but what do you think, Mr Satterthwaite? Really *think*?'

Mr Satterthwaite looked this way and that. There was no escape. Egg Lytton Gore had got him securely cornered on the fishing quay. Merciless, these modern young women – and terrifyingly alive.

'Sir Charles has put this idea into your head,' he said.

'No, he hasn't. It was there already. It's been there from the beginning. It was so frightfully sudden.'

'He was an old man, and his health wasn't very good –'

Egg cut the recital short.

'That's all tripe. He had neuritis and a touch of rheumatoid arthritis. That doesn't make you fall down in a fit. He never had fits. He was the sort of gentle creaking gate that would have lived to be ninety. What did you think of the inquest?'

'It all seemed quite – er – normal.'

'What did you think of Dr MacDougal's evidence? Frightfully technical, and all that – close description of the organs – but didn't it strike you that behind all that bombardment of words he was hedging? What he said amounted to this: that there was nothing to show death had not arisen from natural causes. He didn't say it was the result of natural causes.'

'Aren't you splitting hairs a little, my dear?'

'The point is that *he* did – he was puzzled, but he had nothing to go upon, so he had to take refuge in medical caution. What did Sir Bartholomew Strange think?'

Mr Satterthwaite repeated some of the physician's dictums.

'Pooh-poohed it, did he?' said Egg thoughtfully. 'Of course, he's a cautious man – I suppose a Harley Street big bug has to be.'

'There was nothing in the cocktail glass but gin and vermouth,' Mr Satterthwaite reminded her.

'That seems to settle it. All the same, something that happened after the inquest made me wonder –'

'Something Sir Bartholomew said to you?'

Mr Satterthwaite began to feel a pleasant curiosity.

'Not to me – to Oliver. Oliver Manders – he was at dinner that night, but perhaps you don't remember him.'

'Yes, I remember him very well. Is he a great friend of yours?'

'Used to be. Now we scrap most of the time. He's gone into his uncle's office in the city, and he's getting – well, a bit oily, if you know what I mean. Always talks of chucking it and being a journalist – he writes rather well. But I don't think it's any more than talk now. He wants to get rich. I think everybody is rather disgusting about money, don't you, Mr Satterthwaite?'

Her youth came home to him then – the crude, arrogant childishness of her.

'My dear,' he said, 'so many people are disgusting about so many things.'

'Most people are swine, of course,' agreed Egg cheerfully. 'That's why I'm really cut up about old Mr Babbington. Because you see, he really was rather a pet. He prepared me for confirmation and all that, and though of course a lot of that business is all bunkum, he really was rather sweet about it. You see, Mr Satterthwaite, I really believe in Christianity – not like Mother does, with little books and early service, and things – but intelligently and as a matter of history. The Church is all clotted up with the Pauline tradition – in fact the Church is a mess – but Christianity itself is all right. That's why I can't be a communist like Oliver. In practice our beliefs would work out much the same, things in common and ownership by all, but the difference – well, I needn't go into that. But the Babbingtons really *were* Christians; they didn't poke and pry and condemn, and they were never unkind about people or things. They were pets – and there was Robin . . .'

'Robin?'

'Their son . . . He was out in India and got killed . . . I – I had rather a pash on Robin . . .'

Egg blinked. Her gaze went out to sea . . .

Then her attention returned to Mr Satterthwaite and the present.

'So, you see, I feel rather strongly about this. Supposing it wasn't a natural death . . .'

'My dear child!'

'Well, it's damned odd! You must admit it's damned odd.'

'But surely you yourself have just practically admitted that the Babbingtons hadn't an enemy in the world.'

'That's what's so queer about it. I can't think of any conceivable motive . . .'

'Fantastic! There was nothing in the cocktail.'

'Perhaps someone jabbed him with a hypodermic.'

'Containing the arrow poison of the South American Indians,' suggested Mr Satterthwaite, gently ridiculing.

Egg grinned.

'That's it. The good old untraceable stuff. Oh, well, you're all very superior about it. Some day, perhaps, you'll find out we are right.'

'We?'

'Sir Charles and I.' She flushed slightly.

Mr Satterthwaite thought in the words and metre of his generation when *Quotations for All Occasions* was to be found in every bookcase.

> *'Of more than twice her years,*
> *Seam'd with an ancient swordcut on the cheek,*
> *And bruised and bronzed, she lifted up her eyes*
> *And loved him, with that love which was her doom.'*

He felt a little ashamed of himself for thinking in quotations – Tennyson, too, was very little thought of nowadays. Besides, though Sir Charles was bronzed, he was not scarred, and Egg Lytton Gore, though doubtless capable of a healthy passion, did not look at all likely to perish of love and drift about rivers on a barge. There was nothing of the lily maid of Astolat about her.

'Except,' thought Mr Satterthwaite, 'her youth . . .'

Girls were always attracted to middle-aged men with interesting pasts. Egg seemed to be no exception to this rule.

'Why hasn't he ever married?' she asked abruptly.

'Well . . .' Mr Satterthwaite paused. His own answer, put bluntly, would have been, 'Caution,' but he realized that such a word would be unacceptable to Egg Lytton Gore.

Sir Charles Cartwright had had plenty of affairs with women, actresses and others, but he had always managed to steer clear of matrimony. Egg was clearly seeking for a more romantic explanation.

'That girl who died of consumption – some actress, name began with an M – wasn't he supposed to be very fond of her?'

Mr Satterthwaite remembered the lady in question. Rumour had coupled Charles Cartwright's name with hers, but only very slightly, and Mr Satterthwaite did not for a moment believe that Sir Charles had remained unmarried in order to be faithful to her memory. He conveyed as much tactfully.

'I suppose he's had lots of affairs,' said Egg.

'Er – h'm – probably,' said Mr Satterthwaite, feeling Victorian.

'I like men to have affairs,' said Egg. 'It shows they're not queer or anything.'

Mr Satterthwaite's Victorianism suffered a further pang. He was at a loss for a reply. Egg did not notice his discomfiture. She went on musingly.

'You know, Sir Charles is really cleverer than you'd think. He poses a lot, of course, dramatises himself; but behind all that he's got brains. He's far better sailing a boat than you'd ever think, to hear him talk. You'd think, to listen to him, that it was all pose, but it isn't. It's the same about this business. You think it's all done for effect – that he wants to play the part of the great detective. All I say is: I think he'd play it rather well.'

'Possibly,' agreed Mr Satterthwaite.

The inflection of his voice showed his feelings clearly enough. Egg pounced on them and expressed them in words.

'But your view is that "Death of a Clergyman" isn't a thriller. It's merely "Regrettable Incident at a Dinner Party". Purely a social catastrophe. What did M. Poirot think? *He* ought to know.'

'M. Poirot advised us to wait for the analysis of the cocktail; but in his opinion everything was quite all right.'

'Oh, well,' said Egg, 'he's getting old. He's a back number.' Mr Satterthwaite winced. Egg went on, unconscious of brutality: 'Come home and have tea with Mother. She likes you. She said so.'

Delicately flattered, Mr Satterthwaite accepted the invitation.

On arrival Egg volunteered to ring up Sir Charles and explain the non-appearance of his guest.

Mr Satterthwaite sat down in the tiny sitting-room with its faded chintzes and its well-polished pieces of old furniture. It was a Victorian room, what Mr Satterthwaite called in his own mind a lady's room, and he approved of it.

His conversation with Lady Mary was agreeable, nothing brilliant, but pleasantly chatty. They spoke of Sir Charles. Did Mr Satterthwaite know him well? Not intimately, Mr Satterthwaite said. He had a financial interest in one of Sir Charles's plays some years ago. They had been friends ever since.

'He has great charm,' said Lady Mary, smiling. 'I feel it as well as Egg. I suppose you've discovered that Egg is suffering badly from hero worship?'

Mr Satterthwaite wondered if, as a mother, Lady Mary was not made slightly uneasy by that hero worship. But it did not seem so.

'Egg sees so little of the world,' she said, sighing. 'We are so badly off. One of my cousins presented her and took her to a few things in town, but since then she has hardly been away from here, except for an occasional visit. Young people, I feel, should see plenty of people and places – especially people. Otherwise – well, propinquity is sometimes a dangerous thing.'

Mr Satterthwaite agreed, thinking of Sir Charles and the sailing, but that this was not what was in Lady Mary's mind, she showed a moment or two later.

'Sir Charles's coming has done a lot for Egg. It has widened her horizon. You see, there are very few young people down here – especially men. I've always been afraid that Egg might marry someone simply from being thrown with one person only and seeing no one else.'

Mr Satterthwaite had a quick intuition.

'Are you thinking of young Oliver Manders?'

Lady Mary blushed in ingenuous surprise.

'Oh, Mr Satterthwaite, I don't know how you knew! I *was* thinking of him. He and Egg were together a lot at one time, and I know I'm old-fashioned, but I don't like some of his ideas.'

'Youth must have its fling,' said Mr Satterthwaite.

Lady Mary shook her head.

'I've been so afraid – it's quite suitable, of course, I know all about him, and his uncle, who has recently taken him into his firm, is a very rich man; it's not that – it's silly of me – but –'

She shook her head, unable to express herself further.

Mr Satterthwaite felt curiously intimate. He said quietly and plainly:

'All the same, Lady Mary, you wouldn't like your girl to marry a man twice her own age.'

Her answer surprised him.

'It might be safer so. If you do that, at least you know where you are. At that age a man's follies and sins are definitely behind him; they are not – still to come . . .'

Before Mr Satterthwaite could say any more, Egg rejoined them.

'You've been a long time, darling,' said her mother.

'I was talking to Sir Charles, my sweet. He's all alone in his glory.' She turned reproachfully to Mr Satterthwaite. 'You didn't tell me the house-party had flitted.'

'They went back yesterday – all but Sir Bartholomew Strange. He was staying till tomorrow, but he was recalled to London by an urgent telegram this morning. One of his patients was in a critical condition.'

'It's a pity,' said Egg. 'Because I meant to study the house-party. I might have got a clue.'

'A clue to what, darling?'

'Mr Satterthwaite knows. Oh, well, it doesn't matter. Oliver's still here. We'll rope him in. He's got brains when he likes.'

When Mr Satterthwaite arrived back at Crow's Nest he found his host sitting on the terrace overlooking the sea.

'Hullo, Satterthwaite. Been having tea with the Lytton Gores?'

'Yes. You don't mind?'

'Of course not. Egg telephoned . . . Odd sort of girl, Egg . . .'

'Attractive,' said Mr Satterthwaite.

'H'm, yes, I suppose she is.'

He got up and walked a few aimless steps.

'I wish to God,' he said suddenly and bitterly, 'that I'd never come to this cursed place.'

CHAPTER 5
....
FLIGHT FROM A LADY

Mr Satterthwaite thought to himself: 'He's got it badly.'

He felt a sudden pity for his host. At the age of fifty-two, Charles Cartwright, the gay debonair breaker of hearts, had fallen in love. And, as he himself realized, his case was doomed to disappointment. Youth turns to youth.

'Girls don't wear their hearts on their sleeves,' thought Mr Satterthwaite. 'Egg makes a great parade of her feeling for Sir Charles. She wouldn't if it really meant anything. Young Manders is the one.'

Mr Satterthwaite was usually fairly shrewd in his assumptions.

Still, there was probably one factor that he did not take into account, because he was unaware of it himself. That was the enhanced value placed by age on youth. To Mr Satterthwaite, an elderly man, the fact that Egg might prefer a middle-aged man to a young one was frankly incredible. Youth was to him so much the most magical of all gifts.

He felt strengthened in his beliefs when Egg rang up after dinner and demanded permission to bring Oliver along and 'have a consultation'.

Certainly a handsome lad, with his dark, heavy-lidded eyes and easy grace of movement. He had, it seemed, permitted himself to be brought – a tribute to Egg's energy; but his general attitude was lazily sceptical.

'Can't you talk her out of it, sir?' he said to Sir Charles. 'It's this appallingly healthy bucolic life she leads that makes her so energetic. You know, Egg, you really are detestably hearty. And your tastes are childish – crime – sensation – and all that bunk.'

'You're a sceptic, Manders?'

'Well, sir, really. That dear old bleating fellow. It's fantastic to think of anything else but natural causes.'

'I expect you're right,' said Sir Charles.

Mr Satterthwaite glanced at him. What part was Charles Cartwright playing tonight. Not the ex-Naval man – not the international detective. No, some new and unfamiliar rôle.

It came as a shock to Mr Satterthwaite when he realized what that rôle was. Sir Charles was playing second fiddle. Second fiddle to Oliver Manders.

He sat back with his head in shadow watching those two, Egg and Oliver, as they disputed – Egg hotly, Oliver languidly.

Sir Charles looked older than usual – old and tired.

More than once Egg appealed to him – hotly and confidently – but his response was lacking.

It was eleven o'clock when they left. Sir Charles went out on the terrace with them and offered the loan of an electric torch to help them down the stony path.

But there was no need of a torch. It was a beautiful moonlit night. They set off together, their voices growing fainter as they descended.

Moonlight or no moonlight, Mr Sattherthwaite was not going to risk a chill. He returned to the Ship-room. Sir Charles stayed out on the terrace a little while longer.

When he came in he latched the window behind him, and striding to a side table poured himself out a whisky and soda.

'Satterthwaite,' he said, 'I'm leaving here tomorrow for good.'

'What?' cried Mr Satterthwaite, astonished.

A kind of melancholy pleasure at the effect he had produced showed for a minute on Charles Cartwright's face.

'It's the Only Thing To Do,' he said, obviously speaking in capital letters. 'I shall sell this place. What it has meant to me no one will ever know.' His voice dropped, lingeringly . . . effectively.

After an evening of second fiddle, Sir Charles's egoism was taking its revenge. This was the great Renunciation Scene, so often played by him in sundry and divers dramas. Giving Up the Other Man's Wife, Renouncing the Girl he Loved.

There was a brave flippancy in his voice as he went on.

'Cut your losses – it's the only way . . . Youth to youth . . . They're made for each other, those two . . . I shall clear out . . .'

'Where to?' asked Mr Satterthwaite.

The actor made a careless gesture.

'Anywhere. What does it matter?' He added with a slight change of voice, 'Probably Monte Carlo.' And then, retrieving what his sensitive taste could not but feel to be a slight anticlimax, 'In the heart of the desert or the heart of the crowd – what does it matter? The inmost core of man is solitary – alone. I have always been – a lonely soul . . .'

It was clearly an exit line.

He nodded to Mr Satterthwaite and left the room.

Mr Satterthwaite got up and prepared to follow his host to bed.

'But it won't be the heart of a desert,' he thought to himself with a slight chuckle.

On the following morning Sir Charles begged Mr Satterthwaite to forgive him if he went up to town that day.

'Don't cut your visit short, my dear fellow. You were staying till tomorrow, and I know you're going on to the Harbertons at Tavistock. The car will take you there. What I feel is that, having come to my decision, I mustn't look back. No, I mustn't look back.'

Sir Charles squared his shoulders with manly resolution, wrung Mr Satterthwaite's hand with fervour and delivered him over to the capable Miss Milray.

Miss Milray seemed prepared to deal with the situation as she had dealt with any other. She expressed no surprise or emotion at Sir Charles's overnight decision. Nor could Mr Satterthwaite draw her out on the point. Neither sudden deaths nor sudden changes of plan could excite Miss Milray. She accepted whatever happened as a fact and proceeded to cope with it in an efficient way. She telephoned to the house agents, despatched wires abroad, and wrote busily on her typewriter. Mr Satterthwaite escaped from the depressing spectacle of so much efficiency by strolling down to the quay. He was walking aimlessly along when he was seized by the arm from behind, and turned to confront a white-faced girl.

'What's all this?' demanded Egg fiercely.

'All what?' parried Mr Satterthwaite.

'It's all over the place that Sir Charles is going away – that he's going to sell Crow's Nest.'

'Quite true.'

'He is going away?'

'He's gone.'

'Oh!' Egg relinquished his arm. She looked suddenly like a very small child who has been cruelly hurt.

Mr Satterthwaite did not know what to say.

'Where has he gone?'

'Abroad. To the South of France.'

'Oh!'

Still he did not know what to say. For clearly there was more than hero worship here . . .

Pitying her, he was turning over various consolatory words in his mind when she spoke again – and startled him.

'Which of those damned bitches is it?' asked Egg fiercely.

Mr Satterthwaite stared at her, his mouth fallen open in surprise. Egg took him by the arm again and shook him violently.

'You must know,' she cried. 'Which of them? The grey-haired one or the other?'

'My dear, I don't know what you're talking about.'

'You do. You must. Of course it's some woman. He liked me – I know he liked me. One of those women the other night must have seen it, too, and determined to get him away from me. I hate women. Lousy cats. Did you see her clothes – that one with the green hair? They made me gnash my teeth with envy. A woman who has clothes like that has a pull – you can't deny it. She's quite old and ugly as sin, really, but what does it matter. She makes everyone else look like a dowdy curate's wife. Is it her? Or is it the other one with the grey hair? She's amusing – you can see that. She's got masses of S.A. And he called her Angie. It can't be the one like a wilted cabbage. Is it the smart one or is it Angie?'

'My dear, you've got the most extraordinary ideas into your head. He – er – Charles Cartwright isn't the least interested in either of those women.'

'I don't believe you. They're interested in him, anyway . . .'

'No, no, no, you're making a mistake. This is all imagination.'

'Bitches,' said Egg. 'That's what they are!'

'You mustn't use that word, my dear.'

'I can think of a lot worse things to say than that.'

'Possibly, possibly, but pray don't do so. I can assure you that you are labouring under a misapprehension.'

'Then why has he gone away – like this?'

Mr Satterthwaite cleared his throat.

'I fancy he – er – thought it best.'

Egg stared at him piercingly.

'Do you mean – because of *me*?'

'Well – something of the kind, perhaps.'

'And so he's legged it. I suppose I did show my hand a bit plainly . . . Men do hate being chased, don't they? Mums is right, after all . . . You've no idea how sweet she is when she talks about men. Always in the third person – so Victorian and polite. "A man hates being run after; a girl should always let the man make the running." Don't you think it's a sweet expression – make the running? Sounds the opposite of what it means. Actually that's just what Charles has done – made the running. He's running away from me. He's afraid. And the devil of it is, I can't go after him. If I did I suppose he'd take a boat to the wilds of Africa or somewhere.'

'Hermione,' said Mr Satterthwaite, 'are you serious about Sir Charles?'

The girl flung him an impatient glance.

'Of course I am.'

'What about Oliver Manders?'

Egg dismissed Oliver Manders with an impatient whisk of the head. She was following out a train of thought of her own.

'Do you think I might write to him? Nothing alarming. Just chatty girlish stuff . . . you know, put him at his ease, so that he'd get over his scare?'

She frowned.

'What a fool I've been. Mums would have managed it much better. They knew how to do the trick, those Victorians. All blushing retreat. I've been all wrong about it. I actually thought he needed encouraging. He seemed – well, he seemed to need a bit of help. Tell me,' she turned abruptly on Mr Satterthwaite, 'did he see me do my kissing act with Oliver last night?'

'Not that I know of. When –?'

'All in the moonlight. As we were going down the path. I thought he was still looking from the terrace. I thought perhaps if he saw me and Oliver – well, I thought it might wake him up a bit. Because he did like me. I could swear he liked me.'

'Wasn't that a little hard on Oliver?'

Egg shook her head decisively.

'Not in the least. Oliver thinks it's an honour for any girl to be kissed by him. It was damned bad for his conceit, of course; but one can't think of everything. I wanted to ginger up Charles. He's been different lately – more standoffish.'

'My dear child,' said Mr Satterthwaite, 'I don't think you realize quite why Sir Charles went away so suddenly. He thought that you cared for Oliver. He went away to save himself further pain.'

Egg whisked round. She caught hold of Mr Satterthwaite by the shoulders and peered into his face.

'Is that true? Is that really true? The mutt! The boob! Oh –!'

She released Mr Satterthwaite suddenly and moved along beside him with a skipping motion.

'Then he'll come back,' she said. 'He'll come back. If he doesn't –'

'Well, if he doesn't?'

Egg laughed.

'I'll get him back somehow. You see if I don't.'

It seemed as though allowing for difference of language Egg and the lily maid of Astolat had much in common, but Mr Satterthwaite felt that Egg's methods would be more practical than those of Elaine, and that dying of a broken heart would form no part of them.

SECOND ACT • CERTAINTY

SIR CHARLES RECEIVES A LETTER

Mr Satterthwaite had come over for the day to Monte Carlo. His round of house-parties was over, and the Riviera in September was rather a favourite haunt of his.

He was sitting in the gardens enjoying the sun and reading a two-days-old *Daily Mail*.

Suddenly a name caught his attention. *Strange. Death of Sir Bartholomew Strange.* He read the paragraph through:

> *We much regret having to announce the death of Sir Bartholomew Strange, the eminent nerve specialist. Sir Bartholomew was entertaining a party of friends at his house in Yorkshire. Sir Bartholomew appeared to be in perfect health and spirits, and his demise occurred quite suddenly at the end of dinner. He was chatting with his friends and drinking a glass of port when he had a sudden seizure and died before medical aid could be summoned. Sir Bartholomew will be deeply regretted. He was . . .*

Here followed a description of Sir Bartholomew's career and work.

Mr Satterthwaite let the paper slip from his hand. He was very disagreeably impressed. A vision of the physician as he had seen him last flashed across his mind – big, jocund, in the pink of condition. And now – dead. Certain words detached themselves from their context and floated about disagreeably in Mr Satterthwaite's mind. 'Drinking a glass of port.' 'Sudden seizure . . . Died before medical aid could be summoned . . .'

Port, not a cocktail, but otherwise curiously reminiscent of that death in Cornwall. Mr Satterthwaite saw again the convulsed face of the mild old clergyman . . .

Supposing that after all . . .

He looked up to see Sir Charles Cartwright coming towards him across the grass.

'Satterthwaite, by all that's wonderful! Just the man I'd have chosen to see. Have you seen about poor old Tollie?'

'I was just reading it now.'

Sir Charles dropped into a chair beside him. He was immaculately got up in yachting costume. No more grey flannels and old sweaters. He was the sophisticated yachtsman of the South of France.

'Listen, Satterthwaite, Tollie was as sound as a bell. Never had anything wrong with him. Am I being a complete fanciful ass, or does this business remind you of – of –?'

'Of that business at Loomouth? Yes, it does. But of course we may be mistaken. The resemblance may be only superficial. After all, sudden deaths occur the whole time from a variety of causes.'

Sir Charles nodded his head impatiently. Then he said:

'I've just got a letter – from Egg Lytton Gore.'

Mr Satterthwaite concealed a smile.

'The first you've had from her?'

Sir Charles was unsuspecting.

'No. I had a letter soon after I got here. It followed me about a bit. Just giving me the news and all that. I didn't answer it . . . Dash it all, Satterthwaite, I didn't dare answer it . . . The girl had no idea, of course, but I didn't want to make a fool of myself.'

Mr Satterthwaite passed his hand over his mouth where the smile still lingered.

'And this one?' he asked.

'This is different. It's an appeal for help . . .'

'Help?' Mr Satterthwaite's eyebrows went up.

'She was there – you see – in the house – when it happened.'

'You mean she was staying with Sir Bartholomew Strange at the time of his death?'

'Yes.'

'What does she say about it?'

Sir Charles had taken a letter from his pocket. He hesitated for a moment, then he handed it to Mr Satterthwaite.

'You'd better read it for yourself.'

Mr Satterthwaite opened out the sheet with lively curiosity.

'Dear Sir Charles, – I don't know when this will get to you. I do hope soon. I'm so worried, I don't know what to do. You'll have seen, I expect, in the papers that Sir Bartholomew Strange is dead. Well, he died just the same way as Mr Babbington. It can't be a coincidence – it can't – it can't . . . I'm worried to death . . .

'Look here, can't you come home and do something? It sounds a bit crude put like that, but you did have suspicions before, and nobody would listen to you, and now it's your own friend who's been killed; and perhaps if you don't come back nobody will ever find out the truth, and I'm sure you could. I feel it in my bones . . .

'And there's something else. I'm worried, definitely, about someone . . . He had absolutely nothing to do with it, I know that, but things might look a bit odd. Oh, I can't explain in a letter. But won't you come back? You could find out the truth. I know you could.

'Yours in haste,
'EGG.'

'Well?' demanded Sir Charles impatiently. 'A bit incoherent of course; she wrote it in a hurry. But what about it?'

Mr Satterthwaite folded the letter slowly to give himself a minute or two before replying.

He agreed that the letter was incoherent, but he did not think it had been written in a hurry. It was, in his view, a very careful production. It was designed to appeal to Sir Charles's vanity, to his chivalry, and to his sporting instincts.

From what Mr Satterthwaite knew of Sir Charles, that letter was a certain draw.

'Who do you think she means by "someone", and "he"?' he asked.

'Manders, I suppose.'

'Was he there, then?'

'Must have been. I don't know why. Tollie never met him except on that one occasion at my house. Why he should ask him to stay, I can't imagine.'

'Did he often have those big house-parties?'

'Three or four times a year. Always one for the St Leger.'

'Did he spend much time in Yorkshire?'

'Had a big sanatorium – nursing home, whatever you like to call it. He bought Melfort Abbey (it's an old place), restored it and built a sanatorium in the grounds.'

'I see.'

Mr Satterthwaite was silent for a minute or two. Then he said: 'I wonder who else there was in the house-party?'

Sir Charles suggested that it might be in one of the other newspapers, and they went off to institute a newspaper hunt.

'Here we are,' said Sir Charles.

He read aloud:

> 'Sir Bartholomew Strange is having his usual house-party for the St Leger. Amongst the guests are Lord and Lady Eden, Lady Mary Lytton Gore, Sir Jocelyn and Lady Campbell, Captain and Mrs Dacres, and Miss Angela Sutcliffe, the well-known actress.'

He and Mr Satterthwaite looked at each other.

'The Dacres and Angela Sutcliffe,' said Sir Charles. 'Nothing about Oliver Manders.'

'Let's get today's *Continental Daily Mail*,' said Mr Satterthwaite. 'There might be something in that.'

Sir Charles glanced over the paper. Suddenly he stiffened.

'My God, Satterthwaite, listen to this:

> 'SIR BARTHOLOMEW STRANGE.
> 'At the inquest today on the late Sir Bartholomew Strange, a verdict of Death by Nicotine Poisoning was returned, there being no evidence to show how or by whom the poison was administered.'

He frowned.

'Nicotine poisoning. Sounds mild enough – not the sort of thing to make a man fall down in a fit. I don't understand all this.'

'What are you going to do?'

'Do? I'm going to book a berth on the Blue Train tonight.'

'Well,' said Mr Satterthwaite, 'I might as well do the same.'

'You?' Sir Charles wheeled round on him, surprised.

'This sort of thing is rather in my line,' said Mr Satterthwaite modestly. 'I've – er – had a little experience. Besides, I know the Chief Constable in that part of the world rather well – Colonel Johnson. That will come in useful.'

'Good man,' cried Sir Charles. 'Let's go round to the Wagon Lits offices.'

Mr Satterthwaite thought to himself:

'The girl's done it. She's got him back. She said she would. I wonder just exactly how much of her letter was genuine.'

Decidedly, Egg Lytton Gore was an opportunist.

When Sir Charles had gone off to the Wagon Lits offices, Mr Satterthwaite strolled slowly through the gardens. His mind was still pleasantly engaged with the problem of Egg Lytton Gore. He admired her resource and her driving power, and stifled that slightly Victorian side of his nature which disapproved of a member of the fairer sex taking the initiative in affairs of the heart.

Mr Satterthwaite was an observant man. In the midst of his cogitations on the female sex in general, and Egg Lytton Gore in particular, he was unable to resist saying to himself:

'Now where have I seen that particular shaped head before?'

The owner of the head was sitting on a seat gazing thoughtfully ahead of him. He was a little man whose moustaches were out of proportion to his size.

A discontented-looking English child was standing nearby, standing first on one foot, then the other, and occasionally meditatively kicking the lobelia edging.

'Don't do that, darling,' said her mother, who was absorbed in a fashion paper.

'I haven't anything to do,' said the child.

The little man turned his head to look at her, and Mr Satterthwaite recognized him.

'M. Poirot,' he said. 'This is a very pleasant surprise.'

M. Poirot rose and bowed.

'*Enchanté, monsieur.*'

They shook hands, and Mr Satterthwaite sat down.

'Everyone seems to be in Monte Carlo. Not half an hour ago I ran across Sir Charles Cartwright, and now you.'

'Sir Charles, he also is here?'

'He's been yachting. You know that he gave up his house at Loomouth?'

'Ah, no, I did not know it. I am surprised.'

'I don't know that I am. I don't think Cartwright is really the kind of man who likes to live permanently out of the world.'

'Ah, no, I agree with you there. I was surprised for another reason. It seemed to me that Sir Charles had a particular reason for staying in Loomouth – a very charming reason, eh? Am I not right? The little demoiselle who calls herself, so amusingly, the egg?'

His eyes were twinkling gently.

'Oh, so you noticed that?'

'Assuredly I noticed. I have the heart very susceptible to lovers – you too, I think. And *la jeunesse*, it is always touching.'

He sighed.

'I think,' said Mr Satterthwaite, 'that actually you have hit on Sir Charles's reason for leaving Loomouth. He was running away.'

'From Mademoiselle Egg? But it is obvious that he adores her. Why, then, run?'

'Ah,' said Mr Satterthwaite, 'you don't understand our Anglo-Saxon complexes.'

M. Poirot was following his own line of reasoning.

'Of course,' he said, 'it is a good move to pursue. Run from a woman – immediately she follows. Doubtless Sir Charles, a man of much experience, knows that.'

Mr Satterthwaite was rather amused.

'I don't think it was quite that way,' he said. 'Tell me, what are you doing out here? A holiday?'

'My time is all holidays nowadays. I have succeeded. I am rich. I retire. Now I travel about seeing the world.'

'Splendid,' said Mr Satterthwaite.

'*N'est-ce pas?*'

'Mummy,' said the English child, 'isn't there anything to *do*?'

'Darling,' said her mother reproachfully, 'isn't it lovely to have come abroad and to be in the beautiful sunshine?'

'Yes, but there's nothing to do.'

'Run about – amuse yourself. Go and look at the sea.'

'*Maman*,' said a French child, suddenly appearing. '*Joue avec moi.*'

A French mother looked up from her book.

'*Amuse toi avec ta balle, Marcelle.*'

Obediently the French child bounced her ball with a gloomy face.

'*Je m'amuse,*' said Hercule Poirot; and there was a very curious expression on his face.

Then, as if in answer to something he read in Mr Satterthwaite's face, he said:

'But yet, you have the quick perceptions. It is as you think –'

He was silent for a minute or two, then he said:

'See you, as a boy I was poor. There were many of us. We had to get on in the world. I entered the Police Force. I worked hard. Slowly I rose in that Force. I began to make a name for myself. I made a name for myself. I began to acquire an international reputation. At last, I was due to retire. There came the War. I was injured. I came, a sad and weary refugee, to England. A kind lady gave me hospitality. She died – not naturally; no, she was killed. *Eh bien*, I set my wits to work. I employed my little grey cells. I discovered her murderer. I found that I was not yet finished. No, indeed, my powers were stronger than ever. Then began my second career, that of a private inquiry agent in England. I have solved many fascinating and baffling problems. Ah, monsieur, I have lived! The psychology of human nature, it is wonderful. I grew rich. Some day, I said to myself, I will have all the money I need. I will realize all my dreams.'

He laid a hand on Mr Satterthwaite's knee.

'My friend, *beware of the day when your dreams come true.* That child near us, doubtless she too has dreamt of coming abroad – of the excitement – of how different everything would be. You understand?'

'I understand,' said Mr Satterthwaite, 'that you are *not* amusing yourself.'

Poirot nodded.

'Exactly.'

There were moments when Mr Satterthwaite looked like Puck. This was one of them. His little wrinkled face twitched impishly. He hesitated. Should he? Should he not?

Slowly he unfolded the newspaper he was still carrying.

'Have you seen this, M. Poirot?'

With his forefinger he indicated the paragraph he meant.

The little Belgian took the paper. Mr Satterthwaite watched

him as he read. No change came over his face, but the Englishman had the impression that his body stiffened, as does that of a terrier when it sniffs a rathole.

Hercule Poirot read the paragraph twice, then he folded the paper and returned it to Mr Satterthwaite.

'That is interesting,' he said.

'Yes. It looks, does it not, as though Sir Charles Cartwright had been right and we had been wrong.'

'Yes,' said Poirot. 'It seems as though we had been wrong . . . I will admit it, my friend, I could not believe that so harmless, so friendly an old man could have been murdered . . . Well, it may be that I was wrong . . . Although, see you, this other death may be coincidence. Coincidences do occur – the most amazing coincidences. I, Hercule Poirot, have known coincidences that would surprise you . . .'

He paused, and went on:

'Sir Charles Cartwright's instinct may have been right. He is an artist – sensitive – impressionable – he feels things, rather than reasons about them . . . Such a method in life is often disastrous – but it is sometimes justified. I wonder where Sir Charles is now.'

Mr Satterthwaite smiled.

'I can tell you that. He is in the office of the Wagon Lits Co. He and I are returning to England tonight.'

'Aha!' Poirot put immense meaning into the exclamation. His eyes, bright, inquiring, roguish, asked a question. 'What zeal he has, our Sir Charles. He is determined, then, to play this rôle, the rôle of the amateur policeman? Or is there another reason?'

Mr Satterthwaite did not reply, but from his silence Poirot seemed to deduce an answer.

'I see,' he said. 'The bright eyes of Mademoiselle are concerned in this. It is not only crime that calls?'

'She wrote to him,' said Mr Satterthwaite, 'begging him to return.'

Poirot nodded.

'I wonder now,' he said. 'I do not quite understand –'

Mr Satterthwaite interrupted.

'You do not understand the modern English girl? Well, that is not surprising. I do not always understand them myself. A girl like Miss Lytton Gore –'

In his turn Poirot interrupted.

'Pardon. You have misunderstood me. I understand Miss Lytton Gore very well. I have met such another – many such others. You call the type modern; but it is – how shall I say? – age-long.'

Mr Satterthwaite was slightly annoyed. He felt that he – and only he – understood Egg. This preposterous foreigner knew nothing about young English womanhood.

Poirot was still speaking. His tone was dreamy – brooding.

'A knowledge of human nature – what a dangerous thing it can be.'

'A useful thing,' corrected Mr Satterthwaite.

'Perhaps. It depends upon the point of view.'

'Well –' Mr Satterthwaite hesitated – got up. He was a little disappointed. He had cast the bait and the fish had not risen. He felt that his own knowledge of human nature was at fault. 'I will wish you a pleasant holiday.'

'I thank you.'

'I hope that when you are next in London you will come and see me.' He produced a card. 'This is my address.'

'You are most amiable, Mr Satterthwaite. I shall be charmed.'

'Goodbye for the present, then.'

'Goodbye, and *bon voyage*.'

Mr Satterthwaite moved away. Poirot looked after him for a moment or two, then once more he stared straight ahead of him, looking out over the blue Mediterranean.

So he sat for at least ten minutes.

The English child reappeared.

'I've looked at the sea, Mummy. What shall I do next?'

'An admirable question,' said Hercule Poirot under his breath.

He rose and walked slowly away – in the direction of the Wagon Lits offices.

CHAPTER 2
....

THE MISSING BUTLER

Sir Charles and Mr Satterthwaite were sitting in Colonel Johnson's study. The chief constable was a big red-faced man with a barrack-room voice and a hearty manner.

He had greeted Mr Satterthwaite with every sign of pleasure and was obviously delighted to make the acquaintance of the famous Charles Cartwright.

'My missus is a great playgoer. She's one of your – what do the Americans call it? – fans. That's it – fans. I like a good play myself – good clean stuff that is, some of the things they put on the stage nowadays – faugh!'

Sir Charles, conscious of rectitude in this respect – he had never put on 'daring' plays, responded suitably with all his easy charm of manner. When they came to mention the object of their visit Colonel Johnson was only too ready to tell them all he could.

'Friend of yours, you say? Too bad – too bad. Yes, he was very popular round here. That sanatorium of his is very highly spoken of, and by all accounts Sir Bartholomew was a first-rate fellow, as well as being at the top of his profession. Kind, generous, popular all round. Last man in the world you'd expect to be murdered – and murder is what it looks like. There's nothing to indicate suicide, and anything like accident seems out of the question.'

'Satterthwaite and I have just come back from abroad,' said Sir Charles. 'We've only seen snippets here and there in the papers.'

'And naturally you want to know all about it. Well, I'll tell you exactly how the matter stands. I think there's no doubt the butler's the man we've got to look for. He was a new man – Sir Bartholomew had only had him a fortnight, and the moment after the crime he disappears – vanishes into thin air. That looks a bit fishy, doesn't it? Eh, what?'

'You've no notion where he went?'

Colonel Johnson's naturally red face got a little redder.

'Negligence on our part, you think. I admit it damn' well looks like it. Naturally the fellow was under observation – just the same as everyone else. He answered our questions quite satisfactorily – gave the London agency which obtained him the place. Last employer, Sir Horace Bird. All very civil spoken, no signs of panic. Next thing was he'd gone – and the house under observation. I've hauled my men over the coals, but they swear they didn't bat an eyelid.'

'Very remarkable,' said Mr Satterthwaite.

'Apart from everything else,' said Sir Charles thoughtfully, 'it seems a damn' fool thing to do. As far as he knew, the man wasn't suspected. By bolting he draws attention to himself.'

'Exactly. And not a hope of escape. His description's been circulated. It's only a matter of days before he's pulled in.'

'Very odd,' said Sir Charles. 'I don't understand it.'

'Oh, the reason's clear enough. He lost his nerve. Got the wind up suddenly.'

'Wouldn't a man who had the nerve to commit murder have the nerve to sit still afterward?'

'Depends. Depends. I know criminals. Chicken-livered, most of them. He thought he was suspected, and he bolted.'

'Have you verified his own account of himself?'

'Naturally, Sir Charles. That's plain routine work. London Agency confirms his story. He had a written reference from Sir Horace Bird, recommending him warmly. Sir Horace himself is in East Africa.'

'So the reference might have been forged?'

'Exactly,' said Colonel Johnson, beaming upon Sir Charles, with the air of a schoolmaster congratulating a bright pupil. 'We've wired to Sir Horace, of course, but it may be some little time before we get a reply. He's on safari.'

'When did the man disappear?'

'Morning after the death. There was a doctor present at the dinner – Sir Jocelyn Campbell – bit of a toxicologist, I understand; he and Davis (local man) agreed over the case, and our people were called in immediately. We interviewed everybody that night. Ellis (that's the butler) went to his room as usual and was missing in the morning. His bed hadn't been slept in.'

'He slipped away under cover of the darkness?'

'Seems so. One of the ladies staying there, Miss Sutcliffe, the actress – you know her, perhaps?'

'Very well, indeed.'

'Miss Sutcliffe has made a suggestion to us. She suggested that the man had left the house through a secret passage.' He blew his nose apologetically. 'Sounds rather Edgar Wallace stuff, but it seems there was such a thing. Sir Bartholomew was rather proud of it. He showed it to Miss Sutcliffe. The end of it comes out among some fallen masonry about half a mile away.'

'That would be a possible explanation, certainly,' agreed Sir Charles. 'Only – would the butler know of the existence of such a passage?'

'That's the point, of course. My missus always says servants know everything. Daresay she's right.'

'I understand the poison was nicotine,' said Mr Satterthwaite.

'That's right. Most unusual stuff to use, I believe. Comparatively rare. I understand if a man's a heavy smoker, such as the doctor was, it would tend to complicate matters. I mean, he might have died of nicotine poisoning in a natural way. Only, of course, this business was too sudden for that.'

'How was it administered?'

'We don't know,' admitted Colonel Johnson. 'That's going to be the weak part of the case. According to medical evidence, it could only have been swallowed a few minutes previous to death.'

'They were drinking port, I understand?'

'Exactly. Seems as though the stuff was in the port; but it wasn't. We analysed his glass. That glass had contained port, and nothing but port. The other wine glasses had been cleared, of course, but they were all on a tray in the pantry, unwashed, and not one of them contained anything it shouldn't. As for what he ate, it was the same as everybody else had. Soup, grilled sole, pheasant and chipped potatoes, chocolate soufflé, soft roes on toast. His cook's been with him fifteen years. No, there doesn't seem to be any way he could have been given the stuff, and yet there it is in the stomach. It's a nasty problem.'

Sir Charles wheeled round on Mr Satterthwaite.

'The same thing,' he said excitedly. 'Exactly the same as before.'

He turned apologetically to the chief constable.

'I must explain. A death occurred at my house in Cornwall –'

Colonel Johnson looked interested.

'I think I've heard about that. From a young lady – Miss Lytton Gore.'

'Yes, she was there. She told you about it?'

'She did. She was very set on her theory. But, you know, Sir Charles, I can't believe there's anything in that theory. It doesn't explain the flight of the butler. Your man didn't disappear by any chance?'

'Haven't got a man – only a parlourmaid.'

'She couldn't have been a man in disguise?'

Thinking of the smart and obviously feminine Temple, Sir Charles smiled.

Colonel Johnson also smiled apologetically.

'Just an idea,' he said. 'No, I can't say I put much reliance in Miss Lytton Gore's theory. I understand the death in question was an elderly clergyman. Who would want to put an old clergyman out of the way?'

'That's just the puzzling part of it,' said Sir Charles.

'I think you'll find it's just coincidence. Depend on it, the butler's our man. Very likely he's a regular criminal. Unluckily we can't find any of his fingerprints. We had a fingerprint expert go over his bedroom and the butler's pantry, but he had no luck.'

'If it was the butler, what motive can you suggest?'

'That, of course, is one of our difficulties,' admitted Colonel Johnson. 'The man might have been there with intent to steal, and Sir Bartholomew might have caught him out.'

'Both Sir Charles and Mr Satterthwaite remained courteously silent. Colonel Johnson himself seemed to feel that the suggestion lacked plausibility.

'The fact of the matter is, one can only theorize. Once we've got John Ellis under lock and key and have found out who he is, and whether he's ever been through our hands before – well, the motive may be as clear as day.'

'You've been through Sir Bartholomew's papers, I suppose?'

'Naturally, Sir Charles. We've given that side of the case every attention. I must introduce you to Superintendent Crossfield, who has charge of the case. A most reliable man. I pointed out to him, and he was quick to agree with me, that Sir Bartholomew's profession might have had something to do with the crime.

A doctor knows many professional secrets. Sir Bartholomew's papers were all neatly filed and docketed – his secretary, Miss Lyndon, went through them with Crossfield.'

'And there was nothing?'

'Nothing at all suggestive, Sir Charles.'

'Was anything missing from the house – silver, jewellery, anything like that?'

'Nothing whatsoever.'

'Who exactly was staying in the house?'

'I've got a list – now where is it? Ah, I think Crossfield has it. You must meet Crossfield; as a matter of fact, I'm expecting him any minute now to report' – as a bell went – 'that's probably the man now.'

Superintendent Crossfield was a large, solid-looking man, rather slow of speech, but with a fairly keen blue eye.

He saluted his superior officer, and was introduced to the two visitors.

It is possible that had Mr Satterthwaite been alone he would have found it hard to make Crossfield unbend. Crossfield didn't hold with gentlemen from London – amateurs coming down with 'ideas'. Sir Charles, however, was a different matter. Superintendent Crossfield had a childish reverence for the glamour of the stage. He had twice seen Sir Charles act, and the excitement and rapture of seeing this hero of the footlights in a flesh-and-blood manner made him as friendly and loquacious as could be wished.

'I saw you in London, sir, I did. I was up with the wife. *Lord Aintree's Dilemma* – that's what the play was. In the pit, I was – and the house was crowded out – we had to stand two hours beforehand. But nothing else would do for the wife. "I must see Sir Charles Cartwright in *Lord Aintree's Dilemma*," she said. At the Pall Mall Theatre, it was.'

'Well,' said Sir Charles, 'I've retired from the stage now, as you know. But they still know my name at the Pall Mall.' He took out a card and wrote a few words on it. 'You give this to the people at the box office next time you and Mrs Crossfield are having a jaunt to town, and they'll give you a couple of the best seats going.'

'I take that very kindly of you, Sir Charles – very kindly,

indeed. My wife will be all worked up when I tell her about this.'

After this Superintendent Crossfield was as wax in the ex-actor's hands.

'It's an odd case, sir. Never come across a case of nicotine poisoning before in all my experience. No more has our Doctor Davis.'

'I always thought it was a kind of disease you got from over-smoking.'

'To tell the truth, so did I, sir. But the doctor says that the pure alkaloid is an odourless liquid, and that a few drops of it are enough to kill a man almost instantaneously.'

Sir Charles whistled.

'Potent stuff.'

'As you say, sir. And yet it's in common use, as you might say. Solutions are used to spray roses with. And of course it can be extracted from ordinary tobacco.'

'Roses,' said Sir Charles. 'Now, where have I heard –?'

He frowned, then shook his head.

'Anything fresh to report, Crossfield?' asked Colonel Johnson.

'Nothing definite, sir. We've had reports that our man Ellis has been seen at Durham, at Ipswich, at Balham, at Land's End, and a dozen other places. That's all got to be sifted out for what it's worth.' He turned to the other two. 'The moment a man's description is circulated as wanted, he's seen by someone all over England.'

'What is the man's description?' asked Sir Charles.

Johnson took up a paper.

'John Ellis, medium height, say five-foot seven, stoops slightly, grey hair, small side whiskers, dark eyes, husky voice, tooth missing in upper jaw, visible when he smiles, no special marks or characteristics.'

'H'm,' said Sir Charles. 'Very nondescript, bar the side whiskers and the tooth, and the first will be off by now, and you can't rely on his smiling.'

'The trouble is,' said Crossfield, 'that nobody observes any-thing. The difficulty I had in getting anything but the vaguest description out of the maids at the Abbey. It's always the same. I've had descriptions of one and the same man, and he's been called tall, thin, short, stout, medium height, thickset, slender – not one in fifty really uses their eyes properly.'

'You're satisfied in your own mind, Superintendent, that Ellis is the man? . . .'

'Why else did he bolt, sir? You can't get away from that.'

'That's the stumbling block,' said Sir Charles thoughtfully.

Crossfield turned to Colonel Johnson and reported the measures that were being taken. The Colonel nodded approval and then asked the Superintendent for the list of inmates of the Abbey on the night of the crime. This was handed to the two new inquirers. It ran as follows:

MARTHA LECKIE, *cook.*
BEATRICE CHURCH, *upper-housemaid.*
DORIS COKER, *under-housemaid.*
VICTORIA BALL, *between-maid.*
ALICE WEST, *parlourmaid.*
VIOLET BASSINGTON, *kitchenmaid.*
(Above have all been in service of deceased for some time and bear good character. Mrs Leckie has been there for fifteen years.)
GLADYS LYNDON – *secretary, thirty-three, has been secretary to Sir Bartholomew Strange for three years, can give no information as to likely motive.*
Guests:
LORD AND LADY EDEN, *187 Cadogan Square.*
SIR JOCELYN and LADY CAMPBELL, *1256 Harley Street.*
MISS ANGELA SUTCLIFFE, *28 Cantrell Mansions, S.W.3.*
CAPTAIN and MRS DACRES, *3 St John's House, W.1. (Mrs Dacres carries on business as Ambrosine, Ltd, Brook Street.)*
LADY MARY and MISS HERMIONE LYTTON GORE, *Rose Cottage, Loomouth.*
MISS MURIEL WILLS, *5 Upper Cathcart Road, Tooting.*
MR OLIVER MANDERS, *Messrs Speier & Ross, Old Broad Street, E.C.2.*

'H'm,' said Sir Charles. 'The Tooting touch was omitted by the papers. I see young Manders was there, too.'

'That's by way of being an accident, sir,' said Superintendent Crossfield. 'The young gentleman ran his car into a wall just by the Abbey, and Sir Bartholomew, who I understood was slightly acquainted with him, asked him to stay the night.'

'Careless thing to do,' said Sir Charles cheerfully.

'It was that, sir,' said the Superintendent. 'In fact, I fancy myself the young gentleman must have had one over the eight, as the saying goes. What made him ram the wall just where he did I can't imagine, if he was sober at the time.'

'Just high spirits, I expect,' said Sir Charles.

'Spirits it was, in my opinion, sir.'

'Well, thank you very much, Superintendent. Any objection to our going and having a look at the Abbey, Colonel Johnson?'

'Of course not, my dear sir. Though I'm afraid you won't learn much more there than I can tell you.'

'Anybody there?'

'Only the domestic staff, sir,' said Crossfield. 'The house-party left immediately after the inquest, and Miss Lyndon has returned to Harley Street.'

'We might, perhaps, see Dr – er – Davis, too?' suggested Mr Satterthwaite.

'Good idea.'

They obtained the doctor's address, and having thanked Colonel Johnson warmly for his kindness, they left.

CHAPTER 3
....
WHICH OF THEM?

As they walked along the street, Sir Charles said:

'Any ideas, Satterthwaite?'

'What about you?' asked Mr Satterthwaite. He liked to reserve judgment until the last possible moment.

Not so Sir Charles. He spoke emphatically:

'They're wrong, Satterthwaite. They're all wrong. They've got the butler on the brain. The butler's done a bunk – ergo, the butler's the murderer. It doesn't fit. No, it doesn't fit. You can't leave that other death out of account – the one down at my place.'

'You're still of the opinion that the two are connected?'

Mr Satterthwaite asked the question, though he had already answered it in the affirmative in his own mind.

'Man, they *must* be connected. Everything points to it . . . We've got to find the common factor – someone who was present on both occasions –'

'Yes,' said Mr Satterthwaite. 'And that's not going to be as simple a matter as one might think, on the face of it. We've got too many common factors. Do you realize, Cartwright, that practically every person who was present at the dinner at your house was present here?'

Sir Charles nodded.

'Of course I've realized that – but do you realize what deduction one can draw from it?'

'I don't quite follow you, Cartwright?'

'Dash it all, man, do you suppose that's coincidence? No, it was *meant*. Why are all the people who were at the first death present at the second? Accident? Not on your life. It was plan – design – Tollie's plan.'

'Oh!' said Mr Satterthwaite. 'Yes, it's possible . . .'

'It's certain. You didn't know Tollie as well as I did, Satterthwaite. He was a man who kept his own counsel, and a very patient man. In all the years I've known him I've never known Tollie give utterance to a rash opinion or judgment.

'Look at it this way: Babbington's murdered – yes, *murdered* – I'm not going to hedge, or mince terms – murdered one evening in my house. Tollie ridicules me gently for my suspicions in the matter, but all the time he's got suspicions of his own. He doesn't talk about them – that's not his way. But quietly, in his own mind, he's building up a case. I don't know what he had to build upon. It can't, I think, be a case against any one particular person. He believed that one of those people was responsible for the crime, and he made a plan, a test of some kind to find out which person it was.'

'What about the other guests, the Edens and the Campbells?'

'Camouflage. It made the whole thing less obvious.'

'What do you think the plan was?'

'Sir Charles shrugged his shoulders – an exaggerated foreign gesture. He was Aristide Duval, that master mind of the Secret Service. His left foot limped as he walked.

'How can we know? I am not a magician. I cannot guess. But there *was* a plan . . . It went wrong, because the murderer was just one degree cleverer than Tollie thought . . . He struck first . . .'

'He?'

'Or she. Poison is as much a woman's weapon as a man's – more so.'

Mr Satterthwaite was silent. Sir Charles said:

'Come now, don't you agree? Or are you on the side of public opinion? "*The butler's the man. He done it.*"'

'What's your explanation of the butler?'

'I haven't thought about him. In my view he doesn't matter . . . I could suggest an explanation.'

'Such as?'

'Well, say that the police are right so far – Ellis is a professional criminal, working in, shall we say, with a gang of burglars. Ellis obtains this post with false credentials. Then Tollie is murdered. What is Ellis's position? A man is killed, and in the house is a man whose fingerprints are at Scotland Yard, and who is known to the police. Naturally he gets the wind up and bolts.'

'By the secret passage?'

'Secret passage be damned. He dodged out of the house while one of the fat-headed constables who were watching the house was taking forty winks.'

'It certainly seems more probable.'

'Well, Satterthwaite, what's your view?'

'Mine?' said Mr Satterthwaite. 'Oh, it's the same as yours. It has been all along. The butler seems to me a very clumsy red herring. I believe that Sir Bartholomew and poor old Babbington were killed by the same person.'

'One of the house-party?'

'One of the house-party.'

There was silence for a minute or two, and then Mr Satterthwaite asked casually:

'Which of them do you think it was?'

'My God, Satterthwaite, how can I tell?'

'You can't tell, of course,' said Mr Satterthwaite mildly. 'I just thought you might have some idea – you know, nothing scientific or reasoned. Just an ordinary guess.'

'Well, I haven't . . .' He thought for a minute and then burst out: 'You know, Satterthwaite, the moment you begin to *think* it seems impossible that any of them did it.'

'I suppose your theory is right,' mused Mr Satterthwaite. 'As to the assembling of the suspects, I mean. We've got to take it into account that there were certain definite exclusions. Yourself and myself and Mrs Babbington, for instance. Young Manders, too, he was out of it.'

'Manders?'

'Yes, his arrival on the scene was an accident. He wasn't asked or expected. That lets him out of the circle of suspects.'

'The dramatist woman, too – Anthony Astor.'

'No, no, she was there. Miss Muriel Wills of Tooting.'

'So she was – I'd forgotten the woman's name was Wills.'

He frowned. Mr Satterthwaite was fairly good at reading people's thoughts. He estimated with fair accuracy what was passing through the actor's mind. When the other spoke, Mr Satterthwaite mentally patted himself on the back.

'You know, Satterthwaite, you're right. I don't think it was definitely suspected people that he asked – because, after all, Lady Mary and Egg were there . . . No, he wanted to stage some reproduction of the first business, perhaps . . . He suspected someone, but he wanted other eye-witnesses there to confirm matters. Something of that kind . . .'

'Something of the kind,' agreed Mr Satterthwaite. 'One can only generalize at this stage. Very well, the Lytton Gores are out of it, you and I and Mrs Babbington and Oliver Manders are out of it. Who is left? Angela Sutcliffe?'

'Angie? My dear fellow. She's been a friend of Tollie's for years.'

'Then it boils down to the Dacres . . . In fact, Cartwright, you suspect the Dacres. You might just as well have said so when I asked you.'

Sir Charles looked at him. Mr Satterthwaite had a mildly triumphant air.

'I suppose,' said Cartwright slowly, 'that I do. At least, I don't suspect them . . . They just seem rather more possible than anyone else. I don't know them very well, for one thing. But for the life of me, I can't see why Freddie Dacres, who spends his life on the racecourse, or Cynthia, who spends her time designing fabulously expensive clothes for women, should have any desire to remove a dear, insignificant old clergyman . . .'

He shook his head; then his face brightened.

'There's the Wills woman. I forgot her again. What is there about her that continually makes you forget her? She's the most damnably nondescript creature I've ever seen.'

Mr Satterthwaite smiled.

'I rather fancy she might embody Burns's famous line – "A chiel's amang ye takin' notes." I rather fancy that Miss Wills spends her time taking notes. There are sharp eyes behind that pair of glasses. I think you'll find that anything worth noticing in this affair has been noticed by Miss Wills.'

'Do you?' said Sir Charles doubtfully.

'The next thing to do,' said Mr Satterthwaite, 'is to have some lunch. After that, we'll go out to the Abbey and see what we can discover on the spot.'

'You seem to be taking very kindly to this, Satterthwaite,' said Sir Charles, with a twinkle of amusement.

'The investigation of crime is not new to me,' said Mr Satterthwaite. 'Once when my car broke down and I was staying at a lonely inn –'

He got no further.

'I remember,' said Sir Charles, in his high, clear carrying actor's voice, 'when I was touring in 1921 . . .'

Sir Charles won.

CHAPTER 4

THE EVIDENCE OF THE SERVANTS

Nothing could have been more peaceful than the grounds and building of Melfort Abbey as the two men saw it that afternoon in the September sunshine. Portions of the Abbey were fifteenth century. It had been restored and a new wing added on to it. The new Sanatorium was out of sight of the house, with grounds of its own.

Sir Charles and Mr Satterthwaite were received by Mrs Leckie, the cook, a portly lady, decorously gowned in black, who was tearful and voluble. Sir Charles she already knew, and it was to him she addressed most of her conversation.

'You'll understand, I'm sure, sir, what it's meant to me. The master's death and all. Policemen all over the place, poking their noses here and there – would you believe it, even the dustbins they had to have their noses in, and questions! – they wouldn't have done with asking questions. Oh, that I should have lived to see such a thing – the doctor, such a quiet gentleman as he always was, and made Sir Bartholomew, too, which a proud day it was to all of us, as Beatrice and I well remember, though she's been here two years less than I have. And such questions as that police fellow (for gentleman I will not call him, having been accustomed to gentlemen and their ways and knowing what's what), fellow, I say, whether or not he is a superintendent –' Mrs Leckie paused, took breath and extricated herself from the somewhat complicated conversational morass into which she had fallen. 'Questions, that's what I say, about all the maids in the house, and good girls they are, every one of them – not that I'd say that Doris gets up when she should do in the morning. I have to speak about it at least once a week, and Vickie, she's inclined to be impertinent, but, there, with the young ones you can't expect the training – their mothers don't give it to them nowadays – but good girls they are, and no police superintendent shall make me say otherwise. "Yes," I said to him, "you needn't think I'm going to say anything against my girls. They're good girls, they are, and as to having anything to do with murder, why it's right-down wicked to suggest such a thing."'

Mrs Leckie paused.

'Mr Ellis, now – that's different. I don't know anything about Mr Ellis, and couldn't answer for him in any way, he having been brought from London, and strange to the place, while Mr Baker was on holiday.'

'Baker?' asked Mr Satterthwaite.

'Mr Baker had been Sir Bartholomew's butler for the last seven years, sir. He was in London most of the time, in Harley Street. You'll remember him, sir?' She appealed to Sir Charles, who nodded. 'Sir Bartholomew used to bring him up here when he had a party. But he hadn't been so well in his health, so Sir Bartholomew said, and he gave him a couple of months' holiday, paid for him, too, in a place near the sea down near Brighton – a real kind gentleman the doctor was – and he took Mr Ellis on temporary for the time being, and so, as I said to that superintendent, I can't say anything about Mr Ellis, though, from all he said himself, he seems to have been with the best families, and he certainly had a gentlemanly way with him.'

'You didn't find anything – unusual about him?' asked Sir Charles hopefully.

'Well, it's odd your saying that, sir, because, if you know what I mean, I did and I didn't.'

'Sir Charles looked encouraging, and Mrs Leckie went on:

'I couldn't exactly say what it was, sir, but there was *some*thing –'

There always is – after the event – thought Mr Satterthwaite to himself grimly. However much Mrs Leckie had despised the police, she was not proof against suggestion. If Ellis turned out to be the criminal, well, Mrs Leckie would have noticed *something*.

'For one thing, he was standoffish. Oh, quite polite, quite the gentleman – as I said, he'd been used to good houses. But he kept himself to himself, spent a lot of time in his own room; and he was – well, I don't know how to describe it, I'm sure – he was, well, there was *something* –'

'You didn't suspect he wasn't – not really a butler?' suggested Mr Satterthwaite.

'Oh, he'd been in service, right enough, sir. The things he knew – and about well-known people in society, too.'

'Such as?' suggested Sir Charles gently.

But Mrs Leckie became vague, and non-committal. She was not going to retail servants' hall gossip. Such a thing would have offended her sense of fitness.

To put her at her ease, Mr Satterthwaite said:

'Perhaps you can describe his appearance.'

Mrs Leckie brightened.

'Yes, indeed, sir. He was a very respectable-looking man – side-whiskers and grey hair, stooped a little, and he was growing stout – it worried him, that did. He had a rather shaky hand, too, but not from the cause you might imagine. He was a most abstemious man – not like many I've known. His eyes were a bit weak, I think, sir, the light hurt them – especially a bright light, used to make them water something cruel. Out with us he wore glasses, but not when he was on duty.'

'No special distinguishing marks?' asked Sir Charles. 'No scars? Or broken fingers? Or birth marks?'

'Oh, no, sir, nothing of that kind.'

'How superior detective stories are to life,' sighed Sir Charles. 'In fiction there is always some distinguishing characteristic.'

'He had a tooth missing,' said Mr Satterthwaite.

'I believe so, sir; I never noticed it myself.'

'What was his manner on the night of the tragedy?' asked Mr Satterthwaite in a slightly bookish manner.

'Well, really, sir, I couldn't say. I was busy, you see, in my kitchen. I hadn't time for noticing things.'

'No, no, quite so.'

'When the news came out that the master was dead we were struck all of a heap. I cried and couldn't stop, and so did Beatrice. The young ones, of course, were excited like, though very upset. Mr Ellis naturally wasn't so upset as we were, he being new, but he behaved very considerate, and insisted on Beatrice and me taking a little glass of port to counteract the shock. And to think that all the time it was he – the villain –'

Words failed Mrs Leckie, her eyes shone with indignation.

'He disappeared that night, I understand?'

'Yes, sir, went to his room like the rest of us, and in the morning he wasn't there. That's what set the police on him, of course.'

'Yes, yes, very foolish of him. Have you any idea how he left the house?'

'Not the slightest. It seems the police were watching the house all night, and they never saw him go – but, there, that's what the police are, human like anyone else, in spite of the airs they give themselves, coming into a gentleman's house and nosing round.'

'I hear there's some question of a secret passage,' Sir Charles said.

Mrs Leckie sniffed.

'That's what the police say.'

'Is there such a thing?'

'I've heard mention of it,' Mrs Leckie agreed cautiously.

'Do you know where it starts from?'

'No, I don't, sir. Secret passages are all very well, but they're not things to be encouraged in the servants' hall. It gives the girls ideas. They might think of slipping out that way. My girls go out by the back door and in by the back door, and then we know where we are.'

'Splendid, Mrs Leckie. I think you're very wise.'

Mrs Leckie bridled in the sun of Sir Charles's approval.

'I wonder,' he went on, 'if we might just ask a few questions of the other servants?'

'Of course, sir; but they can't tell you anything more than I can.'

'Oh, I know. I didn't mean so much about Ellis as about Sir Bartholomew himself – his manner that night, and so on. You see, he was a friend of mine.'

'I know, sir. I quite understand. There's Beatrice, and there's Alice. She waited at table, of course.'

'Yes, I'd like to see Alice.'

Mrs Leckie, however, had a belief in seniority. Beatrice Church, the upper-housemaid, was the first to appear.

She was a tall thin woman, with a pinched mouth, who looked aggressively respectable.

After a few unimportant questions, Sir Charles led the talk to the behaviour of the house-party on the fatal evening. Had they all been terribly upset? What had they said or done?

A little animation entered into Beatrice's manner. She had the usual ghoulish relish for tragedy.

'Miss Sutcliffe, she quite broke down. A very warm-hearted lady, she's stayed here before. I suggested bringing her a little drop of brandy, or a nice cup of tea, but she wouldn't hear of it. She took some aspirin, though. Said she was sure she couldn't sleep. But she was sleeping like a little child the next morning when I brought her her early tea.'

'And Mrs Dacres?'

'I don't think anything would upset that lady much.'

From Beatrice's tone, she had not liked Cynthia Dacres.

'Just anxious to get away, she was. Said her business would suffer. She's a big dressmaker in London, so Mr Ellis told us.'

A big dressmaker, to Beatrice, meant 'trade', and trade she looked down upon.

'And her husband?'

Beatrice sniffed.

'Steadied his nerves with brandy, he did. Or unsteadied them, some would say.'

'What about Lady Mary Lytton Gore?'

'A very nice lady,' said Beatrice, her tone softening. 'My great aunt was in service with her father at the Castle. A pretty young girl she was, so I've always heard. Poor she may be, but you can see she's someone – and so considerate, never giving trouble and always speaking so pleasant. Her daughter's a nice young lady, too. They didn't know Sir Bartholomew well, of course, but they were very distressed.'

'Miss Wills?'

Some of Beatrice's rigidity returned.

'I'm sure I couldn't say, sir, what Miss Wills thought about it.'

'Or what you thought about her?' asked Sir Charles. 'Come now, Beatrice, be human.'

An unexpected smile dinted Beatrice's wooden cheeks. There was something appealingly schoolboyish in Sir Charles's manner. She was not proof against the charm that nightly audiences had felt so strongly.

'Really, sir, I don't know what you want me to say.'

'Just what you thought and felt about Miss Wills.'

'Nothing, sir, nothing at all. She wasn't, of course –'

Beatrice hesitated.

'Go on, Beatrice.'

'Well, she wasn't quite the "class" of the others, sir. She couldn't help it, I know,' went on Beatrice kindly. 'But she did things a real lady wouldn't have done. She pried, if you know what I mean, sir, poked and pried about.'

Sir Charles tried hard to get this statement amplified, but Beatrice remained vague. Miss Wills had poked and pried, but asked to produce a special instance of the poking, Beatrice seemed unable to do so. She merely repeated that Miss Wills pried into things that were no business of hers.

They gave it up at last, and Mr Satterthwaite said:

'Young Mr Manders arrived unexpectedly, didn't he?'

'Yes, sir, he had an accident with his car – just by the lodge gates, it was. He said it was a bit of luck its happening just here. The house was full, of course, but Miss Lyndon had a bed made up for him in the little study.'

'Was everyone very surprised to see him?'

'Oh, yes, sir, naturally, sir.'

Asked her opinion of Ellis, Beatrice was non-committal. She'd seen very little of him. Going off the way he did looked bad, though why he should want to harm the master she couldn't imagine. Nobody could.

'What was he like, the doctor, I mean? Did he seem to be looking forward to the house-party? Had he anything on his mind?'

'He seemed particularly cheerful, sir. Smiled to himself, he did, as though he had some joke on. I even heard him make a joke with Mr Ellis, a thing he'd never done with Mr Baker. He was usually a bit brusque with the servants, kind always, but not speaking to them much.'

'What did he say?' asked Mr Satterthwaite eagerly.

'Well, I forget exactly now, sir. Mr Ellis had come up with a telephone message, and Sir Bartholomew asked him if he was sure he'd got the names right, and Mr Ellis said quite sure – speaking respectful, of course. And the doctor he laughed and said, "You're a good fellow, Ellis, a first-class butler. Eh, Beatrice, what do you think?" And I was so surprised, sir, at the master speaking like that – quite unlike his usual self – that I didn't know what to say.'

'And Ellis?'

'He looked kind of disapproving, sir, as though it was the kind of thing he hadn't been used to. Stiff like.'

'What was the telephone message?' asked Sir Charles.

'The message, sir? Oh, it was from the Sanatorium – about a patient who had arrived there and had stood the journey well.'

'Do you remember the name?'

'It was a queer name, sir.' Beatrice hesitated. 'Mrs de Rushbridger – something like that.'

'Ah, yes,' said Sir Charles soothingly. 'Not an easy name to get right on the telephone. Well, thank you very much, Beatrice. Perhaps we could see Alice now.'

When Beatrice had left the room Sir Charles and Mr Satter-thwaite compared notes by an interchange of glances.

'Miss Wills poked and pried, Captain Dacres got drunk, Mrs Dacres displayed no emotion. Anything there? Precious little.'

'Very little indeed,' agreed Mr Satterthwaite.

'Let's pin our hopes on Alice.'

Alice was a demure, dark-eyed young woman of thirty. She was only too pleased to talk.

She herself didn't believe Mr Ellis had anything to do with it. He was too much the gentleman. The police had suggested he was just a common crook. Alice was sure he was nothing of the sort.

'You're quite certain he was an ordinary honest-to-God butler?' asked Sir Charles.

'Not ordinary, sir. He wasn't like any butler I've ever worked with before. He arranged the work different.'

'But you don't think he poisoned your master.'

'Oh, sir, I don't see how he could have done. I was waiting at table with him, and he couldn't have put anything in the master's food without my seeing him.'

'And the drink?'

'He went round with the wine, sir. Sherry first, with the soup, and then hock and claret. But what could he have done, sir? If there'd been anything in the wine he'd have poisoned everybody – or all those who took it. It's not as though the master had anything that nobody else had. The same thing with the port. All the gentlemen had port, and some of the ladies.'

'The wine glasses were taken out on a tray?'

'Yes, sir, I held the tray and Mr Ellis put the glasses on it, and I carried the tray out to the pantry, and there they were, sir, when the police came to examine them. The port glasses were still on the table. And the police didn't find anything.'

'You're quite sure that the doctor didn't have anything to eat or drink at dinner that nobody else had?'

'Not that I saw, sir. In fact, I'm sure he didn't.'

'Nothing that one of the guests gave him –'

'Oh, no, sir.'

'Do you know anything about a secret passage, Alice?'

'One of the gardeners told me something about it. Comes out

in the wood where there's some old walls and things tumbled down. But I've never seen any opening to it in the house.'

'Ellis never said anything about it?'

'Oh, no, sir, he wouldn't know anything about it, I'm sure.'

'Who do you really think killed your master, Alice?'

'I don't know, sir. I can't believe anyone did . . . I feel it must have been some kind of accident.'

'H'm. Thank you, Alice.'

'If it wasn't for the death of Babbington,' said Sir Charles as the girl left the room, 'we could make her the criminal. She's a good-looking girl . . . And she waited at table . . . No, it won't do. Babbington was murdered; and anyway Tollie never noticed good-looking girls. He wasn't made that way.'

'But he was fifty-five,' said Mr Satterthwaite thoughtfully.

'Why do you say that?'

'It's the age a man loses his head badly about a girl – even if he hasn't done so before.'

'Dash it all, Satterthwaite, *I'm* – er – getting on for fifty-five.'

'I know,' said Satterthwaite.

And before his gentle twinkling gaze Sir Charles's eyes fell. Unmistakably he blushed . . .

CHAPTER 5

IN THE BUTLER'S ROOM

'How about an examination of Ellis's room?' asked Mr Satterthwaite, having enjoyed the spectacle of Sir Charles's blush to the full.

The actor seized at the diversion.

'Excellent, excellent. Just what I was about to suggest myself.'

'Of course the police have already searched it thoroughly.'

'The police –'

Aristide Duval waved the police away scornfully. Anxious to forget his momentary discomfiture, he flung himself with renewed vigour into his part.

'The police are blockheads,' he said sweepingly. 'What have they looked for in Ellis's room? Evidences of his guilt. We shall look for evidences of his innocence – an entirely different thing.'

'You're completely convinced of Ellis's innocence?'

'If we're right about Babbington, he *must* be innocent.'

'Yes, besides –'

Mr Satterthwaite did not finish his sentence. He had been about to say that if Ellis was a professional criminal who had been detected by Sir Bartholomew and had murdered him in consequence the whole affair would become unbearably dull. Just in time he remembered that Sir Bartholomew had been a friend of Sir Charles Cartwright's and was duly appalled by the callousness of the sentiments he had nearly revealed.

At first sight Ellis's room did not seem to offer much promise of discovery. The clothes in the drawers and hanging in the cupboard were all neatly arranged. They were well cut, and bore different tailors' marks. Clearly cast-offs given him in different situations. The underclothing was on the same scale. The boots were neatly polished and arranged on trees.

Mr Satterthwaite picked up a boot and murmured, 'Nines, just so, nines.' But, since there were no footprints in the case, that didn't seem to lead anywhere.

It seemed clear from its absence that Ellis had departed in his butler's kit, and Mr Satterthwaite pointed out to Sir Charles that that seemed rather a remarkable fact.

'Any man in his senses would have changed into an ordinary suit.'

'Yes, it's odd that . . . Looks almost, though that's absurd, as if he *hadn't* gone at all . . . Nonsense, of course.'

They continued their search. No letters, no papers, except a cutting from a newspaper regarding a cure for corns, and a paragraph relating to the approaching marriage of a duke's daughter.

There was a small blotting-book and a penny bottle of ink on a side table – no pen. Sir Charles held up the blotting-book to the mirror, but without result. One page of it was very much used – a meaningless jumble, and the ink looked to both men old.

'Either he hasn't written any letters since he was here, or he hasn't blotted them,' deduced Mr Satterthwaite. 'This is an old blotter. Ah, yes –' With some gratification he pointed to a barely decipherable 'L. Baker' amidst the jumble.

'I should say Ellis hadn't used this at all.'

'That's rather odd, isn't it?' said Sir Charles slowly.

'What do you mean?'

'Well, a man usually writes letters . . .'

'Not if he's a criminal.'

'No, perhaps you're right . . . There must have been something fishy about him to make him bolt as he did . . . All we say is that he didn't murder Tollie.'

They hunted round the floor, raising the carpet, looking under the bed. There was nothing anywhere, except a splash of ink beside the fireplace. The room was disappointingly bare.

They left it in a somewhat disconcerted fashion. Their zeal as detectives was momentarily damped.

Possibly the thought passed through their minds that things were arranged better in books.

They had a few words with the other members of the staff, scared-looking juniors in awe of Mrs Leckie and Beatrice Church, but they elicited nothing further.

Finally they took their leave.

'Well, Satterthwaite,' said Sir Charles as they strolled across the park (Mr Satterthwaite's car had been instructed to pick them up at the lodge) 'anything strike you – anything at all?'

Mr Satterthwaite thought. He was not to be hurried into an answer – especially as he felt something *ought* to have struck him. To confess that the whole expedition had been a waste of time was an unwelcome idea. He passed over in his mind the evidence of one servant after another – the information was extraordinarily meagre.

As Sir Charles had summed it up just now, Miss Wills had poked and pried, Miss Sutcliffe had been very upset, Mrs Dacres had not been upset at all, and Captain Dacres had got drunk. Very little there, unless Freddie Dacres's indulgence showed the deadening of a guilty conscience. But Freddie Dacres, Mr Satterthwaite knew, quite frequently got drunk.

'Well?' repeated Sir Charles impatiently.

'Nothing,' confessed Mr Satterthwaite reluctantly. 'Except – well, I think we are entitled to assume from the clipping we found that Ellis suffered from corns.'

Sir Charles gave a wry smile.

'That seems quite a reasonable deduction. Does it – er – get us anywhere?'

Mr Satterthwaite confessed that it did not.

'The only other thing—' he said and then stopped.

'Yes? Go on, man. Anything may help.'

'It struck me as a little odd the way that Sir Bartholomew chaffed his butler – you know what the housemaid told us. It seems somehow uncharacteristic.'

'It *was* uncharacteristic,' said Sir Charles with emphasis. 'I knew Tollie well – better than you did – and I can tell you that he wasn't a facetious sort of man. He'd never have spoken like that unless – well, unless for some reason he wasn't quite normal at the time. You're right, Satterthwaite, that is a point. Now where does it get us?'

'Well,' began Mr Satterthwaite; but it was clear that Sir Charles's question had been merely a rhetorical one. He was anxious, not to hear Mr Satterthwaite's views, but to air his own.

'You remember when that incident occurred, Satterthwaite? *Just after Ellis had brought him a telephone message.* I think it's a fair deduction to assume that it was that telephone message which was the cause of Tollie's sudden unusual hilarity. You may remember I asked the housemaid woman what that message had been.'

Mr Satterthwaite nodded.

'It was to say that a woman named Mrs de Rushbridger had arrived at the Sanatorium,' he said, to show that he, too, had paid attention to the point. 'It doesn't sound particularly thrilling.'

'It doesn't sound so, certainly. But, if our reasoning is correct, *there must be some significance in that message.*'

'Ye-es,' said Mr Satterthwaite doubtfully.

'Indubitably,' said Sir Charles. 'We've got to find out what that significance was. It just crosses my mind that it may have been a code message of some kind – a harmless sounding natural thing, but which really meant something entirely different. If Tollie had been making inquiries into Babbington's death, this may have had something to do with those inquiries. Say, even, that he employed a private detective to find out a certain fact. He may have told him in the event of this particular suspicion being justified to ring up and use that particular phrase which would convey no hint of the truth to anyone taking it. That would explain his jubilation, it might explain his asking Ellis if he was sure of the name – he himself knowing well there was no such person, really. In fact, the slight lack of balance a person shows when they have brought off what can be described as a long shot.'

'You think there's no such person as Mrs de Rushbridger?'

'Well, I think we ought to find out for certain.'

'How?'

'We might run along to the Sanatorium now and ask the Matron.'

'She may think it rather odd.'

Sir Charles laughed.

'You leave it to me,' he said.

They turned aside from the drive and walked in the direction of the Sanatorium.

Mr Satterthwaite said:

'What about you, Cartwright? Does anything strike you at all? Arising out of our visit to the house, I mean.'

Sir Charles answered slowly.

'Yes, there is something – the devil of it is, I can't remember what.'

Mr Satterthwaite stared at him in surprise. The other frowned.

'How can I explain? There was something – something which at the moment struck me as wrong – as unlikely – only – I hadn't the time to think about it then. I put it aside in my own mind.'

'And now you can't remember what it was?'

'No – only that at some moment I said to myself, "That's odd."'

'Was it when we were questioning the servants? Which servant?'

'I tell you I can't remember. And the more I think the less I shall remember . . . If I leave it alone, it may come back to me.'

They came into view of the Sanatorium, a big white modern building, divided from the park by palings. There was a gate through which they passed, and they rang the front-door bell and asked for the Matron.

The Matron, when she came, was a tall, middle-aged woman,

with an intelligent face and a capable manner. Sir Charles she clearly knew by name as a friend of the late Sir Bartholomew Strange.

Sir Charles explained that he had just come back from abroad, had been horrified to hear of his friend's death and of the terrible suspicions entertained, and had been up to the house to learn as many details as he could. The Matron spoke in moving terms of the loss Sir Bartholomew would be to them, and of his fine career as a doctor. Sir Charles professed himself anxious to know what was going to happen to the Sanatorium. The Matron explained that Sir Bartholomew had had two partners, both capable doctors, one was in residence at the Sanatorium.

'Bartholomew was very proud of this place, I know,' said Sir Charles.

'Yes, his treatments were a great success.'

'Mostly nerve cases, isn't it?'

'Yes.'

'That reminds me – fellow I met out at Monte had some kind of relation coming here. I forget her name now – odd sort of name – Rushbridger – Rusbrigger – something like that.'

'Mrs de Rushbridger, you mean?'

'That's it. Is she here now?'

'Oh, yes. But I'm afraid she won't be able to see you – not for some time yet. She's having a very strict rest cure.' The Matron smiled just a trifle archly. 'No letters, no exciting visitors . . .'

'I say, she's not very bad, is she?'

'Rather a bad nervous breakdown – lapses of memory, and severe nervous exhaustion. Oh, we shall get her right in time.'

The Matron smiled reassuringly.

'Let me see, haven't I heard Tollie – Sir Bartholomew – speak of her? She was a friend of his as well as a patient, wasn't she?'

'I don't think so, Sir Charles. At least the doctor never said so. She has recently arrived from the West Indies – really, it was very funny, I must tell you. Rather a difficult name for a servant to remember – the parlourmaid here is rather stupid. She came and said to me, "Mrs West India has come," and of course I suppose Rushbridger *does* sound rather like West India – but it was rather a coincidence her having just come from the West Indies.'

'Rather – rather – most amusing. Her husband over, too?'

'He's still out there.'

'Ah, quite – quite. I must be mixing her up with someone else. It was a case the doctor was specially interested in?'

'Cases of amnesia are fairly common, but they're always interesting to a medical man – the variations, you know. Two cases are seldom alike.'

'Seems all very odd to me. Well, thank you, Matron, I'm glad to have had a little chat with you. I know how much Tollie thought of you. He often spoke about you,' finished Sir Charles mendaciously.

'Oh, I'm glad to hear that.' The Matron flushed and bridled. 'Such a splendid man – such a loss to us all. We were absolutely shocked – well, stunned would describe it better. Murder! Who ever would murder Dr Strange, I said. It's incredible. That awful butler. I hope the police catch him. And no motive or anything.'

Sir Charles shook his head sadly and they took their departure, going round by the road to the spot where the car awaited them.

In revenge for his enforced quiescence during the interview with the Matron, Mr Satterthwaite displayed a lively interest in the scene of Oliver Manders' accident, plying the lodge keeper, a slow-witted man of middle age, with questions.

Yes, that was the place, where the wall was broken away. On a motor cycle the young gentleman was. No, he didn't see it happen. He heard it, though, and come out to see. The young gentleman was standing there – just where the other gentleman was standing now. He didn't seem to be hurt. Just looking rueful-like at his bike – and a proper mess that was. Just asked what the name of the place might be, and when he heard it was Sir Bartholomew Strange's he said, 'That's a piece of luck,' and went on up to the house. A very calm young gentleman he seemed to be – tired like. How he come to have such an accident, the lodge keeper couldn't see, but he supposed them things went wrong sometimes.

'It was an odd accident,' said Mr Satterthwaite thoughtfully.

He looked at the wide straight road. No bends, no dangerous crossroads, nothing to cause a motor cyclist to swerve suddenly into a ten-foot wall. Yes, an odd accident.

'What's in your mind, Satterthwaite?' asked Sir Charles curiously.

'Nothing,' said Mr Satterthwaite, 'nothing.'

'It's odd, certainly,' said Sir Charles, and he, too, stared at the scene of the accident in a puzzled manner.

They got into the car and drove off.

Mr Satterthwaite was busy with his thoughts. Mrs de Rushbridger – Cartwright's theory wouldn't work – it wasn't a code message – there *was* such a person. But could there be something about the woman herself? Was she perhaps a witness of some kind, or was it just because she was an interesting case that Bartholomew Strange had displayed this unusual elation? Was she, perhaps, an attractive woman? To fall in love at the age of fifty-five did (Mr Satterthwaite had observed it many a time) change a man's character completely. It might, perhaps, make him facetious, where before he had been aloof –

His thoughts were interrupted. Sir Charles leant forward.

'Satterthwaite,' he said, 'do you mind if we turn back?'

'Without waiting for a reply, he took up the speaking tube and gave the order. The car slowed down, stopped, and the chauffeur began to reverse into a convenient lane. A minute or two later they were bowling along the road in the opposite direction.

'What is it?' asked Mr Satterthwaite.

'I've remembered,' said Sir Charles, 'what struck me as odd. It was the ink-stain on the floor in the butler's room.'

CHAPTER 6
CONCERNING AN INK-STAIN

Mr Satterthwaite stared at his friend in surprise.

'The ink-stain?' What do you mean, Cartwright?'

'You remember it?'

'I remember there was an ink-stain, yes.'

'You remember its position?'

'Well – not exactly.'

'It was close to the skirting board near the fireplace.'

'Yes, so it was. I remember now.'

'How do you think that stain was caused, Satterthwaite?'

'It wasn't a big stain,' he said at last. 'It couldn't have been an upset ink-bottle. I should say in all probability that the man dropped his fountain pen there – there was no pen in the room, you remember.' (He shall see I notice things just as much as he does, thought Mr Satterthwaite.) 'So it seems clear the man must have had a fountain pen if he ever wrote at all – and there's no evidence that he ever did.'

'Yes, there is, Satterthwaite. There's the ink-stain.'

'He mayn't have been writing,' snapped Satterthwaite. 'He may have just dropped the pen on the floor.'

'But there wouldn't have been a stain unless the top had been off the pen.'

'I daresay you're right,' said Mr Satterthwaite. 'But I can't see what's odd about it.'

'Perhaps there isn't anything odd,' said Sir Charles. 'I can't tell till I get back and see for myself.'

They were turning in at the lodge gates. A few minutes later they had arrived at the house and Sir Charles was allaying the curiosity caused by his return by inventing a pencil left behind in the butler's room.

'And now,' said Sir Charles, shutting the door of Ellis's room behind them, having with some skill shaken off the helpful Mrs Leckie, 'let's see if I'm making an infernal fool of myself, or whether there's anything in my idea.'

In Mr Satterthwaite's opinion the former alternative was by far the more probable, but he was much too polite to say so. He sat down on the bed and watched the other.

'Here's our stain,' said Sir Charles, indicating the mark with his foot. 'Right up against the skirting board at the opposite side of the room to the writing-table. Under what circumstances would a man drop a pen just there?'

'You can drop a pen anywhere,' said Mr Satterthwaite.

'You can hurl it across the room, of course,' agreed Sir Charles. 'But one doesn't usually treat one's pen like that. I don't know, though. Fountain pens are damned annoying things. Dry up and refuse to write just when you want them to. Perhaps that's the solution of the matter. Ellis lost his temper, said, "Damn the thing," and hurled it across the room.'

'I think there are plenty of explanations,' said Mr Satterthwaite.

'He may have simply laid the pen on the mantelpiece and it rolled off.'

Sir Charles experimented with a pencil. He allowed it to roll off the corner of the mantelpiece. The pencil struck the ground at least a foot from the mark and rolled inwards towards the gas fire.

'Well,' said Mr Satterthwaite. 'What's your explanation?'

'I'm trying to find one.'

From his seat on the bed Mr Satterthwaite now witnessed a thoroughly amusing performance.

Sir Charles tried dropping the pencil from his hand as he walked in the direction of the fireplace. He tried sitting on the edge of the bed and writing there and then dropping the pencil. To get the pencil to fall on the right spot it was necessary to stand or sit jammed up against the wall in a most unconvincing attitude.

'That's impossible,' said Sir Charles aloud. He stood considering the wall, the stain and the prim little gas fire.

'If he were burning papers, now,' he said thoughtfully. 'But one doesn't burn papers in a gas fire –'

Suddenly he drew in his breath.

A minute later Mr Satterthwaite was realizing Sir Charles's profession to the full.

Charles Cartwright had become Ellis the butler. He sat writing at the writing-table. He looked furtive, every now and then he raised his eyes, shooting them shiftily from side to side. Suddenly he seemed to hear something – Mr Satterthwaite could even guess what that something was – footsteps along the passage. The man had a guilty conscience. He attached a certain meaning to those footsteps. He sprang up, the paper on which he had been writing in one hand, his pen in the other. He darted across the room to the fireplace, his head half turned, still alert – listening – afraid. He tried to shove the papers under the gas fire – in order to use both hands he cast down the pen impatiently. Sir Charles's pencil, the 'pen' of the drama, fell accurately on the ink-stain . . .

'Bravo,' said Mr Satterthwaite, applauding generously.

So good had the performance been that he was left with the impression that so and only so could Ellis have acted.

'You see?' said Sir Charles, resuming his own personality and speaking with modest elation. 'If the fellow heard the police or what he thought was the police coming and had to hide what he was writing – well, where could he hide it? Not in a drawer or under the mattress – if the police searched the room, that would be found at once. He hadn't time to take up a floor board. No, behind the gas fire was the only chance.'

'The next thing to do,' said Mr Satterthwaite, 'is to see whether there *is* anything hidden behind the gas fire.'

'Exactly. Of course, it may have been a false alarm, and he may have got the things out again later. But we'll hope for the best.'

'Removing his coat and turning up his shirt sleeves, Sir Charles lay down on the floor and applied his eye to the crack under the gas fire.

'There's something under there,' he reported. 'Something white. How can we get it out? We want something like a woman's hatpins.'

'Women don't have hatpins any more,' said Mr Satterthwaite sadly. 'Perhaps a penknife.'

But a penknife proved unavailing.

In the end Mr Satterthwaite went out and borrowed a knitting needle from Beatrice. Though extremely curious to know what he wanted it for, her sense of decorum was too great to permit her to ask.

The knitting needle did the trick. Sir Charles extracted half a dozen sheets of crumpled writing-paper, hastily crushed together and pushed in.

With growing excitement he and Mr Satterthwaite smoothed them out. They were clearly several different drafts of a letter – written in a small, neat clerkly handwriting.

> *This is to say* (began the first) *that the writer of this does not wish to cause unpleasantness, and may possibly have been mistaken in what he thought he saw tonight, but –*

Here the writer had clearly been dissatisfied, and had broken off to start afresh.

> *John Ellis, butler, presents his compliments, and would be glad of*

*a short interview touching the tragedy tonight before going to the
police with certain information in his possession –*

Still dissatisfied, the man had tried again.

*John Ellis, butler, has certain facts concerning the death of the doctor
in his possession. He has not yet given these facts to the police –*

In the next one the use of the third person had been abandoned.

*I am badly in need of money. A thousand pounds would make all
the difference to me. There are certain things I could tell the police,
but do not want to make trouble –*

The last one was even more unreserved.

*I know how the doctor died. I haven't said anything to the police
– yet. If you will meet me –*

This letter broke off in a different way – after the 'me' the
pen had tailed off in a scrawl, and the last five words were all
blurred and blotchy. Clearly it was when writing this that Ellis
had heard something that alarmed him. He had crumpled up
the papers and dashed to conceal them.

Mr Satterthwaite drew a deep breath.

'I congratulate you, Cartwright,' he said. 'Your instinct about
that ink-stain was right. Good work. Now let's see exactly where
we stand.'

He paused a minute.

'Ellis, as we thought, is a scoundrel. He wasn't the murderer,
but he knew who the murderer was, and he was preparing to
blackmail him or her –'

'Him or her,' interrupted Sir Charles. 'Annoying we don't know
which. Why couldn't the fellow begin one of his effusions Sir or
Madam, then we'd know where we are. Ellis seems to have been
an artistic sort of fellow. He was taking a lot of trouble over his

blackmailing letter. If only he'd given us one clue – as to whom that letter was addressed.'

'Never mind,' said Mr Satterthwaite. 'We are getting on. You remember you said that what we wanted to find in this room was a proof of Ellis's innocence. Well, we've found it. These letters show that he was innocent – of the murder, I mean. He was a thorough-paced scoundrel in other ways. But he didn't murder Sir Bartholomew Strange. Somebody else did that. Someone who murdered Babbington also. I think even the police will have to come round to our view now.'

'You're going to tell them about this?'

Sir Charles's voice expressed dissatisfaction.

'I don't see that we can do otherwise. Why?'

'Well –' Sir Charles sat down on the bed. His brow furrowed itself in thought. 'How can I put it best? At the moment we know something that nobody else does. The police are looking for Ellis. They think he's the murderer. Everyone knows that they think he's the murderer. So the real criminal must be feeling pretty good. He (or she) will be not exactly off his or her guard, but feeling – well, comfortable. Isn't it a pity to upset that state of things? Isn't that just our chance? I mean our chance of finding a connection between Babbington and one of these people. They don't know that anyone has connected this death with Babbington's death. They'll be unsuspicious. It's a chance in a hundred.'

'I see what you mean,' said Mr Satterthwaite. 'And I agree with you. It is a chance. But, all the same, I don't think we can take it. It is our duty as citizens to report this discovery of ours to the police at once. We have no right to withhold it from them.'

Sir Charles looked at him quizzically.

'You're the pattern of a good citizen, Satterthwaite. I've no doubt the orthodox thing must be done – but I'm not nearly such a good citizen as you are. I should have no scruples in keeping this find to myself for a day or two – only a day or two – eh? No? Well, I give in. Let us be pillars of law and order.'

'You see,' explained Mr Satterthwaite, 'Johnson is a friend of mine, and he was very decent about it all – let us into all the police were doing – gave us full information, and all that.'

'Oh, you're right,' sighed Sir Charles. 'Quite right. Only, after all, no one but me thought of looking under that gas stove. The idea never occurred to one of those thick-headed policemen . . . But have it your own way. I say, Satterthwaite, where do you think Ellis is now?'

'I presume,' said Mr Satterthwaite, 'that he got what he wanted. He was paid to disappear, and he did disappear – most effectually.'

'Yes,' said Sir Charles. 'I suppose that is the explanation.'

He gave a slight shiver.

'I don't like this room, Satterthwaite. Come out of it.'

CHAPTER 7
PLAN OF CAMPAIGN

Sir Charles and Mr Satterthwaite arrived back in London the following evening.

The interview with Colonel Johnson had had to be very tactfully conducted. Superintendent Crossfield had not been too pleased that mere 'gentlemen' should have found what he and his assistants had missed. He was at some pains to save his face.

'Very creditable, indeed, sir. I confess I never thought of looking under the gas fire. As a matter of fact, it beats me what set you looking there.'

The two men had not gone into a detailed account of how theorizing from an ink-blot had led to the discovery. 'Just nosing around,' was how Sir Charles had put it.

'Still, look you did,' continued the Superintendent, 'and were justified. Not that what you've found is much surprise to me. You see, it stands to reason that if Ellis wasn't the murderer, he must have disappeared for some reason or other, and it's been in the back of my mind all along that blackmail might have been his line of business.'

One thing did arise from their discovery. Colonel Johnson was going to communicate with the Loomouth police. The death of Stephen Babbington ought certainly to be investigated.

'And if they find he died from nicotine poisoning, even Crossfield will admit the two deaths are connected,' said Sir Charles when they were speeding towards London.

He was still a little disgruntled at having had to hand over his discovery to the police.

Mr Satterthwaite had soothed him by pointing out that the information was not to be made public or given to the press.

'The guilty person will have no misgivings. The search for Ellis will still be continued.'

Sir Charles admitted that that was true.

On arrival in London, he explained to Mr Satterthwaite, he proposed to get in touch with Egg Lytton Gore. Her letter had been written from an address in Belgrave Square. He hoped that she might still be there.

Mr Satterthwaite gravely approved this course. He himself was anxious to see Egg. It was arranged that Sir Charles should ring her up as soon as they reached London.

Egg proved to be still in town. She and her mother were staying with relatives and were not returning to Loomouth for about a week. Egg was easily prevailed upon to come out and dine with the two men.

'She can't come here very well, I suppose,' said Sir Charles, looking round his luxurious flat. 'Her mother mightn't like it, eh? Of course we could have Miss Milray, too – but I'd rather not. To tell the truth, Miss Milray cramps my style a bit. She's so efficient that she gives me an inferiority complex.'

Mr Satterthwaite suggested his house. In the end it was arranged to dine at the Berkeley. Afterwards, if Egg liked, they could adjourn elsewhere.

Mr Satterthwaite noticed at once that the girl was looking thinner. Her eyes seemed larger and more feverish, her chin more decided. She was pale and had circles under her eyes. But her charm was as great as ever, her childish eagerness just as intense.

She said to Sir Charles, 'I knew you'd come . . .'

Her tone implied: 'Now that you've come everything will be all right . . .'

Mr Satterthwaite thought to himself: 'But she wasn't sure he'd come – she wasn't sure at all. She's been on tenterhooks. She's been fretting herself to death.' And he thought: 'Doesn't the man realize? Actors are usually vain enough . . . Doesn't he know the girl's head over ears in love with him?'

It was, he thought, an odd situation. That Sir Charles was overwhelmingly in love with the girl, he had no doubt whatever. She was equally in love with him. And the link between them – the link to which each of them clung frenziedly – was a crime – a double crime of a revolting nature.

During dinner little was said. Sir Charles talked about his experiences abroad. Egg talked about Loomouth. Mr Satterthwaite encouraged them both whenever the conversation seemed likely to flag. When dinner was over they went to Mr Satterthwaite's house.

Mr Satterthwaite's house was on Chelsea Embankment. It was a large house, and contained many beautiful works of art. There were pictures, sculpture, Chinese porcelain, prehistoric pottery, ivories, miniatures and much genuine Chippendale and Hepplewhite furniture. It had an atmosphere about it of mellowness and understanding.

Egg Lytton Gore saw nothing, noticed nothing. She flung off her evening coat on to a chair and said:

'At last. Now tell me all about it.'

She listened with vivid interest whilst Sir Charles narrated their adventures in Yorkshire, drawing in her breath sharply when he described the discovery of the blackmailing letters.

'What happened after that we can only conjecture,' finished Sir Charles. 'Presumably Ellis was paid to hold his tongue and his escape was facilitated.'

But Egg shook her head.

'Oh, no,' she said. 'Don't you see? *Ellis is dead.*'

Both men were startled, but Egg reiterated her assertion.

'Of course he's dead. That's why he's disappeared so successfully that no one can find a trace of him. He knew too much, and so he was killed. Ellis is the third murder.'

Although neither of the two men had considered the possibility before, they were forced to admit that it did not entirely ring false.

'But look here, my dear girl,' argued Sir Charles, 'it's all very well to say Ellis is dead. Where's the body? There's twelve stone or so of solid butler to be accounted for.'

'I don't know where the body is,' said Egg. 'There must be lots of places.'

'Hardly,' murmured Mr Satterthwaite. 'Hardly . . .'

'Lots,' reiterated Egg. 'Let me see . . .' She paused for a moment. 'Attics, there are masses of attics that no one ever goes into. He's probably in a trunk in the attic.'

'Rather unlikely,' said Sir Charles. 'But possible, of course. It might evade discovery – for – er – a time.'

It was not Egg's way to avoid unpleasantness. She dealt immediately with the point in Sir Charles's mind.

'Smell goes up, not down. You'd notice a decaying body in the cellar much sooner than in the attic. And, anyway, for a long time people would think it was a dead rat.'

'If your theory were correct, it would point definitely to a man as the murderer. A woman couldn't drag a body round the house. In fact, it would be a pretty good feat for a man.'

'Well, there are other possibilities. There's a secret passage there, you know. Miss Sutcliffe told me so, and Sir Bartholomew told me he would show it to me. The murderer might have given Ellis the money and shown him the way to get out of the house – gone down the passage with him and killed him there. A woman could do that. She could stab him, or something, from behind. Then she'd just leave the body there and go back, and no one would ever know.'

Sir Charles shook his head doubtfully, but he no longer disputed Egg's theory.

Mr Satterthwaite felt sure that the same suspicion had come to him for a moment in Ellis's room when they had found the letters. He remembered Sir Charles's little shiver. The idea that Ellis might be dead had come to him then . . .

Mr Satterthwaite thought: 'If Ellis is dead, then we're dealing with a very dangerous person . . . Yes, a very dangerous person . . .' And suddenly he felt a cold chill of fear down his spine . . .

A person who had killed three times wouldn't hesitate to kill again . . .

They were in danger, all three of them – Sir Charles, and Egg, and he . . .

If they found out too much . . .

He was recalled by the sound of Sir Charles's voice.

'There's one thing I didn't understand in your letter, Egg.

You spoke of Oliver Manders being in danger – of the police suspecting him. I can't see that they attach the least suspicion to him.'

It seemed to Mr Satterthwaite that Egg was very slightly discomposed. He even fancied that she blushed.

'Aha,' said Mr Satterthwaite to himself. 'Let's see how you get out of this, young lady.'

'It was silly of me,' said Egg. 'I got confused. I thought that Oliver arriving as he did, with what might have been a trumped-up excuse – well, I thought the police were sure to suspect him.'

Sir Charles accepted the explanation easily enough.

'Yes,' he said. 'I see.'

Mr Satterthwaite spoke.

'Was it a trumped-up excuse?' he said.

Egg turned on him.

'What do you mean?'

'It was an odd sort of accident,' said Mr Satterthwaite. 'I thought if it was a trumped-up excuse you might know.'

Egg shook her head.

'I don't know. I never thought about it. But why should Oliver pretend to have an accident if he didn't?'

'He might have had reasons,' said Sir Charles. 'Quite natural ones.'

He was smiling at her. Egg blushed crimson.

'Oh, no,' she said. '*No*.'

Sir Charles sighed. It occurred to Mr Satterthwaite that his friend had interpreted that blush quite wrongly. Sir Charles seemed a sadder and older man when he spoke again.

'Well,' he said, 'if our young friend is in no danger, where do I come in?'

Egg came forward quickly and caught him by the coat sleeve.

'You're not going away again. You're not going to give up? You're going to find out the truth – *the truth*. I don't believe anybody but you could find out the truth. You can. You will.'

She was tremendously in earnest. The waves of her vitality seemed to surge and eddy in the old-world air of the room.

'You believe in me?' said Sir Charles. He was moved.

'Yes, yes, yes. We're going to get at the truth. You and I together.'

'And Satterthwaite.'

'Of course, and Mr Satterthwaite,' said Egg without interest.

Mr Satterthwaite smiled covertly. Whether Egg wanted to include him or not, he had no intention of being left out. He was fond of mysteries, and he liked observing human nature, and he had a soft spot for lovers. All three tastes seemed likely to be gratified in this affair.

Sir Charles sat down. His voice changed. He was in command, directing a production.

'First of all we've got to clarify the situation. Do we, or do we not, believe that the same person killed Babbington and Bartholomew Strange?'

'Yes,' said Egg.

'Yes,' said Mr Satterthwaite.

'Do we believe that the second murder sprang directly from the first? I mean, do we believe that Bartholomew Strange was killed in order to prevent his revealing the facts of the first murder, or his suspicion about it?'

'Yes,' said Egg and Mr Satterthwaite again, but in unison this time.

'Then it is the *first* murder we must investigate, not the second –'

Egg nodded.

'In my mind, until we discover the *motive* for the first murder, we can hardly hope to discover the murderer. The motive presents extraordinary difficulty. Babbington was a harmless, pleasant, gentle old man without, one would say, an enemy in the world. Yet he was killed – and there must have been some *reason* for the killing. We've got to find that reason.'

He paused and then said in his ordinary everyday voice:

'Let's get down to it. What reasons are there for killing people? First, I suppose, gain.'

'Revenge,' said Egg.

'Homicidal mania,' said Mr Satterthwaite. 'The *crime passionel* would hardly apply in this case. But there's fear.'

Charles Cartwright nodded. He was scribbling on a piece of paper.

'That about covers the ground,' he said. 'First, *Gain*. Does anyone gain by Babbington's death? Has he any money – or expectation of money?'

'I should think it very unlikely,' said Egg.

'So should I, but we'd better approach Mrs Babbington on the point.'

'Then there's revenge. Did Babbington do any injury to anyone – perhaps in his young days? Did he marry the girl that some other man wanted? We'll have to look into that, too.'

'Then homicidal mania. Were both Babbington and Tollie killed by a lunatic? I don't think that theory will hold water. Even a lunatic has some kind of reasonableness in his crimes. I mean a lunatic might think himself divinely appointed to kill doctors, or to kill clergymen, but not to kill both. I think we can wash out the theory of homicidal mania. There remains *fear*.

'Now, frankly, that seems to me far the most likely solution. Babbington knew something about somebody – or he recognized somebody. He was killed to prevent him telling what that something was.'

'I can't see what someone like Mr Babbington could know that was damaging about anybody who was there that night.'

'Perhaps,' said Sir Charles, 'it was something that he didn't know that he knew.'

He went on, trying to make his meaning clear.

'It's difficult to say just what I mean. Suppose, for instance (this is only an instance) that Babbington saw a certain person in a certain place at a certain time. As far as he knows, there's no reason why that person shouldn't be there. But suppose also that that person had concocted a very clever alibi for some reason showing that at that particular time he was somewhere else a hundred miles away. Well, at any minute old Babbington, in the most innocent way in the world, might give the show away.'

'*I* see,' said Egg. 'Say there's a murder committed in London, and Babbington sees the man who did it at Paddington Station, but the man has proved that he didn't do it by having an alibi showing that he was at Leeds at the time. Then Babbington might give the whole show away.'

'That's what I mean exactly. Of course that's only an instance. It might be anything. Someone he saw that evening whom he'd known under a different name –'

'It might be something to do with a marriage,' said Egg. 'Clergymen do lots of marriages. Somebody who'd committed bigamy.'

'Or it might have to do with a birth or a death,' suggested Mr Satterthwaite.

'It's a very wide field,' said Egg, frowning. 'We'll have to get at it the other way. Work back from the people who were there. Let's make a list. Who was at your house, and who was at Sir Bartholomew's.'

She took the paper and pencil from Sir Charles.

'The Dacres, they were at both. That woman like a wilted cabbage, what's her name – Wills. Miss Sutcliffe.'

'You can leave Angela out of it,' said Sir Charles. 'I've known her for years.'

Egg frowned mutinously.

'We can't do that sort of thing,' she said. 'Leave people out because we know them. We've got to be business-like. Besides, I don't know anything about Angela Sutcliffe. She's just as likely to have done it as anyone else, so far as I can see – more likely. All actresses have pasts. I think, on the whole, she's the most likely person.'

She gazed defiantly at Sir Charles. There was an answering spark in his eyes.

'In that case we mustn't leave out Oliver Manders.'

'How could it be Oliver? He'd met Mr Babbington ever so many times before.'

'He was at both places, and his arrival is a little – open to suspicion.'

'Very well,' said Egg. She paused, and then added: 'In that case I'd better put down Mother and myself as well . . . That makes six suspects.'

'I don't think –'

'We'll do it properly, or not at all.' Her eyes flashed.

Mr Satterthwaite made peace by offering refreshment. He rang for drinks.

Sir Charles strolled off into a far corner to admire a head of Negro sculpture. Egg came over to Mr Satterthwaite and slipped a hand through his arm.

'Stupid of me to have lost my temper,' she murmured. 'I *am* stupid – but why should the woman be excepted? Why is he so keen she should be? Oh, dear, why the devil am I so disgustingly jealous?'

Mr Satterthwaite smiled and patted her hand.

'Jealousy never pays, my dear,' he said. 'If you feel jealous, don't show it. By the way, did you really think young Manders might be suspected?'

Egg grinned – a friendly childish grin.

'Of course not. I put that in so as not to alarm the man.' She turned her head. Sir Charles was still moodily studying Negro sculpture. 'You know – I didn't want him to think I really have a pash for Oliver – because I haven't. How difficult everything is! He's gone back now to his "Bless you, my children," attitude. I don't want that at all.'

'Have patience,' counselled Mr Satterthwaite. 'Everything comes right in the end, you know.'

'I'm not patient,' said Egg. 'I want to have things at once, or even quicker.'

Mr Satterthwaite laughed, and Sir Charles turned and came towards them.

As they sipped their drinks, they arranged a plan of campaign. Sir Charles should return to Crow's Nest, for which he had not yet found a purchaser. Egg and her mother would return to Rose Cottage rather sooner than they had meant to do. Mrs Babbington was still living in Loomouth. They would get what information they could from her and then proceed to act upon it.

'We'll succeed,' said Egg. 'I know we'll succeed.'

She leaned forward to Sir Charles, her eyes glowing. She held out her glass to touch his.

'Drink to our success,' she commanded.

Slowly, very slowly, his eyes fixed on hers, he raised his glass to his lips.

'To success,' he said, 'and to the Future . . .'

THIRD ACT • DISCOVERY

CHAPTER I
MRS BABBINGTON

Mrs Babbington had moved into a small fisherman's cottage not far from the harbour. She was expecting a sister home from Japan in about six months. Until her sister arrived she was making no plans for the future. The cottage chanced to be vacant, and she took it for six months. She felt too bewildered by her sudden loss to move away from Loomouth. Stephen Babbington had held the living of St Petroch, Loomouth, for seventeen years. They had been, on the whole, seventeen happy and peaceful years, in spite of the sorrow occasioned by the death of her son Robin. Of her remaining children, Edward was in Ceylon, Lloyd was in South Africa, and Stephen was third officer on the *Angolia*. They wrote frequently and affectionately, but they could offer neither a home nor companionship to their mother.

Margaret Babbington was very lonely . . .

Not that she allowed herself much time for thinking. She was still active in the parish – the new vicar was unmarried, and she spent a good deal of time working in the tiny plot of ground in front of the cottage. She was a woman whose flowers were part of her life.

She was working there one afternoon when she heard the latch of the gate click, and looked up to see Sir Charles Cartwright and Egg Lytton Gore.

Margaret was not surprised to see Egg. She knew that the girl and her mother were due to return shortly. But she was surprised to see Sir Charles. Rumour had insisted that he had left the neighbourhood for good. There had been paragraphs copied from other papers about his doings in the South of France. There had been a board 'TO BE SOLD' stuck up in the garden of Crow's Nest. No one had expected Sir Charles to return. Yet return he had.

Mrs Babbington shook the untidy hair back from her hot forehead and looked ruefully at her earth-stained hands.

'I'm not fit to shake hands,' she said. 'I ought to garden in gloves, I know. I do start in them sometimes; but I always tear them off sooner or later. One can feel things so much better with bare hands.'

She led the way into the house. The tiny sitting-room had been made cosy with chintz. There were photographs and bowls of chrysanthemums.

'It's a great surprise seeing you, Sir Charles. I thought you had given up Crow's Nest for good.'

'I thought I had,' said the actor frankly. 'But sometimes, Mrs Babbington, our destiny is too strong for us.'

Mrs Babbington did not reply. She turned towards Egg, but the girl forestalled the words on her lips.

'Look here, Mrs Babbington. This isn't just a call. Sir Charles and I have got something very serious to say. Only – I – I should hate to upset you.'

Mrs Babbington looked from the girl to Sir Charles. Her face had gone rather grey and pinched.

'First of all,' said Sir Charles, 'I would like to ask you if you have had any communication from the Home Office?'

Mrs Babbington bowed her head.

'I see – well, perhaps that makes what we are about to say easier.'

'Is that what you have come about – this exhumation order?'

'Yes. Is it – I'm afraid it must be – very distressing to you.'

She softened to the sympathy in his voice.

'Perhaps I do not mind as much as you think. To some people the idea of exhumation is very dreadful – not to me. It is not the dead clay that matters. My dear husband is elsewhere – at peace – where no one can trouble his rest. No, it is not that. It is the idea that is a shock to me – the idea, a terrible one, that Stephen did not die a natural death. It seems so impossible – utterly impossible.'

'I'm afraid it must seem so to you. It did to me – to us – at first.'

'What do you mean by at first, Sir Charles?'

'Because the suspicion crossed my mind on the evening of

your husband's death, Mrs Babbington. Like you, however, it seemed to me so impossible that I put it aside.'

'I thought so, too,' said Egg.

'You too,' Mrs Babbington looked at her wonderingly. 'You thought someone could have killed – Stephen?'

The incredulity in her voice was so great that neither of her visitors knew quite how to proceed. At last Sir Charles took up the tale.

'As you know, Mrs Babbington, I went abroad. When I was in the South of France I read in the paper of my friend Bartholomew Strange's death in almost exactly similar circumstances. I also got a letter from Miss Lytton Gore.'

Egg nodded.

'I was there, you know, staying with him at the time. Mrs Babbington, it was exactly the same – *exactly*. He drank some port and his face changed, and – and – well, it was just the same. He died two or three minutes later.'

Mrs Babbington shook her head slowly.

'I can't understand it. Stephen! Sir Bartholomew – a kind and clever doctor! Who could want to harm either of them? It must be a mistake.'

'Sir Bartholomew was proved to have been poisoned, remember,' said Sir Charles.

'Then it must have been the work of a lunatic.'

Sir Charles went on:

'Mrs Babbington, I want to get to the bottom of this. I want to find out the truth. And I feel there is no time to lose. Once the news of the exhumation gets about our criminal will be on the alert. I am assuming, for the sake of saving time, what the result of the autopsy on your husband's body will be. I am taking it that he, too, died of nicotine poisoning. To begin with, did you or he know anything about the use of pure nicotine?'

'I always use a solution of nicotine for spraying roses. I didn't know it was supposed to be poisonous.'

'I should imagine (I was reading up the subject last night) that in both cases the pure alkaloid must have been used. Cases of poisoning by nicotine are most unusual.'

Mrs Babbington shook her head.

'I really don't know anything about nicotine poisoning – except that I suppose inveterate smokers might suffer from it.'

'Did your husband smoke?'

'Yes.'

'Now tell me, Mrs Babbington, you have expressed the utmost surprise that anyone should want to do away with your husband. Does that mean that as far as you know he had no enemies?'

'I am sure Stephen had no enemies. Everyone was fond of him. People tried to hustle him sometimes,' she smiled a little tearfully. 'He was getting on, you know, and rather afraid of innovations, but everybody liked him. You couldn't dislike Stephen, Sir Charles.'

'I suppose, Mrs Babbington, that your husband didn't leave very much money?'

'No. Next to nothing. Stephen was not good at saving. He gave away far too much. I used to scold him about it.'

'I suppose he had no expectations from anyone? He wasn't the heir to any property?'

'Oh, no. Stephen hadn't many relations. He has a sister who is married to a clergyman in Northumberland, but they are very badly off, and all his uncles and aunts are dead.'

'Then it does not seem as though there were anyone who could benefit by Mr Babbington's death?'

'No, indeed.'

'Let us come back to the question of enemies for a minute. Your husband had no enemies, you say; but he may have had as a young man.'

Mrs Babbington looked sceptical.

'I should think it very unlikely. Stephen hadn't a quarrelsome nature. He always got on well with people.'

'I don't want to sound melodramatic,' Sir Charles coughed a little nervously. 'But – er – when he got engaged to you, for instance, there wasn't any disappointed suitor in the offing?'

A momentary twinkle came into Mrs Babbington's eyes.

'Stephen was my father's curate. He was the first young man I saw when I came home from school. I fell in love with him and he with me. We were engaged for four years, and then he got a living down in Kent, and we were able to get married. Ours was a very simple love story, Sir Charles – and a very happy one.'

Sir Charles bowed his head. Mrs Babbington's simple dignity was very charming.

Egg took up the rôle of questioner.

'Mrs Babbington, do you think your husband had met any of the guests at Sir Charles's that night before?'

Mrs Babbington looked slightly puzzled.

'Well, there were you and your mother, my dear, and young Oliver Manders.'

'Yes, but any of the others?'

'We had both seen Angela Sutcliffe in a play in London five years ago. Both Stephen and I were very excited that we were actually going to meet her.'

'You had never actually met her before?'

'No. We've never met any actresses – or actors, for the matter of that – until Sir Charles came to live here. And that,' added Mrs Babbington, 'was a great excitement. I don't think Sir Charles knows what a wonderful thing it was to us. Quite a breath of romance in our lives.'

'You hadn't met Captain and Mrs Dacres?'

'Was he the little man, and the woman with the wonderful clothes?'

'Yes.'

'No. Nor the other woman – the one who wrote plays. Poor thing, she looked rather out of it, I thought.'

'You're sure you'd never seen any of them before?'

'I'm quite sure I hadn't – and so I'm fairly sure Stephen hadn't, either. You see, we do everything together.'

'And Mr Babbington didn't say anything to you – anything at all,' persisted Egg, 'about the people you were going to meet, or about them, when he saw them?'

'Nothing beforehand – except that he was looking forward to an interesting evening. And when we got there – well, there wasn't much time –' Her face twisted suddenly.

Sir Charles broke in quickly.

'You must forgive us badgering you like this. But, you see, we feel that there must be *something*, if only we could get at it. There must be some *reason* for an apparently brutal and meaningless murder.'

'I see that,' said Mrs Babbington. 'If it was murder, there must be some reason . . . But I don't know – I can't imagine – what that reason could be.'

There was silence for a minute or two, then Sir Charles said:

'Can you give me a slight biographical sketch of your husband's career?'

Mrs Babbington had a good memory for dates. Sir Charles's final notes ran thus:

'Stephen Babbington, born Islington, Devon, 1868. Educated St Paul's School and Oxford. Ordained Deacon and received a title to the Parish of Hoxton, 1891. Priested 1892. Was Curate Eslington, Surrey, to Rev. Vernon Lorrimer, 1894–1899. Married Margaret Lorrimer, 1899, and presented to the living of Gilling, Kent. Transferred to living of St Petroch, Loomouth, 1916.'

'That gives us something to go upon,' said Sir Charles. 'Our best chance seems to me the time during which Mr Babbington was Vicar of St Mary's, Gilling. His earlier history seems rather far back to concern any of the people who were at my house that evening.'

Mrs Babbington shuddered.

'Do you really think – that one of them –?'

'I don't know what to think,' said Sir Charles. 'Bartholomew saw something or guessed something, and Bartholomew Strange died the same way, and five –'

'Seven,' said Egg.

'– of these people were also present. One of them must be guilty.'

'But why?' cried Mrs Babbington. 'Why? What motive could there be for anyone killing Stephen?'

'That,' said Sir Charles, 'is what we are going to find out.'

CHAPTER 2

LADY MARY

Mr Satterthwaite had come down to Crow's Nest with Sir Charles. Whilst his host and Egg Lytton Gore were visiting Mrs Babbington, Mr Satterthwaite was having tea with Lady Mary.

Lady Mary liked Mr Satterthwaite. For all her gentleness of

manner, she was a woman who had very definite views on the subject of whom she did or did not like.

Mr Satterthwaite sipped China tea from a Dresden cup, and ate a microscopic sandwich and chatted. On his last visit they had found many friends and acquaintances in common. Their talk today began on the same subject, but gradually drifted into more intimate channels. Mr Satterthwaite was a sympathetic person – he listened to the troubles of other people and did not intrude his own. Even on his last visit it had seemed natural to Lady Mary to speak to him of her preoccupation with her daughter's future. She talked now as she would have talked to a friend of many years' standing.

'Egg is so headstrong,' she said. 'She flings herself into a thing heart and soul. You know, Mr Satterthwaite, I do not like the way she is – well, mixing herself up in this distressing business. It – Egg would laugh at me, I know – but it doesn't seem to be ladylike.'

She flushed as she spoke. Her brown eyes, gentle and ingenuous, looked with childish appeal at Mr Satterthwaite.

'I know what you mean,' he said. 'I confess that I don't quite like it myself. I know that it's simply an old-fashioned prejudice, but there it is. All the same,' he twinkled at her, 'we can't expect young ladies to sit at home and sew and shudder at the idea of crimes of violence in these enlightened days.'

'I don't like to think of murder,' said Lady Mary. 'I never, never dreamed that I should be mixed up in anything of that kind. It was dreadful.' She shivered. 'Poor Sir Bartholomew.'

'You didn't know him very well?' hazarded Mr Satterthwaite.

'I think I'd only met him twice. The first time about a year ago, when he came down to stay with Sir Charles for a weekend, and the second time was on that dreadful evening when poor Mr Babbington died. I was really most surprised when his invitation arrived. I accepted because I thought Egg would enjoy it. She hasn't many treats, poor child, and – well, she had seemed a little down in the mouth, as though she didn't take any interest in anything. I thought a big house-party might cheer her up.'

Mr Satterthwaite nodded.

'Tell me something about Oliver Manders,' he said. 'The young fellow rather interests me.'

'I think he's clever,' said Lady Mary. 'Of course, things have been difficult for him . . .'

She flushed, and then in answer to the plain inquiry of Mr Satterthwaite's glance she went on.

'You see, his father wasn't married to his mother . . .'

'Really? I had no idea of that.'

'Everyone knows about it down here, otherwise I wouldn't have said anything about it. Old Mrs Manders, Oliver's grandmother, lives at Dunboyne, that biggish house on the Plymouth road. Her husband was a lawyer down here. Her son went into a city firm and did very well. He's quite a rich man. The daughter was a good-looking girl, and she became absolutely infatuated with a married man. I blame him very much indeed. Anyway, in the end, after a lot of scandal, they went off together. His wife wouldn't divorce him. The girl died not long after Oliver was born. His uncle in London took charge of him. He and his wife had no children of their own. The boy divided his time between them and his grandmother. He always came down here for his summer holidays.'

She paused and then went on:

'I always felt sorry for him. I still do. I think that terribly conceited manner of his is a good deal put on.'

'I shouldn't be surprised,' said Mr Satterthwaite. 'It's a very common phenomenon. If I ever see anyone who appears to think a lot of themselves and boasts unceasingly, I always know that there's a secret sense of inferiority somewhere.'

'It seems very odd.'

'An inferiority complex is a very peculiar thing. Crippen, for instance, undoubtedly suffered from it. It's at the back of a lot of crimes. The desire to assert one's personality.'

'It seems very strange to me,' murmured Lady Mary.

She seemed to shrink a little. Mr Satterthwaite looked at her with an almost sentimental eye. He liked her graceful figure with the sloping shoulders, the soft brown of her eyes, her complete absence of make-up. He thought:

'She must have been a beauty when she was young . . .'

Not a flaunting beauty, not a rose – no, a modest, charming violet, hiding its sweetness . . .

His thoughts ran serenely in the idiom of his young days . . .

He remembered incidents in his own youth.

Presently he found himself telling Lady Mary about his own love affair – the only love affair he had ever had. Rather a poor love affair by the standards of today, but very dear to Mr Satterthwaite.

He told her about the Girl, and how pretty she was, and of how they had gone together to see the bluebells at Kew. He had meant to propose to her that day. He had imagined (so he put it) that she reciprocated his sentiments. And then, as they were standing looking at the bluebells, she had confided in him . . . He had discovered that she loved another. And he had hidden the thoughts surging in his breast and had taken up the rôle of the faithful Friend.

It was not, perhaps, a very full-blooded romance, but it sounded well in the dim-faded chintz and egg-shell china atmosphere of Lady Mary's drawing-room.

Afterwards Lady Mary spoke of her own life, of her married life, which had not been very happy.

'I was such a foolish girl – girls are foolish, Mr Satterthwaite. They are so sure of themselves, so convinced they know best. People write and talk a lot of a "woman's instinct". I don't believe, Mr Satterthwaite, that there is any such thing. There doesn't seem to be anything that warns girls against a certain type of man. Nothing in themselves, I mean. Their parents warn them, but that's no good – one doesn't believe. It seems dreadful to say so, but there is something attractive to a girl in being told anyone is a bad man. She thinks at once that her love will reform him.'

Mr Satterthwaite nodded gently.

'One knows so little. When one knows more, it is too late.'

She sighed.

'It was all my own fault. My people didn't want me to marry Ronald. He was well born, but he had a bad reputation. My father told me straight out that he was a wrong 'un. I didn't believe it. I believed that, for my sake, he would turn over a new leaf . . .'

She was silent a moment or two, dwelling on the past.

'Ronald was a very fascinating man. My father was quite right about him. I soon found that out. It's an old-fashioned thing to say – but he broke my heart. Yes, he broke my heart. I was always afraid – of what might come out next.'

Mr Satterthwaite, always intensely interested in other people's lives, made a cautious sympathetic noise.

'It may seem a very wicked thing to say, Mr Satterthwaite, but it was a relief when he got pneumonia and died . . . Not that I didn't care for him – I loved him up to the end – but I had no illusions about him any longer. And there was Egg –'

Her voice softened.

Such a funny little thing she was. A regular little roly-poly, trying to stand up and falling over – just like an egg; that's how that ridiculous nickname started . . .'

She paused again.

'Some books that I've read these last few years have brought a lot of comfort to me. Books on psychology. It seems to show that in many ways people can't help themselves. A kind of kink. Sometimes, in the most carefully brought-up families you get it. As a boy Ronald stole money at school – money that he didn't need. I can feel now that he couldn't help himself . . . He was born with a kink . . .'

Very gently, with a small handkerchief, Lady Mary wiped her eyes.

'It wasn't what I was brought up to believe,' she said apologetically. 'I was taught that everyone knew the difference between right and wrong. But somehow – I don't always think that is so.'

'The human mind is a great mystery,' said Mr Satterthwaite gently. 'As yet, we are going groping our way to understanding. Without acute mania it may nevertheless occur that certain natures lack what I should describe as braking power. If you or I were to say, "I hate someone – I wish he were dead," the idea would pass from our minds as soon as the words were uttered. The brakes would work automatically. But, in some people the idea, or obsession, holds. They see nothing but the immediate gratification of the idea formed.'

'I'm afraid,' said Lady Mary, 'that that's rather too clever for me.'

'I apologize. I was talking rather bookishly.'

'Did you mean that young people have too little restraint nowadays? It sometimes worries me.'

'No, no, I didn't mean that at all. Less restraint is, I think, a good thing – wholesome. I suppose you are thinking of Miss – er – Egg.'

'I think you'd better call her Egg,' said Lady Mary, smiling.

'Thank you. Miss Egg does sound rather ridiculous.'

'Egg's very impulsive, and once she has set her mind on a thing nothing will stop her. As I said before, I hate her mixing herself up in all this, but she won't listen to me.'

Mr Satterthwaite smiled at the distress in Lady Mary's tone. He thought to himself:

'I wonder if she realizes for one minute that Egg's absorption in crime is neither more nor less than a new variant of that old, old game – the pursuit of the male by the female? No, she'd be horrified at the thought.'

'Egg says that Mr Babbington was poisoned also. Do you think that is true, Mr Satterthwaite? Or do you think it is just one of Egg's sweeping statements?'

'We shall know for certain after the exhumation.'

'There is to be an exhumation, then?' Lady Mary shivered. 'How terrible for poor Mrs Babbington. I can imagine nothing more awful for any woman.'

'You knew the Babbingtons fairly intimately, I suppose, Lady Mary?'

'Yes, indeed. They are – were – very dear friends of ours.'

'Do you know of anyone who could possibly have had a grudge against the vicar?'

'No, indeed.'

'He never spoke of such a person?'

'No.'

'And they got on well together?'

'They were perfectly mated – happy in each other and in their children. They were badly off, of course, and Mr Babbington suffered from rheumatoid arthritis. Those were their only troubles.'

'How did Oliver Manders get on with the vicar?'

'Well –' Lady Mary hesitated, 'they didn't hit it off very well. The Babbingtons were sorry for Oliver, and he used to go to the vicarage a good deal in the holidays to play with the Babbington boys – though I don't think he got on very well with them. Oliver wasn't exactly a popular boy. He boasted too much of the money he had and the tuck he took back to school, and all the fun he had in London. Boys are rather merciless about that sort of thing.'

'Yes, but later – since he's been grown up?'

'I don't think he and the vicarage people have seen much of each other. As a matter of fact Oliver was rather rude to Mr Babbington one day here, in my house. It was about two years ago.'

'What happened?'

'Oliver made a rather ill-bred attack on Christianity. Mr Babbington was very patient and courteous with him. That only seemed to make Oliver worse. He said, "All you religious people look down your noses because my father and mother weren't married. I suppose you'd call me the child of sin. Well, I admire people who have the courage of their convictions and don't care what a lot of hypocrites and parsons think." Mr Babbington didn't answer, but Oliver went on: "You won't answer that. It's ecclesiasticism and supersitition that's got the whole world into the mess it's in. I'd like to sweep away the churches all over the world." Mr Babbington smiled and said, "And the clergy, too?" I think it was his smile that annoyed Oliver. He felt he was not being taken seriously. He said, "I hate everything the Church stands for. Smugness, security and hypocrisy. Get rid of the whole canting tribe, I say!" And Mr Babbington smiled – he had a very sweet smile – and he said, "My dear boy, if you were to sweep away all the churches ever built or planned, you would still have to reckon with God."'

'What did young Manders say to that?'

'He seemed taken aback, and then he recovered his temper and went back to his usual sneering tired manner.

'He said, "I'm afraid the things I've been saying are rather bad form, padre, and not very easily assimilated by your generation."'

'You don't like young Manders, do you, Lady Mary?'

'I'm sorry for him,' said Lady Mary defensively.

'But you wouldn't like him to marry Egg.'

'Oh, no.'

'I wonder why, exactly?'

'Because – because, he isn't *kind* . . . and because –'

'Yes?'

'Because there's something in him, somewhere, that I don't understand. Something *cold* –'

Mr Satterthwaite looked at her thoughtfully for a minute or two, then he said:

'What did Sir Bartholomew Strange think of him? Did he ever mention him?'

'He said, I remember, that he found young Manders an interesting study. He said that he reminded him of a case he was treating at the moment in his nursing home. I said that I thought Oliver looked particularly strong and healthy, and he said, "Yes, his health's all right, but he's riding for a fall."'

She paused and then said:

'I suppose Sir Bartholomew was a very clever nerve specialist.'

'I believe he was very highly thought of by his own colleagues.'

'I liked him,' said Lady Mary.

'Did he ever say anything to you about Babbington's death?'

'No.'

'He never mentioned it at all?'

'I don't think so.'

'Do you think – it's difficult for you to tell, not knowing him well – but do you think he had anything on his mind?'

'He seemed in very good spirits – even amused by something – some private joke of his own. He told me at dinner that night that he was going to spring a surprise on me.'

'Oh, he did, did he?'

On his way home, Mr Satterthwaite pondered that statement.

What had been the surprise Sir Bartholomew had intended to spring on his guests?

Would it, when it came, have been as amusing as he pretended?

Or did that gay manner mask a quiet but indomitable purpose? Would anyone ever know?

CHAPTER 3

RE-ENTER HERCULE POIROT

'Frankly,' said Sir Charles, 'are we any forrader?'

It was a council of war. Sir Charles, Mr Satterthwaite and Egg Lytton Gore were sitting in the Ship-room. A fire burned in the grate, and outside an equinoctial gale was howling.

Mr Satterthwaite and Egg answered the question simultaneously.

'No,' said Mr Satterthwaite.

'Yes,' said Egg.

Sir Charles looked from one to the other of them. Mr Satterthwaite indicated gracefully that the lady should speak first.

Egg was silent a moment or two, collecting her ideas.

'We *are* further on,' she said at last. 'We are further on because we haven't found out anything. That sounds nonsense, but it isn't. What I mean is that we had certain vague sketchy ideas; we know now that certain of those ideas are definitely washouts.'

'Progress by elimination,' said Sir Charles.

'That's it.'

Mr Satterthwaite cleared his throat. He liked to define things.

'The idea of gain we can now put definitely away,' he said. 'There does not seem to be anybody who (in detective story parlance) could benefit by Stephen Babbington's death. Revenge seems equally out of the question. Apart from his naturally amiable and peace-loving disposition, I doubt if he were *important* enough to make enemies. So we are back at our last rather sketchy idea – fear. By the death of Stephen Babbington, someone gains security.'

'That's rather well put,' said Egg.

Mr Satterthwaite looked modestly pleased with himself. Sir Charles looked a little annoyed. His was the star part, not Satterthwaite's.

'The point is,' said Egg, 'what are we going to do next – actually *do*, I mean. Are we going to sleuth people, or what? Are we going to disguise ourselves and follow them?'

'My dear child,' said Sir Charles, 'I always did set my face against playing old men in beards, and I'm not going to begin now.'

'Then what –?' began Egg.

But she was interrupted. The door opened, and Temple announced:

'Mr Hercule Poirot.'

M. Poirot walked in with a beaming face and greeted three highly astonished people.

'It is permitted,' he said with a twinkle, 'that I assist at this conference? I am right, am I not – it is a conference?'

'My dear fellow, we're delighted to see you.' Sir Charles, recovering from his surprise, shook his guest warmly by the hand and pushed him into a large armchair. 'Where have you sprung from so suddenly?'

'I went to call upon my good friend Mr Satterthwaite in London. They tell me he is away – in Cornwall. *Eh bien*, it leaps to the eye where he has gone. I take the first train to Loomouth, and here I am.'

'Yes,' said Egg. 'But why have you come?'

'I mean,' she went on, flushing a little as she realized the possible discourtesy of her words, 'you have come for some particular reason?'

'I have come,' said Hercule Poirot, 'to admit an error.'

With an engaging smile he turned to Sir Charles and spread out his hands in a foreign gesture.

'Monsieur, it was in this very room that you declared yourself not satisfied. And I – I thought it was your dramatic instinct – I said to myself, he is a great actor, at all costs he must have drama. It seemed, I will admit it, incredible that a harmless old gentleman should have died anything but a natural death. Even now I do not see how poison could have been administered to him, nor can I guess at any motive. It seems absurd – fantastic. And yet – since then, there has been another death, a death under similar circumstances. One cannot attribute it to coincidence. No, there must be a link between the two. And so, Sir Charles, I have come to you to apologize – to say I, Hercule Poirot, was wrong, and to ask you to admit me to your councils.'

Sir Charles cleared his throat rather nervously. He looked a little embarrassed.

'That's extraordinarily handsome of you, M. Poirot. I don't know – taking up a lot of your time – I –'

He stopped, somewhat at a loss. His eyes consulted Mr Satterthwaite.

'It is very good of you—' began Mr Satterthwaite.

'No, no, it is not good of me. It is the curiosity – and, yes, the hurt to my pride. I must repair my fault. My time – that is nothing – why voyage after all? The language may be different, but everywhere human nature is the same. But of course if I am not welcome, if you feel that I intrude –'

Both men spoke at once.

'No, indeed.'

'Rather not.'

Poirot turned his eyes to the girl.

'And Mademoiselle?'

For a minute or two Egg was silent, and on all three men the same impression was produced. *Egg did not want the assistance of M. Poirot . . .*

Mr Satterthwaite thought he knew why. This was the private ploy of Charles Cartwright and Egg Lytton Gore. Mr Satterthwaite had been admitted – on sufferance – on the clear understanding that he was a negligible third party. But Hercule Poirot was different. His would be the leading rôle. Perhaps, even, Sir Charles might retire in his favour. And then Egg's plans would come to naught.

He watched the girl, sympathizing with her predicament. These men did not understand, but he, with his semi-feminine sensitiveness, realized her dilemma. Egg was fighting for her happiness . . .

What would she say?

After all what could she say? How could she speak the thoughts in her mind? *'Go away – go away – your coming may spoil everything – I don't want you here . . .'*

Egg Lytton Gore said the only thing she could say.

'Of course,' she said with a little smile. 'We'd love to have you.'

CHAPTER 4

A WATCHING BRIEF

'Good,' said Poirot. 'We are colleagues. *Eh bien*, you will put me, if you please, *au courant* of the situation.'

He listened with close attention whilst Mr Satterthwaite outlined the steps they had taken since returning to England. Mr Satterthwaite was a good narrator. He had the faculty of creating an atmosphere, of painting a picture. His description of the Abbey, of the servants, of the Chief Constable was admirable. Poirot was warm in his appreciation of the discovery by Sir Charles of the unfinished letters under the gas fire.

'*Ah, mais c'est magnifique, ça!*' he exclaimed ecstatically. 'The deduction, the reconstruction – perfect! You should have been a great detective, Sir Charles, instead of a great actor.'

Sir Charles received these plaudits with becoming modesty – his own particular brand of modesty. He had not received compliments on his stage performances for many years without perfecting a manner of acknowledging them.

'Your observation, too, it was very just,' said Poirot, turning to Mr Satterthwaite. 'That point of yours about his sudden familiarity with the butler.'

'Do you think there is anything in this Mrs de Rushbridger idea?' asked Sir Charles eagerly.

'It is an idea. It suggests – well, it suggests several things, does it not?'

Nobody was quite sure about the several things, but nobody liked to say so, so there was merely an assenting murmur.

Sir Charles took up the tale next. He described his and Egg's visit to Mrs Babbington and its rather negative result.

'And now you're up to date,' he said. 'You know what we do. Tell us: how does it all strike you?'

He leaned forward, boyishly eager.

Poirot was silent for some minutes. The other three watched him.

He said at last:

'Can you remember at all, mademoiselle, what type of port glass Sir Bartholomew had on his table?'

Sir Charles interposed just as Egg was shaking her head vexedly.

'I can tell you that.'

He got up and went to a cupboard, where he took out some heavy cut-glass sherry glasses.

'They were a slightly different shape, of course – more rounded – proper port shape. He got them at old Lammersfield's sale – a whole set of table glass. I admired them, and as there were more than he needed, he passed some of them on to me. They're good, aren't they?'

Poirot took the glass and turned it about in his hand.

'Yes,' he said. 'They are fine specimens. I thought something of that kind had been used.'

'Why?' cried Egg.

Poirot merely smiled at her.

'Yes,' he went on, 'the death of Sir Bartholomew Strange could be explained easily enough; but the death of Stephen Babbington is more difficult. Ah, if only it had been the other way about!'

'What do you mean, the other way about?' asked Mr Satter-thwaite.

Poirot turned to him.

'Consider, my friend. Sir Bartholomew is a celebrated doctor. There might be many reasons for the death of a celebrated doctor. A doctor knows secrets, my friend, important secrets. A doctor has certain powers. Imagine a patient on the border line of sanity. A word from the doctor, and he will be shut away from the world – what a temptation to an unbalanced brain! A doctor may have suspicions about the sudden death of one of his patients – oh, yes, we can find plenty of motives for the death of a doctor.

'Now, as I say, if only it had been the other way about. If Sir Bartholomew Strange had died *first* and then Stephen Babbington. For Stephen Babbington might have seen something – might have suspected something about the first death.'

He sighed and then resumed.

'But one cannot have a case as one would like to have it. One must take a case as it is. Just one little idea I should like to suggest. I suppose it is not possible that Stephen Babbington's death was an accident – that the poison (if poison there was) was intended for Sir Bartholomew Strange, and that, by mistake, the wrong man was killed.'

'That's an ingenious idea,' said Sir Charles. His face, which had brightened, fell again. 'But I don't believe it will work. Babbington came into this room about four minutes before he was taken ill. During that time the only thing that passed his lips was half a cocktail – there was nothing in that cocktail –'

Poirot interrupted him.

'That you have already told me – but suppose, for the sake of argument, that there was something in that cocktail. Could it have been intended for Sir Bartholomew Strange and did Mr Babbington drink it by mistake?'

Sir Charles shook his head.

'Nobody who knew Tollie at all well would have tried poisoning him in a cocktail.'

'Why?'

'Because he never drank them.'

'Never?'

'Never.'

Poirot made a gesture of annoyance.

'Ah – this business – it goes all wrong. It does not make sense . . .'

'Besides,' went on Sir Charles, 'I don't see how any one glass could have been mistaken for another – or anything of that kind. Temple carried them round on a tray and everyone helped themselves to any glass they fancied.'

'True,' murmured Poirot. 'One cannot force a cocktail like one forces a card. What is she like, this Temple of yours? She is the maid who admitted me tonight – yes?'

'That's right. I've had her three or four years – nice steady girl – knows her work. I don't know where she came from – Miss Milray would know all about that.'

'Miss Milray, that is your secretary? The tall woman – somewhat of the Grenadier?'

'Very much of the Grenadier,' agreed Sir Charles.

'I have dined with you before on various occasions, but I do not think I met her until that night.'

'No, she doesn't usually dine with us. It was a question of thirteen, you see.'

Sir Charles explained the circumstances, to which Poirot listened very attentively.

'It was her own suggestion that she should be present? I see.'

He remained lost in thought a minute, then he said:

'Might I speak to this parlourmaid of yours, this Temple?'

'Certainly, my dear fellow.'

Sir Charles pressed a bell. It was answered promptly.

'You rang, sir?'

Temple was a tall girl of thirty-two or three. She had a certain smartness – her hair was well brushed and glossy, but she was not pretty. Her manner was calm and efficient.

'M. Poirot wants to ask you a few questions,' said Sir Charles.

Temple transferred her superior gaze to Poirot.

'We are talking of the night when Mr Babbington died here,' said Poirot. 'You remember that night?'

'Oh, yes, sir.'

'I want to know exactly how cocktails were served.'

'I beg your pardon, sir.'

'I want to know about the cocktails. Did you mix them?'

'No, sir, Sir Charles likes doing that himself. I brought in the bottles – the vermouth, the gin, and all that.'

'Where did you put them?'

'On the table there, sir.'

She indicated a table by the wall.

'The tray with the glasses stood here, sir. Sir Charles, when he had finished mixing and shaking, poured out the cocktails into the glasses. Then I took the tray round and handed it to the ladies and gentlemen.'

'Were all the cocktails on the tray you handed?'

'Sir Charles gave one to Miss Lytton Gore, sir; he was talking to her at the time, and he took his own. And Mr Satterthwaite' – her eyes shifted to him for a moment – 'came and fetched one for a lady – Miss Wills, I think it was.'

'Quite right,' said Mr Satterthwaite.

'The others I handed, sir; I think everyone took one except Sir Bartholomew.'

'Will you be so very obliging, Temple, as to repeat the performance. Let us put cushions for some of the people. I stood here, I remember – Miss Sutcliffe was there.'

With Mr Satterthwaite's help, the scene was reconstructed. Mr Satterthwaite was observant. He remembered fairly well where everyone had been in the room. Then Temple did her round. They ascertained that she had started with Mrs Dacres, gone on to Miss Sutcliffe and Poirot, and had then come to Mr Babbington, Lady Mary and Mr Satterthwaite, who had been sitting together.

This agreed with Mr Satterthwaite's recollection.

Finally Temple was dismissed.

'Pah,' cried Poirot. 'It does not make sense. Temple is the last person to handle those cocktails, but it was impossible for her to tamper with them in any way, and, as I say, one cannot force a cocktail on a particular person.'

'It's instinctive to take the one nearest to you,' said Sir Charles.

'Possibly that might work by handing the tray to the person first – but even then it would be very uncertain. The glasses are close together; one does not look particularly nearer than another. No, no, such a haphazard method could not be adopted. Tell me, Mr Satterthwaite, did Mr Babbington put his cocktail down, or did he retain it in his hand?'

'He put it down on this table.'

'Did anyone come near that table after he had done so?'

'No. I was the nearest person to him, and I assure you I did not tamper with it in any way – even if I could have done so unobserved.'

Mr Satterthwaite spoke rather stiffly. Poirot hastened to apologize.

'No, no, I am not making an accusation – *quelle idée*! But I want to be very sure of my facts. According to the analysis there was nothing out of the way in that cocktail – now it seems that, apart from that analysis there *could* have been nothing put in it. The same results from two different tests. But Mr Babbington ate or drank nothing else, and if he was poisoned by pure nicotine, death would have resulted very rapidly. You see where that leads us?'

'Nowhere, damn it all,' said Sir Charles.

'I would not say that – no, I would not say that. It suggests a very monstrous idea – which I hope and trust cannot be true. No, of course it is not true – the death of Sir Bartholomew proves that . . . And yet –'

He frowned, lost in thought. The others watched him curiously. He looked up.

'You see my point, do you not? Mrs Babbington was not at Melfort Abbey, therefore Mrs Babbington is cleared of suspicion.'

'Mrs Babbington – but no one has even dreamed of suspecting her.'

Poirot smiled beneficently.

'No? It is a curious thing that. The idea occurred to me at once – but at once. If the poor gentleman is not poisoned by the cocktail, then he must have been poisoned a very few minutes before entering the house. What way could there be? A capsule? Something, perhaps, to prevent indigestion. But who, then, could tamper with that? Only a wife. Who might, perhaps, have a motive that no one outside could possibly suspect? Again a wife.'

'But they were devoted to each other,' cried Egg indignantly. 'You don't understand a bit.'

Poirot smiled kindly at her.

'No. That is valuable. You know, but I do not. I see the facts unbiased by any preconceived notions. And let me tell you something, mademoiselle – in the course of my experience I have known five cases of wives murdered by devoted husbands, and twenty-two of husbands murdered by devoted wives. *Les femmes*, they obviously keep up appearances better.'

'I think you're perfectly horrid,' said Egg. 'I know the Babbingtons are not like that. It's – it's monstrous!'

'Murder is monstrous, mademoiselle,' said Poirot, and there was a sudden sternness in his voice.

He went on in a lighter tone.

'But I – who see only the facts – agree that Mrs Babbington did not do this thing. You see, she was not at Melfort Abbey. No, as Sir Charles has already said, the guilt must lie on a person who was present on both occasions – one of the seven on your list.'

There was a silence.

'And how do you advise us to act?' asked Satterthwaite.

'You have doubtless already your plan?' suggested Poirot.

Sir Charles cleared his throat.

'The only feasible thing seems to be a process of elimination,' he said. 'My idea was to take each person on that list and consider them guilty until they are proved innocent. I mean that we are to feel convinced ourselves that there *is* a connection between that person and Stephen Babbington, and we are to use all our ingenuity to find out what that connection can be. If we find no connection, then we pass on to the next person.'

'It is good psychology, that,' approved Poirot. 'And your methods?'

'That we have not yet had time to discuss. We should welcome your advice on that point, M. Poirot. Perhaps you yourself –'

Poirot held up a hand.

'My friend, do not ask me to do anything of an active nature. It is my lifelong conviction that any problem is best solved by thought. Let me hold what is called, I believe, the watching brief. Continue your investigations which Sir Charles is so ably directing –'

'And what about me?' thought Mr Satterthwaite. 'These actors! Always in the limelight playing the star part!'

'You will, perhaps, from time to time require what we may describe as Counsel's opinion. Me, I am the Counsel.'

He smiled at Egg.

'Does that strike you as the sense, mademoiselle?'

'Excellent,' said Egg. 'I'm sure your experience will be very useful to us.'

Her face looked relieved. She glanced at her watch and gave an exclamation.

'I must go home. Mother will have a fit.'

'I'll drive you home,' said Sir Charles.

They went out together.

CHAPTER 5

DIVISION OF LABOUR

'So you see, the fish has risen,' said Hercule Poirot.

Mr Satterthwaite, who had been looking at the door which had just closed behind the other two, gave a start as he turned to Poirot. The latter was smiling with a hint of mockery.

'Yes, yes, do not deny it. Deliberately you showed me the bait that day in Monte Carlo. Is it not so? You showed me the paragraph in the paper. You hoped that it would arouse my interest – that I should occupy myself with the affair.'

'It is true,' confessed Mr Satterthwaite. 'But I thought that I had failed.'

'No, no, you did not fail. You are a shrewd judge of human nature, my friend. I was suffering from ennui – I had – in the words of the child who was playing near us – "nothing to do". You came at the psychological moment. (And, talking of that, how much crime depends, too, on that psychological moment. The crime, the psychology, they go hand in hand.) But let us come back to our muttons. This is a crime very intriguing – it puzzles me completely.'

'Which crime – the first or the second?'

'There is only one – what you call the first and second murder are only the two halves of the same crime. The second half is simple – the motive – the means adopted –'

Mr Satterthwaite interrupted.

'Surely the means present an equal difficulty. There was no poison found in any of the wine, and the food was eaten by everybody.'

'No, no, it is quite different. In the first case it does not seem as though *anybody* could have poisoned Stephen Babbington. Sir Charles, if he had wanted to, could have poisoned *one* of his guests, but not any particular guest. Temple might possibly have slipped something into the last glass on the tray – but Mr Babbington's was not the last glass. No, the murder of Mr Babbington seems so impossible that I still feel that perhaps it *is* impossible – that he died a natural death after all . . . But that we shall soon know. The second case is different. Any one of the guests present, or the butler or parlourmaid, could have poisoned Bartholomew Strange. That presents no difficulty whatever.'

'I don't see –' began Mr Satterthwaite.

Poirot swept on:

'I will prove that to you some time by a little experiment. Let us pass on to another and most important matter. It is vital, you see (and you *will* see, I am sure, you have the sympathetic heart and the delicate understanding), that I must not play the part of what you call the spoilsport.'

'You mean –' began Mr Satterthwaite with the beginning of a smile.

'That Sir Charles must have the star part! He is used to it. And, moreover, it is expected of him by someone else. Am I not right? It does not please mademoiselle at all that I come to concern myself in this matter.'

'You are what we call "quick in the uptake", M. Poirot.'

'Ah, that, it leaps to the eye! I am of a very susceptible nature – I wish to assist a love affair – not to hinder it. You and I, my friend, must work together in this – to the honour and glory of Charles Cartwright; is it not so? When the case is solved –'

'If –' said Mr Satterthwaite mildly.

'When! I do not permit myself to fail.'

'Never?' asked Mr Satterthwaite searchingly.

'There have been times,' said Poirot with dignity, 'when for a short time, I have been what I suppose you would call slow in the take-up. I have not perceived the truth as soon as I might have done.'

'But you've never failed altogether?'

The persistence of Mr Satterthwaite was curiosity, pure and simple. He wondered . . .

'*Eh bien*,' said Poirot. 'Once. Long ago, in Belgium. We will not talk of it . . .'

Mr Satterthwaite, his curiosity (and his malice) satisfied, hastened to change the subject.

'Just so. You were saying that when the case is solved –'

'Sir Charles will have solved it. That is essential. I shall have been a little cog in the wheel,' he spread out his hands. 'Now and then, here and there, I shall say a little word – just one little word – a hint, no more. I desire no honour – no renown. I have all the renown I need.'

Mr Satterthwaite studied him with interest. He was amused by the naïve conceit, the immense egoism of the little man. But he did not make the easy mistake of considering it mere empty boasting. An Englishman is usually modest about what he does well, sometimes pleased with himself over something he does badly; but a Latin has a truer appreciation of his own powers. If he is clever he sees no reason for concealing the fact.

'I should like to know,' said Mr Satterthwaite, 'it would interest me very much – just what do you yourself hope to get out of this business? Is it the excitement of the chase?'

Poirot shook his head.

'No – no – it is not that. Like the *chien de chasse*, I follow the scent, and I get excited, and once on the scent I cannot be called off it. All that is true. But there is more . . . It is – how shall I put it? – a passion for getting at the *truth*. In all the world there is nothing so curious and so interesting and so beautiful as truth . . .'

There was silence for a little while after Poirot's words.

Then he took up the paper on which Mr Satterthwaite had carefully copied out the seven names, and read them aloud.

'Mrs Dacres, Captain Dacres, Miss Wills, Miss Sutcliffe, Lady Mary Lytton Gore, Miss Lytton Gore, Oliver Manders.

'Yes,' he said, 'suggestive, is it not?'

'What is suggestive about it?'

'The order in which the names occur.'

'I don't think there is anything suggestive about it. We just wrote the names down without any particular order about it.'

'Exactly. The list is headed by Mrs Dacres. I deduce from that that she is considered the most likely person to have committed the crime.'

'Not the most likely,' said Mr Satterthwaite. 'The least unlikely would express it better.'

'And a third phrase would express it better still. She is perhaps the person you would all *prefer* to have committed the crime.'

Mr Satterthwaite opened his lips impulsively, then met the gentle quizzical gaze of Poirot's shining green eyes, and altered what he had been about to say.

'I wonder – perhaps, M. Poirot, you are right – unconsciously that may be true.'

'I would like to ask you something, Mr Satterthwaite.'

'Certainly – certainly,' Mr Satterthwaite answered complacently.

'From what you have told me, I gather that Sir Charles and Miss Lytton Gore went together to interview Mrs Babbington.'

'Yes.'

'You did not accompany them?'

'No. Three would have been rather a crowd.'

Poirot smiled.

'And also, perhaps, your inclinations led you elsewhere. You had, as they say, different fish to fry. Where did you go, Mr Satterthwaite?'

'I had tea with Lady Mary Lytton Gore,' said Mr Satterthwaite stiffly.

'And what did you talk about?'

'She was so good as to confide in me some of the troubles of her early married life.'

He repeated the substance of Lady Mary's story. Poirot nodded his head sympathetically.

'That is so true to life – the idealistic young girl who marries the bad hat and will listen to nobody. But did you talk of nothing else? Did you, for instance, not speak of Mr Oliver Manders?'

'As a matter of fact we did.'

'And you learnt about him – what?'

Mr Satterthwaite repeated what Lady Mary had told him. Then he said:

'What made you think we had talked of him?'

'Because you went there for that reason. Oh, yes, do not protest. You may *hope* that Mrs Dacres or her husband committed the crime, but you *think* that young Manders did.'

He stilled Mr Satterthwaite's protests.

'Yes, yes, you have the secretive nature. You have your ideas, but you like keeping them to yourself. I have sympathy with you. I do the same myself . . .'

'I don't suspect him – that's absurd. But I just wanted to know more about him.'

'That is as I say. He is your instinctive choice. I, too, am interested in that young man. I was interested in him on the night of the dinner here, because I saw –'

'What did you see?' asked Mr Satterthwaite eagerly.

'I saw that there were two people at least (perhaps more) who were playing a part. One was Sir Charles.' He smiled. 'He was playing the naval officer, am I not right? That is quite natural. A great actor does not cease to act because he is not on the stage any more. But young Manders, he too was acting. He was playing the part of the bored and blasé young man – but in reality he was neither bored nor blasé – he was very keenly alive. And therefore, my friend, I noticed him.'

'How did you know I'd been wondering about him?'

'In many little ways. You had been interested in that accident of his that brought him to Melfort Abbey that night. You had not gone with Sir Charles and Miss Lytton Gore to see Mrs Babbington. Why? Because you wanted to follow out some line of your own unobserved. You went to Lady Mary's to find out about someone. Who? It could only be someone local. Oliver Manders. And then, most characteristic, you put his name at the bottom of the list. Who are really the least likely suspects in your mind – Lady Mary and Mademoiselle Egg – but you put his name after theirs, because he is your dark horse, and you want to keep him to yourself.'

'Dear me,' said Mr Satterthwaite. 'Am I really that kind of man?'

'*Précisément*. You have shrewd judgment and observation, and you like keeping its results to yourself. Your opinions of people are your private collection. You do not display them for all the world to see.'

'I believe,' began Mr Satterthwaite, but he was interrupted by the return of Sir Charles.

The actor came in with a springing buoyant step.

'Brrr,' he said. 'It's a wild night.'

He poured himself out a whisky and soda.

Mr Satterthwaite and Poirot both declined.

'Well,' said Sir Charles, 'let's map out our plan of campaign. Where's that list, Satterthwaite? Ah, thanks. Now M. Poirot, Counsel's opinion, if you please. How shall we divide up the spadework?'

'How would you suggest yourself, Sir Charles?'

'Well, we might divide these people up – division of labour – eh? First, there's Mrs Dacres. Egg seems rather keen to take her on. She seems to think that anyone so perfectly turned out won't get impartial treatment from mere males. It seems quite a good idea to approach her through the professional side. Satterthwaite and I might work the other gambit as well if it seemed advisable. Then there's Dacres. I know some of his racing pals. I daresay I could pick up something that way. Then there's Angela Sutcliffe.'

'That also seems to be your work, Cartwright,' said Mr

Satterthwaite. 'You know her pretty well, don't you?'

'Yes. That's why I'd rather somebody else tackled her . . . Firstly,' he smiled ruefully, 'I shall be accused of not putting my back into the job, and secondly – well – she's a friend – you understand?'

'*Parfaitement, parfaitement* – you feel the natural delicacy. It is most understandable. This good Mr Satterthwaite – he will replace you in the task.'

'Lady Mary and Egg – they don't count, of course. What about young Manders? His presence on the night of Tollie's death was an accident; still, I suppose we ought to include him.'

'Mr Satterthwaite will look after young Manders,' said Poirot. 'But I think, Sir Charles, you have missed out a name on your list. You have passed over Miss Muriel Wills.'

'So I have. Well, if Satterthwaite takes on Manders, I'll take on Miss Wills. Is that settled? Any suggestions, M. Poirot?'

'No, no – I do not think so. I shall be interested to hear your results.'

'Of course – that goes without saying. Another idea: If we procured photographs of these people we might use them in making inquiries in Gilling.'

'Excellent,' approved Poirot. 'There was something – ah, yes, your friend, Sir Bartholomew, he did not drink cocktails, but he did drink the port?'

'Yes, he had a particular weakness for port.'

'It seems odd to me that he did not taste anything unusual. Pure nicotine has a most pungent and unpleasant taste.'

'You've got to remember,' said Sir Charles, 'that there probably wasn't any nicotine in the port. The contents of the glass were analysed, remember.'

'Ah, yes – foolish of me. But, however it was administered – nicotine has a very disagreeable taste.'

'I don't know that that would matter,' said Sir Charles slowly. 'Tollie had a very bad go of influenza last spring, and it left him with his sense of taste and smell a good deal impaired.'

'Ah, yes,' said Poirot thoughtfully. 'That might account for it. That simplifies things considerably.'

Sir Charles went to the window and looked out.

'Still blowing a gale. I'll send for your things, M. Poirot. The

Rose and Crown is all very well for enthusiastic artists, but I think you'd prefer proper sanitation and a comfortable bed.'

'You are extremely amiable, Sir Charles.'

'Not at all. I'll see to it now.'

He left the room.

Poirot looked at Mr Satterthwaite.

'If I may permit myself a suggestion.'

'Yes?'

Poirot leaned forward, and said in a low voice:

'*Ask young Manders why he faked an accident.* Tell him the police suspect him – and see what he says.'

CHAPTER 6

CYNTHIA DACRES

The showrooms of Ambrosine, Ltd, were very pure in appearance. The walls were a shade just off white – the thick pile carpet was so neutral as to be almost colourless – so was the upholstery. Chromium gleamed here and there, and on one wall was a gigantic geometric design in vivid blue and lemon yellow. The room had been designed by Mr Sydney Sandford – the newest and youngest decorator of the moment.

Egg Lytton Gore sat in an arm-chair of modern design – faintly reminiscent of a dentist's chair, and watched exquisite snake-like young women with beautiful bored faces pass sinuously before her. Egg was principally concerned with endeavouring to appear as though fifty or sixty pounds was a mere bagatelle to pay for a dress.

Mrs Dacres, looking as usual marvellously unreal, was (as Egg put it to herself) doing her stuff.

'Now, do you like this? Those shoulder knots – rather amusing, don't you think? And the waistline's rather penetrating. I shouldn't have the red lead colour, though – I should have it in the new colour – Espanol – most attractive – like mustard, with a dash of cayenne in it. How do you like Vin Ordinaire? Rather absurd, isn't it? Quite penetrating and ridiculous. Clothes simply must not be serious nowadays.'

'It's very difficult to decide,' said Egg. 'You see' – she became confidential – 'I've never been able to afford any clothes before. We were always so dreadfully poor. I remembered how simply marvellous you looked that night at Crow's Nest, and I thought, "Now that I've got money to spend, I shall go to Mrs Dacres and ask her to advise me." I did admire you so much that night.'

'My dear, how charming of you. I simply adore dressing a young girl. It's so important that girls shouldn't look raw – if you know what I mean.'

'Nothing raw about you,' thought Egg ungratefully. 'Cooked to a turn, you are.'

'You've got so much personality,' continued Mrs Dacres. 'You mustn't have anything at all ordinary. Your clothes must be simple and penetrating – and just faintly visible. You understand? Do you want several things?'

'I thought about four evening frocks, and a couple of day things, and a sports suit or two – that sort of thing.'

The honey of Mrs Dacres's manner became sweeter. It was fortunate that she did not know that at that moment Egg's bank balance was exactly fifteen pounds twelve shillings, and that the said balance had got to last her until December.

More girls in gowns filed past Egg. In the intervals of technical conversation, Egg interspersed other matters.

'I suppose you've never been to Crow's Nest since?' she said.

'No. My dear, I couldn't. It was *so* upsetting – and, anyway, I always think Cornwall is rather terribly artisty . . . I simply cannot bear artists. Their bodies are always such a curious shape.'

'It was a shattering business, wasn't it?' said Egg. 'Old Mr Babbington was rather a pet, too.'

'Quite a period piece, I should imagine,' said Mrs Dacres.

'You'd met him before somewhere, hadn't you?'

'That dear old dug-out? Had I? I don't remember.'

'I think I remember his saying so,' said Egg. 'Not in Cornwall, though. I think it was at a place called Gilling.'

'Was it?' Mrs Dacres's eyes were vague. 'No, Marcelle – *Petite Scandale* is what I want – the Jenny model – and after that blue Patou.'

'Wasn't it extraordinary,' said Egg, 'about Sir Bartholomew being poisoned?'

'My dear, it was too penetrating for words! It's done me a world of good. All sorts of dreadful women come and order frocks from me just for the sensation. Now this Patou model would be perfect for you. Look at that perfectly useless and ridiculous frill – it makes the whole thing adorable. Young without being tiresome. Yes, poor Sir Bartholomew's death has been rather a godsend to me. There's just an off-chance, you see, that I might have murdered him. I've rather played up to that. Extraordinary fat women come and positively goggle at me. Too penetrating. And then, you see –'

But she was interrupted by the advent of a monumental American, evidently a valued client.

While the American was unburdening herself of her requirements, which sounded comprehensive and expensive, Egg managed to make an unobtrusive exit, telling the young lady who had succeeded Mrs Dacres that she would think it over before making a final choice.

As she emerged into Bruton Street, Egg glanced at her watch. It was twenty minutes to one. Before very long she might be able to put her second plan into operation.

She walked as far as Berkeley Square, and then slowly back again. At one o'clock she had her nose glued to a window displaying Chinese *objets d'art*.

Miss Doris Sims came rapidly out into Bruton Street and turned in the direction of Berkeley Square. Just before she got there a voice spoke at her elbow.

'Excuse me,' said Egg, 'but can I speak to you a minute?'

The girl turned, surprised.

'You're one of the mannequins at Ambrosine's, aren't you? I noticed you this morning. I hope you won't be frightfully offended if I say I think you've got simply the most perfect figure I've ever seen.'

Doris Sims was not offended. She was merely slightly confused.

'It's very kind of you, I'm sure, madam,' she said.

'You look frightfully good-natured, too,' said Egg. 'That's why I'm going to ask you a favour. Will you have lunch with me at the Berkeley or the Ritz and let me tell you about it?'

After a moment's hesitation Doris Sims agreed. She was curious and she liked good food.

Once established at a table and lunch ordered, Egg plunged into explanations.

'I hope you'll keep this to yourself,' she said. 'You see, I've got a job – writing up various professions for women. I want you to tell me all about the dressmaking business.'

Doris looked slightly disappointed, but she complied amiably enough, giving bald statements as to hours, rates of pay, conveniences and inconveniences of her employment. Egg entered particulars in a little note-book.

'It's awfully kind of you,' she said. 'I'm very stupid at this. It's quite new to me. You see I'm frightfully badly off, and this little bit of journalistic work will make all the difference.'

She went on confidentially.

'It was rather nerve on my part, walking into Ambrosine's and pretending I could buy lots of your models. Really, I've got just a few pounds of my dress allowance to last me till Christmas. I expect Mrs Dacres would be simply wild if she knew.'

Doris giggled.

'I should say she would.'

'Did I do it well?' asked Egg. 'Did I look as though I had money?'

'You did it splendidly, Miss Lytton Gore. Madam thinks you're going to get quite a lot of things.'

'I'm afraid she'll be disappointed,' said Egg.

Doris giggled more. She was enjoying her lunch, and she felt attracted to Egg. 'She may be a Society young lady,' she thought to herself, 'but she doesn't put on airs. She's as natural as can be.'

These pleasant relations once established, Egg found no difficulty in inducing her companion to talk freely on the subject of her employer.

'I always think,' said Egg, 'that Mrs Dacres looks a frightful cat. Is she?'

'None of us like her, Miss Lytton Gore, and that's a fact. But she's clever, of course, and she's got a rare head for business. Not like some Society ladies who take up the dressmaking business and go bankrupt because their friends get clothes and don't pay. She's as hard as nails, Madam is – though I will say she's fair enough – and she's got real taste – she knows what's what, and she's clever at getting people to have the style that suits them.'

'I suppose she makes a lot of money?'

A queer knowing look came into Doris's eye.

'It's not for me to say anything – or to gossip.'

'Of course not,' said Egg. 'Go on.'

'But if you ask me – the firm's not far off Queer Street. There was a Jewish gentleman came to see Madam, and there have been one or two things – it's my belief she's been borrowing to keep going in the hope that trade would revive, and that she's got in deep. Really, Miss Lytton Gore, she looks terrible sometimes. Quite desperate. I don't know what she'd look like without her make-up. I don't believe she sleeps of nights.'

'What's her husband like?'

'He's a queer fish. Bit of a bad lot, if you ask me. Not that we ever see much of him. None of the other girls agree with me, but I believe she's very keen on him still. Of course a lot of nasty things have been said –'

'Such as?' asked Egg.

'Well, I don't like to repeat things. I never have been one for that.'

'Of course not. Go on, you were saying –?'

'Well, there's been a lot of talk among the girls. About a young fellow – very rich and very soft. Not exactly balmy, if you know what I mean – sort of betwixt and between. Madam's been running him for all she was worth. He might have put things right – he was soft enough for anything – but then he was ordered on a sea voyage – suddenly.'

'Ordered by whom – a doctor?'

'Yes, someone in Harley Street. I believe now that it was the same doctor who was murdered up in Yorkshire – poisoned, so they said.'

'Sir Bartholomew Strange?'

'That was the name. Madame was at the house-party, and we girls said among ourselves – just laughing, you know – well, we said, supposing Madame did him in – out of revenge, you know! Of course it was just *fun* –'

'Naturally,' said Egg. 'Girlish fun. I quite understand. You know, Mrs Dacres is quite my idea of a murderess – so hard and remorseless.'

'She's ever so hard – and she's got a wicked temper! When she lets go, there's not one of us dares to come near her. They say her husband's frightened of her – and no wonder.'

'Have you ever heard her speak of anyone called Babbington or of a place in Kent – Gilling?'

'Really, now, I can't call to mind that I have.'

Doris looked at her watch and uttered an exclamation.

'Oh, dear, I must hurry. I shall be late.'

'Goodbye, and thanks so much for coming.'

'It's been a pleasure, I'm sure. Goodbye, Miss Lytton Gore, and I hope the article will be a great success. I shall look out for it.'

'You'll look in vain, my girl,' thought Egg, as she asked for her bill.

Then, drawing a line through the supposed jottings for the article, she wrote in her little note-book:

'*Cynthia Dacres. Believed to be in financial difficulties. Described as having a "wicked temper". Young man (rich) with whom she was believed to be having an affair was ordered on sea voyage by Sir Bartholomew Strange. Showed no reaction at mention of Gilling or at statement that Babbington knew her.*'

'There doesn't seem much there,' said Egg to herself. 'A possible motive for the murder of Sir Bartholomew, but very thin. M. Poirot may be able to make something of that. I can't.'

CHAPTER 7

CAPTAIN DACRES

Egg had not yet finished her programme for the day. Her next move was to St John's House, in which building the Dacres had a flat. St John's House was a new block of extremely expensive flats. There were sumptuous window-boxes and uniformed porters of such magnificence that they looked like foreign generals.

Egg did not enter the building. She strolled up and down on the opposite side of the street. After about an hour of this she calculated that she must have walked several miles. It was half-past five.

Then a taxi drew up at the Mansions, and Captain Dacres alighted from it. Egg allowed three minutes to elapse, then she crossed the road and entered the building.

Egg pressed the door-bell of No. 3. Dacres himself opened the door. He was still engaged in taking off his overcoat.

'Oh,' said Egg. 'How do you do? You do remember me, don't you? We met in Cornwall, and again in Yorkshire.'

'Of course – of course. In at the death both times, weren't we? Come in, Miss Lytton Gore.'

'I wanted to see your wife. Is she in?'

'She's round in Bruton Street – at her dressmaking place.'

'I know. I was there today. I thought perhaps she'd be back by now, and that she wouldn't mind, perhaps, if I came here – only, of course, I suppose I'm being a frightful bother –'

Egg paused appealingly.

Freddie Dacres said to himself:

'Nice looking filly. Damned pretty girl, in fact.'

Aloud he said:

'Cynthia won't be back till well after six. I've just come back from Newbury. Had a rotten day and left early. Come round to the Seventy-Two Club and have a cocktail?'

Egg accepted, though she had a shrewd suspicion that Dacres had already had quite as much alcohol as was good for him.

Sitting in the underground dimness of the Seventy-Two Club, and sipping a Martini, Egg said: 'This is great fun. I've never been here before.'

Freddie Dacres smiled indulgently. He liked a young and pretty girl. Not perhaps as much as he liked some other things – but well enough.

'Upsettin'' sort of time, wasn't it?' he said. 'Up in Yorkshire, I mean. Something rather amusin' about a doctor being poisoned – you see what I mean – wrong way about. A doctor's a chap who poisons other people.'

He laughed uproariously at his own remark and ordered another pink gin.

'That's rather clever of you,' said Egg. 'I never thought of it that way before.'

'Only a joke, of course,' said Freddie Dacres.

'It's odd, isn't it,' said Egg, 'that when we meet it's always at a death.'

'Bit odd,' admitted Captain Dacres. 'You mean the old clergyman chap at what's his name's – the actor fellow's place?'

'Yes. It was very queer the way he died so suddenly.'

'Damn' disturbin',' said Dacres. 'Makes you feel a bit gruey, fellows popping off all over the place. You know, you think "my turn next", and it gives you the shivers.'

'You knew Mr Babbington before, didn't you, at Gilling?'

'Don't know the place. No, I never set eyes on the old chap before. Funny thing is he popped off just the same way as old Strange did. Bit odd, that. Can't have been bumped off, too, I suppose?'

'Well, what do you think?'

Dacres shook his head.

'Can't have been,' he said decisively. 'Nobody murders parsons. Doctors are different.'

'Yes,' said Egg. 'I suppose doctors are different.'

''Course they are. Stands to reason. Doctors are interfering devils.' He slurred the words a little. He leant forward. 'Won't let well alone. Understand?'

'No,' said Egg.

'They monkey about with fellows' lives. They've got a damned sight too much power. Oughtn't to be allowed.'

'I don't quite see what you mean.'

'M' dear girl, I'm *telling* you. Get a fellow shut up – that's what I mean – put him in hell. God, they're cruel. Shut him up and keep the stuff from him – and however much you beg and pray they won't give it you. Don't care a damn what torture you're in. That's doctors for you. I'm telling you – and I *know*.'

His face twitched painfully. His little pinpoint pupils stared past her.

'It's hell, I tell you – hell. And they call it curing you! Pretend they're doing a decent action. Swine!'

'Did Sir Bartholomew Strange –?' began Egg cautiously.

He took the words out of her mouth.

'Sir Bartholomew Strange. Sir Bartholomew Humbug. I'd like to know what goes on in that precious Sanatorium of his. Nerve cases. That's what they say. You're in there and you can't get out. And they say you've gone of your own free will. Free will! Just because they get hold of you when you've got the horrors.'

He was shaking now. His mouth drooped suddenly.

'I'm all to pieces,' he said apologetically. 'All to pieces.' He called to the waiter, pressed Egg to have another drink, and when she refused, ordered one himself.

'That's better,' he said as he drained the glass. 'Got my nerve back now. Nasty business losing your nerve. Mustn't make Cynthia angry. She told me not to talk.' He nodded his head once or twice. 'Wouldn't do to tell the police all this,' he said. 'They might think I'd bumped old Strange off. Eh? You realize, don't you, that someone must have done it? One of us must have killed him. That's a funny thought. Which of us? That's the question.'

'Perhaps *you* know which,' said Egg.

'What d'you say that for? Why should I know?'

He looked at her angrily and suspiciously.

'I don't know anything about it, I tell you. I wasn't going to take that damnable "cure" of his. No matter what Cynthia said – I wasn't going to take it. He was up to something – they were both up to something. But they couldn't fool me.'

He drew himself up.

'I'm a shtrong man, Mish Lytton Gore.'

'I'm sure you are,' said Egg. 'Tell me, do you know anything of a Mrs de Rushbridger who is at the Sanatorium?'

'Rushbridger? Rushbridger? Old Strange said something about her. Now what was it? Can't remember anything.'

He sighed, shook his head.

'Memory's going, that's what it is. And I've got enemies – a lot of enemies. They may be spying on me now.'

He looked round uneasily. Then he leant across the table to Egg.

'What was that woman doing in my room that day?'

'What woman?'

'Rabbit-faced woman. Writes plays. It was the morning after – after he died. I'd just come up from breakfast. She came out of my room and went through the baize door at the end of the passage – went through into the servants' quarters. Odd, eh? Why did she go into my room? What did she think she'd find there? What did she want to go nosing about for, anyway? What's it got to do with her?' He leaned forward confidentially. 'Or do you think it's true what Cynthia says?'

'What does Mrs Dacres say?'

'Says I imagined it. Says I was "seeing things".' He laughed uncertainly. 'I do see things now and again. Pink mice – snakes – all that sort of thing. But seein' a woman's different . . . I *did* see her. She's a queer fish, that woman. Nasty sort of eye she's got. Goes through you.'

He leaned back on the soft couch. He seemed to be dropping asleep.

Egg got up.

'I must be going. Thank you very much, Captain Dacres.'

'Don't thank me. Delighted. Absolutely delighted . . .'

His voice tailed off.

'I'd better go before he passes out altogether,' thought Egg.

She emerged from the smoky atmosphere of the Seventy-Two Club into the cool evening air.

Beatrice, the housemaid, had said that Miss Wills poked and pried. Now came this story from Freddie Dacres. What *had* Miss Wills been looking for? What had she found? Was it possible that Miss Wills *knew* something?

Was there anything in this rather muddled story about Sir Bartholomew Strange? Had Freddie Dacres secretly feared and hated him?

It seemed possible.

But in all this no hint of any guilty knowledge in the Babbington case.

'How odd it would be,' said Egg to herself, 'if he wasn't murdered after all.'

And then she caught her breath sharply as she caught sight of the words on a newspaper placard a few feet away:

'*CORNISH EXHUMATION CASE – RESULT.*'

Hastily she held out a penny and snatched a paper. As she did so she collided with another woman doing the same thing.

As Egg apologized she recognized Sir Charles's secretary, the efficient Miss Milray.

Standing side by side, they both sought the stop-press news. Yes, there it was.

'RESULT OF CORNISH EXHUMATION.'

The words danced before Egg's eyes. Analysis of the organs . . . Nicotine . . .

'So he *was* murdered,' said Egg.

'Oh, dear,' said Miss Milray. 'This is terrible – terrible –'

Her rugged countenance was distorted with emotion. Egg looked at her in surprise. She had always regarded Miss Milray as something less than human.

'It upsets me,' said Miss Milray, in explanation. 'You see, I've known him all my life.'

'Mr Babbington?'

'Yes. You see, my mother lives at Gilling, where he used to be vicar. Naturally it's upsetting.'

'Oh, of course.'

'In fact,' said Miss Milray, 'I don't know what to do.'

She flushed a little before Egg's look of astonishment.

'I'd like to write to Mrs Babbington,' she said quickly. 'Only it doesn't seem quite – well, quite . . . I don't know what I had better do about it.'

Somehow, to Egg, the explanation was not quite satisfying.

CHAPTER 8

ANGELA SUTCLIFFE

'Now, are you a friend or are you a sleuth? I simply must know.'

Miss Sutcliffe flashed a pair of mocking eyes as she spoke. She was sitting in a straight-backed chair, her grey hair becomingly arranged, her legs were crossed and Mr Satterthwaite admired the perfection of her beautifully shod feet and her slender ankles. Miss Sutcliffe was a very fascinating woman, mainly owing to the fact that she seldom took anything seriously.

'Is that quite fair?' asked Mr Satterthwaite.

'My dear man, of course it's fair. Have you come here for the sake of my beautiful eyes, as the French say so charmingly, or have you, you nasty man, come just to pump me about murders?'

'Can you doubt that your first alternative is the correct one?' asked Mr Satterthwaite with a little bow.

'I can and I do,' said the actress with energy. 'You are one of those people who look so mild, and really wallow in blood.'

'No, no.'

'Yes, yes. The only thing I can't make up my mind about is whether it is an insult or a compliment to be considered a potential murderess. On the whole, I think it's a compliment.'

She cocked her head a little on one side and smiled that slow bewitching smile that never failed.

Mr Satterthwaite thought to himself:

'Adorable creature.'

Aloud he said, 'I will admit, dear lady, that the death of Sir Bartholomew Strange has interested me considerably. I have, as you perhaps know, dabbled in such doings before . . .'

He paused modestly, perhaps hoping that Miss Sutcliffe would show some knowledge of his activities. However, she merely asked:

'Tell me one thing – is there anything in what that girl said?'

'Which girl, and what did she say?'

'The Lytton Gore girl. The one who is so fascinated by Charles. (What a wretch Charles is – he will do it!) She thinks that that nice old man down in Cornwall was murdered, too.'

'What do you think?'

'Well, it certainly happened just the same way . . . She's an intelligent girl, you know. Tell me – is Charles serious?'

'I expect your views on the subject are likely to be much more valuable than mine,' said Mr Satterthwaite.

'What a tiresomely discreet man you are,' cried Miss Sutcliffe. 'Now I' – she sighed – 'am appallingly indiscreet . . .'

She fluttered an eyelash at him.

'I know Charles pretty well. I know men pretty well. He seems to me to display all the signs of settling down. There's an air of virtue about him. He'll be handing round the plate and founding a family in record time – that's my view. How dull men are when they decide to settle down! They lose all their charm.'

'I've often wondered why Sir Charles has never married,' said Mr Satterthwaite.

'My dear, he never showed any signs of wanting to marry. He wasn't what they call a marrying man. But he was a very attractive man . . .' She sighed. A slight twinkle showed in her eyes as she looked at Mr Satterthwaite. 'He and I were once – well, why deny what everybody knows? It was very pleasant while it lasted . . . and we're still the best of friends. I suppose that's the reason the Lytton Gore child looks at me so fiercely. She suspects I still have a *tendresse* for Charles. Have I? Perhaps I have. But at any rate I haven't yet written my memoirs describing all my affairs in detail as most of my friends seem to have done. If I did, you know, the girl wouldn't like it. She'd be shocked. Modern girls are easily shocked. Her mother wouldn't be shocked at all. You can't really shock a sweet mid-Victorian. They say so little, but always think the worst . . .'

Mr Satterthwaite contented himself with saying:

'I think you are right in suspecting that Egg Lytton Gore mistrusts you.'

Miss Sutcliffe frowned.

'I'm not at all sure that I'm not a little jealous of her . . . we women are such cats, aren't we? Scratch, scratch, miauw, miauw, purr, purr . . .'

She laughed.

'Why didn't Charles come and catechize me on this business? Too much nice feeling, I suppose. The man must think me guilty . . . Am I guilty, Mr Satterthwaite? What do you think now?'

She stood up and stretched out a hand.

'All the perfumes of Arabia will not sweeten this little hand –'

She broke off.

'No, I'm not Lady Macbeth. Comedy's my line.'

'There seems also a certain lack of motive,' said Mr Satterthwaite.

'True. I liked Bartholomew Strange. We were friends. I had no reason for wishing him out of the way. Because we were friends I'd rather like to take an active part in hunting down his murderer. Tell me if I can help in any way.'

'I suppose, Miss Sutcliffe, you didn't see or hear anything that might have a bearing on the crime?'

'Nothing that I haven't already told the police. The house-party had only just arrived, you know. His death occurred on that first evening.'

'The butler?'

'I hardly noticed him.'

'Any peculiar behaviour on the part of the guests?'

'No. Of course that boy – what's his name? Manders turned up rather unexpectedly.'

'Did Sir Bartholomew Strange seemed surprised?'

'Yes, I think he was. He said to me just before we went in to dinner that it was an odd buisness, "a new method of gate crashing", he called it. "Only," he said, "it's my wall he's crashed, not my gate."'

'Sir Bartholomew was in good spirits?'

'Very good spirits!'

'What about this secret passage you mentioned to the police?'

'I believe it led out of the library. Sir Bartholomew promised to show it to me – but of course the poor man died.'

'How did the subject come up?'

'We were discussing a recent purchase of his – an old walnut bureau. I asked if it had a secret drawer in it. I told him I adored secret drawers. It's a secret passion of mine. And he said, "No, there wasn't a secret drawer that he knew of – but he had got a secret passage in the house."'

'He didn't mention a patient of his, a Mrs de Rushbridger?'

'No.'

'Do you know a place called Gilling, in Kent?'

'Gilling? Gilling, no, I don't think I do. Why?'

'Well, you knew Mr Babbington before, didn't you?'

'Who is Mr Babbington?'

'The man who died, or who was killed, at the Crow's Nest.'

'Oh, the clergyman. I'd forgotten his name. No, I'd never seen him before in my life. Who told you I knew him?'

'Someone who ought to know,' said Mr Satterthwaite boldly.

Miss Sutcliffe seemed amused.

'Dear old man, did they think I'd had an affair with him? Archdeacons are sometimes very naughty, aren't they? So why not vicars? There's the man in the barrel, isn't there? But I must clear the poor man's memory. I'd never seen him before in my life.'

And with that statement Mr Satterthwaite was forced to rest content.

CHAPTER 9

MURIEL WILLS

Five Upper Cathcart Road, Tooting, seemed an incongruous home for a satiric playwright. The room into which Sir Charles was shown had walls of a rather drab oatmeal colour with a frieze of laburnum round the top. The curtains were of rose-coloured velvet, there were a lot of photographs and china dogs, the telephone was coyly hidden by a lady with ruffled skirts, there were a great many little tables and some suspicious-looking brasswork from Birmingham via the Far East.

Miss Wills entered the room so noiselessly that Sir Charles, who was at the moment examining a ridiculously elongated pierrot doll lying across the sofa, did not hear her. Her thin voice saying, 'How d'you do, Sir Charles. This is really a great pleasure,' made him spin round.

Miss Wills was dressed in a limp jumper suit which hung disconsolately on her angular form. Her stockings were slightly wrinkled, and she had on very high-heeled patent leather slippers.

Sir Charles shook hands, accepted a cigarette, and sat down on the sofa by the pierrot doll. Miss Wills sat opposite him. The light from the window caught her pince-nez and made them give off little flashes.

'Fancy you finding me out here,' said Miss Wills. 'My mother will be ever so excited. She just adores the theatre – especially anything romantic. That play where you were a Prince at a University – she's often talked of it. She goes to matinées, you know, and eats chocolates – she's one of that kind. And she does love it.'

'How delightful,' said Sir Charles. 'You don't know how

charming it is to be remembered. The public memory is short!' He sighed.

'She'll be thrilled at meeting you,' said Miss Wills. 'Miss Sutcliffe came the other day, and Mother was thrilled at meeting her.'

'Angela was here?'

'Yes. She's putting on a play of mine, you know: *Little Dog Laughed.*'

'Of course,' said Sir Charles. 'I've read about it. Rather intriguing title.'

'I'm so glad you think so. Miss Sutcliffe likes it, too. It's a kind of modern version of the nursery rhyme – a lot of froth and nonsense – Hey diddle diddle and the dish and the spoon scandal. Of course, it all revolves round Miss Sutcliffe's part – everyone dances to her fiddling – that's the idea.'

Sir Charles said:

'Not bad. The world nowadays is rather like a mad nursery rhyme. And the little dog laughed to see such sport, eh?' And he thought suddenly: 'Of course this woman's the Little Dog. She looks on and laughs.'

The light shifted from Miss Wills' pince-nez, and he saw her pale-blue eyes regarding him intelligently through them.

'This woman,' thought Sir Charles, 'has a fiendish sense of humour.'

Aloud he said:

'I wonder if you can guess what errand has brought me here?'

'Well,' said Miss Wills archly, 'I don't suppose it was only to see poor little me.'

Sir Charles registered for a moment the difference between the spoken and the written word. On paper Miss Wills was witty and cynical, in speech she was arch.

'It was really Satterthwaite put the idea into my head,' said Sir Charles. 'He fancies himself as being a good judge of character.'

'He's very clever about people,' said Miss Wills. 'It's rather his hobby, I should say.'

'And he is strongly of opinion that if there were anything worth noticing that night at Melfort Abbey you would have noticed it.'

'Is that what he said?'

'Yes.'

'I was very interested, I must admit,' said Miss Wills slowly. 'You see, I'd never seen a murder at close hand before. A writer's got to take everything as copy, hasn't she?'

'I believe that's a well-known axiom.'

'So naturally,' said Miss Wills, 'I tried to notice everything I could.'

This was obviously Miss Wills' version of Beatrice's 'poking and prying.'

'About the guests?'

'About the guests.'

'And what exactly did you notice?'

The pince-nez shifted.

'I didn't really find out anything – if I had I'd have told the police, of course,' she added virtuously.

'But you noticed things.'

'I always do notice things. I can't help it. I'm funny that way.' She giggled.

'And you noticed – what?'

'Oh, nothing – that is – nothing that you'd call anything, Sir Charles. Just little odds and ends about people's characters. I find people so very interesting. So typical, if you know what I mean.'

'Typical of what?'

'Of themselves. Oh, I can't explain. I'm ever so silly at saying things.'

She giggled again.

'Your pen is deadlier than your tongue,' said Sir Charles, smiling.

'I don't think it's very nice of you to say deadlier, Sir Charles.'

'My dear Miss Wills, admit that with a pen in your hand you're quite merciless.'

'I think you're horrid, Sir Charles. It's *you* who are merciless to *me*.'

'I must get out of this bog of badinage,' said Sir Charles to himself. He said aloud:

'So you didn't find out anything concrete, Miss Wills?'

'No – not exactly. At least, there was one thing. Something I noticed and ought to have told the police about, only I forgot.'

'What was that?'

'The butler. He had a kind of strawberry mark on his left wrist. I noticed it when he was handing me vegetables. I suppose that's the sort of thing which might come in useful.'

'I should say very useful indeed. The police are trying hard to track down that man Ellis. Really, Miss Wills, you are a very remarkable woman. Not one of the servants or guests mentioned such a mark.'

'Most people don't use their eyes much, do they?' said Miss Wills.

'Where exactly was the mark? And what size was it?'

'If you'll just stretch out your own wrist –' Sir Charles extended his arm. 'Thank you. It was here.' Miss Wills placed an unerring finger on the spot. 'It was about the size, roughly, of a sixpence, and rather the shape of Australia.'

'Thank you, that's very clear,' said Sir Charles, removing his hand and pulling down his cuffs again.

'You think I ought to write to the police and tell them?'

'Certainly I do. It might be most valuable in tracing the man. Dash it all,' went on Sir Charles with feeling, 'in detective stories there's always some identifying mark on the villain. I thought it was a bit hard that real life should prove so lamentably behindhand.'

'It's usually a scar in stories,' said Miss Wills thoughtfully.

'A birthmark's just as good,' said Sir Charles.

He looked boyishly pleased.

'The trouble is,' he went on, 'most people are so indeterminate. There's nothing about them to take hold of.'

Miss Wills looked inquiringly at him.

'Old Babbington, for instance,' went on Sir Charles, 'he had a curiously vague personality. Very difficult to lay hold of.'

'His hands were very characteristic,' said Miss Wills. 'What I call a scholar's hands. A little crippled with arthritis, but very refined fingers and beautiful nails.'

'What an observer you are. Ah, but – of course, you knew him before.'

'Knew Mr Babbington?'

'Yes, I remember his telling me so – where was it he said he had known you?'

Miss Wills shook her head decisively.

'Not me. You must have been mixing me up with someone else – or he was. I'd never met him before.'

'It must be a mistake. I thought – at Gilling –'

He looked at her keenly. Miss Wills appeared quite composed.

'No,' she said.

'Did it ever occur to you, Miss Wills, that he might have been murdered, too?'

'I know you and Miss Lytton Gore think so – or rather *you* think so.'

'Oh – and – er – what do *you* think?'

'It doesn't seem likely,' said Miss Wills.

A little baffled by Miss Wills's clear lack of interest in the subject Sir Charles started on another tack.

'Did Sir Bartholomew mention a Mrs de Rushbridger at all?'

'No, I don't think so.'

'She was a patient in his Home. Suffering from nervous breakdown and loss of memory.'

'He mentioned a case of lost memory,' said Miss Wills. 'He said you could hypnotize a person and bring their memory back.'

'Did he, now? I wonder – could that be significant?'

Sir Charles frowned and remained lost in thought. Miss Wills said nothing.

'There's nothing else you could tell me? Nothing about any of the guests?'

It seemed to him there was just the slightest pause before Miss Wills answered.

'No.'

'About Mrs Dacres? Or Captain Dacres? Or Miss Sutcliffe? Or Mr Manders?'

He watched her very intently as he pronounced each name.

Once he thought he saw the pince-nez flicker, but he could not be sure.

'I'm afraid there's nothing I can tell you, Sir Charles.'

'Oh, well!' He stood up. 'Satterthwaite will be disappointed.'

'I'm so sorry,' said Miss Wills primly.

'I'm sorry, too, for disturbing you. I expect you were busy writing.'

'I was, as a matter of fact.'

'Another play?'

'Yes. To tell you the truth, I thought of using some of the characters at the house-party at Melfort Abbey.'

'What about libel?'

'That's quite all right, Sir Charles, I find people never recognize themselves.' She giggled. 'Not if, as you said just now, one is really merciless.'

'You mean,' said Sir Charles, 'that we all have an exaggerated idea of our own personalities and don't recognize the truth if it's sufficiently brutally portrayed. I was quite right, Miss Wills, you *are* a cruel woman.'

Miss Wills tittered.

'You needn't be afraid, Sir Charles. Women aren't usually cruel to men – unless it's some particular man – they're only cruel to other women.'

'Meaning you've got your analytical knife into some unfortunate female. Which one? Well, perhaps I can guess. Cynthia's not beloved by her own sex.'

Miss Wills said nothing. She continued to smile – rather a catlike smile.

'Do you write your stuff or dictate it?'

'Oh, I write it and send it to be typed.'

'You ought to have a secretary.'

'Perhaps. Have you still got that clever Miss – Miss Milray, wasn't it?'

'Yes, I've got Miss Milray. She went away for a time to look after her mother in the country, but she's back again now. Most efficient woman.'

'So I should think. Perhaps a little impulsive.'

'Impulsive? Miss Milray?'

Sir Charles stared. Never in his wildest flights of fancy had he associated impulse with Miss Milray.

'Only on occasions, perhaps,' said Miss Wills.

Sir Charles shook his head.

'Miss Milray's the perfect robot. Goodbye, Miss Wills. Forgive me for bothering you, and don't forget to let the police know about that thingummybob.'

'The mark on the butler's right wrist? No, I won't forget.'

'Well, goodbye – half a sec. – did you say right wrist? You said left just now.'

'Did I? How stupid of me.'

'Well, which was it?'

Miss Wills frowned and half closed her eyes.

'Let me see. I was sitting so – and he – would you mind, Sir Charles, handing me that brass plate as though it was a vegetable dish. Left side.'

Sir Charles presented the beaten brass atrocity as directed.

'Cabbage, madam?'

'Thank you,' said Miss Wills, 'I'm quite sure now. It was the left wrist, as I said first. Stupid of me.'

'No, no,' said Sir Charles. 'Left and right are always puzzling.'

He said goodbye for the third time.

As he closed the door he looked back. Miss Wills was not looking at him. She was standing where he had left her. She was gazing at the fire, and on her lips was a smile of satisfied malice.

Sir Charles was startled.

'That woman knows something,' he said to himself. 'I'll swear she knows something. And she won't say . . . But what the devil is it she knows?'

CHAPTER 10

OLIVER MANDERS

At the office of Messrs Speier & Ross, Mr Satterthwaite asked for Mr Oliver Manders and sent in his card.

Presently he was ushered into a small room, where Oliver was sitting at a writing-table.

The young man got up and shook hands.

'Good of you to look me up, sir,' he said.

His tone implied:

'I have to say that, but really it's a damned bore.'

Mr Satterthwaite, however, was not easily put off. He sat

down, blew his nose thoughtfully, and, peering over the top of his handkerchief, said:

'Seen the news this morning?'

'You mean the new financial situation? Well, the dollar –'

'Not dollars,' said Mr Satterthwaite. 'Death. The result of the Loomouth exhumation. Babbington was poisoned – by nicotine.'

'Oh, that – yes, I saw that. Our energetic Egg will be pleased. She always insisted it was murder.'

'But it doesn't interest you?'

'My tastes aren't so crude. After all, murder –' he shrugged his shoulders. 'So violent and inartistic.'

'Not always inartistic,' said Mr Satterthwaite.

'No? Well, perhaps not.'

'It depends, does it not, on who commits the murder. You, for instance, would, I am sure, commit a murder in a very artistic manner.'

'Nice of you to say so,' drawled Oliver.

'But frankly, my dear boy, I don't think much of the accident you faked. No more do the police, I understand.'

There was a moment's silence – then a pen dropped to the floor.

Oliver said:

'Excuse me, I don't quite understand you.'

'That rather inartistic performance of yours at Melfort Abbey. I *should* be interested to know – just why you did it.'

There was another silence, then Oliver said:

'You say the police – suspect?'

Mr Satterthwaite nodded.

'It looks a little suspicious, don't you think?' he asked pleasantly. 'But perhaps you have a perfectly good explanation.'

'I've got an explanation,' said Oliver slowly. 'Whether it's a good one or not, I don't know.'

'Will you let me judge?'

There was a pause, then Oliver said:

'I came there – the way I did – at Sir Bartholomew's own suggestion.'

'What?' Mr Satterthwaite was astonished.

'A bit odd, isn't it? But it's true. I got a letter from him suggesting that I should have a sham accident and claim hospitality. He said he couldn't put his reasons in writing, but he would explain them to me at the first opportunity.'

'And did he explain?'

'No, he didn't . . . I got there just before dinner. I didn't see him alone. At the end of dinner he – he died.'

The weariness had gone out of Oliver's manner. His dark eyes were fixed on Mr Satterthwaite. He seemed to be studying attentively the reactions aroused by his words.

'You've got this letter?'

'No, I tore it up.'

'A pity,' said Mr Satterthwaite dryly. 'And you said nothing to the police?'

'No, it all seemed – well, rather fantastic.'

'It is fantastic.'

Mr Satterthwaite shook his head. Had Bartholomew Strange written such a letter? It seemed highly uncharacteristic. The story had a melodramatic touch most unlike the physician's cheerful common sense.

He looked up at the young man. Oliver was still watching him. Mr Satterthwaite thought: 'He's looking to see if I swallow this story.'

He said, 'And Sir Bartholomew gave absolutely no reason for his request?'

'None whatever.'

'An extraordinary story.'

Oliver did not speak.

'Yet you obeyed the summons?'

Something of the weary manner returned.

'Yes, it seemed refreshingly out of the way to a somewhat jaded palate. I was curious, I must confess.'

'Is there anything else?' asked Mr Satterthwaite.

'What do you mean, sir, anything else?'

Mr Satterthwaite did not really know what he meant. He was led by some obscure instinct.

'I mean,' he said, 'is there anything else that might tell – against you?'

There was a pause. Then the young man shrugged his shoulders.

'I suppose I might as well make a clean breast of it. The woman isn't likely to hold her tongue about it.'

Mr Satterthwaite looked a question.

'It was the morning after the murder stuff. I was talking to the Anthony Armstrong woman. I took out my pocket-book and something fell out of it. She picked it up and handed it back to me.'

'And this something?'

'Unfortunately she glanced at it before returning it to me. It was a cutting from a newspaper about nicotine – what a deadly poison it was, and so on.'

'How did you come to have such an interest in the subject?'

'I didn't. I suppose I must have put that cutting in my wallet sometime or other, but I can't remember doing so. Bit awkward, eh?'

Mr Satterthwaite thought: 'A thin story.'

'I suppose,' went on Oliver Manders, 'she went to the police about it?'

Mr Satterthwaite shook his head.

'I don't think so. I fancy she's a woman who likes – well, to keep things to herself. She's a collector of knowledge.'

Oliver Manders leaned forward suddenly.

'I'm innocent, sir, absolutely innocent.'

'I haven't suggested that you are guilty,' said Mr Satterthwaite mildly.

'But someone has – someone must have done. Someone has put the police on to me.'

Mr Satterthwaite shook his head.

'No, no.'

'Then why did you come here today?'

'Partly as the result of my – er – investigations on the spot.' Mr Satterthwaite spoke a little pompously. 'And partly at the suggestion of – a friend.'

'What friend?'

'Hercule Poirot.'

'That man!' The expression burst from Oliver. 'Is he back in England?'

'Yes.'

'Why has he come back?'

Mr Satterthwaite rose.

'Why does a dog go hunting?' he inquired.

And, rather pleased with his retort, he left the room.

CHAPTER 11

POIROT GIVES A SHERRY PARTY

I

Sitting in a comfortable arm-chair in his slightly florid suite at the Ritz, Hercule Poirot listened.

Egg was perched on the arm of a chair, Sir Charles stood in front of the fireplace, Mr Satterthwaite sat a little farther away observing the group.

'It's failure all along the line,' said Egg.

'Poirot shook his head gently.

'No, no, you exaggerate. As regards a link with Mr Babbington, you have drawn the blank – yes; but you have collected other suggestive information.'

'The Wills woman knows something,' said Sir Charles. 'I'll swear she knows something.'

'And Captain Dacres, he too has not the clear conscience. And Mrs Dacres was desperately in want of money, and Sir Bartholomew spoilt her chance of laying hold of some.'

'What do you think of young Manders's story?' asked Mr Satterthwaite.

'It strikes me as peculiar and as being highly uncharacteristic of the late Sir Bartholomew Strange.'

'You mean it's a lie?' asked Sir Charles bluntly.

'There are so many kinds of lies,' said Hercule Poirot.

He was silent for a minute or two, then he said:

'This Miss Wills, she has written a play for Miss Sutcliffe?'

'Yes. The first night is Wednesday next.'

'Ah!'

He was silent again. Egg said:

'Tell us: What shall we do now?'

The little man smiled at her.

'There is only one thing to do – think.'

'Think?' cried Egg. Her voice was disgusted.

Poirot beamed on her.

'But yes, exactly that. *Think!* With thought, all problems can be solved.'

'Can't we do something?'

'For you the action, eh, mademoiselle? But certainly, there are still things you can do. There is, for instance, this place, Gilling, where Mr Babbington lived for so many years. You can make inquiries there. You say that this Miss Milray's mother lives at Gilling and is an invalid. An invalid knows everything. She hears everything and forgets nothing. Make your inquiries of her, it may lead to something – who knows?'

'Aren't *you* going to do anything?' demanded Egg persistently.

Poirot twinkled.

'You insist that I, too, shall be active? *Eh bien.* It shall be as you wish. Only me, I shall not leave this place. I am very comfortable here. But I will tell you what I will do: I will give the party – the Sherry Party – that is fashionable, is it not?'

'A Sherry Party?'

'*Précisément,* and to it I will ask Mrs Dacres, Captain Dacres, Miss Sutcliffe, Miss Wills, Mr Manders and your charming mother, mademoiselle.'

'And me?'

'Naturally, and you. The present company is included.'

'Hurrah,' said Egg. 'You can't deceive me, M. Poirot. Something will happen at that party. It will, won't it?'

'We shall see,' said Poirot. 'But do not expect too much, mademoiselle. Now leave me with Sir Charles, for there are a few things about which I want to ask his advice.'

As Egg and Mr Satterthwaite stood waiting for the lift, Egg said ecstatically:

'It's lovely – just like detective stories. All the people will be there, and then he'll tell us *which* of them did it.'

'I wonder,' said Mr Satterthwaite.

II

The Sherry Party took place on Monday evening. The invitation had been accepted by all. The charming and indiscreet Miss Sutcliffe laughed mischievously as she glanced round.

'Quite the spider's parlour, M. Poirot. And here all we poor little flies have walked in. I'm sure you're going to give us the most marvellous résumé of the case and then suddenly you'll point at me and say, "Thou art the woman", and everyone will say, "She done it", and I shall burst into tears and confess because I'm too terribly suggestible for words. Oh, M. Poirot, I'm so frightened of you.'

'*Quelle histoire*,' cried Poirot. He was busy with a decanter and glasses. He handed her a glass of sherry with a bow. 'This is a friendly little party. Do not let us talk of murders and bloodshed and poison. *Là, là*! these things, they spoil the palate.'

He handed a glass to the grim Miss Milray, who had accompanied Sir Charles and was standing with a forbidding expression on her face.

'*Voilà*,' said Poirot as he finished dispensing hospitality. 'Let us forget the occasion on which we first met. Let us have the party spirit. Eat, drink and be merry, for tomorrow we die. *Ah, malheur*, I have again mentioned death. Madame,' he bowed to Mrs Dacres, 'may I be permitted to wish you good luck and congratulate you on your very charming gown.'

'Here's to you, Egg,' said Sir Charles.

'Cheerio,' said Freddie Dacres.

Everybody murmured something. There was an air of forced gaiety about the proceedings. Everyone was determine to appear gay and unconcerned. Only Poirot himself seemed naturally so. He rambled on happily . . .

'The sherry, I prefer it to the cocktail – and a thousand times to the whisky. Ah, *quel horreur*, the whisky. By drinking the whisky, you ruin, absolutely ruin, the palate. The delicate wines of France, to appreciate them, you must never never – ah *qu'est-ce qu'il y a* –?'

A strange sound had interrupted him – a kind of choking cry. Every eye went to Sir Charles as he stood swaying, his face convulsed. The glass dropped from his hand on to the carpet, he took a few steps blindly, then collapsed.

There was a moment's stupefied silence, then Angela Sutcliffe screamed and Egg started forward.

'Charles,' cried Egg. 'Charles.'

She fought her way blindly forward. Mr Satterthwaite gently held her back.

'Oh, dear God,' cried Lady Mary. '*Not another!*'

Angela Sutcliffe cried out:

'He's been poisoned, too . . . This is awful. Oh, my God, this is too awful . . .'

And suddenly collapsing on to a sofa, she began to sob and laugh – a horrible sound.

Poirot had taken charge of the situation. He was kneeling by the prostrate man. The others drew back while he made his examination. He rose to his feet, mechanically dusting the knees of his trousers. He looked round at the assembly. There was complete silence, except for the smothered sobs of Angela Sutcliffe.

'My friends,' began Poirot.

He got no further, for Egg spat out at him:

'You fool. You absurd play-acting little fool! Pretending to be so great and so wonderful, and to know all about everything. And now you let this happen. Another murder. Under your very nose . . . If you'd let the whole thing alone this wouldn't have happened . . . It's you who have murdered Charles – you – you – you . . .'

She stopped, unable to get out the words.

Poirot nodded his head gravely and sadly.

'It is true, mademoiselle. I confess it. It is I who have murdered Sir Charles. But I, mademoiselle, am a very special kind of murderer. I can kill – and I can restore to life.' He turned and in a different tone of voice, an apologetic everyday voice, he said:

'A magnificent performance, Sir Charles, I congratulate you. Perhaps you would now like to take your curtain.'

With a laugh the actor sprang to his feet and bowed mockingly.

Egg gave a great gasp.

'M. Poirot, you – you *beast*.'

'Charles,' cried Angela Sutcliffe. 'You complete devil . . .'

'But why –?'

'How –?'

'What on earth –?'

By means of his upraised hand, Poirot obtained silence.

'Messieurs, mesdames. I demand pardon of you all. This little farce was necessary to prove to you all, and incidentally, to prove to myself a fact which my reason already told me is true.

'Listen. On this tray of glasses I placed in one glass a tea-spoonful of plain water. That water represented pure nicotine. These glasses are of the same kind as those possessed by Sir Charles Cartwright and by Sir Bartholomew Strange. Owing to the heavy cut glass, a small quantity of a colourless liquid is quite undetectable. Imagine, then, the port glass of Sir Bartholomew Strange. After it was put on the table somebody introduced into it a sufficient quantity of pure nicotine. That might have been done by anybody. The butler, the parlour-maid, or one of the guests who slipped into the dining-room on his or her way downstairs. Dessert arrived, the port is taken round, the glass is filled. Sir Bartholomew drinks – and dies.

'Tonight we have played a third tragedy – a sham tragedy – I asked Sir Charles to play the part of the victim. This he did magnificently. Now suppose for a minute that this was not a farce, but truth. *Sir Charles is dead*. What will be the steps taken by the police?'

Miss Sutcliffe cried:

'Why, the glass, of course.' She nodded to where the glass lay on the floor as it had fallen from Sir Charles's hand. 'You only put water in, but if it had been nicotine –'

'Let us suppose it was nicotine.' Poirot touched the glass gently with his toe. 'You are of opinion that the police would analyse the glass, and that traces of nicotine would be found?'

'Certainly.'

Poirot shook his head gently.

'You are wrong. No nicotine would be found.'

They stared at him.

'You see,' he smiled, '*that* is not the glass from which Sir Charles drank.' With an apologetic grin he extended a glass from the tail pocket of his coat. '*This* is the glass he used.'

He went on:

'It is, you see, the simple theory of the conjuring trick. The attention cannot be in two places at once. To do my conjuring trick I need the attention focused elsewhere. Well, there is a moment, a psychological moment. When Sir Charles falls – dead – every eye in the room is on his dead body. Everyone crowds forward to get near him, and no one, no one at all, looks at Hercule Poirot, and in that moment I exchange the glasses and no one sees . . .

'So you see, I prove my point . . . There was such a moment at Crow's Nest, there was such a moment at Melfort Abbey – and so, there was nothing in the cocktail glass and nothing in the port glass . . .'

Egg cried:

'Who changed them?'

Looking at her, Poirot replied:

'That, we have still to find out . . .'

'You don't know?'

Poirot shrugged his shoulders.

Rather uncertainly, the guests made signs of departure. Their manner was a little cold. They felt they had been badly fooled.

With a gesture of the hand, Poirot arrested them.

'One little moment, I pray of you. There is one thing more that I have to say. Tonight, admittedly, we have played the comedy. But the comedy may be played in earnest – it may become a tragedy. Under certain conditions the murderer may strike a third time . . . I speak now to all of you here present. *If anyone of you knows something – something that may bear in any way on this crime, I implore that person to speak now.* To keep knowledge to oneself at this juncture may be dangerous – so dangerous that death may be the result of silence. Therefore I beg again – *if anyone knows anything, let that person speak now . . .*'

It seemed to Sir Charles that Poirot's appeal was addressed especially to Miss Wills. If so, it had no result. Nobody spoke or answered.

Poirot sighed. His hand fell.

'Be it so, then. I have given warning. I can do no more. Remember, to keep silence is dangerous . . .'

But still nobody spoke.

Awkwardly the guests departed.

Egg, Sir Charles and Mr Satterthwaite were left.

Egg had not yet forgiven Poirot. She sat very still, her cheeks flushed and her eyes angry. She wouldn't look at Sir Charles.

'That was a damned clever bit of work, Poirot,' said Sir Charles appreciatively.

'Amazing,' said Mr Satterthwaite with a chuckle. 'I wouldn't have believed that I wouldn't have seen you do that exchange.'

'That is why,' said Poirot, 'I could take no one into any confidence. The experiment could only be fair this way.'

'Was that the only reason you planned this – to see whether it could be done unnoticed?'

'Well, not quite, perhaps. I had one other aim.'

'Yes?'

'I wanted to watch the expression on one person's face when Sir Charles fell dead.'

'Which person's?' said Egg sharply.

'Ah, that is my secret.'

'And you did watch that person's face?' asked Mr Satterthwaite.

'Yes.'

'Well?'

Poirot did not reply. He merely shook his head.

'Won't you tell us what you saw there?'

Poirot said slowly:

'I saw an expression of the utmost surprise . . .'

Egg drew her breath in sharply.

'You mean,' she said, '*that you know who the murderer is*?'

'You can put it that way if you like, mademoiselle.'

'But then – but then – you know everything?'

Poirot shook his head.

'No; on the contrary I know nothing at all. For, you see, I do not know *why* Stephen Babbington was killed. Until I know that I can prove nothing, I can know nothing . . . It all hinges on that – the motive for Stephen Babbington's death . . .'

There was a knock at the door and a page entered with a telegram on a tray.

Poirot opened it. His face changed. He handed the telegram to Sir Charles. Leaning over Sir Charles's shoulder, Egg read it aloud:

'Please come and see me at once can give you valuable information as to Bartholomew Strange's death – Margaret Rushbridger.'

'Mrs de Rushbridger!' cried Sir Charles. 'We were right after all. She *has* got something to do with the case.'

CHAPTER 12

DAY AT GILLING

I

At once an excited discussion sprang up. An A.B.C. was produced. It was decided that an early train would be better than going by car.

'At last,' said Sir Charles, 'we're going to get that particular part of the mystery cleared up.'

'What do you think the mystery is?' asked Egg.

'I can't imagine. But it can't fail to throw some light on the Babbington affair. If Tollie got those people together on purpose, as I feel pretty sure he did, then the "surprise" he talked of springing on them had something to do with this Rushbridger woman. I think we can assume that, don't you, M. Poirot?'

Poirot shook his head in a perplexed manner.

'This telegram complicates the affair,' he murmured. 'But we must be quick – extremely quick.'

Mr Satterthwaite did not see the need for extreme haste, but he agreed politely.

'Certainly, we will go by the first train in the morning. Er – that is to say, is it necessary for us all to go?'

'Sir Charles and I had arranged to go down to Gilling,' said Egg.

'We can postpone that,' said Sir Charles.

'I don't think we ought to postpone anything,' said Egg. 'There is no need for all four of us to go to Yorkshire. It's absurd. Mass formation. M. Poirot and Mr Satterthwaite go to Yorkshire and Sir Charles and I go to Gilling.'

'I'd rather like to look into this Rushbridger business,' said Sir Charles with a trace of wistfulness. 'You see, I – er – talked to the Matron before – got my foot in, so to speak.'

'That's just why you'd better keep away,' said Egg. 'You involved yourself in a lot of lies, and now this Rushbridger woman has come to herself you'll be exposed as a thorough-paced liar. It's far far more important that you should come to Gilling. If we want to see Miss Milray's mother she'll open out to you much more than she would to anyone else. You're her daughter's employer, and she'll have confidence in you.'

Sir Charles looked into Egg's glowing, earnest face.

'I'll come to Gilling,' he said. 'I think you're quite right.'

'I know I'm right,' said Egg.

'In my opinion an excellent arrangement,' said Poirot briskly. 'As mademoiselle says, Sir Charles is pre-eminently the person to interview this Mrs Milray. Who knows, you may learn from her facts of much more importance than those we shall learn in Yorkshire.'

Matters were arranged on this basis, and the following morning Sir Charles picked up Egg in his car at a quarter to ten. Poirot and Mr Satterthwaite had already left London by train.

It was a lovely crisp morning, with just a touch of frost in the air. Egg felt her spirits rising as they turned and twisted through the various short cuts which Sir Charles's experience had discovered south of the Thames.

At last, however, they were flying smoothly along the Folkestone road. After passing through Maidstone, Sir Charles consulted a map, and they turned off from the main road and were shortly winding through country lanes. It was about a quarter to twelve when they at last reached their objective.

Gilling was a village which the world had left behind. It had an old church, a vicarage, two or three shops, a row of cottages, three or four new council houses and a very attractive village green.

Miss Milray's mother lived in a tiny house on the other side of the green to the church.

As the car drew up Egg asked:

'Does Miss Milray know you are going to see her mother?'

'Oh, yes. She wrote to prepare the old lady.'

'Do you think that was a good thing?'

'My dear child, why not?'

'Oh, I don't know . . . You didn't bring her down with you, though.'

'As a matter of fact, I thought she might cramp my style. She's so much more efficient than I am – she'd probably try to prompt me.'

Egg laughed.

Mrs Milray turned out to be almost ludicrously unlike her

daughter. Where Miss Milray was hard, she was soft, where Miss Milray was angular, she was round. Mrs Milray was an immense dumpling of a woman immovably fixed in an armchair conveniently placed so that she could, from the window, observe all that went on in the world outside.

She seemed pleasurably excited by the arrival of her visitors.

'This is very nice of you, I'm sure, Sir Charles. I've heard so much about you from my Violet.' (Violet! Singularly incongruous name for Miss Milray.) 'You don't know how much she admires you. It's been most interesting for her working with you all these years. Won't you sit down, Miss Lytton Gore? You'll excuse my not getting up. I've lost the use of my limbs for many years now. The Lord's will, and I don't complain, and what I say is one can get used to anything. Perhaps you'd like a little refreshment after your drive down?'

Both Sir Charles and Egg disclaimed the need of refreshment, but Mrs Milray paid no attention. She clapped her hands in an Oriental manner, and tea and biscuits made their appearance. As they nibbled and sipped, Sir Charles came to the object of their visit.

'I expect you've heard, Mrs Milray, all about the tragic death of Mr Babbington who used to be vicar here?'

The dumpling nodded its head in vigorous assent.

'Yes, indeed. I've read all about the exhumation in the paper. And whoever can have poisoned him I can't imagine. A very nice man, he was, everyone liked him here – and her, too. And their little children and all.'

'It is indeed a great mystery,' said Sir Charles. 'We're all in despair about it. In fact, we wondered if you could possibly throw any light upon the matter.'

'Me? But I haven't seen the Babbingtons – let me see – it must be over fifteen years.'

'I know, but some of us have the idea that there might be something in the past to account for his death.'

'I'm sure I don't know what there could be. They led very quiet lives – very badly off, poor things, with all those children.'

Mrs Milray was willing enough to reminisce, but her reminiscences seemed to shed little light on the problem they had set out to solve.

Sir Charles showed her the enlargement of a snapshot which included the Dacres, also an early portrait of Angela Sutcliffe and a somewhat blurred reproduction of Miss Wills cut from a newspaper. Mrs Milray surveyed them all with great interest, but with no signs of recognition.

'I can't say I remember any of them – of course it's a long time ago. But this is a small place. There's not much coming and going. The Agnew girls, the doctor's daughters – they're all married and out in the world, and our present doctor's a bachelor – he's got a new young partner. Then there were the old Miss Cayleys – sat in the big pew – they're all dead many years back. And the Richardsons – he died and she went to Wales. And the village people, of course. But there's not much change there. Violet, I expect, could tell you as much as I could. She was a young girl then and often over at the Vicarage.'

Sir Charles tried to envisage Miss Milray as a young girl and failed.

He asked Mrs Milray if she remembered anyone of the name of Rushbridger, but the name failed to evoke any response.

Finally they took their leave.

Their next move was a scratch lunch in the baker's shop. Sir Charles had hankerings for fleshpots elsewhere, but Egg pointed out that they might get hold of some local gossip.

'And boiled eggs and scones will do you no harm for once,' she said severely. 'Men are so fussy about their food.'

'I always find eggs so depressing,' said Sir Charles meekly.

The woman who served them was communicative enough. She, too, had read of the exhumation in the paper and had been proportionately thrilled by its being 'old vicar'. 'I were a child at the time,' she explained. 'But I remember him.'

She could not, however, tell them much about him.

After lunch they went to the church and looked through the register of births, marriages and deaths. Here again there seemed nothing hopeful or suggestive.

They came out into the churchyard and lingered. Egg read the names on the tombstones.

'What queer names there are,' she said. 'Listen, here's a whole family of Stavepennys and here's a Mary Ann Sticklepath.'

'None of them so queer as mine,' murmured Sir Charles.

'Cartwright? I don't think that's a queer name at all.'

'I didn't mean Cartwright. Cartwright's my acting name, and I finally adopted it legally.'

'What's your real name?'

'I couldn't possibly tell you. It's my guilty secret.'

'Is it as terrible as all that?'

'It's not so much terrible as humorous.'

'Oh – tell it me.'

'Certainly not,' said Sir Charles firmly.

'Please.'

'No.'

'Why not?'

'You'd laugh.'

'I wouldn't.'

'You wouldn't be able to help laughing.'

'Oh, please tell me. Please, please, please.'

'What a persistent creature you are, Egg. Why do you want to know?'

'Because you won't tell me.'

'You adorable child,' said Sir Charles a little unsteadily.

'I'm not a child.'

'Aren't you? I wonder.'

'Tell me,' whispered Egg softly.

A humorous and rueful smile twisted Sir Charles's mouth.

'Very well, here goes. My father's name was Mugg.'

'Not really?'

'Really and truly.'

'H'm,' said Egg. 'That is a bit catastrophic. To go through life as Mugg –'

'Wouldn't have taken me far in my career, I agree. I remember,' went on Sir Charles dreamily, 'I played with the idea (I was young then) of calling myself Ludovic Castiglione – but I eventually compromised on British alliteration as Charles Cartwright.'

'Are you really Charles?'

'Yes, my godfathers and godmothers saw to that.' He hesitated, then said, 'Why don't you say Charles – and drop the Sir?'

'I might.'

'You did yesterday. When – when – you thought I was dead.'

'Oh, then.' Egg tried to make her voice nonchalant.

Sir Charles said abruptly: 'Egg, somehow or other this murder business doesn't seem real any more. Today especially, it seems fantastic. I meant to clear the thing up before – before anything else. I've been superstitious about it. I've associated success in solving problems with – with another kind of success. Oh, damn, why do I beat about the bush? I've made love on the stage so often that I'm diffident about it in real life . . . Is it me or is it young Manders, Egg? I must know. Yesterday I thought it was me . . .'

'You thought right . . .'

'You incredible angel,' cried Sir Charles.

'Charles, Charles, you can't kiss me in a churchyard . . .'

'I shall kiss you anywhere I please . . .'

II

'We've found out nothing,' said Egg later, as they were speeding back to London.

'Nonsense, we've found out the only thing worth finding out . . . What do I care about dead clergymen or dead doctors? You're the only thing that matters . . . You know, my dear, I'm thirty years older than you – are you sure it doesn't matter?'

Egg pinched his arm gently.

'Don't be silly . . . I wonder if the others have found out anything?'

'They're welcome to it,' said Sir Charles generously.

'Charles – you used to be so keen.'

But Sir Charles was no longer playing the part of the great detective.

'Well, it was my own show. Now I've handed over to Moustachios. It's his business.'

'Do you think he really knows who committed the crimes? He said he did.'

'Probably hasn't the faintest idea, but he's got to keep up his professional reputation.'

Egg was silent. Sir Charles said:

'What are you thinking about, darling?'

'I was thinking about Miss Milray. She was so odd in her manner that evening I told you about. She had just bought the paper about the exhumation, and she said she didn't know what to do.'

'Nonsense,' said Sir Charles cheerfully. 'That woman always knows what to do.'

'Do be serious, Charles. She sounded – worried.'

'Egg, my sweet, what do I care for Miss Milray's worries? What do I care for anything but you and me?'

'You'd better pay some attention to the trams!' said Egg. 'I don't want to be widowed before I'm a wife.'

They arrived back at Sir Charles's flat for tea. Miss Milray came out to meet them.

'There is a telegram for you, Sir Charles.'

'Thank you, Miss Milray.' He laughed, a nervous boyish laugh. 'Look here, I must tell you our news. Miss Lytton Gore and I are going to get married.'

There was a moment's pause, and then Miss Milray said:

'Oh! I'm sure – I'm sure you'll be very happy.'

There was a queer note in her voice. Egg noticed it, but before she could formulate her impression Charles Cartwright had swung round to her with a quick exclamation.

'My God, Egg, look at this. It's from Satterthwaite.'

He shoved the telegram into her hands. Egg read it, and her eyes opened wide.

CHAPTER 13

MRS DE RUSHBRIDGER

Before catching their train Hercule Poirot and Mr Satterthwaite had had a brief interview with Miss Lyndon, the late Sir Bartholomew Strange's secretary. Miss Lyndon had been very willing to help, but had had nothing of importance to tell them. Mrs de Rushbridger was only mentioned in Sir Bartholomew's case book in a purely professional fashion. Sir Bartholomew had never spoken of her save in medical terms.

The two men arrived at the Sanatorium about twelve o'clock. The maid who opened the door looked excited and flushed. Mr Satterthwaite asked first for the Matron.

'I don't know whether she can see you this morning,' said the girl doubtfully.

Mr Satterthwaite extracted a card and wrote a few words on it.

'Please take her this.'

They were shown into a small waiting-room. In about five minutes the door opened and the Matron came in. She was looking quite unlike her usual brisk efficient self.

Mr Satterthwaite rose.

'I hope you remember me,' he said. 'I came here with Sir Charles Cartwright just after the death of Sir Bartholomew Strange.'

'Yes, indeed, Mr Satterthwaite, of course I remember; and Sir Charles asked after poor Mrs de Rushbridger then, and it seems such a coincidence.'

'Let me introduce M. Hercule Poirot.'

Poirot bowed and the Matron responded absently. She went on:

'I can't understand how you can have had a telegram as you say. The whole thing seems most mysterious. Surely it can't be connected with the poor doctor's death in any way? There must be some madman about – that's the only way I can account for it. Having the police here and everything. It's really been terrible.'

'The police?' said Mr Satterthwaite, surprised.

'Yes, since ten o'clock they've been here.'

'The police?' said Hercule Poirot.

'Perhaps we could see Mrs de Rushbridger now,' suggested Mr Satterthwaite. 'Since she asked us to come –'

The Matron interrupted him.

'Oh, Mr Satterthwaite, then you don't know!'

'Know what?' demanded Poirot sharply.

'Poor Mrs de Rushbridger. She's dead.'

'Dead?' cried Poirot. '*Mille Tonnerres*! That explains it. Yes, that explains it. I should have seen—' He broke off. 'How did she die?'

'It's most mysterious. A box of chocolates came for her – liqueur chocolates – by post. She ate one – it must have tasted horrible, but she was taken by surprise, I suppose, and she swallowed it. One doesn't like spitting a thing out.'

'*Oui, oui*, and if a liquid runs suddenly down your throat, it is difficult.'

'So she swallowed it and called out and Nurse came rushing, but we couldn't do anything. She died in about two minutes. Then doctor sent for the police, and they came and examined the chocolates. All the top layer had been tampered with, the underneath ones were all right.'

'And the poison employed?'

'They think it's nicotine.'

'Yes,' said Poirot. 'Again nicotine. What a stroke! What an audacious stroke!'

'We are too late,' said Mr Satterthwaite. 'We shall never know now what she had to tell us. Unless – unless – she confided in someone?' He glanced interrogatively at the Matron.

Poirot shook his head.

'There will have been no confidences, you will find.'

'We can ask,' said Mr Satterthwaite. 'One of the nurses, perhaps?'

'By all means ask,' said Poirot; but he did not sound hopeful.

Mr Satterthwaite turned to the Matron who immediately sent for the two nurses, on day and night duty respectively, who had been in attendance on Mrs de Rushbridger, but neither of them could add any information to that already given. Mrs de Rushbridger had never mentioned Sir Bartholomew's death, and they did not even know of the despatching of the telegram.

On a request from Poirot, the two men were taken to the dead woman's room. They found Superintendent Crossfield in charge, and Mr Satterthwaite introduced him to Poirot.

Then the two men moved over to the bed and stood looking down on the dead woman. She was about forty, dark-haired and pale. Her face was not peaceful – it still showed the agony of her death.

Mr Satterthwaite said slowly:

'Poor soul . . .'

He looked across at Hercule Poirot. There was a strange expression on the little Belgian's face. Something about it made Mr Satterthwaite shiver . . .

Mr Satterthwaite said:

'Someone knew she was going to speak, and killed her . . . She was killed in order to prevent her speaking . . .'

Poirot nodded.

'Yes, that is so.'

'She was murdered to prevent her telling us what she knew.'

'Or what she did not know . . . But let us not waste time . . . There is much to be done. *There must be no more deaths*. We must see to that.'

Mr Satterthwaite asked curiously:

'Does this fit in with your idea of the murderer's identity?'

'Yes, it fits . . . But I realize one thing: The murderer is more dangerous than I thought . . . We must be careful.'

Superintendent Crossfield followed them out of the room and learnt from them of the telegram which had been received by them. The telegram had been handed in at Melfort Post Office, and on inquiry there it was elicited that it had been handed in by a small boy. The young lady in charge remembered it, because the message had excited her very much, mentioning, as it did, Sir Bartholomew Strange's death.

After some lunch in company with the superintendent, and after despatching a telegram to Sir Charles, the quest was resumed.

At six o'clock that evening the small boy who had handed in the telegram was found. He told his story promptly. He had been given the telegram by a man dressed in shabby clothes. The man told him that the telegram had been given him by a 'loony lady' in the 'House in the Park'. She had dropped it out of the window wrapped round two half-crowns. The man was afraid to be mixed up in some funny business, and was tramping in the other direction, so he had given the boy two and six and told him to keep the change.

A search would be instituted for the man. In the meantime there seemed nothing more to be done, and Poirot and Mr Satterthwaite returned to London.

It was close on midnight when the two men arrived back in town. Egg had gone back to her mother, but Sir Charles met them, and the three men discussed the situation.

'*Mon ami*,' said Poirot, 'be guided by me. Only one thing will solve this case – the little grey cells of the brain. To rush up and down England, to hope that this person and that will tell us what we want to know – all such methods are amateurish and absurd. The truth can only be seen from within.'

Sir Charles looked slightly sceptical.

'What do you want to do, then?'

'I want to think. I ask of you twenty-four hours – in which to think.'

Sir Charles shook his head with a slight smile.

'Will thinking tell you what it was this woman could have said if she lived?'

'I believe so.'

'It hardly seems possible. However, M. Poirot, you must have it your own way. If you can see through this mystery, it's more than I can. I'm beaten, and I confess it. In any case, I've other fish to fry.'

Perhaps he hoped to be questioned, but if so his expectation was disappointed. Mr Satterthwaite did indeed look up alertly, but Poirot remained lost in thought.

'Well, I must be off,' said the actor. 'Oh, just one thing. I'm rather worried about – Miss Wills.'

'What about her?'

'She's gone.'

Poirot stared at him.

'Gone? Gone where?'

'Nobody knows . . . I was thinking things over after I got your telegram. As I told you at the time, I felt convinced that that woman knew something she hadn't told us. I thought I'd have a last shot at getting it out of her. I drove out to her house – it was about half-past nine when I got there – and asked for her. It appears she left home this morning – went up to London for the day – that's what she said. Her people got a telegram in the evening saying she wasn't returning for a day or so and not to worry.'

'And were they worrying?'

'I gather they were, rather. You see, she hadn't taken any luggage with her.'

'Odd,' murmured Poirot.

'I know. It seems as though – I don't know. I feel uneasy.'

'I warned her,' said Poirot. 'I warned everyone. You remember I said to them, "Speak now."'

'Yes, yes. Do you think that she, too –?'

'I have my ideas,' said Poirot. 'For the moment I prefer not to discuss them.'

'First, the butler – Ellis – then Miss Wills. Where is Ellis?

It's incredible that the police have never been able to lay hands on him.'

'They have not looked for his body in the right place,' said Poirot.

'Then you agree with Egg. You think he is dead?'

'Ellis will never be seen alive again.'

'My God,' burst out Sir Charles. 'It's a nightmare – the whole thing is utterly incomprehensible.'

'No, no. It is sane and logical, on the contrary.'

Sir Charles stared at him.

'You say that?'

'Certainly. You see, I have the orderly mind.'

'I don't understand you.'

Mr Satterthwaite, too, looked curiously at the little detective.

'What kind of a mind have I?' demanded Sir Charles, slightly hurt.

'You have the actor's mind, Sir Charles, creative, original, seeing always dramatic values. Mr Satterthwaite here, he has the playgoer's mind, he observes the characters, he has the sense of atmosphere. But me, I have the prosaic mind. I see only the facts without any dramatic trappings or footlights.'

'Then we're to leave you to it?'

'That is my idea. For twenty-four hours.'

'Good luck to you, then. Goodnight.'

As they went away together Sir Charles said to Mr Satterthwaite:

'That chap thinks a lot of himself.'

He spoke rather coldly.

Mr Satterthwaite smiled. The star part! So that was it. He said:

'What did you mean by saying you had other fish to fry, Sir Charles?'

On Sir Charles's face appeared the sheepish expression that Mr Satterthwaite knew so well from attending weddings in Hanover Square.

'Well, as a matter of fact, I – er – well, Egg and I –'

'I'm delighted to hear it,' said Mr Satterthwaite. 'My best congratulations.'

'Of course I'm years too old for her.'

'She doesn't think so – and she's the best judge.'

'That's very nice of you, Satterthwaite. You know, I'd got it into my head she was fond of young Manders.'

'I wonder what made you think that,' said Mr Satterthwaite innocently.

'Anyway,' said Sir Charles firmly, 'she isn't . . .'

CHAPTER 14
MISS MILRAY

Poirot did not have quite the uninterrupted twenty-four hours for which he had stipulated.

At twenty minutes past eleven on the following morning Egg walked in unannounced. To her amazement she found the great detective engaged in building card houses. Her face showed such lively scorn that Poirot was impelled to defend himself.

'It is not, mademoiselle, that I have become childish in my old age. No. But the building of card houses, I have always found it most stimulating to the mind. It is an old habit of mine. This morning, first thing, I go out and buy the pack of cards. Unfortunately I make an error, they are not real cards. But they do just as well.'

Egg looked more closely at the erection on the table.

She laughed.

'Good heavens, they've sold you Happy Families.'

'What is that you say, the Happy Family?'

'Yes, it's a game. Children play it in the nursery.'

'Ah, well, one can compose the houses just in the same manner.'

Egg had picked up some of the cards from the table and was looking at them affectionately.

'Master Bun, the baker's son – I always loved him. And here's Mrs Mug, the milkman's wife. Oh, dear, I suppose that's me.'

'Why is that funny picture you, mademoiselle?'

'Because of the name.'

Egg laughed at his bewildered face and then began explaining. When she had finished he said:

'Ah, it was that that Sir Charles meant last night. I wondered . . . Mugg – ah, yes, one says in slang, does one not, you are a *mug* –

a fool? Naturally you would change your name. You would not like to be the Lady Mugg, eh?'

Egg laughed. She said:

'Well, wish me happiness.'

'I do wish you happiness, mademoiselle. Not the brief happiness of youth, but the happiness that endures – the happiness that is built upon a rock.'

'I'll tell Charles you call him a rock,' said Egg. 'And now for what I came to see you about. I've been worrying and worrying about that cutting from the paper that Oliver dropped from his wallet. You know, the one Miss Wills picked up and handed back to him. It seems to me that either Oliver is telling a downright lie when he says he doesn't remember its being there, *or else it never was there*. He dropped some odd bit of paper, and that woman pretended it was the nicotine cutting.'

'Why should she have done that, mademoiselle?'

'Because she wanted to get rid of it. She planted it on Oliver.'

'You mean she is the criminal?'

'Yes.'

'What was her motive?'

'It's no good asking me that. I can only suggest that she's a lunatic. Clever people often are rather mad. I can't see any other reason – in fact I can't see any motive anywhere.'

'Decidedly, that is the *impasse*. I should not ask *you* to guess at a motive. It is of myself that I ask that question without ceasing. *What was the motive behind Mr Babbington's death?* When I can answer that the case will be solved.'

'You don't think just madness –?' suggested Egg.

'No, mademoiselle – not madness in the sense you mean. There is a *reason*. I must find that reason.'

'Well, goodbye,' said Egg. 'I'm sorry to have disturbed you, but the idea just occurred to me. I must hurry. I'm going with Charles to the dress rehearsal of *Little Dog Laughed* – you know, the play Miss Wills has written for Angela Sutcliffe. It's the first night tomorrow.'

'*Mon dieu!*' cried Poirot.

'What is it? Has anything happened?'

'Yes, indeed something has happened. An idea. A superb idea. Oh, but I have been blind – blind –'

Egg stared at him. As though realizing his eccentricity, Poirot took a hold on himself. He patted Egg on the shoulder.

'You think I am mad. Not at all. I heard what you said. You go to see *The Little Dog Laughed*, and Miss Sutcliffe acts in it. Go then, and pay no attention to what I have said.'

Rather doubtfully Egg departed. Left to himself, Poirot strode up and down the room muttering under his breath. His eyes shone green as any cat's.

'*Mais oui* – that explains everything. A curious motive – a very curious motive – such a motive as I have never come across before, and yet it is reasonable, and, given the circumstances, natural. Altogether a very curious case.'

He passed the table where his card house still reposed. With a sweep of his hands he swept the cards from the table.

'The happy family, I need it no longer,' he said. 'The problem is solved. It only remains to act.'

He caught up his hat and put on his overcoat. Then he went downstairs and the commissionaire called him a taxi. Poirot gave the address of Sir Charles's flat.

Arrived there, he paid off the taxi, and stepped into the hall. The porter was absent taking up the lift. Poirot walked up the stairs. Just as he arrived on the second floor the door of Sir Charles's flat opened and Miss Milray came out.

She started when she saw Poirot.

'You!'

Poirot smiled.

'Me! Or is it I? *Enfin, moi!*'

Miss Milray said:

'I'm afraid you won't find Sir Charles. He's gone to the Babylon Theatre with Miss Lytton Gore.'

'It is not Sir Charles I seek. It is my stick that I think I have left behind one day.'

'Oh, I see. Well, if you'll ring, Temple will find it for you. I'm sorry I can't stop. I'm on my way to catch a train. I'm going down to Kent – to my mother.'

'I comprehend. Do not let me delay you, mademoiselle.'

He stood aside and Miss Milray passed rapidly down the stairs. She was carrying a small attaché case.

But when she had gone Poirot seemed to forget the purpose

for which he had come. Instead of going on up to the landing, he turned and made his way downstairs again. He arrived at the front door just in time to see Miss Milray getting into a taxi. Another taxi was coming slowly along the kerb. Poirot raised a hand and it came to rest. He got in and directed the driver to follow the other taxi.

No surprise showed on his face when the first taxi went north and finally drew up at Paddington Station, though Paddington is an odd station from which to proceed to Kent. Poirot went to the first-class booking window and demanded a return ticket to Loomouth. The train was due to depart in five minutes. Pulling up his overcoat well about his ears, for the day was cold, Poirot ensconced himself in the corner of a first-class carriage.

They arrived at Loomouth about five o'clock. It was already growing dark. Standing back a little, Poirot heard Miss Milray being greeted by the friendly porter at the little station.

'Well, now, miss, we didn't expect you. Is Sir Charles coming down?'

Miss Milray replied:

'I've come down here unexpectedly. I shall be going back tomorrow morning. I've just come to fetch some things. No, I don't want a cab, thank you. I'll walk up by the cliff path.'

The dusk had deepened. Miss Milray walked briskly up the steep zigzag path. A good way behind came Hercule Poirot. He trod softly like a cat. Miss Milray, on arrival at Crow's Nest, produced a key from her bag and passed through the side door, leaving it ajar. She reappeared a minute or two later. She had a rusty door key and an electric torch in her hand. Poirot drew back a little behind a convenient bush.

Miss Milray passed round behind the house and up a scrambling overgrown path. Hercule Poirot followed. Up and up went Miss Milray until she came suddenly to an old stone tower such as is found often on that coast. This one was of humble and dilapidated appearance. There was, however, a curtain over the dirty window, and Miss Milray inserted her key in the big wooden door.

The key turned with a protesting creak. The door swung with a groan on its hinges. Miss Milray and her torch passed inside.

With an increase of pace Poirot caught up. He passed, in his turn, noiselessly through the door. The light of Miss Milray's torch gleamed fitfully on glass retorts, a bunsen burner – various apparatus.

Miss Milray had picked up a crowbar. She had raised it and was holding it over the glass apparatus when a hand caught her by the arm. She gasped and turned.

The green, catlike eyes of Poirot looked into hers.

'You cannot do that, mademoiselle,' he said. 'For what you seek to destroy is evidence.'

CHAPTER 15

CURTAIN

Hercule Poirot sat in a big arm-chair. The wall lights had been turned out. Only a rose-shaded lamp shed its glow on the figure in the arm-chair. There seemed something symbolic about it – he alone in the light – and the other three, Sir Charles, Mr Satterthwaite and Egg Lytton Gore – Poirot's audience – sitting in the outer darkness.

Hercule Poirot's voice was dreamy. He seemed to be addressing himself to space rather than to his listeners.

'To reconstruct the crime – that is the aim of the detective. To reconstruct a crime you must place one fact upon another just as you place one card on another in building a house of cards. And if the facts will not fit – if the card will not balance – well – you must start your house again, or else it will fall . . .

'As I said the other day, there are three different types of mind: There is the dramatic mind – the producer's mind, which sees the effect of reality that can be produced by mechanical appliances – there is also the mind that reacts easily to dramatic appearances – and there is the young romantic mind – and finally, my friends, there is the prosaic mind – the mind that sees not blue sea and mimosa trees, but the painted backcloth of stage scenery.

'So I come, *mes amis*, to the murder of Stephen Babbington in August last. On that evening Sir Charles Cartwright advanced the theory that Stephen Babbington had been murdered. I did not agree with that theory. I could not believe (a) that such a man as Stephen Babbington was likely to have been murdered, and (b) that it was possible to administer poison to a particular person under the circumstances that had obtained that evening.

'Now here I admit that Sir Charles was right and I was wrong. I was wrong because I was looking at the crime from an entirely false angle. It is only twenty-four hours ago that I suddenly perceived the proper angle of vision – and let me say that from that angle of vision the murder of Stephen Babbington is both *reasonable* and *possible*.

'But I will pass from that point for the moment and take you step by step along the path I myself have trodden. The death of Stephen Babbington I may call the first act of our drama. The curtain fell on that act when we all departed from Crow's Nest.

'What I might call the second act of the drama began in Monte Carlo when Mr Satterthwaite showed me the newspaper account of Sir Bartholomew's death. It was at once clear that I had been wrong and Sir Charles had been right. Both Stephen Babbington and Sir Bartholomew Strange had been murdered and the two murders formed part of one and the same crime. Later a third murder completed the series – the murder of Mrs de Rushbridger. What we need, therefore, is a reasonable common-sense theory which will link those three deaths together – in other words those three crimes were committed by one and the same person, and were to the advantage and benefit of that particular person.

'Now I may say at once that the principal thing that worried me was the fact that the murder of Sir Bartholomew Strange came *after* that of Stephen Babbington. Looking at those three murders without distinction of time and place the probabilities pointed to the murder of Sir Bartholomew Strange being what one might call the central or principal crime, and the other two murders as secondary in character – that is, arising from the connection of those two people with Sir Bartholomew Strange. However, as I remarked before – one cannot have one's crime as one would like to have it. Stephen Babbington had been murdered first and Sir Bartholomew Strange some time later. It seemed, therefore, as though the second crime must necessarily arise out of the first and that accordingly it was the first crime we must examine for the clue to the whole.

'I did indeed so far incline to the theory of probability that I seriously considered the idea of a *mistake* having arisen. Was it possible that Sir Bartholomew Strange was intended as the first victim, and that Mr Babbington was poisoned by mistake? I was forced, however, to abandon that idea. Anybody who knew Sir Bartholomew Strange with any degree of intimacy knew that he disliked the cocktail habit.

'Another suggestion: Had Stephen Babbington been poisoned in mistake for any other member of the original party? I could not find any evidence of such a thing. I was therefore forced back to the conclusion that the murder of Stephen Babbington had been definitely *intended* – and at once I came up against a complete stumbling block – the apparent *impossibility* of such a thing having happened.

'One should always start an investigation with the simplest and most obvious theories. Granting that Stephen Babbington had drunk a poisoned cocktail, who had had the opportunity of poisoning that cocktail? At first sight, it seemed to me that the only two people who could have done so (e.g., who handled the drinks) were Sir Charles Cartwright himself and the parlourmaid Temple. But though either of them could presumably have introduced the poison into the glass, *neither of them had had any opportunity of directing that particular glass into Mr Babbington's hand.* Temple might have done so by adroit handing of the tray so as to offer him the one remaining glass – (not easy, but it might have been done). Sir Charles could have done so by deliberately picking up the particular glass and handing it to him. But neither of these things had occurred. It looked as though *chance* and *chance* alone directed that particular glass to Stephen Babbington.

'Sir Charles Cartwright and Temple had the handling of the cocktails. Were either of those two at Melfort Abbey? They were not. Who had the best chance of tampering with Sir Bartholomew's port glass? The absconding butler, Ellis, and his helper, the parlourmaid. But here, however, the possibility that one of the guests had done so could not be laid aside. It was risky, but it was possible, for any of the house-party to have slipped into the dining-room and put the nicotine into the port glass.

'When I joined you at Crow's Nest you already had a list

drawn up of the people who had been at Crow's Nest and at Melfort Abbey. I may say now that the four names which headed the list – Captain and Mrs Dacres, Miss Sutcliffe and Miss Wills – I discarded immediately.

'It was *impossible* that any of those four people should have known *beforehand* that they were going to meet Stephen Babbington at dinner. The employment of nicotine as a poison showed a carefully thought-out plan, not one that could be put into operation on the spur of the moment. There were three other names on that list – Lady Mary Lytton Gore, Miss Lytton Gore and Mr Oliver Manders. Although not probable, those three were *possible*. They were local people, they might conceivably have motives for the removal of Stephen Babbington, and have chosen the evening of the dinner-party for putting their plans into operation.

'On the other hand, I could find no evidence whatsoever that any of them had actually done such a thing.

'Mr Satterthwaite, I think, reasoned on much the same lines as I had done, and he fixed his suspicions on Oliver Manders. I may say that young Manders was by far the most possible suspect. He displayed all the signs of high nervous tension on that evening at Crow's Nest – he had a somewhat distorted view of life owing to his private troubles – he had a strong inferiority complex, which is a frequent cause of crime, he was at an unbalanced age, he had actually had a quarrel, or shall we say had displayed animosity against Mr Babbington. Then there were the curious circumstances of his arrival at Melfort Abbey. And later we had his somewhat incredible story of the letter from Sir Bartholomew Strange and the evidence of Miss Wills as to his having a newspaper cutting on the subject of nicotine poisoning in his possession.

'Oliver Manders, then, was clearly the person who should be placed at the head of the list of those seven suspects.

'But then, my friends, I was visited by a curious sensation. It seemed clear and logical enough that the person who had committed the crimes *must have been a person who had been present on both occasions*; in other words *a person on that list of seven – but I had the feeling that that obviousness was an arranged obviousness*. It was what any sane and logical person would be *expected* to think. I felt that I was, in fact, looking not at reality but at an artfully painted bit of scenery. A really clever criminal would have realized that *anyone whose name was on that list would necessarily be suspect*, and therefore he or she would arrange for it not to be there.

'In other words, the murderer of Stephen Babbington and Sir Bartholomew Strange *was* present on both occasions – but was not *apparently* so.

'Who had been present on the first occasion and not on the second? Sir Charles Cartwright, Mr Satterthwaite, Miss Milray and Mrs Babbington.

'Could any of those four have been present on the second occasion in some capacity other than their own? Sir Charles and Mr Satterthwaite had been in the South of France, Miss Milray had been in London, Mrs Babbington had been in Loomouth. Of the four, then, Miss Milray and Mrs Babbington seemed indicated. But could Miss Milray have been present at Melfort Abbey unrecognized by any of the company? Miss Milray has very striking features not easily disguised and not easily forgotten. I decided that it was impossible that Miss Milray could have been at Melfort Abbey unrecognized. The same applied to Mrs Babbington.

'For the matter of that could Mr Satterthwaite or Sir Charles Cartwright have been at Melfort Abbey and not been recognized? Mr Satterthwaite just possibly; but when we come to Sir Charles Cartwright we come to a very different matter. Sir Charles is an actor accustomed to playing a part. But what part could he have played?

'And then I came to the consideration of the butler Ellis.

'A very mysterious person, Ellis. A person who appears from nowhere a fortnight before the crime and vanishes afterwards with complete success. Why was Ellis so successful? *Because Ellis did not really exist.* Ellis, again, was a thing of pasteboard and paint and stagecraft – Ellis was not *real*.

'But was it *possible*? After all, the servants at Melfort Abbey knew Sir Charles Cartwright, and Sir Bartholomew Strange was an intimate friend of his. The servants I got over easily enough. The impersonation of the butler risked nothing – if the servants recognized him – why, no harm would be done – the whole thing could be passed off as a joke. If, on the other hand, a fortnight passed without any suspicion being aroused, well, the thing was safe as houses. And I recalled what I had been told of the servants' remarks about the butler. He was "quite the gentleman", and had been "in good houses", and knew several interesting scandals. That was easy enough. But a very significant statement was made by the parlourmaid Alice. She said, "He arranged the work different from any butler I ever knew before." When that remark was repeated to me, it became a confirmation of my theory.

'But Sir Bartholomew Strange was another matter. It is hardly to be supposed that his friend could take him in. He must have known of the impersonation. Had we any evidence of that? Yes. The acute Mr Satterthwaite pounced on one point quite early in the proceedings – the facetious remark of Sir Bartholomew (totally uncharacteristic of his manner to servants) – "You're a first-class butler, aren't you, Ellis?" *A perfectly understandable remark if the butler were Sir Charles Cartwright and Sir Bartholomew was in on the joke.*

'Because that is undoubtedly how Sir Bartholomew saw the matter. The impersonation of Ellis was a joke, possibly even a wager, its culmination was designed to be the successful spoofing of the house-party – hence Sir Bartholomew's remark about a surprise and his cheerful humour. Note, too, that there was still time to draw back. If any of the house-party had spotted Charles Cartwright that first evening at the dinner-table, nothing irrevocable had yet occurred. The whole thing could have been passed off as a joke. But nobody noticed the stooping middle-aged butler, with his belladonna darkened eyes, and his whiskers, and the painted birthmark on his wrist. A very subtle identifying touch that – which completely failed, owing to the lack of observation of most human beings! The birthmark was intended to bulk largely in the description of Ellis – and in all that fortnight no one noticed it! The only person who did was the sharp-eyed Miss Wills, to whom we shall come presently.

'What happened next? Sir Bartholomew died. This time the death was not put down to natural causes. The police came. They questioned Ellis and the others. Later that night "Ellis" left by the secret passage, resumed his own personality, and two days later was strolling about the gardens at Monte Carlo ready to be shocked and surprised by the news of his friend's death.

'This, mind you, was all theory. I had no actual proof, but everything that arose supported that theory. My house of cards was well and truly built. The blackmailing letters discovered in Ellis's room? But it was Sir Charles himself who discovered them!

'And what of the supposed letter from Sir Bartholomew Strange asking young Manders to arrange an accident? Well, what could be easier than for Sir Charles to write that letter in Sir Bartholomew's name? If Manders had not destroyed that letter himself, Sir Charles in the rôle of Ellis can easily do so when he valets the young gentleman. In the same way the newspaper cutting is easily introduced by Ellis into Oliver Manders's wallet.

'And now we come to the third victim – Mrs de Rushbridger. When do we first hear of Mrs de Rushbridger? Immediately after that very awkward chaffing reference to Ellis being the perfect butler – that extremely uncharacteristic utterance of Sir Bartholomew Strange. At all costs attention must be drawn away from Sir Bartholomew's manner to his butler. Sir Charles quickly asks what was the message the butler had brought. It is about this woman – this patient of the doctor's. And immediately Sir Charles throws all his personality into directing attention to this unknown woman and away from the butler. He goes to the Sanatorium and questions the Matron. He runs Mrs de Rushbridger for all he is worth as a red herring.

'We must now examine the part played by Miss Wills in the drama. Miss Wills has a curious personality. She is one of those people who are quite unable to impress themselves on their surroundings. She is neither good-looking nor witty nor clever, not even particularly sympathetic. She is nondescript. But she is extremely observant and extremely intelligent. She takes her revenge on the world with her pen. She has the great art of being able to reproduce character on paper. I do not know if there was anything about the butler that struck Miss Wills as unusual, but I do think that she was the only person at the table who noticed him at all. On the morning after the murder her insatiable curiosity led her to poke and pry, as the housemaid put it. She went into Dacres's room, she went through the baize door into the servants' quarters, led, I think, by the mongoose instinct for finding out.

'She was the only person who occasioned Sir Charles any uneasiness. That is why he was anxious to be the one to tackle her. He was fairly reassured by his interview and distinctly gratified that she had noticed the birthmark. But after that came catastrophe. I don't think that until that minute Miss Wills had connected Ellis the butler with Sir Charles Cartwright. I think she had only been vaguely struck by some resemblance to someone in Ellis. But she was an observer. When dishes were handed to her she had automatically noted – not the face – but the hands that held the dishes.

'It did not occur to her that *Ellis was Sir Charles*. But when Sir Charles was talking to her it did suddenly occur to her that *Sir Charles was Ellis*! And so she asked him to pretend to hand her a dish of vegetables. But it was not whether the birthmark was on the right or left wrist that interested her. She wanted a pretext to study his *hands* – hands held in the same position as those of Ellis the butler.

'And so she leaped to the truth. But she was a peculiar woman. She enjoyed knowledge for its own sake. Besides, she was by no means sure that Sir Charles had murdered his friend. He had masqueraded as a butler, yes – but that did not necessarily make him a murderer. Many an innocent man has kept silence because speech would place him in an awkward position.

'So Miss Wills kept her knowledge to herself – and enjoyed it. But Sir Charles was worried. He did not like that expression of satisfied malice on her face that he saw as he left the room. She knew something. What? Did it affect him? He could not be sure. But he felt that it was something connected with Ellis the butler. First Mr Satterthwaite – now Miss Wills. Attention *must* be drawn away from that vital point. It *must* be focused definitely elsewhere. And he thought of a plan – simple, audacious and, as he fancied, definitely mystifying.

'On the day of my Sherry Party I imagine Sir Charles rose very early, went to Yorkshire and, disguised in shabby clothes, gave the telegram to a small boy to send off. Then he returned to town in time to act the party I had indicated in my little drama.

He did one more thing. *He posted a box of chocolates to a woman he had never seen and of whom he knew nothing* . . .

'You know what happened that evening. From Sir Charles's uneasiness I was fairly sure that Miss Wills had certain suspicions. When Sir Charles did his "death scene" I watched Miss Wills's face. I saw the look of astonishment that showed on it. I knew then that *Miss Wills definitely suspected Sir Charles of being the murderer*. When he appeared to die poisoned like the other two she thought her deductions must be wrong.

'But if Miss Wills suspected Sir Charles, then Miss Wills was in serious danger. A man who has killed twice will kill again. I uttered a very solemn warning. Later that night I communicated with Miss Wills by telephone, and on my advice she left home suddenly the next day. Since then she has been living here in this hotel. That I was wise is proved by the fact that Sir Charles went out to Tooting on the following evening after he had returned from Gilling. He was too late. The bird had flown.

'In the meantime, from his point of view, the plan had worked well. Mrs de Rushbridger had something of importance to tell us. Mrs de Rushbridger was killed before she could speak. How dramatic! How like the detective stories, the plays, the films! Again the cardboard and the tinsel and the painted cloth.

'But I, Hercule Poirot, was not deceived. Mr Satterthwaite said to me she was killed in order that she should not speak. I agreed. He went on to say she was killed before she could tell us what she knew. I said, "*Or what she did* NOT *know*." I think he was puzzled. But he should have seen then the truth. Mrs de Rushbridger was killed because she could, in actual fact, have told us *nothing at all*. Because she had no connection with the crime. If she were to be Sir Charles's successful red herring – she could only be so *dead*. And so Mrs de Rushbridger, a harmless stranger, was murdered . . .

'Yet even in that seeming triumph Sir Charles made a colossal – a childish – error! The telegram was addressed to me, Hercule Poirot, at the Ritz Hotel. But Mrs de Rushbridger had never heard of my connection with the case! No one up in that part of the world knew of it. It was an unbelievably childish error.

'*Eh bien*, then I had reached a certain stage. I knew the

identity of the murderer. But I did not know the motive for the original crime.

'I reflected.

'And once again, more clearly than ever, I saw the death of Sir Bartholomew Strange as the original and purposeful murder. What reason could Sir Charles Cartwright have for the murder of his friend? Could I imagine a motive? I thought I could.'

There was a deep sigh. Sir Charles Cartwright rose slowly to his feet and strolled to the fireplace. He stood there, his hand on his hip, looking down at Poirot. His attitude (Mr Satterthwaite could have told you) was that of Lord Eaglemount as he looks scornfully at the rascally solicitor who has succeeded in fastening an accusation of fraud upon him. He radiated nobility and disgust. He was the aristocrat looking down at the ignoble canaille.

'You have an extraordinary imagination, M. Poirot,' he said. 'It's hardly worth while saying that there's not one single word of truth in your story. How you have the damned impertinence to dish up such an absurd fandangle of lies I don't know. But go on, I am interested. What was my motive for murdering a man whom I had known ever since boyhood?'

Hercule Poirot, the little bourgeois, looked up at the aristocrat. He spoke quickly but firmly.

'Sir Charles, we have a proverb that says, "*Cherchez la femme*." It was *there* that I found my motive. I had seen you with Mademoiselle Lytton Gore. It was clear that you loved her – loved her with that terrible absorbing passion that comes to a middle-aged man and which is usually inspired by an innocent young girl.

'You loved her. She, I could see, had the hero worship for you. You had only to speak and she would fall into your arms. But you did not speak. Why?

'You pretended to your friend, Mr Satterthwaite, that you were the dense lover who cannot recognize his mistress's answering passion. You pretended to think that Miss Lytton Gore was in love with Oliver Manders. But I say, Sir Charles, that you are a man of the world. You are a man with a great experience of women. *You cannot have been deceived.* You knew perfectly well that Miss Lytton Gore cared for you. Why, then, did you not marry her? You wanted to do so.

'It must be that there was some obstacle. What could that obstacle be? It could only be the fact that you already had a wife. But nobody ever spoke of you as a married man. You passed always as a bachelor. The marriage, then, had taken place when you were very young – before you became known as a rising young actor.

'What had happened to your wife? If she were still alive, why did nobody know about her? If you were living apart there was the remedy of divorce. If your wife was a Catholic, or one who disapproved of divorce, she would still be known as living apart from you.

'But there are two tragedies where the law gives no relief. The woman you married might be serving a life sentence in some prison, or she might be confined in a lunatic asylum. *In neither case could you obtain a divorce*, and if it had happened while you were still a boy nobody might know about it.

'If nobody knew, you might marry Miss Lytton Gore without telling her the truth. *But supposing one person knew* – a friend who had known you all your life? Sir Bartholomew Strange was an honourabe, upright physician. He might pity you deeply, he might sympathize with a liaison or an irregular life, but he would not stand by silent and see you enter into a bigamous marriage with an unsuspecting young girl.

'Before you could marry Miss Lytton Gore, Sir Bartholomew Strange must be removed . . .'

Sir Charles laughed.

'And dear old Babbington? Did he know all about it, too?'

'I fancied so at first. But I soon found that there was no evidence to support that theory. Besides, my original stumbling block remained. *Even if it was you who put the nicotine into the cocktail glass, you could not have ensured its reaching one particular person.*

'That was my problem. And suddenly a chance word from Miss Lytton Gore showed me light.

'The poison was not intended especially for Stephen Babbington. It was intended for *any one* of those present, with three exceptions. These exceptions were Miss Lytton Gore, to whom you were careful to hand an innocent glass, yourself, and Sir Bartholomew Strange, who, you knew, did not drink cocktails.'

Mr Satterthwaite cried out:

'But that's nonsense! What's the point of it? There isn't any.'

Poirot turned towards him. Triumph came into his voice.

'Oh, yes, there is. A queer point – a very queer point. The only time I have come across such a motive for murder. The murder of Stephen Babbington was neither more nor less than a *dress rehearsal.*'

'*What*?'

'Yes, Sir Charles was an actor. He obeyed his actor's instinct. He tried out his murder before committing it. No suspicion could possibly attach to him. Not one of those people's deaths could benefit him in any way, and, moreover, as everyone has found, *he could not have been proved to have poisoned any particular person*. And, my friends, the dress rehearsal went well. Mr Babbington dies, and foul play is not even suspected. It is left to Sir Charles to urge that suspicion and he is highly gratified at our refusal to take it seriously. The substitution of the glass, too, that has gone without a hitch. In fact, he can be sure that, when the real performance comes, it will be "all right on the night".

'As you know, events took a slightly different turn. On the second occasion a doctor was present who immediately suspected poison. It was then to Sir Charles's interests to stress the death of Babbington. Sir Bartholomew's death must be presumed to be the outcome of the earlier death. Attention must be focused on the motive for Babbington's murder, not on any motive that might exist for Sir Bartholomew's removal.

'But there was one thing that Sir Charles failed to realize – the efficient watchfulness of Miss Milray. Miss Milray knew that her employer dabbled in chemical experiments in the tower in the garden. Miss Milray paid bills for rose spraying solution, and realized that quite a lot of it had unaccountably disappeared. When she read that Mr Babbington had died of nicotine poisoning, her clever brain leaped at once to the conclusion that Sir Charles had extracted the pure alkaloid from the rose solution.

'And Miss Milray did not know what to do, for she had known Mr Babbington as a little girl, and she was in love, deeply and devotedly as an ugly woman can be, with her fascinating employer.

'In the end she decided to destroy Sir Charles's apparatus. Sir Charles himself had been so cocksure of his success that he had never thought it necessary. She went down to Cornwall, and I followed.'

Again Sir Charles laughed. More than ever he looked a fine gentleman disgusted by a rat.

'Is some old chemical apparatus all your evidence?' he demanded contemptuously.

'No,' said Poirot. 'There is your passport showing the dates when you returned to and left England. And there is the fact that in the Harverton County Asylum there is a woman, Gladys Mary Mugg, the wife of Charles Mugg.'

Egg had so far sat silent – a frozen figure. But now she stirred. A little cry – almost a moan – came from her.

Sir Charles turned superbly.

'Egg, you don't believe a word of this absurd story, do you?' He laughed. His hands were outstretched.

Egg came slowly forward as though hypnotized. Her eyes, appealing, tortured, gazed into her lover's. And then, just before she reached him, she wavered, her glance fell, went this way and that as though seeking for reassurance.

Then with a cry she fell on her knees by Poirot.

'Is this true? Is this true?'

He put both hands on her shoulders, a firm, kindly touch.

'It is true, mademoiselle.'

There was no sound then but Egg's sobs.

Sir Charles seemed suddenly to have aged. It was an old man's face, a leering satyr's face.

'God damn you,' he said.

And never, in all his acting career, had words come with such utter and compelling malignancy.

Then he turned and went out of the room.

Mr Satterthwaite half sprang up from his chair, but Poirot shook his head, his hand still gently stroking the sobbing girl.

'He'll escape,' said Mr Satterthwaite.

Poirot shook his head.

'No, he will only choose his exit. The slow one before the eyes of the world, or the quick one off stage.'

The door opened softly and someone came in. It was Oliver

Manders. His usual sneering expression was gone. He looked white and unhappy.

Poirot bent over the girl.

'See, mademoiselle,' he said gently. 'Here is a friend come to take you home.'

Egg rose to her feet. She looked uncertainly towards Oliver then made a step stumblingly towards him.

'Oliver . . . Take me to Mother. Oh, take me to Mother.'

He put an arm round her and drew her towards the door.

'Yes, dear, I'll take you. Come.'

Egg's legs were trembling so that she could hardly walk. Between them Oliver and Mr Satterthwaite guided her footsteps. At the door she took a hold upon herself and threw back her head.

'I'm all right.'

Poirot made a gesture, and Oliver Manders came back into the room.

'Be very good to her,' said Poirot.

'I will, sir. She's all I care about in the world – you know that. Love for her made me bitter and cynical. But I shall be different now. I'm ready to stand by. And some day, perhaps –'

'I think so,' said Poirot. 'I think she was beginning to care for you when he came along and dazzled her. Hero worship is a real and terrible danger to the young. Some day Egg will fall in love with a friend, and build her happiness upon rock.'

He looked kindly after the young man as he left the room.

Presently Mr Satterthwaite returned.

'M. Poirot,' he said. 'You have been wonderful – absolutely wonderful.'

Poirot put on his modest look.

'It is nothing – nothing. A tragedy in three acts – and now the curtain has fallen.'

'You'll excuse me –' said Mr Satterthwaite.

'Yes, there is some point you want explained to you?'

'There is one thing I want to know.'

'Ask then.'

'Why do you sometimes speak perfectly good English and at other times not?'

Poirot laughed.

'Ah, I will explain. It is true that I can speak the exact, the idiomatic English. But, my friend, to speak the broken English is an enormous asset. It leads people to despise you. They say – a foreigner – he can't even speak English properly. It is not my policy to terrify people – instead I invite their gentle ridicule. Also I boast! An Englishman he says often, "A fellow who thinks as much of himself as that cannot be worth much." That is the English point of view. It is not at all true. And so, you see, I put people off their guard. Besides,' he added, 'it has become a habit.'

'Dear me,' said Mr Satterthwaite, 'quite the cunning of the serpent.'

He was silent for a moment or two, thinking over the case.

'I'm afraid I have not shone over this matter,' he said vexedly.

'On the contrary. You appreciated that important point – Sir Bartholomew's remark about the butler – you realized the astute observation of Miss Wills. In fact, you could have solved the whole thing but for your playgoer's reaction to dramatic effect.'

Mr Satterthwaite looked cheerful.

Suddenly an idea struck him. His jaw fell.

'My goodness,' he cried, 'I've only just realized it. That rascal, with his poisoned cocktail! Anyone might have drunk it. It might have been *me*.'

'There is an even more terrible possibility that you have not considered,' said Poirot.

'Eh?'

'It might have been ME,' said Hercule Poirot.

SAD CYPRESS

To Peter and Peggy McLeod

Come away, come away, death,
   And in sad cypress let me be laid;
Fly away, fly away, breath!
   I am slain by a fair cruel maid.
My shroud of white, stuck all with yew
   O prepare it;
My part of death no one so true;
   Did share it.

Shakespeare

'Elinor Katharine Carlisle. You stand charged upon this indictment with the murder of Mary Gerrard upon the 27th of July last. Are you guilty or not guilty?'

Elinor Carlisle stood very straight, her head raised. It was a graceful head, the modelling of the bones sharp and well defined. The eyes were a deep vivid blue, the hair black. The brows had been plucked to a faint thin line.

There was a silence – quite a noticeable silence.

Sir Edwin Bulmer, Counsel for the Defence, felt a thrill of dismay.

He thought:

'My God, she's going to plead guilty . . . She's lost her nerve . . .'

Elinor Carlisle's lips parted. She said:

'Not guilty.'

Counsel for the Defence sank back. He passed a handkerchief over his brow, realizing that it had been a near shave.

Sir Samuel Attenbury was on his feet, outlining the case for the Crown.

'May it please your lordship, gentlemen of the jury, on the 27th of July, at half-past three in the afternoon, Mary Gerrard died at Hunterbury, Maidensford . . .'

His voice ran on, sonorous and pleasing to the ear. It lulled Elinor almost into unconsciousness. From the simple and concise narrative, only an occasional phrase seeped through to her conscious mind.

'. . . case a peculiarly simple and straightforward one . . .

'. . . It is the duty of the Crown . . . prove motive and opportunity . . .

'. . . No one, as far as can be seen, had any motive to kill this unfortunate girl, Mary Gerrard, except the accused. A young girl of a charming disposition – liked by everybody – without, one would have said, an enemy in the world . . .'

Mary, Mary Gerrard! How far away it all seemed now. Not real any longer . . .

'. . . Your attention will be particularly directed to the following considerations:

1. What opportunities and means had the accused for administering poison?

2. What motive had she for so doing?

'It will be my duty to call before you witnesses who can help you to form a true conclusion on these matters . . .

'. . . As regards the poisoning of Mary Gerrard, I shall endeavour to show you that *no one had any opportunity* to commit this crime except the accused . . .'

Elinor felt as though imprisoned in a thick mist. Detached words came drifting through the fog.

'. . . Sandwiches . . .

'. . . Fish paste . . .

'. . . Empty house . . .'

The words stabbed through the thick enveloping blanket of Elinor's thoughts – pin-pricks through a heavy muffling veil . . .

The court. Faces. Rows and rows of faces! One particular face with a big black moustache and shrewd eyes. Hercule Poirot, his head a little on one side, his eyes thoughtful, was watching her.

She thought: He's trying to see just exactly *why* I did it . . . He's trying to get inside my head to see what I thought – what I felt . . .

Felt . . . ? A little blur – a slight sense of shock . . . Roddy's face – his dear, *dear* face with its long nose, its sensitive mouth . . . Roddy! Always Roddy – always, ever since she could remember . . . since those days at Hunterbury amongst the raspberries and up in the warren and down by the brook. Roddy – Roddy – Roddy . . .

Other faces! Nurse O'Brien, her mouth slightly open, her freckled fresh face thrust forward. Nurse Hopkins looking smug

– smug and implacable. Peter Lord's face – Peter Lord – so kind, so sensible, so – so *comforting*! But looking now – what was it – *lost*? Yes – lost! Minding – minding all this frightfully! While she herself, the star performer, didn't mind at all!

Here she was, quite calm and cold, standing in the dock, accused of murder. She was in court.

Something stirred; the folds of blanket round her brain lightened – became mere wraiths. In *court*! . . . *People* . . .

People leaning forward, their lips parted a little, their eyes agog, staring at her, Elinor, with a horrible ghoulish enjoyment – listening with a kind of slow, cruel relish to what that tall man with the Jewish nose was saying about her.

'The facts in this case are extremely easy to follow and are not in dispute. I shall put them before you quite simply. From the very beginning . . .'

Elinor thought:

'The beginning . . . The beginning? The day that horrible anonymous letter came! *That* was the beginning of it . . .'

PART I

An anonymous letter!

Elinor Carlisle stood looking down at it as it lay open in her hand. She'd never had such a thing before. It gave one an unpleasant sensation. Ill-written, badly spelt, on cheap pink paper.

> *This is to Warn You* (it ran),
> *I'm naming no Names but there's Someone sucking up to your Aunt and if you're not kareful you'll get Cut Out of Everything. Girls Are very Artful and Old Ladies is Soft when Young Ones suck up to Them and Flatter them What I say is You'd best come down and see for Yourself whats Going On its not right you and the Young Gentleman should be Done Out of What's yours – and She's Very Artful and the Old Lady might Pop off at any time.*
> *Well-Wisher*

Elinor was still staring at this missive, her plucked brows drawn together in distaste, when the door opened. The maid announced, 'Mr Welman,' and Roddy came in.

Roddy! As always when she saw Roddy, Elinor was conscious of a slightly giddy feeling, a throb of sudden pleasure, a feeling that it was incumbent upon her to be very matter-of-fact and unemotional. Because it was so very obvious that Roddy, although he loved her, didn't feel about her the way she felt about him. The first sight of him did something to her, twisted her heart round so that it almost hurt. Absurd that a man – an ordinary, yes, a perfectly ordinary young man – should be able to do that to one! That the mere look of him should set the world spinning, that his voice should make you want – just a little – to cry . . . Love surely should be a pleasurable emotion – not something that hurt you by its intensity . . .

One thing was clear: one must be very, very careful to be

off-hand and casual about it all. Men didn't like devotion and adoration. Certainly Roddy didn't.

She said lightly:

'Hallo, Roddy!'

Roddy said:

'Hallo, darling. You're looking very tragic. Is it a bill?'

Elinor shook her head.

Roddy said:

'I thought it might be – midsummer, you know – when the fairies dance, and the accounts rendered come tripping along!'

Elinor said:

'It's rather horrid. It's an anonymous letter.'

Roddy's brows went up. His keen fastidious face stiffened and changed. He said – a sharp, disgusted exclamation:

'No!'

Elinor said again:

'It's rather horrid . . .'

She moved a step towards her desk.

'I'd better tear it up, I suppose.'

She could have done that – she almost did – for Roddy and anonymous letters were two things that ought not to come together. She might have thrown it away and thought no more about it. He would not have stopped her. His fastidiousness was far more strongly developed than his curiosity.

But on impulse Elinor decided differently. She said:

'Perhaps, though, you'd better read it first. Then we'll burn it. It's about Aunt Laura.'

Roddy's eyebrows rose in surprise.

'Aunt Laura?'

He took the letter, read it, gave a frown of distaste, and handed it back.

'Yes,' he said. 'Definitely to be burnt! How extraordinary people are!'

Elinor said:

'One of the servants, do you think?'

'I suppose so.' He hesitated. 'I wonder who – who the person is – the one they mention?'

Elinor said thoughtfully:

'It must be Mary Gerrard, I think.'

Roddy frowned in an effort of remembrance.

'Mary Gerrard? Who's she?'

'The daughter of the people at the lodge. You must remember her as a child? Aunt Laura was always fond of the girl, and took an interest in her. She paid for her schooling and for various extras – piano lessons and French and things.'

Roddy said:

'Oh, yes, I remember her now: scrawny kid, all legs and arms, with a lot of messy fair hair.'

Elinor nodded.

'Yes, you probably haven't seen her since those summer holidays when Mum and Dad were abroad. You've not been down at Hunterbury as often as I have, of course, and she's been abroad *au pair* in Germany lately, but we used to rout her out and play with her when we were all kids.'

'What's she like now?' asked Roddy.

Elinor said:

'She's turned out very nice-looking. Good manners and all that. As a result of her education, you'd never take her for old Gerrard's daughter.'

'Gone all lady-like, has she?'

'Yes. I think, as a result of that, she doesn't get on very well at the lodge. Mrs Gerrard died some years ago, you know, and Mary and her father don't get on. He jeers at her schooling and her "fine ways".'

Roddy said irritably:

'People never dream what harm they may do by "educating" someone! Often it's cruelty, not kindness!'

Elinor said:

'I suppose she *is* up at the house a good deal . . . She reads aloud to Aunt Laura, I know, since she had her stroke.'

Roddy said:

'Why can't the nurse read to her?'

Elinor said with a smile:

'Nurse O'Brien's got a brogue you can cut with a knife! I don't wonder Aunt Laura prefers Mary.'

Roddy walked rapidly and nervously up and down the room for a minute or two. Then he said:

'You know, Elinor, I believe we ought to go down.'

Elinor said with a slight recoil:

'Because of this –?'

'No, no – not at all. Oh, damn it all, one must be honest, *yes*! Foul as that communication is, there *may* be some truth behind it. I mean, the old girl is pretty ill –'

'Yes, Roddy.'

He looked at her with his charming smile – admitting the fallibility of human nature. He said:

'And the money *does* matter – to you and me, Elinor.'

She admitted it quickly.

'Oh, it does.'

He said seriously:

'It's not that I'm mercenary. But, after all, Aunt Laura herself has said over and over again that you and I are her only family ties. You're her own niece, her brother's child, and I'm her husband's nephew. She's always given us to understand that at her death all she's got would come to one or other – or more probably both – of us. And – and it's a pretty large sum, Elinor.'

'Yes,' said Elinor thoughtfully. 'It must be.'

'It's no joke keeping up Hunterbury.' He paused. 'Uncle Henry was what you'd call, I suppose, comfortably off when he met your Aunt Laura. But she was an heiress. She and your father were both left very wealthy. Pity your father speculated and lost most of his.'

Elinor sighed.

'Poor Father never had much business sense. He got very worried over things before he died.'

'Yes, your Aunt Laura had a much better head than he had. She married Uncle Henry and they bought Hunterbury, and she told me the other day that she'd been exceedingly lucky always in her investments. Practically nothing had slumped.'

'Uncle Henry left all he had to her when he died, didn't he?' Roddy nodded.

'Yes, tragic his dying so soon. And she's never married again. Faithful old bean. And she's always been very good to us. She's treated me as if I was her nephew by blood. If I've been in a hole she's helped me out; luckily I haven't done that *too* often!'

'She's been awfully generous to me, too,' said Elinor gratefully.

Roddy nodded.

'Aunt Laura,' he said, 'is a brick. But, you know, Elinor, perhaps without meaning to do so, you and I live pretty extravagantly, considering what our means really are!'

She said ruefully:

'I suppose we do . . . Everything costs so much – clothes and one's face – and just silly things like cinemas and cocktails – and even gramophone records!'

Roddy said:

'Darling, you *are* one of the lilies of the field, aren't you? You toil not, neither do you spin!'

Elinor said:

'Do you think I ought to, Roddy?'

He shook his head.

'I like you as you are: delicate and aloof and ironical. I'd hate you to go all earnest. I'm only saying that if it weren't for Aunt Laura you probably would be working at some grim job.'

He went on:

'The same with me. I've got a job, of sorts. Being with Lewis & Hume is not too arduous. It suits me. I preserve my self-respect by having a job; but – mark this – but I don't worry about the future because of my expectations – from Aunt Laura.'

Elinor said:

'We sound rather like human leeches!'

'Nonsense! We've been given to understand that some day we shall have money – that's all. Naturally, that fact influences our conduct.'

Elinor said thoughtfully:

'Aunt Laura has never told us definitely just *how* she has left her money?'

Roddy said:

'That doesn't matter! In all probability she's divided it between us; but if that isn't so – if she's left all of it or most of it to you as her own flesh and blood – why, then, darling, I shall share in it, because I'm going to marry you – and if the old pet thinks the majority should go to me as the male representative of the Welmans, that's still all right, because *you're* marrying *me*.'

He grinned at her affectionately. He said:

'Lucky we happen to love each other. You do love me, don't you, Elinor?'

'Yes.'

She said it coldly, almost primly.

'Yes!' Roddy mimicked her. 'You're adorable, Elinor. That little air of yours – aloof – untouchable – *la Princesse Lointaine*. It's that quality of yours that made me love you, I believe.'

Elinor caught her breath. She said, 'Is it?'

'Yes.' He frowned. 'Some women are so – oh, I don't know – so damned possessive – so – so dog-like and devoted – their emotions slopping all over the place! I'd hate that. With you I never know – I'm never sure – any minute you might turn round in that cool, detached way of yours and say you'd changed your mind – quite coolly, like that – without batting an eyelash! You're a fascinating creature, Elinor. You're like a work of art – so – so – *finished*!'

He went on:

'You know, I think ours will be the perfect marriage . . . We both love each other enough and not too much. We're good friends. We've got a lot of tastes in common. We know each other through and through. We've all the advantages of cousinship without the disadvantages of blood relationship. I shall never get tired of you, because you're such an elusive creature. *You* may get tired of *me*, though. I'm such an ordinary sort of chap –'

Elinor shook her head. She said:

'I shan't get tired of you, Roddy – never.'

'My sweet!'

He kissed her.

He said:

'Aunt Laura has a pretty shrewd idea of how it is with us, I think, although we haven't been down since we finally fixed it up. It rather gives us an excuse, doesn't it, for going down?'

'Yes. I was thinking the other day –'

Roddy finished the sentence for her:

'– That we hadn't been down as often as we might. I thought that, too. When she first had her stroke we went down almost every other week-end. And now it must be almost two months since we were there.'

Elinor said:

'We'd have gone if she'd asked for us – at once.'

'Yes, of course. And we know that she likes Nurse O'Brien and is well looked after. All the same, perhaps we *have* been a bit slack. I'm talking now not from the money point of view – but the sheer human one.'

Elinor nodded.

'I know.'

'So that filthy letter has done some good, after all! We'll go down to protect our interests *and* because we're fond of the old dear!'

He lit a match and set fire to the letter which he took from Elinor's hand.

'Wonder who wrote it?' he said. 'Not that it matters . . . Someone who was "on our side", as we used to say when we were kids. Perhaps they've done us a good turn, too. Jim Partington's mother went out to the Riviera to live, had a handsome young Italian doctor to attend her, became quite crazy about him and left him every penny she had. Jim and his sisters tried to upset the will, but couldn't.'

Elinor said:

.'Aunt Laura likes the new doctor who's taken over Dr Ransome's practice – but not to that extent! Anyway, that horrid letter mentioned a girl. It must be Mary.'

Roddy said:

'We'll go down and see for ourselves . . .'

II

Nurse O'Brien rustled out of Mrs Welman's bedroom and into the bathroom. She said over her shoulder:

'I'll just pop the kettle on. You could do with a cup of tea before you go on, I'm sure, Nurse.'

Nurse Hopkins said comfortably:

'Well, dear, I can *always* do with a cup of tea. I always say there's nothing like a nice cup of tea – a strong cup!'

Nurse O'Brien said as she filled the kettle and lit the gas-ring:

'I've got everything here in this cupboard – teapot and cups and sugar – and Edna brings me up fresh milk twice a day. No need to be forever ringing bells. 'Tis a fine gas-ring, this; boils a kettle in a flash.'

Nurse O'Brien was a tall red-haired woman of thirty with flashing white teeth, a freckled face and an engaging smile. Her cheerfulness and vitality made her a favourite with her patients. Nurse Hopkins, the District Nurse who came every morning to assist with the bed-making and toilet of the heavy old lady, was a homely-looking middle-aged woman with a capable air and a brisk manner.

She said now approvingly:

'Everything's very well done in this house.'

The other nodded.

'Yes, old-fashioned, some of it, no central heating, but plenty of fires and all the maids are very obliging girls and Mrs Bishop looks after them well.'

Nurse Hopkins said:

'These girls nowadays – I've no patience with 'em – don't know what they want, most of them – and can't do a decent day's work.'

'Mary Gerrard's a nice girl,' said Nurse O'Brien. 'I really don't know what Mrs Welman would do without her. You saw how she asked for her now? Ah, well, she's a lovely creature, I will say, and she's got a way with her.'

Nurse Hopkins said:

'I'm sorry for Mary. That old father of hers does his best to spite the girl.'

'Not a civil word in his head, the old curmudgeon,' said Nurse O'Brien. 'There, the kettle's singing. I'll wet the tea as soon as it comes to the boil.'

The tea was made and poured, hot and strong. The two nurses sat with it in Nurse O'Brien's room next door to Mrs Welman's bedroom.

'Mr Welman and Miss Carlisle are coming down,' said Nurse O'Brien. 'There was a telegram came this morning.'

'There now, dear,' said Nurse Hopkins. 'I thought the old lady was looking excited about something. It's some time since they've been down, isn't it?'

'It must be two months and over. Such a nice young gentleman, Mr Welman. But very proud-looking.'

Nurse Hopkins said:

'I saw *her* picture in the *Tatler* the other day – with a friend at Newmarket.'

Nurse O'Brien said:

'She's very well known in society, isn't she? And always has such lovely clothes. Do you think she's really good-looking, Nurse?'

Nurse Hopkins said:

'Difficult to tell what these girls really look like under their make-up! In my opinion, she hasn't got anything like the looks Mary Gerrard has!'

Nurse O'Brien pursed her lips and put her head on one side.

'You may be right now. But Mary hasn't got the *style*!'

Nurse Hopkins said sententiously:

'Fine feathers make fine birds.'

'Another cup of tea, Nurse?'

'Thank you, Nurse. I don't mind if I do.'

Over their steaming cups the women drew a little closer together.

Nurse O'Brien said:

'An odd thing happened last night. I went in at two o'clock to settle my dear comfortably, as I always do, and she was lying there awake. But she must have been dreaming, for as soon as I got into the room she said, "The photograph. I must have the photograph."

'So I said, "Why, of course, Mrs Welman. But wouldn't you rather wait till morning?" And she said, "No, I want to look at it now." So I said, "Well, where *is* this photograph? Is it the one of Mr Roderick you're meaning?" And she said, "Roderick? No. *Lewis*." And she began to struggle, and I went to lift her and she got out her keys from the little box beside her bed and told me to unlock the second drawer of the tall-boy, and there, sure enough, was a big photograph in a silver frame. *Such* a handsome man. And "*Lewis*" written across the corner. Old-fashioned, of course, must have been taken many years ago. I took it to her and she held it there, staring at it a long time. And she just murmured. "*Lewis – Lewis.*" Then she sighed and gave it to me and told me to put it back. And would you believe it, when I turned round again she'd gone off as sweetly as a child.'

Nurse Hopkins said:

'Was it her husband, do you think?'

Nurse O'Brien said:

'It was not! For this morning I asked Mrs Bishop, careless-like, what was the late Mr Welman's first name, and it was Henry, she told me!'

The two women exchanged glances. Nurse Hopkins had a long nose, and the end of it quivered a little with pleasurable emotion. She said thoughtfully:

'Lewis – Lewis. I wonder, now. I don't recall the name anywhere round these parts.'

'It would be many years ago, dear,' the other reminded her.

'Yes, and, of course, I've only been here a couple of years. I wonder now –'

Nurse O'Brien said:

'A *very* handsome man. Looked as though he might be a cavalry officer!'

Nurse Hopkins sipped her tea. She said:

'That's very interesting.'

Nurse O'Brien said romantically:

'Maybe they were boy and girl together and a cruel father separated them . . .'

Nurse Hopkins said with a deep sigh:

'Perhaps he was killed in the war . . .'

III

When Nurse Hopkins, pleasantly stimulated by tea and romantic speculation, finally left the house, Mary Gerrard ran out of the door to overtake her.

'Oh, Nurse, may I walk down to the village with you?'

'Of course you can, Mary, my dear.'

Mary Gerrard said breathlessly:

'I *must* talk to you. I'm so worried about everything.'

The older woman looked at her kindly.

At twenty-one, Mary Gerrard was a lovely creature with a kind of wild-rose unreality about her: a long delicate neck, pale golden hair lying close to her exquisitely shaped head in soft natural waves, and eyes of a deep vivid blue.

Nurse Hopkins said:

'What's the trouble?'

'The trouble is that the time is going on and on and I'm not *doing* anything!'

Nurse Hopkins said drily:

'Time enough for that.'

'No, but it is so – so unsettling. Mrs Welman has been wonderfully kind, giving me all that expensive schooling. I do feel now that I ought to be starting to earn my own living. I ought to be training for something.'

Nurse Hopkins nodded sympathetically.

'It's such a waste of everything if I don't. I've tried to – to explain what I feel to Mrs Welman, but – it's difficult – she doesn't seem to understand. She keeps saying there's plenty of time.'

Nurse Hopkins said:

'She's a sick woman, remember.'

Mary flushed a contrite flush.

'Oh, I know. I suppose I oughtn't to bother her. But it *is* worrying – and Father's so – so *beastly* about it! Keeps jibing at me for being a fine lady! But indeed *I* don't want to sit about doing nothing!'

'I know you don't.'

'The trouble is that training of any kind is nearly always expensive. I know German pretty well now, and I might do something with that. But I think really I want to be a hospital nurse. I do like nursing and sick people.'

Nurse Hopkins said unromantically:

'You've got to be as strong as a horse, remember!'

'I am strong! And I really *do* like nursing. Mother's sister, the one in New Zealand, was a nurse. So it's in my blood, you see.'

'What about massage?' suggested Nurse Hopkins. 'Or Norland? You're fond of children. There's good money to be made in massage.'

Mary said doubtfully:

'It's expensive to train for it, isn't it? I hoped – but of course that's very greedy of me – she's done so much for me already.'

'Mrs Welman, you mean? Nonsense. In my opinion, she owes you that. She's given you a slap-up education, but not the kind that leads to anything much. You don't want to teach?'

'I'm not clever enough.'

Nurse Hopkins said:

'There's brains and brains! If you take my advice, Mary, you'll be patient for the present. In my opinion, as I said, Mrs Welman owes it to you to help you get a start at making your living. And I've no doubt she means to do it. But the truth of the matter is, she's got fond of you, and she doesn't want to lose you.'

Mary said:

'Oh!' She drew in her breath with a little gasp. 'Do you really think that's it?'

'I haven't the least doubt of it! There she is, poor old lady, more or less helpless, paralysed one side and nothing and nobody much to amuse her. It means a lot to her to have a fresh, pretty young thing like you about the house. You've a very nice way with you in a sick-room.'

Mary said softly:

'If you really think so – that makes me feel better . . . Dear Mrs Welman, I'm very, *very* fond of her! She's been so good to me always. I'd do *anything* for her!'

Nurse Hopkins said drily:

'Then the best thing you can do is to stay where you are and stop worrying! It won't be for long.'

Mary said, 'Do you mean –?'

Her eyes looked wide and frightened.

The District Nurse nodded.

'She's rallied wonderfully, but it won't be for long. There will be a second stroke and then a third. I know the way of it only too well. You be patient, my dear. If you keep the old lady's last days happy and occupied, that's a better deed than many. The time for the other will come.'

Mary said:

'You're very kind.'

Nurse Hopkins said:

'Here's your father coming out from the lodge – and not to pass the time of day pleasantly, I should say!'

They were just nearing the big iron gates. On the steps of the lodge an elderly man with a bent back was painfully hobbling down the two steps.

Nurse Hopkins said cheerfully:

'Good morning, Mr Gerrard.'

Ephraim Gerrard said crustily:

'Ah!'

'Very nice weather,' said Nurse Hopkins.

Old Gerrard said crossly:

'May be for you. 'Tisn't for me. My lumbago's been at me something cruel.'

Nurse Hopkins said cheerfully:

'That was the wet spell last week, I expect. This hot dry weather will soon clear *that* away.'

Her brisk professional manner appeared to annoy the old man.

He said disagreeably:

'Nurses – nurses, you'm all the same. Full of cheerfulness over other people's troubles. Little *you* care! And there's Mary talks about being a nurse, too. Should have thought she'd want to be something better than *that*, with her French and her German and her piano-playing and all the things she's learned at her grand school and her travels abroad.'

Mary said sharply:

'Being a hospital nurse would be quite good enough for me!'

'Yes, and you'd sooner do nothing at all, wouldn't you? Strutting about with your airs and your graces and your fine-lady-do-nothing ways. Laziness, that's what *you* like, my girl!'

Mary protested, tears springing to her eyes:

'It isn't true, Dad. You've no right to say that!'

Nurse Hopkins intervened with a heavy, determinedly humorous air.

'Just a bit under the weather, aren't we, this morning? You don't really mean what you say, Gerrard. Mary's a good girl and a good daughter to you.'

Gerrard looked at his daughter with an air of almost active malevolence.

'She's no daughter of mine – nowadays – with her French and her history and her mincing talk. Pah!'

He turned and went into the lodge again.

Mary said, the tears still standing in her eyes:

'You do see, Nurse, don't you, how difficult it is? He's so

unreasonable. He's never really liked me even when I was a little girl. Mum was always standing up for me.'

Nurse Hopkins said kindly:

'There, there, don't worry. These things are sent to try us! Goodness, I must hurry. Such a round as I've got this morning.'

And as she stood watching the brisk retreating figure, Mary Gerrard thought forlornly that nobody was any real good or could really help you. Nurse Hopkins, for all her kindness, was quite content to bring out a little stock of platitudes and offer them with an air of novelty.

Mary thought disconsolately:

'What *shall* I do?'

CHAPTER 2

I

Mrs Welman lay on her carefully built-up pillows. Her breathing was a little heavy, but she was not asleep. Her eyes – eyes still deep and blue like those of her niece Elinor, looked up at the ceiling. She was a big, heavy woman, with a handsome, hawk-like profile. Pride and determination showed in her face.

The eyes dropped and came to rest on the figure sitting by the window. They rested there tenderly – almost wistfully.

She said at last:

'Mary –'

The girl turned quickly.

'Oh, you're awake, Mrs Welman.'

Laura Welman said:

'Yes, I've been awake some time . . .'

'Oh, I didn't know. I'd have –'

Mrs Welman broke in:

'No, that's all right. I was thinking – thinking of many things.'

'Yes, Mrs Welman?'

The sympathetic look, the interested voice, made a tender look come into the older woman's face. She said gently:

'I'm very fond of you, my dear. You're very good to me.'

'Oh, Mrs Welman, it's *you* who have been good to *me*. If it hadn't been for you, I don't know what I should have done! You've done *everything* for me.'

'I don't know . . . I don't know, I'm sure . . .' The sick woman moved restlessly, her right arm twitched – the left remaining inert and lifeless. 'One means to do the best one can; but it's so difficult to know what is best – what is *right*. I've been too sure of myself always . . .'

Mary Gerrard said:

'Oh, no, I'm sure you *always* know what is best and right to do.'

But Laura Welman shook her head.

'No – no. It worries me. I've had one besetting sin always, Mary: I'm proud. Pride can be the devil. It runs in our family. Elinor has it, too.'

Mary said quickly:

'It will be nice for you to have Miss Elinor and Mr Roderick down. It will cheer you up a lot. It's quite a time since they were here.'

Mrs Welman said softly:

'They're good children – very good children. And fond of me, both of them. I always know I've only got to send and they'll come at any time. But I don't want to do that too often. They're young and happy – the world in front of them. No need to bring them near decay and suffering before their time.'

Mary said, 'I'm sure they'd *never* feel like that, Mrs Welman.'

Mrs Welman went on, talking perhaps more to herself than to the girl:

'I always hoped they might marry. But I tried never to suggest anything of the kind. Young people are so contradictory. It would have put them off! I had an idea, long ago when they were children, that Elinor had set her heart on Roddy. But I wasn't at all sure about *him*. He's a funny creature. Henry was like that – very reserved and fastidious . . . Yes, Henry . . .'

She was silent for a little, thinking of her dead husband.

She murmured:

'So long ago . . . so very long ago . . . We had only been married five years when he died. Double pneumonia . . . We were happy – yes, very happy; but somehow it all seems very

unreal, that happiness. I was an odd, solemn, undeveloped girl
– my head full of ideas and hero-worship. No *reality* . . .'

Mary murmured:

'You must have been very lonely – afterwards.'

'After? Oh, yes – terribly lonely. I was twenty-six . . . and now
I'm over sixty. A long time, my dear . . . a long, long time . . .'
She said with sudden brisk acerbity, 'And now *this*!'

'Your illness?'

'Yes. A stroke is the thing I've always dreaded. The indignity of
it all! Washed and tended like a baby! Helpless to do anything for
yourself. It maddens me. The O'Brien creature is good-natured
– I will say that for her. She doesn't mind my snapping at her
and she's not more idiotic than most of them. But it makes a lot
of difference to me to have *you* about, Mary.'

'Does it?' The girl flushed. 'I – I'm so glad, Mrs Welman.'

Laura Welman said shrewdly:

'You've been worrying, haven't you? About the future. You
leave it to me, my dear. I'll see to it that you shall have the means
to be independent and take up a profession. But be patient for a
little – it means too much to me to have you here.'

'Oh, Mrs Welman, of course – of *course*! I wouldn't leave you
for the world. Not if you want me –'

'I do want you . . .' The voice was unusually deep and full.
'You're – you're quite like a daughter to me, Mary. I've seen
you grow up here at Hunterbury from a little toddling thing –
seen you grow into a beautiful girl . . . I'm proud of you, child.
I only hope I've done what was best for you.'

Mary said quickly:

'If you mean that your having been so good to me and having
educated me above – well, above my station – if you think it's
made me dissatisfied or – or – given me what Father calls fine-lady
ideas, indeed that isn't true. I'm just ever so grateful, that's all.
And if I'm anxious to start earning my living, it's only because I
feel it's right that I should, and not – and not – well, do nothing
after all you've done for me. I – I shouldn't like it to be thought
that I was sponging on you.'

Laura Welman said, and her voice was suddenly sharp-edged:

'So that's what Gerrard's been putting into your head? Pay no
attention to your father, Mary; there never has been and never

will be any question of your sponging on me! I'm asking you to stay here a little longer solely on my account. Soon it will be over . . . If they went the proper way about things, my life could be ended here and now – none of this long-drawn-out tomfoolery with nurses and doctors.'

'Oh, no, Mrs Welman, Dr Lord says you may live for years.'

'I'm not at all anxious to, thank you! I told him the other day that in a decently civilized state, all there would be to do would be for me to intimate to him that I wished to end it, and he'd finish me off painlessly with some nice drug. "And if you'd any courage, Doctor," I said, "you'd do it, anyway!"'

Mary cried:

'Oh! What did he say?'

'The disrespectful young man merely grinned at me, my dear, and said he wasn't going to risk being hanged. He said, "If you'd left me all your money, Mrs Welman, that would be different, of course!" Impudent young jackanapes! But I like him. His visits do me more good than his medicines.'

'Yes, he's very nice,' said Mary. 'Nurse O'Brien thinks a lot of him and so does Nurse Hopkins.'

Mrs Welman said:

'Hopkins ought to have more sense at her age. As for O'Brien, she simpers and says, "Oh, doctor," and tosses those long streamers of hers whenever he comes near her.'

'Poor Nurse O'Brien.'

Mrs Welman said indulgently:

'She's not a bad sort, really, but all nurses annoy me; they always will think that you'd like a "nice cup of tea" at five in the morning!' She paused. 'What's that? Is it the car?'

Mary looked out of the window.

'Yes, it's the car. Miss Elinor and Mr Roderick have arrived.'

II

Mrs Welman said to her niece:

'I'm very glad, Elinor, about you and Roddy.'

Elinor smiled at her.

'I thought you would be, Aunt Laura.'

The older woman said, after a moment's hesitation:

'You do – care about him, Elinor?'

Elinor's delicate brows lifted.

'Of course.'

Laura Welman said quickly:

'You must forgive me, dear. You know, you're very reserved. It's very difficult to know what you're thinking or feeling. When you were both much younger I thought you were perhaps beginning to care for Roddy – too much . . .'

Again Elinor's delicate brows were raised.

'Too much?'

The older woman nodded.

'Yes. It's not wise to care too much. Sometimes a very young girl does do just that . . . I was glad when you went abroad to Germany to finish. Then, when you came back, you seemed quite indifferent to him – and, well, I was sorry for that, too! I'm a tiresome old woman, difficult to satisfy! But I've always fancied that you had, perhaps, rather an intense nature – that kind of temperament runs in our family. It isn't a very happy one for its possessors . . . But, as I say, when you came back from abroad so indifferent to Roddy, I was sorry about that, because I had always hoped you two would come together. And now you have, and so everything is all right! And you *do* really care for him?'

Elinor said gravely:

'I care for Roddy enough and not too much.'

Mrs Welman nodded approval.

'I think, then, you'll be happy. Roddy needs love – but he doesn't like violent emotion. He'd shy off from possessiveness.'

Elinor said with feeling:

'You know Roddy very well!'

Mrs Welman said:

'If Roddy cares for you just a *little* more than you care for him – well, that's all to the good.'

Elinor said sharply:

'Aunt Agatha's Advice column. "*Keep your boy friend guessing! Don't let him be too sure of you!*"'

Laura Welman said sharply:

'Are you unhappy, child? Is anything wrong?'

'No, no, nothing.'

Laura Welman said:

'You just thought I was being rather – cheap? My dear, you're young and sensitive. Life, I'm afraid, *is* rather cheap . . .'

Elinor said with some slight bitterness:

'I suppose it is.'

Laura Welman said:

'My child – you *are* unhappy? What is it?'

'Nothing – absolutely nothing.' She got up and went to the window. Half turning, she said:

'Aunt Laura, tell me, honestly, do you think love is ever a happy thing?'

Mrs Welman's face became grave.

'In the sense you mean, Elinor – no, probably not . . . To care passionately for another human creature brings always more sorrow than joy; but all the same, Elinor, one would not be without that experience. Anyone who has never really loved has never really lived . . .'

The girl nodded.

She said:

'Yes – you understand – you've known what it's like –'

She turned suddenly, a questioning look in her eyes:

'Aunt Laura –'

The door opened and red-haired Nurse O'Brien came in.

She said in a sprightly manner:

'Mrs Welman, here's Doctor come to see you.'

III

Dr Lord was a young man of thirty-two. He had sandy hair, a pleasantly ugly freckled face and a remarkably square jaw. His eyes were a keen, piercing light blue.

'Good morning, Mrs Welman,' he said.

'Good morning, Dr Lord. This is my niece, Miss Carlisle.'

A very obvious admiration sprang into Dr Lord's transparent face. He said, 'How do you do?' The hand that Elinor extended to him he took rather gingerly as though he thought he might break it.

Mrs Welman went on:

'Elinor and my nephew have come down to cheer me up.'

'Splendid!' said Dr Lord. 'Just what you need! It will do you a lot of good, I am sure, Mrs Welman.'

He was still looking at Elinor with obvious admiration.

Elinor said, moving towards the door:

'Perhaps I shall see you before you go, Dr Lord?'

'Oh – er – yes, of course.'

She went out, shutting the door behind her. Dr Lord approached the bed, Nurse O'Brien fluttering behind him.

Mrs Welman said with a twinkle:

'Going through the usual bag of tricks, Doctor: pulse, respiration, temperature? What humbugs you doctors are!'

Nurse O'Brien said with a sigh:

'Oh, Mrs Welman. What a thing, now, to be saying to the doctor!'

Dr Lord said with a twinkle:

'Mrs Welman sees through me, Nurse! All the same, Mrs Welman, I've got to do my stuff, you know. The trouble with me is I've never learnt the right bedside manner.'

'Your bedside manner's all right. Actually you're rather proud of it.'

Peter Lord chuckled and remarked:

'That's what *you* say.'

After a few routine questions had been asked and answered, Dr Lord leant back in his chair and smiled at his patient.

'Well,' he said. 'You're going on splendidly.'

Laura Welman said: 'So I shall be up and walking round the house in a few weeks' time?'

'Not quite so quickly as that.'

'No, indeed. You humbug! What's the good of living stretched out like this, and cared for like a baby?'

Dr Lord said:

'What's the good of life, anyway? That's the real question. Ever read about that nice mediæval invention, the Little Ease? You couldn't stand, sit or lie in it. You'd think anyone condemned to that would die in a few weeks. Not at all. One man lived for sixteen years in an iron cage, was released and lived to a hearty old age.'

Laura Welman said:

'What's the point of this story?'

Peter Lord said:

'The point is that one's got an *instinct* to live. One doesn't live because one's *reason* assents to living. People who, as we say, "would be better dead", don't want to die! People who apparently have got everything to live for just let themselves fade out of life because they haven't got the energy to fight.'

'Go on.'

'There's nothing more. You're one of the people who really *want* to live, whatever you say about it! And if your body wants to live, it's no good your brain dishing out the other stuff.'

Mrs Welman said with an abrupt change of subject:

'How do you like it down here?'

Peter Lord said, smiling:

'It suits me fine.'

'Isn't it a bit irksome for a young man like you? Don't you want to specialize? Don't you find a country GP practice rather boring?'

Lord shook his sandy head.

'No, I like my job. I like *people*, you know, and I like ordinary everyday diseases. I don't really want to pin down the rare bacillus of an obscure disease. I like measles and chicken-pox and all the rest of it. I like seeing how different bodies react to them. I like seeing if I can't improve on recognized treatment. The trouble with me is I've got absolutely no ambition. I shall stay here till I grow side-whiskers and people begin saying, "Of course, we've always had Dr Lord, and he's a nice old man: but he *is* very old-fashioned in his methods and perhaps we'd better call in young so-and-so, who's so very up to date . . ."'

'H'm,' said Mrs Welman. 'You seem to have got it all taped out!'

Peter Lord got up.

'Well,' he said. 'I must be off.'

Mrs Welman said:

'My niece will want to speak to you, I expect. By the way, what do you think of her? You haven't seen her before.'

Dr Lord went suddenly scarlet. His very eyebrows blushed. He said:

'I – oh! she's very good-looking, isn't she? And – eh – clever and all that, I should think.'

Mrs Welman was diverted. She thought to herself:

'How very young he is, really . . .'

Aloud she said:

'You ought to get married.'

IV

Roddy had wandered into the garden. He had crossed the broad sweep of lawn and along a paved walk and had then entered the walled kitchen-garden. It was well-kept and well-stocked. He wondered if he and Elinor would live at Hunterbury one day. He supposed that they would. He himself would like that. He preferred country life. He was a little doubtful about Elinor. Perhaps she'd like living in London better . . .

A little difficult to know where you were with Elinor. She didn't reveal much of what she thought and felt about things. He liked that about her . . . He hated people who reeled off their thoughts and feelings to you, who took it for granted that you wanted to know all their inner mechanism. Reserve was always more interesting.

Elinor, he thought judicially, was really quite perfect. Nothing about her ever jarred or offended. She was delightful to look at, witty to talk to – altogether the most charming of companions.

He thought complacently to himself:

'I'm damned lucky to have got her. Can't think what she sees in a chap like me.'

For Roderick Welman, in spite of his fastidiousness, was not conceited. It did honestly strike him as strange that Elinor should have consented to marry him.

Life stretched ahead of him pleasantly enough. One knew pretty well where one was; that was always a blessing. He supposed that Elinor and he would be married quite soon – that is, if Elinor wanted to; perhaps she'd rather put it off for a bit. He mustn't rush her. They'd be a bit hard-up at first. Nothing to worry about, though. He hoped sincerely that Aunt Laura wouldn't die for a long time to come. She was a dear and had always been nice to him, having him there for holidays, always interested in what he was doing.

His mind shied away from the thought of her actual death (his mind usually did shy away from any concrete unpleasantness). He didn't like to visualize anything unpleasant too clearly . . . But – er – afterwards – well, it would be very pleasant to live here, especially as there would be plenty of money to keep it up. He wondered exactly how his aunt had left it. Not that it really mattered. With some women it would matter a good deal whether husband or wife had the money. But not with Elinor. She had plenty of tact and she didn't care enough about money to make too much of it.

He thought: 'No, there's nothing to worry about – whatever happens!'

He went out of the walled garden by the gate at the far end. From there he wandered into the little wood where the daffodils were in spring. They were over now, of course. But the green light was very lovely where the sunlight came filtering through the trees.

Just for a moment an odd restlessness came to him – a rippling of his previous placidity. He felt: 'There's something – something I haven't got – something I want – I want – I want . . .'

The golden green light, the softness in the air – with them came a quickened pulse, a stirring of the blood, a sudden impatience.

A girl came through the trees towards him – a girl with pale, gleaming hair and a rose-flushed skin.

He thought, 'How beautiful – how unutterably beautiful.'

Something gripped him; he stood quite still, as though frozen into immobility. The world, he felt, was spinning, was topsy-turvy, was suddenly and impossibly and gloriously crazy!

The girl stopped suddenly, then she came on. She came up to him where he stood, dumb and absurdly fish-like, his mouth open.

She said with a little hesitation:

'Don't you remember me, Mr Roderick? It's a long time of course. I'm Mary Gerrard, from the lodge.'

Roddy said:

'Oh – oh – you're Mary Gerrard?'

She said: 'Yes.'

Then she went on rather shyly:

'I've changed, of course, since you saw me.'

He said: 'Yes, you've changed. I – I wouldn't have recognized you.'

He stood staring at her. He did not hear footsteps behind him. Mary did and turned.

Elinor stood motionless a minute. Then she said:

'Hello, Mary.'

Mary said:

'How do you do, Miss Elinor? It's nice to see you. Mrs Welman has been looking forward to you coming down.'

Elinor said:

'Yes – it's a long time. I – Nurse O'Brien sent me to look for you. She wants to lift Mrs Welman up, and she says you usually do it with her.'

Mary said: 'I'll go at once.'

She moved off, breaking into a run. Elinor stood looking after her. Mary ran well, grace in every movement.

Roddy said softly: 'Atalanta . . .'

Elinor did not answer. She stood quite still for a minute or two. Then she said:

'It's nearly lunch-time. We'd better go back.'

They walked side by side towards the house.

V

'Oh! Come on, Mary. It's Garbo, and a grand film – all about Paris. And a story by a tiptop author. There was an opera of it once.'

'It's frightfully nice of you, Ted, but I really won't.'

Ted Bigland said angrily:

'I can't make you out nowadays, Mary. You're different – altogether different.'

'No, I'm not, Ted.'

'You are! I suppose because you've been away to that grand school and to Germany. You're too good for us now.'

'It's not true, Ted. I'm not like that.'

She spoke vehemently.

The young man, a fine sturdy specimen, looked at her appraisingly in spite of his anger.

'Yes, you are. You're almost a lady, Mary.'

Mary said with sudden bitterness:

'Almost isn't much good, is it?'

He said with sudden understanding:

'No, I reckon it isn't.'

Mary said quickly:

'Anyway, who cares about that sort of thing nowadays? Ladies and gentlemen, and all that!'

'It doesn't matter like it did – no,' Ted assented, but thoughtfully. 'All the same, there's a *feeling*. Lord, Mary, you *look* like a duchess or a countess or something.'

Mary said:

'That's not saying much. I've seen countesses looking like old-clothes women!'

'Well, you know what I mean.'

A stately figure of ample proportions, handsomely dressed in black, bore down upon them. Her eyes gave them a sharp glance. Ted moved aside a step or two. He said:

'Afternoon, Mrs Bishop.'

Mrs Bishop inclined her head graciously.

'Good afternoon, Ted Bigland. Good afternoon, Mary.'

She passed on, a ship in full sail.

Ted looked respectfully after her.

Mary murmured.

'Now, she really is like a duchess!'

'Yes – she's got a manner. Always makes me feel hot inside my collar.'

Mary said slowly:

'She doesn't like me.'

'Nonsense, my girl.'

'It's true. She doesn't. She's always saying sharp things to me.'

'Jealous,' said Ted, nodding his head sapiently. 'That's all it is.'

Mary said doubtfully:

'I suppose it might be that . . .'

'That's it, depend upon it. She's been housekeeper at Hunterbury for years, ruling the roost and ordering everyone about and now old Mrs Welman takes a fancy to you, and it puts her out! That's all it is.'

Mary said, a shade of trouble on her forehead:

'It's silly of me, but I can't bear it when anyone doesn't like me. I want people to like me.'

'Sure to be women who don't like you, Mary! Jealous cats who think you're too good-looking!'

Mary said:

'I think jealousy's horrible.'

Ted said slowly:

'Maybe – *but it exists all right*. Say, I saw a lovely film over at Alledore last week. Clark Gable. All about one of these millionaire blokes who neglected his wife; and then she pretended she'd done the dirty on him. And there was another fellow . . .'

Mary moved away. She said:

'Sorry, Ted, I must go. I'm late.'

'Where are you going?'

'I'm going to have tea with Nurse Hopkins.'

Ted made a face.

'Funny taste. That woman's the biggest gossip in the village! Pokes that long nose of hers into everything.'

Mary said:

'She's been very kind to me always.'

'Oh, I'm not saying there's any harm in her. But she talks.'

Mary said:

'Goodbye, Ted.'

She hurried off, leaving him standing gazing resentfully after her.

VI

Nurse Hopkins occupied a small cottage at the end of the village. She herself had just come in and was untying her bonnet strings when Mary entered.

'Ah, there you are. I'm a bit late. Old Mrs Caldecott was bad again. Made me late with my round of dressings. I saw you with Ted Bigland at the end of the street.'

Mary said rather dispiritedly:

'Yes . . .'

Nurse Hopkins looked up alertly from where she was stooping to light the gas-ring under the kettle.

Her long nose twitched.

'Was he saying something particular to you, my dear?'

'No. He just asked me to go to the cinema.'

'*I* see,' said Nurse Hopkins promptly. 'Well, of course, he's a nice young fellow and doesn't do too badly at the garage, and his father does rather better than most of the farmers round here. All the same, my dear, you don't seem to me cut out for Ted Bigland's wife. Not with your education and all. As I was saying, if I was you I'd go in for massage when the time comes. You get about a bit and see people that way; and your time's more or less your own.'

Mary said:

'I'll think it over. Mrs Welman spoke to me the other day. She was very sweet about it. It was just exactly as you said it was. She doesn't want me to go away just now. She'd miss me, she said. But she told me not to worry about the future, that she meant to help me.'

Nurse Hopkins said dubiously:

'Let's hope she's put that down in black and white! Sick people are odd.'

Mary asked:

'Do you think Mrs Bishop really dislikes me – or is it only my fancy?'

Nurse Hopkins considered a minute.

'She puts on a sour face, I must say. She's one of those who don't like seeing young people having a good time or anything done for them. Thinks, perhaps, Mrs Welman is a bit too fond of you, and resents it.'

She laughed cheerfully.

'I shouldn't worry if I was you, Mary, my dear. Just open that paper bag, will you? There's a couple of doughnuts in it.'

CHAPTER 3

I

Your Aunt had second stroke last night No cause immediate anxiety but suggest you should come down if possible Lord.

II

Immediately on receipt of the telegram Elinor had rung up Roddy, and now they were in the train together bound for Hunterbury.

Elinor had not seen much of Roddy in the week that had elapsed since their visit. On the two brief occasions when they had met, there had been an odd kind of constraint between them.

Roddy had sent her flowers – a great sheaf of long stemmed roses. It was unusual on his part. At a dinner they had had together he had seemed more attentive than usual, consulting her preferences in food and drink, being unusually assiduous in helping her on and off with her coat. A little, Elinor thought, as though he were playing a part in a play – the part of the devoted fiancé . . .

Then she had said to herself:

'Don't be an idiot. Nothing's wrong . . . You imagine things! It's that beastly brooding, possessive mind of yours.'

Her manner to him had been perhaps a shade more detached, more aloof than usual.

Now, in this sudden emergency, the constraint passed, they talked together naturally enough.

Roddy said:

'Poor old dear, and she was so well when we saw her the other day.'

Elinor said:

'I do mind so terribly for *her*. I know how she hated being ill, anyway, and now I suppose she'll be more helpless still, and she'll simply loathe that! One does feel, Roddy, that people ought to be set free – if they themselves really want it.'

Roddy said:

'I agree. It's the only civilized thing to do. You put animals out of their pain. I suppose you don't do it with human beings simply because, human nature being what it is, people would get shoved off for their money by their fond relations – perhaps when they weren't really bad at all.'

Elinor said thoughtfully:

'It would be in the doctors' hands, of course.'

'A doctor might be a crook.'

'You could trust a man like Dr Lord.'

Roddy said carelessly:

'Yes, he seems straightforward enough. Nice fellow.'

III

Dr Lord was leaning over the bed. Nurse O'Brien hovered behind him. He was trying, his forehead puckered, to understand the slurred sounds coming from his patient's mouth.

He said:

'Yes, yes. Now, don't get excited. Take plenty of time. Just raise this right hand a little when you mean *yes*. There's something you're worried about?'

He received the affirmatory sign.

'Something urgent? Yes. Something you want *done*? Someone sent for? Miss Carlisle? And Mr Welman? They're on their way.'

Again Mrs Welman tried incoherently to speak. Dr Lord listened attentively.

'You wanted them to come, but it's not that? Someone else? A relation? No? Some business matter? I see. Something to do with money? *Lawyer*? That's right, isn't it? You want to see your lawyer? Want to give him instructions about something?

'Now, now – that's all right. Keep calm. Plenty of time. What's that you're saying – Elinor?' He caught the garbled name. 'She knows what lawyer? And she will arrange with him? Good. She'll be here in about half an hour. I'll tell her what you want and I'll come up with her and we'll get it all straight. Now, don't worry any more. Leave it all to me. I'll see that things are arranged the way you want them to be.'

He stood a moment watching her relax, then he moved quietly away and went out on the landing. Nurse O'Brien followed him. Nurse Hopkins was just coming up the stairs. He nodded to her. She said breathlessly:

'Good evening, Doctor.'

'Good evening, Nurse.'

He went with the two of them into Nurse O'Brien's room next door and gave them their instructions. Nurse Hopkins would remain on overnight and take charge with Nurse O'Brien.

'Tomorrow I'll have to get hold of a second resident nurse. Awkward, this diphtheria epidemic over at Stamford. The nursing homes there are working short-handed as it is.'

Then, having given his orders, which were listened to with

reverent attention (which sometimes tickled him), Dr Lord went downstairs, ready to receive the niece and nephew who, his watch told him, were due to arrive at any minute now.

In the hall he encountered Mary Gerrard. Her face was pale and anxious. She asked:

'Is she better?'

Dr Lord said:

'I can ensure her a peaceful night – that's about all that can be done.'

Mary said brokenly:

'It seems so cruel – so unfair –'

He nodded sympathetically enough.

'Yes, it does seem like that sometimes. I believe –'

He broke off.

'That's the car.'

He went out into the hall. Mary ran upstairs.

Elinor exclaimed as she came into the drawing-room:

'Is she very bad?'

Roddy was looking pale and apprehensive.

The doctor said gravely:

'I'm afraid it will be rather a shock to you. She's badly paralysed. Her speech is almost unrecognizable. By the way, she's definitely worried about something. It's to do with sending for her lawyer. You know who he is, Miss Carlisle?'

Elinor said quickly:

'Mr Seddon – of Bloomsbury Square. But he wouldn't be there at this time of the evening, and I don't know his home address.'

Dr Lord said reassuringly:

'Tomorrow will be in plenty of time. But I'm anxious to set Mrs Welman's mind at rest as soon as possible. If you will come up with me now, Miss Carlisle, I think together we shall be able to reassure her.'

'Of course. I will come up at once.'

Roddy said hopefully:

'You don't want me?'

He felt faintly ashamed of himself, but he had a nervous dread of going up to the sick-room, of seeing Aunt Laura lying there inarticulate and helpless.

Dr Lord reassured him promptly.

'Not the least need, Mr Welman. Better not to have too many people in the room.'

Roddy's relief showed plainly.

Dr Lord and Elinor went upstairs. Nurse O'Brien was with the patient.

Laura Welman, breathing deeply and stertorously, lay as though in a stupor. Elinor stood looking down on her, shocked by the drawn, twisted face.

Suddenly Mrs Welman's right eyelid quivered and opened. A faint change came over her face as she recognized Elinor.

She tried to speak.

'*Elinor . . .*' The word would have been meaningless to anyone who had not guessed at what she wanted to say.

Elinor said quickly:

'I'm here, Aunt Laura. You're worried about something? You want me to send for Mr Seddon?'

Another of those hoarse raucous sounds. Elinor guessed at the meaning. She said:

'Mary Gerrard?'

Slowly the right hand moved shakily in assent.

A long burble of sound came from the sick woman's lips. Dr Lord and Elinor frowned helplessly. Again and again it came. Then Elinor got a word.

'*Provision*? You want to make *provision* for her in your will? You want her to have some money? I see, dear Aunt Laura. That will be quite simple. Mr Seddon will come down tomorrow and everything shall be arranged exactly as you wish.'

The sufferer seemed relieved. The look of distress faded from that appealing eye. Elinor took her hand in hers and felt a feeble pressure from the fingers.

Mrs Welman said with a great effort:

'*You – all – you . . .*'

Elinor said: 'Yes, yes, leave it all to me. I will see that everything you want is done!'

She felt the pressure of the fingers again. Then it relaxed. The eyelids drooped and closed.

Dr Lord laid a hand on Elinor's arm and drew her gently away out of the room. Nurse O'Brien resumed her seat near the bed.

Outside on the landing Mary Gerrard was talking to Nurse Hopkins. She started forward.

'Oh, Dr Lord, can I go in to her, please?'

He nodded.

'Keep quite quiet, though, and don't disturb her.'

Mary went into the sick-room.

Dr Lord said:

'Your train was late. You –' He stopped.

Elinor had turned her head to look after Mary. Suddenly she became aware of his abrupt silence. She turned her head and looked at him inquiringly. He was staring at her, a startled look in his face. The colour rose in Elinor's cheeks.

She said hurriedly:

'I beg your pardon. What did you say?'

Peter Lord said slowly:

'What was I saying? I don't remember. Miss Carlisle, you were splendid in there!' He spoke warmly. 'Quick to understand, reassuring, everything you should have been.'

The very faintest of sniffs came from Nurse Hopkins.

Elinor said:

'Poor darling. It upset me terribly seeing her like that.'

'Of course. But you didn't show it. You must have great self-control.'

Elinor said, her lips set very straight:

'I've learnt not – to show my feelings.'

The doctor said slowly:

'All the same the mask's bound to slip once in a while.'

Nurse Hopkins had bustled into the bathroom. Elinor said, raising her delicate eyebrows and looking full at him:

'The mask?'

Dr Lord said:

'The human face is, after all, nothing more nor less than a mask.'

'And underneath?'

'Underneath is the primitive human man or woman.'

She turned away quickly and led the way downstairs.

Peter Lord followed, puzzled and unwontedly serious.

Roddy came out into the hall to meet them.

'Well?' he asked anxiously.

Elinor said:

'Poor darling. It's very sad to see her . . . I shouldn't go, Roddy – till – till – she asks for you.'

Roddy asked:

'Did she want anything – special?'

Peter Lord said to Elinor:

'I must be off now. There's nothing more I can do for the moment. I'll look in early tomorrow. Goodbye, Miss Carlisle. Don't – don't worry too much.'

He held her hand in his for a moment or two. He had a strangely reassuring and comforting clasp. He looked at her, Elinor thought, rather oddly as though – as though he was sorry for her.

As the door shut behind the doctor, Roddy repeated his question.

Elinor said:

'Aunt Laura is worried about – about certain business matters. I managed to pacify her and told her Mr Seddon would certainly come down tomorrow. We must telephone him first thing.'

Roddy asked:

'Does she want to make a new will?'

Elinor answered:

'She didn't say so.'

'What did she –?'

He stopped in the middle of the question.

Mary Gerrard was running down the stairs. She crossed the hall and disappeared through the door to the kitchen quarters.

Elinor said in a harsh voice:

'Yes? What is it you wanted to ask?'

Roddy said vaguely:

'I – what? I've forgotten what it was.'

He was staring at the door through which Mary Gerrard had gone.

Elinor's hands closed. She could feel her long, pointed nails biting into the flesh of her palms.

She thought:

'I can't bear it – I can't bear it . . . it's not imagination . . . it's true . . . Roddy – Roddy I *can't* lose you . . .'

And she thought:

'What did that man – the doctor – *what did he see in my face upstairs?* He saw something . . . *Oh, God, how awful life is – to feel as I feel now. Say something, fool. Pull yourself together!*'

Aloud she said, in her calm voice:

'About meals, Roddy. I'm not very hungry. I'll sit with Aunt Laura and the nurses can both come down.'

Roddy said in alarm:

'And have dinner with *me*?'

Elinor said coldly:

'They won't bite you!'

'But what about you? You must have something. Why don't *we* dine first, and let them come down afterwards?'

Elinor said:

'No, the other way's better.' She added wildly, 'They're so touchy, you know.'

She thought:

'*I can't sit through a meal with him – alone – talking – behaving as usual . . .*'

She said impatiently:

'Oh, do let me arrange things my own way!'

CHAPTER 4

I

It was no mere housemaid who wakened Elinor the following morning. It was Mrs Bishop in person, rustling in her old-fashioned black, and weeping unashamedly.

'Oh, Miss Elinor, she's gone . . .'

'What?'

Elinor sat up in bed.

'Your dear aunt. Mrs Welman. My dear mistress. Passed away in her sleep.'

'Aunt Laura? Dead?'

Elinor stared. She seemed unable to take it in.

Mrs Bishop was weeping now with more abandon.

'To think of it,' she sobbed. 'After all these years! Eighteen years I've been here. But indeed it doesn't seem like it . . .'

Elinor said slowly:

'So Aunt Laura died in her sleep – quite peacefully . . . What a blessing for her!'

Mrs Bishop wept.

'So *sudden*. The doctor saying he'd call again this morning and everything just as usual.'

Elinor said rather sharply:

'It wasn't exactly *sudden*. After all, she's been ill for some time. I'm just so thankful she's been spared more suffering.'

Mrs Bishop said tearfully that there was indeed that to be thankful for. She added:

'Who'll tell Mr Roderick?'

Elinor said:

'I will.'

She threw on a dressing-gown and went along to his door and tapped. His voice answered, saying, 'Come in.'

She entered.

'Aunt Laura's dead, Roddy. She died in her sleep.'

Roddy, sitting up in bed, drew a deep sigh.

'Poor dear Aunt Laura! Thank God for it, I say. I couldn't have borne to see her go on lingering in the state she was yesterday.'

Elinor said mechanically:

'I didn't know you'd seen her?'

He nodded rather shamefacedly.

'The truth is, Elinor, I felt the most awful coward, because I'd funked it! I went along there yesterday evening. The nurse, the fat one, left the room for something – went down with a hot-water bottle, I think – and I slipped in. She didn't know I was there, of course. I just stood a bit and looked at her. Then, when I heard Mrs Gamp stumping up the stairs again, I slipped away. But it was – pretty terrible!'

Elinor nodded.

'Yes, it was.'

Roddy said:

'She'd have hated it like hell – every minute of it!'

'I know.'

Roddy said:

'It's marvellous the way you and I always see alike over things.'

Elinor said in a low voice:

'Yes it is.'

He said:

'We're both feeling the same thing at this minute: *just utter thankfulness that she's out of it all . . .*'

II

Nurse O'Brien said:

'What is it, Nurse? Can't you find something?'

Nurse Hopkins, her face rather red, was hunting through the little attaché-case that she had laid down in the hall the preceding evening.

She grunted:

'Most annoying. How I came to do such a thing I can't imagine!'

'What is it?'

Nurse Hopkins replied not very intelligibly:

'It's Eliza Rykin – that sarcoma, you know. She's got to have double injections – night and morning – morphine. Gave her the last tablet in the old tube last night on my way here, and I could swear I had the new tube in here, too.'

'Look again. Those tubes are so small.'

Nurse Hopkins gave a final stir to the contents of the attaché-case.

'No, it's not here! I must have left it in my cupboard after all! Really, I did think I could trust my memory better than *that*. I could have sworn I took it out with me!'

'You didn't leave the case anywhere, did you, on the way here?'

'Of course not!' said Nurse Hopkins sharply.

'Oh, well, dear,' said Nurse O'Brien, 'it must be all *right*?'

'Oh, yes! The only place I've laid my case down was here in this hall, and nobody *here* would pinch anything! Just my memory, I suppose. But it vexes me, if you understand, Nurse. Besides, I shall have to go right home first to the other end of the village and back again.'

Nurse O'Brien said:

'Hope you won't have too tiring a day, dear, after last night. Poor old lady. I didn't think she would last long.'

'No, nor I. I daresay *Doctor* will be surprised!'

Nurse O'Brien said with a tinge of disapproval:

'He's always so *hopeful* about his cases.'

Nurse Hopkins, as she prepared to depart, said:

'Ah, he's young! He hasn't our experience.'

On which gloomy pronouncement she departed.

III

Dr Lord raised himself up on his toes. His sandy eyebrows climbed right up his forehead till they nearly got merged in his hair.

He said in surprise:

'So she's conked out – eh?'

'Yes, Doctor.'

On Nurse O'Brien's tongue exact details were tingling to be uttered, but with stern discipline she waited.

Peter Lord said thoughtfully:

'Conked out?'

He stood for a moment thinking, then he said sharply:

'Get me some boiling water.'

Nurse O'Brien was surprised and mystified, but true to the spirit of hospital training, hers not to reason why. If a doctor had told her to go and get the skin of an alligator she would have murmured automatically, 'Yes, Doctor,' and glided obediently from the room to tackle the problem.

IV

Roderick Welman said:

'Do you mean to say that my aunt died *intestate* – that she never made a will at *all*?'

Mr Seddon polished his eyeglasses. He said:

'That seems to be the case.'

Roddy said:

'But how extraordinary!'

Mr Seddon gave a deprecating cough.

'Not so extraordinary as you might imagine. It happens oftener than you would think. There's a kind of superstition about it. People *will* think they've got plenty of time. The mere fact of making a will seems to bring the possibility of death nearer to them. Very odd – but there it is!'

Roddy said:

'Didn't you ever – er – expostulate with her on the subject?'

Mr Seddon replied drily:

'Frequently.'

'And what did she say?'

Mr Seddon sighed.

'The usual things. That there was plenty of time! That she didn't intend to die just yet! That she hadn't made up her mind definitely, exactly how she wished to dispose of her money!'

Elinor said:

'But surely, after her first stroke –?'

Mr Seddon shook his head.

'Oh, no, it was worse then. She wouldn't hear the subject mentioned!'

Roddy said:

'Surely that's very odd?'

Mr Seddon said again:

'Oh, no. Naturally, her illness made her much more nervous.'

Elinor said in a puzzled voice:

'But she wanted to die . . .'

Polishing his eyeglasses, Mr Seddon said:

'Ah, my dear Miss Elinor, the human mind is a very curious piece of mechanism. Mrs Welman may have *thought* she wanted to die; but side by side with that feeling there ran the hope that she would recover absolutely. And because of that hope, I think she felt that to make a will would be unlucky. It isn't so much that she didn't mean to make one, as that she was eternally putting it off.'

'*You* know,' went on Mr Seddon, suddenly addressing Roddy in an almost personal manner, 'how one puts off and avoids a thing that is distasteful – that you don't want to face?'

Roddy flushed. He muttered:

'Yes, I – I – yes, of course. I know what you mean.'

'Exactly,' said Mr Seddon. 'Mrs Welman always *meant* to make a will, but tomorrow was always a better day to make it than today! She kept telling herself that there was plenty of time.'

Elinor said slowly:

'So that's why she was so upset last night – and in such a panic that you should be sent for . . .'

Mr Seddon replied:

'Undoubtedly!'

Roddy said in a bewildered voice:

'But what happens now?'

'To Mrs Welman's estate?' The lawyer coughed. 'Since Mrs Welman died intestate, all her property goes to her next of kin – that is, to Miss Elinor Carlisle.'

Elinor said slowly.

'All to *me*?'

'The Crown takes a certain percentage,' Mr Seddon explained.

He went into details.

He ended:

'There are no settlements or trusts. Mrs Welman's money was hers absolutely to do with as she chose. It passes, therefore, straight to Miss Carlisle. Er – the death duties, I am afraid, will be somewhat heavy, but even after their payment, the fortune will still be a considerable one, and it is very well invested in sound gilt-edged securities.'

Elinor said:

'But Roderick –'

Mr Seddon said with a little apologetic cough:

'Mr Welman is only Mrs Welman's *husband's* nephew. There is no blood relationship.'

'Quite,' said Roddy.

Elinor said slowly:

'Of course, it doesn't much matter which of us gets it, as we're going to be married.'

But she did not look at Roddy.

It was Mr Seddon's turn to say, 'Quite!'

He said it rather quickly.

V

'But it doesn't matter, does it?' Elinor said.

She spoke almost pleadingly.

Mr Seddon had departed.

Roddy's face twitched nervously.

He said:

'You ought to have it. It's quite right you should. For heaven's sake, Elinor, don't get it into your head that I grudge it to you. *I* don't want the damned money!'

Elinor said, her voice slightly unsteady:

'We did agree, Roddy, in London that it wouldn't matter which of us it was, as – as we were going to be married . . . ?'

He did not answer. She persisted:

'Don't you remember saying that, Roddy?'

He said:

'Yes.'

He looked down at his feet. His face was white and sullen, there was pain in the taut lines of his sensitive mouth.

Elinor said with a sudden gallant lift of the head:

'It doesn't matter – *if we're going to be married . . . But are we, Roddy?*'

He said:

'Are we what?'

'Are we going to marry each other?'

'I understood that was the idea.'

His tone was indifferent, with a slight edge to it. He went on:

'Of course, Elinor, if you've other ideas now . . .'

Elinor cried out:

'Oh, Roddy, can't you be *honest*?'

He winced.

Then he said in a low, bewildered voice:

'I don't know what's happened to me . . .'

Elinor said in a stifled voice:

'I do . . .'

He said quickly:

'Perhaps it's true, that. I don't after all, quite like the idea of living on my wife's money . . .'

Elinor, her face white, said:

'It's not that . . . It's something else . . .' She paused, then she said, 'It's – Mary, isn't it?'

Roddy murmured unhappily:

'I suppose so. How did you know?'

Elinor said, her mouth twisting sideways in a crooked smile:

'It wasn't difficult . . . Every time you look at her – it's there in your face for anyone to read . . .'

Suddenly his composure broke.

'Oh, Elinor – I don't know what's the matter! I think I'm going mad! It happened when I saw her – that first day – in the wood . . . just her face – it's – it's turned everything upside down. *You* can't understand that . . .'

Elinor said:

'Yes, I can. Go on.'

Roddy said helplessly:

'I didn't want to fall in love with her . . . I was quite happy with you. Oh, Elinor, what a cad I am, talking like this to you . . .'

Elinor said:

'Nonsense. Go on. Tell me . . .'

He said brokenly:

'You're wonderful . . . Talking to you helps frightfully. I'm so terribly fond of you, Elinor! You must believe that. This other thing is like an enchantment! It's upset everything: my conception of life – and my enjoyment of things – and – all the decent ordered reasonable things . . .'

Elinor said gently:

'Love – isn't very reasonable . . .'

Roddy said miserably:

'No . . .'

Elinor said, and her voice trembled a little:

'Have you said anything to her?'

Roddy said:

'This morning – like a fool – I lost my head –'

Elinor said:

'Yes?'

Roddy said:

'Of course she – she shut me up at once! She was shocked. Because of Aunt Laura and – of *you* –'

Elinor drew the diamond ring off her finger. She said:

'You'd better take it back, Roddy.'

Taking it, he murmured without looking at her:

'Elinor, you've no idea what a beast I feel.'

Elinor said in her calm voice:

'Do you think she'll marry you?'

He shook his head.

'I've no idea. Not – not for a long time. I don't think she cares for me now; but she might come to care . . .'

Elinor said:

'I think you're right. You must give her time. Not see her for a bit, and then – start afresh.'

'Darling Elinor! You're the best friend anyone ever had.' He took her hand suddenly and kissed it. 'You know, Elinor, I *do* love you – just as much as ever! Sometimes Mary seems just like a dream. I might wake up from it – and find she wasn't there . . .'

Elinor said:

'If Mary wasn't there . . .'

Roddy said with sudden feeling:

'Sometimes I wish she wasn't . . . You and I, Elinor, *belong*. We do belong, don't we?'

Slowly she bent her head.

She said:

'Oh, yes – we belong.'

She thought:

'*If Mary wasn't there . . .*'

CHAPTER 5

I

Nurse Hopkins said with emotion:

'It was a beautiful funeral!'

Nurse O'Brien responded:

'It was, indeed. And the flowers! Did you ever see such beautiful flowers? A harp of white lilies there was, and a cross of yellow roses. Beautiful.'

Nurse Hopkins sighed and helped herself to buttered teacake. The two nurses were sitting in the Blue Tit Café.

Nurse Hopkins went on:

'Miss Carlisle is a generous girl. She gave me a nice present, though she'd no call to do so.'

'She's a fine generous girl,' agreed Nurse O'Brien warmly. 'I do detest stinginess.'

Nurse Hopkins said:

'Well, it's a grand fortune she's inherited.'

Nurse O'Brien said, 'I wonder . . .' and stopped.

Nurse Hopkins said, 'Yes?' encouragingly.

''Twas strange the way the old lady made no will.'

'It was wicked,' Nurse Hopkins said sharply. 'People ought to be forced to make wills! It only leads to unpleasantness when they don't.'

'I'm wondering,' said Nurse O'Brien, 'if she *had* made a will, how she'd have left her money?'

Nurse Hopkins said firmly:

'I know *one* thing.'

'What's that?'

'She'd have left a sum of money to Mary – Mary Gerrard.'

'Yes, indeed, and that's true,' agreed the other. She added excitedly, 'Wasn't I after telling you that night of the state she was in, poor dear, and the doctor doing his best to calm her down. Miss Elinor was there holding her auntie's hand and swearing by God Almighty,' said Nurse O'Brien, her Irish imagination suddenly running away with her, 'that the lawyer should be sent for and everything done accordingly. "Mary! Mary!" the poor old lady said. "Is it Mary Gerrard you're meaning?" says Miss Elinor, and straightaway she swore that Mary should have her rights!'

Nurse Hopkins said rather doubtfully:

'Was it like that?'

Nurse O'Brien replied firmly:

'That was the way of it, and I'll tell you this, Nurse Hopkins: In my opinion, if Mrs Welman had lived to make that will, it's likely there might have been surprises for all! Who knows she mightn't have left every penny she possessed to Mary Gerrard!'

Nurse Hopkins said dubiously:

'I don't think she'd do that. I don't hold with leaving your money away from your own flesh and blood.'

Nurse O'Brien said oracularly:

'There's flesh and blood and flesh and blood.'

Nurse Hopkins responded instantly:

'Now, what might you mean by *that*?'

Nurse O'Brien said with dignity:

'I'm not one to gossip! And I wouldn't be blackening anyone's name that's dead.'

Nurse Hopkins nodded her head slowly and said:

'That's right. I agree with you. Least said soonest mended.'

She filled up the teapot.

Nurse O'Brien said:

'By the way, now, did you find that tube of morphine all right when you got home?'

Nurse Hopkins frowned. She said:

'No. It beats me to know what can have become of it, but I think it may have been this way: I *might* have set it down on the edge of the mantelpiece as I often do while I lock the cupboard, and it *might* have rolled and fallen into the wastepaper basket that was all full of rubbish and that was emptied out into the dustbin just as I left the house.' She paused. 'It *must* be that way, for I don't see what else could have become of it.'

'I see,' said Nurse O'Brien. 'Well, dear, that must have been it. It's not as though you'd left your case about anywhere else – only just in the hall at Hunterbury – so it seems to me that what you suggested just now must be so. It's gone into the rubbish bin.'

'That's right,' said Nurse Hopkins eagerly. 'It couldn't be any other way, could it?'

She helped herself to a pink sugar cake. She said, 'It's not as though . . .' and stopped.

The other agreed quickly – perhaps a little too quickly.

'I'd not be worrying about it any more if I was you,' she said comfortably.

Nurse Hopkins said:

'I'm *not* worrying . . .'

II

Young and severe in her black dress, Elinor sat in front of Mrs Welman's massive writing-table in the library. Various papers were spread out in front of her. She had finished interviewing the servants and Mrs Bishop. Now it was Mary Gerrard who entered the room and hesitated a minute by the doorway.

'You wanted to see me, Miss Elinor?' she said.

Elinor looked up.

'Oh, yes, Mary. Come here and sit down, will you?'

Mary came and sat in the chair Elinor indicated. It was turned a little towards the window, and the light from it fell on her face, showing the dazzling purity of the skin and bringing out the pale gold of the girl's hair.

Elinor held one hand shielding her face a little. Between the fingers she could watch the other girl's face.

She thought:

'Is it possible to hate anyone so much and not show it?'

Aloud she said in a pleasant, businesslike voice:

'I think you know, Mary, that my aunt always took a great interest in you and would have been concerned about your future.'

Mary murmured in her soft voice:

'Mrs Welman was very good to me always.'

Elinor went on, her voice cold and detached:

'My aunt, if she had had time to make a will, would have wished, I know, to leave several legacies. Since she died without making a will, the responsibility of carrying out her wishes rests on me. I have consulted with Mr Seddon, and by his advice we have drawn up a schedule of sums for the servants according to their length of service, etc.' She paused. 'You, of course, don't come quite into that class.'

She half-hoped, perhaps, that those words might hold a sting, but the face she was looking at showed no change. Mary accepted the words at their face value and listened to what more was to come.

Elinor said:

'Though it was difficult for my aunt to speak coherently, she was able to make her meaning understood that last evening. She definitely wanted to make some provision for your future.'

Mary said quietly:

'That was very good of her.'

Elinor said brusquely:

'As soon as probate is granted, I am arranging that two thousand pounds should be made over to you – that sum to be yours to do with absolutely as you please.'

Mary's colour rose.

'Two thousand pounds? Oh, Miss Elinor, that *is* good of you! I don't know what to say.'

Elinor said sharply:

'It isn't particularly good of me, and please don't say any-thing.'

Mary flushed.

'You don't know what a difference it will make to me,' she murmured.

Elinor said:

'I'm glad.'

She hesitated. She looked away from Mary to the other side of the room. She said with a slight effort:

'I wonder – have you any plans?'

Mary said quickly:

'Oh, yes. I shall train for something. Massage, perhaps. That's what Nurse Hopkins advises.'

Elinor said:

'That sounds a very good idea. I will try and arrange with Mr Seddon that some money shall be advanced to you as soon as possible – at once, if that is feasible.'

'You're very, *very* good, Miss Elinor,' said Mary gratefully.

Elinor said curtly:

'It was Aunt Laura's wish.' She hesitated, then said, 'Well, that's all, I think.'

This time the definite dismissal in the words pierced Mary's sensitive skin. She got up, said quietly, 'Thank you very much, Miss Elinor,' and left the room.

Elinor sat quite still, staring ahead of her. Her face was quite impassive. There was no clue in it as to what was going on in her mind. But she sat there, motionless, for a long time . . .

III

Elinor went at last in search of Roddy. She found him in the morning-room. He was standing staring out of the window. He turned sharply as Elinor came in.

She said:

'I've got through it all! Five hundred for Mrs Bishop – she's been here such years. A hundred for the cook and fifty each for Milly and Olive. Five pounds each to the others. Twenty-five for Stephens, the head gardener; and there's old Gerrard, of course, at the Lodge. I haven't done anything about him yet. It's awkward. He'll have to be pensioned off, I suppose?'

She paused and then went on rather hurriedly:

'I'm settling two thousand on Mary Gerrard. Do you think that's what Aunt Laura would have wished? It seemed to me about the right sum.'

Roddy said without looking at her:

'Yes, exactly right. You've always got excellent judgement, Elinor.'

He turned to look out of the window again.

Elinor held her breath for a minute, then she began to speak with nervous haste, the words tumbling out incoherently:

'There's something more: I want to – it's only right – I mean, *you've* got to have your proper share, Roddy.'

As he wheeled round, anger on his face, she hurried on:

'No, *listen*, Roddy. This is just bare justice! The money that was your uncle's – that he left to his wife – naturally he always assumed it would come to you. Aunt Laura meant it to, too. I know she did, from lots of things she said. If *I* have *her* money, *you* should have the amount that was *his* – it's only right. I – I can't bear to feel I've robbed you – just because Aunt Laura funked making a will. You must – you *must* see sense about this!'

Roderick's long, sensitive face had gone dead white.

He said:

'My God, Elinor, do you want to make me feel an utter cad? Do you think for one moment I could – could take this money from you?'

'I'm not *giving* it to you. It's just – fair.'

Roddy cried out:

'I don't want your money!'

'It isn't mine!'

'It's yours by law – and that's all that matters! For God's sake, don't let's be anything but strictly businesslike! I won't take a penny from you. You're not going to do the Lady Bountiful to me!'

Elinor cried out:

'Roddy!'

He made a quick gesture.

'Oh, my dear, I'm sorry. I don't know what I'm saying. I feel so bewildered – so utterly lost . . .'

Elinor said gently:

'Poor Roddy . . .'

He had turned away again and was playing with the blind tassel of the window. He said in a different tone, a detached one:

'Do you know what – Mary Gerrard proposes doing?'

'She's going to train as a masseuse, so she says.'

He said, 'I see.'

There was a silence. Elinor drew herself up; she flung back her head. Her voice when she spoke was suddenly compelling.

She said:

'Roddy, I want you to listen to me carefully!'

He turned to her, slightly surprised.

'Of course, Elinor.'

'I want you, if you will, to follow my advice.'

'And what is your advice?'

Elinor said calmly:

'You are not particularly tied? You can always get a holiday, can't you?'

'Oh, yes.'

'Then do – just that. Go abroad somewhere for – say, three months. Go by yourself. Make new friends and see new places. Let's speak quite frankly. At this moment you think you're in love with Mary Gerrard. Perhaps you are. But it isn't a moment for approaching her – you know that only too well. Our engagement is definitely broken off. Go abroad, then, as a free man, and at the end of the three months, as a free man, make up your mind. You'll know then whether you – really love Mary or whether it was only a temporary infatuation. And if you are quite sure you *do* love her – well, then, come back and go to her and tell her so, and that you're quite sure about it, and perhaps then she'll listen.'

Roddy came to her. He caught her hand in his.

'Elinor, you're wonderful! So clear-headed! So marvellously impersonal! There's no trace of pettiness or meanness about you. I admire you more than I can ever say. I'll do exactly what you suggest. Go away, cut free from everything – and find out whether I've got the genuine disease or if I've just been making the most ghastly fool of myself. Oh, Elinor, my dear, you don't know how truly fond I am of you. I do realize you were always a thousand times too good for me. Bless you, dear, for all your goodness.'

Quickly, impulsively, he kissed her cheek and went out of the room.

It was as well, perhaps, that he did not look back and see her face.

IV

It was a couple of days later that Mary acquainted Nurse Hopkins with her improved prospects.

That practical woman was warmly congratulatory.

'That's a great piece of luck for you, Mary,' she said. 'The old lady may have meant well by you, but unless a thing's down in black and white, intentions don't go for much! You might easily have got nothing at all.'

'Miss Elinor said that the night Mrs Welman died she told her to do something for me.'

Nurse Hopkins snorted.

'Maybe she did. But there's many would have forgotten conveniently afterwards. Relations are like that. I've seen a few things, *I* can tell you! People dying and saying they know they can leave it to their dear son or their dear daughter to carry out their wishes. Nine times out of ten, dear son and dear daughter find some very good reason to do nothing of the kind. Human nature's human nature, and nobody likes parting with money if they're not legally compelled to! I tell you, Mary, my girl, you've been lucky. Miss Carlisle's straighter than most.'

Mary said slowly:

'And yet – somehow – I feel she doesn't like me.'

'With good reason, I should say,' said Nurse Hopkins bluntly. 'Now, don't look so innocent, Mary! Mr Roderick's been making sheep's eyes at you for some time now.'

Mary went red.

Nurse Hopkins went on:

'He's got it badly, in my opinion. Fell for you all of a sudden. What about you, my girl? Got any feelings for him?'

Mary said hesitatingly:

'I – I don't know. I don't think so. But of course, he's very nice.'

'H'm,' said Nurse Hopkins. 'He wouldn't be *my* fancy! One of those men who are finicky and a bundle of nerves. Fussy about their food, too, as likely as not. Men aren't much at the best of times. Don't be in too much of a hurry, Mary, my dear. With your looks you can afford to pick and choose. Nurse O'Brien passed the remark to me the other day that you ought to go on the films. They like blondes, I've always heard.'

Mary said, with a slight frown creasing her forehead:

'Nurse, what do you think I ought to do about Father? He thinks I ought to give some of this money to him.'

'Don't you do anything of the kind,' said Nurse Hopkins wrathfully. 'Mrs Welman never meant that money for him. It's my opinion he'd have lost his job years ago if it hadn't been for you. A lazier man never stepped!'

Mary said:

'It seems funny when she'd all that money that she never made a will to say how it was to go.'

Nurse Hopkins shook her head.

'People are like that. You'd be surprised. Always putting it off.'

Mary said:

'It seems downright silly to me.'

Nurse Hopkins said with a faint twinkle:

'Made a will yourself, Mary?'

Mary stared at her.

'Oh, no.'

'And yet you're over twenty-one.'

'But I – I haven't got anything to leave – at least I suppose I have now.'

Nurse Hopkins said sharply:

'Of course you have. And a nice tidy little sum, too.'

Mary said:

'Oh, well, there's no hurry . . .'

'There you go,' said Nurse Hopkins drily. 'Just like everyone else. Because you're a healthy young girl isn't a reason why you shouldn't be smashed up in a charabanc or a bus, or run over in the street any minute.'

Mary laughed. She said:

'I don't even know how to make a will.'

'Easy enough. You can get a form at the post office. Let's go and get one right away.'

In Nurse Hopkins' cottage, the form was spread out and the important matter discussed. Nurse Hopkins was enjoying herself thoroughly. A will, as she said, was next best to a death, in her opinion.

Mary said:

'Who'd get the money if I didn't make a will?'

Nurse Hopkins said rather doubtfully:

'Your father, I suppose.'

Mary said sharply:

'He shan't have it. I'd rather leave it to my auntie in New Zealand.'

Nurse Hopkins said cheerfully:

'It wouldn't be much use leaving it to your father, anyway – *he's* not long for this world, I should say.'

Mary had heard Nurse Hopkins make this kind of pronouncement too often to be impressed by it.

'I can't remember my auntie's address. We've not heard from her for years.'

'I don't suppose that matters,' said Nurse Hopkins. 'You know her Christian name?'

'Mary. Mary Riley.'

'That's all right. Put down you leave everything to Mary Riley, sister of the late Eliza Gerrard of Hunterbury, Maidensford.'

Mary bent over the form, writing. As she came to the end she shivered suddenly. A shadow had come between her and the sun. She looked up to see Elinor Carlisle standing outside the window looking in. Elinor said:

'What are you doing so busily?'

Nurse Hopkins said with a laugh:

'She's making her will, that's what she's doing.'

'Making her will?' Suddenly Elinor laughed – a strange laugh – almost hysterical.

She said:

'So you're making your will, Mary. *That's funny. That's very funny* . . .'

Still laughing, she turned away and walked rapidly along the street.

Nurse Hopkins stared.

'Did you ever? What's come to her?'

V

Elinor had not taken more than half a dozen steps – she was still laughing – when a hand fell on her arm from behind. She stopped abruptly and turned.

Dr Lord looked straight at her, his brow creased into a frown.

He said peremptorily:

'What were you laughing at?'

Elinor said:

'Really – I don't know.'

Peter Lord said:

'That's rather a silly answer!'

Elinor flushed. She said:

'I think I must be nervous – or something. I looked in at the District Nurse's cottage and – and Mary Gerrard was writing out her will. It made me laugh; I don't know why!'

Lord said abruptly:

'*Don't you?*'

Elinor said:

'It was silly of me – I tell you – I'm nervous.'

Peter Lord said:

'I'll write you out a tonic.'

Elinor said incisively:

'How useful!'

He grinned disarmingly.

'Quite useless, I agree. But it's the only thing one can do when people won't tell one what is the matter with them!'

Elinor said:

'There's nothing the matter with me.'

Peter Lord said calmly:

'There's quite a lot the matter with you.'

Elinor said:

'I've had a certain amount of nervous strain, I suppose . . .'

He said:

'I expect you've had quite a lot. But that's not what I'm talking about.' He paused. 'Are you – are you staying down here much longer?'

'I'm leaving tomorrow.'

'You won't – live down here?'

Elinor shook her head.

'No – never. I think – I think – I shall sell the place if I can get a good offer.'

Dr Lord said rather flatly:

'I see . . .'

Elinor said:

'I must be getting home now.'

She held out her hand firmly. Peter Lord took it. He held it. He said very earnestly:

'Miss Carlisle, will you please tell me what was in your mind when you laughed just now?'

She wrenched her hand away quickly.

'What should there be in my mind?'

'That's what I'd like to know.'

His face was grave and a little unhappy.

Elinor said impatiently:

'It just struck me as funny, that was all!'

'That Mary Gerrard was making a will? Why? Making a will is a perfectly sensible procedure. Saves a lot of trouble. Sometimes, of course, it *makes* trouble!'

Elinor said impatiently:

'Of course – everyone should make a will. I didn't mean that.'

Dr Lord said:

'Mrs Welman ought to have made a will.'

Elinor said with feeling:

'Yes, indeed.'

The colour rose in her face.

Dr Lord said unexpectedly:

'What about you?'

'*Me?*'

'Yes, you said just now everyone should make a will! Have *you*?'

Elinor stared at him for a minute, then she laughed.

'How extraordinary!' she said. 'No, I haven't. I hadn't thought of it! I'm just like Aunt Laura. Do you know, Dr Lord, I shall go home and write to Mr Seddon about it at once.'

Peter Lord said:
'Very sensible.'

VI

In the library Elinor had just finished a letter:

> Dear Mr Seddon, – Will you draft a will for me to sign? Quite a simple one. I want to leave everything to Roderick Welman absolutely.
>
> Yours sincerely,
> Elinor Carlisle

She glanced at the clock. The post would be going in a few minutes.

She opened the drawer of the desk, then remembered she had used the last stamp that morning.

There were some in her bedroom, though, she was almost sure.

She went upstairs. When she re-entered the library with the stamp in her hand, Roddy was standing by the window.

He said:

'So we leave here tomorrow. Good old Hunterbury. We've had some good times here.'

Elinor said:

'Do you mind its being sold?'

'Oh, no, no! I quite see it's the best thing to be done.'

There was a silence. Elinor picked up her letter, glanced through it to see if it was all right. Then she sealed and stamped it.

CHAPTER 6

Letter from Nurse O'Brien to Nurse Hopkins, July 14th:

Laborough Court

> Dear Hopkins, – Have been meaning to write to you for some days now. This is a lovely house and the pictures, I believe, quite famous.

But I can't say it's as comfortable as Hunterbury was, if you know what I mean. Being in the dead country it's difficult to get maids, and the girls they have got are a raw lot, and some of them not too obliging, and though I'm sure I'm never one to give trouble, meals sent up on a tray should at least be hot, and no facilities for boiling a kettle, and the tea not always made with boiling water! Still, all that's neither here nor there. The patient's a nice quiet gentleman – double pneumonia, but the crisis is past and doctor says going on well.

What I've got to tell you that will really interest you is the very queerest coincidence you ever knew. In the drawing-room, on the grand piano, there's a photograph in a big silver frame; and would you believe it, it's the same photograph that I told you about – the one signed Lewis that old Mrs Welman asked for. Well, of course, I was intrigued – and who wouldn't be? And I asked the butler who it was, which he answered at once saying it was Lady Rattery's brother – Sir Lewis Rycroft. He lived, it seems, not far from here and he was killed in the War. Very sad, wasn't it? I asked casual like was he married, and the butler said yes, but that Lady Rycroft went into a lunatic asylum, poor thing, soon after the marriage. She was still alive, he said. Now, isn't that interesting? And we were quite wrong, you see, in all our ideas. They must have been very fond of each other, he and Mrs W., and unable to marry because of the wife being in an asylum. Just like the pictures, isn't it? And her remembering all those years and looking at his photograph just before she died. He was killed in 1917, the butler said. Quite a romance, that's what I feel.

Have you seen that new picture with Myrna Loy? I saw it was coming to Maidensford this week. No cinema anywhere near here! Oh, it's awful to be buried in the country. No wonder they can't get decent maids!

Well, goodbye for the present, dear, write and tell me all the news.

Yours sincerely,
Eileen O'Brien

Letter from Nurse Hopkins to Nurse O'Brien, July 14th:

Rose Cottage

Dear O'Brien, – Everything goes on here much as usual. Hunterbury is deserted – all the servants gone and a board up: For Sale. I saw Mrs Bishop the other day, she is staying with her sister who lives about a mile away. She was very upset, as you can imagine, at the place being sold. It seems she made sure Miss Carlisle would marry Mr Welman and live there. Mrs B. says that the engagement is off! Miss Carlisle went away to London soon after you left. She was very *peculiar in her manner once or twice. I really didn't know what to make of her! Mary Gerrard has gone to London and is starting to train for a masseuse. Very sensible of her, I think. Miss Carlisle's going to settle two thousand pounds on her, which I call very handsome and more than what many would do.*

By the way, it's funny how things come about. Do you remember telling me something about a photograph signed Lewis *that Mrs Welman showed you? I was having a chat the other day with Mrs Slattery (she was housekeeper to old Dr Ransome who had the practice before Dr Lord), and of course she's lived here all her life and knows a lot about the gentry round about. I just brought the subject up in a casual manner, speaking of Christian names and saying that the name of Lewis was uncommon and amongst others she mentioned Sir Lewis Rycroft over at Forbes Park. He served in the War in the 17th Lancers and was killed towards the end of the War. So I said* he was a great friend of Mrs Welman's at Hunterbury, wasn't he? *And at once she gave me a* look *and said,* Yes, very *close friends they'd been, and* some said more than friends, *but that she herself wasn't one to* talk – *and why shouldn't they be friends? So I said but surely Mrs Welman was a* widow *at the time, and she said Oh yes,* she was a widow. *So, dear, I saw* at once *she meant something by* that, *so I said it was odd then, that they'd never married, and she said at once, "They couldn't marry. He'd got a* wife *in a* lunatic asylum!" *So now, you see, we know* all *about it! Curious the way things come about, isn't it? Considering the easy way you get divorces nowadays, it does seem a shame that insanity shouldn't have been a ground for it then.*

Do you remember a good-looking young chap, Ted Bigland, who used to hang around after Mary Gerrard a lot? He's been at me for her address in London, but I haven't given it to him. In my opinion, Mary's a cut above Ted Bigland. I don't know if you realized it, dear, but Mr R – W – was very taken with her. A pity, because it's made trouble. Mark my words, that's the reason for the engagement between him and Miss Carlisle being off. And, if you ask me, it's hit her badly. I don't know what she saw in him, I'm sure – he wouldn't have been my cup of tea, but I hear from a reliable source that she's always been madly in love with him. It does seem a mix-up, doesn't it? And she's got all that money, too. I believe he was always led to expect his aunt would leave him something substantial.

Old Gerrard at the Lodge is failing rapidly – has had several nasty dizzy spells. He's just as rude and cross-grained as ever. He actually said the other day that Mary wasn't his daughter. 'Well,' I said, 'I'd be ashamed to say a thing like that about your wife if I were you.' He just looked at me and said, 'You're nothing but a fool. You don't understand.' Polite, wasn't it? I took him up pretty sharply, I can tell you. His wife was lady's maid to Mrs Welman before her marriage, I believe.

I saw The Good Earth last week. It was lovely! Women have to put up with a lot in China, it seems.

Yours ever,
Jessie Hopkins

Post-card from Nurse Hopkins to Nurse O'Brien:

Fancy our letters just crossing! Isn't this weather awful?

Post-card from Nurse O'Brien to Nurse Hopkins:

Got your letter this morning. What a coincidence!

Letter from Roderick Welman to Elinor Carlisle, July 15th:

Dear Elinor, – Just got your letter. No, really, I have no feelings about Hunterbury being sold. Nice of you to consult me. I think you're doing the wisest thing if you don't fancy living there, which you obviously don't. You may have some difficulty in getting rid of it, though. It's a biggish place for present-day needs, though, of course, it's been modernized and is up to date, with good servants' quarters, and gas and electric light and all that. Anyway, I hope you'll have luck!

The heat here is glorious. I spend hours in the sea. Rather a funny crowd of people, but I don't mix much. You told me once that I wasn't a good mixer. I'm afraid it's true. I find most of the human race extraordinarily repulsive. They probably reciprocate this feeling.

I have long felt that you are one of the only really satisfactory representatives of humanity. Am thinking of wandering on to the Dalmatian coast in a week or two. Address c/o Thomas Cook, Dubrovnik, from the 22nd onwards. If there's anything I can do, let me know.

Yours, with admiration and gratitude,
Roddy

Letter from Mr Seddon of Messrs Seddon, Blatherwick & Seddon to Miss Elinor Carlisle, July 20th:

104 Bloomsbury Square

Dear Miss Carlisle, – I certainly think you should accept Major Somervell's offer of twelve thousand five hundred (£12,500) for Hunterbury. Large properties are extremely difficult to sell at the moment, and the price offered seems to be most advantageous. The offer depends, however, on immediate possession, and I know Major Somervell has been seeing other properties in the neighbourhood, so I would advise immediate acceptance.

Major Somervell is willing, I understand, to take the place furnished for three months, by which time the legal formalities should be accomplished and the sale can go through.

As regards the lodge-keeper, Gerrard, and the question of pensioning him off, I hear from Dr Lord that the old man is seriously ill and not expected to live.

Probate has not yet been granted, but I have advanced one hundred pounds to Miss Mary Gerrard pending the settlement.

Yours sincerely,
Edmund Seddon

Letter from Dr Lord to Miss Elinor Carlisle, July 24th:

Dear Miss Carlisle, – Old Gerrard passed away today. Is there anything I can do for you in any way? I hear you have sold the house to our new MP, Major Somervell.

> *Yours sincerely,*
> *Peter Lord*

Letter from Elinor Carlisle to Mary Gerrard, July 25th:

Dear Mary, – I am so sorry to hear of your father's death.

I have had an offer for Hunterbury – from a Major Somervell. He is anxious to get in as soon as possible. I am going down there to go through my aunt's papers and clear up generally. Would it be possible for you to get your father's things moved out of the Lodge as quickly as possible? I hope you are doing well and not finding your massage training too strenuous.

> *Yours very sincerely,*
> *Elinor Carlisle*

Letter from Mary Gerrard to Nurse Hopkins, July 25th:

Dear Nurse Hopkins, – Thank you so much for writing to me about Father. I'm glad he didn't suffer. Miss Elinor writes me that the house is sold and that she would like the Lodge cleared out as soon as possible. Could you put me up if I came down tomorrow for the funeral? Don't bother to answer if that's all right.

> *Yours affectionately,*
> *Mary Gerrard*

CHAPTER 7

I

Elinor Carlisle came out of the King's Arms on the morning of Thursday, July 27th, and stood for a minute or two looking up and down the main street of Maidensford.

Suddenly, with an exclamation of pleasure, she crossed the road.

There was no mistaking that large dignified presence, that serene gait as of a galleon in full sail.

'Mrs Bishop!'

'Why, Miss Elinor! This *is* a surprise! I'd no notion you were in these parts! If I'd known you were coming to Hunterbury I'd have been there myself! Who's doing for you there? Have you brought someone down from London?'

Elinor shook her head.

'I'm not staying at the house. I am staying at the King's Arms.'

Mrs Bishop looked across the road and sniffed dubiously.

'It is *possible* to stay there, I've heard,' she allowed. 'It's clean, I know. And the cooking, they say, is fair, but it's hardly what *you're* accustomed to, Miss Elinor.'

Elinor said, smiling:

'I'm really quite comfortable. It's only for a day or two. I have to sort out things at the house. All my aunt's personal things; and then there are a few pieces of furniture I should like to have in London.'

'The house is really sold, then?'

'Yes. To a Major Somervell. Our new Member. Sir George Kerr died, you know, and there's been a bye-election.'

'Returned unopposed,' said Mrs Bishop grandly. 'We've never had anyone but a Conservative for Maidenford.'

Elinor said:

'I'm glad someone has bought the house who really wants to live in it. I should have been sorry if it had been turned into a hotel or built upon.'

Mrs Bishop shut her eyes and shivered all over her plump aristocratic person.

'Yes, indeed, that would have been dreadful – quite dreadful. It's bad enough as it is to think of Hunterbury passing into the hands of strangers.'

Elinor said:

'Yes, but, you see, it would have been a very large house for me to live in – alone.'

Mrs Bishop sniffed.

Elinor said quickly:

'I meant to ask you: Is there any especial piece of furniture that you might care to have? I should be very glad for you to have it, if so.'

Mrs Bishop beamed. She said graciously:

'Well, Miss Elinor, that is very thoughtful of you – very kind, I'm sure. If it's not taking a liberty . . . ?'

She paused and Elinor said:

'Oh, no.'

'I have always had a great admiration for the secretaire in the drawing-room. Such a *handsome* piece.'

Elinor remembered it, a somewhat flamboyant piece of inlaid marqueterie. She said quickly:

'Of course you shall have it, Mrs Bishop. Anything else?'

'No, indeed, Miss Elinor. You have already been extremely generous.'

Elinor said:

'There are some chairs in the same style as the secretaire. Would you care for those?'

Mrs Bishop accepted the chairs with becoming thanks. She explained:

'I am staying at the moment with my sister. Is there anything I can do for you up at the house, Miss Elinor? I could come up there with you, if you like.'

'No, thank you.'

Elinor spoke quickly, rather abruptly.

Mrs Bishop said:

'It would be no trouble, I assure you – a pleasure. Such a melancholy task going through all dear Mrs Welman's things.'

Elinor said:

'Thank you, Mrs Bishop, but I would rather tackle it alone. One can do some things better alone –'

Mrs Bishop said stiffly:

'As you please, of course.'

She went on:

'That daughter of Gerrard's is down here. The funeral was yesterday. She's staying with Nurse Hopkins. I did hear *they* were going up to the Lodge this morning.'

Elinor nodded. She said:

'Yes, I asked Mary to come down and see to that. Major Somervell wants to get in as soon as possible.'

'I see.'

Elinor said:

'Well, I must be getting on now. So glad to have seen you, Mrs Bishop. I'll remember about the secretaire and the chairs.'

She shook hands and passed on.

She went into the baker's and bought a loaf of bread. Then she went into the dairy and bought half a pound of butter and some milk.

Finally she went into the grocer's.

'I want some paste for sandwiches, please.'

'Certainly, Miss Carlisle.' Mr Abbott himself bustled forward, elbowing aside his junior apprentice.

'What would you like? Salmon and shrimp? Turkey and tongue? Salmon and sardine? Ham and tongue?'

He whipped down pot after pot and arrayed them on the counter.

Elinor said with a faint smile:

'In spite of their names, I always think they taste much alike.'

Mr Abbott agreed instantly.

'Well, perhaps they do, in a way. Yes, in a way. But, of course, they're very tasty – very tasty.'

Elinor said:

'One used to be rather afraid of eating fish pastes. There have been cases of ptomaine poisoning from them, haven't there?'

Mr Abbot put on a horrified expression.

'I can assure you this is an excellent brand – *most* reliable – we never have any complaints.'

Elinor said:

'I'll have one of salmon and anchovy and one of salmon and shrimp. Thank you.'

II

Elinor Carlisle entered the grounds of Hunterbury by the back gate.

It was a hot, clear summer's day. There were sweetpeas in flower. Elinor passed close by a row of them. The undergardener, Horlick, who was remaining on to keep the place in order, greeted her respectfully.

'Good morning, miss. I got your letter. You'll find the side door open, miss. I've unfastened the shutters and opened most of the windows.'

Elinor said:

'Thank you, Horlick.'

As she moved on, the young man said nervously, his Adam's apple jerking up and down in spasmodic fashion:

'Excuse me, miss –'

Elinor turned back. 'Yes?'

'Is it true that the house is sold? I mean, is it really settled?'

'Oh, yes!'

Horlick said nervously:

'I was wondering, miss, if you would say a word for me – to Major Somervell, I mean. He'll be wanting gardeners. Maybe he'll think I'm too young for head gardener, but I've worked under Mr Stephens for four years now, and I reckon I know a tidyish bit, and I've kept things going fairly well since I've been here, single-handed.'

Elinor said quickly:

'Of course I will do all I can for you, Horlick. As a matter of fact, I intended to mention you to Major Somervell and tell him what a good gardener you are.'

Horlick's face grew dusky red.

'Thank you, miss. That's very kind of you. You can understand it's been a bit of a blow, like – Mrs Welman dying, and then the place being sold off so quick – and I – well, the fact of the matter is I was going to get married this autumn, only one's got to be sure . . .'

He stopped.

Elinor said kindly:

'I hope Major Somervell will take you on. You can rely on me to do all I can.'

Horlick said again:

'Thank you, miss. We all hoped, you see, as how the place would be kept on by the family. Thank you, miss.'

Elinor walked on.

Suddenly, rushing over her like the stream from a broken dam, a wave of anger, of wild resentment, swept over her.

'*We all hoped the place would be kept on by the family . . .*'

She and Roddy could have lived here! *She and Roddy . . .* Roddy would have wanted that. It was what she herself would have wanted. They had always loved Hunterbury, both of them.

Dear Hunterbury . . . In the years before her parents had died, when they had been in India, she had come here for holidays. She had played in the woods, rambled by the stream, picked sweetpeas in great flowering armloads, eaten fat green gooseberries and dark red luscious raspberries. Later, there had been apples. There had been places, secret lairs, where she had curled up with a book and read for hours.

She had loved Hunterbury. Always, at the back of her mind, she had felt sure of living there permanently some day. Aunt Laura had fostered that idea. Little words and phrases:

'Some day, Elinor, you may like to cut down those yews. They are a little gloomy, perhaps!'

'One might have a water garden here. Some day, perhaps, *you* will.'

And Roddy? Roddy, too, had looked forward to Hunterbury being his home. It had lain, perhaps, behind his feeling for her, Elinor. He had felt, subconsciously, that it was fitting and right that they two should be together at Hunterbury.

And they *would* have been together there. They would have been together *here* – *now* – not packing up the house for selling, but redecorating it, planning new beauties in house and garden, walking side by side in gentle proprietary pleasure, happy – yes, *happy* together – but for the fatal accident of a girl's wild-rose beauty . . .

What did Roddy know of Mary Gerrard? Nothing – less than nothing! What did he care for her – for the real Mary? She had, quite possibly, admirable qualities, but did Roddy know anything about them? It was the old story – Nature's hoary old joke!

Hadn't Roddy himself said it was an 'enchantment'?

Didn't Roddy himself – *really* – want to be free of it?

If Mary Gerrard were to – die, for instance, wouldn't Roddy some day acknowledge: 'It was all for the best. I see that now. We had nothing in common . . .'

He would add, perhaps, with gentle melancholy:

'She was a lovely creature . . .'

Let her be that to him – yes – an exquisite memory – a thing of beauty and a joy for ever . . .

If anything were to happen to Mary Gerrard, Roddy would come back to her – Elinor . . . She was quite sure of that!

If anything were to happen to Mary Gerrard . . .

Elinor turned the handle of the side door. She passed from the warm sunlight into the shadow of the house. She shivered.

It felt cold in here, dark, sinister . . . It was as though Something was there, waiting for her, in the house . . .

She walked along the hall and pushed the baize door that led into the butler's pantry.

It smelt slightly musty. She pushed up the window, opening it wide.

She laid down her parcels – the butter, the loaf, the little glass bottle of milk. She thought:

'Stupid! I meant to get coffee.'

She looked in the canisters on a shelf. There was a little tea in one of them, but no coffee.

She thought: 'Oh, well, it doesn't matter.'

She unwrapped the two glass jars of fish paste.

She stood staring at them for a minute. Then she left the pantry and went upstairs. She went straight to Mrs Welman's room. She began on the big tallboy, opening drawers, sorting, arranging, folding clothes in little piles . . .

III

In the Lodge Mary Gerrard was looking round rather help-lessly.

She hadn't realized, somehow, how cramped it all was.

Her past life rushed back over her in a flood. Mum making clothes for her dolls. Dad always cross and surly. Disliking her. Yes, disliking her . . .

She said suddenly to Nurse Hopkins:

'Dad didn't say anything – send me any message before he died, did he?'

Nurse Hopkins said cheerfully and callously:

'Oh, dear me, no. He was unconscious for an hour before he passed away.'

Mary said slowly:

'I feel perhaps I ought to have come down and looked after him. After all, he *was* my father.'

Nurse Hopkins said with a trace of embarrassment:

'Now, just you listen to me, Mary: whether he was your father or not doesn't enter into it. Children don't care much about their parents in these days, from what I can see, and a good many parents don't care for their children, either. Miss Lambert, at the secondary school, says that's as it should be. According to her, family life is all wrong, and children should be brought up by the state. That's as may be – just a glorified orphanage, it sounds to me – but, anyway, it's a waste of breath to go back over the past and sentimentalize. We've got to get on with living – that's our job and not too easy, either, sometimes!'

Mary said slowly:

'I expect you're right. But I feel perhaps it was my fault we didn't get *on* better.'

Nurse Hopkins said robustly:

'Nonsense.'

The word exploded like a bomb.

It quelled Mary. Nurse Hopkins turned to more practical matters.

'What are you going to do with the furniture? Store it? Or sell it?'

Mary said doubtfully:

'I don't know. What do you think?'

Running a practical eye over it, Nurse Hopkins said:

'Some of it's quite good and solid. You might store it and furnish a little flat of your own in London some day. Get rid of the rubbish. The chairs are good – so's the table. And that's a nice bureau – it's the kind that's out of fashion, but it's solid mahogany, and they say Victorian stuff will come in again one day. I'd get rid of that great wardrobe, if I were you. Too big to fit in anywhere. Takes up half the bedroom as it is.'

They made a list between them of pieces to be kept or let go.

Mary said:

'The lawyer's been very kind – Mr Seddon, I mean. He advanced me some money, so that I could get started with my training fees and other expenses. It will be a month or so before the money can be definitely made over to me, so he said.'

Nurse Hopkins said:

'How do you like your work?'

'I think I shall like it very much. It's rather strenuous at first. I come home tired to death.'

Nurse Hopkins said grimly:

'I thought I was going to die when I was a probationer at St Luke's. I felt I could never stick it for three years. But I did.'

They had sorted through the old man's clothes. Now they came to a tin box full of papers.

Mary said:

'We must go through these, I suppose.'

They sat down one on each side of the table.

Nurse Hopkins grumbled as she started with a handful.

'Extraordinary what rubbish people keep! Newspaper cuttings! Old letters. All sorts of things!'

Mary said, unfolding a document:

'Here's Dad's and Mum's marriage certificate. At St Albans, 1919.'

Nurse Hopkins said:

'Marriage lines, that's the old-fashioned term. Lots of the people in this village use that term yet.'

Mary said in a stifled voice:

'But, Nurse –'

'What's the matter?'

Mary Gerrard said in a shaky voice:

'Don't you see? This is 1939. And I'm twenty-one. In 1919 I was a year old. That means – that means – that my father and mother weren't married till – till – *afterwards*.'

Nurse Hopkins frowned. She said robustly:

'Well, after all, what of it? Don't go worrying about that, at *this* time of day!'

'But, Nurse, I can't help it.'

Nurse Hopkins spoke with authority:

'There's many couples that don't go to church till a bit after they should do so. But so long as they do it in the end, what's the odds? That's what I say!'

Mary said in a low voice:

'Is that why – do you think – my father never liked me? Because, perhaps, my mother *made* him marry her?'

Nurse Hopkins hesitated. She bit her lip, then she said:

'It wasn't quite like that, I imagine.' She paused. 'Oh, well, if

you're going to worry about it, you may as well know the truth:
You aren't Gerrard's daughter at all.'

Mary said:

'Then *that* was why!'

Nurse Hopkins said: 'Maybe.'

Mary said, a red spot suddenly burning in each cheek:

'I suppose it's wrong of me, but I'm glad! I've always felt
uncomfortable because I didn't care for my father, but if he
wasn't my father, well, that makes it all right! How did you
know about it?'

Nurse Hopkins said:

'Gerrard talked about it a good deal before he died. I shut him
up pretty sharply, but he didn't care. Naturally, *I* shouldn't have
said anything to you about it if this hadn't cropped up.'

Mary said slowly:

'I wonder who my real father was . . .'

Nurse Hopkins hesitated. She opened her mouth, then shut it
again. She appeared to be finding it hard to make up her mind
on some point.

Then a shadow fell across the room, and the two women looked
round to see Elinor Carlisle standing at the window.

Elinor said:

'Good morning.'

Nurse Hopkins said:

'Good morning, Miss Carlisle. Lovely day, isn't it?'

Mary said:

'Oh – good morning, Miss Elinor.'

Elinor said:

'I've been making some sandwiches. Won't you come up and
have some? It's just on one o'clock, and it's such a bother to have
to go home for lunch. I got enough for three on purpose.'

Nurse Hopkins said in pleased surprise:

'Well, I must say, Miss Carlisle, that's extremely thoughtful
of you. It *is* a nuisance to have to break off what you're doing
and come all the way back from the village. I hoped we might
finish this morning. I went round and saw my cases early. But,
there, turning out takes you longer than you think.'

Mary said gratefully:

'Thank you, Miss Elinor, it's very kind of you.'

The three of them walked up the drive to the house. Elinor had left the front door open. They passed inside into the cool of the hall. Mary shivered a little. Elinor looked at her sharply.

She said:

'What is it?'

Mary said:

'Oh, nothing – just a shiver. It was coming in – out of the sun . . .'

Elinor said in a low voice:

'That's queer. That's what I felt this morning.'

Nurse Hopkins said in a loud, cheerful voice and with a laugh:

'Come, now, you'll be pretending there are ghosts in the house next. *I* didn't feel anything!'

Elinor smiled. She led the way into the morning-room on the right of the front door. The blinds were up and the windows open. It looked cheerful.

Elinor went across the hall and brought back from the pantry a big plate of sandwiches. She handed it to Mary, saying:

'Have one?'

Mary took one. Elinor stood watching her for a moment as the girl's even white teeth bit into the sandwich.

She held her breath for a minute, then expelled it in a little sigh.

Absent-mindedly she stood for a minute with the plate held to her waist, then at the sight of Nurse Hopkins' slightly parted lips and hungry expression she flushed and quickly proffered the plate to the older woman.

Elinor took a sandwich herself. She said apologetically:

'I meant to make some coffee, but I forgot to get any. There's some beer on that table, though, if anyone likes that?'

Nurse Hopkins said sadly:

'If only I'd thought to bring along some tea now.'

Elinor said absently:

'There's a little tea still in the canister in the pantry.'

Nurse Hopkins' face brightened.

'Then I'll just pop out and put the kettle on. No milk, I suppose?'

Elinor said:

'Yes, I brought some.'

'Well, then, that's all right,' said Nurse Hopkins and hurried out.

Elinor and Mary were alone together.

A queer tension crept into the atmosphere. Elinor, with an obvious effort, tried to make conversation. Her lips were dry. She passed her tongue over them. She said, rather stiffly:

'You – like your work in London?'

'Yes, thank you. I – I'm very grateful to you –'

A sudden harsh sound broke from Elinor. A laugh so discordant, so unlike her that Mary stared at her in surprise.

Elinor said:

'You needn't be so grateful!'

Mary, rather embarrassed, said:

'I didn't mean – that is –'

She stopped.

Elinor was staring at her – a glance so searching, so, yes, strange that Mary flinched under it.

She said:

'Is – is anything wrong?'

Elinor got up quickly. She said, turning away:

'What should be wrong?'

Mary murmured.

'You – you looked –'

Elinor said with a little laugh:

'Was I staring? I'm so sorry. I do sometimes – when I'm thinking of something else.'

Nurse Hopkins looked in at the door and remarked brightly, 'I've put the kettle on,' and went out again.

Elinor was taken with a sudden fit of laughter.

'Polly put the kettle on, Polly put the kettle on, Polly put the kettle on – we'll all have tea! Do you remember playing that, Mary, when we were children?'

'Yes, indeed I do.'

Elinor said:

'*When we were children* . . . It's a pity, Mary isn't it, that one can never go back? . . .'

Mary said:

'Would you like to go back?'

Elinor said with force:

'Yes . . . *yes* . . .'

Silence fell between them for a little while.

Then Mary said, her face flushing:

'Miss Elinor, you mustn't think –'

She stopped, warned by the sudden stiffening of Elinor's slender figure, the uplifted line of her chin.

Elinor said in a cold, steel-like voice:

'What mustn't I think?'

Mary murmured:

'I – I've forgotten what I was going to say.'

Elinor's body relaxed – as at a danger past.

Nurse Hopkins came in with a tray. On it was a brown teapot, and milk and three cups.

She said, quite unconscious of anti-climax:

'Here's the tea!'

She put the tray in front of Elinor. Elinor shook her head.

'I won't have any.'

She pushed the tray along towards Mary.

Mary poured out two cups.

Nurse Hopkins sighed with satisfaction.

'It's nice and strong.'

Elinor got up and moved over to the window. Nurse Hopkins said persuasively:

'Are you sure you won't have a cup, Miss Carlisle? Do you good.'

Elinor murmured, 'No, thank you.'

Nurse Hopkins drained her cup, replaced it in the saucer and murmured:

'I'll just turn off the kettle. I put it on in case we needed to fill up the pot again.'

She bustled out.

Elinor wheeled round from the window.

She said, and her voice was suddenly charged with a desperate appeal:

'Mary . . .'

Mary Gerrard answered quickly:

'Yes?'

Slowly the light died out of Elinor's face. The lips closed. The desperate pleading faded and left a mere mask – frozen and still.

She said:

'Nothing.'

The silence came down heavily on the room.

Mary thought:

'How queer everything is today. As though – as though we were waiting for something.'

Elinor moved at last.

She came from the window and picked up the tea-tray, placing on it the empty sandwich plate.

Mary jumped up.

'Oh, Miss Elinor, let me.'

Elinor said sharply:

'No, you stay here. I'll do this.'

She carried the tray out of the room. She looked back, once, over her shoulder at Mary Gerrard by the window, young and alive and beautiful . . .

IV

Nurse Hopkins was in the pantry. She was wiping her face with a handkerchief. She looked up sharply as Elinor entered. She said:

'My word, it's hot in here!'

Elinor answered mechanically:

'Yes, the pantry faces south.'

Nurse Hopkins relieved her of the tray.

'You let me wash up, Miss Carlisle. You're not looking quite the thing.'

Elinor said:

'Oh, I'm all right.'

She picked up a dish-cloth.

'I'll dry.'

Nurse Hopkins slipped off her cuffs. She poured hot water from the kettle into the papier-mâché basin.

Elinor said idly, looking at her wrist:

'You've pricked yourself.'

Nurse Hopkins laughed.

'On the rose trellis at the Lodge – a thorn. I'll get it out presently.'

The rose trellis at the Lodge . . . Memory poured in waves over Elinor. She and Roddy quarrelling – the Wars of the Roses. She and Roddy quarrelling – and making it up. Lovely, laughing, happy days. A sick wave of revulsion passed over her. What had she come to now? What black abyss of hate – of evil . . . She swayed a little as she stood.

She thought:

'I've been mad – quite mad.'

Nurse Hopkins was staring at her curiously.

'Downright odd, she seemed . . .' so ran Nurse Hopkins' narrative later. 'Talking as if she didn't know what she was saying, and her eyes so bright and queer.'

The cups and saucers rattled in the basin. Elinor picked up an empty fish-paste pot from the table and put it into the basin. As she did so she said, and marvelled at the steadiness of her voice:

'I've sorted out some clothes upstairs, Aunt Laura's things. I thought, perhaps, Nurse, you could advise me where they would be useful in the village.'

Nurse Hopkins said briskly:

'I will indeed. There's Mrs Parkinson, and old Nellie, and that poor creature who's not quite all there at Ivy Cottage. Be a godsend to them.'

She and Elinor cleared up the pantry. Then they went upstairs together.

In Mrs Welman's room clothes were folded in neat bundles: underclothing, dresses, and certain articles of handsome clothing, velvet tea-gowns, a musquash coat. The latter, Elinor explained, she thought of giving to Mrs Bishop. Nurse Hopkins nodded assent.

She noticed that Mrs Welman's sables were laid on the chest of drawers.

'Going to have them remodelled for herself,' she thought to herself.

She cast a look at the big tallboy. She wondered if Elinor had found that photograph signed 'Lewis', and what she had made of it, if so.

'Funny,' she thought to herself, 'the way O'Brien's letter crossed mine. I never dreamt a thing like that could happen. Her hitting on that photo just the day I wrote to her about Mrs Slattery.'

She helped Elinor sort through the clothing and volunteered to tie it up in separate bundles for the different families and see to their distribution herself.

She said:

'I can be getting on with that while Mary goes down to the Lodge and finishes up there. She's only got a box of papers to go through. Where is the girl, by the way? Did she go down to the Lodge?'

Elinor said:

'I left her in the morning-room . . .'

Nurse Hopkins said:

'She'd not be there all this time.' She glanced at her watch. 'Why, it's nearly an hour we've been up here!'

She bustled down the stairs. Elinor followed her.

They went into the morning-room.

Nurse Hopkins exclaimed:

'Well, I never, she's fallen asleep.'

Mary Gerrard was sitting in a big arm-chair by the window. She had dropped down a little in it. There was a queer sound in the room: stertorous, laboured breathing.

Nurse Hopkins went across and shook the girl.

'Wake up, my dear –'

She broke off. She bent lower, pulled down an eyelid. Then she started shaking the girl in grim earnest.

She turned on Elinor. There was something menacing in her voice as she said:

'What's all this?'

Elinor said:

'I don't know what you mean. Is she ill?'

Nurse Hopkins said:

'Where's the phone? Get hold of Dr Lord as soon as you can.'

Elinor said:

'What's the matter?'

'The matter? The girl's ill. She's dying.'

Elinor recoiled a step.

'*Dying?*'

Nurse Hopkins said:

'She's been poisoned . . .'

Her eyes, hard with suspicion, glared at Elinor.

PART II

Hercule Poirot, his egg-shaped head gently tilted to one side, his eyebrows raised inquiringly, his fingertips joined together, watched the young man who was striding so savagely up and down the room, his pleasant freckled face puckered and drawn.

Hercule Poirot said:

'*Eh bien*, my friend, what *is* all this?'

Peter Lord stopped dead in his pacing.

He said:

'M. Poirot. You're the only man in the world who can help me. I've heard Stillingfleet talk about you; he's told me what you did in that Benedict Farley case. How every mortal soul thought it was suicide and you showed that it was murder.'

Hercule Poirot said:

'Have you, then, a case of suicide among your patients about which you are not satisfied?'

Peter Lord shook his head.

He sat down opposite Poirot.

He said:

'There's a young woman. She's been arrested and she's going to be tried for murder! I want you to find evidence that will prove that she didn't do it!'

Poirot's eyebrows rose a little higher. Then he assumed a discreet and confidential manner.

He said:

'You and this young lady – you are affianced – yes? You are in love with each other?'

Peter Lord laughed – a sharp, bitter laugh.

He said:

'No, it's not like that! She has the bad taste to prefer a long-nosed supercilious ass with a face like a melancholy horse! Stupid of her, but there it is!'

Poirot said:

'I see.'

Lord said bitterly:

'Oh, yes, you see all right! No need to be so tactful about it. I fell for her straightaway. And because of that I don't want her hanged. See?'

Poirot said:

'What is the charge against her?'

'She's accused of murdering a girl called Mary Gerrard, by poisoning her with morphine hydrochloride. You've probably read the account of the inquest in the papers.'

Poirot said:

'And the motive?'

'Jealousy!'

'And in your opinion she didn't do it?'

'No, of course not.'

Hercule Poirot looked at him thoughtfully for a moment or two, then he said:

'What is it exactly that you want me to do? To investigate this matter?'

'I want you to get her off.'

'I am not a defending counsel, *mon cher*.'

'I'll put it more clearly: *I want you to find evidence that will enable her counsel to get her off.*'

Hercule Poirot said:

'You put this a little curiously.'

Peter Lord said:

'Because I don't wrap it up, you mean? It seems simple enough to me. *I want this girl acquitted.* I think *you* are the only man who can do it!'

'You wish me to look into the facts? To find out the truth? To discover what really happened?'

'I want you to find any facts that will tell in her favour.'

Hercule Poirot, with care and precision, lighted a very tiny cigarette. He said:

'But is it not a little unethical what you say there? To arrive at the truth, yes, that always interests me. But the truth is a two-edged weapon. Supposing that I find facts *against* the lady? Do you demand that I suppress them?'

Peter Lord stood up. He was very white. He said:

'That's impossible! Nothing that you could find could be more against her than the facts are already! They're utterly and completely damning! There's any amount of evidence against her black and plain for all the world to see! You couldn't find anything that would damn her more completely than she is already! I'm asking you to use all your ingenuity – Stillfleet says you're damned ingenious – to ferret out a loophole, a possible alternative.'

Hercule Poirot said:

'Surely her lawyers will do that?'

'Will they?' the young man laughed scornfully. 'They're licked before they start! Think it's hopeless! They've briefed Bulmer, K.C. – the forlorn hope man; that's a giveaway in itself! Big orator – sob stuff – stressing the prisoner's youth – all that! But the judge won't let him get away with it. Not a hope!'

Hercule Poirot said:

'Supposing she *is* guilty – do you still want to get her acquitted?'

Peter Lord said quietly:

'Yes.'

Hercule Poirot moved in his chair. He said:

'You interest me . . .'

After a minute or two he said:

'You had better, I think, tell me the exact facts of the case.'

'Haven't you read anything about it in the papers?'

Hercule Poirot waved a hand.

'A mention of it – yes. But the newspapers, they are so inaccurate, I never go by what they say.'

Peter Lord said:

'It's quite simple. Horribly simple. This girl, Elinor Carlisle, had just come into a place near here – Hunterbury Hall – and a fortune from her aunt, who died intestate. Aunt's name was Welman. Aunt had a nephew by marriage Roderick Welman. He was engaged to Elinor Carlisle – long-standing business, known each other since children. There was a girl down at Hunterbury: Mary Gerrard, daughter of the lodgekeeper. Old Mrs Welman had made a lot of fuss about her, paid for her education, etc. Consequence is, girl was to outward seeming a lady. Roderick

Welman, it seems, fell for her. In consequence, engagement was broken off.

'Now we come to the doings. Elinor Carlisle put up the place for sale and a man called Somervell bought it. Elinor came down to clear out her aunt's personal possessions and so on. Mary Gerrard, whose father had just died, was clearing out the Lodge. That brings us to the morning of July 27th.

'Elinor Carlisle was staying at the local pub. In the street she met the former housekeeper, Mrs Bishop. Mrs Bishop suggested coming up to the house to help her. Elinor refused – rather over-vehemently. Then she went into the grocer's shop and bought some fish paste, and there she made a remark about food-poisoning. You see? Perfectly innocent thing to do; but, of course, it tells against her! She went up to the house, and about one o'clock she went down to the Lodge, where Mary Gerrard was busy with the District Nurse, a Nosey Parker of a woman called Hopkins, helping her, and told them that she had some sandwiches ready up at the house. They came up to the house with her, ate sandwiches, and about an hour or so later I was sent for and found Mary Gerrard unconscious. Did all I could, but it was no good. Autopsy revealed large dose of morphine had been taken a short time previously. And the police found a scrap of a label with morphia hydrochlor on it just where Elinor Carlisle had been spreading the sandwiches.'

'What else did Mary Gerrard eat or drink?'

'She and the District Nurse drank tea with the sandwiches. Nurse made it and Mary poured it out. Couldn't have been anything there. Of course, I understand Counsel will make a song and dance about sandwiches, too, saying all three ate them, therefore *impossible* to ensure that only one person should be poisoned. They said that in the Hearne case, you remember.'

Poirot nodded. He said:

'But actually it is very simple. You make your pile of sandwiches. *In one of them is the poison.* You hand the plate. In our state of civilization it is a foregone conclusion that the person to whom the plate is offered will take *the sandwich that is nearest to them.* I presume that Elinor Carlisle handed the plate to Mary Gerrard first?'

'Exactly.'

'Although the nurse, who was an older woman, was in the room?'

'Yes.'

'That does not look very good.'

'It doesn't mean a thing, really. You don't stand on ceremony at a picnic lunch.'

'Who cut the sandwiches?'

'Elinor Carlisle.'

'Was there anyone else in the house?'

'No one.'

Poirot shook his head.

'It is bad, that. And the girl had *nothing* but the tea and the sandwiches?'

'Nothing. Stomach contents tell us that.'

Poirot said:

'It is suggested that Elinor Carlisle hoped the girl's death would be taken for food poisoning? How did she propose to explain the fact that only *one* member of the party was affected?'

Peter Lord said:

'It does happen that way sometimes. Also, there were two pots of paste – both much alike in appearance. The idea would be that one pot was all right and that by a coincidence all the bad paste was eaten by Mary.'

'An interesting study in the laws of probability,' said Poirot. 'The mathematical chances against that happening would be high, I fancy. But another point, if food poisoning was to be suggested: *Why not choose a different poison?* The symptoms of morphine are not in the least like those of food poisoning. Atropine, surely, would have been a better choice!'

Peter Lord said slowly:

'Yes, that's true. But there's something more. That damned District Nurse swears she lost a tube of morphine!'

'When?'

'Oh, weeks earlier, the night old Mrs Welman died. The nurse says she left her case in the hall and found a tube of morphine missing in the morning. All bunkum, I believe. Probably smashed it at home some time before and forgot about it.'

'She has only remembered it *since* the death of Mary Gerrard?'

Peter Lord said reluctantly:

'As a matter of fact, she *did* mention it at the time – to the nurse on duty.'

Hercule Poirot was looking at Peter Lord with some interest. He said gently:

'I think, *mon cher*, there is something else – something that you have not yet told me.'

Peter Lord said:

'Oh, well, I suppose you'd better have it all. They're applying for an exhumation order and going to dig up old Mrs Welman.'

Poirot said:

'*Eh bien?*'

Peter Lord said:

'When they do, *they'll probably find what they're looking for – morphine!*'

'You knew that?'

Peter Lord, his face white under the freckles, muttered:

'I suspected it.'

Hercule Poirot beat with his hand on the arm of his chair. He cried out:

'*Mon Dieu*, I do not understand you! You *knew* when she died that she had been murdered?'

Peter Lord shouted:

'Good lord, no! I never dreamt of such a thing! I thought she'd taken it herself.'

Poirot sank back in his chair.

'Ah! You thought *that* . . .'

'Of course I did! She'd talked to me about it. Asked me more than once if I couldn't "finish her off". She hated illness, the helplessness of it – the – what she called the *indignity* of lying there tended like a baby. And she was a very determined woman.'

He was silent a moment, then he went on:

'I was surprised at her death. I hadn't expected it. I sent the nurse out of the room and made as thorough an investigation as I could. Of course, it was impossible to be sure without an autopsy. Well, what was the good of that? *If* she'd taken a short-cut, why make a song and dance about it and create a scandal? Better sign the certificate and let her be buried in peace. After all, I couldn't be sure. I decided wrong, I suppose.

But I never dreamed for one moment of foul play. I was quite sure she'd done it herself.'

Poirot asked:

'How do you think she had got hold of the morphine?'

'I hadn't the least idea. But, as I tell you, she was a clever, resourceful woman, with plenty of ingenuity and remarkable determination.'

'Would she have got it from the nurses?'

Peter Lord shook his head.

'Never on your life! You don't know nurses!'

'From her family?'

'Possibly. Might have worked on their feelings.'

Hercule Poirot said:

'You have told me that Mrs Welman died intestate. If she had lived, would she have made a will?'

Peter Lord grinned suddenly.

'Putting your finger with fiendish accuracy on all the vital spots, aren't you? Yes, she was going to make a will; very agitated about it. Couldn't speak intelligently, but made her wishes clear. Elinor Carlisle was to have telephoned the lawyer first thing in the morning.'

'So Elinor Carlisle knew that her aunt wanted to make a will? And if her aunt died without making one, Elinor Carlisle inherited everything?'

Peter Lord said quickly:

'She didn't know that. She'd no idea her aunt had never made a will.'

'That, my friend, is what she *says*. She *may* have known.'

'Look here, Poirot, are you the Prosecuting Counsel?'

'At the moment, yes. I must know the full strength of the case against her. Could Elinor Carlisle have taken the morphine from the attaché-case?'

'Yes. So could anyone else. Roderick Welman. Nurse O'Brien. Any of the servants.'

'Or Dr Lord?'

Peter Lord's eyes opened wide. He said:

'Certainly . . . But what would be the idea?'

'Mercy, perhaps.'

Peter Lord shook his head.

'Nothing doing there! You'll have to believe me!'

Hercule Poirot leaned back in his chair. He said:

'Let us entertain a supposition. Let us say that Elinor Carlisle did take that morphine from the attaché-case and did administer it to her aunt. Was anything said about the loss of the morphine?'

'Not to the household. The two nurses kept it to themselves.'

Poirot said:

'What, in your opinion, will be the action of the Crown?'

'You mean if they find morphine in Mrs Welman's body?'

'Yes.'

Peter Lord said grimly:

'It's possible that if Elinor is acquitted of the present charge she will be rearrested and charged with the murder of her aunt.'

Poirot said thoughtfully:

'The motives are different; that is to say, in the case of Mrs Welman the motive would have been *gain*, whereas in the case of Mary Gerrard the motive is supposed to be *jealousy*.'

'That's right.'

Poirot said:

'What line does the defence propose to take?'

Peter Lord said:

'Bulmer proposes to take the line that there was no motive. He'll put forward the theory that the engagement between Elinor and Roderick was a family business, entered into for family reasons, to please Mrs Welman, and that the moment the old lady was dead Elinor broke it off of her own accord. Roderick Welman will give evidence to that effect. I think he almost believes it!'

'Believes that Elinor did not care for him to any great extent?'

'Yes.'

'In which case,' said Poirot, 'she would have no reason for murdering Mary Gerrard.'

'Exactly.'

'But in that case, who *did* murder Mary Gerrard?'

'As you say.'

Poirot shook his head.

'*C'est difficile.*'

Peter Lord said vehemently:

'That's just it! If *she* didn't, *who did*? There's the tea; but both Nurse Hopkins and Mary drank that. The defence will try to suggest that Mary Gerrard took the morphine herself after the other two had left the room – that she committed suicide, in fact.'

'Had she any reason for committing suicide?'

'None whatever.'

'Was she of a suicidal type?'

'No.'

Poirot said:

'What was she like, this Mary Gerrard?'

Peter Lord considered:

'She was – well, she was a nice kid. Yes, definitely a nice kid.'

Poirot sighed. He murmured:

'This Roderick Welman, did he fall in love with her because she was a nice kid?'

Peter Lord smiled.

'Oh, I get what you mean. She was beautiful, all right.'

'And you yourself? You had no feeling for her?'

Peter Lord stared.

'Good lord, no.'

Hercule Poirot reflected for a moment or two, then he said:

'Roderick Welman says that there was affection between him and Elinor Carlisle, but nothing stronger. Do you agree to that?'

'How the hell should I know?'

Poirot shook his head.

'You told me when you came into this room that Elinor Carlisle had the bad taste to be in love with a long-nosed, supercilious ass. That, I presume, is a description of Roderick Welman. So, according to you, she *does* care for him.'

Peter Lord said in a low, exasperated voice:

'She cares for him all right! Cares like hell!'

Poirot said:

'Then there *was* a motive . . .'

Peter Lord swerved round on him, his face alight with anger.

'Does it matter? She might have done it, yes! *I don't care if she did.*'

Poirot said:

'Aha!'

'But I don't want her hanged, I tell you! Supposing she *was* driven desperate? Love's a desperate and twisting business. It can turn a worm into a fine fellow – and it can bring a decent, straight man down to the dregs! Suppose she *did* do it. Haven't you got any pity?'

Hercule Poirot said:

'I do not approve of murder.'

Peter Lord stared at him, looked away, stared again and finally burst out laughing.

'Of all the things to say – so prim and smug, too! Who's asking you to approve? I'm not asking you to tell lies! Truth's truth, isn't it? If you find something that tells in an accused person's favour, you wouldn't be inclined to suppress it because she's guilty, would you?'

'Certainly not.'

'Then why the hell can't you do what I ask you?'

Hercule Poirot said:

'My friend, I am perfectly prepared to do so . . .'

CHAPTER 2

Peter Lord stared at him, took out a handkerchief, wiped his face and threw himself down in a chair.

'Whoof!' he said. 'You got me all worked up! I didn't see in the least what you were getting at!'

Poirot said:

'I was examining the case against Elinor Carlisle. Now I know it. Morphine was administered to Mary Gerrard; and, as far as I can see, it *must* have been given in the sandwiches. Nobody touched those sandwiches *except Elinor Carlisle*. Elinor Carlisle had a *motive* for killing Mary Gerrard, and she is, in your opinion, *capable* of killing Mary Gerrard, and in all probability she *did* kill Mary Gerrard. I see no reason for believing otherwise.

'That, *mon ami*, is one side of the question. Now we will proceed to stage two. We will dismiss all those considerations from our mind and we will approach the matter from the opposite angle: *If Elinor Carlisle did not kill Mary Gerrard, who did?* Or did Mary Gerrard commit suicide?'

Peter Lord sat up. A frown creased his forehead. He said:

'You weren't quite accurate just now.'

'I? *Not accurate?*'

Poirot sounded affronted.

Peter Lord pursued relentlessly:

'No. You said nobody but Elinor Carlisle touched those sandwiches. You don't know that.'

'There was no one else in the house.'

'*As far as we know.* But you are excluding a short period of time. *There was a time during which Elinor Carlisle left the house to go down to the Lodge.* During that period of time the sandwiches were on a plate in the pantry, and somebody *could* have tampered with them.'

Poirot drew a deep breath.

He said:

'You are right, my friend. I admit it. There *was* a time during which somebody could have had access to the plate of sandwiches. We must try to form some idea *who that somebody could be*; that is to say, *what kind of person . . .*'

He paused.

'Let us consider this Mary Gerrard. *Someone*, not Elinor Carlisle, desires her death. *Why?* Did anyone stand to gain by her death? Had she money to leave?'

Peter Lord shook his head.

'Not now. In another month she would have had two thousand pounds. Elinor Carlisle was making that sum over to her because she believed her aunt would have wished it. But the old lady's estate isn't wound up yet.'

Poirot said:

'Then we can wash out the money angle. Mary Gerrard was beautiful, you say. With that there are always complications. She had admirers?'

'Probably. I don't know much about it.'

'Who would know?'

Peter Lord grinned.

'I'd better put you on to Nurse Hopkins. She's the town crier. She knows everything that goes on in Maidensford.'

'I was going to ask you to give me your impressions of the two nurses.'

'Well, O'Brien's Irish, good nurse, competent, a bit silly, could be spiteful, a bit of a liar – the imaginative kind that's not so much deceitful, but just has to make a good story out of everything.'

Poirot nodded.

'Hopkins is a sensible, shrewd, middle-aged woman, quite kindly and competent, but a sight too much interested in other people's business!'

'If there had been trouble over some young man in the village, would Nurse Hopkins know about it?'

'You bet!'

He added slowly:

'All the same, I don't believe there can be anything very obvious in that line. Mary hadn't been home long. She'd been away in Germany for two years.'

'She was twenty-one?'

'Yes.'

'There may be some German complication.'

Peter Lord's face brightened.

He said eagerly:

'You mean that some German fellow may have had it in for her? He may have followed her over here, waited his time, and finally achieved his object?'

'It sounds a little melodramatic,' said Hercule Poirot doubtfully.

'But it's *possible*?'

'Not very probable, though.'

Peter Lord said:

'I don't agree. Someone *might* get all het up about the girl, and see red when she turned him down. He may have fancied she treated him badly. It's an idea.'

'It is an idea, yes,' said Hercule Poirot, but his tone was not encouraging.

Peter Lord said pleadingly:

'Go on, M. Poirot.'

'You want me, I see, to be the conjurer. To take out of the empty hat rabbit after rabbit.'

'You can put it that way if you like.'

'There *is* another possibility,' said Hercule Poirot.

'Go on.'

'*Someone* abstracted a tube of morphine from Nurse Hopkins' case that evening in June. *Suppose Mary Gerrard saw the person who did it?*'

'She would have said so.'

'No, no, *mon cher*. Be reasonable. If Elinor Carlisle, or Roderick Welman, or Nurse O'Brien, or even any of the servants, were to open that case and abstract a little glass tube, what would anyone think? Simply that the person in question had been sent by the nurse to fetch something from it. The matter would pass straight out of Mary Gerrard's mind again, but it is possible that, later, she *might* recollect the fact and might mention it casually to the person in question – oh, without the least suspicion in the world. But to the person guilty of the murder of Mrs Welman, imagine the effect of that remark! Mary had seen: Mary must be silenced at all costs! I can assure you, my friend, that anyone who has once committed a murder finds it only too easy to commit another!'

Peter Lord said with a frown:

'I've believed all along that Mrs Welman took the stuff herself . . .'

'But she was paralysed – helpless – she had just had a second stroke.'

'Oh, I know. My idea was that, having got hold of morphine somehow or other, she kept it by her in a receptacle close at hand.'

'But in that case she must have got hold of the morphine *before* her second attack and the nurse missed it afterwards.'

'Hopkins may only have missed the morphine that morning. It might have been *taken* a couple of days before, and she hadn't noticed it.'

'How would the old lady have got hold of it?'

'I don't know. Bribed a servant, perhaps. If so, that servant's never going to tell.'

'You don't think either of the nurses were bribable?'

Lord shook his head.

'Not on your life! To begin with, they're both very strict about their professional ethics – and in addition they'd be scared to death to do such a thing. They'd know the danger to themselves.'

Poirot said:

'That is so.'

He added thoughtfully:

'It looks, does it not, as though we return to our muttons? Who is the most likely person to have taken that morphine tube? *Elinor Carlisle.* We may say that she wished to make sure of inheriting a large fortune. We may be more generous and say that she was actuated by pity, that she took the morphine and administered it in compliance with her aunt's often-repeated request; but *she* took it – *and Mary Gerrard saw her do it.* And so we are back at the sandwiches and the empty house, and we have Elinor Carlisle once more – but this time with a different motive: to save her neck.'

Peter Lord cried out:

'That's fantastic. I tell you, she isn't that kind of person! Money doesn't really mean anything to her – or to Roderick Welman, either, I'm bound to admit. I've heard them both say as much!'

'You have? That is very interesting. That is the kind of statement I always look upon with a good deal of suspicion myself.'

Peter Lord said:

'Damn you, Poirot, must you always twist everything round so that it comes back to that girl?'

'It is not I that twist things round: they come round of themselves. It is like the pointer at the fair. It swings round, and when it comes to rest it points always at the same name – *Elinor Carlisle.*'

Peter Lord said:

'No!'

Hercule Poirot shook his head sadly.

Then he said:

'Has she relations, this Elinor Carlisle? Sisters, cousins? A father or mother?'

'No. She's an orphan – alone in the world . . .'

'How pathetic it sounds! Bulmer, I am sure, will make great play with that! Who, then, inherits her money if she dies?'

'I don't know. I haven't thought.'

Poirot said reprovingly:

'One should always think of these things. Has she made a will, for instance?'

Peter Lord flushed. He said uncertainly:

'I – I don't know.'

Hercule Poirot looked at the ceiling and joined his fingertips. He remarked:

'It would be well, you know, to tell me.'

'Tell you what?'

'Exactly what is in your mind – no matter how damaging it may happen to be to Elinor Carlisle.'

'How do you know –?'

'Yes, yes, I know. There is *something* – some incident in your mind! It will be as well to tell me, otherwise I shall imagine it is something worse than it is!'

'It's nothing, really –'

'We will agree it is nothing. But let me hear what it is.'

Slowly, unwillingly, Peter Lord allowed the story to be dragged from him – that scene of Elinor leaning in at the window of Nurse Hopkins' cottage, and of her laughter.

Poirot said thoughtfully:

'She said that, did she, "*So you're making your will, Mary? That's funny – that's very funny.*" And it was very clear to you what was in her mind . . . She had been thinking, perhaps, *that Mary Gerrard was not going to live long . . .*'

Peter Lord said:

'I only imagined that. I don't know.'

Poirot said:

'No, you did not only imagine it . . .'

CHAPTER 3

Hercule Poirot sat in Nurse Hopkins' cottage.

Dr Lord had brought him there, had introducd him and had then, at a glance from Poirot, left him to a tête-à-tête.

Having, to begin with, eyed his foreign appearance somewhat askance, Nurse Hopkins was now thawing rapidly.

She said with a faintly gloomy relish:

'Yes, it's a terrible thing. One of the most terrible things I've ever known. Mary was one of the most beautiful girls you've ever seen. Might have gone on the films any time! And a nice steady girl, too, and not stuck-up, as she might have been with all the notice taken of her.'

Poirot, inserting a question adroitly, said:

'You mean the notice taken of her by Mrs Welman?'

'That's what I mean. The old lady had taken a tremendous fancy to her – really, a tremendous fancy.'

Hercule Poirot murmured:

'Surprising, perhaps?'

'That depends. It might be quite natural, really. I mean . . .' Nurse Hopkins bit her lip and looked confused. 'What I mean is, Mary had a very pretty way with her: nice soft voice and pleasant manners. And it's my opinion it does an elderly person good to have a young face about.'

Hercule Poirot said:

'Miss Carlisle came down occasionally, I suppose, to see her aunt?'

Nurse Hopkins said sharply:

'Miss Carlisle came down when it suited her.'

Poirot murmured:

'You do not like Miss Carlisle.'

Nurse Hopkins cried out:

'I should hope not, indeed! A poisoner! A cold-blooded poisoner!'

'Ah,' said Hercule Poirot, 'I see you have made up your mind.'

Nurse Hopkins said suspiciously:

'What do you mean? Made up my mind?'

'You are quite sure that it was she who administered morphine to Mary Gerrard?'

'Who else could have done it, I should like to know? You're not suggesting that *I* did?'

'Not for a moment. But her guilt has not yet been proved, remember.'

Nurse Hopkins said with calm assurance:

'She did it all right. Apart from anything else, you could see it in her face. Queer she was, all the time. And taking me away upstairs and keeping me there – delaying as long as possible. And then when I turned on her, after finding Mary like that, it was there in her face as plain as anything. She knew I knew!'

Hercule Poirot said thoughtfully:

'It is certainly difficult to see who else could have done it. Unless of course, she did it herself.'

'What do you mean, *did it herself*? Do you mean that Mary committed suicide? I never heard such nonsense!'

Hercule Poirot said:

'One can never tell. The heart of a young girl, it is very sensitive, very tender.' He paused. 'It would have been possible, I suppose? She could have slipped something into her tea without your noticing her?'

'Slipped it into her cup, you mean?'

'Yes. You weren't watching her all the time.'

'I wasn't watching her – no. Yes, I suppose she *could* have done that . . . But it's all nonsense! What would she want to do a thing like that for?'

Hercule Poirot shook his head with a resumption of his former manner.

'A young girl's heart . . . as I say, so sensitive. An unhappy love-affair, perhaps –'

Nurse Hopkins gave a snort.

'Girls don't kill themselves for love-affairs – not unless they're in the family way – and Mary wasn't *that*, let me tell you!' She glared at him belligerently.

'And she was not in love?'

'Not she. Quite fancy free. Keen on her job and enjoying her life.'

'But she must have had admirers, since she was such an attractive girl.'

Nurse Hopkins said:

'She wasn't one of these girls who are all S.A. and IT. She was a quiet girl!'

'But there were young men, no doubt, in the village who admired her.'

'There was Ted Bigland, of course,' said Nurse Hopkins.

Poirot extracted various details as to Ted Bigland.

'Very gone on Mary, he was,' said Nurse Hopkins. 'But, as I told her, she was a cut above him.'

Poirot said:

'He must have been angry when she would not have anything to do with him?'

'He was sore about it, yes,' admitted Nurse Hopkins. 'Blamed *me* for it, too.'

'He thought it was your fault?'

'That's what he said. I'd a perfect right to advise the girl. After all, I know something of the world. I didn't want the girl to throw herself away.'

Poirot said gently:

'What made you take so much interest in the girl?'

'Well, I don't know . . .' Nurse Hopkins hesitated. She looked shy and a little ashamed of herself. 'There was something – well – romantic about Mary.'

Poirot murmured:

'About *her*, perhaps, but not about her circumstances. She was the lodge-keeper's daughter, wasn't she?'

Nurse Hopkins said:

'Yes – yes, of course. At least –'

She hesitated, looked at Poirot, who was gazing at her in the most sympathetic manner.

'As a matter of fact,' said Nurse Hopkins, in a burst of confidence, 'she wasn't old Gerrard's daughter at all. He told me so. Her father was a gentleman.'

Poirot murmured:

'I see . . . And her mother?'

Nurse Hopkins hesitated, bit her lip, and then went on:

'Her mother had been a lady's maid to old Mrs Welman. She married Gerrard after Mary was born.'

'As you say, quite a romance – a mystery romance.'

Nurse Hopkins' face lit up.

'Wasn't it? One can't help taking an interest in people when one knows something that nobody else does about them. Just by chance I happened to find out a good deal. As a matter of fact, it was Nurse O'Brien who set me on the track; but that's another story. But, as you say, it's interesting knowing past history. There's many a tragedy that goes unguessed at. It's a sad world.'

Poirot sighed and shook his head.

Nurse Hopkins said with sudden alarm:

'But I oughtn't to have gone talking like this. I wouldn't have a word of this get out for anything! After all, it's nothing to do with the case. As far as the world is concerned, Mary was Gerrard's daughter, and there mustn't be a hint of anything else. Damaging her in the eyes of the world after she's dead! He married her mother, and that's enough.'

Poirot murmured:

'But you know, perhaps, who her real father was?'

Nurse Hopkins said reluctantly:

'Well, perhaps I do; but, then again, perhaps I don't. That is, I don't *know* anything. I could take a guess. Old sins have long shadows, as they say! But I'm not one to talk, and I shan't say another word.'

Poirot tactfully retired from the fray and attacked another subject.

'There is something else – a delicate matter. But I am sure I can rely on your discretion.'

Nurse Hopkins bridled. A broad smile appeared on her homely face.

Poirot continued:

'I speak of Mr Roderick Welman. He was, so I hear, attracted by Mary Gerrard.'

Nurse Hopkins said:

'Bowled over by her!'

'Although at the time he was engaged to Miss Carlisle?'

'If you ask me,' said Nurse Hopkins, 'he was never really sweet on Miss Carlisle. Not what I'd call *sweet* on her.'

Poirot asked, using an old-fashioned term:

'Did Mary Gerrard – er – encourage his advances?'

Nurse Hopkins said sharply:

'She behaved very well. Nobody could say she led him on!'

Poirot said:

'Was she in love with him?'

Nurse Hopkins said sharply:

'No, she wasn't.'

'But she liked him?'

'Oh, yes, she *liked* him well enough.'

'And I suppose, in time, something might have come of it?'

Nurse Hopkins admitted that.

'That may be. But Mary wouldn't have done anything in a hurry. She told him down here he had no business to speak like that to her when he was engaged to Miss Elinor. And when he came to see her in London she said the same.'

Poirot asked with an air of engaging candour:

'What do you think yourself of Mr Roderick Welman?'

Nurse Hopkins said:

'He's a nice enough young fellow. Nervy, though. Looks as though he might be dyspeptic later on. Those nervy ones often are.'

'Was he very fond of his aunt?'

'I believe so.'

'Did he sit with her much when she was so ill?'

'You mean when she had that second stroke? The night before she died when they came down? I don't believe he even went into her room!'

'Really.'

Nurse Hopkins said quickly:

'She didn't ask for him. And, of course, we'd no idea the end was so near. There are a lot of men like that, you know: fight shy of a sick-room. They can't help it. And it's not heartlessness. They just don't want to be upset in their feelings.'

Poirot nodded comprehendingly.

He said:

'Are you *sure* Mr Welman did not go into his aunt's room before she died?'

'Well not while *I* was on duty! Nurse O'Brien relieved me at 3 a.m., and she may have fetched him before the end; but, if so, she didn't mention it to me.'

Poirot suggested:

'He may have gone into her room when you were absent?'

Nurse Hopkins snapped:

'I don't leave my patients unattended, Mr Poirot.'

'A thousand apologies. I did not mean that. I thought perhaps you might have had to boil water, or to run downstairs for some necessary stimulant.'

Mollified, Nurse Hopkins said:

'I did go down to change the bottles and get them refilled. I knew there'd be a kettle on the boil down in the kitchen.'

'You were away long?'

'Five minutes, perhaps.'

'Ah, yes, then Mr Welman *may* have just looked in on her then?'

'He must have been very quick about it if he did.'

Poirot sighed. He said:

'As you say, men fight shy of illness. It is the women who are the ministering angels. What should we do without them? Especially women of your profession – a truly noble calling.'

Nurse Hopkins, slightly red in the face, said:

'It's very kind of you to say that. I've never thought of it that way myself. Too much hard work in nursing to think about the noble side of it.'

Poirot said:

'And there is nothing else you can tell me about Mary Gerrard?'

There was an appreciable pause before Nurse Hopkins answered:

'I don't know of anything.'

'Are you quite sure?'

Nurse Hopkins said rather incoherently:

'You don't understand. I was *fond* of Mary.'

'And there is nothing more you can tell me?'

'No, there is not! And that's flat.'

CHAPTER 4

In the awesome majesty of Mrs Bishop's black-clad presence Hercule Poirot sat humbly insignificant.

The thawing of Mrs Bishop was no easy matter. For Mrs Bishop, a lady of Conservative habits and views, strongly disapproved of foreigners. And a foreigner most indubitably Hercule Poirot was. Her responses were frosty and she eyed him with disfavour and suspicion.

Dr Lord's introduction of him had done little to soften the situation.

'I am sure,' said Mrs Bishop when Dr Lord had gone, 'Dr

Lord is a very clever doctor and means well. Dr Ransome, his predecessor, had been here *many* years!'

Dr Ransome, that is to say, could be trusted to behave in a manner suitable to the county. Dr Lord, a mere irresponsible youngster, an upstart who had taken Dr Ransome's place, had only one recommendation: 'cleverness' in his profession.

Cleverness, the whole demeamour of Mrs Bishop seemed to say, is not enough!

Hercule Poirot was persuasive. He was adroit. But charm he never so wisely, Mrs Bishop remained aloof and implacable.

The death of Mrs Welman had been very sad. She had been much respected in the neighbourhood. The arrest of Miss Carlisle was 'Disgraceful!' and believed to be the result of 'these new-fangled police methods'. The views of Mrs Bishop upon the death of Mary Gerrard were vague in the extreme. 'I couldn't say, I'm sure,' being the most she could be brought to say.

Hercule Poirot played his last card. He recounted with naïve pride a recent visit of his to Sandringham. He spoke with admiration of the graciousness and delightful simplicity and kindness of Royalty.

Mrs Bishop, who followed daily in the court circular the exact movements of Royalty, was overborne. After all, if They had sent for Mr Poirot . . . Well, naturally, that made All the Difference. Foreigner or no foreigner, who was she, Emma Bishop, to hold back where Royalty had led the way?

Presently she and M. Poirot were engaged in pleasant conversation on a really interesting theme – no less than the selection of a suitable future husband for Princess Elizabeth.

Having finally exhausted all possible candidates as Not Good Enough, the talk reverted to less exalted circles.

Poirot observed sententiously:

'Marriage, alas, is fraught with dangers and pitfalls!'

Mrs Bishop said:

'Yes, indeed – with this nasty divorce,' rather as though she were speaking of a contagious disease such as chickenpox.

'I expect,' said Poirot, 'that Mrs Welman, before her death, must have been anxious to see her niece suitably settled in life?'

Mrs Bishop bowed her head.

'Yes, indeed. The engagement between Miss Elinor and Mr Roderick was a great relief to her. It was a thing she had always hoped for.'

Poirot ventured:

'The engagement was perhaps entered into partly from a wish to please her?'

'Oh, no, I wouldn't say *that*, Mr Poirot. Miss Elinor has always been devoted to Mr Roddy – always was, as a tiny tot – quite beautiful to see. Miss Elinor has a very loyal and devoted nature!'

Poirot murmured:

'And he?'

Mrs Bishop said austerely:

'Mr Roderick was devoted to Miss Elinor.'

Poirot said:

'Yet the engagement, I think, was broken off?'

The colour rose in Mrs Bishop's face. She said:

'Owing, Mr Poirot, to the machinations of a snake in the grass.'

Poirot said, appearing suitably impressed:

'Indeed?'

Mrs Bishop, her face becoming redder still, explained:

'In this country, Mr Poirot, there is a certain Decency to be observed when mentioning the Dead. But that young woman, Mr Poirot, was Underhand in her Dealings.'

Poirot looked at her thoughtfully for a moment.

Then he said with an apparent lack of guile:

'You surprise me. I had been given the impression that she was a very simple and unassuming girl.'

Mrs Bishop's chin trembled a little.

'She was Artful, Mr Poirot. People were Taken In by her. That Nurse Hopkins, for instance! Yes, and my poor dear mistress too!'

Poirot shook his head sympathetically and made a clacking noise with his tongue.

'Yes, indeed,' said Mrs Bishop, stimulated by these encouraging noises. 'She was failing, poor dear, and that young woman Wormed her way into her Confidence. *She* knew which side of her bread was buttered. Always hovering about, reading to her, bringing her little nosegays of flowers. It was Mary this and Mary that and "Where's Mary?" all the time! The money she spent on the girl, too! Expensive schools and finishing places abroad – and the girl nothing but old Gerrard's daughter! *He* didn't like it, I can tell you! Used to complain of her Fine Lady ways. Above Herself, that's what *She* was.'

This time Poirot shook his head and said commiseratingly:

'Dear, dear.'

'And then Making Up to Mr Roddy the way she did! He was too simple to see through Her. And Miss Elinor, a nice-minded young lady as she is, of course she wouldn't realize what was Going On. But Men, they are all alike: easily caught by flattery and a pretty face!'

Poirot sighed.

'She had, I suppose, admirers of her own class?' he asked.

'Of course she had. There was Rufus Bigland's son Ted – as nice a boy as you could find. But oh, no, my fine lady was too good for *him*! I'd no patience with such airs and graces!'

Poirot said:

'Was he not angry about her treatment of him?'

'Yes, indeed. He accused her of carrying on with Mr Roddy. I know *that* for a *fact*. I don't blame the boy for feeling sore!'

'Nor I,' said Poirot. 'You interest me extremely, Mrs Bishop. Some people have the knack of presenting a character clearly and vigorously in a few words. It is a great gift. I have at last a clear picture of Mary Gerrard.'

'Mind you,' said Mrs Bishop, 'I'm not saying a word *against* the girl! I wouldn't do such a thing – and she in her grave. But there's no doubt that she caused a lot of trouble!'

Poirot murmured:

'Where would it have ended, I wonder?'

'That's what *I* say!' said Mrs Bishop. 'You can take it from me, Mr Poirot, that if my dear mistress hadn't died when she did – awful as the shock was at the time, I see now that it was a Mercy in Disguise – I don't know what might have been the end of it!'

Poirot said invitingly:

'You mean?'

Mrs Bishop said solemnly:

'I've come across it time and again. My own sister was in service where it happened. Once when old Colonel Randolph died and left every penny away from his poor wife to a hussy living at Eastbourne – and once old Mrs Dacres – left it to the organist of the church – one of those long-haired young men – and she with married sons and daughters.'

Poirot said:

'You mean, I take it, that Mrs Welman might have left all her money to Mary Gerrard?'

'It wouldn't have surprised me!' said Mrs Bishop. 'That's what the young woman was working up to, I've no doubt. And if I ventured to say a word, Mrs Welman was ready to bite my head off, though I'd been with her nearly twenty years. It's an ungrateful world, Mr Poirot. You try to do your duty and it is not appreciated.'

'Alas,' sighed Poirot, 'how true that is!'

'But Wickedness doesn't always flourish,' said Mrs Bishop.

Poirot said:

'True. Mary Gerrard is dead . . .'

Mrs Bishop said comfortably:

'She's gone to her reckoning, and we mustn't judge her.'

Poirot mused:

'The circumstances of her death seem quite inexplicable.'

'These police and their new-fangled ideas,' said Mrs Bishop. 'Is it likely that a well-bred, nicely brought-up young lady like Miss Elinor would go about poisoning anyone? Trying to drag *me* into it, too, saying *I* said her manner was peculiar!'

'But was it not peculiar?'

'And why shouldn't it be?' Mrs Bishop's bust heaved with a flash of jet. 'Miss Elinor's a young lady of feelings. She was going to turn out her aunt's things – and that's always a painful business.'

Poirot nodded sympathetically.

He said:

'It would have made it much easier for her if you had accompanied her.'

'I wanted to, Mr Poirot, but she took me up quite sharp. Oh, well, Miss Elinor was always a very proud and reserved young lady. I wish, though, that I *had* gone with her.'

Poirot murmured:

'You did not think of following her up to the house?'

Mrs Bishop reared her head majestically.

'I don't go where I'm not wanted, Mr Poirot.'

Poirot looked abashed. He murmured:

'Besides, you had doubtless matters of importance to attend to that morning?'

'It was a very warm day, I remember. Very sultry.' She sighed. 'I walked to the cemetery to place a few flowers on Mrs Welman's grave, a token of respect, and I had to rest there quite a long time. Quite overcome by the heat, I was. I got home late for lunch, and my sister was quite upset when she saw the State of Heat I was in! Said I never should have done it on a day like that.'

Poirot looked at her with admiration.

He said:

'I envy you, Mrs Bishop. It is pleasant indeed to have nothing with which to reproach oneself after a death. Mr Roderick Welman, I fancy, must blame himself for not going in to see his aunt that night, though naturally he could not know she was going to pass away so soon.'

'Oh, but you're quite wrong, Mr Poirot. I can tell you that for a fact. Mr Roddy *did* go into his aunt's room. I was just outside on the landing myself. I'd heard that nurse go off downstairs, and I thought maybe I'd better make sure the mistress wasn't needing anything, for you know what nurses are: always staying downstairs to gossip with the maids, or else worrying them to death by asking them for things. Not that Nurse Hopkins was as bad as that red-haired Irish nurse. Always chattering and making trouble, *she* was! But, as I say, I thought I'd just see everything was all right, and it was then that I saw Mr Roddy slip into his aunt's room. I don't know whether she knew him or not; but anyway he hasn't got anything to *reproach* himself with!'

Poirot said:

'I am glad. He is of a somewhat nervous disposition.'

'Just a trifle cranky. He always has been.'

Poirot said:

'Mrs Bishop, you are evidently a woman of great understanding. I have formed a high regard for your judgement. What do you think is the truth about the death of Mary Gerrard?'

Mrs Bishop snorted.

'Clear enough, I should think! One of those nasty pots of paste of Abbott's. Keeps them on those shelves for months! My second cousin was took ill and nearly died once, with tinned crab!'

Poirot objected:

'But what about the morphine found in the body?'

Mrs Bishop said grandly:

'*I* don't know anything about morphine! I know what *doctors* are: Tell them to look for something, and they'll find it! Tainted fish paste isn't *good* enough for *them*!'

Poirot said:

'You do not think it possible that she committed suicide?'

'She?' Mrs Bishop snorted. 'No indeed. Hadn't she made up her mind to marry Mr Roddy? Catch *her* committing suicide!'

CHAPTER 5

Since it was a Sunday, Hercule Poirot found Ted Bigland at his father's farm.

There was little difficulty in getting Ted Bigland to talk. He seemed to welcome the opportunity – as though it was a relief.

He said thoughtfully:

'So you're trying to find out who killed Mary? It's a black mystery, that.'

Poirot said:

'You do not believe that Miss Carlisle killed her, then?'

Ted Bigland frowned – a puzzled, almost childlike frown it was.

He said slowly:

'Miss Elinor's a lady. She's the kind – well, you couldn't imagine her doing anything like that – anything *violent*, if you know what I mean. After all, 'tisn't likely, is it, sir, that a nice young lady would go and do a thing of that kind?'

Hercule Poirot nodded in a contemplative manner.

He said:

'No, it is not likely . . . But when it comes to jealousy –'

He paused, watching the good-looking, fair young giant before him.

Ted Bigland said:

'Jealousy? I know things happen that way; but it's usually drink and getting worked up that makes a fellow see red and run amok. Miss Elinor – a nice quiet young lady like that –'

Poirot said:

'*But Mary Gerrard died* . . . and she did not die a natural death. Have you any idea – is there anything you can tell me to help me find out – who killed Mary Gerrard?'

Slowly the other shook his head.

He said:

'It doesn't seem right. It doesn't seem *possible*, if you take my meaning, that anyone could have killed Mary. She was – she was like a flower.'

And suddenly, for a vivid minute, Hercule Poirot had a new conception of the dead girl . . . In that halting rustic voice the girl Mary lived and bloomed again. '*She was like a flower.*'

II

There was suddenly a poignant sense of loss, of something exquisite destroyed . . .

In his mind phrase after phrase succeeded each other. Peter Lord's '*She was a nice kid.*' Nurse Hopkins' '*She could have gone on the films any time.*' Mrs Bishop's venomous '*No patience with her airs and graces.*' And now last, putting to shame, laying aside those other views, the quiet wondering: '*She was like a flower.*'

Hercule Poirot said:

'But, then . . . ?'

He spread out his hands in a wide, appealing foreign gesture.

Ted Bigland nodded his head. His eyes had still the dumb, glazed look of an animal in pain.

He said:

'I know, sir. I know what you say's true. She didn't die natural. But I've been wondering . . .'

He paused.

Poirot said:

'Yes?'

Ted Bigland said slowly:

'I've been wondering if in some way it couldn't have been an *accident*?'

'An accident? But what kind of an accident?'

'I know, sir. I know. It doesn't sound like sense. But I keep thinking and thinking, and it seems to me it must have been that way. Something that wasn't meant to happen or something that was all a mistake. Just – well, just an *accident*!'

He looked pleadingly at Poirot, embarrassed by his own lack of eloquence.

Poirot was silent a moment or two. He seemed to be considering. He said at last:

'It is interesting that you feel that.'

Ted Bigland said deprecatingly:

'I dare say it doesn't make sense to you, sir. I can't figure out any *how* and *why* about it. It's just a *feeling* I've got.'

Hercule Poirot said:

'Feeling is sometimes an important guide . . . You will pardon me, I hope, if I seem to tread on painful ground, but you cared very much for Mary Gerrard, did you not?'

A little dark colour came up in the tanned face.

Ted said simply:

'Everyone knows that around here, I reckon.'

'You wanted to marry her?'

'Yes.'

'But she – was not willing?'

Ted's face darkened a little. He said, with a hint of surpressed anger:

'Mean well, people do, but they shouldn't muck up people's lives by interfering. All this schooling and going abroad! It changed Mary. I don't mean spoilt her, or that she was stuck-up – she wasn't. But it . . . oh, it bewildered her! She didn't know where she was any more. She was – well, put it crudely – she was too good for *me*; but she still wasn't good enough for a real gentleman like Mr Welman.'

Hercule Poirot said, watching him:

'You don't like Mr Welman?'

Ted Bigland said with simple violence:

'Why the hell should I? Mr Welman's all right. I've nothing against him. He's not what I call much of a *man*! I could pick him up and break him in two. He's got brains, I suppose . . . But that's not much help to you if your car breaks down, for instance.

You may know the principle that makes a car run; but it doesn't stop you from being as helpless as a baby when all that's needed is to take the mag out and give it a wipe.'

Poirot said:

'Of course, you work in a garage?'

Ted Bigland nodded.

'Henderson's, down the road.'

'You were there on the morning when – this thing happened?'

Ted Bigland said:

'Yes, testing out a car for a gentleman. A choke somewhere, and I couldn't locate it. Ran it round for a bit. Seems odd to think of now. It was a lovely day, some honeysuckle still in the hedges . . . Mary used to like honeysuckle. We used to go picking it together before she went away abroad . . .'

Again there was that puzzled child-like wonder on his face.

Hercule Poirot was silent.

With a start Ted Bigland came out of his trance.

He said:

'Sorry, sir, forget what I said about Mr Welman. I was sore – because of his hanging round after Mary. He ought to have left her alone. She wasn't his sort – not really.'

Poirot said:

'Do you think she cared for him?'

Again Ted Bigland frowned.

'I don't – not really. But she might have done. I couldn't say.'

Poirot asked:

'Was there any other man in Mary's life? Anyone, for instance, she had met abroad?'

'I couldn't say, sir. She never mentioned anybody.'

'Any enemies – here in Maidensford?'

'You mean anyone who had it in for her?' He shook his head. 'Nobody knew her very well. But they all liked her.'

Poirot said:

'Did Mrs Bishop, the housekeeper at Hunterbury, like her?'

Ted gave a sudden grin. He said:

'Oh, that was just spite! The old dame didn't like Mrs Welman taking such a fancy to Mary.'

Poirot asked:

'Was Mary Gerrard happy when she was down here? Was she fond of old Mrs Welman?'

'She'd have been happy enough, I dare say, if Nurse had let her alone. Nurse Hopkins, I mean. Putting ideas into her head of earning a living and going off to do massage.'

'She was fond of Mary, though?'

'Oh, yes, she was *fond* enough of her; but she's the kind who always knows what's best for everyone!'

Poirot said slowly:

'Supposing that Nurse Hopkins knows something – something, let us say, that would throw a discreditable light on Mary – do you think she would keep it to herself?'

Ted Bigland looked at him curiously.

'I don't quite get your meaning, sir?'

'Do you think that if Nurse Hopkins knew something against Mary Gerrard she would hold her tongue about it?'

Ted Bigland said:

'I doubt if that woman could hold her tongue about anything! She's the greatest gossip in the village. But if she'd hold her tongue about *anybody*, it would probably be about Mary.' He added, his curiosity getting the better of him, 'I'd like to know *why* you ask that?'

Hercule Poirot said:

'One has, in talking to people, a certain impression. Nurse Hopkins was, to all seeming, perfectly frank and outspoken, but I formed the impression – very strongly – that she was keeping *something* back. It is not necessarily an *important* thing. It may have no bearing on the crime. *But there is something that she knows which she has not told.* I also formed the impression that this something – whatever it is – is something definitely damaging or detrimental to the character of Mary Gerrard . . .'

Ted shook his head helplessly.

Hercule Poirot sighed:

'Ah, well. I shall learn what it is in time.'

CHAPTER 6

Poirot looked with interest at the long, sensitive face of Roderick Welman.

Roddy's nerves were in a pitiable condition. His hands twitched, his eyes were bloodshot, his voice was husky and irritable.

He said, looking down at the card:

'Of course, I know your name, M. Poirot. But I don't see what Dr Lord thinks you can do in this matter! And, anyway, what business is it of *his*? He attended my aunt, but otherwise he's a complete stranger. Elinor and I had not even met him until we went down there this June. Surely it is Seddon's business to attend to all this sort of thing?'

Hercule Poirot said:

'Technically that is correct.'

Roddy went on unhappily:

'Not that Seddon gives me much confidence. He's so confoundedly gloomy.'

'It is a habit, that, of lawyers.'

'Still,' said Roddy, cheering up a little, 'we've briefed Bulmer. He's supposed to be pretty well at the top of the tree, isn't he?'

Hercule Poirot said:

'He has a reputation for leading forlorn hopes.'

Roddy winced palpably.

Poirot said:

'It does not displease you, I hope, that I should endeavour to be of assistance to Miss Elinor Carlisle?'

'No, no, of course not. But –'

'But what can I do? It is that, that you would ask?'

A quick smile flashed across Roddy's worried face – a smile so suddenly charming that Hercule Poirot understood the subtle attraction of the man.

Roddy said apologetically:

'It sounds a little rude, put like that. But, really, of course, that *is* the point. I won't beat about the bush. What *can* you do, M. Poirot?'

Poirot said:

'I can search for the truth.'

'Yes.' Roddy sounded a little doubtful.

Poirot said:

'I might discover facts that would be helpful to the accused.'

Roddy sighed.

'If you only could!'

Hercule Poirot went on:

'It is my earnest desire to be helpful. Will you assist me by telling me just exactly what you think of the whole business?'

Roddy got up and walked restlessly up and down.

'What can I say? The whole thing's so absurd – so fantastic! The mere idea of Elinor – Elinor, whom I've known since she was a child – actually doing such a melodramatic thing as poisoning someone. It's quite laughable, of course! But how on earth explain that to a jury?'

Poirot said stolidly:

'You consider it quite impossible that Miss Carlisle should have done such a thing?'

'Oh quite! That goes without saying! Elinor's an exquisite creature – beautifully poised and balanced – no violence in her nature. She's intellectual, sensitive and altogether devoid of animal passions. But get twelve fat-headed fools in a jury-box, and God knows what they can be made to believe! After all, let's be reasonable: they're not there to judge character; they're there to sift evidence. Facts – facts – *facts*. And the facts are unfortunate!'

Hercule Poirot nodded thoughtfully.

He said:

'You are a person, Mr Welman, of sensibility and intelligence. The facts condemn Miss Carlisle. Your knowledge of her acquits her. *What, then, really happened?* What *can* have happened?'

Roddy spread out his hands in exasperation.

'That's the devil of it all! I suppose the nurse couldn't have done it?'

'She was never near the sandwiches – oh, I have made the inquiries very minutely – and she could not have poisoned the tea without poisoning herself as well. I have made quite sure of that. Moreover, *why* should she wish to kill Mary Gerrard?'

Roddy cried out:

'Why should *anyone* wish to kill Mary Gerrard?'

'That,' said Poirot, 'seems to be the unanswerable question in this case. *No one* wished to kill Mary Gerrard.' (He added in his own mind: '*Except Elinor Carlisle*.') 'Therefore, the next step logically would seem to be: Mary Gerrard was not killed! But that, alas, is not so. She *was* killed!'

He added, slightly melodramatically:

> '*But she is in her grave, and oh,*
> *The difference to me!*'

'I beg your pardon,' said Roddy.

Hercule Poirot explained:

'Wordsworth. I read him much. Those lines express, perhaps, what you feel?'

'I?'

Roddy looked stiff and unapproachable.

Poirot said:

'I apologize – I apologize deeply! It is so hard – to be a detective and also a *pukka sahib*. As it is so well expressed in your language, there are things that one does not say. But, alas, a detective is forced to say them! He must ask questions: about people's private affairs, about their feelings!'

Roddy said:

'Surely all this is quite unnecessary?'

Poirot said quickly and humbly:

'If I might just understand the position? Then we will pass from the unpleasant subject and not refer to it again. It is fairly widely known, Mr Welman, that you – admired Mary Gerrard? That is, I think, true?'

Roddy got up and stood by the window. He played with the blind tassel. He said:

'Yes.'

'You fell in love with her?'

'I suppose so.'

'Ah, and you are now heart-broken by her death –'

'I – I suppose – I mean – well, really, M. Poirot –'

He turned – a nervous, irritable, sensitive creature at bay.

Hercule Poirot said:

'If you could just tell me – just show me clearly – then it would be finished with.'

Roddy Welman sat down in a chair. He did not look at the other man. He spoke in a series of jerks.

'It's very difficult to explain. Must we go into it?'

Poirot said:

'One cannot always turn aside and pass by from the unpleasant-nesses of life, Mr Welman! You say you *suppose* you cared for this girl. You are not sure, then?'

Roddy said:

'I don't know . . . She was so lovely. Like a dream . . . That's what it seems like now. A dream! Not real! All that – my seeing her first – my – well, my infatuation for her! A kind of madness! And now everything is finished – gone . . . as though – as though it had never happened.'

Poirot nodded his head . . .

He said:

'Yes, I understand . . .'

He added:

'You were not in England yourself at the time of her death?'

'No, I went abroad on July 9th and returned on August 1st. Elinor's telegram followed me about from place to place. I hurried home as soon as I got the news.'

Poirot said:

'It must have been a great shock to you. You had cared for the girl very much.'

Roddy said, and there was bitterness and exasperation in his voice:

'Why should these things happen to one? It's not as though one *wished* them to happen! It is contrary to all – to all one's ordered expectation of life!'

Hercule Poirot said:

'Ah, but life is like that! It does not permit you to arrange and order it as you will. It will not permit you to escape emotion, to live by the intellect and by reason! You cannot say, "I will feel so much and no more." Life, Mr Welman, whatever else it is, is not *reasonable*!'

Roderick Welman murmured:

'So it seems . . .'

Poirot said:

'A spring morning, a girl's face – and the well-ordered sequence of existence is routed.'

Roddy winced and Poirot went on:

'Sometimes it is little more than that – a *face*. What did you really know of Mary Gerrard, Mr Welman?'

Roddy said heavily:

'What did I know? So little; I see that now. She was sweet, I think, and gentle; but really, I know nothing – nothing at all . . . That's why, I suppose, I don't miss her . . .'

His antagonism and resentment were gone now. He spoke naturally and simply. Hercule Poirot, as he had a knack of doing, had penetrated the other's defences. Roddy seemed to feel a certain relief in unburdening himself.

He said:

'Sweet – gentle – not very clever. Sensitive, I think, and kind. She had a refinement that you would not expect to find in a girl of her class.'

'Was she the kind of girl who would make enemies unconsciously?'

Roddy shook his head vigorously.

'No, no, I can't imagine anyone disliking her – really disliking her, I mean. Spite is different.'

Poirot said quickly.

'Spite? So there was spite, you think?'

Roddy said absently:

'Must have been – to account for that letter.'

Poirot said sharply:

'What letter?'

Roddy flushed and looked annoyed. He said:

'Oh, nothing important.'

Poirot repeated:

'What letter?'

'An anonymous letter.'

He spoke reluctantly.

'When did it come? To whom was it written?'

Rather unwillingly Roddy explained.

Hercule Poirot murmured:

'It is interesting, that. Can I see it, this letter?'

'Afraid you can't. As a matter of fact, I burnt it.'

'Now, why did you do that, Mr Welman?'

Roddy said rather stiffly:

'It seemed the natural thing to do at the time.'

Poirot said:

'And in consequence of this letter, you and Miss Carlisle went hurriedly down to Hunterbury?'

'We went down, yes. I don't know about *hurriedly*.'

'But you were a little uneasy, were you not? Perhaps even, a little alarmed?'

Roddy said even more stiffly:

'I won't admit that.'

Hercule Poirot cried:

'But surely that was only natural! Your inheritance – that which was promised you – was in jeopardy! Surely it is natural that you should be unquiet about the matter! Money, it is very important!'

'Not as important as you make out.'

Poirot said:

'Such unworldliness is indeed remarkable!'

Roddy flushed. He said:

'Oh, of course, the money *did* matter to us. We weren't completely indifferent to it. But our main object was to – to see my aunt and make sure she was all right.'

Poirot said:

'You went down there with Miss Carlisle. At that time your aunt had not made a will. Shortly afterwards she had another attack of her illness. She then wished to make a will, but, conveniently for Miss Carlisle, perhaps, she dies that night before that will can be made.'

'Look here, what are you hinting at?'

Roddy's face was wrathful.

Poirot answered him like a flash:

'You have told me, Mr Welman, as regards the death of Mary Gerrard, that the motive attributed to Elinor Carlisle is absurd – that she was, emphatically, not that kind of a person. But there is now another interpretation. Elinor Carlisle had reason to fear that she might be disinherited in favour of an outsider. The letter has warned her – her aunt's broken murmurings confirm that fear. In the hall below is an attaché-case with various drugs and medical supplies. It is easy to abstract a tube of morphine. And afterwards, so I have learned, *she sits in the sick-room alone with her aunt while you and the nurses are at dinner . . .*'

Roddy cried:

'Good God, M. Poirot, what are you suggesting now? That Elinor killed Aunt Laura? Of all the ridiculous ideas!'

Poirot said:

'But you know, do you not, that an order to exhume Mrs Welman's body has been applied for?'

'Yes, I know. But they won't find anything!'

'Suppose they do?'

'They won't!' Roddy spoke positively.

Poirot shook his head.

'I am not so sure. And there was only *one* person, you realize, who would benefit by Mrs Welman's dying at that moment . . .'

Roddy sat down. His face was white and he was shaking a little. He stared at Poirot. Then he said:

'I thought – you were on *her* side . . .'

Hercule Poirot said:

'Whatever side one is on, one must face *facts*! I think, Mr Welman, that you have so far preferred in life to avoid facing an awkward truth whenever it is possible.'

Roddy said:

'Why harrow oneself by looking on the worst side?'

Hercule Poirot replied gravely:

'Because it is something necessary . . .'

He paused a minute and then said:

'Let us face the possibility that your aunt's death may be found to be due to the administration of morphine. What then?'

Roddy shook his head helplessly.

'I don't know.'

'But you must try to *think*. Who could have given it to her? You must admit that Elinor Carlisle had the best opportunity to do so?'

'What about the nurses?'

'Either of them could have done so, certainly. But Nurse Hopkins was concerned about the disappearance of the tube at the time and mentioned it openly. There was no need for her to do so. The death certificate had been signed. Why call attention to the missing morphine if she were guilty? It will probably bring her censure for carelessness as it is, and if she poisoned Mrs Welman it was surely idiotic to draw attention to the morphine. Besides, what could she gain by Mrs Welman's death? Nothing. The same applies to Nurse O'Brien. She could have administered morphine, could have taken it from Nurse Hopkins' case; but, again – *why should she?*'

Roddy shook his head.

'All that's true enough.'

Poirot said:

'Then there is *yourself.*'

Roddy started like a nervous horse.

'Me?'

'Certainly. *You* could have abstracted the morphine. *You* could have given it to Mrs Welman! You were alone with her for a short period that night. But, again, *why should you*? If she lived to make a will, it is at least probable that you would have been mentioned in it. So again, you see, there is no motive. Only two people had a motive.'

Roddy's eyes brightened.

'*Two* people?'

'Yes. One was Elinor Carlisle.'

'And the other?'

Poirot said slowly:

'The other was the writer of that anonymous letter.'

Roddy looked incredulous.

Poirot said:

'*Somebody* wrote that letter – somebody who hated Mary Gerrard or at least disliked her – somebody who was, as they say, "on your side". Somebody, that is, *who did not want Mary Gerrard to benefit at Mrs Welman's death*. Now, have you any idea, Mr Welman, who the writer of that letter could be?'

Roddy shook his head.

'I've no idea at all. It was an illiterate letter, misspelt, cheap-looking.'

Poirot waved a hand.

'There is nothing much to that! It might easily have been written by an educated person who chose to disguise the fact.

That is why I wish you had the letter still. People who try to write in an uneducated manner usually give themselves away.'

Roddy said thoughtfully:

'Elinor and I thought it might be one of the servants.'

'Had you any idea which of them?'

'No – no idea whatsoever.'

'Could it, do you think, have been Mrs Bishop, the house-keeper?'

Roddy looked shocked.

'Oh, no, she's a most respectable, high-and-mighty creature. Writes beautifully involved and ornate letters with long words in them. Besides, I'm sure she would never –'

As he hesitated, Poirot cut in:

'She did not like Mary Gerrard!'

'I suppose she didn't. I never noticed anything, though.'

'But perhaps, Mr Welman, you do not notice very much?'

Roddy said slowly:

'You don't think, M. Poirot, that my aunt could have taken that morphine herself?'

Poirot said slowly:

'It is an idea, yes.'

Roddy said:

'She hated her – her helplessness, you know. Often said she wished she could die.'

Poirot said:

'But, then, she could not have risen from her bed, gone downstairs and helped herself to the tube of morphine from the nurse's case?'

Roddy said slowly:

'No, but somebody could have got it for her.'

'Who?'

'Well, one of the nurses.'

'No, neither of the nurses. They would understand the danger to themselves far too well! The nurses are the last people to suspect.'

'Then – somebody else . . .'

He started, opened his mouth, shut it again.

Poirot said quietly:

'You have remembered something, have you not?'

Roddy said doubtfully:

'Yes – but –'

'You wonder if you ought to tell me?'

'Well, yes . . .'

Poirot said, a curious smile tilting the corners of his mouth:

'When did Miss Carlisle say it?'

Roddy drew a deep breath.

'By Jove, you are a wizard! It was in the train coming down. We'd had the telegram, you know, saying Aunt Laura had had another stroke. Elinor said how terribly sorry she was for her, how the poor dear hated being ill, and that now she would be more helpless still and that it would be absolute hell for her. Elinor said, "One does feel that people *ought* to be set free if they themselves really want it."'

'And you said – what?'

'I agreed.'

Poirot spoke very gravely:

'Just now, Mr Welman, you scouted the possibility of Miss Carlisle having killed your aunt for monetary gain. Do you also scout the possibility that she may have killed Mrs Welman *out of compassion*?'

Roddy said:

'I – I – no, I can't . . .'

Hercule Poirot bowed his head.

He said:

'Yes, I thought – I was sure – that you would say that . . .'

CHAPTER 7

In the offices of Messrs Seddon, Blatherwick & Seddon, Hercule Poirot was received with extreme caution, not to say distrust.

Mr Seddon, a forefinger stroking his closely shaven chin, was non-committal and his shrewd grey eyes appraised the detective thoughtfully.

'Your name is familiar to me, M. Poirot, of course. But I am at a loss to understand your position in this case.'

Hercule Poirot said:

'I am acting, Monsieur, in the interests of your client.'

'Ah – indeed? And who – er – engaged you in that capacity?'

'I am here at the request of Dr Lord.'

Mr Seddon's eyebrows rose very high.

'Indeed! That seems to me very irregular – very irregular. Dr Lord, I understand, has been subpœnaed as a witness for the prosecution.'

Hercule Poirot shrugged his shoulders.

'Does that matter?'

Mr Seddon said:

'The arrangements for Miss Carlisle's defence are entirely in our hands. I really do not think we need any outside assistance in this case.'

Poirot asked:

'Is that because your client's innocence will be so easily proved?'

Mr Seddon winced. Then he became wrathful in a dry legal fashion.

'That,' he said, 'is a most improper question. Most improper.'

Hercule Poirot said:

'The case against your client is a very strong one . . .'

'I really fail to see, M. Poirot, how you know anything about it.'

Poirot said:

'Although I am actually retained by Dr Lord, I have here a note from Mr Roderick Welman.'

He handed it over with a bow.

Mr Seddon perused the few lines it contained and remarked grudgingly:

'That, of course, throws a new complexion on the matter. Mr Welman has made himself responsible for Miss Carlisle's defence. We are acting at his request.'

He added with visible distaste:

'Our firm does very little in – er – criminal procedure, but I felt it my duty to my – er – late client – to undertake the defence of her niece. I may say we have already briefed Sir Edwin Bulmer, K.C.'

Poirot said, and his smile was suddenly ironic:

'No expense will be spared. Very right and proper!'

Looking over his glasses, Mr Seddon said:

'Really, M. Poirot –'

Poirot cut into his protest.

'Eloquence and emotional appeal will not save your client. It will need more than that.'

Mr Seddon said drily:

'What do you advise?'

'There is always the truth.'

'Quite so.'

'But in this case will the truth help us?'

Mr Seddon said sharply:

'That, again, is a most improper remark.'

Poirot said:

'There are certain questions to which I should like answers.'

Mr Seddon said cautiously:

'I cannot, of course, guarantee to answer without the consent of my client.'

'Naturally. I understand that.' He paused and then said, 'Has Elinor Carlisle any enemies?'

Mr Seddon showed a faint surprise.

'As far as I know, none.'

'Did the late Mrs Welman, at any period of her life, make a will?'

'Never. She always put it off.'

'Has Elinor Carlisle made a will?'

'Yes.'

'Recently? Since her aunt's death?'

'Yes.'

'To whom has she left her property?'

'That, M. Poirot, is confidential. I cannot tell you without authorization from my client.'

Poirot said:

'Then I shall have to interview your client!'

Mr Seddon said with a cold smile:

'That, I fear, will not be easy.'

Poirot rose and made a gesture.

'Everything,' he said, 'is easy to Hercule Poirot.'

CHAPTER 8

Chief Inspector Marsden was affable.

'Well, M. Poirot,' he said. 'Come to set me right about one of my cases?'

Poirot murmured deprecatingly:

'No, no. A little curiosity on my part, that is all.'

'Only too happy to satisfy it. Which case is it?'

'Elinor Carlisle.'

'Oh, yes, girl who poisoned Mary Gerrard. Coming up for trial in two weeks' time. Interesting case. She did in the old woman too, by the way. Final report isn't in yet, but it seems there's no doubt of it. Morphia. Cold-blooded bit of goods. Never turned a hair at the time of her arrest or after. Giving nothing away. But we've got the goods on her all right. She's for it.'

'You think she did it?'

Marsden, an experienced, kindly looking man, nodded his head affirmatively.

'Not a doubt of it. Put the stuff in the top sandwich. She's a cool customer.'

'You have no doubts? No doubts at all?'

'Oh, no! I'm quite sure. It's a pleasant feeling when you *are* sure! We don't like making mistakes any more than anyone else would. We're not just out to get a conviction, as some people think. This time I can go ahead with a clear conscience.'

Poirot said slowly:

'I see.'

The Scotland Yard man looked at him curiously.

'Is there anything on the other side?'

Slowly Poirot shook his head.

'As yet, no. So far everything I have found out about the case points to Elinor Carlisle's being guilty.'

Inspector Marsden said with cheerful certainty:

'*She's* guilty, all right.'

Poirot said:

'I should like to see her.'

Inspector Marsden smiled indulgently. He said:

'Got the present Home Secretary in your pocket, haven't you? That will be easy enough.'

CHAPTER 9

Peter Lord said:
'Well?'
Hercule Poirot said:
'No, it is not very well.'
Peter Lord said heavily:
'You haven't got hold of anything?'
Poirot said slowly:
'Elinor Carlisle killed Mary Gerrard out of jealousy . . . Elinor Carlisle killed her aunt so as to inherit her money . . . Elinor Carlisle killed her aunt out of compassion . . . My friend, you may make your choice!'
Peter Lord said:
'You're talking nonsense!'
Hercule Poirot said:
'Am I?'
Lord's freckled face looked angry. He said:
'What *is* all this?'
Hercule Poirot said:
'Do you think it is possible, that?'
'Do I think what is possible?'
'That Elinor Carlisle was unable to bear the sight of her aunt's misery and helped her out of existence.'
'Nonsense!'
'Is it nonsense? You have told me yourself that the old lady asked *you* to help her.'
'She didn't mean it seriously. She knew I wouldn't do anything of the sort.'
'Still, the idea was in her mind. Elinor Carlisle *might* have helped her.'
Peter Lord strolled up and down. He said at last:
'One can't deny that that sort of thing is possible. But Elinor Carlisle is a level-headed, clear-thinking kind of young woman. I don't think she'd be so carried away by pity as to lose sight

of the risk. And she'd realize exactly what the risk was. She'd be liable to stand accused of murder.'

'So you don't think she would do it?'

Peter Lord said slowly:

'I think a woman might do such a thing for her husband; or for her child; or for her mother, perhaps. I don't think she'd do it for an aunt, though she might be fond of that aunt. And I think in any case she'd only do it if the person in question was actually suffering unbearable pain.'

Poirot said thoughtfully:

'Perhaps you are right.'

Then he added:

'Do you think Roderick Welman's feelings could have been sufficiently worked upon to induce *him* to do such a thing?'

Peter Lord replied scornfully:

'He wouldn't have the guts!'

Poirot murmured:

'I wonder. In some ways, *mon cher*, you underestimate that young man.'

'Oh, he's clever and intellectual and all that, I dare say.'

'Exactly,' said Poirot. 'And he has charm, too ... Yes, I felt that.'

'Did you? I never have!'

Then Peter Lord said earnestly:

'Look here, Poirot, isn't there *anything*?'

Poirot said:

'They are not fortunate so far, my investigations! They lead always back to the same place. No one stood to gain by Mary Gerrard's death. No one hated Mary Gerrard – *except* Elinor Carlisle. There is only one question that we might perhaps ask ourselves. We might say, perhaps: *Did anyone hate Elinor Carlisle?*'

Slowly Dr Lord shook his head.

'Not that I know of ... You mean – that someone might have framed her for the crime?'

Poirot nodded. He said:

'It is a very far-fetched speculation, that, and there is nothing to support it ... except, perhaps, the very completeness of the case against her.'

He told the other of the anonymous letter.

'You see,' he said, 'that makes it possible to outline a very strong case against her. She was warned that she might be completely cut out of her aunt's will – that this girl, a stranger, might get all the money. So, when her aunt in her halting speech was asking for a lawyer, Elinor took no chances, and saw to it that the old lady should die that night!'

Peter Lord cried:

'What about Roderick Welman? He stood to lose, too!'

Poirot shook his head.

'No, it was to his advantage that the old lady should make a will. If she died intestate, he got nothing, remember. Elinor was the next of kin.'

Lord said:

'But he was going to marry Elinor!'

Poirot said, 'True. But remember that immediately afterwards the engagement was broken off – that he showed her clearly that he wished to be released from it.'

Peter Lord groaned and held his head. He said:

'It comes back to her, then. Every time!'

'Yes. Unless . . .'

He was silent for a minute. Then he said:

'There is *something* . . .'

'Yes?'

'Something – some little piece of the puzzle that is missing. It is something – of that I am certain – that concerns Mary Gerrard. My friend, you hear a certain amount of gossip, of scandal, down here. Have you ever heard anything against her?'

'Against Mary Gerrard? Her character, you mean?'

'Anything. Some bygone story about her. Some indiscretion on her part. A hint of scandal. A doubt of her honesty. A malicious rumour concerning her. Anything – anything at all – but something that definitely is *damaging to her* . . .'

Peter Lord said slowly:

'I hope you're not going to suggest that line . . . Trying to rake up things about a harmless young woman who's dead and can't defend herself . . . And, anyway, I don't believe you can do it!'

'She was like the female Sir Galahad – a blameless life?'

'As far as I know, she was. I never heard anything else.'

Poirot said gently:

'You must not think, my friend, that I would stir the mud where no mud is . . . No, no, it is not like that at all. But the good Nurse Hopkins is not an adept at hiding her feelings. She was fond of Mary, and there is something about Mary she does not want known; that is to say, there is something against Mary that she is afraid I will find out. She does not think that it has any bearing on the crime. But, then, she is convinced that the crime was committed by Elinor Carlisle, and clearly this fact, whatever it is, has nothing to do with Elinor. But, you see, my friend, it is imperative that I should know *everything*. For it may be that there is a wrong done by Mary to some third person, and in that case, that third person might have a motive for desiring her death.'

Peter Lord said:

'But surely, in that case, Nurse Hopkins would realize that, too.'

Poirot said:

'Nurse Hopkins is quite an intelligent woman within her limitations, but her intellect is hardly the equal of *mine*. *She* might not see, but Hercule Poirot would!'

Peter Lord said, shaking his head:

'I'm sorry. I don't know anything.'

Poirot said thoughtfully:

'No more does Ted Bigland – and he has lived here all his life and Mary's. No more does Mrs Bishop; for if she knew anything unpleasant about the girl, she would not have been able to keep it to herself! *Eh bien*, there is one more hope.'

'Yes?'

'I am seeing the other nurse, Nurse O'Brien, today.'

Peter Lord said, shaking his head:

'She doesn't know much about this part of the world. She was only here for a month or two.'

Poirot said:

'I am aware of that. But, my friend, Nurse Hopkins, we have been told, has the long tongue. She has not gossiped in the village, where such talk might have done Mary Gerrard harm. But I doubt if she could refrain from giving at least a hint about something that was occupying her mind to a stranger and a colleague! Nurse O'Brien *may* know something.'

CHAPTER 10

Nurse O'Brien tossed her red head and smiled widely across the tea-table at the little man opposite her.

She thought to herself:

'It's the funny little fellow he is – and his eyes green like any cat's, and with all that Dr Lord saying he's the clever one!'

Hercule Poirot said:

'It is a pleasure to meet someone so full of health and vitality. Your patients, I am sure, must all recover.'

Nurse O'Brien said:

'I'm not one for pulling a long face, and not many of my patients die on me, I'm thankful to say.'

Poirot said:

'Of course, in Mrs Welman's case, it was a merciful release.'

'Ah! It was that, the poor dear.' Her eyes were shrewd as she looked at Poirot and asked:

'Is it about that you want to talk to me? I was after hearing that they're digging her up.'

Poirot said:

'You yourself had no suspicion at the time?'

'Not the least in the world, though indeed I might have had, with the face Dr Lord had on him that morning, and him sending me here, there and everywhere for things he didn't need! But he signed the certificate, for all that.'

Poirot began, 'He had his reasons –' but she took the words out of his mouth.

'Indeed and he was right. It does a doctor no good to think things and offend the family, and then if he's wrong it's the end of him, and no one would be wishing to call him in any more. A doctor's got to be *sure*!'

Poirot said:

'There is a suggestion that Mrs Welman might have committed suicide.'

'She? And her lying there helpless? Just lift one hand, that was all *she* could do!'

'Someone might have helped her?'

'Ah! I see now what you're meaning. Miss Carlisle, or Mr Welman, or maybe Mary Gerrard?'

'It would be possible, would it not?'

Nurse O'Brien shook her head. She said:

'They'd not dare – any of them!'

Poirot said slowly:

'Perhaps not.'

Then he said:

'When was it Nurse Hopkins missed the tube of morphine?'

'It was that very morning. "I'm sure I had it here," she said. Very sure she was at first; but you know how it is, after a while your mind gets confused, and in the end she made sure she'd left it at home.'

Poirot murmured:

'And even then you had no suspicion?'

'Not the least in the world! Sure, it never entered my head for a moment that things weren't as they should be. And even now 'tis only a suspicion they have.'

'The thought of that missing tube never caused either you or Nurse Hopkins an uneasy moment?'

'Well, I wouldn't say that . . . I do remember that it came into my head – and into Nurse Hopkins' head, too, I believe – in the Blue Tit Café, we were at the time. And I saw the thought pass into her mind from mine. "It couldn't be any other way than that I left it on the mantelpiece and it fell into the dustbin, could it?" she says. And "No, indeed, that was the way of it," I said to her; and neither of us saying what was in our minds and the fear that was on us.'

Hercule Poirot asked:

'And what do you think now?'

Nurse O'Brien said:

'If they find morphine in her there'll be little doubt who took that tube, nor what it was used for – though I'll not be believing she sent the old lady the same road till it's proved there's morphine in her.'

Poirot said:

'You have no doubt at all that Elinor Carlisle killed Mary Gerrard?'

'There's no question of it at all, in my opinion! Who else had the reason or the wish to do it?'

'That is the question,' said Poirot.

Nurse O'Brien went on dramatically:

'Wasn't I there that night when the old lady was trying to speak, and Miss Elinor promising her that everything should be done decently and according to her wishes? And didn't I see her face looking after Mary as she went down the stairs one day, and the black hate that was on it? 'Twas murder she had in her heart that minute.'

Poirot said:

'If Elinor Carlisle killed Mrs Welman, why did she do it?'

'Why? For the money, of course. Two hundred thousand pounds, no less. That's what she got by it, and that's why she did it – if she did it. She's a bold, clever young lady, with no fear in her, and plenty of brains.'

Hercule Poirot said:

'If Mrs Welman had lived to make a will, how do you think she'd have left her money?'

'Ah, it's not for me to be saying that,' said Nurse O'Brien, betraying, however, every symptom of being about to do so. 'But it's my opinion that every penny the old lady had would have gone to Mary Gerrard.'

'Why?' said Hercule Poirot.

The simple monosyllable seemed to upset Nurse O'Brien.

'Why? Is it *why* you're asking? Well – I'd say that that would be the way of it.'

Poirot murmured:

'Some people might say that Mary Gerrard had played her cards very cleverly, that she had managed so to ingratiate herself with the old woman, as to make her forget the ties of blood and affection.'

'They might that,' said Nurse O'Brien slowly.

Poirot asked:

'*Was* Mary Gerrard a clever, scheming girl?'

Nurse O'Brien said, still rather slowly:

'I'll not think that of her . . . All she did was natural enough, with no thought of scheming. She wasn't that kind. And there's reasons often for these things that never get made public . . .'

Hercule Poirot said softly:

'You are, I think, a very discreet woman, Nurse O'Brien.'

'I'm not one to be talking of what doesn't concern me.'

Watching her very closely, Poirot went on:

'You and Nurse Hopkins, you have agreed together, have you not, that there are some things which are best not brought out into the light of day.'

Nurse O'Brien said:

'What would you be meaning by that?'

Poirot said quickly:

'Nothing to do with the crime – or crimes. I mean – the other matter.'

Nurse O'Brien said, nodding her head:

'What would be the use of raking up mud and an old story, and she a decent elderly woman with never a breath of scandal about her, and dying respected and looked up to by everybody.'

Hercule Poirot nodded in assent. He said cautiously:

'As you say, Mrs Welman was much respected in Maidensford.'

The conversation had taken an unexpected turn, but his face expressed no surprise or puzzlement.

Nurse O'Brien went on:

'It's so long ago, too. All dead and forgotten. I've a soft heart for a romance myself, and I do say and I always have said that it's hard for a man who's got a wife in an asylum to be tied all his life with nothing but death that can free him.'

Poirot murmured, still in bewilderment:

'Yes, it is hard . . .'

Nurse O'Brien said:

'Did Nurse Hopkins tell you how her letter crossed mine?'

Poirot said truthfully:

'She did not tell me *that*.'

''Twas an odd coincidence. But there, that's always the way of it! Once you hear a name, maybe, and a day or two later you'll come across it again, and so on and so on. That I should be seeing the self-same photograph on the piano and at the same minute Nurse Hopkins was hearing all about it from the doctor's housekeeper.'

'That,' said Poirot, 'is very interesting.'

He murmured tentatively:

'Did Mary Gerrard know – about this?'

'Who'd be telling her?' said Nurse O'Brien. 'Not I – and not Hopkins. After all, what good would it be to her?'

She flung up her red head and gazed at him steadily.

Poirot said with a sigh:

'What, indeed?'

CHAPTER 11

Elinor Carlisle . . .

Across the width of the table that separated them Poirot looked at her searchingly.

They were alone together. Through a glass wall a warder watched them.

Poirot noted the sensitive intelligent face with the square, white forehead, and the delicate modelling of the ears and nose. Fine lines; a proud, sensitive creature, showing breeding, self-restraint and – something else – a capacity for passion.

He said:

'I am Hercule Poirot. I have been sent to you by Dr Peter Lord. He thinks that I can help you.'

Elinor Carlisle said:

'Peter Lord . . .' Her tone was reminiscent. For a moment she smiled a little wistfully. She went on formally: 'It was kind of him, but I do not think there is anything you can do.'

Hercule Poirot said:

'Will you answer my questions?'

She sighed. She said:

'Believe me – really – it would be better not to ask them. I am in good hands. Mr Seddon has been most kind. I am to have a very famous counsel.'

Poirot said:

'He is not so famous as I am!'

Elinor Carlisle said with a touch of weariness:

'He has a great reputation.'

'Yes, for defending criminals. I have a great reputation – for demonstrating innocence.'

She lifted her eyes at last – eyes of a vivid, beautiful blue. They looked straight into Poirot's. She said:

'Do you believe I am innocent?'

Hercule Poirot said:

'Are you?'

Elinor smiled, an ironic little smile. She said:

'Is that a sample of your questions? It is very easy, isn't it, to answer Yes?'

He said unexpectedly:

'You are very tired, are you not?'

Her eyes widened a little. She answered:

'Why, yes – that more than anything. How did you know?'

Hercule Poirot said:

'I knew . . .'

Elinor said:

'I shall be glad when it is – over.'

Poirot looked at her for a minute in silence. Then he said:

'I have seen your – cousin, shall I call him for convenience? – Mr Roderick Welman.'

Into the white proud face the colour crept slowly up. He knew then that one question of his was answered without his asking it.

She said, and her voice shook very slightly:

'You've seen Roddy?'

Poirot said:

'He is doing all he can for you.'

'I know.'

Her voice was quick and soft.

Poirot said:

'Is he poor or rich?'

'Roddy? He has not very much money of his own.'

'And he is extravagant?'

She said, almost absently:

'Neither of us ever thought it mattered. We knew that some day . . .'

She stopped.

Poirot said quickly:

'You counted on your inheritance? That is understandable.'

He went on:

'You have heard, perhaps, the result of the autopsy on your aunt's body. She died of morphine poisoning.'

Elinor Carlisle said coldly:

'I did not kill her.'

'Did you help her to kill herself?'

'Did I help –? Oh, I see. No, I did not.'

'Did you know that your aunt had not made a will?'

'No, I had no idea of that.'

Her voice was flat now – dull. The answer was mechanical, uninterested.

Poirot said:

'And you yourself, have you made a will?'

'Yes.'

'Did you make it the day Dr Lord spoke to you about it?'

'Yes.'

Again that swift wave of colour.

Poirot said:

'How have you left your fortune, Miss Carlisle?'

Elinor said quietly:

'I have left everything to Roddy – to Roderick Welman.'

Poirot said:

'Does he know that?'

She said quickly:

'Certainly not.'

'You didn't discuss it with him?'

'Of course not. He would have been horribly embarrassed and would have disliked what I was doing very much.'

'Who else knows the contents of your will?'

'Only Mr Seddon – and his clerks, I suppose.'

'Did Mr Seddon draw up the will for you?'

'Yes. I wrote to him that same evening – I mean the evening of the day Dr Lord spoke to me about it.'

'Did you post your letter yourself?'

'No. It went in the box from the house with the other letters.'

'You wrote it, put it in an envelope, sealed it, stamped it and put it in the box – *comme ça*? You did not pause to reflect? To read it over?'

Elinor said, staring at him:

'I read it over – yes. I had gone to look for some stamps. When I came back with them, I just re-read the letter to be sure I had put it clearly.'

'Was anyone in the room with you?'

'Only Roddy.'

'Did he know what you were doing?'

'I told you – no.'

'Could anyone have read that letter when you were out of the room?'

'I don't know . . . One of the servants, you mean? I suppose they could have if they had chanced to come in while I was out of the room.'

'And before Mr Roderick Welman entered it?'

'Yes.'

Poirot said:

'And he could have read it, too?'

Elinor's voice was clear and scornful. She said:

'I can assure you, M. Poirot, that my "cousin", as you call him, does not read other people's letters.'

Poirot said:

'That is the accepted idea, I know. You would be surprised how many people do the things that "are not done".'

Elinor shrugged her shoulders.

Poirot said in a casual voice:

'Was it on that day that the idea of killing Mary Gerrard first came to you?'

For the third time colour swept over Elinor Carlisle's face. This time it was a burning tide. She said:

'Did Peter Lord tell you that?'

Poirot said gently:

'It *was* then, wasn't it? When you looked through the window and saw her making her will. It was then, was it not, that it struck you how funny it would be – and how convenient – if Mary Gerrard should happen to die . . .'

Elinor said in a low suffocated voice:

'He knew – he looked at me and he knew . . .'

Poirot said:

'Dr Lord knows a good deal . . . He is no fool, that young man with the freckled face and the red hair . . .'

Elinor said in a low voice:

'Is it true that he sent you to – help me?'

'It is true, Mademoiselle.'

She sighed and said:

'I don't understand. No, I don't understand.'

Poirot said:

'Listen, Miss Carlisle. It is necessary that you tell me just what happened that day when Mary Gerrard died: where you went, what you did; more than that, I want to know even what you thought.'

She stared at him. Then slowly a queer little smile came to her lips. She said:

'You must be an incredibly simple man. Don't you realize how easy it is for me to lie to you?'

Hercule Poirot said placidly:

'It does not matter.'

She was puzzled.

'Not matter?'

'No. For lies, Mademoiselle, tell a listener just as much as truth can. Sometimes they tell more. Come, now, commence. You met your housekeeper, the good Mrs Bishop. She wanted to come and help you. You would not let her. Why?'

'I wanted to be alone.'

'Why?'

'*Why? Why?* Because I wanted to – to think.'

'You wanted to imagine – yes. And then what did you do next?'

Elinor, her chin raised defiantly, said:

'I bought some paste for sandwiches.'

'Two pots?'

'Two.'

'And you went to Hunterbury. What did you do there?'

'I went up to my aunt's room and began to go through her things.'

'What did you find?'

'Find?' She frowned. 'Clothes – old letters – photographs – jewellery.'

Poirot said:

'No secrets?'

'Secrets? I don't understand you.'

'Then let us proceed. What next?'

Elinor said:

'I came down to the pantry and I cut sandwiches . . .'

Poirot said softly:

'And you thought – what?'

Her blue eyes flushed suddenly. She said:

'I thought of my namesake, Eleanor of Aquitaine . . .'

Poirot said:

'I understand perfectly.'

'Do you?'

'Oh, yes. I know the story. She offered Fair Rosamund, did she not, the choice of a dagger *or a cup of poison*. Rosamund chose the poison . . .'

Elinor said nothing. She was white now.

Poirot said:

'But perhaps, this time, *there was to be no choice* . . . Go on, Mademoiselle, what next?'

Elinor said:

'I put the sandwiches ready on a plate and I went down to the Lodge. Nurse Hopkins was there as well as Mary. I told them I had some sandwiches up at the house.'

Poirot was watching her. He said softly:

'Yes, and you all came up to the house together, did you not?'

'Yes. We – ate the sandwiches in the morning-room.'

Poirot said in the same soft tone:

'Yes, yes – *still in the dream* . . . And then . . .'

'Then?' She stared. 'I left her – standing by the window. I went out into the pantry. It was still like you say – *in a dream* . . . Nurse was there washing up . . . I gave her the paste-pot.'

'Yes – yes. And what happened then? What did you think of next?'

Elinor said dreamily:

'There was a mark on Nurse's wrist. I mentioned it and she said it was a thorn from the rose trellis by the Lodge. *The roses by the Lodge* . . . Roddy and I had a quarrel once – long ago – about the Wars of the Roses. I was Lancaster and he was York. He liked white roses. I said they weren't real – they didn't even smell! I liked red roses, big and dark and velvety and smelling of summer . . . We quarrelled in the most idiotic way. You see, it all came back to me – there in the pantry – and something –

something broke – the black hate I'd had in my heart – it went away – with remembering how we were together as children. I didn't hate Mary any more. I didn't want her to die . . .'

She stopped.

'But later, when we went back into the morning-room, she was dying . . .'

She stopped. Poirot was staring at her very intently. She flushed and said:

'Will you ask me – again – *did I kill Mary Gerrard?*'

Poirot rose to his feet. He said quickly:

'I shall ask you – nothing. There are things I do not want to know . . .'

CHAPTER 12

I

Dr Lord met the train at the station as requested.

Hercule Poirot alighted from it. He looked very Londonified and was wearing pointed patent leather shoes.

Peter Lord scrutinized his face anxiously, but Hercule Poirot was giving nothing away.

Peter Lord said:

'I've done my best to get answers to your questions. First, Mary Gerrard left here for London on July 10th. Second, I haven't got a housekeeper – a couple of giggling girls run my house. I think you must mean Mrs Slattery, who was Ransome's (my predecessor's) housekeeper. I can take you to her this morning if you like. I've arranged that she shall be in.'

Poirot said:

'Yes, I think it would be as well if I saw her first.'

'Then you said you wanted to go to Hunterbury, I could come with you there. It beats me why you haven't been there already. I can't think why you wouldn't go when you were down here before. I should have thought the first thing to be done in a case like this was to visit the place where the crime took place.'

Holding his head a little on one side, Hercule Poirot inquired:

'Why?'

'Why?' Peter Lord was rather disconcerted by the question. 'Isn't it the usual thing to do?'

Hercule Poirot said:

'One does not practise detection with a textbook! One uses one's natural intelligence.'

Peter Lord said:

'You might find a clue of some sort there.'

Poirot sighed:

'You read too much detective fiction. Your police force in this country is quite admirable. I have no doubt that they searched the house and grounds most carefully.'

'For evidence *against* Elinor Carlisle – not for evidence in her favour.'

Poirot sighed:

'My dear friend, it is not a monster – this police force! Elinor Carlisle was arrested because sufficient evidence was found to make out a case against her – a very strong case, I may say. It was useless for me to go over ground when the police had gone over it already.'

'But you do want to go there now?' objected Peter.

Hercule Poirot nodded his head. He said:

'Yes – now it is necessary. Because now I know *exactly what I am looking for*. One must understand with the cells of one's brain before one uses one's eyes.'

'Then you *do* think there might be – something – there still?'

Poirot said gently:

'I have a little idea we shall find something – yes.'

'Something to prove Elinor's innocence?'

'Ah, I did not say that.'

Peter Lord stopped dead.

'You don't mean you *still* think she's guilty?'

Poirot said gravely:

'You must wait, my friend, before you get an answer to that question.'

II

Poirot lunched with the doctor in a pleasant square room with a window open on to the garden.

Lord said:

'Did you get what you wanted out of old Slattery?'

Poirot nodded.

'Yes.'

'What *did* you want with her?'

'Gossip! Talk about old days. Some crimes have their roots in the past. I think this one had.'

Peter Lord said irritably:

'I don't understand a word you are talking about.'

Poirot smiled. He said:

'This fish is deliciously fresh.'

Lord said impatiently:

'I dare say. I caught it myself before breakfast this morning. Look here, Poirot, am I to have any idea what you're driving at? Why keep me in the dark?'

The other shook his head.

'Because as yet there is no light. I am always brought up short by the fact that there was no one who had any reason to kill Mary Gerrard – except Elinor Carlisle.'

Peter Lord said:

'You can't be sure of that. She'd been abroad for some time, remember.'

'Yes, yes, I have made the inquiries.'

'You've been to Germany yourself?'

'Myself, no.' With a slight chuckle he added: 'I have my spies!'

'Can you depend on other people?'

'Certainly. It is not for me to run here and there, doing amateurishly the things that for a small sum someone else can do with professional skill. I can assure you, *mon cher*, I have several irons on the fire. I have some useful assistants – one of them a former burglar.'

'What do you use him for?'

'The last thing I have used him for was a very thorough search of Mr Welman's flat.'

'What was he looking for?'

Poirot said:

'One always likes to know exactly what lies have been told one.'

'Did Welman tell you a lie?'

'Definitely.'

'Who else has lied to you?'

'Everybody, I think: Nurse O'Brien romantically; Nurse Hopkins stubbornly; Mrs Bishop venomously. You yourself –'

'Good God!' Peter Lord interrupted him unceremoniously. 'You don't think I've lied to you, do you?'

'Not yet,' Poirot admitted.

Dr Lord sank back in his chair. He said:

'You're a disbelieving sort of fellow, Poirot.'

Then he said:

'If you've finished, shall we set off for Hunterbury? I've got some patients to see later, and then there's the surgery.'

'I am at your disposal, my friend.'

They set off on foot, entering the grounds by the back drive. Half-way up it they met a tall, good-looking young fellow wheeling a barrow. He touched his cap respectfully to Dr Lord.

'Good morning, Horlick. This is Horlick, the gardener, Poirot. He was working here that morning.'

Horlick said:

'Yes, sir, I was. I saw Miss Elinor that morning and talked to her.'

Poirot asked:

'What did she say to you?'

'She told me the house was as good as sold, and that rather took me aback, sir; but Miss Elinor said as how she'd speak for me to Major Somervell, and that maybe he'd keep me on – if he didn't think me too young, perhaps, as head – seeing as how I'd had good training under Mr Stephens, here.'

Dr Lord said:

'Did she seem much the same as usual, Horlick?'

'Why, yes, sir, except that she looked a bit excited like – and as though she had something on her mind.'

Hercule Poirot said:

'Did you know Mary Gerrard?'

'Oh, yes, sir. But not very well.'

Poirot said:

'What was she like?'

Horlick looked puzzled.

'Like sir? Do you mean to look at?'

'Not exactly. I mean, what kind of a girl was she?'

'Oh, well, sir, she was a very superior sort of a girl. Nice spoken and all that. Thought a lot of herself, I should say. You see, old Mrs Welman had made a lot of fuss over her. Made her father wild, that did. He was like a bear with a sore head about it.'

Poirot said:

'By all that I've heard, he had not the best of tempers, that old one?'

'No, indeed, he hadn't. Always grumbling, and crusty as they make them. Seldom had a civil word for you.'

Poirot said:

'You were here on that morning. Whereabouts were you working?'

'Mostly in the kitchen garden, sir.'

'You cannot see the house from there?'

'No, sir.'

Peter Lord said:

'If anybody had come up to the house – up to the pantry window – you wouldn't have seen them?'

'No, I wouldn't, sir.'

Peter Lord said:

'When did you go to your dinner?'

'One o'clock, sir.'

'And you didn't see anything – any man hanging about – or a car outside – anything like that?'

The man's eyebrows rose in slight surprise.

'Outside the back gate, sir? There was your car there – nobody else's.'

Peter Lord cried:

'*My* car: It wasn't my car! I was over Withenbury direction that morning. Didn't get back till after two.'

Horlick looked puzzled.

'I made sure it was your car, sir,' he said doubtfully.

Peter Lord said quickly:

'Oh, well, it doesn't matter. Good morning, Horlick.'

He and Poirot moved on. Horlick stared after them for a minute or two, then slowly resumed his progress with the wheelbarrow.

Peter Lord said softly – but with great excitement:

'Something – at last. Whose car was it standing in the lane that morning?'

Poirot said:

'What make is your car, my friend?'

'A Ford ten – sea-green. They're pretty common, of course.'

'And you are sure that it was not yours? You haven't mistaken the day?'

'Absolutely certain. I was over at Withenbury, came back late, snatched a bit of lunch, and then the call came through about Mary Gerrard and I rushed over.'

Poirot said softly:

'Then it would seem, my friend, that we have come upon something tangible at last.'

Peter Lord said:

'*Someone was here that morning* . . . someone who was not Elinor Carlisle, nor Mary Gerrard, nor Nurse Hopkins . . .'

Poirot said:

'This is very interesting. Come, let us make our investigations. Let us see, for instance, supposing a man (or woman) were to wish to approach the house unseen, how they would set about it.'

Half-way along the drive a path branched off through some shrubbery. They took this and at a certain turn in it Peter Lord clutched Poirot's arm, pointing to a window.

He said:

'That's the window of the pantry where Elinor Carlisle was cutting the sandwiches.'

Poirot murmured:

'And from here, *anyone could see her cutting them.* The window was open, if I remember rightly?'

Peter Lord said:

'It was wide open. It was a hot day, remember.'

Hercule Poirot said musingly:

'Then if anyone wished to watch unseen what was going on, somewhere about here would be a good spot.'

The two men cast about. Peter Lord said:

'There's a place here – behind these bushes. Some stuff's been trampled down here. It's grown up again now, but you can see plainly enough.'

Poirot joined him. He said thoughtfully:

'Yes, this is a good place. It is concealed from the path, and that opening in the shrubs gives one a good view of the window. Now, what did he do, our friend who stood here? Did he perhaps smoke?'

They bent down, examining the ground and pushing aside the leaves and branches.

Suddenly Hercule Poirot uttered a grunt.

Peter Lord straightened up from his own search.

'What is it?'

'A match-box, my friend. An empty match-box, trodden heavily into the ground, sodden and decayed.'

With care and delicacy he salved the object. He displayed it at last on a sheet of notepaper taken from his pocket.

Peter Lord said:

'It's foreign. My god! *German matches!*'

Hercule Poirot said:

'And Mary Gerrard had recently come from Germany!'

Peter Lord said exultantly:

'We've got something now! You can't deny it.'

Hercule Poirot said slowly:

'Perhaps . . .'

'But, damn it all, man. Who on earth round here would have had foreign matches?'

Hercule Poirot said:

'I know – I know.'

His eyes, perplexed eyes, went to the gap in the bushes and the view of the window.

He said:

'It is not quite so simple as you think. There is one great difficulty. Do you not see it yourself?'

'What? Tell me.'

Poirot sighed.

'If you do not see for yourself . . . But come, let us go on.'

They went on to the house. Peter Lord unlocked the back door with a key.

He led the way through the scullery to the kitchen, through that, along a passage where there was a cloakroom on one side and the butler's pantry on the other. The two men looked round the pantry.

It had the usual cupboards with sliding glass doors for glass and china. There was a gas-ring and two kettles and canisters marked Tea and Coffee on a shelf above. There was a sink and draining-board and a papier-mâché washing-up bowl. In front of the window was a table.

Peter Lord said:

'It was on this table that Elinor Carlisle cut the sandwiches. The fragment of the morphine label was found in this crack in the floor under the sink.'

Poirot said thoughtfully:

'The police are careful searchers. They do not miss much.'

Peter Lord said violently:

'There's no evidence that Elinor ever handled that tube! I tell you, someone was watching her from the shrubbery outside. She went down to the Lodge and he saw his chance and slipped in, uncorked the tube, crushed some tablets of morphine to powder and put them into the top sandwich.

He never noticed that he'd torn a bit off the label of the tube, and that it had fluttered down the crack. He hurried away, started up his car and went off again.'

Poirot sighed.

'And still you do not see! It is extraordinary how dense an intelligent man can be.'

Peter Lord demanded angrily:

'Do you mean to say that you don't believe someone stood in those bushes watching the window?'

Poirot said:

'Yes, I believe that . . .'

'Then we've got to find whoever it was!'

Poirot murmured:

'We shall not have to look far, I fancy.'

'Do you mean you *know*?'

'I have a very shrewd idea.'

Peter Lord said slowly:

'Then your minions who made inquiries in Germany *did* bring you something . . .'

Hercule Poirot said, tapping his forehead:

'My friend, it is all here, in my head . . . Come, let us look over the house.'

III

They stood at last in the room where Mary Gerrard had died.

The house had a strange atmosphere in it: it seemed alive with memories and forebodings.

Peter Lord flung up one of the windows.

He said with a slight shiver:

'This place feels like a tomb . . .'

Poirot said:

'If walls could speak . . . It is all here, is it not, here in the house – the beginning of the whole story.'

He paused and then said softly:

'It was here in this room that Mary Gerrard died.'

Peter Lord said:

'They found her sitting in that chair by the window . . .'

Hercule Poirot said thoughtfully:

'A young girl – beautiful – romantic? Did she scheme and intrigue? Was she a superior person who gave herself airs? Was she gentle and sweet, with no thought of intrigue . . . just a young thing beginning life . . . a girl like a flower? . . .'

'Whatever she was,' said Peter Lord, 'someone wished her dead.'

Hercule Poirot murmured:

'I wonder . . .'

Lord stared at him.

'What do you mean?'

Poirot shook his head.

'Not yet.'

He turned about.

'We have been all through the house. We have seen all that there is to be seen here. Let us go down to the Lodge.'

Here again all was in order: the rooms dusty, but neat and emptied of personal possessions. The two men stayed only a few minutes. As they came out into the sun, Poirot touched the leaves of a pillar rose growing up a trellis. It was pink and sweet-scented.

He murmured:

'Do you know the name of this rose? It is Zephyrine Drouhin, my friend.'

Peter Lord said irritably:

'What of it?'

Hercule Poirot said:

'When I saw Elinor Carlisle, she spoke to me of roses. It was then that I began to see – not daylight, but the little glimpse of light that one gets in a train when one is about to come out of a tunnel. It is not so much daylight, but the promise of daylight.'

Peter Lord said harshly:

'What did she tell you?'

'She told me of her childhood, of playing here in this garden, and of how she and Roderick Welman were on different sides. They were enemies, for he preferred the white rose of York – cold and austere – and she, so she told me, loved red roses, the red rose of Lancaster. Red roses that have scent and colour and passion and warmth. And that, my friend, is the difference between Elinor Carlisle and Roderick Welman.'

Peter Lord said:

'Does that explain – anything?'

Poirot said:

'It explains Elinor Carlisle – who is passionate and proud and who loved desperately a man who was incapable of loving her . . .'

Peter Lord said:

'I don't understand you . . .'

Poirot said:

'But I understand *her* . . . I understand both of them. Now my friend, we will go back once more to that little clearing in the shrubbery.'

They went there in silence. Peter Lord's freckled face was troubled and angry.

When they came to the spot, Poirot stood motionless for some time, and Peter Lord watched him.

Then suddenly the little detective gave a vexed sigh.

He said:

'It is so simple, really. Do you not see, my friend, the fatal fallacy in your reasoning? According to your theory someone, a man, presumably, who had known Mary Gerrard in Germany came here intent on killing her. But *look*, my friend, *look*! Use the two eyes of your body, since the eyes of the mind do not seem to serve you. What do you see from here: a window, is it not? And at that window – a girl. A girl cutting sandwiches. That is to say, Elinor Carlisle. But think for a minute of this: *What on earth was to tell the watching man that those sandwiches were going to be offered to Mary Gerrard?* No one knew that *but Elinor Carlisle – herself – nobody!* Not even Mary Gerrard, nor Nurse Hopkins.

'So what follows – if a man stood here watching, and if he afterwards went to that window and climbed in and tampered with the sandwiches? What did he think and believe? He thought, he must have thought, *that the sandwiches were to be eaten by Elinor Carlisle herself* . . .'

CHAPTER 13

Poirot knocked at the door of Nurse Hopkins' cottage. She opened it to him with her mouth full of Bath bun.

She said sharply:

'Well, Mr Poirot, what do you want *now*?'

'I may enter?'

Somewhat grudgingly Nurse Hopkins drew back and Poirot was permitted to cross the threshold. Nurse Hopkins was hospitable with the teapot, and a minute later Poirot was regarding with some dismay a cup of inky beverage.

'Just made – nice and strong!' said Nurse Hopkins.

Poirot stirred his tea cautiously and took one heroic sip.

He said:

'Have you any idea why I have come here?'

'I couldn't say, I'm sure, until you tell me. I don't profess to be a mind-reader.'

'I have come to ask you for the truth.'

Nurse Hopkins uprose in wrath.

'And what's the meaning of that, I should like to know? A truthful woman I've always been. Not one to shield myself in any way. I spoke up about that missing tube of morphine at the inquest when many a one in my place would have sat tight and said nothing. For well enough did I know that I should get censured for carelessness in leaving my case about; and, after all, it's a thing might happen to anybody! I was blamed for that – and it won't do me any good in my profession, I can tell you. But that didn't make any difference to me! I knew something that had a bearing on the case, and so I spoke out. And I'll thank you, Mr Poirot, to keep any nasty insinuations to yourself! There's not a thing about Mary Gerrard's death that I haven't been open and above-board as daylight about, and if *you* think differently, I'd be obliged if you'd give chapter and verse for it! I've concealed nothing – nothing at all! And I'm prepared to take the oath and stand up in court and say so.'

Poirot did not attempt to interrupt. He knew only too well the technique of dealing with an angry woman. He allowed Nurse Hopkins to flare up and simmer down. Then he spoke – quietly and mildly.

He said:

'I did not suggest that there is anything about the crime which you have not told.'

'Then what did you suggest, I'd like to know?'

'I asked you to tell the truth – not about the death, but about the *life* of Mary Gerrard.'

'Oh!' Nurse Hopkins seemed momentarily taken aback. She said, 'So that's what you're getting at? But it's got nothing to do with the murder.'

'I did not say that it had, I said that you were withholding knowledge concerning her.'

'Why shouldn't I – if it's nothing to do with the crime?'

Poirot shrugged his shoulders.

'Why should you?'

Nurse Hopkins, very red in the face, said:

'Because it's common decency! They're all dead now – everyone concerned. And it's no business of anyone else's!'

'If it is only surmise – perhaps not. But if you have *actual knowledge*, that is different.'

Nurse Hopkins said slowly:

'I don't know exactly what you mean . . .'

Poirot said:

'I will help you. I have had hints from Nurse O'Brien and I have had a long conversation with Mrs Slattery, who has a very good memory for events that happened over twenty years ago. I will tell you exactly what I have learned. Well, over twenty years ago there was a love-affair between two people. One of them was Mrs Welman, who had been a widow for some years and who was a woman capable of a deep and passionate love. The other party was Sir Lewis Rycroft, who had the great misfortune to have a wife who was hopelessly insane. The law in those days gave no promise of relief by divorce, and Lady Rycroft, whose physical health was excellent, might live to be ninety. The *liaison* between those two people was, I think, guessed at, but they were both discreet and careful to keep up appearances. Then Sir Lewis Rycroft was killed in action.'

'Well?' said Nurse Hopkins.

'I suggest,' said Poirot, 'that there was a child born after his death, and that that child was Mary Gerrard.'

Nurse Hopkins said:

'You seem to know all about it!'

Poirot said:

'That is what I *think*. But it is possible that you have got definite proof that that is so.'

Nurse Hopkins sat silent a minute or two, frowning, then abruptly she rose, went across the room, opened a drawer and took out an envelope. She brought it across to Poirot.

She said:

'I'll tell you how this came into my hands. Mind, I'd had my suspicions. The way Mrs Welman looked at the girl, for one thing, and then hearing the gossip on top of it. And old Gerrard told me when he was ill that Mary wasn't his daughter.

'Well, after Mary died I finished clearing up the Lodge, and in a drawer amongst some of the old man's things I came across this letter. You see what's written on it.'

Poirot read the superscription written in faded ink:

'For Mary – to be sent to her after my death.'

Poirot said:

'This writing is not recent?'

'It wasn't Gerrard who wrote that,' explained Nurse Hopkins. 'It was Mary's mother, who died fourteen years ago. She meant this for the girl, but the old man kept it among his things and so she never saw it – and I'm thankful she didn't! She was able to hold up her head to the end, and she'd no cause to feel ashamed.'

She paused and then said:

'Well, it was sealed up, but when I found it I'll admit to you that I opened it and read it then and there, which I dare say I should not have done. But Mary was dead, and I guessed more or less at what was inside it and I didn't see that it was any concern of anyone else's. All the same, I haven't liked to destroy it, because I didn't feel somehow it would be right to do that. But, there, you'd better read it yourself.'

Poirot drew out the sheet of paper covered in small angular writing:

This is the truth I've written down here in case it should ever be needed. I was lady's maid to Mrs Welman at Hunterbury, and very kind to me she was. I got into trouble, and she stood by me and took me back into her service when it was all over; but the baby died. My mistress and Sir Lewis Rycroft were fond of each other, but they couldn't marry, because he had a wife already and she was in a madhouse, poor lady. He was a fine gentleman and devoted to Mrs Welman. He was killed, and she told me soon after that she was going to have a child. After that she went up to Scotland and took me with her. The child was born there – at Ardlochrie. Bob Gerrard, who had washed his hands of me and flung me off when I had my trouble, had been writing to me again. The arrangement was that we should marry and live at the Lodge and he should think that the baby was mine. If we lived on the place it would seem natural that Mrs Welman should be interested in the child and she'd see to educating her and giving her a place in the world. She thought it would be better for Mary never to know the truth. Mrs Welman gave us both a handsome sum of money; but I would have helped her without that. I've been quite happy with Bob, but he never took to Mary. I've held my tongue and never said anything to anybody, but I think it's right in case I die that I should put this down in black and white.

Eliza Gerrard (*born* Eliza Riley)

Hercule Poirot drew a deep breath and folded up the letter again.

Nurse Hopkins said anxiously:

'What are you going to do about it? They're all dead now! It's no good raking up these things. Everyone looked up to Mrs Welman in these parts; there's never been anything said against her. All this old scandal – it would be cruel. The same with Mary. She was a sweet girl. Why should anyone have to know she was a bastard? Let the dead rest in peace in their graves, that's what I say.'

Poirot said:

'One has to consider the living.'

Nurse Hopkins said:

'But this has got nothing to do with the murder.'

Hercule Poirot said gravely:

'It may have a great deal to do with it.'

He went out of the cottage, leaving Nurse Hopkins with her mouth open, staring after him.

He had walked some way when he became aware of hesitating footsteps just behind him. He stopped and turned round.

It was Horlick, the young gardener from Hunterbury. He was looking the picture of embarrassment and twisting his cap round and round in his hands.

'Excuse me, sir. Could I have a word with you?'

Horlick spoke with a kind of gulp.

'Certainly. What is it?'

Horlick twisted the cap even more fiercely. He said, averting his eyes and looking the picture of misery and embarrassment:

'It's about that car.'

'The car that was outside the back gate that morning?'

'Yes, sir. Dr Lord said this morning that it wasn't his car – *but it was, sir.*'

'You know that for a fact?'

'Yes, sir. Because of the number, sir. It was MSS 2022. I noticed it particular – MSS 2022. You see, we know it in the village, and always call it Miss Tou-Tou! I'm quite sure of it, sir.'

Poirot said with a faint smile:

'But Dr Lord says he was over at Withenbury that morning.'

Horlick said miserably:

'Yes, sir. I heard him. But it *was* his car, sir . . . I'll take my oath on that.'

Poirot said gently:

'Thank you, Horlick, that's just exactly what you may have to do . . .'

PART III

I

Was it very hot in the court? Or very cold? Elinor Carlisle could not be quite sure. Sometimes she felt burning, as though with fever, and immediately after she shivered.

She had not heard the end of the Prosecuting Counsel's speech. She had gone back to the past – gone slowly through the whole business again, from the day when that miserable letter came to the moment when that smooth-faced police officer had said with horrible fluency:

'You are Elinor Katharine Carlisle. I have here a warrant for your arrest upon the charge of murdering Mary Gerrard by administering poison to her on the 27th of July last, and I must warn you that anything you say will be taken down in writing and may be used as evidence at your trial.'

Horrible, frightening fluency . . . She felt caught up in a smooth-running, well-oiled machine – inhuman, passionless.

And now here she was, standing in the dock in the open glare of publicity, with hundreds of eyes that were neither impersonal nor inhuman, feasting upon her and gloating . . .

Only the jury did not look at her. Embarrassed, they kept their eyes studiously turned away . . . She thought: 'It's because – soon – they know what they're going to say . . .'

II

Dr Lord was giving evidence. Was this Peter Lord – that freckled, cheery young doctor who had been so kind and so friendly at Hunterbury? He was very stiff now. Sternly professional. His answers came monotonously: He had been summoned by telephone to Hunterbury Hall; too late for anything to be done; Mary Gerrard had died a few minutes after his arrival; death consistent, in his opinion, with morphia poisoning in one of its less common forms – the 'foudroyante' variety.

Sir Edwin Bulmer rose to cross-examine.

'You were the late Mrs Welman's regular medical attendant?'

'I was.'

'During your visits to Hunterbury in June last, you had occasion to see the accused and Mary Gerrard together?'

'Several times.'

'What would you say was the manner of the accused to Mary Gerrard?'

'Perfectly pleasant and natural.'

Sir Edwin Bulmer said with a slight disdainful smile:

'You never saw any signs of this "jealous hatred" we have heard so much about?'

Peter Lord, his jaw set, said firmly:

'No.'

Elinor thought:

'But he did – he did . . . He told a lie for me there . . . He knew . . .'

Peter Lord was succeeded by the police surgeon. His evidence was longer, more detailed. Death was due to morphia poisoning of the 'foudroyante' variety. Would he kindly explain that term? With some enjoyment he did so. Death from morphine poisoning might occur in several different ways. The most common was a period of intense excitement followed by drowsiness and narcosis, pupils of eyes contracted. Another not so common form had been named by the French, 'foudroyante.' In these cases deep sleep supervened in a very short time – about ten minutes; the pupils of the eyes were usually dilated . . .

III

The court had adjourned and sat again. There had been some hours of expert medical testimony.

Dr Alan Garcia, the distinguished analyst, full of learned terms, spoke with gusto of the stomach contents: Bread, fish paste, tea, presence of morphia . . . more learned terms and various decimal points. Amount taken by the deceased estimated to be about four grains. Fatal dose could be as low as one grain.

Sir Edwin rose, still bland.

'I should like to get it quite clear. You found in the stomach nothing but bread, butter, fish paste, tea and morphia. There were no other foodstuffs?'

'None.'

'That is to say, the deceased had eaten nothing but sandwiches and tea for some considerable time?'

'That is so.'

'Was there anything to show in what particular vehicle the morphia had been administered?'

'I don't quite understand.'

'I will simplify that question. The morphia could have been taken in the fish paste, or in the bread, or in the butter on the bread, or in the tea, or in the milk that had been added to the tea?'

'Certainly.'

'There was no special evidence that the morphia was in the fish paste rather than in any of the other mediums?'

'No.'

'And, in fact, the morphia *might* have been taken separately – that is to say, not in any vehicle at all? It could have been simply swallowed in its tablet form?'

'That is so, of course.'

'Sir Edwin sat down.

Sir Samuel re-examined.

'Nevertheless, you are of the opinion that, however the morphia was taken, it was taken at the same time as the other food and drink?'

'Yes.'

'Thank you.'

IV

Inspector Brill had taken the oath with mechanical fluency. He stood there, soldierly and stolid, reeling off his evidence with practised ease.

'Summoned to the house . . . The accused said, "It must have been bad fish paste." . . . search of the premises . . . one jar of fish paste washed out was standing on the draining-board in the pantry, another half full . . . further search of pantry kitchen . . .'

'What did you find?'

'In a crack behind the table, between the floorboards, I found a tiny scrap of paper.'

The exhibit went to the jury.

'What did you take it to be?'

'A fragment torn off a printed label – such as are used on glass tubes of morphia.'

Counsel for the Defence arose with leisurely ease.

He said:

'You found this scrap in a crack in the flooring?'

'Yes.'

'Part of a label?'

'Yes.'

'Did you find the rest of that label?'

'No.'

'You did not find any glass tube or any bottle to which that label might have been affixed?'

'No.'

'What was the state of that scrap of paper when you found it? Was it clean or dirty?'

'It was quite fresh.'

'What do you mean, quite fresh?'

'There was surface dust on it from the flooring, but it was quite clean otherwise.'

'It could not have been there for any length of time?'

'No, it had found its way there quite recently.'

'You would say, then, that it had come there on the actual day you found it – not earlier?'

'Yes.'

With a grunt Sir Edwin sat down.

V

Nurse Hopkins in the box, her face red and self-righteous.

All the same, Elinor thought, Nurse Hopkins was not so frightening as Inspector Brill. It was the inhumanity of Inspector Brill that was so paralysing. He was so definitely part of a great machine. Nurse Hopkins had human passions, prejudices.

'Your name is Jessie Hopkins?'

'Yes.'

'You are a certificated District Nurse and you reside at Rose Cottage, Hunterbury?'

'Yes.'

'Where were you on the 28th of June last?'

'I was at Hunterbury Hall.'

'You had been sent for?'

'Yes. Mrs Welman had had a stroke – the second. I went to assist Nurse O'Brien until a second nurse could be found.'

'Did you take a small attaché-case with you?'

'Yes.'

'Tell the jury what was in it.'

'Bandages, dressings, a hypodermic syringe and certain drugs, including a tube of morphine hydrochloride.'

'For what purpose was it there?'

'One of the cases in the village had to have hypodermic injections of morphia morning and evening.'

'What were the contents of the tube?'

'There were twenty tablets, each containing half-grain morphine hydrochloride.'

'What did you do with your attaché-case?'

'I laid it down in the hall.'

'That was on the evening of the 28th. When did you next have occasion to look in the case?'

'The following morning about nine o'clock, just as I was preparing to leave the house.'

'Was anything missing?'

'The tube of morphine was missing.'

'Did you mention this loss?'

'I spoke of it to Nurse O'Brien, the nurse in charge of the patient.'

'This case was lying in the hall, where people were in the habit of passing to and fro?'

'Yes.'

Sir Samuel paused. Then he said:

'You knew the dead girl Mary Gerrard intimately?'

'Yes.'

'What was your opinion of her?'

'She was a very sweet girl – and a good girl.'

'Was she of a happy disposition?'

'Very happy.'

'She had no troubles that you know of?'

'No.'

'At the time of her death was there anything whatever to worry her or make her unhappy about the future?'

'Nothing.'

'She would have had no reason to have taken her own life?'

'No reason at all.'

It went on and on – the damning story. How Nurse Hopkins had accompanied Mary to the Lodge, the appearance of Elinor, her excitable manner, the invitation to sandwiches, the plate being handed first to Mary. Elinor's suggestion that everything be washed up, and her further suggestion that Nurse Hopkins should come upstairs with her and assist in sorting out clothes.

There were frequent interruptions and objections from Sir Edwin Bulmer.

Elinor thought:

'Yes, it's all true – and she believes it. She's certain I did it. And every word she says is the truth – that's what's so horrible. It's all true.'

Once more, as she looked across the court, she saw the face of Hercule Poirot regarding her thoughtfully – almost kindly. *Seeing her with too much knowledge* . . .

The piece of cardboard with the scrap of label pasted on to it was handed to the witness.

'Do you know what this is?'

'It's a bit of a label.'

'Can you tell the jury what label?'

'Yes – it's a part of a label off a tube of hypodermic tablets. Morphine tablets half-grain – like the one I lost.'

'You are sure of that?'

'Of course I'm sure. It's off my tube.'

The judge said:

'Is there any special mark on it by which you can identify it as the label of the tube you lost?'

'No, my lord, but it must be the same.'

'Actually, all you can say is that it is exactly similar?'

'Well, yes, that's what I mean.'

The court adjourned.

CHAPTER 2

I

It was another day.

Sir Edwin Bulmer was on his feet cross-examining. He was not at all bland now. He said sharply:

'This attaché-case we've heard so much about. On June 28th it was left in the main hall of Hunterbury all night?'

Nurse Hopkins agreed:

'Yes.'

'Rather a careless thing to do, wasn't it?'

Nurse Hopkins flushed.

'Yes, I suppose it was.'

'Are you in the habit of leaving dangerous drugs lying about where anyone could get at 'em?'

'No, of course not.'

'Oh! you're not? But you did it on this occasion?'

'Yes.'

'And it's a fact, isn't it, that *anybody in the house* could have got at that morphia if they'd wanted to?'

'I suppose so.'

'No suppose about it. It is so, isn't it?'

'Well – yes.'

'It wasn't only Miss Carlisle who could have got at it? Any of the servants could. Or Dr Lord. Or Mr Roderick Welman. Or Nurse O'Brien. Or Mary Gerrard herself.'

'I suppose so – yes.'

'It is so, isn't it?'

'Yes.'

'Was anyone aware you'd got morphia in that case?'

'I don't know.'

'Well, did you talk about it to anyone?'

'No.'

'So, as a matter of fact, Miss Carlisle couldn't have known that there was any morphia there?'

'She might have looked to see.'

'That's very unlikely, isn't it?'

'I don't know, I'm sure.'

'There were people who'd be more likely to know about the morphia than Miss Carlisle. Dr Lord, for instance. He'd know. You were administering this morphia under his orders, weren't you?'

'Of course.'

'Mary Gerrard knew you had it there, too?'

'No, she didn't.'

'She was often in your cottage, wasn't she?'

'Not very often.'

'I suggest to you that she was there very frequently, and that she, of all the people in the house, would be the most likely to guess that there was morphia in your case.'

'I don't agree.'

Sir Edwin paused a minute.

'You told Nurse O'Brien in the morning that the morphia was missing?'

'Yes.'

'I put it to you that what you really said was: "I have left the morphia at home. I shall have to go back for it."'

'No, I didn't.'

'You didn't suggest that the morphia had been left on the mantelpiece in your cottage?'

'Well, when I couldn't find it I thought that must have been what had happened.'

'In fact, you didn't really know what you'd done with it!'

'Yes, I did. I put it in the case.'

'Then why did you suggest on the morning of June 29th that you had left it at home?'

'Because I thought I might have done.'

'I put it to you that you're a very careless woman.'

'That's not true.'

'You make rather inaccurate statements sometimes, don't you?'

'No, I don't. I'm very careful what I say.'

'Did you make a remark about a prick from a rose tree on July 27th – the day of Mary Gerrard's death?'

'I don't see what that's got to do with it!'

The judge said:

'Is that relevant, Sir Edwin?'

'Yes, my lord, it is an essential part of the defence, and I intend to call witnesses to prove that that statement was a lie.'

He resumed:

'Do you still say you pricked your wrist on a rose tree on July 27th?'

'Yes, I did.'

Nurse Hopkins looked defiant.

'When did you do that?'

'Just before leaving the Lodge and coming up to the house on the morning of July 27th.'

Sir Edwin said sceptically:

'And what rose tree was this?'

'A climbing one just outside the Lodge, with pink flowers.'

'You're sure of that?'

'I'm quite sure.'

Sir Edwin paused and then asked:

'You persist in saying the morphia was in the attaché-case when you came to Hunterbury on June 28th?'

'I do. I had it with me.'

'Supposing that presently Nurse O'Brien goes into the box and swears that you said you had probably left it at home?'

'It was in my case. I'm sure of it.'

Sir Edwin sighed.

'You didn't feel at all uneasy about the disappearance of the morphia?'

'Not – uneasy – no.'

'Oh, so you were quite at ease, notwithstanding the fact that a large quantity of a dangerous drug had disappeared?'

'I didn't think at the time anyone had taken it.'

'I see. You just couldn't remember for the moment what you had done with it?'

'Not at all. It was in the case.'

'Twenty half-grain tablets – that is, ten grains of morphia. Enough to kill several people, isn't it?'

'Yes.'

'But you are not uneasy – and you don't even report the loss officially?'

'I thought it was all right.'

'I put it to you that if the morphia had really disappeared the way it did you would have been bound, as a conscientious person, to report the loss officially.'

Nurse Hopkins, very red in the face, said:

'Well, I didn't.'

'That was surely a piece of criminal carelessness on your part? You don't seem to take your responsibilities very seriously. Did you often mislay these dangerous drugs?'

'It never happened before.'

It went on for some minutes. Nurse Hopkins, flustered, red in the face, contradicting herself . . . an easy prey to Sir Edwin's skill.

'Is it a fact that on Thursday, July 6th, the dead girl, Mary Gerrard, made a will?'

'She did.'

'Why did she do that?'

'Because she thought it was the proper thing to do. And so it was.'

'Are you sure it wasn't because she was depressed and uncertain about her future?'

'Nonsense.'

'It showed, though, that the idea of death was present in her mind – that she was brooding on the subject.'

'Not at all. She just thought it was the proper thing to do.'

'Is this the will? Signed by Mary Gerrard, witnessed by Emily Biggs and Roger Wade, confectioners' assistants, and leaving everything of which she died possessed to Mary Riley, sister of Eliza Riley?'

'That's right.'

It was handed to the jury.

'To your knowledge, had Mary Gerrard any property to leave?'

'Not then, she hadn't.'

'But she was shortly going to have?'

'Yes.'

'Is it not a fact that a considerable sum of money – two thousand pounds – was being given to Mary by Miss Carlisle?'

'Yes.'

'There was no compulsion on Miss Carlisle to do this? It was entirely a generous impulse on her part?'

'She did it of her own free will, yes.'

'But surely, if she had hated Mary Gerrard, as is suggested, she would not of her own free will have handed over to her a large sum of money.'

'That's as may be.'

'What do you mean by that answer?'

'I don't mean anything.'

'Exactly. Now, had you heard any local gossip about Mary Gerrard and Mr Roderick Welman?'

'He was sweet on her.'

'Have you any evidence of that?'

'I just knew it, that's all.'

'Oh – you "just knew it". That's not very convincing to the jury, I'm afraid. Did you say on one occasion Mary would have nothing to do with him because he was engaged to Miss Elinor and she said the same to him in London?'

'That's what she told me.'

Sir Samuel Attenbury re-examined:

'When Mary Gerrard was discussing with you the wording of this will, did the accused look in through the window?'

'Yes, she did.'

'What did she say?'

'She said, "So you're making your will, Mary. That's funny." And she laughed. Laughed and laughed. And it's my opinion,' said the witness viciously, 'that it was at that moment the idea came into her head. The idea of making away with the girl! She'd murder in her heart that very minute.'

The judge spoke sharply:

'Confine yourself to answering the questions that are asked you. The last part of that answer is to be struck out . . .'

Elinor thought:

'How queer . . . When anyone says what's true, they strike it out . . .'

She wanted to laugh hysterically.

II

Nurse O'Brien was in the box.

'On the morning of June 29th did Nurse Hopkins make a statement to you?'

'Yes. She said she had a tube of morphine hydrochloride missing from her case.'

'What did you do?'

'I helped her to hunt for it.'

'But you could not find it?'

'No.'

'To your knowledge, was the case left overnight in the hall?'

'It was.'

'Mr Welman and the accused were both staying in the house at the time of Mrs Welman's death – that is, on June 28th to 29th?'

'Yes.'

'Will you tell us of an incident that occurred on June 29th – the day after Mrs Welman's death?'

'I saw Mr Roderick Welman with Mary Gerrard. He was telling her he loved her, and he tried to kiss her.'

'He was at the time engaged to the accused?'

'Yes.'

'What happened next?'

'Mary told him to think shame of himself, and him engaged to Miss Elinor!'

'In your opinion, what was the feeling of the accused towards Mary Gerrard?'

'She hated her. She would look after her as though she'd like to destroy her.'

Sir Edwin jumped up.

Elinor thought: 'Why do they wrangle about it? What does it *matter*?'

Sir Edwin Bulmer cross-examined.

'Is it not a fact that Nurse Hopkins said she thought she had left the morphia at home?'

'Well, you see, it was this way: After –'

'Kindly answer my question. Did she not say that she had probably left the morphia at home?'

'Yes.'

'She was not really worried at the time about it?'

'No, not then.'

'Because she thought she had left it at home. So naturally she was not uneasy.'

'She couldn't imagine anyone taking it.'

'Exactly. It wasn't till after Mary Gerrard's death from morphia that her imagination got to work.'

The judge interrupted:

'I think, Sir Edwin, that you have already been over that point with the former witness.'

'As your lordship pleases.'

'Now, regarding the attitude of the accused to Mary Gerrard, there was no quarrel between them at any time?'

'No quarrel, no.'

'Miss Carlisle was always quite pleasant to the girl?'

'Yes. 'Twas the way she looked at her.'

'Yes – yes – yes. But we can't go by that sort of thing. You're Irish, I think?'

'I am that.'

'And the Irish have rather a vivid imagination, haven't they?'

Nurse O'Brien cried excitedly:

'Every word I've told you is the truth.'

III

Mr Abbott, the grocer, in the box. Flustered – unsure of himself (slightly thrilled, though, at his importance). His evidence was short. The purchase of two pots of fish paste. The accused had said, 'There's a lot of food poisoning with fish paste.' She had seemed excited and queer.

No cross-examination.

CHAPTER 3

I

Opening speech for the Defence:

'Gentlemen of the Jury, I might, if I like, submit to you that there is no case against the accused. The onus of proof is on the Prosecution, and so far, in my opinion – and, I have no doubt, yours – they have proved exactly nothing at all! The Prosecution avers that Elinor Carlisle, having obtained possession of morphine (which everyone else in the house had had equal opportunity of purloining, and as to which there exists considerable doubt whether it was ever in the house at all), proceeds to poison Mary Gerrard. Here the Prosecution has relied solely on opportunity. It has sought to prove motive, but I submit that that is just what it has not been able to do. For, members of the jury, there is no motive! The Prosecution has spoken of a broken engagement. I ask you – a broken engagement! If a broken engagement is a cause for murder, why are we not having murders committed every day? And this engagement, mark you, was not an affair of desperate passion, it was an engagement entered into mainly for family reasons. Miss Carlisle and Mr Welman had grown up together; they had always been fond of each other, and gradually they drifted into a warmer attachment; but I intend to prove to you it was at best a very luke-warm affair.'

(Oh Roddy – Roddy. A luke-warm affair?)

'Moreover, this engagement was broken off, not by Mr Welman – but by the prisoner. I submit to you that the engagement between Elinor Carlisle and Roderick Welman was entered into mainly to please old Mrs Welman. When she died, both parties realized that their feelings were not strong enough to justify them in entering upon matrimony. They remained, however, good friends. Moreover, Elinor Carlisle, who had inherited her aunt's fortune, in the kindliness of her nature, was planning to settle a considerable sum of money on Mary Gerrard. And this is the girl she is accused of poisoning! The thing is farcical.

'The only thing that there is against Elinor Carlisle is the circumstances under which the poisoning took place.

'The Prosecution has said in effect:

'No one but Elinor Carlisle could have killed Mary Gerrard. Therefore they have had to search about for a possible motive. But, as I have said to you, they have been unable to find any motive because there was none.

'Now, is it true that no one but Elinor Carlisle could have killed Mary Gerrard? No, it is not. There is the possibility that Mary Gerrard committed suicide. There is the possibility that someone tampered with the sandwiches while Elinor Carlisle was out of the house at the Lodge. There is a third possibility. It is a fundamental law of evidence that if it can be shown that there is an alternative theory which is possible and consistent with the evidence, the accused must be acquitted. I propose to show you that there was another person who had not only an equal opportunity to poison Mary Gerrard, but who had a far better motive for doing so. I propose to call evidence to show you that there was another person who had access to the morphine, and who had a very good motive for killing Mary Gerrard, and I can show that that person had an equally good opportunity of doing so. I submit to you that no jury in the world will convict this woman of murder when there is no evidence against her except that of opportunity, and when it can be shown that there is not only evidence of opportunity against another person, but an overwhelming motive. I shall also call witness to prove that there has been deliberate perjury on the part of one of the witnesses for the Crown. But first I will call the prisoner, that she may tell you her own story, and that you may see for yourself how entirely unfounded the charges against her are.'

II

She had taken the oath. She was answering Sir Edwin's questions in a low voice. The judge leaned forward. He told her to speak louder . . .

Sir Edwin was talking gently and encouragingly – all the questions to which she had rehearsed the answers.

'You were fond of Roderick Welman?'

'Very fond. He was like a brother to me – or a cousin. I always thought of him as a cousin.'

The engagement . . . drifted into it . . . very pleasant to marry someone you had known all your life . . .

'Not, perhaps, what might be called a passionate affair?'

(Passionate? Oh, Roddy . . .)

'Well, no . . . you see we knew each other so well . . .'

'After the death of Mrs Welman was there a slightly strained feeling between you?'

'Yes, there was.'

'How did you account for this?'

'I think it was partly the money.'

'The money?'

'Yes. Roderick felt uncomfortable. He thought people might think he was marrying me for that . . .'

'The engagement was not broken off on account of Mary Gerrard?'

'I did think Roderick was rather taken with her, but I didn't believe it was anything serious.'

'Would you have been upset if it had been?'

'Oh, no. I should have thought it rather unsuitable, that is all.'

'Now, Miss Carlisle. Did you or did you not take a tube of morphine from Nurse Hopkins' attaché-case on June 28th?'

'I did not.'

'Have you at any time had morphine in your possession?'

'Never.'

'Were you aware that your aunt had not made a will?'

'No. It came as a great surprise to me.'

'Did you think she was trying to convey to you a message on the night of June 28th when she died?'

'I understood that she had made no provision for Mary Gerrard, and was anxious to do so.'

'And in order to carry out her wishes, you yourself were prepared to settle a sum of money on the girl?'

'Yes. I wanted to carry out Aunt Laura's wishes. And I was grateful for the kindness Mary had shown to my aunt.'

'On July 26th did you come down from London to Maidensford and stay at the King's Arms?'

'Yes.'

'What was your purpose in coming down?'

'I had an offer for the house, and the man who had bought it wanted possession as quickly as possible. I had to look through my aunt's personal things and settle things up generally.'

'Did you buy various provisions on your way to the Hall on July 27th?'

'Yes. I thought it would be easier to have a picnic lunch there than to come back to the village.'

'Did you then go on to the house, and did you sort through your aunt's personal effects?'

'I did.'

'And after that?'

'I came down to the pantry and cut some sandwiches. I then went down to the Lodge and invited the District Nurse and Mary Gerrard to come up to the house.'

'Why did you do this?'

'I wished to save them a hot walk back to the village and back again to the Lodge.'

'It was, in fact, a natural and kindly action on your part. Did they accept the invitation?'

'Yes. They walked up to the house with me.'

'Where were the sandwiches you had cut?'

'I left them in the pantry on a plate.'

'Was the window open?'

'Yes.'

'Anyone could have got into the pantry while you were absent?'

'Certainly.'

'If anybody had observed you from outside while you were cutting the sandwiches, what would they have thought?'

'I suppose that I was preparing to have a picnic lunch.'

'They could not know, could they, that anyone was to share the lunch?'

'No. The idea of inviting the other two only came to me when I saw what a quantity of food I had.'

'So that if anyone had entered the house during your absence and placed morphine in one of those sandwiches, it would be *you* they were attempting to poison?'

'Well, yes, it would.'

'What happened when you had all arrived back at the house?'

'We went into the morning-room. I fetched the sandwiches and handed them to the other two.'

'Did you drink anything with them?'

'I drank water. There was beer on a table; but Nurse Hopkins and Mary preferred tea. Nurse Hopkins went into the pantry and made it. She brought it in on a tray and Mary poured it out.'

'Did you have any?'

'No.'

'But Mary Gerrard and Nurse Hopkins both drank tea?'

'Yes.'

'What happened next?'

'Nurse Hopkins went and turned the gas-ring off.'

'Leaving you alone with Mary Gerrard?'

'Yes.'

'What happened next?'

'After a few minutes I picked up the tray and the sandwich plate and carried them into the pantry. Nurse Hopkins was there, and we washed them together.'

'Did Nurse Hopkins have her cuffs off at the time?'

'Yes. She was washing the things, while I dried them.'

'Did you make a certain remark to her about a scratch on her wrist?'

'I asked her if she had pricked herself.'

'What did she reply?'

'She said, "It was a thorn from the rose tree outside the Lodge. I'll get it out presently."'

'What was her manner at the time?'

'I think she was feeling the heat. She was perspiring and her face was a queer colour.'

'What happened after that?'

'We went upstairs, and she helped me with my aunt's things.'

'What time was it when you went downstairs again?'

'It must have been an hour later.'

'Where was Mary Gerrard?'

'She was sitting in the morning-room. She was breathing very queerly and was in a coma. I rang up the doctor on Nurse Hopkins' instructions. He arrived just before she died.'

Sir Edwin squared his shoulders dramatically.

'*Miss Carlisle, did you kill Mary Gerrard?*'

(That's your cue! Head up, eyes straight.)

'*No!*'

III

Sir Samuel Attenbury. A sick beating at one's heart. Now – now she was at the mercy of an enemy! No more gentleness, no more questions to which she knew the answers!

But he began quite mildly.

'You were engaged to be married, you have told us, to Mr Roderick Welman?'

'Yes.'

'You were fond of him?'

'Very fond.'

'I put it to you that you were deeply in love with Roderick Welman and that you were wildly jealous of his love for Mary Gerrard?'

'No.' (Did it sound properly indignant, that 'no'?)

Sir Samuel said menacingly:

'I put it to you that you deliberately planned to put this girl out of the way, in the hope that Roderick Welman would return to you.'

'Certainly not.' (Disdainful – a little weary. That was better.)

The questions went on. It was just like a dream . . . a bad dream . . . a nightmare . . .

Question after question . . . horrible, hurting questions . . . Some of them she was prepared for, some took her unawares . . .

Always trying to remember her part. Never once to let go, to say:

'Yes, I did hate her . . . Yes, I did want her dead . . . Yes, all the time I was cutting the sandwiches I was thinking of her dying . . .'

To remain calm and cool and answer as briefly and passionlessly as possible . . .

Fighting . . .

Fighting every inch of the way . . .

Over now . . . The horrible man with the Jewish nose was sitting down. And the kindly, unctuous voice of Sir Edwin Bulmer was asking a few more questions. Easy, pleasant questions, designed to remove any bad impression she might have made under cross-examination . . .

She was back again in the dock. Looking at the jury, wondering . . .

IV

Roddy. Roddy standing there, blinking a little, hating it all. Roddy – looking somehow – not quite *real*.

But nothing's real any more. Everything is whirling round in a devilish way. Black's white, and top is bottom and east is west . . . And I'm not Elinor Carlisle; I'm 'the accused'. And, whether they hang me or whether they let me go, nothing will ever be the same again. If there were just something – just one sane thing to hold on to . . .

(Peter Lord's face, perhaps, with its freckles and its extraordinary air of being just the same as usual . . .)

Where had Sir Edwin got to now?

'Will you tell us what were the state of Miss Carlisle's feelings towards you?'

Roddy answered in his precise voice:

'I should say she was deeply attached to me, but certainly not passionately in love with me.'

'You considered your engagement satisfactory?'

'Oh, quite. We had a good deal in common.'

'Will you tell the jury, Mr Welman, exactly why that engagement was broken off?'

'Well, after Mrs Welman died it pulled us up, I think, with a bit of a shock. I didn't like the idea of marrying a rich woman when I myself was penniless. Actually the engagement was dissolved by mutual consent. We were both rather relieved.'

'Now, will you tell us just what your relations were with Mary Gerrard?'

(Oh, Roddy, poor Roddy, how you must hate all this!)

'I thought her very lovely.'

'Were you in love with her?'

'Just a little.'

'When was the last time you saw her?'

'Let me see. It must have been the 5th or 6th of July.'

Sir Edwin said, a touch of steel in his voice:

'You saw her after that, I think.'

'No, I went abroad – to Venice and Dalmatia.'

'You returned to England – when?'

'When I received a telegram – let me see – on the 1st of August, it must have been.'

'But you were actually in England on July 27th, I think.'

'No.'

'Come, now, Mr Welman. You are on oath, remember. Is it not a fact that your passport shows that you returned to England on July 25th and left it again on the night of the 27th?'

Sir Edwin's voice held a subtly menacing note. Elinor frowned, suddenly jerked back to reality. Why was Counsel bullying his own witness?

Roderick had turned rather pale. He was silent for a minute or two, then he said with an effort:

'Well – yes, that is so.'

'Did you go and see this girl Mary Gerrard in London on the 25th at her lodgings?'

'Yes, I did.'

'Did you ask her to marry you?'

'Er – er – yes.'

'What was her answer?'

'She refused.'

'You are not a rich man, Mr Welman?'

'No.'

'And you are rather heavily in debt?'

'What business is that of yours?'

'Were you not aware of the fact that Miss Carlisle had left all her money to you in the event of her death?'

'This is the first I have heard of it.'

'Were you in Maidensford on the morning of July 27th?'

'I was not.'

Sir Edwin sat down.

Counsel for the Prosecution said:

'You say that in your opinion the accused was not deeply in love with you.'

'That is what I said.'

'Are you a chivalrous man, Mr Welman?'

'I don't know what you mean.'

'If a lady were deeply in love with you and you were not in

love with her, would you feel it incumbent upon you to conceal the fact?'

'Certainly not.'

'Where did you go to school, Mr Welman?'

'Eton.'

Sir Samuel said with a quiet smile:

'That is all.'

V

Alfred James Wargrave.

'You are a rose-grower and live at Emsworth, Berks?'

'Yes.'

'Did you on October 20th go to Maidensford and examine a rose tree growing at the Lodge at Hunterbury Hall?'

'I did.'

'Will you describe this tree?'

'It was a climbing rose – Zephyrine Drouhin. It bears a sweetly scented pink flower. It has no thorns.'

'It would be impossible to prick oneself on a rose tree of this description?'

'It would be quite impossible. It is a thornless tree.'

No cross-examination.

VI

'You are James Arthur Littledale. You are a qualified chemist and employed by the wholesale chemists, Jenkins & Hale?'

'I am.'

'Will you tell me what this scrap of paper is?'

The exhibit was handed to him.

'It is a fragment of one of our labels.'

'What kind of label?'

'The label we attach to tubes of hypodermic tablets.'

'Is there enough here for you to say definitely what drug was in the tube to which this label was attached?'

'Yes. I should say quite definitely that the tube in question contained hypodermic tablets of apomorphine hydrochloride 1/20 grain.'

'Not morphine hydrochloride?'

'No, it could not be that.'

'Why not?'

'On such a tube the word Morphine is spelt with a capital M. The end of the line of the m here, seen under my magnifying-glass, shows plainly that it is part of a small m, not a capital M.'

'Please let the jury examine it with the glass. Have you labels here to show what you mean?'

The labels were handed to the jury.

Sir Edwin resumed:

'You say this is from a tube of apomorphine hydrochloride? What exactly is apomorphine hydrochloride?'

'The formula is $C_{17}H_{17}NO_2$. It is a derivative of morphine prepared by saponifying morphine by heating it with dilute hydrochloric acid in sealed tubes. The morphine loses one molecule of water.'

'What are the special properties of apomorphine?'

Mr Littledale said quietly:

'Apomorphine is the quickest and most powerful emetic known. It acts within a few minutes.'

'So if anybody had swallowed a lethal dose of morphine and were *to inject a dose of apomorphine hypodermically within a few minutes*, what would result?'

'Vomiting would take place almost immediately and the morphine would be expelled from the system.'

'Therefore, if two people were to share the same sandwich *or drink from the same pot of tea*, and one of them were then to inject a dose of apomorphine hypodermically, what would be the result, supposing the shared food or drink to have contained morphine?'

'The food or drink together with the morphine would be vomited by the person who injected the apomorphine.'

'And that person would suffer no ill-results?'

'No.'

There was suddenly a stir of excitement in court and order for silence from the judge.

VII

'You are Amelia Mary Sedley and you reside ordinarily at 17 Charles Street, Boonamba, Auckland?'

'Yes.'

'Do you know a Mrs Draper?'

'Yes. I have known her for over twenty years.'

'Do you know her maiden name?'

'Yes. I was at her marriage. Her name was Mary Riley.'

'Is she a native of New Zealand?'

'No, she came out from England.'

'You have been in court since the beginning of these proceedings?'

'Yes, I have.'

'Have you seen this Mary Riley – or Draper – in court?'

'Yes.'

'Where did you see her?'

'Giving evidence in this box.'

'Under what name?'

'Jessie Hopkins.'

'And you are quite sure that this Jessie Hopkins is the woman you know as Mary Riley or Draper?'

'Not a doubt of it.'

A slight commotion at the back of the court.

'When did you last see Mary Draper – until today?'

'Five years ago. She went to England.'

Sir Edwin said with a bow:

'Your witness.'

Sir Samuel, rising with a slightly perplexed face, began:

'I suggest to you, Mrs – Sedley, that you may be mistaken.'

'I'm not mistaken.'

'You may have been misled by a chance resemblance.'

'I know Mary Draper well enough.'

'Nurse Hopkins is a certificated District Nurse.'

'Mary Draper was a hospital nurse before her marriage.'

'You understand, do you not, that you are accusing a Crown witness of perjury?'

'I understand what I'm saying.'

VIII

'Edward John Marshall, you lived for some years in Auckland, New Zealand, and now reside at 14 Wren Street, Deptford?'

'That's right.'

'Do you know Mary Draper?'

'I've known her for years in New Zealand.'

'Have you seen her today in court?'

'I have. She called herself Hopkins; but it was Mrs Draper all right.'

The judge lifted his head. He spoke in a small, clear, penetrating voice:

'It is desirable, I think, that the witness Jessie Hopkins should be recalled.'

A pause, a murmur.

'Your lordship, Jessie Hopkins left the court a few minutes ago.'

IX

'Hercule Poirot.'

Hercule Poirot entered the box, took the oath, twirled his moustache and waited, with his head a little on one side. He gave his name and address and calling.

'M. Poirot, do you recognize this document?'

'Certainly.'

'How did it originally come into your possession?'

'It was given me by the District Nurse, Nurse Hopkins.'

Sir Edwin said:

'With your permission, my lord, I will read this aloud, and it can then go to the jury.'

CHAPTER 4

I

Closing speech for the Defence.

'Gentlemen of the jury, the responsibility now rests with you. It is for you to say if Elinor Carlisle is to go forth free from the court. If, after the evidence you have heard, you are satisfied that Elinor Carlisle poisoned Mary Gerrard, then it is your duty to pronounce her guilty.

'But if it should seem to you that there is equally strong evidence, and perhaps far stronger evidence against another person, then it is your duty to free the accused without more ado.

'You will have realized by now that the facts of the case are very different from what they originally appeared to be.

'Yesterday, after the dramatic evidence given by M. Hercule Poirot, I called other witnesses to prove beyond any reasonable doubt that the girl Mary Gerrard was the illegitimate daughter of Laura Welman. That being true, it follows, as his lordship will doubtless instruct you, that Mrs Welman's next of kin was not her niece, Elinor Carlisle, but her illegitimate daughter who went by the name of Mary Gerrard. And therefore Mary Gerrard at Mrs Welman's death inherited a vast fortune. That, gentlemen, is the crux of the situation. A sum in the neighbourhood of two hundred thousand pounds was inherited by Mary Gerrard. But she herself was unaware of the fact. She was also unaware of the true identity of the woman Hopkins. You may think, gentlemen, that Mary Riley or Draper may have had some perfectly legitimate reason for changing her name to Hopkins. If so, why has she not come forward to state what the reason was?

'All that we do know is this: That at Nurse Hopkins' instigation, Mary Gerrard made a will leaving everything she had to "Mary Riley, sister of Eliza Riley". We know that Nurse Hopkins, by reason of her profession, had access to morphine and to apomorphine and was well acquainted with their properties. Furthermore, it has been proved that Nurse Hopkins was not speaking the truth when she said that her wrist had been pricked by a thorn from a thornless rose tree. Why did she lie, if it were not that she wanted hurriedly *to account for the mark just made by the hypodermic needle*? Remember, too, that the accused has stated on oath that Nurse Hopkins, when she joined her in the pantry, was looking ill, and her face was of a greenish colour – comprehensible enough if she had just been violently sick.

'I will underline yet another point: *If* Mrs Welman had lived twenty-four hours longer, she would have made a will; and in all probability that will would have made a suitable provision for Mary Gerrard, but would not have left her the bulk of her

fortune, since it was Mrs Welman's belief that her unacknow-
ledged daughter would be happier if she remained in another
sphere of life.

'It is not for me to pronounce on the evidence against another
person, except to show that this other person had equal opportunities and a far stronger motive for the murder.

'Looked at from that point of view, gentlemen of the jury, I
submit to you that the case against Elinor Carlisle falls to the
ground . . .'

II

From Mr Justice Beddingfield's summing-up:

'. . . You must be perfectly satisfied that this woman did, in fact,
administer a dangerous dose of morphia to Mary Gerrard on July
27th. If you are not satisfied, you must acquit the prisoner.

'The Prosecution has stated that the only person who had
the opportunity to administer poison to Mary Gerrard was the
accused. The Defence has sought to prove that there were other
alternatives. There is the theory that Mary Gerrard committed
suicide, but the only evidence in support of that theory is the fact
that Mary Gerrard made a will shortly before she died. There is
not the slightest proof that she was depressed or unhappy or in
a state of mind likely to lead her to take her own life. It has also
been suggested that the morphine might have been introduced
into the sandwiches by someone entering the pantry during the
time that Elinor Carlisle was at the Lodge. In that case, the poison
was intended for Elinor Carlisle, and Mary Gerrard's death was a
mistake. The third alternative suggested by the Defence is that
another person had an equal opportunity to administer morphine,
and that in the latter case the poison was introduced into the tea
and not into the sandwiches. In support of that theory the Defence
has called the witness Littledale, who has sworn that the scrap of
paper found in the pantry was part of a label on a tube containing
tablets of apomorphine hydrochloride, a very powerful emetic.
You have had an example of both types of labels submitted to
you. In my view, the police were guilty of gross carelessness in
not checking the original fragment more closely and in jumping
to the conclusion that it was a morphine label.

'The witness Hopkins has stated that she pricked her wrist on a rose tree at the Lodge. The witness Wargrave has examined that tree, and it has no thorns on it. You have to decide what caused the mark on Nurse Hopkins' wrist and why she should tell a lie about it . . .

'If the Prosecution has convinced you that the accused and no other committed the crime, then you must find the accused guilty.

'If the alternative theory suggested by the Defence is possible and consistent with the evidence, the accused must be acquitted.

'I will ask you to consider the verdict with courage and diligence, weighing only the evidence that has been put before you.'

III

Elinor was brought back into the court.

The jury filed in.

'Gentlemen of the jury, are you agreed upon your verdict?'

'Yes.'

'Look upon the prisoner at the bar, and say whether she is guilty or not guilty.'

'*Not guilty . . .*'

CHAPTER 5

They had brought her out by a side door.

She had been aware of faces welcoming her . . . Roddy . . . the detective with the big moustaches . . .

But it was to Peter Lord that she turned.

'I want to get away . . .'

She was with him now in the smooth Daimler, driving rapidly out of London.

He had said nothing to her. She had sat in the blessed silence.

Every minute taking her farther and farther away.

A new life . . .

That was what she wanted . . .

A new life.

She said suddenly:

'I – I want to go somewhere quiet . . . where there won't be any *faces* . . .'

Peter Lord said quietly:

'That's all arranged. You're going to a sanatorium. Quiet place. Lovely gardens. No one will bother you – or get at you.'

She said with a sigh:

'Yes – that's what I want . . .'

It was being a doctor, she supposed, that made him understand. He knew – and didn't bother her. So blessedly peaceful to be here with him, going away from it all, out of London . . . to a place that was *safe* . . .

She wanted to forget – forget everything . . . None of it was real any longer. It was all gone, vanished, finished with – the old life and the old emotions. She was a new, strange, defenceless creature, very crude and raw, beginning all over again. Very strange and very afraid . . .

But it was comforting to be with Peter Lord . . .

They were out of London now, passing through suburbs.

She said at last:

'It was all you – all you . . .'

Peter Lord said:

'It was Hercule Poirot. The fellow's a kind of magician!'

But Elinor shook her head. She said obstinately:

'It was *you*. *You* got hold of him and made him do it!'

Peter grinned.

'I made him do it all right . . .'

Elinor said:

'Did you know I hadn't done it, or weren't you sure?'

Peter said simply:

'I was never quite sure.'

Elinor said:

'That's why I nearly said: "guilty" right at the beginning . . . because, you see, I *had* thought of it . . . I thought of it that day when I laughed outside the cottage.'

Peter said:

'Yes, I knew.'

She said wonderingly:

'It seems so queer now . . . like a kind of possession. That day I bought the paste and cut the sandwiches I was pretending to myself, I was thinking: "I've mixed poison with this, and when she eats she will die – and then Roddy will come back to me."'

Peter Lord said:

'It helps some people to pretend that sort of thing to themselves. It isn't a bad thing, really. You take it out of yourself in a fantasy. Like sweating a thing out of your system.'

Elinor said:

'Yes, that's true. Because it went – suddenly! The blackness, I mean! When that woman mentioned the rose tree outside the Lodge – it all swung back into – into being normal again . . .'

Then with a shiver she said:

'Afterwards when we went into the morning-room and she was dead – dying, at least – I felt then: Is there much difference between *thinking* and *doing* murder?'

Peter Lord said:

'All the difference in the world!'

'Yes, but is there?'

'Of course there is! Thinking murder doesn't really do any harm. People have silly ideas about that; they think it's the same as *planning* murder! It isn't. If you think murder long enough, you suddenly come through the blackness and feel that it's all rather silly!'

Elinor cried:

'Oh! you *are* a comforting person . . .'

Peter Lord said rather incoherently:

'Not at all. Just common sense.'

Elinor said, and there were suddenly tears in her eyes:

'Every now and then – in court – I looked at you. It gave me courage. You looked so – so *ordinary*.'

Then she laughed. 'That's rude!'

He said:

'I understand. When you're in the middle of a nightmare something ordinary is the only hope. Anyway, ordinary things are the best, I've always thought so.'

For the first time since she had entered the car she turned her head and looked at him.

The sight of his face didn't hurt her as Roddy's face always hurt her; it gave her no sharp pang of pain and pleasure mixed; instead, it made her feel warm and comforted.

She thought:

'How nice his face is . . . nice and funny – and, yes, comforting . . .'

They drove on.

They came at last to a gateway and a drive that wound upwards till it reached a quiet white house on the side of a hill.

He said:

'You'll be quite safe here. No one will bother you.'

Impulsively she laid her hand on his arm.

She said:

'You – you'll come and see me?'

'Of course.'

'Often?'

Peter Lord said:

'As often as you want me.'

She said:

'Please come – *very often* . . .'

CHAPTER 6

Hercule Poirot said:

'So you see, my friend, the lies people tell are just as useful as the truth?'

Peter Lord said:

'Did everyone tell you lies?'

Hercule Poirot nodded.

'Oh, yes! For one reason or another, you comprehend. The one person to whom truth was an obligation and who was sensitive and scrupulous concerning it – that person was the one who puzzled me most!'

Peter Lord murmured:

'Elinor herself!'

'Precisely. The evidence pointed to her as the guilty party. And she herself, with her sensitive and fastidious conscience, did nothing to dispel that assumption. Accusing herself of the will, if not the deed, she came very near to abandoning a distasteful and sordid fight and pleading guilty in court to a crime she had not committed.'

Peter Lord breathed a sigh of exasperation.

'Incredible.'

Poirot shook his head.

'Not at all. She condemned herself – because she judged herself by a more exacting standard than ordinary humanity applies!'

Peter Lord said thoughtfully:

'Yes, she's like that.'

Hercule Poirot went on:

'From the moment that I started my investigations there was always the strong possibility that Elinor Carlisle was guilty of the crime of which she was accused. But I fulfilled my obligations towards you and I discovered that a fairly strong case could be made out against another person.'

'Nurse Hopkins?'

'Not to begin with. Roderick Welman was the first person to attract my attention. In his case, again, we start with a lie. He told me that he left England on July 9th and returned on August 1st. But Nurse Hopkins had mentioned casually that Mary Gerrard had rebuffed Roderick. Welman's advances both in Maidensford "and again when she saw him in London". Mary Gerrard, you informed me, went to London on July 10th – *a day after* Roderick Welman had left England. When then did Mary Gerrard have an interview with Roderick Welman in London? I set my burglarious friend to work, and by an examination of Welman's passport I discovered that he had been in England from July 25th to the 27th. *And he had deliberately lied about it.*

'There had always been that period of time in my mind when the sandwiches were on a plate in the pantry and Elinor Carlisle was down at the Lodge. But all along I realized that in that case Elinor must have been the intended victim, not Mary. Had Roderick Welman any motive for killing Elinor Carlisle? Yes, a very good one. She had made a will leaving him her entire fortune; and by adroit questioning I discovered that Roderick Welman could have made himself acquainted with that fact.'

Peter Lord said:

'And why did you decide that he was innocent?'

'Because of one more lie. Such a silly stupid negligible little lie, too. Nurse Hopkins said that she had scratched her wrist on a rose tree, that she had got a thorn in it. And I went and saw the rose tree, and *it had no thorns* . . . So clearly Nurse Hopkins had told a lie – and the lie was so silly and so seemingly pointless that it focused my attention upon her.

'I began to wonder about Nurse Hopkins. Up till then she had struck me as a perfectly credible witness, consistent throughout, with a strong bias against the accused arising naturally enough out of her affection for the dead girl. But now, with that silly pointless little lie in my mind, I considered Nurse Hopkins and her evidence very carefully, and I realized something that I had not been clever enough to see before. Nurse Hopkins knew something about Mary Gerrard which she was very anxious should come out.'

Peter Lord said in surprise:

'I thought it was the other way round?'

'Ostensibly, yes. She gave a very fine performance of someone who knows something and isn't going to tell! But when I thought it over carefully I realized that every word she had said on the subject had been uttered with diametrically the opposite end in view. My conversation with Nurse O'Brien confirmed that belief. Hopkins had used her very cleverly without Nurse O'Brien being conscious of the fact.

'It was clear then that Nurse Hopkins had a game of her own to play. I contrasted the two lies, hers and Roderick Welman's. Was either of them capable of an innocent explanation?

'In Roderick's case, I answered immediately: Yes. Roderick Welman is a very sensitive creature. To admit that he had been unable to keep to his plan of staying abroad, and had been compelled to slink back and hang round the girl, who would have nothing to do with him, would have been most hurtful to his pride. Since there was no question of his having been near the scene of the murder or of knowing anything about it, he took the line of least resistance and avoided unpleasantness (a most characteristic trait!) by ignoring that hurried visit to England and simply stating that he returned on August 1st when the news of the murder reached him.

'Now as to Nurse Hopkins, could there be an innocent explanation of her lie? The more I thought of it, the more extraordinary it seemed to me. *Why* should Nurse Hopkins find it necessary to lie because she had a mark on her wrist? What was the significance of that mark?

'I began to ask myself certain questions. Who did the morphine that was stolen belong to? Nurse Hopkins. Who could have administered that morphine to old Mrs Welman? Nurse Hopkins. Yes, but why call attention to its disappearance? There could be only one answer to that if Nurse Hopkins was guilty: because the other murder, the murder of Mary Gerrard, was already planned, and a scapegoat had been selected, but that scapegoat must be shown to *have had a chance of obtaining morphine*.

'Certain other things fitted in. The anonymous letter written to Elinor. That was to create bad feeling between Elinor and Mary. The idea doubtless was that Elinor would come down and object to Mary's influence over Mrs Welman. The fact that Roderick Welman fell violently in love with Mary was, of course, a totally unforeseen circumstance – but one that Nurse Hopkins was quick to appreciate. Here was a perfect motive for the scapegoat, Elinor.

'But what was the *reason* for the two crimes? What motive could there be for Nurse Hopkins to do away with Mary Gerrard? I began to see a light – oh, very dim as yet. Nurse Hopkins had a good deal of influence over Mary, and one of the ways she had used that influence was to induce the girl *to make a will*. But the will did not benefit Nurse Hopkins. It benefited an aunt of Mary's who lived in New Zealand. And then I remembered a chance remark that someone in the village had made to me. That aunt had been a hospital nurse.

'The light was not quite so dim now. The pattern – the design of the crime – was becoming apparent. The next step was easy. I visited Nurse Hopkins once more. We both played the comedy very prettily. In the end she allowed herself to be persuaded to tell what she had been aiming to tell all along! Only she tells it, perhaps, just a little sooner than she meant to do! But the opportunity is so good that she cannot resist. And, after all, the truth has got to be known some time. So, with well-feigned reluctance, she produces the letter. And then, my friend, it is no longer conjecture. I *know*! The letter gives her away.'

Peter Lord frowned and said:

'How?'

'*Mon cher*! The superscription on that letter was as follows: "For Mary, to be sent to her after my death." But the gist of the contents made it perfectly plain that Mary *Gerrard* was not to know the truth. Also, the word *sent* (not *given*) on the envelope was illuminating. It was not Mary *Gerrard* to whom that letter was written, but another Mary. It was to her sister, Mary *Riley*, in New Zealand, that Eliza Riley wrote the truth.

'Nurse Hopkins did not find that letter at the Lodge after Mary Gerrard's death. She had had it in her possession for many years. She received it in New Zealand, where it was sent to her after her sister's death.'

He paused.

'Once one had seen the truth with the eyes of the mind the rest was easy. The quickness of air travel made it possible for a witness who knew Mary Draper well in New Zealand to be present in court.'

Peter Lord said:

'Supposing you had been wrong and Nurse Hopkins and Mary Draper had been two entirely different people?'

Poirot said coldly:

'I am never wrong!'

Peter Lord laughed:

Hercule Poirot went on:

'My friend, we know something now of this woman Mary Riley or Draper. The police of New Zealand were unable to get sufficient evidence for a conviction, but they had been watching her for some time when she suddenly left the country. There was a patient of hers, an old lady, who left her "dear Nurse Riley" a very snug little legacy, and whose death was somewhat of a puzzle to the doctor attending her. Mary Draper's husband insured his life in her favour for a considerable sum, and his death was sudden and unaccountable. Unfortunately for her, though he had made out a cheque to the Insurance Company, he had forgotten to post it. Other deaths may lie at her door. It is certain she is a remorseless and unscrupulous woman.

'One can imagine that her sister's letter suggested possibilities to her resourceful mind. When New Zealand became too hot, as you say, to hold her, and she came to this country and resumed her profession in the name of Hopkins (a former colleague of hers in hospital who died abroad), Maidensford was her objective. She may perhaps have contemplated some form of blackmail. But old

Mrs Welman was not the kind of woman to allow herself to be blackmailed, and Nurse Riley, or Hopkins, very wisely did not attempt anything of the sort. Doubtless she made inquiries and discovered that Mrs Welman was a very wealthy woman, and some chance word of Mrs Welman's may have revealed the fact that the old lady had not made a will.

'So, on that June evening, when Nurse O'Brien retailed to her colleague that Mrs Welman was asking for her lawyer, Hopkins did not hesitate. Mrs Welman must die intestate so that her illegitimate daughter would inherit her money. Hopkins had already made friends with Mary Gerrard and acquired a good deal of influence over the girl. All that she had to do now was to persuade the girl to make a will leaving her money to her mother's sister; and she inspired the wording of that will very carefully. There was no mention of the relationship: just "Mary Riley, sister of the late Eliza Riley". Once that was signed, Mary Gerrard was doomed. The woman only had to wait for a suitable opportunity. She had, I fancy, already planned the method of the crime, with the use of the apomorphine to secure her own alibi. She may have meant to get Elinor and Mary to her cottage, but when Elinor came down to the Lodge and asked them both to come up and have sandwiches she realized at once that a perfect opportunity had arisen. The circumstances were such that Elinor was practically certain to be convicted.'

Peter Lord said slowly:

'If it hadn't been for you – she would have been convicted.'

Hercule Poirot said quickly:

'No, it is you, my friend, she has to thank for her life.'

'I? I didn't do anything. I tried –'

He broke off. Hercule Poirot smiled a little.

'*Mais oui*, you tried very hard, did you not? You were impatient because I did not seem to you to be getting anywhere. And you were afraid, too, that she might, after all, be guilty. And so, with great impertinence, you also told me the lies! But, *mon cher*, you were not very clever about it. In future I advise you to stick to the measles and the whooping cough and leave crime detection alone.'

Peter Lord blushed.

He said:

'Did you know – all the time?'

Poirot said severely:

'You lead me by the hand to a clearing in the shrubs, and you assist me to find a German matchbox that you have just put there! *C'est l'enfantillage!*'

Peter Lord winced.

He groaned:

'Rub it in!'

Poirot went on:

'You converse with the gardener and lead him to say that he saw your car in the road; and then you give a start and pretend that it was *not* your car. And you look hard at me to make sure that I realize that someone, a stranger, must have been there that morning.'

'I was a damned fool,' said Peter Lord.

'What were you doing at Hunterbury that morning?'

Peter Lord blushed.

'It was just sheer idiocy . . . I – I'd heard she was down. I went up to the house on the chance of seeing her. I didn't mean to speak to her. I – I just wanted to – well – see her. From the path in the shrubbery I saw her in the pantry cutting bread and butter –'

'Charlotte and the poet Werther. Continue, my friend.'

'Oh, there's nothing to tell. I just slipped into the bushes and stayed there watching her till she went away.'

Poirot said gently:

'Did you fall in love with Elinor Carlisle the first time you saw her?'

There was a long silence.

'I suppose so.'

Then Peter Lord said:

'Oh, well, I suppose she and Roderick Welman will live happy ever afterwards.'

Hercule Poirot said:

'My dear friend, you suppose nothing of the sort!'

'Why not? She'll forgive him the Mary Gerrard business. It was only a wild infatuation on his part, anyway.'

Hercule Poirot said:

'It goes deeper than that . . . There is, sometimes, a deep

chasm between the past and the future. When one has walked in the valley of the shadow of death, and come out of it into the sunshine – then, *mon cher*, it is a new life that begins . . . The past will not serve . . .'

He waited a minute and then went on:

'A new life . . . That is what Elinor Carlisle is beginning now – and it is you who have given her that life.'

'No.'

'Yes. It was your determination, your arrogant insistence that compelled me to do as you asked. Admit now, it is to you she turns in gratitude, is it not?'

Peter Lord said slowly:

'Yes, she's very grateful – now . . . She asked me to go and see her – often.'

'Yes, she needs you.'

Peter Lord said violently:

'Not as she needs – him!'

Hercule Poirot shook his head.

'She never *needed* Roderick Welman. She loved him, yes, unhappily – even desperately.'

Peter Lord, his face set and grim, said harshly:

'She will never love me like that.'

Hercule Poirot said softly:

'Perhaps not. But she needs you, my friend, because it is only with you that she can begin the world again.'

Peter Lord said nothing.

Hercule Poirot's voice was very gentle as he said:

'Can you not accept *facts*? She loved Roderick Welman. What of it? With you, *she can be happy* . . .'

EVIL UNDER THE SUN

To John
In memory of our last season in Syria

I

When Captain Roger Angmering built himself a house in the year 1782 on the island off Leathercombe Bay, it was thought the height of eccentricity on his part. A man of good family such as he was should have had a decorous mansion set in wide meadows with, perhaps, a running stream and good pasture.

But Captain Roger Angmering had only one great love, the sea. So he built his house – a sturdy house too, as it needed to be, on the little windswept gull-haunted promontory – cut off from land at each high tide.

He did not marry, the sea was his first and last spouse, and at his death the house and island went to a distant cousin. That cousin and his descendants thought little of the bequest. Their own acres dwindled, and their heirs grew steadily poorer.

In 1922 when the great cult of the Seaside for Holidays was finally established and the coast of Devon and Cornwall was no longer thought too hot in the summer, Arthur Angmering found his vast inconvenient late Georgian house unsaleable, but he got a good price for the odd bit of property acquired by the seafaring Captain Roger.

The sturdy house was added to and embellished. A concrete causeway was laid down from the mainland to the island. 'Walks' and 'Nooks' were cut and devised all round the island. There were two tennis courts, sun-terraces leading down to a little bay embellished with rafts and diving boards. The Jolly Roger Hotel, Smugglers' Island, Leathercombe Bay, came triumphantly into being. And from June till September (with a short season at Easter) the Jolly Roger Hotel was usually packed to the attics. It was enlarged and improved in 1934 by the addition of a cocktail bar, a bigger dining-room and some extra bathrooms. The prices went up.

People said:

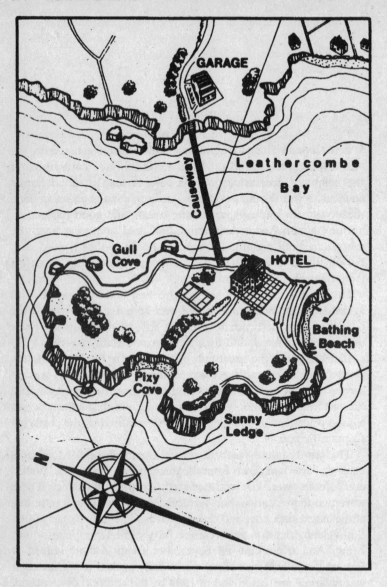

'Ever been to Leathercombe Bay? Awfully jolly hotel there, on a sort of island. Very comfortable and no trippers or charabancs. Good cooking and all that. You ought to go.'

And people did go.

II

There was one very important person (in his own estimation at least) staying at the Jolly Roger. Hercule Poirot, resplendent in a white duck suit, with a panama hat tilted over his eyes, his moustaches magnificently befurled, lay back in an improved type of deck-chair and surveyed the bathing beach. A series of terraces led down to it from the hotel. On the beach itself were floats, lilos, rubber and canvas boats, balls and rubber toys. There was a long springboard and three rafts at varying distances from the shore.

Of the bathers, some were in the sea, some were lying stretched out in the sun, and some were anointing themselves carefully with oil.

On the terrace immediately above, the non-bathers sat and commented on the weather, the scene in front of them, the news in the morning papers and any other subject that appealed to them.

On Poirot's left a ceaseless flow of conversation poured in a gentle monotone from the lips of Mrs Gardener while at the same time her needles clacked as she knitted vigorously. Beyond her, her husband, Odell C. Gardener, lay in a hammock chair, his hat tilted forward over his nose, and occasionally uttered a brief statement when called upon to do so.

On Poirot's right, Miss Brewster, a tough athletic woman with grizzled hair and a pleasant weather-beaten face, made gruff comments. The result sounded rather like a sheepdog whose short stentorian barks interrupted the ceaseless yapping of a Pomeranian.

Mrs Gardener was saying:

'And so I said to Mr Gardener, why, I said, sight-seeing is all very well, and I do like to do a place thoroughly. But, after all, I said, we've done England pretty well and all I want now is to get to some quiet spot by the seaside and just relax. That's what I said, wasn't it, Odell? Just *relax*. I feel I must relax, I said. That's so, isn't it, Odell?'

Mr Gardener, from behind his hat, murmured:

'Yes, darling.'

Mrs Gardener pursued the theme.

'And so, when I mentioned it to Mr Kelso, at Cook's – He's arranged all our itinerary for us and been *most* helpful in every way. I don't really know what we'd have done without him! – well, as I say, when I mentioned it to him, Mr Kelso said that we couldn't do better than come here. A most picturesque spot, he said, quite out of the world, and at the same time very comfortable and most exclusive in every way. And, of course, Mr Gardener, he chipped in there and said what about the sanitary arrangements? Because, if you'll believe me, M. Poirot, a sister of Mr Gardener's went to stay at a guesthouse once, very exclusive they said it was, and in the heart of the moors, but would you believe me, *nothing but an earth closet*! So naturally that made Mr Gardener suspicious of these out-of-the-world places, didn't it, Odell?'

'Why, yes, darling,' said Gardener.

'But Mr Kelso reassured us at once. The sanitation, he said, was absolutely the latest word, and the cooking was excellent. And I'm sure that's so. And what I like about it is, it's *intime*, if you know what I mean. Being a small place we all talk to each other and everybody knows everybody. If there is a fault about the British it is that they're inclined to be a bit stand-offish until they've known you a couple of years. After that nobody could be nicer. Mr Kelso said that interesting people came here, and I see he was right. There's you, M. Poirot and Miss Darnley. Oh! I was just tickled to death when I found out who you were, wasn't I, Odell?'

'You were, darling.'

'Ha!' said Miss Brewster, breaking in explosively. 'What a thrill, eh, M. Poirot?'

Hercule Poirot raised his hands in deprecation. But it was no more than a polite gesture. Mrs Gardener flowed smoothly on.

'You see, M. Poirot, I'd heard a lot about you from Cornelia Robson who was. Mr Gardener and I were at Badenhof in May. And of course Cornelia told us all about that business in Egypt when Linnet Ridgeway was killed. She said you were wonderful and I've always been simply crazy to meet you, haven't I, Odell?'

'Yes, darling.'

'And then Miss Darnley, too. I get a lot of my things at Rose Mond's and of course she *is* Rose Mond, isn't she? I think her clothes are ever so clever. Such a marvellous line. That dress I had on last night was one of hers. She's just a lovely woman in every way, I think.'

From beyond Miss Brewster, Major Barry, who had been sitting with protuberant eyes glued to the bathers, grunted out:

'Distinguished lookin' gal!'

Mrs Gardener clacked her needles.

'I've just got to confess one thing, M. Poirot. It gave me a kind of a *turn* meeting you here – not that I wasn't just thrilled to meet you, because I was. Mr Gardener knows that. But it just came to me that you might be here – well, *professionally*. You know what I mean? Well, I'm just terribly sensitive, as Mr Gardener will tell you, and I just couldn't bear it if I was to be mixed up in crime of any kind. You see –'

Mr Gardener cleared his throat. He said:

'You see, M. Poirot, Mrs Gardener is very sensitive.'

The hands of Hercule Poirot shot into the air.

'But let me assure you, Madame, that I am here simply in the same way that you are here yourselves – to enjoy myself – to spend the holiday. I do not think of crime even.'

Miss Brewster said again, giving her short gruff bark:

'No bodies on Smugglers' Island.'

Hercule Poirot said:

'Ah! but that, it is not strictly true.' He pointed downward. 'Regard them there, lying out in rows. What are they? They are not men and women. There is nothing personal about them. They are just – bodies!'

Major Barry said appreciatively:

'Good-looking fillies, some of 'em. Bit on the thin side, perhaps.'

Poirot cried:

'Yes, but what appeal is there? What mystery? I, I am old, of the old school, When I was young, one saw barely the ankle. The glimpse of a foamy petticoat, how alluring! The gentle swelling of the calf – a knee – a beribboned garter –'

'Naughty, naughty!' said Major Barry hoarsely.

'Much more sensible – the things we wear nowadays,' said Miss Brewster.

'Why, yes, M. Poirot,' said Mrs Gardener. 'I do think, you know, that our girls and boys nowadays lead a much more natural healthy life. They just romp about together and they – well, they –' Mrs Gardener blushed slightly for she had a nice mind – 'they think nothing *of* it, if you know what I mean?'

'I do know,' said Hercule Poirot. 'It is deplorable!'

'Deplorable?' squeaked Mrs Gardener.

'To remove all the romance – all the mystery! Today everything is *standardized*!' He waved a hand towards the recumbent figures. 'That reminds me very much of the Morgue in Paris.'

'M. Poirot!' Mrs Gardener was scandalized.

'Bodies – arranged on slabs – like butcher's meat!'

'But M. Poirot, isn't that too far-fetched for words?'

Hercule Poirot admitted:

'It may be, yes.'

'All the same,' Mrs Gardener knitted with energy, 'I'm inclined to agree with you on one point. These girls that lie out like that in the sun will grow hair on their legs and arms. I've said so to Irene – that's my daughter, M. Poirot. Irene, I said to her, if you lie out like that in the sun, you'll have hair all over you, hair on your arms and hair on your legs and hair on your bosom, and what will you look like then? I said to her. Didn't I, Odell?'

'Yes, darling,' said Mr Gardener.

Everyone was silent, perhaps making a mental picture of Irene when the worst had happened.

Mrs Gardener rolled up her knitting and said:

'I wonder now –'

Mr Gardener said:

'Yes, darling?'

He struggled out of the hammock chair and took Mrs Gardener's knitting and her book. He asked:

'What about joining us for a drink, Miss Brewster?'

'Not just now, thanks.'

The Gardeners went up to the hotel.

Miss Brewster said:

'American husbands are wonderful!'

III

Mrs Gardener's place was taken by the Reverend Stephen Lane.

Mr Lane was a tall vigorous clergyman of fifty odd. His face was tanned and his dark grey flannel trousers were holidayfied and disreputable.

He said with enthusiasm:

'Marvellous country! I've been from Leathercombe Bay to Harford and back over the cliffs.'

'Warm work walking today,' said Major Barry who never walked.

'Good exercise,' said Miss Brewster. 'I haven't been for my row yet. Nothing like rowing for your stomach muscles.'

The eyes of Hercule Poirot dropped somewhat ruefully to a certain protuberance in his middle.

Miss Brewster, noting the glance, said kindly:

'You'd soon get that off, M. Poirot, if you took a rowing-boat out every day.'

'*Merci, Mademoiselle.* I detest boats!'

'You mean small boats?'

'Boats of all sizes!' He closed his eyes and shuddered. 'The movement of the sea, it is not pleasant.'

'Bless the man, the sea is as calm as a mill pond today.'

Poirot replied with conviction:

'There is no such thing as a really calm sea. Always, always, there is motion.'

'If you ask me,' said Major Barry, 'seasickness is nine-tenths nerves.'

'There,' said the clergyman, smiling a little, 'speaks the good sailor – eh, Major?'

'Only been ill once – and that was crossing the Channel! Don't think about it, that's my motto.'

'Seasickness is really a very odd thing,' mused Miss Brewster. 'Why should some people be subject to it and not others? It seems so unfair. And nothing to do with one's ordinary health. Quite sickly people are good sailors. Someone told me once it was something to do with one's spine. Then there's the way some people can't stand heights. I'm not very good myself, but Mrs Redfern is far worse. The other day, on the cliff path to

Harford, she turned quite giddy and simply clung to me. She told me she once got stuck halfway down that outside staircase on Milan Cathedral. She'd gone up without thinking but coming down did for her.'

'She'd better not go down the ladder to Pixy Cove, then,' observed Lane.

Miss Brewster made a face.

'I funk that myself. It's all right for the young. The Cowan boys and the young Mastermans, they run up and down and enjoy it.'

Lane said.

'Here comes Mrs Redfern now, coming up from her bathe.'

Miss Brewster remarked:

'M. Poirot ought to approve of her. She's no sun-bather.'

Young Mrs Redfern had taken off her rubber cap and was shaking out her hair. She was an ash blonde and her skin was of that dead fairness that goes with that colouring. Her legs and arms were very white.

With a hoarse chuckle, Major Barry said:

'Looks a bit uncooked among the others, doesn't she?'

Wrapping herself in a long bath-robe Christine Redfern came up the beach and mounted the steps towards them.

She had a fair serious face, pretty in a negative way and small dainty hands and feet.

She smiled at them and dropped down beside them, tucking her bath-wrap round her.

Miss Brewster said:

'You have earned M. Poirot's good opinion. He doesn't like the sun-tanning crowd. Says they're like joints of butcher's meat, or words to that effect.'

Christine Redfern smiled ruefully. She said:

'I wish I *could* sun-bathe! But I don't go brown. I only blister and get the most frightful freckles all over my arms.'

'Better than getting hair all over them like Mrs Gardener's Irene,' said Miss Brewster. In answer to Christine's inquiring glance she went on: 'Mrs Gardener's been in grand form this morning. Absolutely non-stop. "Isn't that so, Odell?" "Yes, darling."' She paused and then said: 'I wish, though, M. Poirot, that you'd played up to her a bit. Why didn't you? Why didn't you tell her that you were down here investigating a particularly gruesome murder, and that the murderer, a homicidal maniac, was certainly to be found among the guests of the hotel?'

Hercule Poirot sighed. He said:

'I very much fear she would have believed me.'

Major Barry gave a wheezy chuckle. He said:

'She certainly would.'

Emily Brewster said:

'No, I don't believe even Mrs Gardener would have believed in a crime staged here. This isn't the sort of place you'd get a body!'

Hercule Poirot stirred a little in his chair. He protested. He said:

'But why not, Mademoiselle? Why should there not be what you call a "body" here on Smugglers' Island?'

Emily Brewster said:

'I don't know. I suppose some places *are* more unlikely than others. This isn't the kind of spot –' She broke off, finding it difficult to explain her meaning.

'It is romantic, yes,' agreed Hercule Poirot. 'It is peaceful. The sun shines. The sea is blue. But you forget, Miss Brewster, there is evil everywhere under the sun.'

The clergyman stirred in his chair. He leaned forward. His intensely blue eyes lighted up.

Miss Brewster shrugged her shoulders.

'Oh! of course I realize that, but all the same –'

'But all the same this still seems to you an unlikely setting for crime? You forget one thing, Mademoiselle.'

'Human nature, I suppose?'

'That, yes. That, always. But that was not what I was going to say. I was going to point out to you that here everyone is on holiday.'

Emily Brewster turned a puzzled face to him.

'I don't understand.'

Hercule Poirot beamed kindly at her. He made dabs in the air with an emphatic forefinger.

'Let us say, you have an enemy. If you seek him out in his flat, in his office, in the street – *eh bien*, you must have a *reason* – you must account for yourself. But here at the seaside it is necessary for no one to account for himself. You are at Leathercombe Bay, why? *Parbleu!* it is August – one goes to the seaside in August – one is on one's holiday. It is quite natural, you see, for you to be here and for Mr Lane to be here and for Major Barry to be here and for Mrs Redfern and her husband to be here. Because it is the custom in England to go to the seaside in August.'

'Well,' admitted Miss Brewster, 'that's certainly a very ingenious idea. But what about the Gardeners? They're American.'

Poirot smiled.

'Even Mrs Gardener, as she told us, feels the need to *relax*. Also, since she is "doing" England, she must certainly spend a fortnight at the seaside – as a good tourist, if nothing else. She enjoys watching people.'

Mrs Redfern murmured:

'You like watching the people too, I think?'

'Madame, I will confess it. I do.'

She said thoughtfully: 'You see – a good deal.'

IV

There was a pause. Stephen Lane cleared his throat and said with a trace of self-consciousness.

'I was interested, M. Poirot, in something you said just now. You said that there was evil done everywhere under the sun. It was almost a quotation from Ecclesiastes.' He paused and then quoted himself: '*Yea, also the heart of the sons of men is full of evil, and madness is in their heart while they live.*' His face lit up with an almost fanatical light. 'I was glad to hear you say that. Nowadays, no one believes in evil. It is considered, at most, a mere negation of good. Evil, people say, is done by those who know no better – who are undeveloped – who are to be pitied rather than blamed. But M. Poirot, evil is *real*! It is a *fact*! I believe in Evil like I believe in Good. It exists! It is powerful! It walks the earth!'

He stopped. His breath was coming fast. He wiped his forehead with his handkerchief and looked suddenly apologetic.

'I'm sorry. I got carried away.'

Poirot said calmly:

'I understand your meaning. Up to a point I agree with you. Evil does walk the earth and can be recognized as such.'

Major Barry cleared his throat.

'Talking of that sort of thing, some of these fakir fellers in India –'

Major Barry had been long enough at the Jolly Roger for everyone to be on their guard against his fatal tendency to embark on long Indian stories. Both Miss Brewster and Mrs Redfern burst into speech.

'That's your husband swimming in now, isn't it, Mrs Redfern? How magnificent his crawl stroke is. He's an awfully good swimmer.'

At the same moment Mrs Redfern said:

'Oh look! What a lovely little boat that is out there with the red sails. It's Mr Blatt's, isn't it?'

The sailing boat with the red sails was just crossing the end of the bay.

Major Barry grunted:

'Fanciful idea, red sails,' but the menace of the story about the fakir was avoided.

Hercule Poirot looked with appreciation at the young man who had just swum to shore. Patrick Redfern was a good specimen of humanity. Lean, bronzed with broad shoulders and narrow thighs, there was about him a kind of infectious enjoyment and gaiety – a native simplicity that endeared him to all women and most men.

He stood there shaking the water from him and raising a hand in gay salutation to his wife.

She waved back calling out:

'Come up here, Pat.'

'I'm coming.'

He went a little way along the beach to retrieve the towel he had left there.

It was then that a woman came down past them from the hotel to the beach.

Her arrival had all the importance of a stage entrance.

Moreover, she walked as though she knew it. There was no self-consciousness apparent. It would seem that she was too used to the invariable effect her presence produced.

She was tall and slender. She wore a simple backless white bathing dress and every inch of her exposed body was tanned a beautiful even shade of bronze. She was as perfect as a statue. Her hair was a rich flaming auburn curling richly and intimately into her neck. Her face had that slight hardness which is seen when thirty years have come and gone, but the whole effect of her was one of youth – of superb and triumphant vitality. There was a Chinese immobility about her face, and an upward slant of the dark blue eyes. On her head she wore a fantastic Chinese hat of jade green cardboard.

There was that about her which made every other woman on the beach seem faded and insignificant. And with equal inevitability, the eye of every male present was drawn and riveted on her.

The eyes of Hercule Poirot opened, his moustache quivered appreciatively, Major Barry sat up and his protuberant eyes bulged even farther with excitement; on Poirot's left the Reverend Stephen Lane drew in his breath with a little hiss and his figure stiffened.

Major Barry said in a hoarse whisper:

'Arlena Stuart (that's who she was before she married Marshall) – I saw her in *Come and Go* before she left the stage. Something worth looking at, eh?'

Christine Redfern said slowly and her voice was cold: 'She's handsome – yes. I think – she looks rather a beast!'

Emily Brewster said abruptly:

'You talked about evil just now, M. Poirot. Now to my mind that woman's a personification of evil! She's a bad lot through and through. I happen to know a good deal about her.'

Major Barry said reminiscently:

'I remember a gal out in Simla. *She* had red hair too. Wife of a subaltern. Did she set the place by the ears? I'll say she did! Men went mad about her! All the women, of course, would have liked to gouge her eyes out! She upset the apple cart in more homes than one.'

He chuckled reminiscently.

'Husband was a nice quiet fellow. Worshipped the ground she walked on. Never saw a thing – or made out he didn't.'

Stephen Lane said in a low voice full of intense feeling:

'Such women are a menace – a menace to –'

He stopped.

Arlena Stuart had come to the water's edge. Two young men, little more than boys, had sprung up and come eagerly towards her. She stood smiling at them.

Her eyes slid past them to where Patrick Redfern was coming along the beach.

It was, Hercule Poirot thought, like watching the needle of a compass. Patrick Redfern was deflected, his feet changed their direction. The needle, do what it will, must obey the law of magnetism and turn to the north. Patrick Redfern's feet brought him to Arlena Stuart.

She stood smiling at him. Then she moved slowly along the beach by the side of the waves. Patrick Redfern went with her. She stretched herself out by a rock. Redfern dropped to the shingle beside her.

Abruptly, Christine Redfern got up and went into the hotel.

V

There was an uncomfortable little silence after she had left.

Then Emily Brewster said:

'It's rather too bad. She's a nice little thing. They've only been married a year or two.'

'Gal I was speaking of,' said Major Barry, 'the one in Simla. She upset a couple of really happy marriages. Seemed a pity, what?'

'There's a type of woman,' said Miss Brewster, 'who *likes* smashing up homes.' She added after a minute or two, 'Patrick Redfern's a fool!'

Hercule Poirot said nothing. He was gazing down the beach, but he was not looking at Patrick Redfern and Arlena Stuart.

Miss Brewster said:

'Well, I'd better go and get hold of my boat.'

She left them.

Major Barry turned his boiled gooseberry eyes with mild curiosity on Poirot.

'Well, Poirot,' he said. 'What are you thinking about? You've not opened your mouth. What do you think of the siren? Pretty hot?'

Poirot said:

'C'est possible.'

'Now then, you old dog. I know you Frenchmen!'

Poirot said coldly:

'I am *not* a Frenchman!'

'Well, don't tell me you haven't got an eye for a pretty girl! What do you think of her, eh?'

Hercule Poirot said:

'She is not young.'

'What does that matter? A woman's as old as she looks! *Her* looks are all right.'

Hercule Poirot nodded. He said:

'Yes, she is beautiful. But it is not beauty that counts in the end. It is not beauty that makes every head (except one) turn on the beach to look at her.'

'It's IT, my boy,' said the Major. 'That's what it is – IT.'

Then he said with sudden curiosity.

'What are you looking at so steadily?'

Hercule Poirot replied: 'I am looking at the exception. At the one man who did not look up when she passed.'

Major Barry followed his gaze to where it rested on a man of about forty, fair-haired and sun-tanned. He had a quiet pleasant face and was sitting on the beach smoking a pipe and reading *The Times*.

'Oh, *that*!' said Major Barry. 'That's the husband, my boy. That's Marshall.'

Hercule Poirot said:

'Yes, I know.'

Major Barry chuckled. He himself was a bachelor. He was accustomed to think of The Husband in three lights only – as 'the Obstacle', 'the Inconvenience' or 'the Safeguard'.

He said:

'Seems a nice fellow. Quiet. Wonder if my *Times* has come?'

He got up and went up towards the hotel.

Poirot's glance shifted slowly to the face of Stephen Lane.

Stephen Lane was watching Arlena Marshall and Patrick Redfern. He turned suddenly to Poirot. There was a stern fanatical light in his eyes.

He said:

'That woman is evil through and through. Do you doubt it?'

Poirot said slowly:

'It is difficult to be sure.'

Stephen Lane said:

'But, man alive, don't you feel it in the air? All round you? The presence of Evil.'

Slowly, Hercule Poirot nodded his head.

CHAPTER 2

I

When Rosamund Darnley came and sat down by him, Hercule Poirot made no attempt to disguise his pleasure.

As he has since admitted, he admired Rosamund Darnley as much as any woman he had ever met. He liked her distinction, the graceful lines of her figure, the alert proud carriage of her head. He liked the neat sleek waves of her dark hair and the ironic quality of her smile.

She was wearing a dress of some navy blue material with touches of white. It looked very simple owing to the expensive severity of its line. Rosamund Darnley as Rose Mond Ltd was one of London's best-known dressmakers.

She said:

'I don't think I like this place. I'm wondering why I came here!'

'You have been here before, have you not?'

'Yes, two years ago, at Easter. There weren't so many people then.'

Hercule Poirot looked at her. He said gently:

'Something has occurred to worry you. That is right, is it not?'

She nodded. Her foot swung to and fro. She stared down at it. She said:

'I've met a ghost. That's what it is.'

'A ghost, Mademoiselle?'

'Yes.'

'The ghost of what? Or of whom?'

'Oh, the ghost of myself.'

Poirot asked gently:

'Was it a painful ghost?'

'Unexpectedly painful. It took me back, you know . . .'

She paused, musing. Then she said.

'Imagine my childhood. No, you can't! You're not English!'

Poirot asked:

'Was it a very English childhood?'

'Oh, incredibly so! The country – a big shabby house – horses, dogs – walks in the rain – wood fires – apples in the orchard – lack of money – old tweeds – evening dresses that went on from year to year – a neglected garden – with Michaelmas daisies coming out like great banners in the autumn . . .'

Poirot asked gently:

'And you want to go back?'

Rosamund Darnley shook her head. She said:

'One can't go back, can one? That – never. But I'd like to have gone on – a different way.'

Poirot said:

'I wonder.'

Rosamund Darnley laughed.

'So do I, really!'

Poirot said:

'When I was young (and that, Mademoiselle, is indeed a long time ago) there was a game entitled, "*If not yourself, who would you be?*" One wrote the answer in young ladies' albums. They had gold edges and were bound in blue leather. The answer? Mademoiselle, is not really very easy to find.'

Rosamund said:

'No – I suppose not. It would be a big risk. One wouldn't like to take on being Mussolini or Princess Elizabeth. As for one's friends, one knows too much about them. I remember once meeting a charming husband and wife. They were so courteous and delightful to one another and seemed on such good terms after years of marriage that I envied the woman. I'd have changed places with her willingly. Somebody told me afterwards that in private they'd never spoken to each other for eleven years!'

She laughed.

'That shows, doesn't it, that you never know?'

After a moment or two Poirot said:

'Many people, Mademoiselle, must envy you.'

Rosamund Darnley said coolly:

'Oh, yes. Naturally.'

She thought about it, her lips curved upward in their ironic smile.

'Yes, I'm really the perfect type of the successful woman! I enjoy the artistic satisfaction of the successful creative artist (I really do like designing clothes) and the financial satisfaction of the successful business woman. I'm very well off, I've a good figure, a passable face, and a not too malicious tongue.'

She paused. Her smiled widened.

'Of course – I haven't got a husband! I've failed there, haven't I, M. Poirot?'

Poirot said gallantly:

'Mademoiselle, if you are not married, it is because none of my sex have been sufficiently eloquent. It is from choice, not necessity, that you remain single.'

Rosamund Darnley said:

'And yet, like all men, I'm sure you believe in your heart that no woman is content unless she is married and has children.'

Poirot shrugged his shoulders.

'To marry and have children, that is the common lot of women. Only one woman in a hundred – more, in a thousand, can make for herself a name and a position as you have done.'

Rosamund grinned at him.

'And yet, all the same, I'm nothing but a wretched old maid! That's what I feel today, at any rate. I'd be happier with twopence a year and a big silent brute of a husband and a brood of brats running after me. That's true, isn't it?'

Poirot shrugged his shoulders.

'Since you say so, then, yes, Mademoiselle.'

Rosamund laughed, her equilibrium suddenly restored. She took out a cigarette and lit it.

She said:

'You certainly know how to deal with women, M. Poirot. I now feel like taking the opposite point of view and arguing with you in favour of careers for women. Of course I'm damned well off as I am – and I know it!'

'Then everything in the garden – or shall we say at the seaside? is lovely, Mademoiselle.'

'Quite right.'

Poirot, in his turn, extracted his cigarette case and lit one of those tiny cigarettes which it was his affection to smoke.

Regarding the ascending haze with a quizzical eye, he murmured:

'So Mr – no, Captain Marshall is an old friend of yours, Mademoiselle?'

Rosamund sat up. She said:

'Now how do you know that? Oh, I suppose Ken told you.'

Poirot shook his head.

'Nobody has told me anything. After all, Mademoiselle, I am a detective. It was the obvious conclusion to draw.'

Rosamund Darnley said: 'I don't see it.'

'But consider!' The little man's hands were eloquent. 'You have been here a week. You are lively, gay, without a care. Today, suddenly, you speak of ghosts, of old times. What has happened? For several days there have been no new arrivals until last night when Captain Marshall and his wife and daughter arrive. Today the change! It is obvious!'

Rosamund Darnley said:

'Well, it's true enough. Kenneth Marshall and I were more or less children together. The Marshalls lived next door to us. Ken was always nice to me – although condescending, of course, since he was four years older. I've not seen anything of him for a long time. It must be – fifteen years at least.'

Poirot said thoughtfully:

'A long time.'

Rosamund nodded.

There was a pause and then Hercule Poirot said:

'He is sympathetic, yes?'

Rosamund said warmly:

'Ken's a dear. One of the best. Frightfully quiet and reserved. I'd say his only fault is a *penchant* for making unfortunate marriages.'

Poirot said in a tone of great understanding: 'Ah –'

Rosamund Darnley went on.

'Kenneth's a fool – an utter fool where women are concerned! Do you remember the Martingdale case?'

Poirot frowned.

'Martingdale? Martingdale? Arsenic, was it not?'

'Yes. Seventeen or eighteen years ago. The woman was tried for the murder of her husband.'

'And he was proved to have been an arsenic eater and she was acquitted?'

'That's right. Well, after her acquittal, Ken married her. That's the sort of damn silly thing he does.'

Hercule Poirot murmured:

'But if she was innocent?'

Rosamund Darnley said impatiently:

'Oh, I dare say she *was* innocent. Nobody really knows! But there are plenty of women to marry in the world without going out of your way to marry one who's stood her trial for murder.'

Poirot said nothing. Perhaps he knew that if he kept silence Rosamund Darnley would go on. She did so.

'He was very young, of course, only just twenty-one. He was crazy about her. She died when Linda was born – a year after their marriage. I believe Ken was terribly cut up by her death. Afterwards he racketed around a lot – trying to forget, I suppose.'

She paused.

'And then came this business of Arlena Stuart. She was in Revue at the time. There was the Codrington divorce case. Lady Codrington divorced Codrington, citing Arlena Stuart. They say Lord Codrington was absolutely infatuated with her. It was understood they were to be married as soon as the decree was made absolute. Actually, when it came to it, he didn't marry her. Turned her down flat. I believe she actually sued him for breach of promise. Anyway, the thing made a big stir at the time. The next thing that happens is that Ken goes and marries her. The fool – the complete fool!'

Hercule Poirot murmured:

'A man might be excused such a folly – she is beautiful, Mademoiselle.'

'Yes, there's no doubt of that. There was another scandal about three years ago. Old Sir Roger Erskine left her every penny of his money. I should have thought that would have opened Ken's eyes if anything would.'

'And did it not?'

Rosamund Darnley shrugged her shoulders.

'I tell you I've seen nothing of him for years. People say, though, that he took it with absolute equanimity. Why, I should like to know? Has he got an absolutely blind belief in her?'

There might be other reasons.'

'Yes. Pride! Keeping a stiff upper lip! I don't know what he really feels about her. Nobody does.'

'And she? What does she feel about him?'

Rosamund stared at him.

She said:

'She? She's the world's first gold-digger. And a man-eater as well! If anything personable in trousers comes within a hundred yards of her, it's fresh sport for Arlena! She's that kind.'

Poirot nodded his head slowly in complete agreement.

'Yes,' he said. 'That is true what you say . . . Her eyes look for one thing only – men.'

Rosamund said:

'She's got her eye on Patrick Redfern now. He's a good-looking man – and rather the simple kind – you know, fond of his wife, and not a philanderer. That's the kind that's meat and drink to Arlena. I like little Mrs Redfern – she's nice-looking in her fair washed-out way – but I don't think she'll stand a dog's chance against that man-eating tiger, Arlena.'

Poirot said:

'No, it is as you say.'

He looked distressed.

Rosamund said:

'Christine Redfern was a school teacher, I believe. She's the kind that thinks that mind has a pull over matter. She's got a rude shock coming to her.'

Poirot shook his head vexedly.

Rosamund got up. She said:

'It's a shame, you know.' She added vaguely: 'Somebody ought to do something about it.'

II

Linda Marshall was examining her face dispassionately in her bedroom mirror. She disliked her face very much. At this minute it seemed to her to be mostly bones and freckles. She noted with distaste her heavy bush of soft brown hair (mouse, she called it in her own mind), her greenish-grey eyes, her high cheek-bones and the long aggressive line of the chin. Her mouth and teeth weren't perhaps quite so bad – but what were teeth after all? And was that a spot coming on the side of her nose?

She decided with relief that it wasn't a spot. She thought to herself:

'It's awful to be sixteen – simply *awful*.'

One didn't, somehow, know where one was. Linda was as awkward as a young colt and as prickly as a hedgehog. She was conscious the whole time of her ungainliness and of the fact that she was neither one thing nor the other. It hadn't been so bad at school. But now she had left school. Nobody seemed to know quite what she was going to do next. Her father talked vaguely of sending her to Paris next winter. Linda didn't want to go to Paris – but then she didn't want to be at home either. She'd never realized properly, somehow, until now, how very much she disliked Arlena.

Linda's young face grew tense, her green eyes hardened.

Arlena . . .

She thought to herself:

'She's a beast – a *beast* . . .'

Stepmothers! It was rotten to have a stepmother, everybody said so. And it was true! Not that Arlena was unkind to her. Most of the time she hardly noticed the girl. But when she did, there was a contemptuous amusement in her glance, in her words. The finished grace and poise of Arlena's movements emphasized Linda's own adolescent clumsiness. With Arlena about, one felt, shamingly, just how immature and crude one was.

But it wasn't that only. No, it wasn't only that.

Linda groped haltingly in the recesses of her mind. She wasn't very good at sorting out her emotions and labelling them. It was something that Arlena *did* to people – to the house –

'She's bad,' thought Linda with decision. 'She's quite, quite bad.'

But you couldn't even leave it at that. You couldn't just elevate your nose with a sniff of moral superiority and dismiss her from your mind.

It was something she did to people. Father, now, Father was quite different . . .

She puzzled over it. Father coming down to take her out from school. Father taking her once for a cruise. And Father at home – with Arlena there. All – all sort of bottled up and not – and not *there*.

Linda thought:

'And it'll go on like this. Day after day – month after month. I can't bear it.'

Life stretched before her – endless – in a series of days darkened and poisoned by Arlena's presence. She was childish enough still to have little sense of proportion. A year, to Linda, seemed like an eternity.

A big dark burning wave of hatred against Arlena surged up in her mind. She thought:

'I'd like to kill her. Oh! I wish she'd die . . .'

She looked out above the mirror on to the sea below.

This place was really rather fun. Or it could be fun. All those beaches and coves and queer little paths. Lots to explore. And places where one could go off by oneself and muck about. There were caves, too, so the Cowan boys had told her.

Linda thought:

'If only Arlena would go away, I could enjoy myself.'

Her mind went back to the evening of their arrival. It had been exciting coming from the mainland. The tide had been up over the causeway. They had come in a boat. The hotel had looked exciting, unusual. And then on the terrace a tall dark woman had jumped up and said:

'Why, Kenneth!'

And her father, looking frightfully surprised, had exclaimed: 'Rosamund!'

Linda considered Rosamund Darnley severely and critically in the manner of youth.

She decided that she approved of Rosamund. Rosamund, she

thought, was sensible. And her hair grew nicely – as though it fitted her – most people's hair didn't fit them. And her clothes were nice. And she had a kind of funny amused face – as though it were amused at herself, not at you. Rosamund had been nice to her, Linda. She hadn't been gushing or *said* things. (Under the term of 'saying things' Linda grouped a mass of miscellaneous dislikes.) And Rosamund hadn't looked as though she thought Linda a fool. In fact she'd treated Linda as though she was a real human being. Linda so seldom felt like a real human being that she was deeply grateful when anyone appeared to consider her one.

Father, too, had seemed pleased to see Miss Darnley.

Funny – he'd looked quite different, all of a sudden. He'd looked – he'd looked – Linda puzzled it out – why, *young*, that was it! He'd laughed – a queer boyish laugh. Now Linda came to think of it, she'd very seldom heard him laugh.

She felt puzzled. It was as though she'd got a glimpse of quite a different person. She thought:

'I wonder what Father was like when he was my age . . .'

But that was too difficult. She gave it up.

An idea flashed across her mind.

What fun it would have been if they'd come here and found Miss Darnley here – just she and Father.

A vista opened out just for a minute. Father, boyish and laughing, Miss Darnley, herself – and all the fun one could have on the island – bathing – caves –

The blackness shut down again.

Arlena. One couldn't enjoy oneself with Arlena about. Why not? Well, she, Linda, couldn't anyway. You couldn't be happy when there was a person there you – hated. Yes, hated. She hated Arlena.

Very slowly again that black burning wave of hatred rose up again.

Linda's face went very white. Her lips parted a little. The pupils of her eyes contracted. And her fingers stiffened and clenched themselves . . .

III

Kenneth Marshall tapped on his wife's door. When her voice answered, he opened the door and went in.

Arlena was just putting the finishing touches to her toilet. She was dressed in glittering green and looked a little like a mermaid. She was standing in front of the glass applying mascara to her eyelashes. She said:

'Oh, it's you, Ken.'

'Yes. I wondered if you were ready.'

'Just a minute.'

Kenneth Marshall strolled to the window. He looked out on the sea. His face, as usual, displayed no emotion of any kind. It was pleasant and ordinary.

Turning round, he said:

'Arlena?'

'Yes?'

'You've met Redfern before, I gather?'

Arlena said easily:

'Oh yes, darling. At a cocktail party somewhere. I thought he was rather a pet.'

'So I gather. Did you know that he and his wife were coming down here?'

Arlena opened her eyes very wide.

'Oh no, darling. It was the *greatest* surprise!'

Kenneth Marshall said quietly:

'I thought, perhaps, that that was what put the idea of this place into your head. You were very keen we should come here.'

Arlena put down the mascara. She turned towards him. She smiled – a soft seductive smile. She said:

'Somebody told me about this place. I think it was the Rylands. They said it was simply too marvellous – so unspoilt! Don't you like it?'

Kenneth Marshall said:

'I'm not sure.'

'Oh, darling, but you adore bathing and lazing about. I'm sure you'll simply adore it here.'

'I can see that you mean to enjoy yourself.'

Her eyes widened a little. She looked at him uncertainly.

Kenneth Marshall said:

'I suppose the truth of it is that you told young Redfern that you were coming here?'

Arlena said:

'Kenneth darling, you're not going to be horrid, are you?'

Kenneth Marshall said:

'Look here, Arlena. I know what you're like. They're rather a nice young couple. That boy's fond of his wife, really. Must you upset the whole blinking show?'

Arlena said:

'It's so unfair blaming *me*. *I* haven't done anything – anything at all. I can't help it if –'

He prompted her.

'If what?'

Her eyelids fluttered.

'Well, of course. I know people do go crazy about me. But it's not my doing. They just get like that.'

'So you do admit that young Redfern is crazy about you?'

Arlena murmured:

'It's really rather stupid of him.'

She moved a step towards her husband.

'But you know, don't you, Ken, that I don't really care for anyone but you?'

She looked up at him through her darkened lashes.

It was a marvellous look – a look that few men could have resisted.

Kenneth Marshall looked down at her gravely. His face was composed. His voice quiet. He said:

'I think I know you pretty well, Arlena . . .'

IV

When you came out of the hotel on the south side the terraces and the bathing beach were immediately below you. There was also a path that led off round the cliff on the south-west side of the island. A little way along it, a few steps led down to a series of recesses cut into the cliff and labelled on the hotel map of the island as Sunny Ledge. Here cut out of the cliff were niches with seats in them.

To one of these, immediately after dinner, came Patrick

Redfern and his wife. It was a lovely clear night with a bright moon.

The Redferns sat down. For a while they were silent.

At last Patrick Redfern said:

'It's a glorious evening, isn't it, Christine?'

'Yes.'

Something in her voice may have made him uneasy. He sat without looking at her.

Christine Redfern asked in her quiet voice:

'Did you know that woman was going to be here?'

He turned sharply. He said:

'I don't know what you mean.'

'I think you do.'

'Look here, Christine. I don't know what has come over you –'

She interrupted. Her voice held feeling now. It trembled.

'Over *me*? It's what has come over *you*!'

'Nothing's come over me.'

'Oh! Patrick! it *has*! You insisted so on coming here. You were quite vehement. I wanted to go to Tintagel again where – where we had our honeymoon. You were bent on coming here.'

'Well, why not? It's a fascinating spot.'

'Perhaps. But you wanted to come here because *she* was going to be here.'

'She? Who is she?'

'Mrs Marshall. You – you're infatuated with her.'

'For God's sake, Christine, don't make a fool of yourself. It's not like you to be jealous.'

His bluster was a little uncertain. He exaggerated it.

She said:

'We've been so happy.'

'Happy? Of course we've been happy! We *are* happy. But we shan't go on being happy if I can't even speak to another woman without you kicking up a row.'

'It's not like that.'

'Yes, it is. In marriage one has got to have – well – friendships with other people. This suspicious attitude is all wrong. I – I can't speak to a pretty woman without your jumping to the conclusion that I'm in love with her –'

He stopped. He shrugged his shoulders.

Christine Redfern said:

'You *are* in love with her . . .'

'Oh, don't be a fool, Christine! I've – I've barely spoken to her.'

'That's not true.'

'Don't for goodness' sake get into the habit of being jealous of every pretty woman we come across.'

Christine Redfern said:

'She's not just any pretty woman! She's – she's *different*! She's a bad lot! Yes, she is. She'll do you harm, Patrick, please, *give it up*. Let's go away from here.'

Patrick Redfern stuck out his chin mutinously. He looked, somehow, very young as he said defiantly:

'Don't be ridiculous, Christine. And – and don't let's quarrel about it.'

'I don't want to quarrel.'

'Then behave like a reasonable human being. Come on, let's go back to the hotel.'

He got up. There was a pause, then Christine Redfern got up too.

She said:

'Very well . . .'

In the recess adjoining, on the seat there, Hercule Poirot sat and shook his head sorrowfully.

Some people might have scrupulously removed themselves from earshot of a private conversation. But not Hercule Poirot. He had no scruples of that kind.

'Besides,' as he explained to his friend Hastings at a later date, 'it was a question of murder.'

Hastings said, staring:

'But the murder hadn't happened, then.'

Hercule Poirot sighed. He said:

'But already, *mon cher*, it was very clearly indicated.'

'Then why didn't you stop it?'

And Hercule Poirot, with a sigh, said as he had said once before in Egypt, that if a person is determined to commit murder it is not easy to prevent them. He does not blame himself for what happened. It was, according to him, inevitable.

CHAPTER 3

I

Rosamund Darnley and Kenneth Marshall sat on the short springy turf of the cliff overlooking Gull Cove. This was on the east side of the island. People came here in the morning sometimes to bathe when they wanted to be peaceful.

Rosamund said:

'It's nice to get away from people.'

Marshall murmured inaudibly:

'M – m, yes.'

He rolled over, sniffing at the short turf.

'Smells good. Remember the downs at Shipley?'

'Rather.'

'Pretty good, those days.'

'Yes.'

'You've not changed much, Rosamund.'

'Yes, I have. I've changed enormously.'

'You've been very successful and you're rich and all that, but you're the same old Rosamund.'

Rosamund murmured:

'I wish I were.'

'What's that?'

'Nothing. It's a pity, isn't it, Kenneth, that we can't keep the nice natures and high ideals that we had when we were young?'

'I don't know that your nature was ever particularly nice, my child. You used to get into the most frightful rages. You half-choked me once when you flew at me in a temper.'

Rosamund laughed. She said:

'Do you remember the day that we took Toby down to get water rats?'

They spent some minutes in recalling old adventures.

Then there came a pause.

Rosamund's fingers played with the clasp of her bag. She said at last:

'Kenneth?'

'Um.' His reply was indistinct. He was still lying on his face on the turf.

'If I say something to you that is probably outrageously impertinent will you never speak to me again?'

He rolled over and sat up.

'I don't think,' he said seriously, 'that I would ever regard anything you said as impertinent. You see, you *belong*.'

She nodded in acceptance of all that last phrase meant. She concealed only the pleasure it gave her.

'Kenneth, why don't you get a divorce from your wife?'

His face altered. It hardened – the happy expression died out of it. He took a pipe from his pocket and began filling it.

Rosamund said:

'I'm sorry if I've offended you.'

He said quietly:

'You haven't offended me.'

'Well then, why don't you?'

'You don't understand, my dear girl.'

'Are you – so frightfully fond of her?'

'It's not just a question of that. You see, I married her.'

'I know. But she's – pretty notorious.'

He considered that for a moment, ramming in the tobacco carefully.

'Is she? I suppose she is.'

'You *could* divorce her, Ken.'

'My dear girl, you've got no business to say a thing like that. Just because men lose their heads about her a bit isn't to say that she loses hers.'

Rosamund bit off a rejoinder. Then she said:

'You could fix it so that she divorced you – if you prefer it that way.'

'I dare say I could.'

'You ought to, Ken. Really, I mean it. There's the child.'

'Linda?'

'Yes, Linda.'

'What's Linda to do with it?'

'Arlena's not good for Linda. She isn't really. Linda, I think, *feels* things a good deal.'

Kenneth Marshall applied a match to his pipe. Between puffs he said:

'Yes – there's something in that. I suppose Arlena and Linda aren't very good for each other. Not the right thing for a girl perhaps. It's a bit worrying.'

Rosamund said:

'I like Linda – very much. There's something – fine about her.'

Kenneth said:

'She's like her mother. She takes things hard like Ruth did.'

Rosamund said:

'Then don't you think – really – that you ought to get rid of Arlena?'

'Fix up a divorce?'

'Yes. People are doing that all the time.'

Kenneth Marshall said with sudden vehemence:

'Yes, and that's just what I hate.'

'Hate?' She was startled.

'Yes. Sort of attitude to life there is nowadays. If you take on a thing and don't like it, then you get yourself out of it as quick as possible! Dash it all, there's got to be such a thing as good faith. If you marry a woman and engage yourself to look after her, well it's up to you to do it. It's your show. You've taken it on. I'm sick of quick marriage and easy divorce. Arlena's my wife, that's all there is to it.'

Rosamund leaned forward. She said in a low voice:

'So it's like that with you? "Till death do us part"?'

Kenneth Marshall nodded his head.

He said:

'That's just it.'

Rosamund said:

'I see.'

II

Mr Horace Blatt, returning to Leathercombe Bay down a narrow twisting lane, nearly ran down Mrs Redfern at a corner.

As she flattened herself into the hedge, Mr Blatt brought his Sunbeam to a halt by applying the brakes vigorously.

'Hullo-ullo-ullo,' said Mr Blatt cheerfully.

He was a large man with a red face and a fringe of reddish hair round a shining bald spot.

It was Mr Blatt's apparent ambition to be the life and soul of any place he happened to be in. The Jolly Roger Hotel, in his opinion, given somewhat loudly, needed brightening up. He was puzzled at the way people seemed to melt and disappear when he himself arrived on the scene.

'Nearly made you into strawberry jam, didn't I?' said Mr Blatt gaily.

Christine Redfern said:

'Yes, you did.'

'Jump in,' said Mr Blatt.

'Oh, thanks – I think I'll walk.'

'Nonsense,' said Mr Blatt. 'What's a car for?'

Yielding to necessity Christine Redfern got in.

Mr Blatt restarted the engine which had stopped owing to the suddenness with which he had previously pulled up.

Mr Blatt inquired:

'And what are you doing walking about all alone? That's all wrong, a nice-looking girl like you.'

Christine said hurriedly:

'Oh! I like being alone.'

Mr Blatt gave her a terrific dig with his elbow, nearly sending the car into the hedge at the same time.

'Girls always say that,' he said. 'They don't mean it. You know, that place, the Jolly Roger, wants a bit of livening up. Nothing jolly about it. No *life* in it. Of course there's a good amount of duds staying there. A lot of kids, to begin with and a lot of old fogeys too. There's that old Anglo-Indian bore and that athletic parson and those yapping Americans and that foreigner with the moustache – makes me laugh that moustache of his! I should say he's a hairdresser, something of that sort.'

Christine shook her head.

'Oh no, he's a detective.'

Mr Blatt nearly let the car go into the hedge again.

'A detective? D'you mean he's in *disguise*?'

Christine smiled faintly.

She said:

'Oh no, he really *is* like that. He's Hercule Poirot. You must have heard of him.'

Mr Blatt said:

'Didn't catch his name properly. Oh yes, I've *heard* of him.

But I thought he was dead. Dash it, he *ought* to be dead. What's he after down here?'

'He's not after anything – he's just on a holiday.'

'Well, I suppose that might be so,' Mr Blatt seemed doubtful about it. 'Looks a bit of a bounder, doesn't he?'

'Well,' said Christine and hesitated. 'Perhaps a little peculiar.'

'What I say is,' said Mr Blatt, 'what's wrong with Scotland Yard? Buy British every time for me.'

He reached the bottom of the hill and with a triumphant fanfare of the horn ran the car into the Jolly Roger's garage which was situated, for tidal reasons, on the mainland opposite the hotel.

III

Linda Marshall was in the small shop which catered for the wants of visitors to Leathercombe Bay. One side of it was devoted to shelves on which were books which could be borrowed for the sum of twopence. The newest of them was ten years old, some were twenty years old and others older still.

Linda took first one and then another doubtfully from the shelf and glanced into it. She decided that she couldn't possibly read *The Four Feathers* or *Vice Versa*. She took out a small squat volume in brown calf.

The time passed . . .

With a start Linda shoved the book back in the shelf as Christine Redfern's voice said:

'What are you reading, Linda?'

Linda said hurriedly:

'Nothing. I'm looking for a book.'

She pulled out *The Marriage of William Ashe* at random and advanced to the counter fumbling for twopence.

Christine said:

'Mr Blatt just drove me home – after nearly running over me first. I really felt I couldn't walk all across the causeway with him, so I said I had to buy some things.'

Linda said:

'He's awful, isn't he? Always saying how rich he is and making the most terrible jokes.'

Christine said:

'Poor man. One really feels rather sorry for him.'

Linda didn't agree. She didn't see anything to be sorry for in Mr Blatt. She was young and ruthless.

She walked with Christine Redfern out of the shop and down towards the causeway.

She was busy with her own thoughts. She liked Christine Redfern. She and Rosamund Darnley were the only bearable people on the island in Linda's opinion. Neither of them talked much to her for one thing. Now, as they walked, Christine didn't say anything. That, Linda thought, was sensible. If you hadn't anything worth saying why go chattering all the time?

She lost herself in her own perplexities.

She said suddenly:

'Mrs Redfern, have you ever felt that everything's so awful – so terrible – that you'll – oh, *burst* . . . ?'

The words were almost comic, but Linda's face, drawn and anxious, was not. Christine Redfern, looking at her at first vaguely, with scarcely comprehending eyes, certainly saw nothing to laugh at . . .

She caught her breath sharply.

She said:

'Yes – yes – I have felt – just that . . .'

IV

Mr Blatt said:

'So you're the famous sleuth, eh?'

They were in the cocktail bar, a favourite haunt of Mr Blatt's.

Hercule Poirot acknowledged the remark with his usual lack of modesty.

Mr Blatt went on.

'And what are you doing down here – on a job?'

'No, no. I repose myself. I take the holiday.'

Mr Blatt winked.

'You'd say that anyway, wouldn't you?'

Poirot replied:

'Not necessarily.'

Horace Blatt said:

'Oh! Come now. As a matter of fact you'd be safe enough with *me*. *I* don't repeat all I hear! Learnt to keep my mouth shut years ago. Shouldn't have got on the way I have if I hadn't known how to do that. But you know what most people are – yap, yap, yap about everything they hear! Now you can't afford that in your trade! That's why you've got to keep it up that you're here holiday-making and nothing else.'

Poirot asked:

'And why should you suppose the contrary?'

Mr Blatt closed one eye.

He said:

'I'm a man of the world. I know the cut of a fellow's jib. A man like you would be at Deauville or Le Touquet or down at Juan les Pins. That's your – what's the phrase? – spiritual home.'

Poirot sighed. He looked out of the window. Rain was falling and mist encircled the island. He said:

'It is possible that you are right! There, at least, in wet weather there are the distractions.'

'Good old Casino!' said Mr Blatt. 'You know, I've had to work pretty hard most of my life. No time for holidays or kickshaws. I meant to make good and I have made good. Now I can do what I please. My money's as good as any man's. I've seen a bit of life in the last few years, I can tell you.'

Poirot murmured:

'Ah, yes?'

'Don't know why I came to this place,' Mr Blatt continued.

Poirot observed:

'I, too, wondered?'

'Eh, what's that?'

Poirot waved an eloquent hand.

'I, too, am not without observation. I should have expected *you* most certainly to choose Deauville or Biarritz.'

'Instead of which, we're both here, eh?'

Mr Blatt gave a hoarse chuckle.

'Don't really know why I came here,' he mused. 'I think, you know, it sounded *romantic*. Jolly Roger Hotel, Smugglers' Island. That kind of address tickles you up, you know. Makes you think of when you were a boy. Pirates, smuggling, all that.'

He laughed, rather self-consciously.

'I used to sail quite a bit as a boy. Not this part of the world. Off the East coast. Funny how a taste for that sort of thing never quite leaves you. I could have a tip-top yacht if I liked, but somehow I don't really fancy it. I like mucking about in that little yawl of mine. Redfern's keen on sailing, too. He's been out with me once or twice. Can't get hold of him now – always hanging round that red-haired wife of Marshall's.'

He paused, then lowering his voice, he went on:

'Mostly a dried up lot of sticks in this hotel! Mrs Marshall's about the only lively spot! I should think Marshall's got his hands full looking after her. All sorts of stories about her in her stage days – *and* after! Men go crazy about her. You'll see, there'll be a spot of trouble one of these days.'

Poirot asked: 'What kind of trouble?'

Horace Blatt replied:

'That depends. I'd say, looking at Marshall, that he's a man with a funny kind of temper. As a matter of fact, I know he is. Heard something about him. I've met that quiet sort. Never know where you are with that kind. Redfern had better look out –'

He broke off, as the subject of his words came into the bar. He went on speaking loudly and self-consciously.

'And, as I say, sailing round this coast is good fun. Hullo, Redfern, have one with me? What'll you have? Dry Martini? Right. What about you, M. Poirot?'

Poirot shook his head.

Patrick Redfern sat down and said:

'Sailing? It's the best fun in the world. Wish I could do more of it. Used to spend most of my time as a boy in a sailing dinghy round this coast.'

Poirot said:

'Then you know this part of the world well?'

'Rather! I knew this place before there was a hotel on it. There were just a few fishermen's cottages at Leathercombe Bay and a tumbledown old house, all shut up, on the island.'

'There was a house here?'

'Oh, yes, but it hadn't been lived in for years. Was practically falling down. There used to be all sorts of stories of secret passages from the house to Pixy's Cave. We were always looking for that secret passage, I remember.'

Horace Blatt spilt his drink. He cursed, mopped himself and asked:

'What is this Pixy's Cave?'

Patrick said:

'Oh, don't you know it? It's on Pixy Cove. You can't find the entrance to it easily. It's among a lot of piled up boulders at one end. Just a long thin crack. You can just squeeze through it. Inside it widens out into quite a big cave. You can imagine what fun it was to a boy! An old fisherman showed it to me. Nowadays, even the fishermen don't know about it. I asked one the other day why the place was called Pixy Cove and he couldn't tell me.'

Hercule Poirot said:

'But I still do not understand. What is this pixy?'

Patrick Redfern said:

'Oh! that's typically Devonshire. There's the pixy's cave at Sheepstor on the Moor. You're supposed to leave a pin, you know, as a present for the pixy. A pixy is a kind of moor spirit.'

Hercule Poirot said:

'Ah! but it is interesting, that.'

Patrick Redfern went on.

'There's a lot of pixy lore on Dartmoor still. There are tors that are said to be pixy ridden, and I expect that farmers coming home after a thick night still complain of being pixy led.'

Horace Blatt said:

'You mean when they've had a couple?'

Patrick Redfern said with a smile:

'That's certainly the commonsense explanation!'

Blatt looked at his watch. He said:

'I'm going in to dinner. On the whole, Redfern, pirates are my favourites, not pixies.'

Patrick Redfern said with a laugh as the other went out:

'Faith, I'd like to see the old boy pixy led himself!'

Poirot observed meditatively:

'For a hard-bitten business man, M. Blatt seems to have a very romantic imagination.'

Patrick Redfern said:

'That's because he's only half educated. Or so my wife says. Look at what he reads! Nothing but thrillers or Wild West stories.'

Poirot said:

'You mean that he has still the mentality of a boy?'

'Well, don't you think so, sir?'

'Me, I have not seen very much of him.'

'I haven't either. I've been out sailing with him once or twice – but he doesn't really like having anyone with him. He prefers to be on his own.'

Hercule Poirot said:

'That is indeed curious. It is singularly unlike his practice on land.'

Redfern laughed. He said:

'I know. We all have a bit of trouble keeping out of his way. He'd like to turn this place into a cross between Margate and Le Touquet.'

Poirot said nothing for a minute or two. He was studying the laughing face of his companion very attentively. He said suddenly and unexpectedly:

'I think, M. Redfern, that you enjoy living.'

Patrick stared at him, surprised.

'Indeed I do. Why not?'

'Why not indeed,' agreed Poirot. 'I make you my felicitation on the fact.'

Smiling a little, Patrick Redfern said:

'Thank you, sir.'

'That is why, as an older man, a very much older man, I venture to offer you a piece of advice.'

'Yes, sir?'

'A very wise friend of mine in the Police Force said to me years ago: "Hercule, my friend, if you would know tranquillity, avoid women."'

Patrick Redfern said:

'I'm afraid it's a bit late for that, sir. I'm married, you know.'

'I do know. Your wife is a very charming, a very accomplished woman. She is, I think, very fond of you.'

Patrick Redfern said sharply:

'I'm very fond of her.'

'Ah,' said Hercule Poirot, 'I am delighted to hear it.'

Patrick's brow was suddenly like thunder.

'Look here, M. Poirot, what are you getting at?'

'*Les Femmes.*' Poirot leaned back and closed his eyes. 'I know something of them. They are capable of complicating life unbearably. And the English, they conduct their affairs indescribably. If it was necessary for you to come here, M. Redfern, why, in the name of heaven, did you bring your wife?'

Patrick Redfern said angrily:

'I don't know what you mean.'

Hercule Poirot said calmly:

'You know perfectly. I am not so foolish as to argue with an infatuated man. I utter only the word of caution.'

'You've been listening to these damned scandal-mongers. Mrs Gardener, the Brewster woman – nothing to do but to clack their tongues all day. Just because a woman's good-looking – they're down on her like a sack of coals.'

Hercule Poirot got up. He murmured:

'Are you really as young as all that?'

Shaking his head, he left the bar. Patrick Redfern stared angrily after him.

V

Hercule Poirot paused in the hall on his way from the dining-room. The doors were open – a breath of soft night air came in.

The rain had stopped and the mist had dispersed. It was a fine night again.

Hercule Poirot found Mrs Redfern in her favourite seat on the cliff ledge. He stopped by her and said:

'This seat is damp. You should not sit here. You will catch the chill.'

'No, I shan't. And what does it matter anyway.'

'Tscha, tscha, you are not a child! You are an educated woman. You must look at things sensibly.'

She said coldly:

'I can assure you I never take cold.'

Poirot said:

'It has been a wet day. The wind blew, the rain came down, and the mist was everywhere so that one could not see through it. *Eh bien*, what is it like now? The mists have rolled away, the sky is clear and up above the stars shine. That is like life, Madame.'

Christine said in a low fierce voice:

'Do you know what I am most sick of in this place?'

'What, Madame?'

'Pity.'

She brought the word out like the flick of a whip.

She went on:

'Do you think I don't know? That I can't see? All the time people are saying: "Poor Mrs Redfern – that poor little woman." And anyway I'm not little, I'm tall. They say little because they are sorry for me. And I can't bear it!'

Cautiously, Hercule Poirot spread his handkerchief on the seat and sat down. He said thoughtfully:

'There is something in that.'

'That woman –' said Christine and stopped.

Poirot said gravely:

'Will you allow me to tell you something, Madame? Something that is as true as the stars above us? The Arlena Stuarts – or Arlena Marshalls – of this world – do not count.'

Christine Redfern said:

'Nonsense.'

'I assure you, it is true. Their Empire is of the moment and for the moment. To count – really and truly to count – a woman must have goodness or brains.'

Christine said scornfully:

'Do you think men care for goodness or brains?'

Poirot said gravely:

'Fundamentally, yes.'

Christine laughed shortly.

'I don't agree with you.'

Poirot said:

'Your husband loves you, Madame. I know it.'

'You can't know it.'

'Yes, yes. I know it. I have seen him looking at you.'

Suddenly she broke down. She wept stormily and bitterly against Poirot's accommodating shoulder.

She said:

'I can't bear it . . . I can't bear it . . .'

Poirot patted her arm. He said soothingly:

'Patience – only patience.'

She sat up and pressed her handkerchief to her eyes. She said in a stifled voice:

'It's all right. I'm better now. Leave me. I'd – I'd rather be alone.'

He obeyed and left her sitting there while he himself followed the winding path down to the hotel.

He was nearly there when he heard the murmur of voices.

He turned a little aside from the path. There was a gap in the bushes.

He saw Arlena Marshall and Patrick Redfern beside her. He heard the man's voice, with the throb in it of emotion.

'I'm crazy about you – crazy – you've driven me mad . . . You do care a little – you do care?'

He saw Arlena Marshall's face – it was, he thought, like a sleek happy cat – it was animal, not human. She said softly:

'Of course, Patrick darling, I adore you. You know that . . .'

For once Hercule Poirot cut his eavesdropping short. He went back to the path and on down to the hotel.

A figure joined him suddenly. It was Captain Marshall.

Marshall said:

'Remarkable night, what? After that foul day.' He looked up at the sky. 'Looks as though we should have fine weather tomorrow.'

CHAPTER 4

I

The morning of the 25th of August dawned bright and cloudless. It was a morning to tempt even an inveterate sluggard to rise early.

Several people rose early that morning at the Jolly Roger.

It was eight o'clock when Linda, sitting at her dressing-table, turned a little thick calf bound volume face downwards, sprawling it open and looked at her own face in the mirror.

Her lips were set tight together and the pupils of her eyes contracted.

She said below her breath:

'I'll do it . . .'

She slipped out of her pyjamas and into her bathing-dress. Over it she flung on a bath-robe and laced espadrilles on her feet.

She went out of her room and along the passage. At the end of it a door on to the balcony led to an outside staircase leading directly down to the rocks below the hotel. There was a small iron ladder clamped on to the rocks leading down into the water which was used by many of the hotel guests for a before-breakfast dip as taking up less time than going down to the main bathing beach.

As Linda started down from the balcony she met her father coming up. He said:

'You're up early. Going to have a dip?'

Linda nodded.

They passed each other.

Instead of going on down the rocks, however, Linda skirted round the hotel to the left until she came to the path down to the causeway connecting the hotel with the mainland. The tide was high and the causeway under water, but the boat that took hotel guests across was tied to a little jetty. The man in charge of it was absent at the moment. Linda got in, untied it and rowed herself across.

She tied up the boat on the other side, walked up the slope, past the hotel garage and along until she reached the general shop.

The woman had just taken down the shutters and was engaged in sweeping out the floor. She looked amazed at the sight of Linda.

'Well, Miss, you *are* up early.'

Linda put her hand in the pocket of her bath-wrap and brought out some money. She proceeded to make her purchases.

II

Christine Redfern was standing in Linda's room when the girl returned.

'Oh, there you are,' Christine exclaimed. 'I thought you couldn't be really up yet.'

Linda said:

'No, I've been bathing.'

Noticing the parcel in her hand, Christine said with surprise:

'The post has come early today.'

Linda flushed. With her habitual nervous clumsiness the parcel slipped from her hand. The flimsy string broke and some of the contents rolled over the floor.

Christine exclaimed:

'What have you been buying *candles* for?'

But to Linda's relief she did not wait for an answer, but went on, as she helped to pick the things up from the floor.

'I came in to ask whether you would like to come with me to Gull Cove this morning. I want to sketch there.'

Linda accepted with alacrity.

In the last few days she had accompanied Christine Redfern more than once on sketching expeditions. Christine was a most indifferent artist, but it is possible that she found the excuse of painting a help to her pride since her husband now spent most of his time with Arlena Marshall.

Linda Marshall had been increasingly morose and bad tempered. She liked being with Christine who, intent on her work, spoke very little. It was, Linda felt, nearly as good as being by oneself, and in a curious way she craved for company of some kind. There was a subtle kind of sympathy between her and the elder woman, probably based on the fact of their mutual dislike of the same person.

Christine said:

'I'm playing tennis at twelve, so we'd better start fairly early. Half-past ten?'

'Right. I'll be ready. Meet you in the hall.'

III

Rosamund Darnley, strolling out of the dining-room after a very late breakfast, was cannoned into by Linda as the latter came tearing down the stairs.

'Oh! sorry, Miss Darnley.'

Rosamund said: 'Lovely morning, isn't it? One can hardly believe it after yesterday.'

'I know. I'm going with Mrs Redfern to Gull Cove. I said I'd meet her at half-past ten. I thought I was late.'

'No, it's only twenty-five past.'

'Oh! good.'

She was panting a little and Rosamund looked at her curiously.

'You're not feverish, are you, Linda?'

The girls' eyes were very bright and she had a vivid patch of colour in each cheek.

'Oh! *no*. I'm never feverish.'

Rosamund smiled and said:

'It's such a lovely day I got up for breakfast. Usually I have it in bed. But today I came down and faced eggs and bacon like a man.'

'I know – it's heavenly after yesterday. Gull Cove is nice in the morning. I shall put a lot of oil on and get really brown.'

Rosamund said:

'Yes, Gull Cove is nice in the morning. And it's more peaceful than the beach here.'

Linda said, rather shyly:

'Come too.'

Rosamund shook her head.

She said:

'Not this morning. I've other fish to fry.'

Christine Redfern came down the stairs.

She was wearing beach pyjamas of a loose floppy pattern with long sleeves and wide legs. They were made of some green material with a yellow design. Rosamund's tongue itched to tell her that yellow and green were the most unbecoming colours possible for her fair, slightly anaemic complexion. It always annoyed Rosamund when people had no clothes sense.

She thought: 'If I dressed that girl, *I'd* soon make her husband sit up and take notice. However much of a fool Arlena is, she does know how to dress. This wretched girl looks just like a wilting lettuce.'

Aloud she said:

'Have a nice time. I'm going to Sunny Ledge with a book.'

IV

Hercule Poirot breakfasted in his room as usual off coffee and rolls.

The beauty of the morning, however, tempted him to leave the hotel earlier than usual. It was ten o'clock, at least half an hour before his usual appearance, when he descended to the bathing beach. The beach itself was empty save for one person.

That person was Arlena Marshall.

Clad in her white bathing-dress, the green Chinese hat on her head, she was trying to launch a white wooden float. Poirot came gallantly to the rescue, completely immersing a pair of white suède shoes in doing so.

She thanked him with one of those sideways glances of hers.

Just as she was pushing off, she called him.

'M. Poirot?'

Poirot leaped to the water's edge.

'Madame.'

Arlena Marshall said:

'Do something for me, will you?'

'Anything.'

She smiled at him. She murmured:

'Don't tell any one where I am.' She made her glance appealing. 'Every one *will* follow me about so. I just want for once to be *alone*.'

She paddled off vigorously.

Poirot walked up the beach. He murmured to himself:

'*Ah ça, jamais!* That, *par example*, I do not believe.'

He doubted if Arlena Stuart, to give her her stage name, had ever wanted to be alone in her life.

Hercule Poirot, that man of the world, knew better. Arlena Marshall was doubtless keeping a rendezvous, and Poirot had a very good idea with whom.

Or thought he had, but there he found himself proved wrong.

For just as she floated rounded the point of the bay and disappeared out of sight, Patrick Redfern closely followed by Kenneth Marshall, came striding down the beach from the hotel.

Marshall nodded to Poirot, ''Morning, Poirot. Seen my wife anywhere about?'

Poirot's answer was diplomatic.

'Has Madame then risen so early?'

Marshall said:

'She's not in her room.' He looked up at the sky. 'Lovely day. I shall have a bathe right away. Got a lot of typing to do this morning.'

Patrick Redfern, less openly, was looking up and down the beach. He sat down near Poirot and prepared to wait for the arrival of his lady.

Poirot said:

'And Madame Redfern? Has she too risen early?'

Patrick Redfern said:

'Christine? Oh, she's going off sketching. She's rather keen on art just now.'

He spoke impatiently, his mind clearly elsewhere. As time passed he displayed his impatience for Arlena's arrival only too crudely. At every footstep he turned an eager head to see who it was coming down from the hotel.

Disappointment followed disappointment.

First Mr and Mrs Gardener complete with knitting and book and then Miss Brewster arrived.

Mrs Gardener, industrious as ever, settled herself in her chair, and began to knit vigorously and talk at the same time.

'Well. M. Poirot. The beach seems very deserted this morning. Where *is* everybody?'

Poirot replied that the Mastermans and the Cowans, two families with young people in them, had gone off on an all-day sailing excursion.

'Why that certainly does make all the difference, not having them about laughing and calling out. And only one person bathing, Captain Marshall.'

Marshall had just finished his swim. He came up the beach swinging his towel.

'Pretty good in the sea this morning,' he said. 'Unfortunately I've got a lot of work to do. Must go and get on with it.'

'Why, if that isn't too bad, Captain Marshall. On a beautiful day like this, too. My, wasn't yesterday too terrible? I said to Mr Gardener that if the weather was going to continue like that we'd just have to leave. It's the melancholy, you know, with the mist right up around the island. Gives you a kind of ghostly feeling, but then I've always been very susceptible to atmosphere ever since I was a child. Sometimes, you know, I'd feel I just had to scream and scream. And that, of course, was very trying to my parents. But my mother was a lovely woman and she said to my father, "Sinclair, if the child feels like that, we must let her do it. Screaming is her way of expressing herself." And of course, my father agreed. He was devoted to my mother and just did everything she said. They were a perfectly lovely couple, as

I'm sure Mr Gardener will agree. They were a very remarkable couple, weren't they, Odell?'

'Yes, darling,' said Mr Gardener.

'And where's your girl this morning, Captain Marshall?'

'Linda? I don't know. I expect she's mooning round the island somewhere.'

'You know, Captain Marshall, that girl looks kind of peaky to me. She needs feeding up and very very sympathetic treatment.'

Kenneth Marshall said curtly:

'Linda's all right.'

He went up to the hotel.

Patrick Redfern did not go into the water. He sat about, frankly looking up towards the hotel. He was beginning to look a shade sulky.

Miss Brewster was brisk and cheerful when she arrived.

The conversation was much as it had been on a previous morning. Gentle yapping from Mrs Gardener and short staccato barks from Miss Brewster.

She remarked at last: 'Beach seems a bit empty. Everyone off on excursions?'

Mrs Gardener said:

'I was saying to Mr Gardener only this morning that we simply must make an excursion to Dartmoor. It's quite near and the associations are all so romantic. And I'd like to see that convict prison – Princetown, isn't it? I think we'd better fix up right away and go there tomorrow, Odell.'

Mr Gardener said:

'Yes, darling.'

Hercule Poirot said to Miss Brewster.

'You are going to bathe, Mademoiselle?'

'Oh I've had my morning dip before breakfast. Somebody nearly brained me with a bottle, too. Chucked it out of one of the hotel windows.'

'Now that's a very dangerous thing to do,' said Mrs Gardener. 'I had a very dear friend who got concussion by a toothpaste tin falling on him in the street – thrown out of a thirty-fifth storey window it was. A most dangerous thing to do. He got very substantial damages.' She began to hunt among her skeins of wool. 'Why, Odell, I don't believe I've got that second shade of purple wool. It's in the second drawer of the bureau in our bedroom or it might be the third.'

'Yes, darling.'

Mr Gardener rose obediently and departed on his search.

Mrs Gardener went on:

'Sometimes, you know, I do think that maybe we're going a little too far nowadays. What with all our great discoveries and all the electrical waves there must be in the atmosphere, I do think it leads to a great deal of mental unrest, and I just feel that maybe the time has come for a new message to humanity. I don't know, M. Poirot, if you've ever interested yourself in the prophecies from the Pyramids.'

'I have not,' said Poirot.

'Well, I do assure you that they're very, very interesting. What with Moscow being exactly a thousand miles due north of – now what was it? – would it be Nineveh? – but anyway you take a circle and it just shows the most surprising things – and one can just see that there must have been special guidance, and that those ancient Egyptians couldn't have thought of what they did all by themselves. And when you've gone into the theory of the numbers and their repetition, why it's all just so clear that I can't see how anyone can doubt the truth of it for a moment.'

Mrs Gardener paused triumphantly but neither Poirot nor Miss Emily Brewster felt moved to argue the point.

Poirot studied his white suède shoes ruefully.

Emily Brewster said:

'You been paddling with your shoes on, M. Poirot?'

Poirot murmured:

'Alas! I was precipitate.'

Emily Brewster lowered her voice. She said:

'Where's our vamp this morning? She's late.'

Mrs Gardener, raising her eyes from her knitting to study Patrick Redfern, murmured:

'He looks just like a thundercloud. Oh dear, I do feel the whole thing is such a pity. I wonder what Captain Marshall thinks about it all. He's such a nice quiet man – very British and unassuming. You just never know what he's thinking about things.'

Patrick Redfern rose and began to pace up and down the beach.

Mrs Gardener murmured:

'Just like a tiger.'

Three pairs of eyes watched his pacing. Their scrutiny seemed to make Patrick Redfern uncomfortable. He looked more than sulky now. He looked in a flaming temper.

In the stillness a faint chime from the mainland came to their ears.

Emily Brewster murmured:

'Wind's from the east again. That's a good sign when you can hear the church clock strike.'

Nobody said any more until Mr Gardener returned with a skein of brilliant magenta wool.

'Why, Odell, what a long time you have been?'

'Sorry darling, but you see it wasn't in your bureau at all. I found it on your wardrobe shelf.'

'Why, isn't that too extraordinary? I could have declared I put it in that bureau drawer. I do think it's fortunate that I've never had to give evidence in a court case. I'd just worry myself to death in case I wasn't remembering a thing just right.'

Mr Gardener said:

'Mrs Gardener is very conscientious.'

V

It was some five minutes later that Patrick Redfern said:

'Going for your row this morning, Miss Brewster? Mind if I come with you?'

Miss Brewster said heartily:

'Delighted.'

'Let's row right round the island,' proposed Redfern.

Miss Brewster consulted her watch.

'Shall we have time? Oh yes, it's not half-past eleven yet. Come on, then, let's start.'

They went down the beach together.

Patrick Redfern took first turn at the oars. He rowed with a powerful stroke. The boat leapt forward.

Emily Brewster said approvingly:

'Good. We'll see if you can keep that up.'

He laughed into her eyes. His spirits had improved.

'I shall probably have a fine crop of blisters by the time we get back.' He threw up his head, tossing back his black hair. 'God, it's a marvellous day! If you do get a real summer's day in England there's nothing to beat it.'

Emily Brewster said gruffly:

'Can't beat England anyway in my opinion. Only place in the world to live in.'

'I'm with you.'

They rounded the point of the bay to the west and rowed under the cliffs. Patrick Redfern looked up.

'Any one on Sunny Ledge this morning? Yes, there's a sunshade. Who is it, I wonder?'

Emily Brewster said:

'It's Miss Darnley, I think. She's got one of those Japanese affairs.'

They rowed up the coast. On their left was the open sea.

Emily Brewster said:

'We ought to have gone the other way round. This way we've got the current against us.'

'There's very little current. I've swum out here and not noticed it. Anyway we couldn't go the other way, the causeway wouldn't be covered.'

'Depends on the tide, of course. But they always say that bathing from Pixy Cove is dangerous if you swim out too far.'

Patrick was rowing vigorously still. At the same time he was scanning the cliffs attentively.

Emily Brewster thought suddenly:

'He's looking for the Marshall woman. That's why he wanted to come with me. She hasn't shown up this morning and he's wondering what she's up to. Probably she's done it on purpose. Just a move in the game – to make him keener.'

They rounded the jutting point of rock to the south of the little bay named Pixy's Cove. It was quite a small cove, with rocks dotted fantastically about the beach. It faced nearly north-west and the cliff overhung it a good deal. It was a favourite place for picnic teas. In the morning, when the sun was off, it was not popular and there was seldom anyone there.

On this occasion, however, there was a figure on the beach.

Patrick Redfern's stroke checked and recovered.

He said in a would-be casual tone:

'Hullo, who's that?'

Miss Brewster said dryly:

'It looks like Mrs Marshall.'

Patrick Redfern said, as though struck by the idea.

'So it does.'

He altered his course, rowing inshore.

Emily Brewster protested.

'We don't want to land here, do we?'

Patrick Redfern said quickly:

'Oh, plenty of time.'

His eyes looked into hers – something in them, a naïve pleading look rather like that of an importunate dog, silenced Emily Brewster. She thought to herself:

'Poor boy, he's got it badly. Oh well, it can't be helped. He'll get over it in time.'

The boat was fast approaching the beach.

Arlena Marshall was lying face downwards on the shingle, her arms outstretched. The white float was drawn up nearby.

Something was puzzling Emily Brewster. It was as though she was looking at something she knew quite well but which was in one respect quite wrong.

It was a minute or two before it came to her.

Arlena Marshall's attitude was the attitude of a sun-bather. So had she lain many a time on the beach by the hotel, her bronzed body outstretched and the green cardboard hat protecting her head and neck.

But there was no sun on Pixy's Beach and there would be none for some hours yet. The overhanging cliff protected the beach from the sun in the morning. A vague feeling of apprehension came over Emily Brewster.

The boat grounded on the shingle. Patrick Redfern called:

'Hullo, Arlena.'

And then Emily Brewster's foreboding took definite shape. For the recumbent figure did not move or answer.

Emily saw Patrick Redfern's face change. He jumped out of the boat and she followed him. They dragged the boat ashore then set off up the beach to where that white figure lay so still and unresponsive near the bottom of the cliff.

Patrick Redfern got there first but Emily Brewster was close behind him.

She saw, as one sees in a dream, the bronzed limbs, the white backless bathing-dress – the red curl of hair escaping under the jade-green hat – saw something else too – the curious unnatural angle of the outspread arms. Felt, in that minute, that this body had not *lain* down but had been thrown . . .

She heard Patrick's voice – a mere frightened whisper. He knelt down beside that still form – touched the hand – the arm . . .

He said in a low shuddering whisper:

'*My God, she's dead . . .*'

And then, as he lifted the hat a little, peered at the neck:

'*Oh, God, she's been strangled . . . murdered.*'

VI

It was one of those moments when time stands still.

With an odd feeling of unreality Emily Brewster heard herself saying:

'We musn't touch anything . . . Not until the police come.'

Redfern's answer came mechanically.

'No – no – of course not.' And then in a deep agonized whisper. 'Who? *Who?* Who could have done that to Arlena. She can't have – have been murdered. It can't be true!'

Emily Brewster shook her head, not knowing quite what to answer.

She heard him draw in his breath – heard the low controlled rage in his voice as he said:

'My God, if I get my hands on the foul fiend who did this.'

Emily Brewster shivered. Her imagination pictured a lurking murderer behind one of the boulders. Then she heard her voice saying:

'Whoever did it wouldn't be hanging about. We must get the police. Perhaps –' she hesitated – 'one of us ought to stay with – with the body.'

Patrick Redfern said:

'I'll stay.'

Emily Brewster drew a little sigh of relief. She was not the kind of woman who would ever admit to feeling fear, but she was secretly thankful not to have to remain on that beach alone with the faint possibility of a homicidal maniac lingering close at hand.

She said:

'Good. I'll be as quick as I can. I'll go in the boat. Can't face that ladder. There's a constable at Leathercombe Bay.'

Patrick Redfern murmured mechanically:

'Yes – yes, whatever you think best.'

As she rowed vigorously away from the shore, Emily Brewster saw Patrick drop down beside the dead woman and bury his head in his hands. There was something so forlorn about his attitude that she felt an unwilling sympathy. He looked like a dog watching by its dead master. Nevertheless her robust common sense was saying to her:

'Best thing that could have happened for him and his wife – and for Marshall and the child – but I don't suppose *he* can see it that way, poor devil.'

Emily Brewster was a woman who could always rise to an emergency.

CHAPTER 5

I

Inspector Colgate stood back by the cliff waiting for the police-surgeon to finish with Arlena's body. Patrick Redfern and Emily Brewster stood a little to one side.

Dr Neasden rose from his knees with a quick deft movement. He said:

'Strangled – and by a pretty powerful pair of hands. She doesn't seem to have put up much of a struggle. Taken by surprise. H'm – well – nasty business.'

Emily Brewster had taken one look and then quickly averted her eyes from the dead woman's face. That horrible purple convulsed countenance.

Inspector Colgate asked:

'What about time of death?'

Neasden said irritably:

'Can't say definitely without knowing more about her. Lots of factors to take into account. Let's see, it's quarter to one now. What time was it when you found her?'

Patrick Redfern, to whom the question was addressed, said vaguely:

'Some time before twelve. I don't know exactly.'

Emily Brewster said:

'It was exactly a quarter to twelve when we found she was dead.'

'Ah, and you came here in the boat. What time was it when you caught sight of her lying here?'

Emily Brewster considered.

'I should say we rounded the point about five or six minutes earlier.' She turned to Redfern. 'Do you agree?'

He said vaguely:

'Yes – yes – about that, I should think.'

Neasden asked the Inspector in a low voice:

'This the husband? Oh! I see, my mistake. Thought it might be. He seems rather done in over it.'

He raised his voice officially.

'Let's put it at twenty minutes to twelve. She cannot have been killed very long before that. Say between then and eleven – quarter to eleven at the earliest outside limit.'

The Inspector shut his notebook with a snap.

'Thanks,' he said. 'That ought to help us considerably. Puts it within very narrow limits – less than an hour all told.'

He turned to Miss Brewster.

'Now then, I think it's all clear so far. You're Miss Emily Brewster and this is Mr Patrick Redfern, both staying at the Jolly Roger Hotel. You identify this lady as a fellow guest of yours at the hotel – the wife of a Captain Marshall?'

Emily Brewster nodded.

'Then, I think,' said Inspector Colgate, 'that we'll adjourn to the hotel.'

He beckoned to a constable.

'Hawkes, you stay here and don't allow anyone on to this cove. I'll be sending Phillips along later.'

II

'Upon my soul!' said Colonel Weston. 'This is a surprise finding you here!'

Hercule Poirot replied to the Chief Constable's greeting in a suitable manner. He murmured:

'Ah, yes, many years have passed since that affair at St Loo.'

'I haven't forgotten it, though,' said Weston. 'Biggest surprise of my life. The thing I've never got over, though, is the way you got round me about that funeral business. Absolutely unorthodox, the whole thing. Fantastic!'

'*Tout de même, mon Colonel*,' said Poirot. 'It produced the goods, did it not?'

'Er – well, possibly. I dare say we should have got there by more orthodox methods.'

'It is possible,' agreed Poirot diplomatically.

'And here you are in the thick of another murder,' said the Chief Constable. 'Any ideas about this one?'

Poirot said slowly:

'Nothing definite – but it is interesting.'

'Going to give us a hand?'

'You would permit it, yes?'

'My dear fellow, delighted to have you. Don't know enough yet to decide whether it's a case for Scotland Yard or not. Off-hand it looks as though our murderer must be pretty well within a limited radius. On the other hand, all these people are strangers down here. To find out about them and their motives you've got to go to London.'

Poirot said:

'Yes, that is true.'

'First of all,' said Weston, 'we've got to find out who last saw the dead woman alive. Chambermaid took her her breakfast at nine. Girl in the bureau downstairs saw her pass through the lounge and go out about ten.'

'My friend,' said Poirot, 'I suspect that I am the man you want.'

'You saw her this morning? What time?'

'At five minutes past ten. I assisted her to launch her float from the bathing beach.'

'And she went off on it?'

'Yes.'

'Alone?'

'Yes.'

'Did you see which direction she took?'

'She paddled round that point there to the right.'

'In the direction of Pixy's Cove, that is?'

'Yes.'

'And the time then was –?'

'I should say she actually left the beach at a quarter past ten.'

Weston considered.

'That fits in well enough. How long should you say that it would take her to paddle round to the Cove?'

'Ah me, I am not an expert. I do not go in boats or expose myself on floats. Perhaps half an hour?'

'That's about what I think,' said the Colonel. 'She wouldn't be hurrying, I presume. Well, if she arrived there at a quarter to eleven, that fits in well enough.'

'At what time does your doctor suggest she died?'

'Oh, Neasden doesn't commit himself. He's a cautious chap. A quarter to eleven is his earliest outside limit.'

Poirot nodded. He said:

'There is one other point that I must mention. As she left, Mrs Marshall asked me not to say I had seen her.'

Weston stared.

He said:

'H'm, that's rather suggestive, isn't it?'

Poirot murmured.

'Yes. I thought so myself.'

Weston tugged at his moustache. He said:

'Look here, Poirot. You're a man of the world. What sort of a woman was Mrs Marshall?'

A faint smile came to Poirot's lips.

He asked:

'Have you not already heard?'

The Chief Constable said dryly:

'I know what the women say of her. They would. How much truth is there in it? *Was* she having an affair with this fellow Redfern?'

'I should say undoubtedly *yes*.'

'He followed her down here, eh?'

'There is reason to suppose so.'

'And the husband? Did he know about it? What did he feel?'

Poirot said slowly:

'It is not easy to know what Captain Marshall feels or thinks. He is a man who does not display his emotions.'

Weston said sharply:

'But he might have 'em, all the same.'

Poirot nodded. He said:

'Oh yes, he might have them.'

III

The Chief Constable was being as tactful as it was in his nature to be with Mrs Castle.

Mrs Castle was the owner and proprietress of the Jolly Roger Hotel. She was a woman of forty odd with a large bust, rather violent henna red hair, and an almost offensively refined manner of speech.

She was saying:

'That such a thing should happen in my hotel! Ay am sure it has always been the quayettest place imaginable! The people who come here are such naice people. No *rowdiness* – if you know what ay mean. Not like the big hotels in St Loo.'

'Quite so, Mrs Castle,' said Colonel Weston. 'But accidents happen in the best regulated – er households.'

'Ay'm sure Inspector Colgate will bear me out,' said Mrs Castle, sending an appealing glance towards the Inspector who was sitting looking very official. 'As to the laycensing laws, ay am *most* particular. There has never been *any* irregularity!'

'Quite, quite,' said Weston. 'We're not blaming you in any way, Mrs Castle.'

'But it does so reflect upon an establishment,' said Mrs Castle, her large bust heaving. 'When ay think of the noisy gaping crowds. Of course no one but hotel guests are allowed upon the island – but all the same they will no doubt come and *point* from the shore.'

She shuddered.

Inspector Colgate saw his chance to turn the conversation to good account.

He said:

'In regard to that point you've just raised. Access to the island. How do you keep people off?'

'Ay am *most* particular about it.'

'Yes, but what measures do you take? *What* keeps 'em off? Holiday crowds in summer time swarm everywhere like flies.'

Mrs Castle shrugged slightly again.

She said:

'That is the fault of the charabancs. Ay have seen eighteen at one time parked by the quay at Leathercombe Bay. Eighteen!'

'Just so. How do you stop them coming here?'

'There are notices. And then, of course, at high tide, we are cut off.'

'Yes, but at low tide?'

Mrs Castle explained. At the island end of the causeway there was a gate. This said 'Jolly Roger Hotel. Private. No entry except to Hotel.' The rocks rose sheer out of the sea on either side there and could not be climbed.

'Anyone could take a boat, though, I suppose, and row round and land on one of the coves? You couldn't stop them doing that. There's a right of access to the foreshore. You can't stop people being on the beach between low and high watermark.'

But this, it seemed, very seldom happened. Boats could be obtained at Leathercombe Bay harbour, but from there it was a long row to the island, and there was also a strong current just outside Leathercombe Bay harbour.

There were notices, too, on both Gull Cove and Pixy Cove by the ladder. She added that George or William were always on the look out at the bathing beach proper which was the nearest to the mainland.

'Who are George and William?'

'George attends to the bathing beach. He sees to the costumes and the floats. William is the gardener. He keeps the paths and marks the tennis courts and all that.'

Colonel Weston said impatiently:

'Well, that seems clear enough. That's not to say that nobody could have come from outside, but anyone who did so took a risk – the risk of being noticed. We'll have a word with George and William presently.'

Mrs Castle said:

'Ay do not care for trippers – a very noisy crowd, and they frequently leave orange peel and cigarette boxes on the causeway and down by the rocks, but all the same ay never thought one of them would turn out to be a murderer. Oh dear! it really is too terrible for words. A lady like Mrs Marshall murdered and what's so horrible, actually – er – strangled . . .'

Mrs Castle could hardly bring herself to say the word. She brought it out with the utmost reluctance.

Inspector Colgate said soothingly:

'Yes, it's a nasty business.'

'And the newspapers. *My* hotel in the newspapers!'

Colgate said, with a faint grin.

'Oh well, it's advertisement, in a way.'

Mrs Castle drew herself up. Her bust heaved and whalebone creaked. She said icily:

'That is not the kind of advertisement ay care about, Mr Colgate.'

Colonel Weston broke in. He said:

'Now then, Mrs Castle, you've got a list of the guests staying here, as I asked you?'

'Yes, sir.'

Colonel Weston pored over the hotel register. He looked over to Poirot who made the fourth member of the group assembled in the manageress's office.

'This is where you'll probably be able to help us presently.'

He read down the names.

'What about servants?'

Mrs Castle produced a second list.

'There are four chambermaids, the head waiter and three under him and Henry in the bar. William does the boots and shoes. Then there's the cook and two under her.'

'What about the waiters?'

'Well, sir, Albert, the Mater Dotel, came to me from the Vincent at Plymouth. He was there for some years. The three under him have been here for three years – one of them four.

They are very naise lads and most respectable. Henry has been here since the hotel opened. He is quite an institution.'

Weston nodded. He said to Colgate:

'Seems all right. You'll check up on them, of course. Thank you, Mrs Castle.'

'That will be all you require?'

'For the moment, yes.'

Mrs Castle creaked out of the room.

Weston said:

'First thing to do is to talk with Captain Marshall.'

IV

Kenneth Marshall sat quietly answering the questions put to him. Apart from a slight hardening of his features he was quite calm. Seen here, with the sunlight falling on him from the window, you realized that he was a handsome man. Those straight features, the steady blue eyes, the firm mouth. His voice was low and pleasant.

Colonel Weston was saying:

'I quite understand, Captain Marshall, what a terrible shock this must be to you. But you realize that I am anxious to get the fullest information as soon as possible.'

Marshall nodded.

He said:

'I quite understand. Carry on.'

'Mrs Marshall was your second wife?'

'Yes.'

'And you have been married how long?'

'Just over four years.'

'And her name before she was married?'

'Helen Stuart. Her acting name was Arlena Stuart.'

'She was an actress?'

'She appeared in Revue and musical shows.'

'Did she give up the stage on her marriage?'

'No. She continued to appear. She actually retired only about a year and a half ago.'

'Was there any special reason for her retirement?'

Kenneth Marshall appeared to consider.

'No,' he said. 'She simply said that she was tired of it all.'

'It was not – er – in obedience to your special wish?'

Marshall raised his eyebrows.

'Oh, no.'

'You were quite content for her to continue acting after your marriage?'

Marshall smiled very faintly.

'I should have preferred her to give it up – that, yes. But I made no fuss about it.'

'It caused no point of dissension between you?'

'Certainly not. My wife was free to please herself.'

'And – the marriage was a happy one?'

Kenneth Marshall said coldly:

'Certainly.'

Colonel Weston paused a minute. Then he said:

'Captain Marshall, have you any idea who could possibly have killed your wife?'

The answer came without the least hesitation.

'None whatever.'

'Had she any enemies?'

'Possibly.'

'Ah?'

The other went on quickly. He said:

'Don't misunderstand me, sir. My wife was an actress. She was also a very good-looking woman. In both capacities she aroused a certain amount of jealousy and envy. There were fusses over parts – there was rivalry from other women – there was a good deal, shall we say, of general envy, hatred, malice, and all uncharitableness! But that is not to say that there was anyone who was capable of deliberately murdering her.'

Hercule Poirot spoke for the first time. He said:

'What you really mean, Monsieur, is that her enemies were mostly or entirely, *women*?'

Kenneth Marshall looked across at him.

'Yes,' he said. 'That is so.'

The Chief Constable said:

'You know of no man who had a grudge against her?'

'No.'

'Was she previously acquainted with anyone in this hotel?'

'I believe she had met Mr Redfern before – at some cocktail party. Nobody else to my knowledge.'

Weston paused. He seemed to deliberate as to whether to pursue the subject. Then he decided against that course. He said:

'We now come to this morning. When was the last time you saw your wife?'

Marshall paused a minute, then he said:

'I looked in on my way down to breakfast –'

'Excuse me, you occupied separate rooms?'

'Yes.'

'And what time was that?'

'It must have been about nine o'clock.'

'What was she doing?'

'She was opening her letters.'

'Did she say anything?'

'Nothing of any particular interest. Just goodmorning – and that it was a nice day – that sort of thing.'

'What was her manner? Unusual at all?'

'No, perfectly normal.'

'She did not seem excited, or depressed, or upset in any way?'

'I certainly didn't notice it.'

Hercule Poirot said:

'Did she mention at all what were the contents of her letters?'

Again a faint smile appeared on Marshall's lips. He said:

'As far as I can remember, she said they were all bills.'

'Your wife breakfasted in bed?'

'Yes.'

'Did she always do that?'

'Invariably.'

Hercule Poirot said:

'What time did she usually come downstairs?'

'Oh! between ten and eleven – usually nearer eleven.'

Poirot went on:

'If she was to descend at ten o'clock exactly, that would be rather surprising?'

'Yes. She wasn't often down as early as that.'

'But she was this morning. Why do you think that was, Captain Marshall?'

Marshall said unemotionally:

'Haven't the least idea. Might have been the weather – extra fine day and all that.'

'You missed her?'

Kenneth Marshall shifted a little in his chair. He said:

'Looked in on her again after breakfast. Room was empty. I was a bit surprised.'

'And then you came down on the beach and asked me if I had seen her?'

'Er – yes.' He added with a faint emphasis in his voice. 'And you said you hadn't . . .'

The innocent eyes of Hercule Poirot did not falter. Gently he caressed his large and flamboyant moustache.

Weston asked:

'Had you any special reason for wanting to find your wife this morning?'

Marshall shifted his glance amiably to the Chief Constable. He said:

'No, just wondered where she was, that's all.'

Weston paused. He moved his chair slightly. His voice fell into a different key. He said:

'Just now, Captain Marshall, you mentioned that your wife had a previous acquaintance with Mr Patrick Redfern. How well did your wife know Mr Redfern?'

Kenneth Marshall said:

'Mind if I smoke?' He felt through his pockets. 'Dash! I've mislaid my pipe somewhere.'

Poirot offered him a cigarette which he accepted. Lighting it, he said:

'You were asking about Redfern. My wife told me she had come across him at some cocktail party or other.'

'He was, then, just a casual acquaintance?'

'I believe so.'

'Since then –' the Chief Constable paused. 'I understand that that acquaintanceship has ripened into something rather closer.'

Marshall said sharply:

'You understand that, do you? Who told you so?'

'It is the common gossip of the hotel.'

For a moment Marshall's eyes went to Hercule Poirot. They dwelt on him with a kind of cold anger. He said:

'Hotel gossip is usually a tissue of lies!'

'Possibly. But I gather that Mr Redfern and your wife gave some grounds for the gossip.'

'What grounds?'

'They were constantly in each other's company.'

'Is that all?'

'You do not deny that that was so?'

'May have been. I really didn't notice.'

'You did not – excuse me, Captain Marshall – object to your wife's friendship with Mr Redfern?'

'I wasn't in the habit of criticizing my wife's conduct.'

'You did not protest or object in any way?'

'Certainly not.'

'Not even though it was becoming a subject of scandal and an estrangement was growing up between Mr Redfern and his wife?'

Kenneth Marshall said coldly:

'I mind my own business and I expect other people to mind theirs. I don't listen to gossip and tittle tattle.'

'You won't deny that Mr Redfern admired your wife?'

'He probably did. Most men did. She was a very beautiful woman.'

'But you yourself were persuaded that there was nothing serious in the affair?'

'I never thought about it, I tell you.'

'And suppose we have a witness who can testify that they were on terms of the greatest intimacy?'

Again those blue eyes went to Hercule Poirot. Again an expression of dislike showed on that usually impassive face.

Marshall said:

'If you want to listen to these tales, listen to 'em. My wife's dead and can't defend herself.'

'You mean that you, personally, don't believe them?'

For the first time a faint dew of sweat was observable on Marshall's brow. He said:

'I don't propose to believe anything of the kind.'

He went on:

'Aren't you getting a good way from the essentials of this business? What I believe or don't believe is surely not relevant to the plain fact of murder?'

Hercule Poirot answered before either of the others could speak. He said:

'You do not comprehend, Captain Marshall. There is no such thing as a plain fact of murder. Murder springs, nine times out of ten, out of the character and circumstances of the murdered person. *Because* the victim was the kind of person he or she was, *therefore* was he or she murdered! Until we can understand fully and completely *exactly what kind of a person Arlena Marshall was*, we shall not be able to see clearly exactly *the kind of person who murdered her*. From that springs the necessity of our questions.'

Marshall turned to the Chief Constable. He said:

'That your view, too?'

Weston boggled a little. He said:

'Well, up to a point – that is to say –'

Marshall gave a short laugh. He said:

'Thought you wouldn't agree. This character stuff is M. Poirot's speciality, I believe.'

Poirot said, smiling:

'You can at least congratulate yourself on having done nothing to assist me!'

'What do you mean?'

'What have you told us about your wife? Exactly nothing at all. You have told us only what everyone could see for themselves. That she was beautiful and admired. Nothing more.'

Kenneth Marshall shrugged his shoulders. He said simply:

'You're crazy.'

He looked towards the Chief Constable and said with emphasis:

'Anything else, sir, that *you'd* like me to tell you?'

'Yes, Captain Marshall, your own movements this morning, please.'

Kenneth Marshall nodded. He had clearly expected this.

He said:

'I breakfasted downstairs about nine o'clock as usual and read the paper. As I told you I went up to my wife's room afterwards and found she had gone out. I came down to the beach, saw M.

Poirot and asked if he had seen her. Then I had a quick bathe and went up to the hotel again. It was then, let me see, about twenty to eleven – yes, just about that. I saw the clock in the lounge. It was just after twenty minutes to. I went up to my room, but the chambermaid hadn't quite finished it. I asked her to finish as quickly as she could. I had some letters to type which I wanted to get off by the post. I went downstairs again and had a word or two with Henry in the bar. I went up again to my room at ten minutes to eleven. There I typed my letters. I typed until ten minutes to twelve. I then changed into tennis kit as I had a date to play tennis at twelve. We'd booked the court the day before.'

'Who was we?'

'Mrs Redfern, Miss Darnley, Mr Gardener and myself. I came down at twelve o'clock and went up to the court. Miss Darnley was there and Mr Gardener. Mrs Redfern arrived a few minutes later. We played tennis for an hour. Just as we came into the hotel afterwards I – I – got the news.'

'Thank you, Captain Marshall. Just as a matter of form, is there anyone who can corroborate the fact that you were typing in your room between – er – ten minutes to eleven and ten minutes to twelve?'

Kenneth Marshall said with a faint smile:

'Have you got some idea that I killed my own wife? Let me see now. The chambermaid was about doing the rooms. She must have heard the typewriter going. And then there are the letters themselves. With all this upset I haven't posted them. I should imagine they are as good evidence as anything.'

He took three letters from his pocket. They were addressed, but not stamped. He said:

'Their contents, by the way, are strictly confidential. But when it's a case of murder, one is forced to trust in the discretion of the police. They contain lists of figures and various financial statements. I think you will find that if you put one of your men on to type them out, he won't do it in much under an hour.'

He paused.

'Satisfied, I hope?'

Weston said smoothly.

'It is no question of suspicion. Everyone on the island will be asked to account for his or her movements between a quarter to eleven and twenty minutes to twelve this morning.'

Kenneth Marshall said:

'Quite.'

Weston said:

'One more thing, Captain Marshall. Do you know anything about the way your wife was likely to have disposed of any property she had?'

'You mean a will? I don't think she ever made a will.'

'But you are not sure?'

'Her solicitors are Barkett, Markett & Applegood, Bedford Square. They saw to all her contracts, etc. But I'm fairly certain she never made a will. She said once that doing a thing like that would give her the shivers.'

'In that case, if she has died intestate, you, as her husband, succeed to her property.'

'Yes, I suppose I do.'

'Had she any near relatives?'

'I don't think so. If she had, she never mentioned them. I know that her father and mother died when she was a child and she had no brothers or sisters.'

'In any case, I suppose, she had nothing very much to leave?'

Kenneth Marshall said coldly:

'On the contrary. Only two years ago, Sir Robert Erskine, who was an old friend of hers, died and left her most of his fortune. It amounted, I think, to about fifty thousand pounds.'

Inspector Colgate looked up. An alertness came into his glance. Up to now he had been silent. Now he asked:

'Then actually, Captain Marshall, your wife was a rich woman?'

Kenneth Marshall shrugged his shoulders.

'I suppose she was really.'

'And you still say she did not make a will?'

'You can ask the solicitors. But I'm pretty certain she didn't. As I tell you, she thought it unlucky.'

There was a pause then Marshall added:

'Is there anything further?'

Weston shook his head.

'Don't think so – eh Colgate? No. Once more, Captain Marshall, let me offer you all my sympathy in your loss.'

Marshall blinked. He said jerkily:

'Oh – thanks.'

He went out.

V

The three men looked at each other.

Weston said:

'Cool customer. Not giving anything away, is he? What do you make of him, Colgate?'

The Inspector shook his head.

'It's difficult to tell. He's not the kind that shows anything. That sort makes a bad impression in the witness-box, and yet it's a bit unfair on them really. Sometimes they're as cut up as anything and yet can't show it. That kind of manner made the jury bring in a verdict of Guilty against Wallace. It wasn't the evidence. They just couldn't believe that a man could lose his wife and talk and act so coolly about it.'

Weston turned to Poirot.

'What do you think, Poirot?'

Hercule Poirot raised his hands.

He said:

'What can one say? He is the closed box – the fastened oyster. He has chosen his rôle. He has heard nothing, he has seen nothing, he knows nothing!'

'We've got a choice of motives,' said Colgate. 'There's jealousy and there's the money motive. Of course, in a way, a husband's the obvious suspect. One naturally thinks of him first. If he knew his missus was carrying on with the other chap –'

Poirot interrupted.

He said:

'I think he knew that.'

'Why do you say so?'

'Listen, my friend. Last night I had been talking with Mrs Redfern on Sunny Ledge. I came down from there to the hotel and on my way I saw those two together – Mrs Marshall and Patrick Redfern. And a moment or two after I met Captain Marshall. His face was very stiff. It says nothing – but nothing at all! It is almost *too* blank, if you understand me. Oh! he knew all right.'

Colgate grunted doubtfully.

He said:

'Oh well, if you think so –'

'I am sure of it! But even then, what does that tell us? What did Kenneth Marshall *feel* about his wife?'

Colonel Weston said:

'Takes her death coolly enough.'

Poirot shook his head in a dissatisfied manner.

Inspector Colgate said:

'Sometimes these quiet ones are the most violent underneath, so to speak. It's all bottled up. He may have been madly fond of her – and madly jealous. But he's not the kind to show it.'

Poirot said slowly:

'That is possible – yes. He is a very interesting character this Captain Marshall. I interest myself in him greatly. And in his *alibi*.'

'Alibi by typewriter,' said Weston with a short bark of a laugh. 'What have you got to say about that, Colgate?'

Inspector Colgate screwed up his eyes. He said:

'Well, you know, sir, I rather fancy that alibi. It's not too good, if you know what I mean. It's – well, it's *natural*. And if we find the chambermaid was about, and did hear the typewriter going, well then, it seems to me that it's all right and that we'll have to look elsewhere.'

'H'm,' said Colonel Weston. 'Where are you going to look?'

VI

For a minute or two the three men pondered the question.

Inspector Colgate spoke first. He said:

'It boils down to this – was it an outsider, or a guest at the hotel? I'm not eliminating the servants entirely, mind, but I don't expect for a minute that we'll find any of them had a hand in it. No, it's a hotel guest, or it's someone from right outside. We've got to look at it this way. First of all – motive. There's gain. The only person to gain by her death was the lady's husband, it seems. What other motives are there? First and foremost – jealousy. It seems to me – just looking at it – that if ever you've got a *crime passionnel* – (he bowed to Poirot) this is one.'

Poirot murmured as he looked up at the ceiling:

'There are so many passions.'

Inspector Colgate went on:

'Her husband wouldn't allow that she had any enemies – real enemies, that is, but I don't believe for a minute that that's so! I should say that a lady like her would – well, would make some pretty bad enemies – eh, sir, what do you say?'

Poirot responded. He said:

'*Mais oui*, that is so. Arlena Marshall would make enemies. But in my opinion, the enemy theory is not tenable, for you see, Inspector, Arlena Marshall's enemies would, I think, as I said just now, always be *women*.'

Colonel Weston grunted and said:

'Something in that. It's the women who've got their knife into her here all right.'

Poirot went on.

'It seems to be hardly possible that this crime was committed by a woman. What does the medical evidence say?'

Weston grunted again. He said:

'Neasden's pretty confident that she was strangled by a man. Big hands – powerful grip. It's just possible, of course, that an unusually athletic woman might have done it – but it's damned unlikely.'

Poirot nodded.

'Exactly. Arsenic in a cup of tea – a box of poisoned chocolates – a knife – even a pistol – but strangulation – no! It is a man we have to look for.'

'And immediately,' he went on, 'it becomes more difficult. There are two people here in this hotel who have a motive for wishing Arlena Marshall out of the way – but both of them are women.'

Colonel Weston asked:

'Redfern's wife is one of them, I suppose?'

'Yes. Mrs Redfern might have made up her mind to kill Arlena Stuart. She had, let us say, ample cause. I think, too, that it would be possible for Mrs Redfern to commit a murder. But not this kind of murder. For all her unhappiness and jealousy, she is not, I should say, a woman of strong passions. In love, she would be devoted and loyal – not passionate. As I said just now – arsenic in the teacup, possibly – strangulation, no. I am sure, also, that she is physically incapable of committing this crime, her hands and feet are small, below the average.'

Weston nodded. He said:

'This isn't a woman's crime. No, a man did this.'

Inspector Colgate coughed.

'Let me put forward a solution, sir. Say that prior to meeting this Mr Redfern the lady had had another affair with someone – call him X. She turns X down for Mr Redfern. X is mad with rage and jealousy. He follows her down here, stays somewhere in the neighbourhood, comes over to the island, does her in. It's a possibility!'

Weston said:

'It's *possible*, all right. And if it's true, it ought to be easy to prove. Did he come on foot or in a boat? The latter seems more likely. If so, he must have hired a boat somewhere. You'd better make inquiries.'

He looked across at Poirot.

'What do you think of Colgate's suggestion?'

Poirot said slowly:

'It leaves, somehow, too much to chance. And besides – somewhere the picture is not true. I cannot, you see, imagine this man . . . the man who is mad with rage and jealousy.'

Colgate said:

'People *did* go potty about her, though, sir. Look at Redfern.'

'Yes, yes . . . But all the same –'

Colgate looked at him questioningly.

Poirot shook his head.

He said, frowning:

'Somewhere, there is something that we have missed . . . .'

CHAPTER 6

I

Colonel Weston was poring over the hotel register.
He read aloud:

'Major and Mrs Cowan,
Miss Pamela Cowan,
Master Robert Cowan,
Master Evan Cowan,
  Rydal's Mount, Leatherhead.
Mr and Mrs Masterman,
Mr Edward Masterman,
Miss Jennifer Masterman,
Mr Roy Masterman,
Master Frederick Masterman,
  5 Marlborough Avenue, London, N.W.
Mr and Mrs Gardener,
  New York.
Mr and Mrs Redfern,
  Crossgates, Seldon, Princes Risborough.
Major Barry,
  18 Cardon St., St James, London, S.W.1.
Mr Horace Blatt,
  5 Pickersgill Street, London, E.C.2.
M. Hercule Poirot,
  Whitehaven Mansions, London, W.1.
Miss Rosamund Darnley,
  8 Cardigan Court, W.1.
Miss Emily Brewster,
  Southgates, Sunbury-on-Thames.
Rev. Stephen Lane,
  London.
Captain and Mrs Marshall,
Miss Linda Marshall,
  73 Upcott Mansions, London, S.W.7.'

He stopped.

Inspector Colgate said:

'I think, sir, that we can wash out the first two entries. Mrs Castle tells me that the Mastermans and the Cowans come here regularly every summer with their children. This morning they went off on an all-day excursion sailing, taking lunch with them. They left just after nine o'clock. A man called Andrew Baston took them. We can check up from him, but I think we can put them right out of it.'

Weston nodded.

'I agree. Let's eliminate everyone we can. Can you give us a pointer on any of the rest of them, Poirot?'

Poirot said:

'Superficially, that is easy. The Gardeners are a middle-aged married couple, pleasant, travelled. All the talking is done by the lady. The husband is acquiescent. He plays tennis and golf and has a form of dry humour that is attractive when one gets him to oneself.'

'Sounds quite O.K.'

'Next – the Redferns. Mr Redfern is young, attractive to women, a magnificent swimmer, a good tennis player and accomplished dancer. His wife I have already spoken of to you. She is quiet, pretty in a washed-out way. She is, I think, devoted to her husband. She has something that Arlena Marshall did not have.'

'What is that?'

'Brains.'

Inspector Colgate sighed. He said:

'Brains don't count for much when it comes to an infatuation, sir.'

'Perhaps not. And yet I do truly believe that in spite of his infatuation for Mrs Marshall, Patrick Redfern really cares for his wife.'

'That may be, sir. It wouldn't be the first time that's happened.'

Poirot murmured.

'That is the pity of it! It is always the thing women find hardest to believe.'

He went on:

'Major Barry. Retired Indian Army. An admirer of women. A teller of long and boring stories.'

Inspector Colgate sighed.

'You needn't go on. I've met a few, sir.'

'Mr Horace Blatt. He is, apparently, a rich man. He talks a good deal – about Mr Blatt. He wants to be everybody's friend. It is sad. For nobody likes him very much. And there is something else. Mr Blatt last night asked me a good many questions. Mr Blatt was uneasy. Yes, there is something not quite right about Mr Blatt.'

He paused and went on with a change of voice:

'Next comes Miss Rosamund Darnley. Her business name is Rose Mond Ltd. She is a celebrated dressmaker. What can I say of her? She has brains and charm and chic. She is very pleasing to look at.' He paused and added. 'And she is a very old friend of Captain Marshall's.'

Weston sat up in his chair.

'Oh, she is, is she?'

'Yes. They had not met for some years.'

Weston asked:

'Did she know he was going to be down here?'

'She says not.'

Poirot paused and then went on.

'Who comes next? Miss Brewster. I find her just a little alarming.' He shook his head. 'She has a voice like a man's. She is gruff and what you call hearty. She rows boats and has a handicap of four at golf.' He paused. 'I think, though, that she has a good heart.'

Weston said:

'That leaves only the Reverend Stephen Lane. Who's the Reverend Stephen Lane?'

'I can only tell you one thing. He is a man who is in a condition of great nervous tension. Also he is, I think, a fanatic.'

Inspector Colgate said:

'Oh, that kind of person.'

Weston said:

'And that's the lot!' He looked at Poirot. 'You seem very lost in thought, my friend?'

Poirot said:

'Yes. Because, you see, when Mrs Marshall went off this morning and asked me not to tell anyone I had seen her. I jumped at once in my own mind to a certain conclusion. I thought that her friendship with Patrick Redfern had made trouble between her and her husband. I thought that she was going to meet Patrick Redfern somewhere, and that she did not want her husband to know where she was.'

He paused.

'But that, you see, was where I was wrong. Because, although her husband appeared almost immediately on the beach and asked if I had seen her, Patrick Redfern arrived also – and was most patently and obviously looking for her! And therefore, my friends, I am asking myself, *who was it that Arlena Marshall went off to meet*?'

Inspector Colgate said:

'That fits in with *my* idea. A man from London or somewhere.'

Hercule Poirot shook his head. He said:

'But, my friend, according to your theory, Arlena Marshall had broken with this mythical man. Why, then, should she take such trouble and pains to meet him?'

Inspector Colgate shook his head. He said:

'Who do *you* think it was?'

'That is just what I cannot imagine. We have just read through the list of hotel guests. They are all middle-aged – dull. Which of them would Arlena Marshall prefer to Patrick Redfern? No, that is impossible. And yet, all the same, she *did* go to meet someone – and that someone was not Patrick Redfern.'

Weston murmured:

'You don't think she just went off by herself?'

Poirot shook his head.

'*Mon cher*,' he said. 'It is very evident that you never met the dead woman. Somebody once wrote a learned treatise on the difference that solitary confinement would mean to Beau Brummel or to a man like Newton. Arlena Marshall, my dear friend, would practically not exist in solitude. She only lived in the light of a man's admiration. No, Arlena Marshall went to meet *someone* this morning. *Who was it?*'

II

Colonel Weston sighed, shook his head and said:

'Well, we can go into theories later. Got to get through these interviews now. Got to get it down in black and white where everyone was. I suppose we'd better see the Marshall girl now. She might be able to tell us something useful.'

Linda Marshall came into the room clumsily, knocking against the doorpost. She was breathing quickly and the pupils of her eyes were dilated. She looked like a startled young colt. Colonel Weston felt a kindly impulse towards her.

He thought:

'Poor kid – she's nothing but a kid after all. This must have been a pretty bad shock to her.'

He drew up a chair and said in a reassuring voice.

'Sorry to put you through this, Miss – Linda, isn't it?'

'Yes, Linda.'

Her voice had that indrawn breathy quality that is often characteristic of schoolgirls. Her hands rested helplessly on the table in front of him – pathetic hands, big and red, with large bones and long wrists. Weston thought:

'A kid oughtn't to be mixed up in this sort of thing.'

He said reassuringly.

'There's nothing very alarming about all this. We just want you to tell us anything you know that might be useful, that's all.'

Linda said:

'You mean – about Arlena?'

'Yes. Did you see her this morning at all?'

The girl shook her head.

'No. Arlena always gets down rather late. She has breakfast in bed.'

Hercule Poirot said:

'And you, Mademoiselle?'

'Oh, I get up. Breakfast in bed's so *stuffy*.'

Weston said:

'Will you tell us what you did this morning?'

'Well, I had a bathe first and then breakfast, and then I went with Mrs Redfern to Gull Cove.'

Weston said:

'What time did you and Mrs Redfern start?'

'She said she'd be waiting for me in the hall at half-past ten. I was afraid I was going to be late, but it was all right. We started off at about three minutes to the half-hour.'

Poirot said:

'And what did you do at Gull Cove?'

'Oh, I oiled myself and sunbathed and Mrs Redfern sketched. Then, later, I went into the sea and Christine went back to the hotel to get changed for tennis.'

Weston said, keeping his voice quite casual:

'Do you remember what time that was?'

'When Mrs Redfern went back to the hotel? Quarter to twelve.'

'Sure of that time – quarter to twelve?'

Linda, opening her eyes wide, said:

'Oh *yes*. I looked at my watch.'

'The watch you have on now?'

Linda glanced down at her wrist.

'Yes.'

Weston said:

'Mind if I see?'

She held out her wrist. He compared the watch with his own and with the hotel clock on the wall.

He said, smiling:

'Correct to a second. And after that you had a bathe?'

'Yes.'

'And you got back to the hotel – when?'

'Just about one o'clock. And – and then – I heard – about Arlena . . .'

Her voice changed.

Colonel Weston said:

'Did you – er – get on with your stepmother all right?'

She looked at him for a minute without replying. Then she said:

'Oh yes.'

Poirot asked:

'Did you like her, Mademoiselle?'

Linda said again:

'Oh yes.' She added: 'Arlena was quite kind to me.'

Weston said with rather uneasy facetiousness.

'Not the cruel stepmother, eh?'

Linda shook her head without smiling.

Weston said:

'That's good. That's good. Sometimes, you know, there's a bit of difficulty in families – jealousy – all that. Girl and her father great pals and then she resents it a bit when he's all wrapped up in the new wife. You didn't feel like that, eh?'

Linda stared at him. She said with obvious sincerity:

'Oh no.'

Weston said:

'I suppose your father was – er – very wrapped up in her?'

Linda said simply:

'I don't know.'

Weston went on:

'All sorts of difficulties, as I say, arise in families. Quarrels – rows – that sort of thing. If husband and wife get ratty with each other, that's a bit awkward for a daughter too. Anything of that sort?'

Linda said clearly:

'Do you mean, did Father and Arlena quarrel?'

'Well – yes.'

Weston thought to himself:

'Rotten business – questioning a child about her father. Why is one a policeman? Damn it all, it's got to be done, though.'

Linda said positively:

'Oh no.' She added: 'Father doesn't quarrel with people. He's not like that at all.'

Weston said:

'Now, Miss Linda, I want you to think very carefully. Have you any idea at all who might have killed your stepmother? Is there anything you've ever heard or anything you know that could help us on that point?'

Linda was silent a minute. She seemed to be giving the question a serious unhurried consideration. She said at last.

'No, I don't know who could have wanted to kill Arlena.' She added: 'Except, of course, Mrs Redfern.'

Weston said:

'You think Mrs Redfern wanted to kill her? Why?'

Linda said:

'Because her husband was in love with Arlena. But I don't think she would really want to *kill* her. I mean she'd just feel that she wished she was dead – and that isn't the same thing at all, is it?'

Poirot said gently:

'No, it is not at all the same.'

Linda nodded. A queer sort of spasm passed across her face. She said:

'And anyway, Mrs Redfern could never do a thing like that – kill anybody. She isn't – she isn't *violent*, if you know what I mean.'

Weston and Poirot nodded. The latter said:

'I know exactly what you mean, my child, and I agree with you. Mrs Redfern is not of those who, as your saying goes, "sees red". She would not be' – he leaned back half closing his eyes, picking his words with care – 'shaken by a storm of feeling – seeing life narrowing in front of her – seeing a hated face – a hated white neck – feeling her hands clench – longing to feel them press into flesh –'

He stopped.

Linda moved jerkily back from the table. She said in a trembling voice:

'Can I go now? Is that all?'

Colonel Weston said:

'Yes, yes, that's all. Thank you, Miss Linda.'

He got up to open the door for her. Then came back to the table and lit a cigarette.

'Phew,' he said. 'Not a nice job, ours. I can tell you I felt a bit of a cad questioning that child about the relations between her father and her stepmother. More or less inviting a daughter to put a rope round her father's neck. All the same, it had to be done. Murder is murder. And she's the person most likely to know the truth of things. I'm rather thankful, though, that she'd nothing to tell us in that line.'

Poirot said:

'Yes, I thought you were.'

Weston said with an embarrassed cough:

'By the way, Poirot, you went a bit far, I thought at the end. All that hands sinking into flesh business! Not quite the sort of idea to put into a kid's head.'

Hercule Poirot looked at him with thoughtful eyes. He said:

'So you thought I put ideas into her head?'

'Well, didn't you? Come now.'

Poirot shook his head.

Weston sheered away from the point. He said:

'On the whole we got very little useful stuff out of her. Except a more or less complete *alibi* for the Redfern woman. If they were together from half-past ten to a quarter to twelve that lets Christine Redfern out of it. Exit the jealous wife suspect.'

Poirot said:

'There are better reasons than that for leaving Mrs Redfern out of it. It would, I am convinced, be physically impossible and mentally impossible for her to strangle anyone. She is cold rather than warm blooded, capable of deep devotion and unswerving constancy, but not of hot blooded passion or rage. Moreover, her hands are far too small and delicate.'

Colgate said:

'I agree with M. Poirot. She's out of it. Dr Neasden says it was a full-sized pair of hands that throttled that dame.'

Weston said:

'Well, I suppose we'd better see the Redferns next. I expect he's recovered a bit from the shock now.'

III

Patrick Redfern had recovered full composure by now. He looked pale and haggard and suddenly very young, but his manner was quite composed.

'You are Mr Patrick Redfern of Crossgates, Seldon, Princes Risborough?'

'Yes.'

'How long had you known Mrs Marshall?'

Patrick Redfern hesitated, then said:

'Three months.'

Weston went on:

'Captain Marshall has told us that you and she met casually at a cocktail party. Is that right?'

'Yes, that's how it came about.'

Weston said:

'Captain Marshall has implied that until you both met down

here you did not know each other well. Is that the truth, Mr Redfern?'

Again Patrick Redfern hesitated a minute. Then he said:

'Well – not exactly. As a matter of fact I saw a fair amount of her one way and another.'

'Without Captain Marshall's knowledge?'

Redfern flushed slightly. He said:

'I don't know whether he knew about it or not.'

Hercule Poirot spoke. He murmured:

'And was it also without your wife's knowledge, Mr Redfern?'

'I believe I mentioned to my wife that I had met the famous Arlena Stuart.'

Poirot persisted.

'But she did not know how often you were seeing her?'

'Well, perhaps not.'

Weston said:

'Did you and Mrs Marshall arrange to meet down here?'

Redfern was silent a minute or two. Then he shrugged his shoulders.

'Oh well,' he said, 'I suppose it's bound to come out now. It's no good my fencing with you. I was crazy about the woman – mad – infatuated – anything you like. She wanted me to come down here. I demurred a bit and then I agreed. I – I – well, I would have agreed to do any mortal thing she liked. She had that kind of effect on people.'

Hercule Poirot murmured:

'You paint a very clear picture of her. She was the eternal Circe. Just that!'

Patrick Redfern said bitterly:

'She turned men into swine all right!' He went on: 'I'm being frank with you, gentlemen. I'm not going to hide anything. What's the use? As I say, I was infatuated with her. Whether she cared for me or not, I don't know. She pretended to, but I think she was one of those women who lose interest in a man once they've got him body and soul. She knew she'd got me all right. This morning, when I found her there on the beach, dead, it was as though' – he paused – 'as though something had hit me straight between the eyes. I was dazed – knocked out!'

Poirot leaned forward. 'And now?'

Patrick Redfern met his eyes squarely.

He said:

'I've told you the truth. What I want to ask is this – *how much of it has got to be made public*? It's not as though it could have any bearing on her death. And if it all comes out, it's going to be pretty rough on my wife.'

'Oh, I know,' he went on quickly. 'You think I haven't thought much about her up to now? Perhaps that's true. But, though I may sound the worst kind of hypocrite, the real truth is that I care for my wife – care for her very deeply. The other' – he twitched his shoulders – 'it was a madness – the kind of idiotic fool thing men do – but Christine is different. She's *real*. Badly as I've treated her, I've known all along, deep down, that she was the person who really counted.' He paused – sighed – and said rather pathetically: 'I wish I could make you believe that.'

Hercule Poirot leant forward. He said:

'But I do believe it. Yes, yes, I do believe it!'

Patrick Redfern looked at him gratefully. He said:

'Thank you.'

Colonel Weston cleared his throat. He said:

'You may take it, Mr Redfern, that we shall not go into irrelevancies. If your infatuation for Mrs Marshall played no part in the murder then there will be no point in dragging it into the case. But what you don't seem to realize is that that – er – intimacy – may have a very direct bearing on the murder. It might establish, you understand, a *motive* for the crime.'

Patrick Redfern said:

'Motive?'

Weston said:

'Yes, Mr Redfern, *motive*! Captain Marshall, perhaps, was unaware of the affair. Suppose that he suddenly found out?'

Redfern said:

'Oh God! You mean he got wise and – and killed her?'

The Chief Constable said rather dryly:

'That solution had not occurred to you?'

Redfern shook his head. He said:

'No – funny. I never thought of it. You see, Marshall's such a quiet chap. I – oh, it doesn't seem likely.'

Weston asked:

'What was Mrs Marshall's attitude to her husband in all this? Was she – well, uneasy – in case it should come to his ears? Or was she indifferent?'

Redfern said slowly:

'She was – a bit nervous. She didn't want him to suspect anything.'

'Did she seem afraid of him?'

'Afraid. No, I wouldn't say that.'

Poirot murmured:

'Excuse me, M. Redfern, there was not, at any time, the question of a divorce?'

Patrick Redfern shook his head decisively.

'Oh no, there was no question of anything like that. There was Christine, you see. And Arlena, I am sure, never thought of such a thing. She was perfectly satisfied married to Marshall. He's – well, rather a big bug in his way –' He smiled suddenly. 'County – all that sort of thing, and quite well off. She never thought of me as a possible *husband*. No, I was just one of a succession of poor mutts – just something to pass the time with. I knew that all along, and yet, queerly enough, it didn't alter my feeling towards her . . .'

His voice trailed off. He sat there thinking.

Weston recalled him to the needs of the moment.

'Now, Mr Redfern, had you any particular appointment with Mrs Marshall this morning?'

Patrick Redfern looked slightly puzzled.

He said:

'Not a particular appointment, no. We usually met every morning on the beach. We used to paddle about on floats.'

'Were you surprised not to find Mrs Marshall there this morning?'

'Yes, I was. Very surprised. I couldn't understand it at all.'

'What did you think?'

'Well, I didn't know what to think. I mean, all the time I thought she would be coming.'

'If she were keeping an appointment elsewhere you had no idea with whom that appointment might be?'

Patrick Redfern merely stared and shook his head.

'When you had a *rendezvous* with Mrs Marshall, where did you meet?'

'Well, sometimes I'd meet her in the afternoon down at Gull Cove. You see the sun is off Gull Cove in the afternoon and so there aren't usually many people there. We met there once or twice.'

'Never on the other cove? Pixy Cove?'

'No. You see Pixy Cove faces west and people go round there in boats or on floats in the afternoon. We never tried to meet in the morning. It would have been too noticeable. In the afternoon people go and have a sleep or mouch around and nobody knows much where any one else is.'

Weston nodded:

Patrick Redfern went on:

'After dinner, of course, on the fine nights, we used to go off for a stroll together to different parts of the island.'

Hercule Poirot murmured:

'Ah, yes!' and Patrick Redfern shot him an inquiring glance.

Weston said:

'Then you can give us no help whatsoever as to the cause that took Mrs Marshall to Pixy Cove this morning?'

Redfern shook his head. He said, and his voice sounded honestly bewildered:

'I haven't the faintest idea! It wasn't like Arlena.'

Weston said:

'Had she any friends down here staying in the neighbourhood?'

'Not that I know of. Oh, I'm sure she hadn't.'

'Now, Mr Redfern, I want you to think very carefully. You knew Mrs Marshall in London. You must be acquainted with various members of her circle. Is there anyone you know of who could have had a grudge against her? Someone, for instance, whom you may have supplanted in her fancy?'

Patrick Redfern thought for some minutes. Then he shook his head.

'Honestly,' he said. 'I can't think of anyone.'

Colonel Weston drummed with his fingers on the table.

He said at last:

'Well, that's that. We seem to be left with three possibilities. That of an unknown killer – some monomaniac – who happened to be in the neighbourhood – and that's a pretty tall order –'

Redfern said, interrupting:

'And yet surely, it's by far the most likely explanation.'

Weston shook his head. He said:

'This isn't one of the "lonely copse" murders. This cove place was pretty inaccessible. Either the man would have to come up from the causeway past the hotel, over the top of the island and down by that ladder contraption, or else he came there by boat. Either way is unlikely for a casual killing.'

Patrick Redfern said:

'You said there were three possibilities.'

'Um – yes,' said the Chief Constable. 'That's to say, there were two people on this island who had a motive for killing her. Her husband, for one, and your wife for another.'

Redfern stared at him. He looked dumbfounded. He said:

'My wife? Christine? D'you mean that *Christine* had anything to do with this?'

He got up and stood there stammering slightly in his incoherent haste to get the words out.

'You're mad – quite mad – Christine? Why, it's *impossible*. It's laughable!'

Weston said:

'All the same, Mr Redfern, jealousy is a very powerful motive. Women who are jealous lose control of themselves completely.'

Redfern said earnestly.

'Not Christine. She's – oh she's not like that. She was unhappy, yes. But she's not the kind of person to – Oh, there's no violence in her.'

Hercule Poirot nodded thoughtfully. Violence. The same word that Linda Marshall had used. As before, he agreed with the sentiment.

'Besides,' went on Redfern confidently. 'It would be absurd. Arlena was twice as strong physically as Christine. I doubt if Christine could strangle a kitten – certainly not a strong wiry creature like Arlena. And then Christine could never have got down that ladder to the beach. She has no head for that sort of thing. And – oh, the whole thing is fantastic!'

Colonel Weston scratched his ear tentatively.

'Well,' he said. 'Put like that it doesn't seem likely. I grant you that. But motive's the first thing we've got to look for.' He added: 'Motive and opportunity.'

IV

When Redfern had left the room, the Chief Constable observed with a slight smile:

'Didn't think it necessary to tell the fellow his wife had got an alibi. Wanted to hear what he'd have to say to the idea. Shook him up a bit, didn't it?'

Hercule Poirot murmured:

'The arguments he advanced were quite as strong as any alibi.'

'Yes. Oh! she didn't do it! She couldn't have done it – physically impossible as you said. Marshall *could* have done it – but apparently he didn't.'

Inspector Colgate coughed. He said:

'Excuse me, sir, I've been thinking about that alibi. It's possible, you know, if he'd thought this thing out, that those letters were got ready *beforehand*.'

Weston said:

'That's a good idea. We must look into –'

He broke off as Christine Redfern entered the room.

She was, as always, calm and a little precise in manner. She was wearing a white tennis frock and a pale blue pullover. It accentuated her fair, rather anaemic prettiness. Yet, Hercule Poirot thought to himself, it was neither a silly face nor a weak one. It had plenty of resolution, courage and good sense. He nodded appreciatively.

Colonel Weston thought:

'Nice little woman. Bit wishy-washy, perhaps. A lot too good for that philandering young ass of a husband of hers. Oh well, the boy's young. Women usually make a fool of you once!'

He said:

'Sit down, Mrs Redfern. We've got to go through a certain amount of routine, you see. Asking everybody for an account of their movements this morning. Just for our records.'

Christine Redfern nodded.

She said in her quiet precise voice.

'Oh yes, I quite understand. Where do you want me to begin?'

Hercule Poirot said:

'As early as possible, Madame. What did you do when you first got up this morning?'

Christine said:

'Let me see. On my way down to breakfast I went into Linda Marshall's room and fixed up with her to go to Gull Cove this morning. We agreed to meet in the lounge at half-past ten.'

Poirot asked:

'You did not bathe before breakfast, Madame?'

'No. I very seldom do.' She smiled. 'I like the sea well warmed before I get into it. I'm rather a chilly person.'

'But your husband bathes then?'

'Oh, yes. Nearly always.'

'And Mrs Marshall, she also?'

A change came over Christine's voice. It became cold and almost acrid.

She said:

'Oh no, Mrs Marshall was the sort of person who never made an appearance before the middle of the morning.'

With an air of confusion, Hercule Poirot said:

'Pardon, Madame, I interrupted you. You were saying that you went to Miss Linda Marshall's room. What time was that?'

'Let me see – half-past eight – no, a little later.'

'And was Miss Marshall up then?'

'Oh yes, she had been out.'

'Out?'

'Yes, she said she'd been bathing.'

There was a faint – a very faint note of embarrassment in Christine's voice. It puzzled Hercule Poirot.

Weston said:

'And then?'

'Then I went down to breakfast.'

'And after breakfast?'

'I went upstairs, collected my sketching box and sketching book and we started out.'

'You and Miss Linda Marshall?'

'Yes.'

'What time was that?'

'I think it was just on half-past ten.'

'And what did you do?'

'We went to Gull Cove. You know, the cove on the east side of the island. We settled ourselves there. I did a sketch and Linda sunbathed.'

'What time did you leave the cove?'

'At a quarter to twelve. I was playing tennis at twelve and had to change.'

'You had your watch with you?'

'No, as a matter of fact I hadn't. I asked Linda the time.'

'I see. And then?'

'I packed up my sketching things and went back to the hotel.'

Poirot said:

'And Mademoiselle Linda?'

'Linda? Oh, Linda went into the sea.'

Poirot said:

'Were you far from the sea where you were sitting?'

'Well, we were well above high-water mark. Just under the cliff – so that I could be a little in the shade and Linda in the sun.'

Poirot said:

'Did Linda Marshall actually enter the sea before you left the beach?'

Christine frowned a little in the effort to remember. She said:

'Let me see. She ran down the beach – I fastened my box – Yes, I heard her splashing in the waves as I was on the path up the cliff.'

'You are sure of that, Madame? That she really entered the sea?'

'Oh yes.'

She stared at him in surprise.

Colonel Weston also stared at him.

Then he said:

'Go on, Mrs Redfern.'

'I went back to the hotel, changed, and went to the tennis courts where I met the others.'

'Who were?'

'Captain Marshall, Mr Gardener and Miss Darnley. We played two sets. We were just going in again when the news came about – about Mrs Marshall.'

Hercule Poirot leant forward. He said:

'And what did you think, Madame, when you heard that news?'

'What did I think?'

Her face showed a faint distaste for the question.

'Yes.'

Christine Redfern said slowly:

'It was – a horrible thing to happen.'

'Ah, yes, your fastidiousness was revolted. I understand that. But what did it mean to *you* – personally?'

She gave him a quick look – a look of appeal. He responded to it. He said in a matter-of-fact voice.

'I am appealing to you, Madame, as a woman of intelligence with plenty of good sense and judgment. You had doubtless during your stay here formed an opinion of Mrs Marshall, of the kind of woman she was?'

Christine said cautiously:

'I suppose one always does that more or less when one is staying in hotels.'

'Certainly, it is the natural thing to do. So I ask you, Madame, were you really very surprised at the manner of her death?'

Christine said slowly:

'I think I see what you mean. No, I was not, perhaps, surprised. Shocked, yes. But she was the kind of woman –'

Poirot finished the sentence for her.

'She was the kind of woman to whom such a thing might happen . . . Yes, Madame, that is the truest and most significant thing that has been said in this room this morning. Laying all – er (he stressed it carefully) *personal* feeling aside, what did you really think of the late Mrs Marshall?'

Christine Redfern said calmly:

'Is it really worth while going into all that now?'

'I think it might be, yes.'

'Well, what shall I say?' Her fair skin was suddenly suffused with colour. The careful poise of her manner was relaxed. For a short space the natural raw woman looked out. 'She's the kind of woman that to my mind is absolutely worthless! She did nothing to justify her existence. She had no mind – no brains. She thought of nothing but men and clothes and admiration. Useless, a parasite!

She was attractive to men, I suppose – Oh, of course, she was. And she lived for that kind of life. And so, I suppose, I wasn't really surprised at her coming to a sticky end. She was the sort of woman who would be mixed up with everything sordid – blackmail – jealousy – violence – every kind of crude emotion. She – she appealed to the worst in people.'

She stopped, panting a little. Her rather short top lip lifted itself in a kind of fastidious disgust. It occured to Colonel Weston that you could not have found a more complete contrast to Arlena Stuart than Christine Redfern. It also occurred to him that if you were married to Christine Redfern, the atmosphere might be so rarefied that the Arlena Stuarts of this world would hold a particular attraction for you.

And then, immediately following on these thoughts, a single word out of the words she had spoken fastened on his attention with particular intensity.

He leaned forward and said:

'Mrs Redfern, why, in speaking of her, did you mention the word *blackmail*?'

CHAPTER 7

I

Christine stared at him, not seeming at once to take in what he meant. She answered almost mechanically.

'I suppose – because she *was* being blackmailed. She was the sort of person who would be.'

Colonel Weston said earnestly:

'But – do you know she was being blackmailed?'

A faint colour rose in the girl's cheeks. She said rather awkwardly:

'As a matter of fact I do happen to know it. I – I overheard something.'

'Will you explain, Mrs Redfern?'

Flushing still more, Christine Redfern said:

'I – I didn't mean to overhear. It was an accident. It was two – no, three nights ago. We were playing bridge.' She turned towards Poirot. 'You remember? My husband and I, M. Poirot and Miss Darnley. I was dummy. It was very stuffy in the card room, and I slipped out of the window for a breath of fresh air. I went down towards the beach and I suddenly heard voices. One – it was Arlena Marshall's – I knew it at once – said: "It's no good pressing me. I can't get any more money now. My husband will suspect something." And then a man's voice said: "I'm not taking any excuses. You've got to cough up." And then Arlena Marshall said: "You blackmailing brute!" And the man said: "Brute or not, you'll pay up, my lady."'

Christine paused.

'I'd turned back and a minute after Arlena Marshall rushed past me. She looked – well, frightfully upset.'

Weston said:

'And the man? Do you know who he was?'

Christine Redfern shook her head.

She said:

'He was keeping his voice low. I barely heard what he said.'

'It didn't suggest the voice to you of anyone you knew?'

She thought again, but once more shook her head. She said:

'No, I don't know. It was gruff and low. It – oh, it might have been anybody's.'

Colonel Weston said:

'Thank you, Mrs Redfern.'

II

When the door had closed behind Christine Redfern Inspector Colgate said:

'Now we are getting somewhere!'

Weston said:

'You think so, eh?'

'Well, it's suggestive, sir, you can't get away from it. Somebody in this hotel was blackmailing the lady.'

Poirot murmured:

'But it is not the wicked blackmailer who lies dead. It is the victim.'

'That's a bit of a setback, I agree,' said the Inspector. 'Black-mailers aren't in the habit of bumping off their victims. But what it does give us is this, it suggests a reason for Mrs Marshall's curious behaviour this morning. She'd got a *rendezvous* with this fellow who was blackmailing her, and she didn't want either her husband or Redfern to know about it.'

'It certainly explains that point,' agreed Poirot.

Inspector Colgate went on:

'And think of the place chosen. The very spot for the purpose. The lady goes off in her float. That's natural enough. It's what she does every day. She goes round to Pixy Cove where no one ever goes in the morning and which will be a nice quiet place for an interview.'

Poirot said:

'But yes, I too was struck by that point. It is as you say, an ideal spot for a *rendezvous*. It is deserted, it is only accessible from the land side by descending a vertical steel ladder which is not everybody's money, *bien entendu*. Moreover most of the beach is invisible from above because of the overhanging cliff. And it has another advantage. Mr Redfern told me of that one day. There is a cave on it, the entrance to which is not easy to find but where anyone could wait unseen.'

Weston said:

'Of course, the Pixy's Cave – remember hearing about it.'

Inspector Colgate said:

'Haven't heard it spoken of for years, though. We'd better have a look inside it. Never know, we might find a pointer of some kind.'

Weston said:

'Yes, you're right, Colgate, we've got the solution to part one of the puzzle. *Why did Mrs Marshall go to Pixy's Cove?* We want the other half of that solution, though. *Who did she go there to meet?* Presumably someone staying in this hotel. None of them fitted as a lover – but a blackmailer's a different proposition.'

He drew the register towards him.

'Excluding the waiters, boots, etc., whom I don't think likely, we've got the following. The American – Gardener, Major Barry, Mr Horace Blatt, and the Reverend Stephen Lane.'

Inspector Colgate said:

'We can narrow it down a bit, sir. We might almost rule out the American, I think. He was on the beach all the morning. That's so, isn't it, M. Poirot?'

Poirot replied:

'He was absent for a short time when he fetched a skein of wool for his wife.'

Colgate said:

'Oh well, we needn't count that.'

Weston said:

'And what about the other three?'

'Major Barry went out at ten o'clock this morning. He returned at one-thirty. Mr Lane was earlier still. He breakfasted at eight. Said he was going for a tramp. Mr Blatt went off for a sail at nine-thirty same as he does most days. Neither of them are back yet.'

'A sail, eh?' Colonel Weston's voice was thoughtful.

Inspector Colgate's voice was responsive. He said:

'Might fit in rather well, sir.'

Weston said:

'Well, we'll have a word with this Major bloke – and let me see, who else is there? Rosamund Darnley. And there's the Brewster woman who found the body with Redfern. What's she like, Colgate?'

'Oh, a sensible party, sir. No nonsense about her.'

'She didn't express any opinions on the death?'

The Inspector shook his head.

'I don't think she'll have anything more to tell us, sir, but we'll have to make sure. Then there are the Americans.'

Colonel Weston nodded. He said: 'Let's have 'em all in and get it over as soon as possible. Never know, might learn something. About the blackmailing stunt if about nothing else.'

III

Mr and Mrs Gardener came into the presence of authority together.

Mrs Gardener explained immediately.

'I hope you'll understand how it is, Colonel Weston (that is the name, I think?).' Reassured on this point she went on: 'But this has been a very bad shock to me and Mr Gardener is always very, very careful of my health –'

Mr Gardener here interpolated:

'Mrs Gardener,' he said, 'is very sensitive.'

'– and he said to me, "Why, Carrie," he said, "naturally I'm coming right along with you." It's not that we haven't the highest admiration for British police methods because we have. I've been told that British police procedure is most refined and delicate, and I've never doubted it, and certainly when I once had a bracelet missing at the Savoy Hotel nothing could have been more lovely and sympathetic than the young man who came to see me about it, and, of course, I hadn't really lost the bracelet at all, but just mislaid it; that's the worst of rushing about so much, it makes you kind of forgetful where you put things –' Mrs Gardener paused, inhaled gently and started off again. 'And what I say is, and I know Mr Gardener agrees with me, that we're only too anxious to do anything to help the British police in every way. So go right ahead and ask me anything at all you want to know –'

Colonel Weston opened his mouth to comply with this invitation, but had momentarily to postpone speech while Mrs Gardener went on.

'That's what I said, Odell, isn't it? And that's so, isn't it?'

'Yes, darling,' said Mr Gardener.

Colonel Weston spoke hastily.

'I understand, Mrs Gardener, that you and your husband were on the beach all the morning?'

For once Mr Gardener was able to get in first.

'That's so,' he said.

'Why, certainly we were,' said Mrs Gardener. 'And a lovely peaceful morning it was, just like any other morning if you get me, perhaps even more so, and not the slightest idea in our minds of what was happening round the corner on that lonely beach.'

'Did you see Mrs Marshall at all today?'

'We did not. And I said to Odell, why wherever can Mrs Marshall have got to this morning? I said. And first her husband coming looking for her and then that good-looking young man, Mr Redfern, and so impatient he was, just sitting there on the beach scowling at everyone and everything. And I said to myself why, when he has that nice pretty little wife of his own, must he go running after that dreadful woman? Because that's just what I felt she was. I always felt that about her, didn't I, Odell?'

'Yes, darling.'

'However that nice Captain Marshall came to marry such a woman I just cannot imagine and with that nice young daughter growing up, and it's so important for girls to have the right influence. Mrs Marshall was not at all the right person – no breeding at all – and I should say a very animal nature. Now if Captain Marshall had had any sense he'd have married Miss Darnley, who's a very very charming woman and a very distinguished one. I must say I admire the way she's gone straight ahead and built up a first-class business as she has. It takes brains to do a thing like that – and you've only got to look at Rosamund Darnley to see she's just frantic with brains. She could plan and carry out any mortal thing she liked. I just admire that woman more than I can say. And I said to Mr Gardener the other day that any one could see she was very much in love with Captain Marshall – crazy about him was what I said, didn't I, Odell?'

'Yes, darling.'

'It seems they knew each other as children, and why now, who knows, it may all come right after all with that woman out of the way. I'm not a narrow-minded woman, Colonel Weston, and it isn't that I disapprove of the stage as such – why, quite a lot of my best friends are actresses – but I've said to Mr Gardener all along that there was something evil about that woman. And you see, I've been proved right.'

She paused triumphantly.

The lips of Hercule Poirot quivered in a little smile. His eyes met for a minute the shrewd grey eyes of Mr Gardener.

Colonel Weston said rather desperately:

'Well, thank you, Mrs Gardener. I suppose there's nothing that either of you has noticed since you've been here that might have a bearing upon the case?'

'Why no, I don't think so.' Mr Gardener spoke with a slow drawl. 'Mrs Marshall was around with young Redfern most of the time – but everybody can tell you that.'

'What about her husband? Did he mind, do you think?'

Mr Gardener said cautiously:

'Captain Marshall is a very reserved man.'

Mrs Gardener confirmed this by saying:

'Why, yes, he is a real Britisher!'

IV

On the slightly apoplectic countenance of Major Barry various emotions seemed contending for mastery. He was endeavouring to look properly horrified but could not subdue a kind of shamefaced gusto.

He was saying in his hoarse, slightly wheezy voice:

'Glad to help you any way I can. 'Course I don't know anythin' about it – nothin' at all. Not acquainted with the parties. But I've knocked about a bit in my time. Lived a lot in the East, you know. And I can tell you that after being in an Indian hill station what you don't know about human nature isn't worth knowin'.'

He paused, took a breath and was off again.

'Matter of fact this business reminds me of a case in Simla. Fellow called Robinson, or was it Falconer? Anyway he was in the East Wilts, or was it the North Surreys? Can't remember now, and anyway it doesn't matter. Quiet chap, you know, great reader – mild as milk you'd have said. Went for his wife one evening in their bungalow. Got her by the throat. She'd been carryin' on with some feller or other and he'd got wise to it. By Jove, he nearly did for her! It was touch and go. Surprised us all! Didn't think he had it in him.'

Hercule Poirot murmured:

'And you see there an analogy to the death of Mrs Marshall?'

'Well, what I mean to say – strangled, you know. Same idea. Feller suddenly sees red!'

Poirot said:

'You think that Captain Marshall felt like that?'

'Oh, look here, I never said that.' Major Barry's face went even redder. 'Never said anything about Marshall. Thoroughly nice chap. Wouldn't say a word against him for the world.'

Poirot murmured:

'Ah, *pardon*, but you *did* refer to the natural reactions of a husband.'

Major Barry said:

'Well, I mean to say, I should think she'd been pretty hot stuff. Eh? Got young Redfern on a string all right. And there were probably others before him. But the funny thing is, you know, that husbands are a dense lot. Amazin'. I've been surprised by it again and again. They see a feller sweet on their wife but they don't see that *she's* sweet on *him*! Remember a case like that in Poona. Very pretty woman, Jove, she led her husband a dance –'

Colonel Weston stirred a little restively. He said:

'Yes, yes, Major Barry. For the moment we've just got to establish the facts. You don't know of anything personally – that you've seen or noticed that might help us in this case?'

'Well, really, Weston, I can't say I do. Saw her and young Redfern one afternoon on Gull Cove' – here he winked knowingly and gave a deep hoarse chuckle – 'very pretty it was, too. But it's not evidence of that kind you're wanting. Ha, ha!'

'You did not see Mrs Marshall at all this morning?'

'Didn't see anybody this morning. Went over to St Loo. Just my luck. Sort of place here where nothin' happens for months and when it does you miss it!'

The Major's voice held a ghoulish regret.

Colonel Weston prompted him.

'You went to St Loo, you say?'

'Yes, wanted to do some telephonin'. No telephone here and that post-office place at Leathercombe Bay isn't very private.'

'Were your telephone calls of a very private nature?'

The Major winked again cheerfully.

'Well, they were and they weren't. Wanted to get through to a pal of mine and get him to put somethin' on a horse. Couldn't get through to him, worse luck.'

'Where did you telephone from?'

'Call box in the G.P.O. at St Loo. Then on the way back I got lost – these confounded lanes – twistin' and turnin' all over the place. Must have wasted an hour over that at least. Damned confusing part of the world. I only got back half an hour ago.'

Colonel Weston said:

'Speak to anyone or meet anyone in St Loo?'

Major Barry said with a chuckle:

'Wantin' me to prove an alibi? Can't think of anythin' useful. Saw about fifty thousand people in St Loo – but that's not to say they'll remember seein' me.'

The Chief Constable said:

'We have to ask these things, you know.'

'Right you are. Call on me at any time. Glad to help you. Very fetchin' woman, the deceased. Like to help you catch the feller who did it. The Lonely Beach Murder – bet you that's what the papers will call it. Reminds me of the time –'

It was Inspector Colgate who firmly nipped this latest reminiscence in the bud and manoeuvred the garrulous Major out of the door.

Coming back he said:

'Difficult to check up on anything in St Loo. It's the middle of the holiday season.'

The Chief Constable said:

'Yes, we can't take him off the list. Not that I seriously believe he's implicated. Dozens of old bores like him going about. Remember one or two of them in my army days. Still – he's a possibility. I leave all that to you, Colgate. Check what time he took the car out – petrol – all that. It's humanly possible that he parked the car somewhere in a lonely spot, walked back here and went to the cove. But it doesn't seem feasible to me. He'd have run too much risk of being seen.'

Colgate nodded.

He said:

'Of course there are a good many charabancs here today. Fine day. They start arriving round about half-past eleven. High tide was at seven. Low tide would be about one o'clock. People would be spread out over the sands and the causeway.'

Weston said:

'Yes. But he'd have to come up from the causeway past the hotel.'

'Not right past it. He could branch off on the path that leads up over the top of the island.'

Weston said doubtfully:

'I'm not saying that he mightn't have done it without being seen. Practically all the hotel guests were on the bathing beach except for Mrs Redfern and the Marshall girl who were down in Gull Cove, and the beginning of that path would only be overlooked by a few rooms of the hotel and there are plenty of chances against anyone looking out of those windows just at that moment. For the matter of that, I dare say it's possible for a man to walk up to the hotel, through the lounge and out again without anyone happening to see him. But what I say is, he couldn't *count* on no one seeing him.'

Colgate said:

'He could have gone round to the cove by boat.'

Weston nodded. He said:

'That's much sounder. If he'd had a boat handy in one of the coves nearby, he could have left the car, rowed or sailed to Pixy Cove, done the murder, rowed back, picked up the car and arrived back with this tale about having been to St Loo and lost his way – a story that he'd know would be pretty hard to disprove.'

'You're right, sir.'

The Chief Constable said:

'Well, I leave it to you, Colgate. Comb the neighbourhood thoroughly. You know what to do. We'd better see Miss Brewster now.'

V

Emily Brewster was not able to add anything of material value to what they already knew.

Weston said after she had repeated her story:

'And there's nothing you know of that could help us in any way?'

Emily Brewster said shortly:

'Afraid not. It's a distressing business. However, I expect you'll soon get to the bottom of it.'

Weston said:

'I hope so, I'm sure.'

Emily Brewster said dryly:

'Ought not to be difficult.'

'Now what do you mean by that, Miss Brewster?'

'Sorry. Wasn't attempting to teach you your business. All I meant was that with a woman of that kind it ought to be easy enough.'

Hercule Poirot murmured:

'That is your opinion?'

Emily Brewster snapped out:

'Of course. *De mortuis nil nisi bonum* and all that, but you can't get away from *facts*. That woman was a bad lot through and through. You've only got to hunt round a bit in her unsavoury past.'

Hercule Poirot said gently:

'You did not like her?'

'I know a bit too much about her.' In answer to the inquiring looks she went on: 'My first cousin married one of the Erskines. You've probably heard that that woman induced old Sir Robert when he was in his dotage to leave most of his fortune to her away from his own family.'

Colonel Weston said:

'And the family – er – resented that?'

'Naturally. His association with her was a scandal anyway, and on top of that, to leave her a sum like fifty thousand pounds shows just the kind of woman she was. I dare say I sound hard, but in my opinion the Arlena Stuarts of this world deserve very little sympathy. I know of something else too – a young fellow who lost his head about her completely – he'd always been a bit wild, naturally his association with her pushed him over the edge. He did something rather fishy with some shares – solely to get money to spend on her – and only just managed to escape prosecution. That woman contaminated everyone she met. Look at the way she was ruining young Redfern. No, I'm afraid I can't have any regret for her death – though of course it would have been better if she'd drowned herself, or fallen over a cliff. Strangling is rather unpleasant.'

'And you think the murderer was someone out of her past?'

'Yes, I do.'

'Someone who came from the mainland with no one seeing him?'

'Why should any one see him? We were all on the beach. I gather the Marshall child and Christine Redfern were down on Gull Cove out of the way. Captain Marshall was in his room in the hotel. Then who on earth was there to see him except possibly Miss Darnley.'

'Where was Miss Darnley?'

'Sitting up on the cutting at the top of the cliff. Sunny Ledge it's called. We saw her there, Mr Redfern and I, when we were rowing round the island.'

Colonel Weston said:

'You may be right, Miss Brewster.'

Emily Brewster said positively:

'I'm sure I'm right. When a woman's neither more nor less than a nasty mess, then she herself will provide the best possible clue. Don't you agree with me, M. Poirot?'

Hercule Poirot looked up. His eyes met her confident grey ones. He said:

'Oh, yes – I agree with that which you have just this minute said. Arlena Marshall herself is the best, the only clue, to her own death.'

Miss Brewster said sharply:

'Well, then!'

She stood there, an erect sturdy figure, her cool self-confident glance going from one man to the other.

Colonel Weston said:

'You may be sure, Miss Brewster, that any clue there may be in Mrs Marshall's past life will not be overlooked.'

Emily Brewster went out.

VI

Inspector Colgate shifted his position at the table. He said in a thoughtful voice:

'She's a determined one, she is. And she'd got her knife into the dead lady, proper, she had.'

He stopped a minute and said reflectively:

'It's a pity in a way that she's got a cast-iron alibi for the whole morning. Did you notice her hands, sir? As big as a man's. And she's a hefty woman – as strong and stronger than many a man, I'd say . . .'

He paused again. His glance at Poirot was almost pleading.

'And you say she never left the beach this morning, M. Poirot?'

Slowly Poirot shook his head. He said:

'My dear Inspector, she came down to the beach before Mrs Marshall could have reached Pixy Cove and she was within my sight until she set off with Mr Redfern in the boat.'

Inspector Colgate said gloomily:

'Then that washes her out.'

He seemed upset about it.

VII

As always, Hercule Poirot felt a keen sense of pleasure at the sight of Rosamund Darnley.

Even to a bare police inquiry into the ugly facts of murder she brought a distinction of her own.

She sat down opposite Colonel Weston and turned a grave and intelligent face to him.

She said:

'You want my name and address? Rosamund Anne Darnley. I carry on a dressmaking business under the name of Rose Mond Ltd at 622 Brook Street.'

'Thank you, Miss Darnley. Now can you tell us anything that may help us?'

'I don't really think I can.'

'Your own movements —'

'I had breakfast about nine-thirty. Then I went up to my room and collected some books and my sunshade and went out to Sunny Ledge. That must have been about twenty-five past ten. I came back to the hotel about ten minutes to twelve, went up and got my tennis racquet and went out to the tennis courts, where I played tennis until lunch-time.'

'You were in the cliff recess, called by the hotel Sunny Ledge, from about half-past ten until ten minutes to twelve?'

'Yes.'

'Did you see Mrs Marshall at all this morning?'

'No.'

'Did you see her from the cliff as she paddled her float round to Pixy Cove?'

'No, she must have gone by before I got there.'

'Did you notice anyone on a float or in a boat at all this morning?'

'No, I don't think I did. You see, I was reading. Of course I looked up from my book from time to time, but as it happened the sea was quite bare each time I did so.'

'You didn't even notice Mr Redfern and Miss Brewster when they went round?'

'No.'

'You were, I think, acquainted with Mr Marshall?'

'Captain Marshall is an old family friend. His family and mine lived next door to each other. I had not seen him, however, for a good many years – it must be something like twelve years.'

'And Mrs Marshall?'

'I'd never exchanged half a dozen words with her until I met her here.'

'Were Captain and Mrs Marshall, as far as you knew, on good terms with each other?'

'On perfectly good terms, I should say.'

'Was Captain Marshall very devoted to his wife?'

Rosamund said:

'He may have been. I can't really tell you anything about that. Captain Marshall is rather old-fashioned – he hasn't got the modern habit of shouting matrimonial woes upon the house-top.'

'Did you like Mrs Marshall, Miss Darnley?'

'No.'

The monosyllable came quietly and evenly. It sounded what it was – a simple statement of fact.

'Why was that?'

A half smile came to Rosamund's lips. She said:

'Surely you've discovered that Arlena Marshall was not popular with her own sex? She was bored to death with women and showed it. Nevertheless I should like to have had the dressing of her. She had a great gift for clothes. Her clothes were always just right and she wore them well. I should like to have had her as a client.'

'She spent a good deal on clothes?'

'She must have done. But then she had money of her own and of course Captain Marshall is quite well off.'

'Did you ever hear or did it ever occur to you that Mrs Marshall was being blackmailed, Miss Darnley?'

A look of intense astonishment came over Rosamund Darnley's expressive face.

She said:

'Blackmailed? Arlena?'

'The idea seems to surprise you.'

'Well, yes, it does rather. It seems so incongruous.'

'But surely it is possible?'

'Everything's possible, isn't it? The world soon teaches one that. But I wondered what any one could blackmail Arlena about?'

'There are certain things, I suppose, that Mrs Marshall might be anxious should not come to her husband's ears?'

'We-ll, yes.'

She explained the doubt in her voice by saying with a half smile:

'I sound sceptical, but then, you see, Arlena was rather notorious in her conduct. She never made much of a pose of respectability.'

'You think, then, that her husband was aware of her – intimacies with other people?'

There was a pause. Rosamund was frowning. She spoke at last in a slow, reluctant voice. She said:

'You know, I don't really know what to think. I've always assumed that Kenneth Marshall accepted his wife, quite frankly, for what she was. That he had no illusions about her. But it may not be so.'

'He may have believed in her absolutely?'

Rosamund said with semi-exasperation:

'Men are such fools. And Kenneth Marshall is unworldly under his sophisticated manner. He *may* have believed in her blindly. He may have thought she was just – admired.'

'And you know of no one – that is, you have heard of no one who was likely to have had a grudge against Mrs Marshall?'

Rosamund Darnley smiled. She said:

'Only resentful wives. And I presume, since she was strangled, that it was a man who killed her.'

'Yes.'

Rosamund said thoughtfully:

'No, I can't think of any one. But then I probably shouldn't know. You'll have to ask someone in her own intimate set.'

'Thank you, Miss Darnley.'

Rosamund turned a little in her chair. She said:

'Hasn't M. Poirot any questions to ask?'

Her faintly ironic smile flashed out at him.

Hercule Poirot smiled and shook his head.

He said:

'I can think of nothing.'

Rosamund Darnley got up and went out.

CHAPTER 8

I

They were standing in the bedroom that had been Arlena Marshall's.

Two big bay windows gave on to a balcony that overlooked the bathing beach and the sea beyond. Sunshine poured into the room, flashing over the bewildering array of bottles and jars on Arlena's dressing-table.

Here there was every kind of cosmetic and unguent known to beauty parlours. Amongst this panoply of woman's affairs three men moved purposefully. Inspector Colgate went about shutting and opening drawers.

Presently he gave a grunt. He had come upon a packet of folded letters. He and Weston ran through them together.

Hercule Poirot had moved to the wardrobe. He opened the door of the hanging cupboard and looked at the multiplicity of gowns and sports suits that hung there. He opened the other side. Foamy lingerie lay in piles. On a wide shelf were hats. Two more beach cardboard hats in lacquer red and pale yellow – a Big Hawaiian straw hat – another of drooping dark-blue linen and three or four little absurdities for which, no doubt, several guiness had been paid apiece – a kind of beret in dark blue – a tuft, no more, of black velvet – a pale grey turban.

Hercule Poirot stood scanning them – a faintly indulgent smile came to his lips. He murmured:

'*Les femmes!*'

Colonel Weston was refolding the letters.

'Three from young Redfern,' he said. 'Damned young ass. He'll learn not to write letters to women in a few more years. Women always keep letters and then swear they've burnt them. There's one other letter here. Same line of country.'

He held it out and Poirot took it.

Darling Arlena, – God, I feel blue. To be going out to China – and perhaps not seeing you again for years and years. I didn't know any man could go on feeling crazy about a woman like I feel about you. Thanks for the cheque. They won't prosecute now. It was a near shave, though, and all because I wanted to make big money for you. Can you forgive me? I wanted to set diamonds in your ears – your lovely ears – and clasp great milk-white pearls round your throat, only they say pearls are no good nowadays. A fabulous emerald, then? Yes, that's the thing. A great emerald, cool and green and full of hidden fire. Don't forget me – but you won't, I know. You're mine – always.

Goodbye – goodbye – goodbye.

J.N.

Inspector Colgate said:

'Might be worth while to find out if J.N. really did go to China. Otherwise – well, he might be the person we're looking for. Crazy about the woman, idealizing her, suddenly finding out he'd been played for a sucker. It sounds to me as though this is the boy Miss Brewster mentioned. Yes, I think this might be useful.'

Hercule Poirot nodded. He said: 'Yes, that letter is important. I find it very important.'

He turned round and stared at the room – at the bottles on the dressing-table – at the open wardrobe and at a big Pierrot doll that lolled insolently on the bed.

They went into Kenneth Marshall's room.

It was next door to his wife's but with no communicating door and no balcony. It faced the same way and had two windows, but it was much smaller. Between the two windows a gilt mirror hung on the wall. In the corner beyond the right-hand window was the dressing-table. On it were two ivory brushes, a clothes brush and a bottle of hair lotion. In the corner by the left-hand window was a writing-table. An open typewriter stood on it and papers were ranged in a stack beside it.

Colgate went through them rapidly.

He said:

'All seems straightforward enough. Ah, here's the letter he mentioned this morning. Dated the 24th – that's yesterday. And here's the envelope postmarked Leathercombe Bay this morning. Seems all square. Now we'll have an idea if he could have prepared that answer of his beforehand.

He sat down.

Colonel Weston said:

'We'll leave you to it, for a moment. We'll just glance through the rest of the rooms. Everyone's been kept out of this corridor until now, and they're getting a bit restive about it.'

They went next into Linda Marshall's room. It faced east, looking out over the rocks down to the sea below.

Weston gave a glance round. He murmured:

'Don't suppose there's anything to see here. But it's possible Marshall might have put something in his daughter's room that he didn't want us to find. Not likely, though. It isn't as though there had been a weapon or anything to get rid of.'

He went out again.

Hercule Poirot stayed behind. He found something that interested him in the grate. Something had been burnt there recently. He knelt down, working patiently. He laid out his finds on a sheet of paper. A large irregular blob of candle grease – some fragments of green paper or cardboard, possibly a pull-off calendar for with it was an unburnt fragment bearing a large figure 5 and a scrap of printing . . . *noble deeds* . . . There was also an ordinary pin and some burnt animal matter which might have been hair.

Poirot arranged them neatly in a row and stared at them.

He murmured:

'*Do noble deeds, not dream them all day long. C'est possible.* But what is one to make of this collection? *C'est fantastique!*'

And then he picked up the pin and his eyes grew sharp and green.

He murmured:

'*Pour l'amour de Dieu!* Is it possible?'

Hercule Poirot got up from where he had been kneeling by the grate.

Slowly he looked round the room and this time there was an entirely new expression on his face. It was grave and almost stern.

To the left of the mantelpiece there were some shelves with a row of books. Hercule Poirot looked thoughtfully along the titles.

A Bible, a battered copy of Shakespeare's plays, *The Marriage of William Ashe*, by Mrs Humphry Ward. *The Young Stepmother*, by Charlotte Yonge. *The Shropshire Lad*. Eliot's *Murder in the Cathedral*. Bernard Shaw's *St Joan*. *Gone With the Wind*, by Margaret Mitchell. *The Burning Court*, by Dickson Carr.

Poirot took out two books. *The Young Stepmother* and *William Ashe*, and glanced inside at the blurred stamp affixed to the title page. As he was about to replace them, his eye caught sight of a book that had been shoved behind the other books. It was a small dumpy volume bound in brown calf.

He took it out and opened it. Very slowly he nodded his head.

He murmured:

'So I was right . . . Yes, I was right. But for the other – is that possible too? No, it is not possible, unless . . .'

He stayed there, motionless, stroking his moustaches whilst his mind ranged busily over the problem.

He said again, softly:

'Unless –'

II

Colonel Weston looked in at the door.

'Hullo, Poirot, still there?'

'I arrive. I arrive,' cried Poirot.

He hurried out into the corridor.

The room next to Linda's was that of the Redferns.

Poirot looked into it, noting automatically the trace of two different individualities – a neatness and tidiness which he associated with Christine, and a picturesque disorder which was characteristic of Patrick. Apart from these sidelights on personality the room did not interest him.

Next to it again was Rosamund Darnley's room, and here he lingered for a moment in the sheer pleasure of the owner's personality.

He noted the few books that lay on the table next to the bed, the expensive simplicity of the toilet set on the dressing-table. And there came gently to his nostrils the elusive expensive perfume that Rosamund Darnley used.

Next to Rosamund Darnley's room at the northern end of the

corridor was an open window leading to a balcony from which an outside stair led down to the rocks below.

Weston said:

'That's the way people go down to bathe before breakfast – that is, if they bathe off the rocks as most of them do.'

Interest came into Hercule Poirot's eyes. He stepped outside and looked down.

Below, a path led to steps cut zigzag leading down the rocks to the sea. There was also a path that led round the hotel to the left. He said:

'One could go down these stairs, go to the left round the hotel and join the main path up from the causeway.'

Weston nodded. He amplified Poirot's statement.

'One could go right across the island without going through the hotel at all.' He added: 'But one might still be seen from a window.'

'What window?'

'Two of the public bathrooms look out that way – north – and the staff bathroom, and the cloakrooms on the ground floor. Also the billiard room.'

Poirot nodded. He said:

'And all the former have frosted glass windows, and one does not play billiards on a fine morning.'

'Exactly.'

Weston paused and said:

'If he did it, that's the way he went.'

'You mean Captain Marshall?'

'Yes. Blackmail, or no blackmail. I still feel it points to him. And his manner – well, his manner is unfortunate.'

Hercule Poirot said dryly:

'Perhaps – but a manner does not make a murderer!'

Weston said:

'Then you think he's out of it?'

Poirot shook his head. He said:

'No, I would not say that.'

Weston said:

'We'll see what Colgate can make out of the typewriting alibi. In the meantime I've got the chambermaid of this floor waiting to be interviewed. A good deal may depend on her evidence.'

The chambermaid was a woman of thirty, brisk, efficient and intelligent. Her answers came readily.

Captain Marshall had come up to his room not long after ten-thirty. She was then finishing the room. He had asked her to be as quick as possible. She had not seen him come back but she had heard the sound of the typewriter a little later. She put it at about five minutes to eleven. She was then in Mr and Mrs Redfern's room. After she had done that she moved on to Miss Darnley's room at the end of the corridor. She could not hear the typewriter from there. She went to Miss Darnley's room, as near as she could say, at just after eleven o'clock. She remembered hearing Leathercombe Church strike the hour as she went in. At a quarter-past eleven she had gone downstairs for her eleven o'clock cup of tea and 'snack'. Afterwards she had gone to do the rooms in the other wing of the hotel. In answer to the Chief Constable's question she explained that she had done the rooms in this corridor in the following order:

Miss Linda Marshall's, the two public bathrooms, Mrs Marshall's room and private bath, Captain Marshall's room. Mr and Mrs Redfern's room and private bath, Miss Darnley's room and private bath. Captain Marshall's and Miss Marshall's rooms had no adjoining bathrooms.

During the time she was in Miss Darnley's room and bathroom she had not heard any one pass the door or go out by the staircase to the rocks, but it was quite likely she wouldn't have heard if any one went quietly.

Weston then directed his questions to the subject of Mrs Marshall.

No, Mrs Marshall wasn't one for rising early as a rule. She, Gladys Narracott, had been surprised to find the door open and Mrs Marshall gone down at just after ten. Something quite unusual, that was.

'Did Mrs Marshall always have her breakfast in bed?'

'Oh yes, sir, always. Not very much of it either. Just tea and orange juice and one piece of toast. Slimming like so many ladies.'

No, she hadn't noticed anything unusual in Mrs Marshall's manner that morning. She'd seemed quite as usual.

Hercule Poirot murmured:

'What did you think of Mrs Marshall, Mademoiselle?'

Gladys Narracott stared at him. She said:

'Well, that's hardly for me to say, is it, sir?'

'But yes, it is for you to say. We are anxious – very anxious – to hear your impression.'

Gladys gave a slightly uneasy glance towards the Chief Constable, who endeavoured to make his face sympathetic and approving, though actually he felt slightly embarrassed by his foreign colleague's methods of approach. He said:

'Er – yes, certainly. Go ahead.'

For the first time Gladys Narracott's brisk efficiency deserted her. Her fingers fumbled with her print dress. She said:

'Well, Mrs Marshall – she wasn't exactly a lady, as you might say. What I mean is she was more like an actress.'

Colonel Weston said:

'She was an actress.'

'Yes, sir, that's what I'm saying. She just went on exactly as she felt like it. She didn't – well, she didn't trouble to be polite if she wasn't feeling polite. And she'd be all smiles one minute and then, if she couldn't find something or the bell wasn't answered at once or her laundry wasn't back, well, be downright rude and nasty about it. None of us you might say *liked* her. But her clothes were beautiful, and, of course, she was a very handsome lady, so it was only natural she should be admired.'

Colonel Weston said:

'I am sorry to have to ask you what I am going to ask you, but it is a very vital matter. Can you tell me how things were between her and her husband?'

Gladys Narracott hesitated a minute.

She said:

'You don't – it wasn't – you don't think as *he* did it?'

Hercule Poirot said quickly:

'Do you?'

'Oh! I wouldn't like to think so. He's such a nice gentleman, Captain Marshall. He couldn't do a thing like that – I'm sure he couldn't.'

'But you are *not* very sure – I hear it in your voice.'

Gladys Narracott said reluctantly:

'You do read such things in the papers! When there's jealousy.

If there's been goings on – and, of course, everyone's been talking about it – about her and Mr Redfern, I mean. And Mrs Redfern such a nice quiet lady! It does seem a shame! And Mr Redfern's a nice gentleman too, but it seems men can't help themselves when it's a lady like Mrs Marshall – one who's used to having her own way. Wives have to put up with a lot, I'm sure.' She sighed and paused. 'But if Captain Marshall found out about it –'

Colonel Weston said sharply:

'Well?'

Gladys Narracott said slowly:

'I did think sometimes that Mrs Marshall was frightened of her husband knowing.'

'What makes you say that?'

'It wasn't anything definite, sir. It was only I felt – that sometimes she was – afraid of him. He was a very quiet gentleman but he wasn't – he wasn't *easy*.'

Weston said:

'But you've nothing definite to go on? Nothing either of them ever said to each other.'

Slowly Gladys Narracott shook her head.

Weston sighed. He went on.

'Now, as to letters received by Mrs Marshall this morning. Can you tell us anything about those?'

'There were about six or seven, sir. I couldn't say exactly.'

'Did you take them up to her?'

'Yes, sir. I got them from the office as usual and put them on her breakfast tray.'

'Do you remember anything about the look of them?'

The girl shook her head.

'They were just ordinary-looking letters. Some of them were bills and circulars, I think, because they were torn up on the tray.'

'What happened to them?'

'They went into the dustbin, sir. One of the police gentlemen is going through that now.'

Weston nodded.

'And the contents of the waste-paper baskets, where are they?'

'They'll be in the dustbin too.'

Weston said: 'H'm – well, I think that is all at present.' He looked inquiringly at Poirot.

Poirot leaned forward.

'When you did Miss Linda Marshall's room this morning, did you do the fireplace?'

'There wasn't anything to do, sir. There had been no fire lit.'

'And there was nothing in the fireplace itself?'

'No sir, it was perfectly all right.'

'What time did you do her room?'

'About a quarter-past nine, sir, when she'd gone down to breakfast.'

'Did she come up to her room after breakfast, do you know?'

'Yes, sir. She came up about a quarter to ten.'

'Did she stay in her room?'

'I think so, sir. She came out, hurrying rather, just before half-past ten.'

'You didn't go into her room again?'

'No, sir. I had finished with it.'

Poirot nodded. He said:

'There is another thing I want to know. What people bathed before breakfast this morning?'

'I couldn't say about the other wing and the floor above. Only about this one.'

'That is all I want to know.'

'Well, sir, Captain Marshall and Mr Redfern were the only ones this morning, I think. They always go down for an early dip.'

'Did you see them?'

'No, sir, but their wet bathing things were hanging over the balcony rail as usual.'

'Miss Linda Marshall did not bathe this morning?'

'No, sir. All her bathing dresses were quite dry.'

'Ah,' said Poirot. 'That is what I wanted to know.'

Gladys Narracott volunteered:

'She does most mornings, sir.'

'And the other three, Miss Darnley, Mrs Redfern and Mrs Marshall?'

'Mrs Marshall never, sir. Miss Darnley has once or twice, I think. Mrs Redfern doesn't often bathe before breakfast – only when it's very hot, but she didn't this morning.'

Again Poirot nodded. Then he asked:

'I wonder if you have noticed whether a bottle is missing from any of the rooms you look after in this wing?'

'A bottle, sir? What kind of a bottle?'

'Unfortunately I do not know. But have you noticed – or would you be likely to notice – if one had gone?'

Gladys said frankly:

'I shouldn't from Mrs Marshall's room, sir, and that's a fact. She has ever so many.'

'And the other rooms?'

'Well, I'm not sure about Miss Darnley. She has a good many creams and lotions. But from the other rooms, yes, I would, sir. I mean if I were to look special. If I were noticing, so to speak.'

'But you haven't actually noticed?'

'No, because I wasn't looking special, as I say.'

'Perhaps you would go and look now, then.'

'Certainly, sir.'

She left the room, her print dress rustling. Weston looked at Poirot. He said: 'What's all this?'

Poirot murmured:

'My orderly mind, that is vexed by trifles! Miss Brewster, this morning, was bathing off the rocks before breakfast, and she says that a bottle was thrown from above and nearly hit her. *Eh bien*, I want to know who threw that bottle and why?'

'My dear man, any one may have chucked a bottle away.'

'Not at all. To begin with, it could only have been thrown from a window on the east side of the hotel – that is, one of the windows of the rooms we have just examined. Now I ask you, if you have an empty bottle on your dressing-table or in your bathroom what do you do with it? I will tell you, you drop it into the waste-paper basket. You do not take the trouble to go out on your balcony and hurl it into the sea! For one thing you might hit someone, for another it would be too much trouble. No, you would only do that *if you did not want any one to see that particular bottle.*'

Weston stared at him.

Weston said:

'I know that Chief Inspector Japp, whom I met over a case

not long ago, always says you have a damned tortuous mind. You're not going to tell me now that Arlena Marshall wasn't strangled at all, but poisoned out of some mysterious bottle with a mysterious drug?'

'No, no, I do not think there was poison in that bottle.'

'Then what was there?'

'I do not know at all. That's why I am interested.'

Gladys Narracott came back. She was a little breathless. She said:

'I'm sorry, sir, but I can't find anything missing. I'm sure there's nothing gone from Captain Marshall's room, or Miss Linda Marshall's room, or Mr and Mrs Redfern's room, and I'm pretty sure there's nothing gone from Miss Darnley's either. But I couldn't say about Mrs Marshall's. As I say, she's got such a lot.'

Poirot shrugged his shoulders.

He said:

'No matter. We will leave it.'

Gladys Narracott said:

'Is there anything more, sir?'

She looked from one to the other of them.

Weston said:

'Don't think so. Thank you.'

Poirot said:

'I thank you, no. You are sure, are you not, that there is nothing – nothing at all, that you have forgotten to tell us?'

'About Mrs Marshall, sir?'

'About anything at all. Anything unusual, out of the way, unexplained, slightly peculiar, rather curious – *enfin*, something that has made you say to yourself or to one of your colleagues: "That's funny!"?'

Gladys said doubtfully:

'Well, not the sort of thing that you would mean, sir.'

Hercule Poirot said:

'Never mind what I mean. You do not know what I mean. It is true, then, that you have said to yourself or to a colleague today, "that is funny!"?'

He brought out the three words with ironic detachment.

Gladys said:

'It was nothing really. Just a bath being run. And I did pass the remark to Elsie, downstairs, that it was funny somebody having a bath round about twelve o'clock.'

'Whose bath, who had a bath?'

'That I couldn't say, sir. We heard it going down the waste from this wing, that's all, and that's when I said what I did to Elsie.'

'You're sure it was a bath? Not one of the hand-basins?'

'Oh! quite sure, sir. You can't mistake bath-water running away.'

Poirot displaying no further desire to keep her, Gladys Narracott was permitted to depart.

Weston said:

'You don't think this bath question is important, do you, Poirot? I mean, there's no point to it. No bloodstains or anything like that to wash off. That's the –' He hesitated.

Poirot cut in:

'That, you would say, is the advantage of strangulation! No bloodstains, no weapon – nothing to get rid of or conceal! Nothing is needed but physical strength – *and the soul of a killer*!'

His voice was so fierce, so charged with feeling, that Weston recoiled a little.

Hercule Poirot smiled at him apologetically.

'No one,' he said, 'the bath is probably of no importance. Anyone may have had a bath. Mrs Redfern before she went to play tennis, Captain Marshall, Miss Darnley. As I say, anyone. There is nothing in that.'

A police constable knocked at the door, and put in his head.

'It's Miss Darnley, sir. She says she'd like to see you again for a minute. There's something she forgot to tell you, she says.'

Weston said:

'We're coming down – now.'

III

The first person they saw was Colgate. His face was gloomy.

'Just a minute, sir.'

Weston and Poirot followed him into Mrs Castle's office.

Colgate said:

'I've been checking-up with Heald on this type-writing business. Not a doubt of it, it couldn't be done under an hour. Longer, if you had to stop and think here and there. That seems to me pretty well to settle it. And look at this letter.'

He held it out.

'*My dear Marshall – Sorry to worry you on your holiday but an entirely unforseen situation has arisen over the Burley and Tender contracts . . .*'

'Etcetera, etcetera,' said Colgate. 'Dated the 24th – that's yesterday. Envelope postmarked yesterday evening E.C.1. and Leathercombe Bay this morning. Same typewriter used on envelope and in letter. And by the contents it was clearly impossible for Marshall to prepare his answer beforehand. The figures arise out of the ones in the letter – the whole thing is quite intricate.'

'H'm,' said Weston gloomily. 'That seems to let Marshall out. We'll have to look elsewhere.' He added: 'I've got to see Miss Darnley again. She's waiting now.'

Rosamund came in crisply. Her smile held an apologetic *nuance*.

She said:

'I'm frightfully sorry. Probably it isn't worth bothering about. But one does forget things so.'

'Yes, Miss Darnley?'

The Chief Constable indicated a chair.

She shook her shapely black head.

'Oh, it isn't worth sitting down. It's simply this. I told you that I spent the morning lying out on Sunny Ledge. That isn't quite accurate. I forgot that once during the morning I went back to the hotel and out again.'

'What time was that, Miss Darnley?'

'It must have been about a quarter-past eleven.'

'You went back to the hotel, you said?'

'Yes, I'd forgotten my glare glasses. At first I thought I wouldn't bother and then my eyes got tired and I decided to go in and get them.'

'You went straight to your room and out again?'

'Yes. At least, as a matter of fact, I just looked in on Ken – Captain Marshall. I heard his machine going and I thought it was so stupid of him to stay indoors typing on such a lovely day. I thought I'd tell him to come out.'

'And what did Captain Marshall say?'

Rosamund smiled rather shamefacedly.

'Well, when I opened the door he was typing so vigorously, and frowning and looking so concentrated, that I just went away quietly. I don't think he even saw me come in.'

'And that was – at what time, Miss Darnley?'

'Just about twenty-past eleven. I noticed the clock in the hall as I went out again.'

IV

'And that puts the lid on it finally,' said Inspector Colgate. 'The chambermaid heard him typing up till five minutes to eleven. Miss Darnley saw him at twenty minutes past, and the woman was dead at a quarter to twelve. He says he spent that hour typing in his room, and it seems quite clear that he *was* typing in his room. That washes Captain Marshall right out.'

He stopped, then looking at Poirot with some curiosity, he asked:

'M. Poirot's looking very serious over something.'

Poirot said thoughtfully:

'I was wondering why Miss Darnley suddenly volunteered this extra evidence.'

Inspector Colgate cocked his head alertly.

'Think there's something fishy about it? That it isn't just a question of "forgetting"?'

He considered for a minute or two, then he said slowly:

'Look here, sir, let's look at it this way. Supposing Miss Darnley wasn't on Sunny Ledge this morning as she says. That story's a lie. Now suppose that *after* telling us her story, she finds that somebody saw her somewhere else or alternatively that someone went to the Ledge and didn't find her there. Then she thinks up this story quick and comes and tells it to us to account for her absence. You'll notice that she was careful to say Captain Marshall didn't *see* her when she looked into his room.'

Poirot murmured:

'Yes, I noticed that.'

Weston said incredulously:

'Are you suggesting that Miss Darnley's mixed up in this? Nonsense, seems absurd to me. Why should she be?'

Inspector Colgate coughed.

He said:

'You'll remember what the American lady, Mrs Gardener, said. She sort of hinted that Miss Darnley was sweet on Captain Marshall. There'd be a motive there, sir.'

Weston said impatiently:

'Arlena Marshall wasn't killed by a woman. It's a man we've got to look for. We've got to stick to the men in the case.'

Inspector Colgate sighed. He said:

'Yes, that's true, sir. We always come back to that, don't we?'

Weston went on:

'Better put a constable on to timing one or two things. From the hotel across the island to the top of the ladder. Let him do it running and walking. Same thing with the ladder itself. And somebody had better check the time it takes to go on a float from the bathing beach to the cove.'

Inspector Colgate nodded.

'I'll attend to all that, sir,' he said confidently.

The Chief Constable said:

'Think I'll go along to the cove now. See if Phillips has found anything. Then there's that Pixy's Cave we've been hearing about. Ought to see if there are any traces of a man waiting in there. Eh, Poirot? What do you think?'

'By all means. It is a possibility.'

Weston said:

'If somebody from outside had nipped over to the island that would be a good hiding-place – if he knew about it. I suppose the locals know?'

Colgate said:

'Don't believe the younger generation would. You see, ever since this hotel was started the coves have been private property. Fishermen don't go there, or picnic parties. And the hotel people aren't local. Mrs Castle's a Londoner.'

Weston said:

'We might take Redfern with us. He told us about it. What about you, M. Poirot?'

Hercule Poirot hesitated. He said, his foreign intonation very pronounced:

'Me, I am like Miss Brewster and Mrs Redfern, I do not like to descend perpendicular ladders.'

Weston said: 'You can go round by boat.'

Again Hercule Poirot sighed.

'My stomach, it is not happy on the sea.'

'Nonsense, man, it's a beautiful day. Calm as a mill pond. You can't let us down, you know.'

Hercule Poirot hardly looked like responding to this British adjuration. But at that moment, Mrs Castle poked her ladylike face and elaborate coiffure round the door.

'Ay'm sure ay hope ay am not intruding,' she said. 'But Mr Lane, the clergyman, you know, has just returned. Ay thought you might like to know.'

'Ah yes, thanks, Mrs Castle. We'll see him right away.'

Mrs Castle came a little farther into the room. She said:

'Ay don't know if it is worth mentioning, but ay *have* heard that the smallest incident should not be ignored –'

'Yes, yes?' said Weston impatiently.

'It is only that there was a lady and gentleman here about one o'clock. Came over from the mainland. For luncheon. They were informed that there had been an accident and that under the circumstances no luncheons could be served.'

'Any idea who they were?'

'Ay couldn't say at all. Naturally no name was given. They expressed disappointment and a certain amount of curiosity as to the nature of the accident. Ay couldn't tell them anything, of course. Ay should say, myself, they were summer visitors of the better class.'

Weston said brusquely:

'Ah well, thank you for telling us. Probably not important but quite right – er – to remember everything.'

'Naturally,' said Mrs Castle, 'ay wish to do my Duty!'

'Quite, quite. Ask Mr Lane to come here.'

V

Stephen Lane strode into the room with his usual vigour.

Weston said:

'I'm the Chief Constable of the County, Mr Lane. I suppose you've been told what has occurred here?'

'Yes – oh yes – I heard as soon as I got here. Terrible . . . Terrible . . .' His thin frame quivered. He said in a low voice: 'All along – ever since I arrived here – I have been conscious – very conscious – of the forces of evil close at hand.'

His eyes, burning eager eyes, went to Hercule Poirot.

He said:

'You remember, M. Poirot? Our conversation some days ago? About the reality of evil?'

Weston was studying the tall, gaunt figure in some perplexity. He found it difficult to make this man out. Lane's eyes came back to him. The clergyman said with a slight smile:

'I dare say that seems fantastic to you, sir. We have left off believing in evil in these days. We have abolished Hell fire! We no longer believe in the Devil! But Satan and Satan's emissaries were never more powerful than they are today!'

Weston said:

'Er – er – yes, perhaps. That, Mr Lane, is your province. Mine is more prosaic – to clear up a case of murder.'

Stephen Lane said:

'An awful word. Murder! One of the earliest sins known on earth – the ruthless shedding of an innocent brother's blood . . .' He paused, his eyes half closed. Then, in a more ordinary voice he said:

'In what way can I help you?'

'First of all, Mr Lane, will you tell me your own movements today?'

'Willingly. I started off early on one of my usual tramps. I am fond of walking. I have roamed over a good deal of the countryside round here. Today I went to St Petrock-in-the-Combe. That is about seven miles from here – a very pleasant walk along winding lanes, up and down the Devon hills and valleys. I took some lunch with me and ate it in a spinney. I visited the church – it has some fragments – only fragments alas, of early glass – also a very interesting painted screen.'

'Thank you, Mr Lane. Did you meet anyone on your walk?'

'Not to speak to. A cart passed me once and a couple of boys on bicycles and some cows. However,' he smiled, 'if you want proof of my statement, I wrote my name in the book at the church. You will find it there.'

'You did not see anyone at the church itself – the Vicar, or the verger?'

Stephen Lane shook his head. He said:

'No, there was no one about and I was the only visitor. St Petrock is a very remote spot. The village itself lies on the far side of it about half a mile farther on.'

Colonel Weston said pleasantly:

'You mustn't think we're – er – doubting what you say. Just a matter of checking-up on everybody. Just routine, you know, routine. Have to stick to routine in cases of this kind.'

Stephen Lane said gently:

'Oh yes, I quite understand.'

Weston went on:

'Now the next point. Is there anything you know that would assist us at all? Anything about the dead woman? Anything that could give us a pointer as to who murdered her? Anything you heard or saw?'

Stephen Lane said:

'I heard nothing. All I can tell you is this: that I knew instinctively as soon as I saw her that Arlena Marshall was a focus of evil. She *was* Evil! Evil personified! Woman can be man's help and inspiration in life – she can also be man's downfall. She can drag a man down to the level of the beast. The dead woman was just such a woman. She appealed to everything base in a man's nature. She was a woman such as Jezebel and Aholibah. Now – she has been struck down in the middle of her wickedness!'

Hercule Poirot stirred. He said:

'Not struck down – *strangled!* Strangled, Mr Lane, by a pair of human hands.'

The clergyman's own hands trembled. The fingers writhed and twitched. He said, and his voice came low and choked:

'That's horrible – horrible – Must you put it like that?'

Hercule Poirot said:

'It is the simple truth. Have you any idea, Mr Lane, whose hands those were?'

The other shook his head. He said: 'I know nothing – nothing . . .'

Weston got up. He said, after a glance at Colgate to which the latter replied by an almost imperceptible nod, 'Well, we must get on to the Cove.'

Lane said:

'Is that where – it happened?'

Weston nodded.

Lane said:

'Can – can I come with you?'

About to return a curt negative, Weston was forestalled by Poirot.

'But certainly,' said Poirot. 'Accompany me there in a boat, Mr Lane. We start immediately.'

CHAPTER 9

I

For the second time that morning Patrick Redfern was rowing a boat into Pixy Cove. The other occupants of the boat were Hercule Poirot, very pale with a hand to his stomach, and Stephen Lane. Colonel Weston had taken the land route. Having been delayed on the way he arrived on the beach at the same time as the boat grounded. A police constable and a plainclothes sergeant were on the beach already. Weston was questioning the latter as the three from the boat walked up and joined him.

Sergeant Phillips said:

'I think I've been over every inch of the beach, sir.'

'Good, what did you find?'

'It's all together here, sir, if you'd like to come and see.'

A small collection of objects was laid out neatly on a rock. There was a pair of scissors, an empty Gold Flake packet, five patent bottle tops, a number of used matches, three pieces of string, one or two fragments of newspaper, a fragment of a smashed pipe, four buttons, the drumstick bone of a chicken and an empty bottle of sun-bathing oil.

Weston looked down appraisingly on the objects.

'H'm,' he said. 'Rather moderate for a beach nowadays! Most people seem to confuse a beach with a public rubbish dump! Empty bottle's been here some time by the way the label's blurred – so have most of the other things, I should say. The scissors are new, though. Bright and shining. *They* weren't out in yesterday's rain! Where were they?'

'Close by the bottom of the ladder, sir. Also this bit of pipe.'

'H'm, probably dropped by someone going up or down. Nothing to say who they belong to?'

'No, sir. Quite an ordinary pair of nail scissors. Pipe's a good quality brier – expensive.'

Poirot murmured thoughtfully:

'Captain Marshall told us, I think, that he had mislaid his pipe.'

Weston said:

'Marshall's out of the picture. Anyway, he's not the only person who smokes a pipe.'

Hercule Poirot was watching Stephen Lane as the latter's hand went to his pocket and away again. He said pleasantly:

'You also smoke a pipe, do you not, Mr Lane?'

The clergyman started. He looked at Poirot.

He said:

'Yes. Oh yes. My pipe is an old friend and companion.' Putting his hand into his pocket again he drew out a pipe, filled it with tobacco and lighted it.

Hercule Poirot moved away to where Redfern was standing, his eyes blank.

He said in a low voice:

'I'm glad – they've taken *her* away . . .'

Stephen Lane asked:

'Where was she found?'

The Sergeant said cheerfully:

'Just about where you're standing, sir.'

Lane moved swiftly aside. He stared at the spot he had just vacated.

The Sergeant went on:

'Place where the float was drawn up agrees with putting the

time she arrived here at 10.45. That's going by the tide. It's turned now.'

'Photography all done?' asked Weston.

'Yes, sir.'

Weston turned to Redfern.

'Now then, man, where's the entrance to this cave of yours?'

Patrick Redfern was still staring down at the beach where Lane had been standing. It was as though he was seeing that sprawling body that was no longer there.

Weston's words recalled him to himself.

He said: 'It's over here.'

He led the way to where a great mass of tumbled-down rocks were massed picturesquely against the cliff side. He went straight to where two big rocks, side by side, showed a straight narrow cleft between them. He said:

'The entrance is here.'

Weston said:

'Here? Doesn't look as though a man could squeeze through.'

'It's deceptive, you'll find, sir. It can just be done.'

Weston inserted himself gingerly into the cleft. It was not as narrow as it looked. Inside, the space widened and proved to be a fairly roomy recess with room to stand upright and to move about.

Hercule Poirot and Stephen Lane joined the Chief Constable. The other stayed outside. Light filtered in through the opening, but Weston had also got a powerful torch which he played freely over the interior.

He observed:

'Handy place. You'd never suspect it from the outside.'

He played the torch carefully over the floor.

Hercule Poirot was delicately sniffing the air.

Noticing this, Weston said:

'Air quite fresh, not fishy or seaweedy, but of course this place is well above high water mark.'

But to Poirot's sensitive nose, the air was more than fresh. It was delicately scented. He knew two people who used that elusive perfume . . .

'Weston's torch came to rest. He said:

'Don't see anything out of the way in here.'

Poirot's eyes rose to a ledge a little way above his head. He murmured:

'One might perhaps see that there is nothing up there?'

Weston said: 'If there's anything up there it would have to be deliberately put there. Still, we'd better have a look.'

Poirot said to Lane:

'You are, I think, the tallest of us, Monsieur. Could we venture to ask you to make sure there is nothing resting on that ledge?'

Lane stretched up, but he could not quite reach to the back of the shelf. Then, seeing a crevice in the rock, he inserted a toe in it and pulled himself up by one hand.

He said:

'Hullo, there's a box up here.'

In a minute or two they were out in the sunshine examining the clergyman's find.

Weston said:

'Careful, don't handle it more than you can help. May be finger-prints.'

It was a dark-green tin box and bore the word Sandwiches on it.

Sergeant Phillips said:

'Left from some picnic or other, I suppose.'

He opened the lid with his handkerchief.

Inside were small tin containers marked salt, pepper, mustard and two larger square tins evidently for sandwiches. Sergeant Phillips lifted the lid of the salt container. It was full to the brim. He raised the next one, commenting:

'H'm, got salt in the pepper one too.'

The mustard compartment also contained salt.

His face suddenly alert, the police sergeant opened one of the bigger square tins. That, too, contained the same white crystalline powder.

Very gingerly, Sergeant Phillips dipped a finger in and applied it to his tongue.

His face changed. He said – and his voice was excited:

'This isn't *salt*, sir. Not by a long way! Bitter taste! Seems to me it's some kind of *drug*.'

II

'The third angle,' said Colonel Weston with a groan.

They were back at the hotel again.

The Chief Constable went on:

'If by any chance there's a dope gang mixed up in this, it opens up several possibilities. First of all, the dead woman may have been in with the gang herself. Think that's likely?'

Hercule Poirot said cautiously:

'It is possible.'

'She may have been a drug addict?'

Poirot shook his head.

He said:

'I should doubt that. She had steady nerves, radiant health, there were no marks of hypodermic injections (not that that proves anything. Some people sniff the stuff). No, I do not think she took drugs.'

'In that case,' said Weston, 'she may have run into the business accidentally, and she was deliberately silenced by the people running the show. We'll know presently just what the stuff is. I've sent it to Neasden. If we're on to some dope ring, they're not the people to stick at trifles –'

He broke off as the door opened and Mr Horace Blatt came briskly into the room.

Mr Blatt was looking hot. He was wiping the perspiration from his forehead. His big hearty voice billowed out and filled the small room.

'Just this minute got back and heard the news! You the Chief Constable? They told me you were in here. My name's Blatt – Horace Blatt. Any way I can help you? Don't suppose so. I've been out in my boat since early this morning. Missed the whole blinking show. The one day that something *does* happen in this out-of-the-way spot, I'm not there. Just like life, that, isn't it? Hullo, Poirot, didn't see you at first. So you're in on this? Oh well, I suppose you would be. Sherlock Holmes *v.* the local police, is that it? Ha, ha! Lestrade – all that stuff. I'll enjoy seeing you do a bit of fancy sleuthing.'

Mr Blatt came to anchor in a chair, pulled out a cigarette case and offered it to Colonel Weston, who shook his head.

He said, with a slight smile:

'I'm an inveterate pipe smoker.'

'Same here. I smoke cigarettes as well – but nothing beats a pipe.'

Colonel Weston said with suddenly geniality:

'Then light up, man.'

Blatt shook his head.

'Not got my pipe on me at the moment. But put me wise about all this. All I've heard so far is that Mrs Marshall was found murdered on one of the beaches here.'

'On Pixy Cove,' said Colonel Weston, watching him.

But Mr Blatt merely asked excitedly:

'And she was strangled?'

'Yes, Mr Blatt.'

'Nasty – very nasty. Mind you, she asked for it! Hot stuff – *très moustarde* – eh, M. Poirot? Any idea who did it, or mustn't I ask that?'

With a faint smile Colonel Weston said:

'Well, you know, it's we who are supposed to ask the questions.'

Mr Blatt waved his cigarette.

'Sorry – sorry – my mistake. Go ahead.'

'You went out sailing this morning. At what time?'

'Left here at a quarter to ten.'

'Was any one with you?'

'Not a soul. All on my little lonesome.'

'And where did you go?'

'Along the coast in the direction of Plymouth. Took lunch with me. Not much wind so I didn't actually get very far.'

After another question or two, Weston asked:

'Now about the Marshalls? Do you know anything that might help us?'

'Well, I've given you my opinion. *Crime passionnel!* All I can tell you is, it wasn't *me*! The fair Arlena had no use for me. Nothing doing in that quarter. She had her own blue-eyed boy! And if you ask me, Marshall was getting wise to it.'

'Have you any evidence for that?'

'Saw him give young Redfern a dirty look once or twice. Dark horse, Marshall. Looks very meek and mild and as though he were half asleep all the time – but that's not his reputation in the City. I've heard a thing or two about him. Nearly had up for assault once. Mind you, the fellow in question had put up a pretty dirty deal. Marshall had trusted him and the fellow had let him down cold. Particularly dirty business, I believe. Marshall went for him and half killed him. Fellow didn't prosecute – too afraid of what might come out. I give you that for what it's worth.'

'So you think it possible,' said Poirot, 'that Captain Marshall strangled his wife?'

'Not at all. Never said anything of the sort. Just letting you know that he's the sort of fellow who could go berserk on occasions.'

Poirot said:

'Mr Blatt, there is reason to believe that Mrs Marshall went this morning to Pixy Cove to meet someone. Have you any idea who that someone might be?'

Mr Blatt winked.

'It's not a guess. It's a certainty. Redfern!'

'It was not Mr Redfern.'

Mr Blatt seemed taken aback. He said hesitatingly:

'Then I don't know . . . No, I can't imagine . . .'

He went on, regaining a little of his aplomb:

'As I said before, it wasn't *me*! No such luck! Let me see, couldn't have been Gardener – his wife keeps far too sharp an eye on him! That old ass Barry? Rot! And it would hardly be the parson. Although, mind you, I've seen his Reverence watching her a good bit. All holy disapproval, but perhaps an eye for the contours all the same! Eh? Lot of hypocrites, most parsons. Did you read that case last month? Parson and the churchwarden's daughter! Bit of an eye-opener.'

Mr Blatt chuckled.

Colonel Weston said coldly:

'There is nothing you can think of that might help us?'

The other shook his head.

'No. Can't think of a thing.' He added: 'This will make a bit of a stir, I imagine. The Press will be on to it like hot cakes. There won't be quite so much of this high-toned exclusiveness about the Jolly Roger in future. Jolly Roger indeed. Precious little jollity about it.'

Hercule Poirot murmured:

'You have not enjoyed your stay here?'

Mr Blatt's red face got slightly redder. He said:

'Well, no, I haven't. The sailing's all right and the scenery and the service and the food – but there's no *matiness* in the place, you know what I mean! What I say is, my money's as good as another man's. We're all here to enjoy ourselves. Then why not get together and *do* it? All these cliques and people sitting by themselves and giving you frosty good-mornings – and good-evenings – and yes, very pleasant weather. No joy de viver. Lot of stuck-up dummies!'

Mr Blatt paused – by now very red indeed.

He wiped his forehead once more and said apologetically:

'Don't pay any attention to me. I get all worked up.'

III

Hercule Poirot murmured:

'And what do we think of Mr Blatt?'

Colonel Weston grinned and said:

'What do *you* think of him? You've seen more of him than I have.'

Poirot said softly:

'There are many of your English idioms that describe him. The rough diamond! The self-made man! The social climber! He is, as you choose to look at it, pathetic, ludicrous, blatant! It is a matter of opinion. But I think, too, that he is something else.'

'And what is that?'

Hercule Poirot, his eyes raised to the ceiling, murmured:

'I think that he is – *nervous*!'

IV

Inspector Colgate said:

'I've got those times worked out. From the hotel to the ladder down to Pixy Cove three minutes. That's walking till you are out of sight of the hotel and then running like hell.'

Weston raised his eyebrows. He said:

'That's quicker than I thought.'

'Down ladder to beach one minute and three-quarters. Up same two minutes. That's P.C. Flint. He's a bit of an athlete.

Walking and taking the ladder in the normal way, the whole business takes close on a quarter of an hour.'

Weston nodded. He said:

'There's another thing we must go into, the pipe question.'

Colgate said:

'Blatt smokes a pipe, so does Marshall, so does the parson. Redfern smokes cigarettes, the American prefers a cigar. Major Barry doesn't smoke at all. There's one pipe in Marshall's room, two in Blatt's, and one in the parson's. Chambermaid says Marshall has two pipes. The other chambermaid isn't a very bright girl. Doesn't know how many pipes the other two have. Says vaguely she's noticed two or three about in their rooms.'

Weston nodded.

'Anything else?'

'I've checked up on the staff. They all seem quite O.K. Henry, in the bar, checks Marshall's statement about seeing him at ten to eleven. William, the beach attendant, was down repairing the ladder on the rocks by the hotel most of the morning. He seems all right. George marked the tennis court and then bedded out some plants round by the dining-room. Neither of them would have seen anyone who came across the causeway to the island.'

'When was the causeway uncovered?'

'Round about 9.30, sir.'

Weston pulled at his moustache.

'It's possible somebody did come that way. We've got a new angle, Colgate.'

He told of the discovery of the sandwich box in the cave.

V

There was a tap on the door.

'Come in,' said Weston.

It was Captain Marshall.

He said:

'Can you tell me what arrangements I can make about the funeral?'

'I think we shall manage the inquest for the day after tomorrow, Captain Marshall.'

'Thank you.'

Inspector Colgate said:

'Excuse me, sir, allow me to return you these.'

He handed over the three letters.

Kenneth Marshall smiled rather sardonically.

He said:

'Has the police department been testing the speed of my typing? I hope my character is cleared.'

Colonel Weston said pleasantly.

'Yes, Captain Marshall, I think we can give you a clean bill of health. Those sheets take fully an hour to type. Moreover you were heard typing them by the chambermaid up till five minutes to eleven and you were seen by another witness at twenty minutes past.'

Captain Marshall murmured:

'Really? That all seems very satisfactory!'

'Yes. Miss Darnley came to your room at twenty minutes past eleven. You were so busy typing that you did not observe her entry.'

Kenneth Marshall's face took on an impassive expression. He said:

'Does Miss Darnley say that?' He paused. 'As a matter of fact she is wrong. I *did* see her, though she may not be aware of the fact. I saw her in the mirror.'

Poirot murmured:

'But you did not interrupt your typing?'

Marshall said shortly:

'No. I wanted to get finished.'

He paused a minute, then, in an abrupt voice, he said:

'Nothing more I can do for you?'

'No, thank you, Captain Marshall.'

Kenneth Marshall nodded and went out.

Weston said with a sigh:

'There goes our most hopeful suspect – cleared! Hullo, here's Neasden.'

The doctor came in with a trace of excitement in his manner. He said:

'That's a nice little death lot you sent me along.'

'What is it?'

'What is it? Diamorphine Hydrochloride. Stuff that's usually called Heroin.'

Inspector Colgate whistled. He said:

'Now we're getting places, all right! Depend upon it, this dope stunt is at the bottom of the whole business.'

CHAPTER 10

....

!

The little crowd of people flocked out of the Red Bull. The brief inquest was over – adjourned for a fortnight.

Rosamund Darnley joined Captain Marshall. She said in a low voice:

'That wasn't so bad, was it, Ken?'

He did not answer at once. Perhaps he was conscious of the staring eyes of the villagers, the fingers that nearly pointed to him and only just did not quite do so!

'*That's 'im, my dear.' 'See, that's 'er 'usband.' 'That be the 'usband.' 'Look, there 'e goes . . .*'

The murmurs were not loud enough to reach his ears, but he was none the less sensitive to them. This was the modern-day pillory. The Press he had already encountered – self-confident, persuasive young men, adept at battering down his wall of silence of 'Nothing to say' that he had endeavoured to erect. Even the curt monosyllables that he had uttered, thinking that they at least could not lead to misapprehension, had reappeared in his morning's papers in a totally different guise. 'Asked whether he agreed that the mystery of his wife's death could only be explained on the assumption that a homicidal murderer had found his way on to the island, Captain Marshall declared that –' and so on and so forth.

Cameras had clicked ceaselessly. Now, at this minute, the well-known sound caught his ear. He half turned – a smiling young man was nodding cheerfully, his purpose accomplished.

Rosamund murmured:

'*Captain Marshall and a friend leaving the Red Bull after the inquest.*'

Marshall winced.

Rosamund said:

'It's no use, Ken! You've got to face it! I don't mean just the fact of Arlena's death – I mean all the attendant beastliness. The staring eyes and gossiping tongues, the fatuous interviews in the papers – and the best way to meet it is to find it funny! Come out with all the old inane cliches and curl a sardonic lip at them.'

He said:

'Is that your way?'

'Yes.' She paused. 'It isn't yours, I know. Protective colouring is your line. Remain rigidly non-active and fade into the background! But you can't do that here – you've no background to fade into. You stand out clear for all to see – like a striped tiger against a white backcloth. *The husband of the murdered woman!*'

'For God's sake, Rosamund –'

She said gently:

'My dear, I'm trying to be good for you!'

They walked for a few steps in silence. Then Marshall said in a different voice:

'I know you are. I'm not really ungrateful, Rosamund.'

They had progressed beyond the limits of the village. Eyes followed them but there was no one very near. Rosamund Darnley's voice dropped as she repeated a variant of her first remark.

'It didn't really go so badly, did it?'

He was silent for a moment, then he said:

'I don't know.'

'What do the police think?'

'They're non-committal.'

After a minute Rosamund said:

'That little man – Poirot – is he really taking an active interest!'

Kenneth Marshall said:

'Seemed to be sitting in the Chief Constable's pocket all right the other day.'

'I know – but is he *doing* anything?'

'How the hell should I know, Rosamund?'

She said thoughtfully:

'He's pretty old. Probably more or less ga ga.'

'Perhaps.'

They came to the causeway. Opposite them, serene in the sun, lay the island.

Rosamund said suddenly:

'Sometimes – things seem unreal. I can't believe, this minute, that it ever happened . . .'

Marshall said slowly:

'I think I know what you mean. Nature is so regardless! One ant the less – that's all it is in Nature!'

Rosamund said:

'Yes – and that's the proper way to look at it really.'

He gave her one very quick glance. Then he said in a low voice:

'Don't worry, my dear. It's all right. *It's all right.*'

II

Linda came down to the causeway to meet them. She moved with the spasmodic jerkiness of a nervous colt. Her young face was marred by deep black shadows under her eyes. Her lips were dry and rough.

She said breathlessly:

'What happened – what – what did they say?'

Her father said abruptly:

'Inquest adjourned for a fortnight.'

'That means they – they haven't decided?'

'Yes. More evidence is needed.'

'But – but what do they think?'

Marshall smiled a little in spite of himself.

'Oh, my dear child – who knows? And whom do you mean by they? The coroner, the jury, the police, the newspaper reporters, the fishing folk of Leathercombe Bay?'

Linda said slowly:

'I suppose I mean – the police.'

Marshall said dryly:

'Whatever the police think, they're not giving it away at present.'

His lips closed tightly after the sentence. He went into the hotel.

As Rosamund Darnley was about to follow suit, Linda said:

'Rosamund!'

Rosamund turned. The mute appeal in the girl's unhappy face touched her. She linked her arm through Linda's and together they walked away from the hotel, taking the path that led to the extreme end of the island.

Rosamund said gently:

'Try not to mind so much, Linda. I know it's all very terrible and a shock and all that, but it's no use brooding over these things. And it can be only the – horror of it, that is worrying you. You weren't in the least *fond* of Arlena, you know.'

She felt the tremor that ran through the girl's body as Linda answered:

'No, I wasn't fond of her . . .'

Rosamund went on:

'Sorrow for a person is different – one can't put *that* behind one. But one *can* get over shock and horror by just not letting your mind *dwell* on it all the time.'

Linda said sharply:

'You don't understand.'

'I think I do, my dear.'

Linda shook her head.

'No, you don't. You don't understand in the least – and Christine doesn't understand either! Both of you have been nice to me, but you can't understand what I'm feeling. You just think it's morbid – that I'm dwelling on it all when I needn't.'

She paused.

'But it isn't that at all. If you knew what I know –'

Rosamund stopped dead. Her body did not tremble – on the contrary it stiffened. She stood for a minute or two, then she disengaged her arm from Linda's.

She said:

'What is it that you know, Linda?'

The girl gazed at her. Then she shook her head.

She muttered:

'Nothing.'

Rosamund caught her by the arm. The grip hurt and Linda winced slightly.

Rosamund said:

'Be careful, Linda. Be damned careful.'

Linda had gone dead white.

She said:

'I *am* very careful – all the time.'

Rosamund said urgently:

'Listen, Linda, what I said a minute or two ago applies just the same – only a hundred times more so. *Put the whole business out of your mind.* Never think about it. Forget – forget . . . You can if you try! Arlena is dead and nothing can bring her back to life . . . Forget everything and live in the future. And above all, *hold your tongue.*'

Linda shrank a little. She said:

'You – you seem to know all about it?'

Rosamund said energetically:

'I don't know *anything*! In my opinion a wandering maniac got on to the island and killed Arlena. That's much the most probable solution. I'm fairly sure that the police will have to accept that in the end. That's what *must* have happened! That's what *did* happen!'

Linda said:

'If Father –'

Rosamund interrupted her.

'Don't talk about it.'

Linda said:

'I've got to say one thing. My mother –'

'Well, what about her?'

'She – she was tried for murder, wasn't she?'

'Yes.'

Linda said slowly:

'And then Father married her. That looks, doesn't it, as though Father didn't really think murder was very wrong – not always, that is.'

Rosamund said sharply:

'Don't say things like that – even to me! The police haven't got anything against your father. He's got an alibi – an alibi that they can't break. He's perfectly safe.'

Linda whispered:

'Did they think at first that Father –?'

Rosamund cried:

'I don't know what they thought! But they know now *that he couldn't have done it.* Do you understand? *He couldn't have done it.*'

She spoke with authority, her eyes commanded Linda's acquiescence. The girl uttered a long fluttering sigh.

Rosamund said:

'You'll be able to leave here soon. You'll forget everything – everything!'

Linda said with sudden unexpected violence.

'*I shall never forget.*'

She turned abruptly and ran back to the hotel. Rosamund stared after her.

III

'There is something I want to know, Madame?'

Christine Redfern glanced up at Poirot in a slightly abstracted manner. She said:

'Yes?'

Hercule Poirot took very little notice of her abstraction. He had noted the way her eyes followed her husband's figure where he was pacing up and down on the terrace outside the bar, but for the moment he had no interest in purely conjugal problems. He wanted information.

He said:

'Yes, Madame. It was a phrase – a chance phrase of yours the other day which roused my attention.'

Christine, her eyes still on Patrick, said:

'Yes? What did I say?'

'It was in answer to a question from the Chief Constable. You described how you went into Miss Linda Marshall's room on the morning of the crime and how you found her absent from it and how she returned there, and it was then that the Chief Constable asked you where she had been.'

Christine said rather impatiently:

'And I said she had been bathing? Is that it?'

'Ah, but you did not say quite that. You did not say "she had been bathing". Your words were, "she said she had been bathing".'

Christine said:

'It's the same thing, surely.'

'No, it is not the same! The form of your answer suggests a certain attitude of mind on your part. Linda Marshall came into the room – she was wearing a bathing-wrap and yet – for some reason – you did not at once assume she had been bathing. That is shown by your words, "she *said* she had been bathing". What was there about her appearance – was it her manner, or something that she was wearing or something she said – that led you to feel surprised when she said she had been bathing?'

Christine's attention left Patrick and focused itself entirely on Poirot. She was interested. She said:

'That's clever of you. It's quite true, now I remember . . . I *was*, just faintly, surprised when Linda said she had been bathing.'

'But why, Madame, why?'

'Yes, why? That's just what I'm trying to remember. Oh yes, I think it was the parcel in her hand.'

'She had a parcel?'

'Yes.'

'You do not know what was in it?'

'Oh yes, I do. The string broke. It was loosely done up in the way they do in the village. It was *candles* – they were scattered on the floor. I helped her to pick them up.'

'Ah,' said Poirot. 'Candles.'

Christine stared at him. She said:

'You seem excited, M. Poirot.'

Poirot asked:

'Did Linda say why she had bought candles?'

Christine reflected.

'No, I don't think she did. I suppose it was to read by at night – perhaps the electric light wasn't good.'

'On the contrary, Madame, there was a bedside electric lamp in perfect order.'

Christine said:

'Then I don't know what she wanted them for.'

Poirot said:

'What was her manner – when the string broke and the candles fell out of the parcel?'

Christine said slowly:

'She was – upset – embarrassed.'

Poirot nodded his head. Then he asked:

'Did you notice a calendar in her room?'

'A calendar? What kind of a calendar?'

Poirot said:

'Possibly a green calendar – with tear-off leaves.'

Christine screwed up her eyes in an effort of memory.

'A green calendar – rather a bright green. Yes, I have seen a calendar like that – but I can't remember where. It may have been in Linda's room, but I can't be sure.'

'But you have definitely seen such a thing.'

'Yes.'

Again Poirot nodded.

Christine said rather sharply:

'What are you hinting at, M. Poirot? What is the meaning of all this?'

For answer Poirot produced a small volume bound in faded brown calf. He said:

'Have you ever seen this before?'

'Why – I think – I'm not sure – yes, Linda was looking into it in the village lending library the other day. But she shut it up and thrust it back quickly when I came up to her. It made me wonder what it was.'

Silently Poirot displayed the title.

A History of Witchcraft, Sorcery and of the Compounding of Untraceable Poisons.

Christine said:

'I don't understand. What does all this mean?'

Poirot said gravely.

'It may mean, Madame, a good deal.'

She looked at him inquiringly, but he did not go on. Instead he asked:

'One more question, Madame, did you take a bath that morning before you went out to play tennis?'

Christine stared again.

'A bath? No. I would have had no time and, anyway, I didn't want a bath – not before tennis. I might have had one after.'

'Did you use your bathroom at all when you came in?'

'I sponged my face and hands, that's all.'

'You did not turn on the bath at all?'

'No, I'm sure I didn't.'

Poirot nodded. He said:

'It is of no importance.'

IV

Hercule Poirot stood by the table where Mrs Gardener was wrestling with a jig-saw. She looked up and jumped.

'Why, M. Poirot, how very quietly you came up beside me! I never heard you. Have you just come back from the inquest? You know, the very thought of that inquest makes me so nervous, I don't know what to do. That's why I'm doing this puzzle. I just felt I couldn't sit outside on the beach as usual. As Mr Gardener knows, when my nerves are all upset, there's nothing like one of these puzzles for calming me. There now, where *does* this white piece fit in? It must be part of the fur rug, but I don't seem to see . . .'

Gently Poirot's hand took the piece from her. He said:

'It fits, Madame, *here*. It is part of the cat.'

'It can't be. It's a black cat.'

'A black cat, yes, but you see the tip of the black cat's tail happens to be white.'

'Why, so it does! How clever of you! But I do think the people who make puzzles are kind of mean. They just go out of their way to deceive you.'

She fitted in another piece and then resumed.

'You know, M. Poirot, I've been watching you this last day or two. I just wanted to watch you detecting if you know what I mean – not that it doesn't sound rather heartless put like that, as though it were all a game – and a poor creature killed. Oh dear, every time *I* think of it I get the shivers! I told Mr Gardener this morning I'd just *got* to get away from here, and now the inquest's over he thinks we'll be able to leave tomorrow, and that's a blessing, I'm sure. But about detecting, I would so like to know your methods – you know, I'd feel privileged if you'd just *explain* it to me.'

Hercule Poirot said:

'It is a little like your puzzle, Madame. One assembles the pieces. It is like a mosaic – many colours and patterns – and every strange-shaped little piece must be fitted into its own place.'

'Now isn't that interesting? Why, I'm sure you explain it just too beautifully.'

Poirot went on:

'And sometimes it is like that piece of your puzzle just now. One arranges very methodically the pieces of the puzzle – one sorts the colours – and then perhaps a piece of one colour that should fit in with – say, the fur rug, fits in instead in a black cat's tail.'

'Why, if that doesn't sound too fascinating! And are there a great many pieces, M. Poirot?'

'Yes, Madame. Almost everyone here in this hotel has given me a piece for my puzzle. You amongst them.'

'Me?' Mrs Gardener's tone was shrill.

'Yes, a remark of yours, Madame, was exceedingly helpful. I might say it was illuminating.'

'Well, if that isn't too lovely! Can't you tell me some more, M. Poirot?'

'Ah! Madame, I reserve the explanations for the last chapter.'

Mrs Gardener murmured:

'If that isn't just too bad!'

V

Hercule Poirot tapped gently on the door of Captain Marshall's room. Inside there was the sound of a typewriter.

A curt 'Come in' came from the room and Poirot entered.

Captain Marshall's back was turned to him. He was sitting typing at the table between the windows. He did not turn his head but his eyes met Poirot's in the mirror that hung on the wall directly in front of him. He said irritably:

'Well, M. Poirot, what is it?'

Poirot said quickly:

'A thousand apologies for intruding. You are busy?'

Marshall said shortly: 'I am rather.'

Poirot said:

'It is one little question that I would like to ask you.'

Marshall said:

'My God, I'm sick of answering questions. I've answered the police questions. I don't feel called upon to answer yours.'

Poirot said:

'Mine is a very simple one. Only this. On the morning of your wife's death, did you have a bath after you finished typing and before you went out to play tennis?'

'A bath? No, of course I didn't! I'd had a bathe only an hour earlier!'

Hercule Poirot said:

'Thank you. That is all.'

'But look here. Oh –' the other paused irresolutely.

Poirot withdrew, gently closing the door.

Kenneth Marshall said:

'The fellow's crazy!'

VI

Just outside the bar Poirot encountered Mr Gardener. He was carrying two cocktails and was clearly on his way to where Mrs Gardener was ensconced with her jig-saw.

He smiled at Poirot in genial fashion.

'Care to join us, M. Poirot?'

Poirot shook his head. He said:

'What did you think of the inquest, Mr Gardener?'

Mr Gardener lowered his voice. He said:

'Seemed kind of indeterminate to me. Your police, I gather, have got something up their sleeves.'

'It is possible,' said Hercule Poirot.

Mr Gardener lowered his voice still further.

'I shall be glad to get Mrs Gardener away. She's a very, very sensitive woman, and this affair has got on her nerves. She's very highly strung.'

Hercule Poirot said:

'Will you permit me, Mr Gardener, to ask you one question?'

'Why, certainly, M. Poirot. Delighted to assist in any way I can.'

Hercule Poirot said:

'You are a man of the world – a man, I think, of considerable acumen. What, frankly, was your opinion of the late Mrs Marshall?'

Mr Gardener's eyebrows rose in surprise. He glanced cautiously round and lowered his voice.

'Well, M. Poirot, I've heard a few things that have been kind of going around, if you get me, especially among the women.'

Poirot nodded. 'But if you ask me I'll tell you my candid opinion and that is that that woman was pretty much of a darned fool!'

Hercule Poirot said thoughtfully:

'Now that is very interesting.'

VII

Rosamund Darnley said: 'So it's my turn, is it?'

'Pardon?'

She laughed.

'The other day the Chief Constable held his inquisition. You sat by. Today, I think, you are conducting your own unofficial inquiry. I've been watching you. First Mrs Redfern, then I caught a glimpse of you through the lounge window where Mrs Gardener is doing her hateful jig-saw puzzle. Now it's my turn.'

Hercule Poirot sat down beside her. They were on Sunny Ledge. Below them the sea showed a deep-glowing green. Farther out it was a pale dazzling blue.

Poirot said:

'You are very intelligent, Mademoiselle. I have thought so ever since I arrived here. It would be a pleasure to discuss this business with you.'

Rosamund Darnley said softly:

'You want to know what I think about the whole thing?'

'It would be most interesting.'

Rosamund said:

'I think it's really very simple. The clue is in the woman's past.'

'The past? Not the present?'

'Oh! not necessarily the very remote past. I look at it like this. Arlena Marshall was attractive, fatally attractive, to men. It's possible, I think, that she also tired of them rather quickly. Amongst her – followers, shall we say – was one who resented that. Oh, don't misunderstand me, it won't be someone who sticks out a mile. Probably some tepid little man, vain and sensitive – the kind of man who broods. I think he followed her down here, waited his opportunity and killed her.'

'You mean that he was an outsider, that he came from the mainland?'

'Yes. He probably hid in that cave until he got his chance.'

Poirot shook his head. He said:

'Would she go there to meet such a man as you describe? No, she would laugh and not go.'

Rosamund said:

'She mayn't have known she was going to meet him. He may have sent her a message in some other person's name.'

Poirot murmured:

'That is possible.'

Then he said:

'But you forget one thing, Mademoiselle. A man bent on murder could not risk coming in broad daylight across the causeway and past the hotel. Someone might have seen him.'

'They might have – but I don't think that it's certain. I think it's quite possible that he could have come without anyone noticing him at all.'

'It would be *possible*, yes, that I grant you. But the point is that he could not *count* on that possibility.'

Rosamund said:

'Aren't you forgetting something? The weather.'

'The weather?'

'Yes. The day of the murder was a glorious day, but the day before, remember, there was rain and thick mist. Anyone could come on to the island then without being seen. He had only to go down to the beach and spend the night in the cave. That mist, M. Poirot, is important.'

Poirot looked at her thoughtfully for a minute or two. He said:

'You know, there is a good deal in what you have just said.'

Rosamund flushed. She said:

'That's my theory, for what it is worth. Now tell me yours.'

'Ah,' said Hercule Poirot. He stared down at the sea.

'*Eh bien*, Mademoiselle. I am a very simple person. I always incline to the belief that the most likely person committed the crime. At the very beginning it seemed to me that one person was very clearly indicated.'

Rosamund's voice hardened a little. She said:

'Go on.'

Hercule Poirot went on.

'But you see, there is what you call a snag in the way! It seems that it was *impossible* for that person to have committed the crime.'

He heard the quick expulsion of her breath. She said rather breathlessly:

'Well?'

Hercule Poirot shrugged his shoulders.

'Well, what do we do about it? That is my problem.' He paused and then went on. 'May I ask you a question?'

'Certainly.'

She faced him, alert and vigilant. But the question that came was an unexpected one.

'When you came in to change for tennis that morning, did you have a bath?'

Rosamund stared at him.

'A bath? What do you mean?'

'That is what I mean. A bath! The receptacle of porcelain, one turns the taps and fills it, one gets in, one gets out and ghoosh – ghoosh – ghoosh, the water goes down the waste-pipe!'

'M. Poirot, are you quite mad?'

'No, I am extremely sane.'

'Well, anyway, I *didn't* take a bath.'

'Ha!' said Poirot. 'So nobody took a bath. That is extremely interesting.'

'But why should anyone take a bath?'

Hercule Poirot said: 'Why, indeed?'

Rosamund said with some exasperation:

'I suppose this is the Sherlock Holmes touch!'

Hercule Poirot smiled.

Then he sniffed the air delicately.

'Will you permit me to be impertinent, Mademoiselle?'

'I'm sure you couldn't be impertinent, M. Poirot.'

'That is very kind of you. Then may I venture to say that the scent you use is delicious – it has a *nuance* – a delicate elusive charm.' He waved his hands, and then added in a practical voice, 'Gabrielle, No 8, I think?'

'How clever you are. Yes, I always use it.'

'So did the late Mrs Marshall. It is chic, eh? And very expensive?'

Rosamund shrugged her shoulders with a faint smile.

Poirot said:

'You sat here where we are now, Mademoiselle, on the morning of the crime. You were seen here, or at least your sunshade was seen by Miss Brewster and Mr Redfern as they passed on the sea. During the morning, Mademoiselle, are you sure you did not happen to go down to Pixy Cove and enter the cave there – the famous Pixy's Cave?'

Rosamund turned her head and stared at him.

She said in a quiet level voice:

'Are you asking me if I killed Arlena Marshall?'

'No, I am asking you if you went into the Pixy's Cave?'

'I don't even know where it is. Why should I go into it? For what reason?'

'On the day of the crime, Mademoiselle, somebody had been in that cave who used Gabrielle No 8.'

Rosamund said sharply:

'You've just said yourself, M. Poirot, that Arlena Marshall used Gabrielle No 8. She was on the beach there that day. Presumably she went into the cave.'

'Why should she go into the cave? It is dark there and narrow and very uncomfortable.'

Rosamund said impatiently:

'Don't ask me for reasons. Since she was actually at the cove she was by far the most likely person. I've told you already I never left this place the whole morning.'

'Except for the time when you went into the hotel to Captain Marshall's room.' Poirot reminded her.

'Yes, of course. I'd forgotten that.'

Poirot said:

'And you were wrong, Mademoiselle, when you thought that Captain Marshall did not see you.'

Rosamund said incredulously:

'Kenneth did see me? Did – did he say so?'

Poirot nodded.

'He saw you, Mademoiselle, in the mirror that hangs over the table.'

Rosamund caught her breath. She said:

'Oh! I see.'

Poirot was no longer looking out to sea. He was looking at Rosamund Darnley's hands as they lay folded in her lap.

They were well-shaped hands, beautifully moulded with very long fingers.

Rosamund, shooting a quick look at him, followed the direction of his eyes. She said sharply:

'What are you looking at my hands for? Do you think – do you think –?'

Poirot said:

'Do I think – what, Mademoiselle?'

Rosamund Darnley said:

'Nothing.'

VIII

It was perhaps an hour later that Hercule Poirot came to the top of the path leading to Gull Cove. There was someone sitting on the beach. A slight figure in a red shirt and dark blue shorts.

Poirot descended the path, stepping carefully in his tight smart shoes.

Linda Marshall turned her head sharply. He thought that she shrank a little.

Her eyes, as he came and lowered himself gingerly to the shingle beside her, rested on him with the suspicion and alertness of a trapped animal. He realized, with a pang, how young and vulnerable she was.

She said:

'What is it? What do you want?'

Hercule Poirot did not answer for a minute or two. Then he said:

'The other day you told the Chief Constable that you were fond of your stepmother and that she was kind to you.'

'Well?'

'That was not true, was it, Mademoiselle?'

'Yes, it was.'

Poirot said:

'She may not have been actively unkind – that I will grant. But you were not fond of her – Oh no – I think you disliked her very much. That was very plain to see.'

Linda said:

'Perhaps I didn't like her very much. But one can't say that when a person is dead. It wouldn't be decent.'

Poirot sighed. He said:

'They taught you that at your school?'

'More or less, I suppose.'

Hercule Poirot said:

'When a person has been murdered, it is more important to be truthful than to be decent.'

Linda said:

'I suppose you *would* say a thing like that.'

'I would say it and I do say it. It is my business, you see, to find out who killed Arlena Marshall.'

Linda muttered:

'I want to forget it all. It's so horrible.'

Poirot said gently:

'*But you can't forget, can you?*'

Linda said:

'I suppose some beastly madman killed her.'

Hercule Poirot murmured:

'No, I do not think it was quite like that.'

Linda caught her breath. She said:

'You sound – as though you *knew*?'

Poirot said:

'Perhaps I do know.' He paused and went on: 'Will you trust me, my child, to do the best I can for you in your bitter trouble?'

Linda sprang up. She said:

'I haven't any trouble. There is nothing you can do for me. I don't know what you are talking about.'

Poirot said, watching her:

'I am talking about *candles* . . .'

He saw the terror leap into her eyes. She cried:

'I won't listen to you. I won't listen.'

She ran across the beach, swift as a young gazelle and went flying up the zigzag path.

Poirot shook his head. He looked grave and troubled.

CHAPTER 11

I

Inspector Colgate was reporting to the Chief Constable.

'I've got on to one thing, sir, and something pretty sensational. It's about Mrs Marshall's money. I've been into it with her lawyers. I'd say it's a bit of a shock to them. I've got proof of the blackmail story. You remember she was left fifty thousand pounds by old Erskine? Well, all that's left of that is about fifteen thousand.'

The Chief Constable whistled.

'Whew, what's become of the rest?'

'That's the interesting point, sir. She's sold out stuff from time to time, and each time she's handled it in cash or negotiable securities – that's to say she's handed out money to someone that she didn't want traced. Blackmail all right.'

The Chief Constable nodded.

'Certainly looks like it. And the blackmailer is here in this hotel. That means it must be one of those three men. Got anything fresh on any of them?'

'Can't say I've got anything definite, sir. Major Barry's a retired Army man, as he says. Lives in a small flat, has a pension and a small income from stocks. *But* he's paid in pretty considerable sums into his account in the last year.'

'That sounds promising. What's his explanation?'

'Says they're betting gains. It's perfectly true that he goes to all the large race meetings. Places his bets on the course too, doesn't run an account.'

The Chief Constable nodded.

'Hard to disprove that,' he said. 'But it's suggestive.'

Colgate went on.

'Next, the Reverend Stephen Lane. He's *bona fide* all right – had a living at St Helen's, Whiteridge, Surrey – resigned his living just over a year ago owing to ill-health. His ill-health amounted to his going into a nursing home for mental patients. He was there for over a year.'

'Interesting,' said Weston.

'Yes, sir. I tried to get as much as I could out of the doctor in charge but you know what these medicos are – it's difficult to pin them down to anything you can get hold of. But as far as I can make out, his reverence's trouble was an obsession about the devil – especially the devil in the guise of a woman – scarlet woman – whore of Babylon.'

'H'm,' said Weston. 'There have been precedents for murder there.'

'Yes, sir. It seems to me that Stephen Lane is at least a possibility. The late Mrs Marshall was a pretty good example of what a clergyman would call a Scarlet Woman – hair and goings on and all. Seems to me it's not impossible he may have felt it his appointed task to dispose of her. That is if he is really batty.'

'Nothing to fit in with the blackmail theory?'

'No, sir, I think we can wash him out as far as that's concerned. Has some private means of his own, but not very much, and no sudden increase lately.'

'What about his story of his movements on the day of the crime?'

'Can't get any confirmation of them. Nobody remembers meeting a parson in the lanes. As to the book at the church, the last entry was three days before and nobody had looked at it for about a fortnight. He could have quite easily gone over the day before, say, or even a couple of days before, and dated his entry the 25th.'

Weston nodded. He said:

'And the third man?'

'Horace Blatt? It's my opinion, sir, that there's definitely something fishy there. Pays income-tax on a sum far exceeding what he makes out of his hardware business. And mind you, he's a slippery customer. He could probably cook up a reasonable statement – he gambles a bit on the Stock Exchange, and he's in with one or two shady deals. Oh, yes, there may be plausible explanations, but there's no getting away from it that he's been making pretty big sums from unexplained sources for some years now.'

'In fact,' said Weston, 'the idea is that Mr Horace Blatt is a successful blackmailer by profession?'

'Either that, sir, or it's dope. I saw Chief Inspector Ridgeway who's in charge of the dope business, and he was no end keen. Seems there's been a good bit of heroin coming in lately. They're on to the small distributors, and they know more or less who's running it the other end, but it's the way it's coming into the country that's baffled them so far.'

Weston said:

'If the Marshall woman's death is the result of her getting mixed up, innocently or otherwise, with the dope-running stunt, then we'd better hand the whole thing over to Scotland Yard. It's their pigeon. Eh? What do you say?'

Inspector Colgate said rather regretfully:

'I'm afraid you're right, sir. If it's dope, then it's a case for the Yard.'

Weston said after a moment or two's thought:

'It really seems the most likely explanation.'

Colgate nodded gloomily.

'Yes, it does. Marshall's right out of it – though I did get some information that might have been useful if his alibi hadn't been so good. Seems his firm is very near the rocks. Not his fault or his partner's, just the general result of the crisis last year and the general state of trade and finance. And as far as he knew, he'd come into fifty thousand pounds if his wife died. And fifty thousand would have been a very useful sum.'

He sighed.

'Seems a pity when a man's got two perfectly good motives for murder, that he can be proved to have had nothing to do with it!'

Weston smiled.

'Cheer up, Colgate. There's still a chance we may distinguish ourselves. There's the blackmail angle still and there's the batty parson, but, personally, I think the dope solution is far the most likely.' He added: 'And if it was one of the dope gang who put her out we'll have been instrumental in helping Scotland Yard to solve the dope problem. In fact, take it all round, one way or another, we've done pretty well.'

An unwilling smile showed on Colgate's face.

He said:

'Well, that's the lot, sir. By the way, I checked up on the writer of that letter we found in her room. The one signed J.N. Nothing doing. He's in China safe enough. Same chap as Miss Brewster was telling us about. Bit of a young scallywag. I've checked up on the rest of Mrs Marshall's friends. No leads there. Everything there is to get, we've got, sir.'

Weston said:

'So now it's up to us.' He paused and then added: 'Seen anything of our Belgian colleague? Does he know all you've told me?'

Colgate said with a grin:

'He's a queer little cuss, isn't he? D'you know what he asked me day before yesterday? He wanted particulars of any cases of strangulation in the last three years.'

Colonel Weston sat up.

'He did, did he? Now I wonder –' he paused a minute. 'When did you say the Reverend Stephen Lane went into that mental home?'

'A year ago last Easter, sir.'

Colonel Weston was thinking deeply. He said:

'There was a case – body of a young woman found somewhere near Bagshot. Going to meet her husband somewhere and never turned up. And there was what the papers called the Lonely Copse Mystery. Both in Surrey if I remember rightly.'

His eyes met those of his Inspector. Colgate said:

'Surrey? My word, sir, it fits, doesn't it? I wonder . . .'

II

Hercule Poirot sat on the turf on the summit of the island.

A little to his left was the beginning of the steel ladder that led down to Pixy Cove. There were several rough boulders near the head of the ladder, he noted, forming easy concealment for anyone who proposed to descend to the beach below. Of the beach itself little could be seen from the top owing to the overhang of the cliff.

Hercule Poirot nodded his head gravely.

The pieces of his jig-saw were fitting into position.

Mentally he went over those pieces, considering each as a detached item.

A morning on the bathing beach some few days before Arlena Marshall's death.

One, two, three, four, five separate remarks uttered on that morning.

The evening of a bridge game. He, Patrick Redfern and Rosamund Darnley had been at the table. Christine had wandered out while dummy and had overheard a certain conversation. Who else had been in the lounge at that time? Who had been absent?

The evening before the crime. The conversation he had had with Christine on the cliff and the scene he had witnessed on his way back to the hotel.

Gabrielle No 8.

A pair of scissors.

A broken pipe stem.

A bottle thrown from a window.

A green calendar.

A packet of candles.

A mirror and a typewriter.

A skein of magenta wool.

A girl's wristwatch.

Bathwater rushing down the waste-pipe.

Each of these unrelated facts must fit into its appointed place. There must be no loose ends.

And then, with each concrete fact fitted into position, on to the next stop: his own belief in the presence of evil on the island.

Evil . . .

He looked down at a typewritten paper in his hands.

Nellie Parsons – found strangled in a lonely copse near Chobham. No clue to her murderer ever discovered.

Nellie Parsons?

Alice Corrigan.

He read very carefully the details of Alice Corrigan's death.

III

To Hercule Poirot, sitting on the ledge overlooking the sea, came Inspector Colgate.

Poirot liked Inspector Colgate. He liked his rugged face, his shrewd eyes, and his slow unhurried manner.

Inspector Colgate sat down. He said, glancing down at the typewritten sheets in Poirot's hand:

'Done anything with those cases, sir?'

'I have studied them – yes.'

Colgate got up, he walked along and peered into the next niche. He came back, saying:

'One can't be too careful. Don't want to be overheard.'

Poirot said:

'You are wise.'

Colgate said:

'I don't mind telling you, M. Poirot, that I've been interested in those cases myself – though perhaps I shouldn't have thought about them if you hadn't asked for them.' He paused: 'I've been interested in one case in particular.'

'Alice Corrigan?'

'Alice Corrigan.' He paused. 'I've been on to the Surrey police about that case – wanted to get all the ins and outs of it.'

'Tell me, my friend. I am interested – very interested.'

'I thought you might be. Alice Corrigan was found strangled in Caesar's Grove on Blackridge Heath – not ten miles from Marley Copse where Nellie Parsons was found – and both those places are within twelve miles of Whiteridge where Mr Lane was vicar.'

Poirot said:

'Tell me more about the death of Alice Corrigan.'

Colgate said:

'The Surrey police didn't at first connect her death with that of Nellie Parsons. That's because they'd pitched on the husband as the guilty party. Don't quite know why except that he was a bit of what the Press calls a "mystery man" – not much known about him – who he was or where he came from. She'd married him against her people's wishes, she'd a bit of money of her own – and she'd insured her life in his favour – all that was enough to raise suspicion, as I think you'll agree, sir?'

Poirot nodded.

'But when it came down to brass tacks the husband was washed right out of the picture. The body was discovered by one of these women hikers – hefty young women in shorts. She was an absolutely competent and reliable witness – games mistress at a school in Lancashire. She noted the time when she found the body – it was exactly four-fifteen – and gave it as her opinion that the woman had been dead quite a short time – not more than ten minutes. That fitted in well enough with the police surgeon's view when he examined the body at 5.45. She left everything as it was and tramped across country to Bagshot police station where she reported the death. Now from three o'clock to four-ten, Edward Corrigan was in the train coming down from London where he'd gone up for the day on business. Four other people were in the carriage with him. From the station he took the local bus, two of his fellow passengers travelling by it also. He got off at the Pine Ridge Café where he'd arranged to meet his wife for tea. Time then was four twenty-five. He ordered tea for them both, but said not to bring it till she came. Then he walked about outside waiting for her. When, by five o'clock she hadn't turned up, he was getting alarmed – thought she might have sprained her ankle. The arrangement was that she was to walk across the moors from the village where they were staying to the Pine Ridge Café and go home by bus. Caesar's Grove is not far from the café, and it's thought that as she was ahead of time she sat down there to admire the view for a bit before going on, and that some tramp or madman came upon her there and caught her unawares. Once the husband was proved to be out of it, naturally they connected up her death with that of Nellie Parsons – that rather flighty servant girl who was found strangled in Marley Copse. They decided that the same man was responsible for both crimes, but they never caught him – and what's more they never came near to catching him! Drew a blank everywhere.'

He paused and then he said slowly:

'And now – here's a third woman strangled – and a certain gentleman we won't name right on the spot.'

He stopped.

His small shrewd eyes came round to Poirot. He waited hopefully.

Poirot's lips moved. Inspector Colgate leaned forward.

Poirot was murmuring:

'– so difficult to know which pieces are part of the fur rug and which are the cat's tail.'

'I *beg* pardon, sir?' said Inspector Colgate, startled.

Poirot said quickly:

'I apologize. I was following a train of thought of my own.'

'What's this about a fur rug and a cat?'

'Nothing – nothing at all.' He paused. 'Tell me, Inspector Colgate, if you suspected someone of telling lies – many, many lies but you had no proof, what would you do?'

Inspector Colgate considered.

'It's difficult, that is. But it's my opinion that if anyone tells enough lies, they're bound to trip up in the end.'

Poirot nodded.

'Yes, that is very true. You see, it is only in my mind that certain statements are lies. I *think* that they are lies, but I cannot *know* that they are lies. But one might perhaps make a test – a test of one little not very noticeable lie. And if that were proved to be a lie – why then, one would know that all the rest were lies, too!'

Inspector Colgate looked at him curiously.

'Your mind works a funny way, doesn't it, sir? But I dare say it comes out all right in the end. If you'll excuse me asking, what put you on to asking about strangulation cases in general?'

Poirot said slowly:

'You have a word in your language – *slick*. This crime seemed to me a very slick crime! It made me wonder if, perhaps, it was not a first attempt.'

Inspector Colgate said:

'I see.'

Poirot went on:

'I said to myself, let us examine past crimes of a similar kind and if there is a crime that closely resembles this one – *eh bien*, we shall have there a very valuable clue.'

'You mean using the same method of death, sir?'

'No, no, I mean more than that. The death of Nellie Parsons for instance tells me nothing. But the death of Alice Corrigan – tell me, Inspector Colgate, do you not notice one striking form of similarity in this crime?'

Inspector Colgate turned the problem over in his mind. He said at last.

'No, sir, I can't say that I do really. Unless it's that in each case the husband has got a cast-iron alibi.'

Poirot said softly:

'Ah, so you *have* noticed that?'

IV

'Ha, Poirot. Glad to see you. Come in. Just the man I want.'

Hercule Poirot responded to the invitation.

The Chief Constable pushed over a box of cigarettes, took one himself and lighted it. Between puffs he said:

'I've decided, more or less, on a course of action. But I'd like your opinion on it before I act decisively.'

Hercule Poirot said:

'Tell me, my friend.'

Weston said:

'I've decided to call in Scotland Yard and hand the case over to them. In my opinion, although there have been grounds for suspicion against one or two people, the whole case hinges on dope smuggling. It seems clear to me that that place, Pixy's Cave, was a definite rendezvous for the stuff.'

Poirot nodded.

'I agree.'

'Good man. And I'm pretty certain who our dope smuggler is. Horace Blatt.'

Again Poirot assented. He said:

'That, too, is indicated.'

'I see our minds have both worked the same way. Blatt used to go sailing in that boat of his. Sometimes he'd invite people to go with him, but most of the time he went out alone. He had some rather conspicuous red sails on that boat, but we've found that he had some white sails as well stowed away. I think he sailed out on a good day to an appointed spot, and was met by another boat – sailing boat or motor yacht – something of the kind and the stuff was handed over. Then Blatt would run ashore into Pixy Cove at a suitable time of day –'

Hercule Poirot smiled:

'Yes, yes, at half-past one. The hour of the British lunch when everyone is quite sure to be in the dining-room. The island is private. It is not a place where outsiders come for picnics. People take their tea sometimes from the hotel to Pixy Cove in the afternoon when the sun is on it, or if they want a picnic they would go somewhere far afield, many miles away.'

The Chief Constable nodded.

'Quite,' he said. 'Therefore, Blatt ran ashore there and stowed the stuff on that ledge in the cave. Somebody else was to pick it up there in due course.'

Poirot murmured:

'There was a couple, you remember, who came to the island for lunch on the day of the murder? That would be a way of getting the stuff. Some summer visitors from a hotel on the Moor or at St Loo come over to Smugglers' Island. They announce that they will have lunch. They walk round the island first. How easy to descend to the beach, pick up the sandwich box, place it, no doubt, in Madame's bathing-bag which she carries – and return for lunch to the hotel – a little late, perhaps, say at ten minutes to two, having enjoyed their walk whilst everyone else was in the dining-room.'

Weston said:

'Yes, it all sounds practicable enough. Now these dope organizations are pretty ruthless. If any one blundered in and got wise to things they wouldn't make any bones about silencing that person. It seems to me that that is the right explanation of Arlena Marshall's death. It's possible that on that morning Blatt was actually at the cove stowing the stuff away. His accomplices were to come for it that very day. Arlena arrives on her float and sees him going into the cave with the box. She asks him about it and he kills her then and there and sheers off in his boat as quick as possible.'

Poirot said:

'You think definitely that Blatt is the murderer?'

'It seems the most probable solution. Of course it's possible that Arlena might have got on to the truth earlier, said something to Blatt about it, and some other member of the gang fixed a fake appointment with her and did her in. As I say, I think the best course is to hand the case over to Scotland Yard. They've a far better chance than we have of proving Blatt's connection with the gang.'

Hercule Poirot nodded thoughtfully.

Weston said:

'You think that's the wise thing to do – eh?'

Poirot was thoughtful. He said at last: 'It may be.'

'Dash it all, Poirot, have you got something up your sleeve, or haven't you?'

Poirot said gravely:

'If I have, I am not sure that I can prove it.'

Weston said:

'Of course, I know that you and Colgate have other ideas. Seems a bit fantastic to me, but I'm bound to admit there may be something in it. But even if you're right. I still think it's a case for the Yard. We'll give them the facts and they can work in with the Surrey police. What I feel is that it isn't really a case for us. It's not sufficiently localized.'

He paused.

'What do you think, Poirot? What do you feel ought to be done about it?'

Poirot seemed lost in thought. At last he said:

'I know what I should like to do.'

'Yes, man.'

Poirot murmured:

'I should like to go for a picnic.'

Colonel Weston stared at him.

CHAPTER 12

I

'A picnic, M. Poirot?'

Emily Brewster stared at him as though he were out of his senses.

Poirot said engagingly:

'It sounds to you, does it not, very outrageous? But indeed it seems to me a most admirable idea. We need something of the every day, the usual, to restore life to the normal. I am most anxious to see something of Dartmoor, the weather is good. It will – how shall I say, it will cheer everybody up! So aid me in this matter. Persuade everyone.'

The idea met with unexpected success. Everyone was at first dubious and then grudgingly admitted it might not be such a bad idea after all.

It was not suggested that Captain Marshall should be asked.

He had himself announced that he had to go to Plymouth that day. Mr Blatt was of the party, enthusiastically so. He was determined to be the life and soul of it. Besides him there was Emily Brewster, the Redferns, Stephen Lane, the Gardeners, who were persuaded to delay their departure by one day, Rosamund Darnley and Linda.

Poirot had been eloquent to Rosamund and had dwelt on the advantage it would be to Linda to have something to take her out of herself. To this Rosamund agreed. She said:

'You're quite right. The shock has been very bad for a child of that age. It has made her terribly jumpy.'

'That is only natural, Mademoiselle. But at any age one soon forgets. Persuade her to come. You can, I know.'

Major Barry had refused firmly. He said he didn't like picnics. 'Lots of baskets to carry,' he said. 'And darned uncomfortable. Eating my food at a table's good enough for me.'

The party assembled at ten o'clock. Three cars had been ordered. Mr Blatt was loud and cheerful, imitating a tourist guide.

'This way, ladies and gentlemen – this way for Dartmoor. Heather and bilberries, Devonshire cream and convicts. Bring your wives, gentlemen, or bring the other thing! Everyone welcome! Scenery guaranteed. Walk up. Walk up.'

At the last minute Rosamund Darnley came down looking concerned. She said:

'Linda's not coming. She says she's got a frightful headache.'

Poirot cried:

'But it will do her good to come. Persuade her, Mademoiselle.'

Rosamund said firmly:

'It's no good. She's absolutely determined. I've given her some aspirin and she's gone to bed.'

She hesitated and said:

'I think, perhaps, I won't go, either.'

'Can't allow that, dear lady, can't allow that,' cried Mr Blatt, seizing her facetiously by the arm. '*La haute Mode* must grace the occasion. No refusals! I've taken you into custody, ha, ha. Sentenced to Dartmoor.'

He led her firmly to the first car. Rosamund threw a black look at Hercule Poirot.

'I'll stay with Linda,' said Christine Redfern. 'I don't mind a bit.'

Patrick said: 'Oh, come on, Christine.'

And Poirot said:

'No, no, you must come, Madame. With a headache one is better alone. Come, let us start.'

The three cars drove off. They went first to the real Pixy's Cave on Sheepstor, and had a good deal of fun looking for the entrance and at last finding it, aided by a picture postcard.

It was precarious going on the big boulders and Hercule Poirot did not attempt it. He watched indulgently while Christine Redfern sprang lightly from stone to stone and observed that her husband was never far from her. Rosamund Darnley and Emily Brewster had joined in the search though the latter slipped once and gave a slight twist to her ankle. Stephen Lane was indefatigable, his long lean figure turning and twisting among the boulders. Mr Blatt contented himself with going a little way and shouting encouragement, also taking photographs of the searchers.

The Gardeners and Poirot remained staidly sitting by the wayside whilst Mrs Gardener's voice upraised itself in a pleasant even-toned monologue, punctuated now and then by the obedient 'Yes, darlings' of her spouse.

'– and what I always have felt, M. Poirot, and Mr Gardener agrees with me, is that snapshots can be very annoying. Unless, that is to say, they are taken among friends. That Mr Blatt has just no sensitiveness of any kind. He just comes right up to everyone and talks away and takes pictures of you and, as I said to Mr Gardener, that really is very ill-bred. That's what I said, Odell, wasn't it?'

'Yes, darling.'

'That group he took of us all sitting on the beach. Well, that's all very well, but he should have asked first. As it was, Miss Brewster was just getting up from the beach, and it certainly makes her look a very peculiar shape.'

'I'll say it does,' said Mr Gardener with a grin.

'And there's Mr Blatt giving round copies to everybody without so much as asking first. He gave one to you, M. Poirot, I noticed.'

Poirot nodded. He said:

'I value that group very much.'

Mrs Gardener went on:

'And look at his behaviour today – so loud and noisy and common. Why, it just makes me shudder. You ought to have arranged to leave that man at home, M. Poirot.'

Hercule Poirot murmured:

'Alas, Madame, that would have been difficult.'

'I should say it would. That man just pushes his way in anywhere. He's just not sensitive at all.'

At this moment the discovery of the Pixy's Cave was hailed from below with loud cries.

The party now drove on, under Hercule Poirot's directions, to a spot where a short walk from the car down a hillside of heather led to a delightful spot by a small river.

A narrow plank bridge crossed the river and Poirot and her husband induced Mrs Gardener to cross it to where a delightful heathery spot free from prickly furze looked an ideal spot for a picnic lunch.

Talking volubly about her sensations when crossing on a plank bridge Mrs Gardener sank down. Suddenly there was a slight outcry.

The others had run across the bridge lightly enough, but Emily Brewster was standing in the middle of the plank, her eyes shut, swaying to and fro.

Poirot and Patrick Redfern rushed to the rescue.

Emily Brewster was gruff and ashamed.

'Thanks, thanks. Sorry. Never was good at crossing running water. Get giddy. Stupid, very.'

Lunch was spread out and the picnic began.

All the people concerned were secretly surprised to find how much they enjoyed this interlude. It was, perhaps, because it afforded an escape from an atmosphere of suspicion and dread. Here, with the trickling of the water, the soft peaty smell in the air and the warm colouring of bracken and heather, a world of murder and police inquiries and suspicion seemed blotted out as though it had never existed. Even Mr Blatt forgot to be the life and soul of the party. After lunch he went to sleep a little distance away and subdued snores testified to his blissful unconsciousness.

It was quite a grateful party of people who packed up the picnic baskets and congratulated Hercule Poirot on his good idea.

The sun was sinking as they returned along the narrow winding lanes. From the top of the hill above Leathercombe Bay they had a brief glimpse of the island with the white hotel on it.

It looked peaceful and innocent in the setting sun.

Mrs Gardener, not loquacious for once, sighed and said:

'I really do thank you, M. Poirot. I feel so calm. It's just wonderful.'

II

Major Barry came out to greet them on arrival.

'Hullo,' he said. 'Had a good day?'

Mrs Gardener said:

'Indeed we did. The moors were just too lovely for anything. So English and old world. And the air delicious and invigorating. You ought to be ashamed of yourself for being so lazy as to stay behind.'

The Major chuckled.

'I'm too old for that kind of thing – sitting on a patch of bog and eating sandwiches.'

A chambermaid had come out of the hotel. She was a little out of breath. She hesitated for a moment then came swiftly up to Christine Redfern.

Hercule Poirot recognized her as Gladys Narracott. Her voice came quick and uneven.

'Excuse me, Madam, but I'm worried about the young lady. About Miss Marshall. I took her up some tea just now and I couldn't get her to wake, and she looks so – so queer somehow.'

Christine looked round helplessly. Poirot was at her side in a moment. His hand under her elbow he said quietly:

'We will go up and see.'

They hurried up the stairs and along the passage to Linda's room.

One glance at her was enough to tell them both that something was very wrong. She was an odd colour and her breathing was hardly perceptible.

Poirot's hand went to her pulse. At the same time he noticed an envelope stuck up against the lamp on the bedside table. It was addressed to himself.

Captain Marshall came quickly into the room. He said:

'What's this about Linda? What's the matter with her?'

A small frightened sob came from Christine Redfern.

Hercule Poirot turned from the bed. He said to Marshall:

'Get a doctor – as quick as you possibly can. But I'm afraid – very much afraid – it may be too late.'

He took the letter with his name on it and ripped open the envelope. Inside were a few lines of writing in Linda's prim schoolgirl hand.

> *I think this is the best way out. Ask Father to try and forgive me. I killed Arlena. I thought I should be glad – but I'm not. I am very sorry for everything.*

III

They were assembled in the lounge – Marshall, the Redferns, Rosamund Darnley and Hercule Poirot.

They sat there silent – waiting . . .

The door opened and Dr Neasden came in. He said curtly:

'I've done all I can. She may pull through – but I'm bound to tell you that there's not much hope.'

He paused. Marshall, his face stiff, his eyes a cold frosty blue, asked:

'How did she get hold of the stuff?'

Neasden opened the door again and beckoned.

The chambermaid came into the room. She had been crying:

Neasden said:

'Just tell us again what you saw.'

Sniffing, the girl said:

'I never thought – I never thought for a minute there was anything wrong – though the young lady did seem rather strange about it.' A slight gesture of impatience from the doctor started her off again. 'She was in the other lady's room. Mrs Redfern's. Your room, Madam. Over at the washstand, and she took up a little bottle. She did give a bit of a jump when I came in, and I thought it was queer her taking things from your room, but then, of course, it might be something she'd lent you.

She just said: "Oh, this is what I'm looking for –" and went out.'

Christine said almost in a whisper.

'My sleeping tablets.'

The doctor said brusquely:

'How did she know about them?'

Christine said:

'I gave her one. The night after it happened. She told me she couldn't sleep. She – I remember her saying – "Will one be enough?" – and I said, Oh yes, they were very strong – that I'd been cautioned never to take more than two at most.' Neasden nodded: 'She made pretty sure,' he said. 'Took six of them.'

Christine sobbed again.

'Oh dear, I feel it's my fault. I should have kept them locked up.'

The doctor shrugged his shoulders.

'It might have been wiser, Mrs Redfern.'

Christine said despairingly:

'She's dying – and it's my fault . . .'

Kenneth Marshall stirred in his chair. He said:

'No, you can't blame yourself. Linda knew what she was doing. She took them deliberately. Perhaps – perhaps it was best.'

He looked down at the crumpled note in his hand – the note that Poirot had silently handed to him.

Rosamund Darnley cried out.

'I don't believe it. I don't believe Linda killed her. Surely it's impossible – on the evidence!'

Christine said eagerly:

'Yes, she *can't* have done it! She must have got overwrought and imagined it all.'

The door opened and Colonel Weston came in. He said:

'What's all this I hear?'

Dr Neasden took the note from Marshall's hand and handed it to the Chief Constable. The latter read it. He exclaimed incredulously:

'What? But this is nonsense – absolute nonsense! It's impossible.' He repeated with assurance. 'Impossible! Isn't it, Poirot?'

Hercule Poirot moved for the first time. He said in a slow sad voice:

'No, I'm afraid it is not impossible.'

Christine Redfern said:

'But I was with her, M. Poirot. I was with her up to a quarter to twelve. I told the police so.'

Poirot said:

'Your evidence gave her an alibi – yes. But what was your evidence based on? It was based on *Linda Marshall's own wristwatch*. You do not know *of your own knowledge* that it was a quarter to twelve when you left her – you only know that she told you so. You said yourself the time seemed to have gone very fast.'

She stared at him, stricken.

He said:

'Now, think, Madame, when you left the beach, did you walk back to the hotel fast or slow?'

'I – well, fairly slowly, I think.'

'Do you remember much about that walk back?'

'Not very much, I'm afraid. I – I was thinking.'

Poirot said:

'I am sorry to ask you this, but will you tell just what you were thinking about during that walk?'

Christine flushed.

'I suppose – if it is necessary . . . I was considering the question of – of leaving here. Just going away without telling my husband. I – I was very unhappy just then, you see.'

Patrick Redfern cried:

'Oh, Christine! I know . . . I know . . .'

Poirot's precise voice cut in.

'Exactly. You were concerned over taking a step of some importance. You were, I should say, deaf and blind to your surroundings. You probably walked very slowly and occasionally stopped for some minutes whilst you puzzled things out.'

Christine nodded.

'How clever you are. It was just like that. I woke up from a kind of dream just outside the hotel and hurried in thinking I should be very late, but when I saw the clock in the lounge I realized I had plenty of time.'

Hercule Poirot said again:

'Exactly.'

He turned to Marshall.

'I must now describe to you certain things I found in your daughter's room after the murder. In the grate was a large blob of melted wax, some burnt hair, fragments of cardboard and paper and an ordinary household pin. The paper and the cardboard might not be relevant, but the other three things were suggestive – particularly when I found tucked away in the bookshelf a volume from the local library here dealing with witchcraft and magic. It opened very easily at a certain page. On that page were described various methods of causing death by moulding in wax a figure supposed to represent the victim. This was then slowly roasted till it melted away – or alternatively you would pierce the wax figure to the heart with a pin. Death of the victim would ensue. I later heard from Mrs Redfern that Linda Marshall had been out early that morning and had bought a packet of candles, and had seemed embarrassed when her purchase was revealed. I had no doubt what had happened after that. Linda had made a crude figure of the candle wax – possibly adorning it with a snip of Arlena's red hair to give the magic force – had then stabbed it to the heart with a pin and finally melted the figure away by lighting strips of cardboard under it.

'It was crude, childish, superstitious, but it revealed one thing: the desire to kill.

'Was there any possibility that there had been more than a desire? Could Linda Marshall have *actually* killed her stepmother?

'At first sight it seemed as though she had a perfect alibi – but in actuality, as I have just pointed out, the time evidence was supplied *by Linda herself*. She could easily have declared the time to be a quarter of an hour later than it really was.

'It was quite possible once Mrs Redfern had left the beach for Linda to follow her up and then strike across the narrow neck of land to the ladder, hurry down it, meet her stepmother there, strangle her and return up the ladder before the boat containing Miss Brewster and Patrick Redfern came in sight. She could then return to Gull Cove, take her bathe and return to the hotel at her leisure.

'But that entailed two things. She must have definite knowledge that Arlena Marshall would be at Pixy Cove and she must be physically capable of the deed.

'Well, the first was quite possible – if Linda Marshall had written a note to Arlena herself in someone else's name. As to the second, Linda has very large strong hands. They are as large as a man's. As to the strength, she is at the age when one is prone to be mentally unbalanced. Mental derangement often is accompanied by unusual strength. There was one other small point. Linda Marshall's mother had actually been accused and tried for murder.'

Kenneth Marshall lifted his head. He said fiercely: 'She was also acquitted.'

'She was acquitted,' Poirot agreed.

Marshall said:

'And I'll tell you this, M. Poirot. Ruth – my wife – was innocent. That I know with complete and absolute certainty. In the intimacy of our life I could not have been deceived. She was an innocent victim of circumstances.'

He paused.

'And I don't believe that Linda killed Arlena. It's ridiculous – absurd!'

Poirot said:

'Do you believe that letter, then, to be a forgery?'

Marshall held out his hand for it and Weston gave it to him. Marshall studied it attentively. Then he shook his head.

'No,' he said unwillingly. 'I believe Linda did write this.'

Poirot said:

'Then if she wrote it, there are only two explanations. Either she wrote it in all good faith, knowing herself to be the murderess or – or, I say – *she wrote it deliberately to shield someone else*, someone whom she feared was suspected.'

Kenneth Marshall said:

'You mean me?'

'It is possible, is it not?'

Marshall considered for a moment or two, then he said quietly:

'No, I think that idea is absurd. Linda may have realized that I was regarded with suspicion at first. But she knew definitely by now that that was over and done with – that the police had accepted my alibi and turned their attention elsewhere.'

Poirot said:

'And supposing that it was not so much that she thought that you were suspected as that she *knew* you were guilty.'

Marshall stared at him. He gave a short laugh.

'That's absurd.'

Poirot said:

'I wonder. There are, you know, several possibilities about Mrs Marshall's death. There is the theory that she was being blackmailed, that she went that morning to meet the blackmailer and that the blackmailer killed her. There is the theory that Pixy Cove and Cave were being used for drug-running, and that she was killed because she accidentally learned something about that. There is a third possibility – that she was killed by a religious maniac. And there is a fourth possibility – you stood to gain a lot of money by your wife's death, Captain Marshall?'

'I've just told you –'

'Yes, yes – I agree that it is impossible that you could have killed your wife – *if you were acting alone*. But supposing someone helped you?'

'What the devil do you mean?'

The quiet man was roused at last. He half rose from his chair. His voice was menacing. There was a hard angry light in his eyes.

Poirot said:

'I mean that this is not a crime that was committed single-handed. Two people were in it. It is quite true that you could not have typed that letter and at the same time gone to the cove – but there would have been time for you to have jotted down that letter in shorthand – and for *someone else* to have typed it in your room while you yourself were absent on your murderous errand.'

Hercule Poirot looked towards Rosamund Darnley. He said:

'Miss Darnley states that she left Sunny Ledge at ten minutes past eleven and saw you typing in your room. But just about that time Mr Gardener went up to the hotel to fetch a skein of wool for his wife. He did not meet Miss Darnley or see her. That is rather remarkable. It looks as though either Miss Darnley never left Sunny Ledge, or else she had left it much earlier and was in your room typing industriously. Another point, you stated that when Miss Darnley looked into your room at a quarter past eleven *you saw her in the mirror*. But on the day of the murder your typewriter and papers were all on the writing-desk across the corner of the room, whereas the mirror was between the windows. So that statement was a deliberate lie. Later, you moved your typewriter to the table under the mirror so as to substantiate your story – but it was too late. I was aware that both you and Miss Darnley had lied.'

Rosamund Darnley spoke. Her voice was low and clear.

She said:

'How devilishly ingenious you are!'

Hercule Poirot said, raising his voice:

'But not so devilish and so ingenious as the man who killed Arlena Marshall! Think back for a moment. Who did I think – who did everybody think – that Arlena Marshall had gone to meet that morning? We all jumped to the same conclusion. *Patrick Redfern*. It was not to meet a blackmailer that she went. Her face alone would have told me that. Oh no, it was a lover she was going to meet – or thought she was going to meet.

'Yes, I was quite sure of that. Arlena Marshall was going to meet Patrick Redfern. But a minute later Patrick Redfern appeared on the beach and was obviously looking for her. So what then?'

Patrick Redfern said with subdued anger:

'Some devil used my name.'

Poirot said:

'You were very obviously upset and surprised by her non-appearance. Almost too obviously, perhaps. It is *my* theory, Mr Redfern, that she went to Pixy Cove to meet *you*, and that she *did* meet you, and that *you killed her there as you had planned to do*.'

Patrick Redfern stared. He said in his high good-humoured Irish voice:

'Is it daft you are? I was with you on the beach until I went round in the boat with Miss Brewster and found her dead.'

Hercule Poirot said:

'You killed her after Miss Brewster had gone off in the boat to fetch the police. Arlena Marshall was not dead when you got to the beach. She was waiting hidden in the cave until the coast could be clear.'

'But the body! Miss Brewster and I both saw the body.'

'*A* body – yes. But not a *dead* body. The *live* body of the woman who helped you, her arms and legs stained with tan, her face hidden by a green cardboard hat. Christine, your wife (or possibly not your wife – but still your partner), helping you to commit this crime as she helped you to commit that crime in the past when she 'discovered' the body of Alice Corrigan at least twenty minutes before Alice Corrigan died – killed by her husband Edward Corrigan – you!'

Christine spoke. Her voice was sharp – cold. She said:

'Be careful, Patrick, don't lose your temper.'

Poirot said:

'You will be interested to hear that both you and your wife Christine were easily recognized and picked out by the Surrey police from a group of people photographed here. They identified you both at once as Edward Corrigan and Christine Deverill, the young woman who found the body.'

Patrick Redfern had risen. His handsome face was transformed, suffused with blood, blind with rage. It was the face of a killer – of a tiger. He yelled:

'You damned interfering murdering lousy little worm!'

He hurled himself forward, his fingers stretching and curling, his voice raving curses, as he fastened his fingers round Hercule Poirot's throat . . .

CHAPTER 13

I

Poirot said reflectively:

'It was on a morning when we were sitting out here that we talked of sun-tanned bodies lying like meat upon a slab, and it was then that I reflected how little difference there was between one body and another. If one looked closely and appraisingly – yes – but to the casual glance? One moderately well-made young woman is very like another. Two brown legs, two brown arms, a little piece of bathing suit in between – just a body lying out in the sun. When a woman walks, when she speaks, laughs, turns her head, moves a hand – then, yes then, there is personality – individuality. But in the sun ritual – no.

'It was that day that we spoke of evil – *evil under the sun* as Mr Lane put it. Mr Lane is a very sensitive person – evil affects him – he perceives its presence – but though he is a good recording instrument, he did not really know exactly where the evil was. To him, evil was focused in the person of Arlena Marshall, and practically everyone present agreed with him.

'But to my mind, though evil was present, it was not centralized in Arlena Marshall at all. It was connected with her, yes – but in a totally different way. I saw her, first, last and all the time, as an eternal and predestined *victim*. Because she was beautiful, because she had glamour, because men turned their heads to look at her, it was assumed that she was the type of woman who wrecked lives and destroyed souls. But I saw her very differently. It was not she who fatally attracted men – it was men who fatally attracted her. She was the type of woman whom men care for easily and of whom they as easily tire. And everything that I was told or found out about her strengthened my conviction on this point. The first thing that was mentioned about her was how the man in whose divorce case she had been cited refused to marry her. It was then that Captain Marshall, one of those incurably chivalrous men, stepped in and asked her to marry him. To a shy retiring man of Captain Marshall's type, a public ordeal of any kind would be the worst torture – hence his love and pity for his first wife who was publicly accused and tried for a murder she had not committed. He married her and found himself amply justified in his estimate of her character. After her death another beautiful woman, perhaps something of the same type (since Linda has red hair which she probably inherited from her mother), is held up to public ignominy. Again Marshall performs a rescue act. But this time he finds little to sustain his infatuation. Arlena is stupid, unworthy of his sympathy and protection, mindless. Nevertheless, I think he always had a fairly true vision of her. Long after he ceased to love her and was irked by her presence, he remained sorry for her. She was to him like a child who cannot get farther than a certain page in the book of life.

'I saw in Arlena Marshall with her passion for men, a predestined prey for an unscrupulous man of a certain type. In Patrick Redfern, with his good looks, his easy assurance, his undeniable charm for women, I recognized at once that type. The adventurer who makes his living, one way or another, out of women. Looking on from my place on the beach I was quite certain that Arlena was Patrick's victim, not the other way about. And I associated that focus of evil with Patrick Redfern, not with Arlena Marshall.

'Arlena had recently come into a large sum of money, left her by an elderly admirer who had not had time to grow tired of her. She was the type of woman who is invariably defrauded of money by some man or other. Miss Brewster mentioned a young man who had been "ruined" by Arlena, but a letter from him which was found in her room, though it expressed a wish (which cost nothing) to cover her with jewels, in actual *fact* acknowledged a cheque from *her* by means of which he hoped to escape prosecution. A clear case of a young waster sponging on her. I have no doubt that Patrick Redfern found it easy to induce her to hand him large sums from time to time "for investment". He probably dazzled her with stories of great opportunities – how he would make her fortune and his own. Unprotected women, living alone, are easy prey to that type of man – and he usually escapes scot free with the booty. If, however, there is a husband, or a brother, or a father about, things are apt to take an unpleasant turn for the swindler. Once Captain Marshall was to find out what had happened to his wife's fortune, Patrick Redfern might expect short shrift.

'That did not worry him, however, because he contemplated quite calmly doing away with her when he judged it necessary – encouraged by having already got away with one murder – that of a young woman whom he had married in the name of Corrigan and whom he had persuaded to insure her life for a large sum.

'In his plans he was aided and abetted by the woman who down here passed as his wife and to whom he was genuinely attached. A young woman as unlike the type of his victims as could well be imagined – cool, calm, passionless, but steadfastly loyal to him and an actress of no mean ability. From the time of her arrival here Christine Redfern played a part, the part of the "poor little wife" – frail, helpless, intellectual rather than athletic. Think of the points she made one after another. Her tendency to blister in the sun and her consequent white skin, her giddiness at heights – stories of getting stuck on Milan Cathedral, etc. An emphasis on her frailty and delicacy – nearly every one spoke of her as a "little woman". She was actually as tall as Arlena Marshall, but with very small hands and feet. She spoke of herself as a former school-teacher, and thereby emphasized an impression of book learning and lack of athletic prowess. Actually, it is quite true that she had worked in a school, but the position she held there was that of *games mistress*, and she was an extremely active young woman who could climb like a cat and run like an athlete.

'The crime itself was perfectly planned and timed. It was, as I mentioned before, a very slick crime. The timing was a work of genius.

'First of all there were certain preliminary scenes – one played on the cliff ledge when they knew me to be occupying the next recess – a conventional jealous wife dialogue between her and her husband. Later she played the same part in a scene with me. At the time I remember a vague feeling of having read all this in a book. It did not seem *real*. Because, of course, it was *not* real. Then came the day of the crime. It was a fine day – an essential. Redfern's first act was to slip out very early – by the balcony door which he unlocked from the inside (if found open it would only be thought someone had gone for an early bathe). Under his bathing-wrap he concealed a green Chinese hat, the duplicate of the one Arlena was in the habit of wearing. He slipped across the island, down the ladder and stowed it away in an appointed place behind some rocks. Part I.

'On the previous evening he had arranged a rendezvous with Arlena. They were exercising a good deal of caution about meeting as Arlena was slightly afraid of her husband. She agreed to go round to Pixy Cove early. Nobody went there in the morning. Redfern was to join her there, taking a chance to slip away unobtrusively. If she heard anyone descending the ladder or a boat came in sight she was to slip inside the Pixy's Cave, the secret of which he had told her, and wait there until the coast was clear. Part II.

'In the meantime Christine went to Linda's room at a time when she judged Linda would have gone for her early morning dip. She would then alter Linda's watch, putting it on twenty minutes. There was, of course, a risk that Linda might notice her watch was wrong, but it did not much matter if she did.

Christine's real alibi was the size of her hands which made it a physical impossibility for her to have committed the crime. Nevertheless, an additional alibi would be desirable. Then in Linda's room she noticed the book on witchcraft and magic, open at a certain page. She read it, and when Linda came in and dropped a parcel of candles she realized what was in Linda's mind. It opened up some new ideas to her. The original idea of the guilty pair had been to cast a reasonable amount of suspicion on Kenneth Marshall, hence the abstracted pipe, a fragment of which was to be planted on the Cove underneath the ladder.

'On Linda's return Christine easily arranged an outing together to Gull Cove. She then returned to her own room, took out from a locked suitcase a bottle of artificial suntan, applied it carefully and threw the empty bottle out of the window where it narrowly escaped hitting Emily Brewster who was bathing. Part II successfully accomplished.

'Christine then dressed herself in a white bathing-suit, and over it a pair of beach trousers and coat with long floppy sleeves which effectually concealed her newly-browned arms and legs.

'At 10.15 Arlena departed for her rendezvous, a minute or two later Patrick Redfern came down and registered surprise, annoyance etc. Christine's task was easy enough. Keeping her own watch concealed she asked Linda at twenty-five past eleven what time it was. Linda looked at her watch and replied that it was a quarter to twelve. She then starts down to the sea and Christine packs up her sketching things. As soon as Linda's back is turned Christine picks up the girl's watch which she has necessarily discarded before going into the sea and alters it back to the correct time. Then she hurries up the cliff path, runs across the narrow neck of land to the top of the ladder, strips off her pyjamas and shoves them and her sketching box behind a rock and swarms rapidly down the ladder in her best gymnastic fashion.

'Arlena is on the beach below wondering why Patrick is so long in coming. She sees or hears someone on the ladder, takes a cautious observation, and to her annoyance sees that inconvenient person – the wife! She hurries along the beach and into the Pixy's Cave.

'Christine takes the hat from its hiding-place, a false red curl pinned underneath the brim at the back, and disposes herself in a sprawling attitude with the hat and curl shielding her face and neck. The timing is perfect. A minute or two later the boat containing Patrick and Emily Brewster comes round the point. Remember it is *Patrick* who bends down and examines the body, *Patrick* who is stunned – shocked – broken down by the death of his lady love! His witness has been carefully chosen. Miss Brewster has not got a good head, she will not attempt to go up the ladder. She will leave the Cove by boat, Patrick naturally being the one to remain with the body – "in case the murderer may still be about". Miss Brewster rows off to fetch the police. Christine, as soon as the boat has disappeared, springs up, cuts the hat into pieces with the scissors Patrick has carefully brought, stuffs them into her bathing-suit and swarms up the ladder in double quick time, slips into her beach-pyjamas and runs back to the hotel. Just time to have a quick bath, washing off the brown suntan application, and into her tennis dress. One other thing she does. She burns the pieces of the green cardboard hat and the hair in Linda's grate, adding a leaf of a calendar so that it may be associated with the cardboard. Not a *Hat* but a *Calendar* has been burnt. As she suspected, Linda has been experimenting in magic – the blob of wax and the pin shows that.

'Then, down to the tennis court, arriving the last, but showing no signs of flurry or haste.

'And, meanwhile, Patrick has gone to the cave. Arlena has seen nothing and heard very little – a boat – voices – she has prudently remained hidden. But now it is Patrick calling.

'"All clear, darling," and she comes out, and his hands fasten round her neck – and that is the end of poor foolish beautiful Arlena Marshall . . .'

His voice died away.

For a moment there was silence, then Rosamund Darnley said with a little shiver:

'Yes, you make one see it all. But that's the story from the other side. You haven't told us how *you* came to get at the truth?'

Hercule Poirot said:

'I told you once that I had a very simple mind. Always, from the beginning, it seemed to me that *the most likely person* had killed Arlena Marshall. And the most likely person was Patrick

Redfern. He was the type, *par excellence* – the type of man who exploits women like her – and the type of the killer – the kind of man who will take a woman's savings and cut her throat into the bargain. Who was Arlena going to meet that morning? By the evidence of her face, her smile, her manner, her words to me – *Patrick Redfern*. And therefore, in the very nature of things, it should be Patrick who killed her.

'But at once I came up, as I told you, against impossibility. Patrick Redfern could not have killed her since he was on the beach and in Miss Brewster's company until the actual discovery of the body. So I looked about for other solutions – and there were several. She could have been killed by her husband – with Miss Darnley's connivance. (They too had both lied as to one point which looked suspicious.) She could have been killed as a result of her having stumbled on the secret of the dope smuggling. She could have been killed, as I said, by a religious maniac, and she could have been killed by her stepdaughter. The latter seemed to me at one time to be the real solution. Linda's manner in her very first interview with the police was significant. An interview that I had with her later assured me of one point. Linda considered herself guilty.'

'You mean she imagined that she had actually killed Arlena?' Rosamund's voice was incredulous.

Hercule Poirot nodded.

'Yes. Remember – she is really little more than a child. She read that book on witchcraft and she half believed it. She hated Arlena. She deliberately made the wax doll, cast her spell, pierced it to the heart, melted it away – *and that very day Arlena dies*. Older and wiser people than Linda have believed fervently in magic. Naturally, she believed that it was all true – that by using magic she had killed her stepmother.'

Rosamund cried:

'Oh, poor child, poor child. And I thought – I imagined – something quite different – that she knew something which would –'

Rosamund stopped. Poirot said:

'I know what it was you thought. Actually your manner frightened Linda still further. She believed that her action had really brought about Arlena's death and that you knew it. Christine

Redfern worked on her too, introducing the idea of the sleeping tablets to her mind, showing her the way to a speedy and painless expiation of her crime. You see, once Captain Marshall was proved to have an alibi, it was vital for a new suspect to be found. Neither she nor her husband knew about the dope smuggling. They fixed on Linda to be the scapegoat.'

Rosamund said:

'What a devil!'

Poirot nodded.

'Yes, you are right. A cold-blooded and cruel woman. For me, I was in great difficulty. Was Linda guilty only of the childish attempt at witchcraft, or had her hate carried her still further – to the actual act? I tried to get her to confess to me. But it was no good. At that moment I was in grave uncertainty. The Chief Constable was inclined to accept the dope smuggling explanation. I couldn't let it go at that. I went over the facts again very carefully. I had, you see, a collection of jig-saw puzzle pieces, isolated happenings – plain facts. The whole must fit into a complete and harmonious pattern. There were the scissors found on the beach – a bottle thrown from a window – a bath that no one would admit to having taken – all perfectly harmless occurrences in themselves, but rendered significant by the fact that no one would admit to them. Therefore, they *must* be of significance. Nothing about them fitted in with the theories of either Captain Marshall's or Linda's, or of a dope gang's being responsible. And yet they *must* have meaning. I went back again to my first solution – that Patrick Redfern had committed the murder. Was there anything in support of that? Yes, the fact that a very large sum of money was missing from Arlena's account. Who had got that money? Patrick Redfern of course. She was the type of woman easily swindled by a handsome young man – but she was not at all the type of woman to be blackmailed. She was far too transparent, not good enough at keeping a secret. The blackmailer story had never rung true to my mind. And yet there *had* been that conversation overheard – ah, but overheard by whom? *Patrick Redfern's wife.* It was her story – unsupported by any outside evidence. Why was it invented? The answer came to me like lightning. To account for the absence of Arlena's money!

'Patrick and Christine Redfern. The two of them were in it together. Christine hadn't got the physical strength to strangle her or the mental make up. No, it was Patrick who had done it – but that was impossible! Every minute of his time was accounted for until the body was found.

'Body – the word stirred something in my mind – bodies lying on the beach – *all alike*. Patrick Redfern and Emily Brewster had got to the Cove and seen *a body* lying there. A body – suppose it was not Arlena's body but somebody else's? The face was hidden by the great Chinese hat.

'But there *was* only one dead body – Arlena's. Then, could it be – a *live* body – someone pretending to be dead? Could it be Arlena herself, inspired by Patrick to play some kind of a joke. I shook my head – no, too risky. A live body – whose? Was there any woman who would help Redfern? Of course – his wife. But she was a white-skinned delicate creature. Ah yes, but suntan can be applied out of bottles – bottles – I had one of my jig-saw pieces. Yes, and afterwards, of course, a bath – to wash that tell-tale stain off before she went out to play tennis. And the scissors? Why, to cut up that duplicate cardboard hat – an unwieldy thing that must be got out of the way, and in the haste the scissors were left behind – the one thing that the pair of murderers forgot.

'But where was Arlena all the time? That again was perfectly clear. Either Rosamund Darnley or Arlena Marshall had been in the Pixy's Cave, the scent they both used told me that. It was certainly not Rosamund Darnley. Then it was Arlena, hiding till the coast should clear.

'When Emily Brewster went off in the boat, Patrick had the beach to himself and full opportunity to commit the crime. Arlena Marshall was killed after a quarter to twelve, but the medical evidence was only concerned with the earliest possible time the crime could have been committed. That Arlena was dead at a quarter to twelve was what was told to the doctor, not what he told the police.

'Two more points had to be settled. Linda Marshall's evidence gave Christine Redfern an alibi. Yes, but that evidence depended on Linda Marshall's wristwatch. All that was needed was to prove that Christine had had two opportunities of tampering with the watch. I found those easily enough. She had been alone in Linda's room that morning – and there was an indirect proof. Linda was heard to say that she was "afraid she was going to be late", but when she got down it was only twenty-five past ten by the lounge clock. The second opportunity was easy – she could alter the watch back again as soon as Linda turned her back and went down to bathe.

'Then there was the question of the ladder. Christine had always declared she had no head for heights. Another carefully prepared lie.

'I had my mosaic now – each piece beautifully fitted into its place. But, unfortunately, I had no definite proof. It was all in my mind.

'It was then that an idea came to me. There was an assurance – a slickness about the crime. I had no doubt that in the future Patrick Redfern would repeat his crime. What about the past? It was remotely possible that this was not his first killing. The method employed, strangulation, was in harmony with his nature – a killer for pleasure as well as for profit. If he was already a murderer I was sure that he would have used the same means. I asked Inspector Colgate for a list of women victims of strangulation. The result filled me with joy. The death of Nellie Parson found strangled in a lonely copse might or might not be Patrick Redfern's work – it might merely have suggested choice of locality to him, but in Alice Corrigan's death I found exactly what I was looking for. In essence the same method. Juggling with time – a murder committed not, as is the usual way, *before* it is supposed to have happened, but *afterwards*. A body supposedly discovered at a quarter past four. A husband with an alibi up to twenty-five past four.

'What really happened? It was said that Edward Corrigan arrived at the Pine Ridge, found his wife not there, *and went out* and *walked up and down*. Actually, of course, he ran full speed to the rendezvous, Caesar's Grove (which you will remember was quite nearby), killed her and returned to the café. The girl hiker who reported the crime was a most respectable young lady, games mistress in a well-known girls' school. Apparently she had no connection with Edward Corrigan. She had to walk some way to report the death. The police surgeon only examined the body at a quarter to six. As in this case the time of death was accepted without question.

'I made one final test. I must know definitely if Mrs Redfern was a liar. I arranged our little excursion to Dartmoor. If anyone has a bad head for heights, they are never comfortable crossing a narrow bridge over running water. Miss Brewster, a genuine sufferer, showed giddiness. But Christine Redfern, unconcerned, ran across without a qualm. It was a small point, but it was a definite test. If she had told one unnecessary lie – then all the other lies were possible. In the meantime Colgate had got the photograph identified by the Surrey Police. I played my hand in the only way I thought likely to succeed. Having lulled Patrick Redfern into security, I turned on him and did my utmost to make him lose his self-control. The knowledge that he had been identified with Corrigan caused him to lose his head completely.'

Hercule Poirot stroked his throat reminiscently.

'What I did,' he said with importance, 'was exceedingly dangerous – but I do not regret it. I succeeded! I did not suffer in vain.'

There was a moment's silence. Then Mrs Gardener gave a deep sigh.

'Why, M. Poirot,' she said. 'It's just been too wonderful – hearing just exactly how you got your results. It's every bit as fascinating as a lecture on criminology – in fact it *is* a lecture on criminology. And to think my magenta wool and that sun-bathing conversation actually had something to do with it? That really makes me too excited for words, and I'm sure Mr Gardener feels the same, don't you, Odell?'

'Yes, darling,' said Mr Gardener.

Hercule Poirot said:

'Mr Gardener too was of assistance to me. I wanted the opinion of a sensible man about Mrs Marshall. I asked Mr Gardener what he thought of her.'

'Is that so,' said Mrs Gardener. 'And what did you say about her, Odell?'

Mr Gardener coughed. He said:

'Well, darling, I never did think very much of her, you know.'

'That's the kind of thing men always say to their wives,' said

Mrs Gardener. 'And if you ask me, even M. Poirot here is what I should call a shade on the indulgent side about her, calling her a natural victim and all that. Of course it's true that she wasn't a cultured woman at all, and as Captain Marshall isn't here I don't mind saying that she always did seem to me kind of dumb. I said so to Mr Gardener, didn't I, Odell?'

'Yes, darling,' said Mr Gardener.

II

Linda Marshall sat with Hercule Poirot on Gull Cove.

She said:

'Of course I'm glad I didn't die after all. But you know, M. Poirot, it's just the same as if I'd killed her, isn't it? I meant to.'

Hercule Poirot said energetically:

'It is not at all the same thing. The wish to kill and the action of killing are two different things. If in your bedroom instead of a little wax figure you had had your stepmother bound and helpless and a dagger in your hand instead of a pin, you would not have pushed it into her heart! Something within you would have said "no". It is the same with me. I enrage myself at an imbecile. I say, "I would like to kick him." Instead, I kick the table. I say, "This table, it is the imbecile, I kick him so." And then, if I have not hurt my toe too much, I feel much better and the table it is not usually damaged. But if the imbecile himself was there I should not kick him. To make the wax figures and stick in the pins, it is silly, yes, it is childish, yes – but it does something useful too. You took the hate out of yourself and put it into that little figure. And with the pin and the fire you destroyed – not your stepmother – but the hate you bore her. Afterwards, even before you heard of her death, you felt cleansed, did you not – you felt lighter – happier?'

Linda nodded. She said:

'How did you know? That's just how I did feel.'

Poirot said:

'Then do not repeat to yourself the imbecilities. Just make up your mind not to hate your next stepmother.'

Linda said startled:

'Do you think I'm going to have another? Oh, I see, you

mean Rosamund. I don't mind her.' She hesitated a minute. 'She's *sensible*.'

It was not the adjective that Poirot himself would have selected for Rosamund Darnley, but he realized that it was Linda's idea of high praise.

III

Kenneth Marshall said:

'Rosamund, did you get some extraordinary idea into your head that I'd killed Arlena.'

Rosamund looked rather shamefaced. She said:

'I suppose I was a damned fool.'

'Of course you were.'

'Yes, but Ken, you are such an oyster. I never knew what you really felt about Arlena. I didn't know if you accepted her as she was and were just frightfully decent about her, or whether you – well, just believed in her blindly. And I thought if it was that, and you suddenly found out that she was letting you down you might go mad with rage. I've heard stories about you. You're always very quiet but you're rather frightening sometimes.'

'So you thought I just took her by the throat and throttled the life out of her?'

'Well – yes – that's just exactly what I did think. And your alibi seemed a bit on the light side. That's when I suddenly decided to take a hand, and made up that silly story about seeing you typing in your room. And when I heard that you said you'd seen me look in – well, that made me quite sure you'd done it. That, and Linda's queerness.'

Kenneth Marshall said with a sigh:

'Don't you realize that I said I'd seen you in the mirror in order to back up *your* story. I – I thought you needed it corroborated.'

Rosamund stared at him.

'You don't mean you thought that I killed your wife?'

Kenneth Marshall shifted uneasily. He mumbled:

'Dash it all, Rosamund, don't you remember how you nearly killed that boy about that dog once? How you hung on to his throat and wouldn't let go.'

'But that was years ago.'

'Yes, I know –'

Rosamund said sharply:

'What earthly motive do you think I had to kill Arlena?'

His glance shifted. He mumbled something again.

Rosamund cried:

'Ken, you mass of conceit! You thought I killed her out of altruism on your behalf, did you? Or – did you think I killed her because I wanted you myself?'

'Not at all,' said Kenneth Marshall indignantly. 'But you know what you said that day – about Linda and everything – and – and you seemed to care what happened to me.'

Rosamund said:

'I've always cared about that.'

'I believe you have. You know, Rosamund – I can't usually talk about things – I'm not good at talking – but I'd like to get this clear. I didn't care for Arlena – only just a little at first – and living with her day after day was a pretty nerve-racking business. In fact it was absolute hell, but I *was* awfully sorry for her. She was such a damned fool – crazy about men – she just couldn't help it – and they always let her down and treated her rottenly. I simply felt I couldn't be the one to give her the final push. I'd married her and it was up to me to look after her as best I could. I think she knew that and was grateful to me really. She was – she was a pathetic sort of creature really.'

Rosamund said gently:

'It's all right, Ken. I understand now.'

Without looking at her Kenneth Marshall carefully filled a pipe. He mumbled:

'You're – pretty good at understanding, Rosamund.'

A faint smile curved Rosamund's ironic mouth. She said:

'Are you going to ask me to marry you now, Ken, or are you determined to wait six months?'

Kenneth Marshall's pipe dropped from his lips and crashed on the rocks below.

He said:

'Damn, that's the second pipe I've lost down here. And I haven't got another with me. How the devil did you know I'd fixed six months as the proper time?'

'I suppose because it *is* the proper time. But I'd rather have something definite now, please. Because in the intervening months you may come across some other persecuted female and rush to the rescue in chivalrous fashion again.'

He laughed.

'You're going to be the persecuted female this time, Rosamund. You're going to give up that damned dress-making business of yours and we're going to live in the country.'

'Don't you know that I make a very handsome income out of my business? Don't you realize that it's *my* business – that I created it and worked it up, and that I'm proud of it! And you've got the damned nerve to come along and say, "Give it all up, dear."'

'I've got the damned nerve to say it, yes.'

'And you think I care enough for you to do it?'

'If you don't,' said Kenneth Marshall, 'you'd be no good to me.'

Rosamund said softly:

'Oh, my dear, I've wanted to live in the country with you all my life. Now – it's going to come true . . .'

THE HOLLOW

For Larry and Danae
With apologies for using their swimming pool
as the scene of a murder

At six thirteen am on a Friday morning Lucy Angkatell's big blue eyes opened upon another day and, as always, she was at once wide awake and began immediately to deal with the problems conjured up by her incredibly active mind. Feeling urgently the need of consultation and conversation, and selecting for the purpose her young cousin, Midge Hardcastle, who had arrived at The Hollow the night before, Lady Angkatell slipped quickly out of bed, threw a négligée round her still graceful shoulders, and went along the passage to Midge's room. Since she was a woman of disconcertingly rapid thought processes, Lady Angkatell, as was her invariable custom, commenced the conversation in her own mind, supplying Midge's answers out of her own fertile imagination.

The conversation was in full swing when Lady Angkatell flung open Midge's door.

'– And so, darling, you really must agree that the weekend *is* going to present difficulties!'

'Eh? Hwah!' Midge grunted inarticulately, aroused thus abruptly from a satisfying and deep sleep.

Lady Angkatell crossed to the window, opening the shutters and jerking up the blind with a brisk movement, letting in the pale light of a September dawn.

'Birds!' she observed, peering with kindly pleasure through the pane. 'So sweet.'

'What?'

'Well, at any rate, the weather isn't going to present difficulties. It looks as though it has set in fine. That's something. Because if a lot of discordant personalities are boxed up indoors, I'm sure you will agree with me that it makes it ten times worse. Round games perhaps, and that would be like last year when I shall never forgive myself about poor Gerda. I said to Henry afterwards it was most thoughtless of me – and one *has* to have her, of course, because it would be so rude to ask John without her, but it really does make things difficult – and the worst of it is that she is so nice – really it seems odd sometimes that anyone so nice as Gerda is should be so devoid of any kind of intelligence, and if that is what they mean by the law of compensation I don't really think it is at all fair.'

'What *are* you talking about, Lucy?'

'The weekend, darling. The people who are coming tomorrow. I have been thinking about it all night and I have been dreadfully bothered about it. So it really is a relief to talk it over with you, Midge. You are always so sensible and practical.'

'Lucy,' said Midge sternly. 'Do you know what time it is?'

'Not exactly, darling. I never do, you know.'

'It's quarter-past six.'

'Yes, dear,' said Lady Angkatell, with no signs of contrition.

Midge gazed sternly at her. How maddening, how absolutely impossible Lucy was! Really, thought Midge, I don't know why we put up with her!

Yet even as she voiced the thought to herself, she was aware of the answer. Lucy Angkatell was smiling, and as Midge looked at her, she felt the extraordinary pervasive charm that Lucy had wielded all her life and that even now, at over sixty, had not failed her. Because of it, people all over the world, foreign potentates, ADCs, Government officials, had endured inconvenience, annoyance and bewilderment. It was the childlike pleasure and delight in her own doings that disarmed and nullified criticism. Lucy had but to open those wide blue eyes and stretch out those fragile hands, and murmur, 'Oh! but I'm so *sorry* . . .' and resentment immediately vanished.

'Darling,' said Lady Angkatell, 'I'm so *sorry*. You should have told me!'

'I'm telling you now – but it's too late! I'm thoroughly awake.'

'What a shame! But you *will* help me, won't you?'

'About the weekend? Why? What's wrong with it?'

Lady Angkatell sat down on the edge of the bed. It was not, Midge thought, like anyone else sitting on your bed. It was as insubstantial as though a fairy had poised itself there for a minute.

Lady Angkatell stretched out fluttering white hands in a lovely, helpless gesture.

'All the wrong people coming – the wrong people to be *together*, I mean – not in themselves. They're all charming really.'

'Who *is* coming?'

Midge pushed thick wiry black hair back from her square forehead with a sturdy brown arm. Nothing insubstantial or fairylike about her.

'Well, John and Gerda. That's all right by itself. I mean, John is delightful – *most* attractive. And as for poor Gerda – well, I mean, we must all be very kind. Very, very kind.'

Moved by an obscure instinct of defence, Midge said:

'Oh, come now, she's not as bad as that.'

'Oh, darling, she's pathetic. Those *eyes*. And she never seems to understand a single word one says.'

'She doesn't,' said Midge. 'Not what you say – but I don't know that I blame her. Your mind, Lucy, goes so fast, that to keep pace with it your conversation takes the most amazing leaps. All the connecting links are left out.'

'Just like a monkey,' said Lady Angkatell vaguely.

'But who else is coming besides the Christows? Henrietta, I suppose?'

Lady Angkatell's face brightened.

'Yes – and I really do feel that she will be a tower of strength. She always is. Henrietta, you know, is really kind – kind all through, not just on top. She will help a lot with poor Gerda. She was simply wonderful last year. That was the time we played limericks, or word-making, or quotations – or one of those things, and we had all finished and were reading them out when we suddenly discovered that poor dear Gerda hadn't even begun. She wasn't even sure what the game was. It was dreadful, wasn't it, Midge?'

'Why anyone ever comes to stay with the Angkatells, I don't know,' said Midge. 'What with the brainwork, and the round games, and your peculiar style of conversation, Lucy.'

'Yes, darling, we must be trying – and it must always be hateful for Gerda, and I often think that if she had any spirit she would stay away – but however, there it was, and the poor dear looked so bewildered and – well – mortified, you know. And

John looked so dreadfully impatient. And I simply couldn't think of how to make things all right again – and it was then that I felt so grateful to Henrietta. She turned right round to Gerda and asked about the pullover she was wearing – really a dreadful affair in faded lettuce green – too depressing and jumble sale, darling – and Gerda brightened up at once, it seems that she had knitted it herself, and Henrietta asked her for the pattern, and Gerda looked so happy and proud. And that is what I mean about Henrietta. She can always *do* that sort of thing. It's a kind of knack.'

'She takes trouble,' said Midge slowly.

'Yes, and she knows what to say.'

'Ah,' said Midge. 'But it goes further than saying. Do you know, Lucy, that Henrietta actually knitted that pullover?'

'Oh, my dear.' Lady Angkatell looked grave. 'And wore it?'

'And wore it. Henrietta carries things through.'

'And was it very dreadful?'

'No. On Henrietta it looked very nice.'

'Well, of course it would. That's just the difference between Henrietta and Gerda. Everything Henrietta does she does well and it turns out right. She's clever about nearly everything, as well as in her own line. I must say, Midge, that if anyone carries us through this weekend, it will be Henrietta. She will be nice to Gerda and she will amuse Henry, and she'll keep John in a good temper and I'm sure she'll be most helpful with David.'

'David Angkatell?'

'Yes. He's just down from Oxford – or perhaps Cambridge. Boys of that age are so difficult – especially when they are intellectual. David is very intellectual. One wishes that they could put off being intellectual until they were rather older. As it is, they always glower at one so and bite their nails and seem to have so many spots and sometimes an Adam's apple as well. And they either won't speak at all, or else are very loud and contradictory. Still, as I say, I am trusting to Henrietta. She is very tactful and asks the right kind of questions, and being a sculptress they respect her, especially as she doesn't just carve animals or children's heads but does advanced things like that curious affair in metal and plaster that she exhibited at the New Artists last year. It looked rather like a Heath Robinson step-ladder. It was called Ascending Thought – or something like that. It is the kind of thing that would impress a boy like David . . . I thought myself it was just silly.'

'Dear Lucy!'

'But some of Henrietta's things I think are quite lovely. That Weeping Ash-tree figure, for instance.'

'Henrietta has a touch of real genius, I think. And she is a very lovely and satisfying person as well,' said Midge.

Lady Angkatell got up and drifted over to the window again. She played absent-mindedly with the blind cord.

'Why acorns, I wonder?' she murmured.

'Acorns?'

'On the blind cord. Like pineapples on gates. I mean, there must be a *reason*. Because it might just as easily be a fir-cone or a pear, but it's always an acorn. Mast, they call it in crosswords – you know, for pigs. So curious, I always think.'

'Don't ramble off, Lucy. You came in here to talk about the weekend and I can't see why you were so anxious about it. If you manage to keep off round games, and try to be coherent when you're talking to Gerda, and put Henrietta on to tame intellectual David, where is the difficulty?'

'Well, for one thing, darling, Edward is coming.'

'Oh, Edward.' Midge was silent for a moment after saying the name.

Then she asked quietly:

'What on earth made you ask Edward for this weekend?'

'I didn't, Midge. That's just it. He asked himself. Wired to know if we could have him. You know what Edward is. How sensitive. If I'd wired back "No," he'd probably never have asked himself again. He's like that.'

Midge nodded her head slowly.

Yes, she thought, Edward was like that. For an instant she saw his face clearly, that very dearly loved face. A face with something of Lucy's insubstantial charm; gentle, diffident, ironic . . .

'Dear Edward,' said Lucy, echoing the thought in Midge's mind.

She went on impatiently:

'If only Henrietta would make up her mind to marry him. She is really fond of him, I know she is. If they had been here some weekend without the Christows ... As it is, John Christow has always the most unfortunate effect on Edward. John, if you know what I mean, becomes so much *more* so and Edward becomes so much *less* so. You understand?'

Again Midge nodded.

'And I can't put the Christows off because this weekend was arranged long ago, but I do feel, Midge, that it is all going to be difficult, with David glowering and biting his nails, and with trying to keep Gerda from feeling out of it, and with John being so positive and dear Edward so negative –'

'The ingredients of the pudding are not promising,' murmured Midge.

Lucy smiled at her.

'Sometimes,' she said meditatively, 'things arrange themselves quite simply. I've asked the Crime man to lunch on Sunday. It will make a distraction, don't you think so?'

'Crime man?'

'Like an egg,' said Lady Angkatell. 'He was in Baghdad, solving something, when Henry was High Commissioner. Or perhaps it was afterwards? We had him to lunch with some other Duty people. He had on a white duck suit, I remember, and a pink flower in his buttonhole, and black patent-leather shoes. I don't remember much about it because I never think it's very interesting who killed who. I mean, once they are dead it doesn't seem to matter why, and to make a fuss about it all seems so silly . . .'

'But have you any crimes down here, Lucy?'

'Oh, no, darling. He's in one of those funny new cottages – you know, beams that bump your head and a lot of very good plumbing and quite the wrong kind of garden. London people like that sort of thing. There's an actress in the other, I believe. They don't live in them all the time like we do. Still,' Lady Angkatell moved vaguely across the room, 'I dare say it pleases them. Midge, darling, it's sweet of you to have been so helpful.'

'I don't think I have been so very helpful.'

'Oh, haven't you?' Lucy Angkatell looked surprised. 'Well, have a nice sleep now and don't get up to breakfast, and when you do get up, do be as rude as ever you like.'

'Rude?' Midge looked surprised. 'Why! Oh!' she laughed. 'I see! Penetrating of you, Lucy. Perhaps I'll take you at your word.'

Lady Angkatell smiled and went out. As she passed the open bathroom door and saw the kettle and gas-ring, an idea came to her.

People were fond of tea, she knew – and Midge wouldn't be called for hours. She would make Midge some tea. She put the kettle on and then went on down the passage.

She paused at her husband's door and turned the handle, but Sir Henry Angkatell, that able administrator, knew his Lucy. He was extremely fond of her, but he liked his morning sleep undisturbed. The door was locked.

Lady Angkatell went on into her own room. She would have liked to have consulted Henry, but later would do. She stood by her open window, looked out for a moment or two, then she yawned. She got into bed, laid her head on the pillow and in two minutes was sleeping like a child.

In the bathroom the kettle came to the boil and went on boiling . . .

'Another kettle gone, Mr Gudgeon,' said Simmons, the housemaid.

Gudgeon, the butler, shook his grey head.

He took the burnt-out kettle from Simmons and, going into the pantry, produced another kettle from the bottom of the plate cupboard where he had a stock of half a dozen.

'There you are, Miss Simmons. Her ladyship will never know.'

'Does her ladyship often do this sort of thing?' asked Simmons.

Gudgeon sighed.

'Her ladyship,' he said, 'is at once kind-hearted and very forgetful, if you know what I mean. But in this house,' he continued, 'I see to it that everything possible is done to spare her ladyship annoyance or worry.'

CHAPTER 2

Henrietta Savernake rolled up a little strip of clay and patted it into place. She was building up the clay head of a girl with swift practised skill.

In her ears, but penetrating only to the edge of her understanding, was the thin whine of a slightly common voice:

'And I do think, Miss Savernake, that I was quite right! "Really," I said, "if *that's* the line you're going to take!" Because I do think, Miss Savernake, that a girl owes it to herself to make a stand about these sort of things – if you know what I mean. "I'm not accustomed," I said, "to having things like that said to me, and I can only say that you must have a very nasty imagination!" One does hate unpleasantness, but I do think I was right to make a stand, don't you, Miss Savernake?'

'Oh, absolutely,' said Henrietta with a fervour in her voice which might have led someone who knew her well to suspect that she had not been listening very closely.

'"And if your wife says things of that kind," I said, "well, I'm sure *I* can't help it!" I don't know how it is, Miss Savernake, but it seems to be trouble wherever I go, and I'm sure it's not *my* fault. I mean, men are so susceptible, aren't they?' The model gave a coquettish little giggle.

'Frightfully,' said Henrietta, her eyes half-closed.

'Lovely,' she was thinking. 'Lovely that plane just below the eyelid – and the other plane coming up to meet it. That angle by the jaw's wrong . . . I must scrape off there and build up again. It's tricky.'

Aloud she said in her warm, sympathetic voice:

'It must have been *most* difficult for you.'

'I do think jealousy's so unfair, Miss Savernake, and so *narrow*, if you know what I mean. It's just envy, if I may say so, because someone's better-looking and younger than they are.'

Henrietta, working on the jaw, said absently: 'Yes, of course.'

She had learned the trick, years ago, of shutting her mind into watertight compartments. She could play a game of bridge, conduct an intelligent conversation, write a clearly constructed letter, all without giving more than a fraction of her essential mind to the task. She was now completely intent on seeing the head of Nausicaa build itself up under her fingers, and the thin, spiteful stream of chatter issuing from those very lovely childish lips penetrated not at all into the deeper recesses of her mind. She kept the conversation going without effort. She was used to models who wanted to talk. Not so much the professional ones – it was the amateurs who, uneasy, at their forced inactivity of limb, made up for it by bursting into garrulous self-revelation. So an inconspicuous part of Henrietta listened and replied, and, very far and remote, the real Henrietta commented, 'Common mean spiteful little piece – but what eyes . . . Lovely lovely lovely eyes . . .'

Whilst she was busy on the eyes, let the girl talk. She would ask her to keep silent when she got to the mouth. Funny when you came to think of it, that that thin stream of spite should come out through those perfect curves.

'Oh, damn,' thought Henrietta with sudden frenzy, 'I'm ruining that eyebrow arch! What the hell's the matter with it? I've over-emphasized the bone – it's sharp, not thick . . .'

She stood back again frowning from the clay to the flesh and blood sitting on the platform.

Doris Saunders went on:

'"Well," I said, "I really don't see why your husband shouldn't give me a present if he likes, and I don't think," I said, "you ought to make insinuations of that kind." It was ever such a nice bracelet, Miss Savernake, reely quite lovely – and of course I dare say the poor fellow couldn't reely afford it, but I do think it was nice of him, and I certainly wasn't going to give it back!'

'No, no,' murmured Henrietta.

'And it's not as though there was anything between us – anything *nasty*, I mean – there was nothing of *that* kind.'

'No,' said Henrietta, 'I'm sure there wouldn't be . . .'

Her brow cleared. For the next half-hour she worked in a kind of fury. Clay smeared itself on her forehead, clung to her hair, as she pushed an impatient hand through it. Her eyes had a blind intense ferocity. It was coming . . . She was getting it . . .

Now, in a few hours, she would be out of her agony – the agony that had been growing upon her for the last ten days.

Nausicaa – she had been Nausicaa, she had got up with

Nausicaa and had breakfast with Nausicaa and gone out with Nausicaa. She had tramped the streets in a nervous excitable restlessness, unable to fix her mind on anything but a beautiful blind face somewhere just beyond her mind's eye – hovering there just not able to be clearly seen. She had interviewed models, hesitated over Greek types, felt profoundly dissatisfied . . .

She wanted something – something to give her the start – something that would bring her own already partially realized vision alive. She had walked long distances, getting physically tired out and welcoming the fact. And driving her, harrying her, was that urgent incessant longing – to *see* –

There was a blind look in her own eyes as she walked. She saw nothing of what was around her. She was straining – straining the whole time to make that face come nearer . . . She felt sick, ill, miserable . . .

And then, suddenly, her vision had cleared and with normal human eyes she had seen opposite her in the bus which she had boarded absent-mindedly and with no interest in its destination – she had seen – yes, *Nausicaa*! A foreshortened childish face, half-parted lips and eyes – lovely vacant, blind eyes.

The girl rang the bell and got out. Henrietta followed her.

She was now quite calm and businesslike. She had got what she wanted – the agony of baffled search was over.

'Excuse me speaking to you. I'm a professional sculptor and to put it frankly, your head is just what I have been looking for.'

She was friendly, charming and compelling as she knew how to be when she wanted something.

Doris Saunders had been doubtful, alarmed, flattered.

'Well, I don't know, I'm sure. If it's just the *head*. Of course, I've never *done* that sort of thing!'

Suitable hesitations, delicate financial inquiry.

'Of course I should insist on your accepting the proper professional fee.'

And so here was Nausicaa, sitting on the platform, enjoying the idea of her attractions, being immortalized (though not liking very much the examples of Henrietta's work which she could see in the studio!) and enjoying also the revelation of her personality to a listener whose sympathy and attention seemed to be so complete.

On the table beside the model were her spectacles . . . the spectacles that she put on as seldom as possible owing to vanity, preferring to feel her way almost blindly sometimes, since she admitted to Henrietta that without them she was so shortsighted that she could hardly see a yard in front of her.

Henrietta had nodded comprehendingly. She understood now the physical reason for that blank and lovely stare.

Time went on. Henrietta suddenly laid down her modelling tools and stretched her arms widely.

'All right,' she said, 'I've finished. I hope you're not too tired?'

'Oh, no, thank you, Miss Savernake. It's been very interesting, I'm sure. Do you mean, it's really done – so soon?'

Henrietta laughed.

'Oh, no, it's not actually finished. I shall have to work on it quite a bit. But it's finished as far as you're concerned. I've got what I wanted – built up the planes.'

The girl came down slowly from the platform. She put on her spectacles and at once the blind innocence and vague confiding charm of the face vanished. There remained now an easy, cheap prettiness.

She came to stand by Henrietta and looked at the clay model.

'Oh,' she said doubtfully, disappointment in her voice. 'It's not very like me, is it?'

Henrietta smiled.

'Oh, no, it's not a portrait.'

There was, indeed, hardly a likeness at all. It was the setting of the eyes – the line of the cheekbones – that Henrietta had seen as the essential keynote of her conception of Nausicaa. This was not Doris Saunders, it was a blind girl about whom a poem could be made. The lips were parted as Doris's were parted, but they were not Doris's lips. They were lips that would speak another language and would utter thoughts that were not Doris's thoughts –

None of the features were clearly defined. It was Nausicaa remembered, not seen . . .

'Well,' said Miss Saunders doubtfully, 'I suppose it'll look better when you've got on with it a bit . . . And you reely don't want me any more?'

'No, thank you,' said Henrietta ('And thank God I don't!'

said her inner mind). 'You've been simply splendid. I'm very grateful.'

She got rid of Doris expertly and returned to make herself some black coffee. She was tired – she was horribly tired. But happy – happy and at peace.

'Thank goodness,' she thought, 'now I can be a human being again.'

And at once her thoughts went to John.

'John,' she thought. Warmth crept into her cheeks, a sudden quick lifting of the heart made her spirits soar.

'Tomorrow,' she thought, 'I'm going to The Hollow ... I shall see John ...'

She sat quite still, sprawled back on the divan, drinking down the hot, strong liquid. She drank three cups of it. She felt vitality surging back.

It was nice, she thought, to be a human being again ... and not that other thing. Nice to have stopped feeling restless and miserable and driven. Nice to be able to stop walking about the streets unhappily, looking for something, and feeling irritable and impatient because, really, you didn't know what you were looking for! Now, thank goodness, there would be only hard work – and who minded hard work?

She put down the empty cup and got up and strolled back to Nausicaa. She looked at it for some time, and slowly a little frown crept between her brows.

It wasn't – it wasn't quite –

What was it that was wrong? ...

Blind eyes.

Blind eyes that were more beautiful than any eyes that could see ... Blind eyes that tore at your heart because they were blind ... Had she got that or hadn't she?

She'd got it, yes – but she'd got something else as well. Something that she hadn't meant or thought about ... The structure was all right – yes, surely. But where did it come from – that faint, insidious suggestion? ...

The suggestion, somewhere, of a common spiteful mind.

She hadn't been listening, not really listening. Yet somehow, in through her ears and out at her fingers, it had worked its way into the clay.

And she wouldn't, she knew she wouldn't, be able to get it out again . . .

Henrietta turned away sharply. Perhaps it was fancy. Yes, surely it was fancy. She would feel quite differently about it in the morning. She thought with dismay:

'How vulnerable one is . . .'

She walked, frowning, up to the end of the studio. She stopped in front of her figure of The Worshipper.

That was all right – a lovely bit of pearwood, graining just right. She'd saved it up for ages, hoarding it.

She looked at it critically. Yes, it was good. No doubt about that. The best thing she had done for a long time – it was for the International Group. Yes, quite a worthy exhibit.

She'd *got* it all right: the humility, the strength in the neck muscles, the bowed shoulders, the slightly upraised face – a featureless face, since worship drives out personality.

Yes, submission, adoration – and that final devotion that is beyond, not this side, idolatry . . .

Henrietta sighed. If only, she thought, John had not been so angry.

It had startled her, that anger. It had told her something about him that he did not, she thought, know himself.

He had said flatly: 'You can't exhibit that!'

And she had said, as flatly: 'I shall.'

She went slowly back to Nausicaa. There was nothing there, she thought, that she couldn't put right. She sprayed it and wrapped it up in the damp cloths. It would have to stand over until Monday or Tuesday. There was no hurry now. The urgency had gone – all the essential planes were there. It only needed patience.

Ahead of her were three happy days with Lucy and Henry and Midge – and John!

She yawned, stretched herself like a cat stretches itself with relish and abandon, pulling out each muscle to its fullest extent. She knew suddenly how very tired she was.

She had a hot bath and went to bed. She lay on her back staring at a star or two through the skylight. Then from there her eyes went to the one light always left on, the small bulb that illuminated the glass mask that had been one of her earliest bits of work. Rather an obvious piece, she thought now. Conventional in its suggestion.

Lucky, thought Henrietta, that one outgrew oneself . . .

And now, sleep! The strong black coffee that she had drunk did not bring wakefulness in its train unless she wished it to do so. Long ago she had taught herself the essential rhythm that could bring oblivion at call.

You took thoughts, choosing them out of your store, and then, not dwelling on them, you let them slip through the fingers of your mind, never clutching at them, never dwelling on them, no concentration . . . just letting them drift gently past.

Outside in the Mews a car was being revved up – somewhere there was hoarse shouting and laughing. She took the sounds into the stream of her semi-consciousness.

The car, she thought, was a tiger roaring . . . yellow and black . . . striped like the striped leaves – leaves and shadows – a hot jungle . . . and then down the river – a wide tropical river . . . to the sea and the liner starting . . . and hoarse voices calling goodbye – and John beside her on the deck . . . she and John starting – blue sea and down into the dining-saloon – smiling at him across the table – like dinner at the Maison Dorée – poor John, so angry! . . . out into the night air – and the car, the feeling of sliding in the gears – effortless, smooth, racing out of London . . . up over Shovel Down . . . the trees . . . tree worship . . . The Hollow . . . Lucy . . . John . . . John . . . Ridgeway's Disease . . . dear John . . .

Passing into unconsciousness now, into a happy beatitude.

And then some sharp discomfort, some haunting sense of guilt pulling her back. Something she ought to have done. Something that she had shirked.

Nausicaa?

Slowly, unwillingly, Henrietta got out of bed. She switched on the lights, went across to the stand and unwrapped the cloths.

She took a deep breath.

Not Nausicaa – Doris Saunders!

A pang went through Henrietta. She was pleading with herself: 'I can get it right – I can get it right . . .'

'Stupid,' she said to herself. 'You know quite well what you've got to do.'

Because if she didn't do it now, at once – tomorrow she wouldn't have the courage. It was like destroying your flesh and blood. It hurt – yes, it hurt.

Perhaps, thought Henrietta, cats feel like this when one of their kittens has something wrong with it and they kill it.

She took a quick, sharp breath, then she seized the clay, twisting it off the armature, carrying it, a large heavy lump, to dump it in the clay bin.

She stood there breathing deeply, looking down at her clay-smeared hands, still feeling the wrench to her physical and mental self. She cleaned the clay off her hands slowly.

She went back to bed feeling a curious emptiness, yet a sense of peace.

Nausicaa, she thought sadly, would not come again. She had been born, had been contaminated and had died.

'Queer,' thought Henrietta, 'how things can seep into you without your knowing it.'

She hadn't been listening – not really listening – and yet knowledge of Doris's cheap, spiteful little mind had seeped into her mind and had, unconsciously, influenced her hands.

And now the thing that had been Nausicaa – Doris – was only clay – just the raw material that would, soon, be fashioned into something else.

Henrietta thought dreamily: 'Is that, then, what *death* is? Is what we call personality just the shaping of it – the impress of somebody's thought? Whose thought? God's?'

That was the idea, wasn't it, of Peer Gynt? Back into the Button Moulder's ladle.

'Where am I myself, the whole man, the true man? Where am I with God's mark upon my brow?'

Did John feel like that? He had been so tired the other night – so disheartened. Ridgeway's Disease . . . Not one of those books told you who Ridgeway was! Stupid, she thought, she would like to know . . . Ridgeway's Disease.

CHAPTER 3

John Christow sat in his consulting-room, seeing his last patient but one for that morning. His eyes, sympathetic and encouraging, watched her as she described – explained – went into details. Now and then he nodded his head, understandingly. He asked questions, gave directions. A gentle glow pervaded the sufferer. Dr Christow was really wonderful! He was so interested – so truly concerned. Even talking to him made one feel stronger.

John Christow drew a sheet of paper towards him and began to write. Better give her a laxative, he supposed. That new American proprietary – nicely put up in cellophane and attractively coated in an unusual shade of salmon pink. Very expensive, too, and difficult to get – not every chemist stocked it. She'd probably have to go to that little place in Wardour Street. That would be all to the good – probably buck her up no end for a month or two, then he'd have to think of something else. There was nothing he could do for her. Poor physique and nothing to be done about it! Nothing to get your teeth into. Not like old mother Crabtree . . .

A boring morning. Profitable financially – but nothing else. God, he was tired! Tired of sickly women and their ailments. Palliation, alleviation – nothing to it but that. Sometimes he wondered if it was worth it. But always then he remembered St Christopher's, and the long row of beds in the Margaret Russell Ward, and Mrs Crabtree grinning up at him with her toothless smile.

He and she understood each other! She was a fighter, not like that limp slug of a woman in the next bed. She was on his side, she wanted to live – though God knew why, considering the slum she lived in, with a husband who drank and a brood of unruly children, and she herself obliged to work day in day out, scrubbing endless floors of endless offices. Hard unremitting drudgery and few pleasures! But she wanted to live – she enjoyed life – just as he, John Christow, enjoyed life! It wasn't the circumstances of life they enjoyed, it was life itself – the zest of existence. Curious – a thing one couldn't explain. He thought to himself that he must talk to Henrietta about that.

He got up to accompany his patient to the door. His hand took hers in a warm clasp, friendly, encouraging. His voice was encouraging too, full of interest and sympathy. She went away revived, almost happy. Dr Christow took such an interest!

As the door closed behind her, John Christow forgot her, he had really been hardly aware of her existence even when she had been there. He had just done his stuff. It was all automatic. Yet, though it had hardly ruffled the surface of his mind, he had given out strength. His had been the automatic response of the healer and he felt the sag of depleted energy.

'God,' he thought again, 'I'm tired.'

Only one more patient to see and then the clear space of the weekend. His mind dwelt on it gratefully. Golden leaves tinged with red and brown, the soft moist smell of autumn – the road down through the woods – the wood fires, Lucy, *most* unique and delightful of creatures – with her curious, elusive will-o'-the-wisp mind. He'd rather have Henry and Lucy than any host and hostess in England. And The Hollow was the most delightful house he knew. On Sunday he'd walk through the woods with Henrietta – up on to the crest of the hill and along the ridge. Walking with Henrietta he'd forget that there were any sick people in the world. Thank goodness, he thought, there's never anything the matter with Henrietta.

And then with a sudden, quick twist of humour:

'She'd never let on to me if there were!'

One more patient to see. He must press the bell on his desk. Yet, unaccountably, he delayed. Already he was late. Lunch would be ready upstairs in the dining-room. Gerda and the children would be waiting. He must get on.

Yet he sat there motionless. He was so tired – so very tired.

It had been growing on him lately, this tiredness. It was at the root of the constantly increasing irritability which he was aware of but could not check. Poor Gerda, he thought, she has a lot to put up with. If only she was not so submissive – so ready to admit herself in the wrong when, half the time, it was *he* who was to blame! There were days when everything that Gerda said or did conspired to irritate him, and mainly, he thought ruefully, it was her virtues that irritated him. It was her patience, her unselfishness, her subordination of her wishes to his, that aroused his ill-humour. And she never resented his quick bursts of temper, never stuck to her own opinion in preference to his, never attempted to strike out a line of her own.

(*Well, he thought, that's why you married her, isn't it? What are you complaining about? After that summer at San Miguel . . .*)

Curious, when you came to think of it, that the very qualities that irritated him in Gerda were the qualities he wanted so badly to find in Henrietta. What irritated him in Henrietta (no, that was the wrong word – it was anger, not irritation, that she inspired) – what angered him there was Henrietta's unswerving rectitude where he was concerned. It was so at variance to her attitude to the world in general. He had said to her once:

'I think you are the greatest liar I know.'

'Perhaps.'

'You are always willing to say anything to people if only it pleases them.'

'That always seems to me more important.'

'More important than speaking the truth?'

'Much more.'

'Then why in God's name can't you lie a little more to *me*?'

'Do you want me to?'

'Yes.'

'I'm sorry, John, but I can't.'

'You must know so often what I want you to say.'

Come now, he mustn't start thinking of Henrietta. He'd be seeing her this very afternoon. The thing to do now was to get on with things! Ring the bell and see this last damned woman. Another sickly creature! One-tenth genuine ailment and nine-tenths hypochondria! Well, why shouldn't she enjoy ill-health if she cared to pay for it? It balanced the Mrs Crabtrees of this world.

But still he sat there motionless.

He was tired – he was so very tired. It seemed to him that he had been tired for a very long time. There was something he wanted – wanted badly.

And there shot into his mind the thought: '*I want to go home.*'

It astonished him. Where had that thought come from? And what did it mean? Home? He had never had a home. His parents had been Anglo-Indians, he had been brought up, bandied about from aunt to uncle, one set of holidays with each. The first permanent home he had had, he supposed, was this house in Harley Street.

Did he think of this house as home? He shook his head. He knew that he didn't.

But his medical curiosity was aroused. What had he meant by that phrase that had flashed out suddenly in his mind?

I want to go home.

There must be something – some image.

He half-closed his eyes – there must be some *background*.

And very clearly, before his mind's eye, he saw the deep blue of the Mediterranean Sea, the palms, the cactus and the prickly pear; he smelt the hot summer dust, and remembered the cool feeling of the water after lying on the beach in the sun. *San Miguel!*

He was startled – a little disturbed. He hadn't thought of San Miguel for years. He certainly didn't want to go back there. All that belonged to a past chapter in his life.

That was twelve – fourteen – fifteen years ago. And he'd done the right thing! His judgment had been absolutely right! He'd been madly in love with Veronica but it wouldn't have done. Veronica would have swallowed him body and soul. She was the complete egoist and she had made no bones about admitting it! Veronica had grabbed most things that she wanted, but she hadn't been able to grab him! He'd escaped. He had, he supposed, treated her badly from the conventional point of view. In plain words, he had jilted her! But the truth was that he intended to live his own life, and that was a thing that Veronica would not have allowed him to do. She intended to live *her* life and carry John along as an extra.

She had been astonished when he had refused to come with her to Hollywood.

She had said disdainfully:

'If you really want to be a doctor you can take a degree over there, I suppose, but it's quite unnecessary. You've got enough to live on, and *I* shall be making heaps of money.'

And he had replied vehemently:

'But I'm *keen* on my profession. I'm going to work with *Radley*.'

His voice – a young enthusiastic voice – was quite awed.
Veronica sniffed.

'That funny snuffy old man?'

'That funny snuffy old man,' John had said angrily, 'has done some of the most valuable research work on Pratt's Disease –'

She had interrupted: Who cared for Pratt's Disease? California, she said, was an enchanting climate. And it was fun to see the world. She added: 'I shall hate it without you. I want you, John – I *need* you.'

And then he had put forward the, to Veronica, amazing suggestion that she should turn down the Hollywood offer and marry him and settle down in London.

She was amused and quite firm. She was going to Hollywood, and she loved John, and John must marry her and come too. She had had no doubts of her beauty and of her power.

He had seen that there was only one thing to be done and he had done it. He had written to her breaking off the engagement.

He had suffered a good deal, but he had had no doubts as to the wisdom of the course he had taken. He'd come back to London and started work with Radley, and a year later he had married Gerda, who was as unlike Veronica in every way as it was possible to be . . .

The door opened and his secretary, Beryl Collins, came in.

'You've still got Mrs Forrester to see.'

He said shortly: 'I know.'

'I thought you might have forgotten.'

She crossed the room and went out at the farther door. Christow's eyes followed her calm withdrawal. A plain girl, Beryl, but damned efficient. He'd had her six years. She never made a mistake, she was never flurried or worried or hurried. She had black hair and a muddy complexion and a determined chin. Through strong glasses, her clear grey eyes surveyed him and the rest of the universe with the same dispassionate attention.

He had wanted a plain secretary with no nonsense about her, and he had got a plain secretary with no nonsense about her, but sometimes, illogically, John Christow felt aggrieved! By all the rules of stage and fiction, Beryl should have been hopelessly devoted to her employer. But he had always known that he cut no ice with Beryl. There was no devotion, no self-abnegation

– Beryl regarded him as a definitely fallible human being. She remained unimpressed by his personality, uninfluenced by his charm. He doubted sometimes whether she even *liked* him.

He had heard her once speaking to a friend on the telephone.

'No,' she had been saying, 'I don't really think he is *much* more selfish than he was. Perhaps rather more thoughtless and inconsiderate.'

He had known that she was speaking of him, and for quite twenty-four hours he had been annoyed about it.

Although Gerda's indiscriminate enthusiasm irritated him, Beryl's cool appraisal irritated him too. In fact, he thought, nearly everything irritates me . . .

Something wrong there. Overwork? Perhaps. No, that was the excuse. This growing impatience, this irritable tiredness, it had some deeper significance. He thought: 'This won't do. I can't go on this way. What's the matter with me? If I could get *away* . . .'

There it was again – the blind idea rushing up to meet the formulated idea of escape.

I want to go home . . .

Damn it all, 404 Harley Street *was* his home!

And Mrs Forrester was sitting in the waiting-room. A tiresome woman, a woman with too much money and too much spare time to think about her ailments.

Someone had once said to him: 'You must get very tired of these rich patients always fancying themselves ill. It must be so satisfactory to get to the poor, who only come when there is something *really* the matter with them!' He had grinned. Funny the things people believed about the Poor with a capital P. They should have seen old Mrs Pearstock, on five different clinics, up every week, taking away bottles of medicine, liniments for her back, linctus for her cough, aperients, digestive mixtures. 'Fourteen years I've 'ad the brown medicine, Doctor, and it's the only thing does me any good. That young doctor last week writes me down a *white* medicine. No good at all! It stands to reason, doesn't it, Doctor? I mean, I've 'ad me brown medicine for fourteen years, and if I don't 'ave me liquid paraffin and them brown pills . . .'

He could hear the whining voice now – excellent physique, sound as a bell – even all the physic she took couldn't really do her any harm!

They were the same, sisters under the skin, Mrs Pearstock from Tottenham and Mrs Forrester of Park Lane Court. You listened and you wrote scratches with your pen on a piece of stiff expensive notepaper, or on a hospital card as the case might be . . .

God, he was tired of the whole business . . .

Blue sea, the faint sweet smell of mimosa, hot dust . . .

Fifteen years ago. All that was over and done with – yes, done with, thank heaven. He'd had the courage to break off the whole business.

Courage? said a little imp somewhere. Is *that* what you call it?

Well, he'd done the sensible thing, hadn't he? It had been a wrench. Damn it all, it had hurt like hell! But he'd gone through with it, cut loose, come home, and married Gerda.

He'd got a plain secretary and he'd married a plain wife. That was what he wanted, wasn't it? He'd had enough of beauty, hadn't he? He'd seen what someone like Veronica could do with her beauty – seen the effect it had on every male within range. After Veronica, he'd wanted safety. Safety and peace and devotion and the quiet, enduring things of life. He'd wanted, in fact, Gerda! He'd wanted someone who'd take her ideas of life from him, who would accept his decisions and who wouldn't have, for one moment, any ideas of her own . . .

Who was it who had said that the real tragedy of life was that you got what you wanted?

Angrily he pressed the buzzer on his desk.

He'd deal with Mrs Forrester.

It took him a quarter of an hour to deal with Mrs Forrester. Once again it was easy money. Once again he listened, asked questions, reassured, sympathized, infused something of his own healing energy. Once more he wrote out a prescription for an expensive proprietary.

The sickly neurotic woman who had trailed into the room left it with a firmer step, with colour in her cheeks, with a feeling that life might possibly after all be worth while.

John Christow leant back in his chair. He was free now – free to go upstairs to join Gerda and the children – free from the preoccupations of illness and suffering for a whole weekend.

But he felt still that strange disinclination to move, that new queer lassitude of the will.

He was tired – tired – tired.

CHAPTER 4

In the dining-room of the flat above the consulting room Gerda Christow was staring at a joint of mutton.

Should she or should she not send it back to the kitchen to be kept warm?

If John was going to be much longer it would be cold – congealed, and that would be dreadful.

But on the other hand the last patient had gone, John would be up in a moment, if she sent it back there would be delay – John was so impatient. 'But surely you knew I was just coming . . .' There would be that tone of suppressed exasperation in his voice that she knew and dreaded. Besides, it would get over-cooked, dried up – John hated over-cooked meat.

But on the other hand he disliked cold food very much indeed.

At any rate the dish was nice and hot.

Her mind oscillated to and fro, and her sense of misery and anxiety deepened.

The whole world had shrunk to a leg of mutton getting cold on a dish.

On the other side of the table her son Terence, aged twelve, said:

'Boracic salts burn with a green flame, sodium salts are yellow.'

Gerda looked distractedly across the table at his square, freckled face. She had no idea what he was talking about.

'Did you know that, Mother?'

'Know what, dear?'

'About salts.'

Gerda's eye flew distractedly to the salt-cellar. Yes, salt and pepper were on the table. That was all right. Last week Lewis had forgotten them and that had annoyed John. There was always something . . .

'It's one of the chemical tests,' said Terence in a dreamy voice. 'Jolly interesting. *I* think.'

Zena, aged nine, with a pretty, vacuous face, whimpered:

'I want my dinner. Can't we start, Mother?'

'In a minute, dear, we must wait for Father.'

'*We* could start,' said Terence. 'Father wouldn't mind. You know how fast he eats.'

Gerda shook her head.

Carve the mutton? But she never could remember which was the right side to plunge the knife in. Of course, perhaps Lewis had put it the right way on the dish – but sometimes she didn't – and John was always annoyed if it was done the wrong way. And, Gerda reflected desperately, it always *was* the wrong way when she did it. Oh, dear, how cold the gravy was getting – a skin was forming on the top of it – and surely he would be coming now.

Her mind went round and round unhappily . . . like a trapped animal.

Sitting back in his consulting-room chair, tapping with one hand on the table in front of him, conscious that upstairs lunch must be ready, John Christow was nevertheless unable to force himself to get up.

San Miguel . . . blue sea . . . smell of mimosa . . . a scarlet tritoma upright against green leaves . . . the hot sun . . . the dust . . . that desperation of love and suffering . . .

He thought: 'Oh, God, not that. Never that again! That's over . . .'

He wished suddenly that he had never known Veronica, never married Gerda, never met Henrietta . . .

Mrs Crabtree, he thought, was worth the lot of them. That had been a bad afternoon last week. He'd been so pleased with the reactions. She could stand .005 by now. And then had come that alarming rise in toxicity and the DL reaction had been negative instead of positive.

The old bean had lain there, blue, gasping for breath – peering up at him with malicious, indomitable eyes.

'Making a bit of a guinea pig out of me, ain't you, dearie? Experimenting – that kinder thing.'

'We want to get you well,' he had said, smiling down at her.

'Up to your tricks, yer mean!' She had grinned suddenly. 'I don't mind, bless yer. You carry on, Doctor! Someone's got to be first, that's it, ain't it? 'Ad me 'air permed, I did, when I was a kid. It wasn't 'alf a difficult business then. Looked like a nigger, I did. Couldn't get a comb through it. But there – I enjoyed the fun. You can 'ave yer fun with me. *I* can stand it.'

'Feel pretty bad, don't you?' His hand was on her pulse. Vitality passed from him to the panting old woman on the bed.

'Orful, I feel. You're about right! 'Asn't gone according to plan – that's it, isn't it? Never you mind. Don't you lose 'eart. I can stand a lot, I can!'

John Christow said appreciatively:

'You're fine. I wish all my patients were like you.'

'I wanter get well – that's why! I wanter get well. Mum, she lived to be eighty-eight – and old Grandma was ninety when she popped off. We're long-livers in our family, we are.'

He had come away miserable, racked with doubt and uncertainty. He'd been so sure he was on the right track. Where had he gone wrong? How diminish the toxicity and keep up the hormone content and at the same time neutralize the pantratin? . . .

He'd been too cocksure – he'd taken it for granted that he'd circumvented all the snags.

And it was then, on the steps of St Christopher's, that a sudden desperate weariness had overcome him – a hatred of all this long, slow, wearisome clinical work, and he'd thought of Henrietta, thought of her suddenly not as herself, but of her beauty and her freshness, her health and her radiant vitality – and the faint smell of primroses that clung about her hair.

And he had gone to Henrietta straight away, sending a curt telephone message home about being called away. He had strode into the studio and taken Henrietta in his arms, holding her to him with a fierceness that was new in their relationship.

There had been a quick, startled wonder in her eyes. She had freed herself from his arms and had made him coffee. And as she moved about the studio she had thrown out desultory questions. Had he come, she asked, straight from the hospital?

He didn't want to talk about the hospital. He wanted to make love to Henrietta and forget that the hospital and Mrs

Crabtree and Ridgeway's Disease and all the rest of the caboodle existed.

But, at first unwillingly, then more fluently, he answered her questions. And presently he was striding up and down, pouring out a spate of technical explanations and surmises. Once or twice he paused, trying to simplify – to explain:

'You see, you have to get a reaction –'

Henrietta said quickly:

'Yes, yes, the DL reaction has to be positive. I understand that. Go on.'

He said sharply, 'How do *you* know about the DL reaction?'

'I got a book –'

'What book? Whose?'

She motioned towards the small book table. He snorted.

'Scobell? Scobell's no good. He's fundamentally unsound. Look here, if you want to read – don't –'

She interrupted him.

'I only want to understand some of the terms you use – enough so as to understand you without making you stop to explain everything the whole time. Go on. I'm following you all right.'

'Well,' he said doubtfully, 'remember Scobell's unsound.' He went on talking. He talked for two hours and a half. Reviewing the setbacks, analysing the possibilities, outlining possible theories. He was hardly conscious of Henrietta's presence. And yet, more than once, as he hesitated, her quick intelligence took him a step on the way, seeing, almost before he did, what he was hesitating to advance. He was interested now, and his belief in himself was creeping back. He had been right – the main theory was correct – and there were ways, more ways than one, of combating the toxic symptoms.

And then, suddenly, he was tired out. He'd got it all clear now. He'd get on to it tomorrow morning. He'd ring up Neill, tell him to combine the two solutions and try that. Yes, try that. By God, he wasn't going to be beaten!

'I'm tired,' he said abruptly. 'My God, I'm tired.'

And he had flung himself down and slept – slept like the dead.

He had awoken to find Henrietta smiling at him in the morning light and making tea and he had smiled back at her.

'Not at all according to plan,' he said.

'Does it matter?'

'No. No. You are rather a nice person, Henrietta.' His eye went to the bookcase. 'If you're interested in this sort of thing, I'll get you the proper stuff to read.'

'I'm not interested in this sort of thing. I'm interested in you, John.'

'You can't read Scobell.' He took up the offending volume. 'The man's a charlatan.'

And she had laughed. He could not understand why his strictures on Scobell amused her so.

But that was what, every now and then, startled him about Henrietta. The sudden revelation, disconcerting to him, that she was able to laugh at him.

He wasn't used to it. Gerda took him in deadly earnest. And Veronica had never thought about anything but herself. But Henrietta had a trick of throwing her head back, of looking at him through half-closed eyes, with a sudden tender half-mocking little smile, as though she were saying: 'Let me have a good look at this funny person called John . . . Let me get a long way away and look at him . . .'

It was, he thought, very much the same as the way she screwed up her eyes to look at her work – or a picture. It was – damn it all – it was *detached*. He didn't want Henrietta to be detached. He wanted Henrietta to think only of him, never to let her mind stray away from him.

('Just what you object to in Gerda, in fact,' said his private imp, bobbing up again.)

The truth of it was that he was completely illogical. He didn't know what he wanted.

('*I want to go home.*' What an absurd, what a ridiculous phrase. It didn't mean anything.)

In an hour or so at any rate he'd be driving out of London – forgetting about sick people with their faint sour 'wrong' smell . . . sniffing wood smoke and pines and soft wet autumn leaves . . . The very motion of the car would be soothing – that smooth, effortless increase of speed.

But it wouldn't, he reflected suddenly, be at all like that because owing to a slightly strained wrist, Gerda would have to drive, and

Gerda, God help her, had never been able to begin to drive a car! Every time she changed gear he would be silent, grinding his teeth together, managing not to say anything because he knew, by bitter experience, that when he did say anything Gerda became immediately worse. Curious that no one had ever been able to teach Gerda to change gear – not even Henrietta. He'd turned her over to Henrietta, thinking that Henrietta's enthusiasm might do better than his own irritability.

For Henrietta loved cars. She spoke of cars with the lyrical intensity that other people gave to spring, or the first snow-drop.

'Isn't he a beauty, John? Doesn't he just purr along?' (For Henrietta's cars were always masculine.) 'He'll do Bale Hill in third – not straining at all – quite effortlessly. Listen to the even way he ticks over.'

Until he had burst out suddenly and furiously:

'Don't you think, Henrietta, you could pay *some* attention to me and forget the damned car for a minute or two!'

He was always ashamed of these outbursts.

He never knew when they would come upon him out of a blue sky.

It was the same thing over her work. He realized that her work was good. He admired it – and hated it – at the same time.

The most furious quarrel he had had with her had arisen over that.

Gerda had said to him one day:

'Henrietta has asked me to sit for her.'

'What?' His astonishment had not, if he came to think of it, been flattering. '*You*?'

'Yes, I'm going over to the studio tomorrow.'

'What on earth does she want you for?'

Yes, he hadn't been very polite about it. But luckily Gerda hadn't realized that fact. She had looked pleased about it. He suspected Henrietta of one of those insincere kindnesses of hers – Gerda, perhaps, had hinted that she would like to be modelled. Something of that kind.

Then, about ten days later, Gerda had shown him triumphantly a small plaster statuette.

It was a pretty thing – technically skilful like all Henrietta's work. It idealized Gerda – and Gerda herself was clearly pleased about it.

'I really think it's rather charming, John.'

'Is that Henrietta's work? It means nothing – nothing at all. I don't see how she came to do a thing like that.'

'It's different, of course, from her abstract work – but I think it's good, John, I really do.'

He had said no more – after all, he didn't want to spoil Gerda's pleasure. But he tackled Henrietta about it at the first opportunity.

'What did you want to make that silly thing of Gerda for? It's unworthy of you. After all, you usually turn out decent stuff.'

Henrietta said slowly:

'I didn't think it was bad. Gerda seemed quite pleased.'

'Gerda was delighted. She would be. Gerda doesn't know art from a coloured photograph.'

'It wasn't bad art, John. It was just a portrait statuette – quite harmless and not at all pretentious.'

'You don't usually waste your time doing that kind of stuff –'

He broke off, staring at a wooden figure about five feet high.

'Hallo, what's this?'

'It's for the International Group. Pearwood. The Worshipper.'

She watched him. He stared and then – suddenly, his neck swelled and he turned on her furiously.

'So that's what you wanted Gerda for? How dare you?'

'I wondered if you'd see . . .'

'See it? Of course I see it. It's *here*.' He placed a finger on the broad heavy neck muscles.

Henrietta nodded.

'Yes, it's the neck and shoulders I wanted – and that heavy forward slant – the submission – that bowed look. It's wonderful!'

'Wonderful? Look here, Henrietta, I won't have it. You're to leave Gerda alone.'

'Gerda won't know. Nobody will know. You know Gerda would never recognize herself here – nobody else would either. And it *isn't* Gerda. It isn't *anybody*.'

'*I* recognized it, didn't I?'

'You're different, John. You – see things.'

'It's the damned cheek of it! I won't have it, Henrietta! I won't have it. Can't you see that it was an indefensible thing to do?'

'Was it?'

'Don't you know it was? Can't you *feel* it was? Where's your usual sensitiveness?'

Henrietta said slowly:

'You don't understand, John. I don't think I could ever make you understand . . . You don't know what it is to want something – to look at it day after day – that line of the neck – those muscles – the angle where the head goes forward – that heaviness round the jaw. I've been looking at them, wanting them – every time I saw Gerda . . . In the end I just had to have them!'

'Unscrupulous!'

'Yes, I suppose just that. But when you want things, in that way, you just have to take them.'

'You mean you don't care a damn about anybody else. You don't care about Gerda –'

'Don't be stupid, John. That's why I made that statuette thing. To please Gerda and make her happy. I'm not inhuman!'

'Inhuman is exactly what you are.'

'Do you think – honestly – that Gerda would ever recognize herself in this?'

John looked at it unwillingly. For the first time his anger and resentment became subordinated to his interest. A strange submissive figure, a figure offering up worship to an unseen deity – the face raised – blind, dumb, devoted – terribly strong, terribly fanatical . . . He said:

'That's rather a terrifying thing that you have made, Henrietta!'

Henrietta shivered slightly.

She said, 'Yes – *I* thought that . . .'

John said sharply:

'What's she looking at – who is it? There in front of her?'

Henrietta hesitated. She said, and her voice had a queer note in it:

'I don't know. But I *think* – she might be looking at *you*, John.'

CHAPTER 5

I

In the dining-room the child Terry made another scientific statement.

'Lead salts are more soluble in cold water than hot. If you add potassium iodide you get a yellow precipitate of lead iodide.'

He looked expectantly at his mother but without any real hope. Parents, in the opinion of young Terence, were sadly disappointing.

'Did you know that, Mother –'

'I don't know anything about chemistry, dear.'

'You could read about it in a book,' said Terence.

It was a simple statement of fact, but there was a certain wistfulness behind it.

Gerda did not hear the wistfulness. She was caught in the trap of her anxious misery. Round and round and round. She had been miserable ever since she woke up this morning and realized that at last this long-dreaded weekend with the Angkatells was upon her. Staying at The Hollow was always a nightmare to her. She always felt bewildered and forlorn. Lucy Angkatell with her sentences that were never finished, her swift inconsequences, and her obvious attempts at kindliness, was the figure she dreaded most. But the others were nearly as bad. For Gerda it was two days of sheer martyrdom – to be endured for John's sake.

For John that morning as he stretched himself had remarked in tones of unmitigated pleasure:

'Splendid to think we'll be getting into the country this weekend. It will do you good, Gerda, just what you need.'

She had smiled mechanically and had said with unselfish fortitude: 'It will be delightful.'

Her unhappy eyes had wandered round the bedroom. The wallpaper, cream striped with a black mark just by the wardrobe, the mahogany dressing-table with the glass that swung too far forward, the cheerful bright blue carpet, the watercolours of the Lake District. All dear familiar things and she would not see them again until Monday.

Instead, tomorrow a housemaid who rustled would come into

the strange bedroom and put down a little dainty tray of early tea by the bed and pull up the blinds, and would then rearrange and fold Gerda's clothes – a thing which made Gerda feel hot and uncomfortable all over. She would lie miserably, enduring these things, trying to comfort herself by thinking, 'Only one morning more.' Like being at school and counting the days.

Gerda had not been happy at school. At school there had been even less reassurance than elsewhere. Home had been better. But even home had not been very good. For they had all, of course, been quicker and cleverer than she was. Their comments, quick, impatient, not quite unkind, had whistled about her ears like a hailstorm. 'Oh, do be quick, Gerda.' 'Butter-fingers, give it to me!' 'Oh don't let Gerda do it, she'll be *ages*.' 'Gerda never takes in anything . . .'

Hadn't they seen, all of them, that that was the way to make her slower and stupider still? She'd got worse and worse, more clumsy with her fingers, more slow-witted, more inclined to stare vacantly at what was said to her.

Until, suddenly, she had reached the point where she had found a way out. Almost accidentally, really, she found her weapon of defence.

She had grown slower still, her puzzled stare had become even blanker. But now, when they said impatiently: 'Oh, Gerda, how stupid you are, don't you understand *that*?' she had been able, behind her blank expression, to hug herself a little in her secret knowledge . . . For she wasn't as stupid as they thought. Often, when she pretended not to understand, she *did* understand. And often, deliberately, she slowed down in her task of whatever it was, smiling to herself when someone's impatient fingers snatched it away from her.

For, warm and delightful, was a secret knowledge of superiority. She began to be, quite often, a little amused. Yes, it was amusing to know more than they thought you knew. To be able to do a thing, but not let anybody know that you could do it.

And it had the advantage, suddenly discovered, that people often did things for you. That, of course, saved you a lot of trouble. And, in the end, if people got into the habit of doing things for you, you didn't have to do them at all, and then people didn't know that you did them badly. And so, slowly, you came round again almost to where you started. To feeling that you could hold your own on equal terms with the world at large.

(But that wouldn't, Gerda feared, hold good with the Angkatells; the Angkatells were always so far ahead that you didn't feel even in the same street with them. How she hated the Angkatells! It was good for John – John liked it there. He came home less tired – and sometimes less irritable.)

Dear John, she thought. John was wonderful. Everyone thought so. Such a clever doctor, so terribly kind to his patients. Wearing himself out – and the interest he took in his hospital patients – all that side of his work that didn't pay at all. John was so *disinterested* – so truly noble.

She had always known, from the very first, that John was brilliant and was going to get to the top of the tree. And he had chosen her, when he might have married somebody far more brilliant. He had not minded her being slow and rather stupid and not very pretty. 'I'll look after you,' he had said. Nicely, rather masterfully. 'Don't worry about things, Gerda, I'll take care of you . . .'

Just what a man ought to be. Wonderful to think John should have chosen her.

He had said with that sudden, very attractive, half-pleading smile of his: 'I like my own way, you know, Gerda.'

Well, that was all right. She had always tried to give in to him in everything. Even lately when he had been so difficult and nervy – when nothing seemed to please him. When, somehow, nothing she did was right. One couldn't blame him. He was so busy, so unselfish –

Oh, dear, that mutton! She ought to have sent it back. Still no sign of John. Why couldn't she, sometimes, decide right? Again those dark waves of misery swept over her. The mutton! This awful weekend with the Angkatells. She felt a sharp pain through both temples. Oh, dear, now she was going to have one of her headaches. And it did so annoy John when she had headaches. He never would give her anything for them, when surely it would be so easy, being a doctor. Instead he always said: 'Don't think about it. No use poisoning yourself with drugs. Take a brisk walk.'

The mutton! Staring at it, Gerda felt the words repeating

themselves in her aching head, 'The mutton, the MUTTON, THE MUTTON . . .'

Tears of self-pity sprang to her eyes. 'Why,' she thought, 'does nothing *ever* go right for me?'

Terence looked across at the table at his mother and then at the joint. He thought: 'Why can't *we* have our dinner? How stupid grown-up people are. They haven't any sense!'

Aloud he said in a careful voice:

'Nicholson Minor and I are going to make nitroglycerine in his father's shrubbery. They live at Streatham.'

'Are you, dear? That will be very nice,' said Gerda.

There was still time. If she rang the bell and told Lewis to take the joint down now –

Terence looked at her with faint curiosity. He had felt instinctively that the manufacture of nitroglycerine was not the kind of occupation that would be encouraged by parents. With base opportunism he had selected a moment when he felt tolerably certain that he had a good chance of getting away with his statement. And his judgement had been justified. If, by any chance, there should be a fuss – if, that is, the properties of nitroglycerine should manifest themselves too evidently, he would be able to say in an injured voice, 'I *told* Mother.'

All the same, he felt vaguely disappointed.

'Even *Mother*,' he thought, 'ought to know about nitroglycerine.'

He sighed. There swept over him that intense sense of loneliness that only childhood can feel. His father was too impatient to listen, his mother was too inattentive. Zena was only a silly kid.

Pages of interesting chemical tests. And who cared about them? Nobody!

Bang! Gerda started. It was the door of John's consulting-room. It was John running upstairs.

John Christow burst into the room, bringing with him his own particular atmosphere of intense energy. He was good-humoured, hungry, impatient.

'God,' he exclaimed as he sat down and energetically sharpened the carving knife against the steel. 'How I hate sick people!'

'Oh, John.' Gerda was quickly reproachful. 'Don't say things like that. *They'll* think you mean it.'

She gestured slightly with her head towards the children.

'I do mean it,' said John Christow. 'Nobody ought to be ill.'

'Father's joking,' said Gerda quickly to Terence.

Terence examined his father with the dispassionate attention he gave to everything.

'I don't think he is,' he said.

'If you hated sick people, you wouldn't be a doctor, dear,' said Gerda, laughing gently.

'That's exactly the reason,' said John Christow. 'No doctors like sickness. Good God, this meat's stone cold. Why on earth didn't you have it sent down to keep hot?'

'Well, dear, I didn't know. You see, I thought you were just coming –'

John Christow pressed the bell, a long, irritated push. Lewis came promptly.

'Take this down and tell Cook to warm it up.'

He spoke curtly.

'Yes, sir.' Lewis, slightly impertinent, managed to convey in the two innocuous words exactly her opinion of a mistress who sat at the dining-table watching a joint of meat grow cold.

Gerda went on rather incoherently:

'I'm so sorry, dear, it's all my fault, but first, you see, I thought you were coming, and then I thought, well, if I did send it back . . .'

John interrupted her impatiently.

'Oh, what does it matter? It isn't important. Not worth making a song and dance about.'

Then he asked:

'Is the car here?'

'I think so. Collie ordered it.'

'Then we can get away as soon as lunch is over.'

Across Albert Bridge, he thought, and then over Clapham Common – the short-cut by the Crystal Palace – Croydon – Purley Way, then avoid the main road – take that right-hand fork up Metherly Hill – along Haverston Ridge – get suddenly right of the suburban belt, through Cormerton, and then up Shovel Down – trees golden red – woodland below one everywhere – the soft autumn smell, and down over the crest of the hill.

Lucy and Henry . . . Henrietta . . .

He hadn't seen Henrietta for four days. When he had last seen her, he'd been angry. She'd had that look in her eyes. Not abstracted, not inattentive – he couldn't quite describe it – that look of *seeing* something – something that wasn't there – something (and that was the crux of it) something that wasn't John Christow!

He said to himself: 'I know she's a sculptor. I know her work's good. But damn it all, can't she put it aside sometimes? Can't she sometimes think of me – and nothing else?'

He was unfair. He knew he was unfair. Henrietta seldom talked of her work – was indeed less obsessed by it than most artists he knew. It was only on very rare occasions that her absorption with some inner vision spoiled the completeness of her interest in him. But it always roused his furious anger.

Once he had said, his voice sharp and hard: 'Would you give all this up if I asked you to?'

'All – what?' Her warm voice held surprise.

'All – this.' He waved a comprehensive hand round the studio.

And immediately he thought to himself: 'Fool! Why did you ask her that?' And again: 'Let her say: "Of course." Let her lie to me! If she'll only say: "Of course I will." It doesn't matter if she means it or not! But let her say it. I *must* have peace.'

Instead she had said nothing for some time. Her eyes had gone dreamy and abstracted. She had frowned a little.

Then she had said slowly:

'I suppose so. If it was *necessary*.'

'Necessary? What do you mean by necessary?'

'I don't really know what I mean by it, John. Necessary, as an amputation might be necessary.'

'Nothing short of a surgical operation, in fact!'

'You are angry. What did you want me to say?'

'You know well enough. One word would have done. *Yes*. Why couldn't you say it? You say enough things to people to please them, without caring whether they're true or not. Why not to me? For God's sake, why not to me?'

And still very slowly she had answered:

'I don't know . . . really, I don't know, John. I can't – that's all. I can't.'

He had walked up and down for a minute or two. Then he said:

'You will drive me mad, Henrietta. I never feel that I have any influence over you at all.'

'Why should you want to have?'

'I don't know. I do.'

He threw himself down on a chair.

'I want to come first.'

'You do, John.'

'No. If I were dead, the first thing you'd do, with the tears streaming down your face, would be to start modelling some damned mourning woman or some figure of grief.'

'I wonder. I believe – yes, perhaps I would. It's rather horrible.'

She had sat there looking at him with dismayed eyes.

II

The pudding was burnt. Christow raised his eyebrows over it and Gerda hurried into apologies.

'I'm sorry, dear. I can't think *why* that should happen. It's my fault. Give me the top and you take the underneath.'

The pudding was burnt because he, John Christow, had stayed sitting in his consulting-room for a quarter of an hour after he need, thinking about Henrietta and Mrs Crabtree and letting ridiculous nostalgic feelings about San Miguel sweep over him. The fault was his. It was idiotic of Gerda to try and take the blame, maddening of her to try and eat the burnt part herself. Why did she always have to make a martyr of herself? Why did Terence stare at him in that slow, interested way? Why, oh why, did Zena have to sniff so continually? Why were they all so damned irritating?

His wrath fell on Zena.

'Why on earth don't you blow your nose?'

'She's got a little cold, I think, dear.'

'No, she hasn't. You're always thinking they have colds! She's all right.'

Gerda sighed. She had never been able to understand why a

doctor, who spent his time treating the ailments of others, could be so indifferent to the health of his own family. He always ridiculed any suggestions of illness.

'I sneezed eight times before lunch,' said Zena importantly.

'Heat sneeze!' said John.

'It's not hot,' said Terence. 'The thermometer in the hall is 55.'

John got up. 'Have we finished? Good, let's get on. Ready to start, Gerda?'

'In a minute, John. I've just a few things to put in.'

'Surely you could have done that *before*. What have you been doing all the morning?'

He went out of the dining-room fuming. Gerda had hurried off into her bedroom. Her anxiety to be quick would make her much slower. But why couldn't she have been ready? His own suitcase was packed and in the hall. Why on earth –

Zena was advancing on him, clasping some rather sticky cards.

'Can I tell your fortune, Daddy? I know how. I've told Mother's and Terry's and Lewis's and Jane's and Cook's.'

'All right.'

He wondered how long Gerda was going to be. He wanted to get away from this horrible house and this horrible street and this city full of ailing, sniffing, diseased people. He wanted to get to woods and wet leaves – and the graceful aloofness of Lucy Angkatell, who always gave you the impression she hadn't even got a body.

Zena was importantly dealing out cards.

'That's you in the middle, Father, the King of Hearts. The person whose fortune's told is always the King of Hearts. And then I deal the others face down. Two on the left of you and two on the right of you and one over your head – that has power over you, and one under your feet – you have power over it. And this one – covers you!

'*Now*.' Zena drew a deep breath. 'We turn them over. On the right of you is the Queen of Diamonds – quite close.'

'Henrietta,' he thought, momentarily diverted and amused by Zena's solemnity.

'And the next one is the knave of clubs – he's some quiet young man.

'On the left of you is the eight of spades – that's a secret enemy. Have you got a secret enemy, Father?'

'Not that I know of.'

'And beyond is the Queen of Spades – that's a much older lady.'

'Lady Angkatell,' he said.

'Now this is what's over your head and has power over you – the Queen of Hearts.'

'Veronica,' he thought. 'Veronica!' And then, 'What a fool I am! Veronica doesn't mean a thing to me now.'

'And this is under your feet and you have power over it – the Queen of Clubs.'

Gerda hurried into the room.

'I'm quite ready now, John.'

'Oh, wait, Mother, wait, I'm telling Daddy's fortune. Just the last card, Daddy – the most important of all. The one that covers you.'

Zena's small sticky fingers turned it over. She gave a gasp.

'Oh – it's the Ace of Spades! That's usually a *death* – but –'

'Your mother,' said John, 'is going to run over someone on the way out of London. Come on, Gerda. Goodbye, you two. Try and behave.'

CHAPTER 6

I

Midge Hardcastle came downstairs about eleven on Saturday morning. She had had breakfast in bed and had read a book and dozed a little and then got up.

It was nice lazing this way. About time she had a holiday! No doubt about it, Madame Alfrege's got on your nerves.

She came out of the front door into the pleasant autumn sunshine. Sir Henry Angkatell was sitting on a rustic seat reading *The Times*. He looked up and smiled. He was fond of Midge.

'Hallo, my dear.'

'Am I very late?'

'You haven't missed lunch,' said Sir Henry, smiling.

Midge sat down beside him and said with a sigh:

'It's nice being here.'

'You're looking rather peaked.'

'Oh, I'm all right. How delightful to be somewhere where no fat women are trying to get into clothes several sizes too small for them!'

'Must be dreadful!' Sir Henry paused and then said, glancing down at his wrist-watch: 'Edward's arriving by the 12.15.'

'Is he?' Midge paused, then said: 'I haven't seen Edward for a long time.'

'He's just the same,' said Sir Henry. 'Hardly ever comes up from Ainswick.'

'Ainswick,' thought Midge. 'Ainswick!' Her heart gave a sick pang. Those lovely days at Ainswick. Visits looked forward to for months! 'I'm going to Ainswick.' Lying awake for nights beforehand thinking about it. And at last – the day! The little country station at which the train – the big London express – had to stop if you gave notice to the guard! The Daimler waiting outside. The drive – the final turn in through the gate and up through the woods till you came out into the open and there the house was – big and white and welcoming. Old Uncle Geoffrey in his patchwork tweed coat.

'Now then, youngsters – enjoy yourselves.' And they had enjoyed themselves. Henrietta over from Ireland. Edward, home from Eton. She herself, from the North-country grimness of a manufacturing town. How like heaven it had been.

But always centring about Edward. Edward, tall and gentle and diffident and always kind. But never, of course, noticing her very much because Henrietta was there.

Edward, always so retiring, so very much of a visitor so that she had been startled one day when Tremlet, the head gardener, had said:

'The place will be Mr Edward's some day.'

'But why, Tremlet? He's not Uncle Geoffrey's son.'

'He's the *heir*, Miss Midge. Entailed, that's what they call it. Miss Lucy, she's Mr Geoffrey's only child, but she can't inherit because she's a female, and Mr Henry, as she married, he's only a second cousin. Not so near as Mr Edward.'

And now Edward lived at Ainswick. Lived there alone and very seldom came away. Midge wondered, sometimes, if Lucy minded. Lucy always looked as though she never minded about anything.

Yet Ainswick had been her home, and Edward was only her first cousin once removed, and over twenty years younger than she was. Her father, old Geoffrey Angkatell, had been a great 'character' in the country. He had had considerable wealth as well, most of which had come to Lucy, so that Edward was a comparatively poor man, with enough to keep the place up, but not much over when that was done.

Not that Edward had expensive tastes. He had been in the diplomatic service for a time, but when he inherited Ainswick he had resigned and come to live on his property. He was of a bookish turn of mind, collected first editions, and occasionally wrote rather hesitating ironical little articles for obscure reviews. He had asked his second cousin, Henrietta Savernake, three times to marry him.

Midge sat in the autumn sunshine thinking of these things. She could not make up her mind whether she was glad she was going to see Edward or not. It was not as though she were what is called 'getting over it'. One simply did not get over any one like Edward. Edward of Ainswick was just as real to her as Edward rising to greet her from a restaurant table in London. She had loved Edward ever since she could remember . . .

Sir Henry's voice recalled her.

'How do you think Lucy is looking?'

'Very well. She's just the same as ever.' Midge smiled a little. 'More so.'

'Ye – es.' Sir Henry drew on his pipe. He said unexpectedly: 'Sometimes, you know, Midge, I get worried about Lucy.'

'Worried?' Midge looked at him in surprise. 'Why?'

Sir Henry shook his head.

'Lucy,' he said, 'doesn't realize that there are things that she can't do.'

Midge stared. He went on:

'She gets away with things. She always has.' He smiled. 'She's flouted the traditions of Government House – she's played merry hell with precedence at dinner parties (and that, Midge, is a black crime!). She's put deadly enemies next to each other at the dinner table, and run riot over the colour question! And instead of raising one big almighty row and setting everyone at loggerheads and bringing disgrace on the British Raj – I'm damned if she hasn't got away with it! That trick of hers – smiling at people and looking as though she couldn't help it! Servants are the same – she gives them any amount of trouble and they adore her.'

'I know what you mean,' said Midge thoughtfully. 'Things that you wouldn't stand from anyone else, you feel are all right if Lucy does them. What is it, I wonder? Charm? Magnetism?'

Sir Henry shrugged his shoulders.

'She's always been the same from a girl – only sometimes I feel it's growing on her. I mean that she doesn't realize that there *are* limits. Why, I really believe, Midge,' he said, amused, 'that Lucy would feel she could get away with murder!'

II

Henrietta got the Delage out from the garage in the Mews and, after a wholly technical conversation with her friend Albert, who looked after the Delage's health, she started off.

'Running a treat, miss,' said Albert.

Henrietta smiled. She shot away down the Mews, savouring the unfailing pleasure she always felt when setting off in the car alone. She much preferred to be alone when driving. In that way she could realize to the full the intimate personal enjoyment that driving a car brought to her.

She enjoyed her own skill in traffic, she enjoyed nosing out new short-cuts out of London. She had routes of her own and when driving in London itself had as intimate a knowledge of its streets as any taxi-driver.

She took now her own newly discovered way southwest, turning and twisting through intricate mazes of suburban streets.

When she came finally to the long ridge of Shovel Down it was half-past twelve. Henrietta had always loved the view from that particular place. She paused now just at the point where the road began to descend. All around and below her were trees, trees whose leaves were turning from gold to brown. It was a world incredibly golden and splendid in the strong autumn sunlight.

Henrietta thought: 'I love autumn. It's so much richer than spring.'

And suddenly one of those moments of intense happiness came

to her – a sense of the loveliness of the world – of her own intense enjoyment of that world.

She thought: 'I shall never be as happy again as I am now – never.'

She stayed there a minute, gazing out over that golden world that seemed to swim and dissolve into itself, hazy and blurred with its own beauty.

Then she came down over the crest of the hill, down through the woods, down the long steep road to The Hollow.

III

When Henrietta drove in, Midge was sitting on the low wall of the terrace, and waved to her cheerfully. Henrietta was pleased to see Midge, whom she liked.

Lady Angkatell came out of the house and said:

'Oh, there you are, Henrietta. When you've taken your car into the stables and given it a bran mash, lunch will be ready.'

'What a penetrating remark of Lucy's,' said Henrietta as she drove round the house, Midge accompanying her on the step. 'You know, I always prided myself on having completely escaped the horsy taint of my Irish forebears. When you've been brought up amongst people who talk nothing but horse, you go all superior about not caring for them. And now Lucy has just shown me that I treat my car exactly like a horse. It's quite true. I do.'

'I know,' said Midge. 'Lucy is quite devastating. She told me this morning that I was to be as rude as I liked whilst I was here.'

Henrietta considered this for a moment and then nodded.

'Of course,' she said. 'The *shop*!'

'Yes. When one has to spend every day of one's life in a damnable little box being polite to rude women, calling them Madam, pulling frocks over their heads, smiling and swallowing their damned cheek whatever they like to say to one – well, one does want to cuss! You know, Henrietta, I always wonder why people think it's so humiliating to go "into service" and that it's grand and independent to be in a shop. One puts up with far more insolence in a shop than Gudgeon or Simmons or any decent domestic does.'

'It must be foul, darling. I wish you weren't so grand and proud and insistent on earning your own living.'

'Anyway, Lucy's an angel. I shall be gloriously rude to everyone this weekend.'

'Who's here?' said Henrietta as she got out of the car.

'The Christows are coming.' Midge paused and then went on, 'Edward's just arrived.'

'Edward? How nice. I haven't seen Edward for ages. Anybody else?'

'David Angkatell. That, according to Lucy, is where you are going to come in useful. You're going to stop him biting his nails.'

'It sounds very unlike me,' said Henrietta. 'I hate interfering with people, and I wouldn't dream of checking their personal habits. What did Lucy really say?'

'It amounted to that! He's got an Adam's apple, too!'

'I'm not expected to do anything about that, am I?' asked Henrietta, alarmed.

'And you're to be kind to Gerda.'

'How I should hate Lucy if I were Gerda!'

'And someone who solves crimes is coming to lunch tomorrow.'

'We're not going to play the Murder Game, are we?'

'I don't think so. I think it is just neighbourly hospitality.'

Midge's voice changed a little.

'Here's Edward coming out to meet us.'

'Dear Edward,' thought Henrietta with a sudden rush of warm affection.

Edward Angkatell was very tall and thin. He was smiling now as he came towards the two young women.

'Hallo, Henrietta, I haven't seen you for over a year.'

'Hallo, Edward.'

How nice Edward was! That gentle smile of his, the little creases at the corners of his eyes. And all his nice knobbly bones. 'I believe it's his *bones* I like so much,' thought Henrietta. The warmth of her affection for Edward startled her. She had forgotten that she liked Edward so much.

IV

After lunch Edward said: 'Come for a walk, Henrietta.'

It was Edward's kind of walk – a stroll.

They went up behind the house, taking a path that zigzagged up through the trees. Like the woods at Ainswick, thought Henrietta. Dear Ainswick, what fun they had had there! She began to talk to Edward about Ainswick. They revived old memories.

'Do you remember our squirrel? The one with the broken paw. And we kept it in a cage and it got well?'

'Of course. It had a ridiculous name – what was it now?'

'Cholmondeley-Marjoribanks!'

'That's it.'

They both laughed.

'And old Mrs Bondy, the housekeeper – she always *said* it would go up the chimney one day.'

'And we were so indignant.'

'And then it *did*.'

'She made it,' said Henrietta positively. 'She put the thought into the squirrel's head.'

She went on:

'Is it all the same, Edward? Or is it changed? I always imagine it just the same.'

'Why don't you come and see, Henrietta? It's a long long time since you've been there.'

'I know.'

Why, she thought, had she let so long a time go by? One got busy – interested – tangled up with people . . .

'You know you're always welcome there at any time.'

'How sweet you are, Edward!'

Dear Edward, she thought, with his *nice* bones.

He said presently:

'I'm glad you're fond of Ainswick, Henrietta.'

She said dreamily: 'Ainswick is the loveliest place in the world.'

A long-legged girl, with a mane of untidy brown hair . . . a happy girl with no idea at all of the things that life was going to do to her . . . a girl who loved trees . . .

To have been so happy and not to have known it! *'If I could go back,'* she thought.

And aloud she said suddenly:

'Is Ygdrasil still there?'

'It was struck by lightning.'

'Oh, no, not *Ygdrasil*!'

She was distressed. Ygdrasil – her own special name for the big oak tree. If the gods could strike down Ygdrasil, then nothing was safe! Better not go back.

'Do you remember your special sign, the Ygdrasil sign?'

'The funny tree like no tree that ever was I used to draw on bits of paper? I still do, Edward! On blotters, and on telephone books, and on bridge scores. I doodle it all the time. Give me a pencil.'

He handed her a pencil and notebook, and laughing, she drew the ridiculous tree.

'Yes,' he said, 'that's Ygdrasil.'

They had come almost to the top of the path. Henrietta sat on a fallen tree-trunk. Edward sat down beside her.

She looked down through the trees.

'It's a little like Ainswick here – a kind of pocket Ainswick. I've sometimes wondered – Edward, do you think that that is why Lucy and Henry came here?'

'It's possible.'

'One never knows,' said Henrietta slowly, 'what goes on in Lucy's head.' Then she asked: 'What have you been doing with yourself, Edward, since I saw you last?'

'Nothing, Henrietta.'

'That sounds very peaceful.'

'I've never been very good at – doing things.'

She threw him a quick glance. There had been something in his tone. But he was smiling at her quietly.

And again she felt that rush of deep affection.

'Perhaps,' she said, 'you are wise.'

'Wise?'

'Not to do things.'

Edward said slowly, 'That's an odd thing for you to say, Henrietta. You, who've been so successful.'

'Do you think of me as successful? How funny.'

'But you are, my dear. You're an artist. You must be proud of yourself; you can't help being.'

'I know,' said Henrietta. 'A lot of people say that to me. They don't understand – they don't understand the first thing about it. *You* don't, Edward. Sculpture isn't a thing you set out to do and succeed in. It's a thing that gets *at* you, that nags at you – and haunts you – so that you've got, sooner or later, to make terms with it. And then, for a bit, you get some peace – until the whole thing starts over again.'

'Do you want to be peaceful, Henrietta?'

'Sometimes I think I want to be peaceful more than anything in the world, Edward!'

'You could be peaceful at Ainswick. I think you could be happy there. Even – even if you had to put up with *me*. What about it, Henrietta? Won't you come to Ainswick and make it your home? It's always been there, you know, waiting for you.'

Henrietta turned her head slowly. She said in a low voice: 'I wish I wasn't so dreadfully fond of you, Edward. It makes it so very much harder to go on saying No.'

'It *is* No, then?'

'I'm sorry.'

'You've said No before – but this time – well, I thought it might be different. You've been happy this afternoon, Henrietta. You can't deny that.'

'I've been very happy.'

'Your face even – it's younger than it was this morning.'

'I know.'

'We've been happy together, talking about Ainswick, thinking about Ainswick. Don't you see what that means, Henrietta?'

'It's *you* who don't see what it means, Edward! We've been living all this afternoon in the past.'

'The past is sometimes a very good place to live.'

'One can't go back. That's the one thing one can't do – go back.'

He was silent for a minute or two. Then he said in a quiet, pleasant and quite unemotional voice:

'What you really mean is that you won't marry me because of John Christow?'

Henrietta did not answer, and Edward went on:

'That's it, isn't it? If there were no John Christow in the world you would marry me.'

Henrietta said harshly, 'I can't imagine a world in which there was no John Christow! That's what *you've* got to understand.'

'If it's like that, why on earth doesn't the fellow get a divorce from his wife and then you could marry?'

'John doesn't want to get a divorce from his wife. And I don't know that I should want to marry John if he did. It isn't – it isn't in the least like you think.'

Edward said in a thoughtful, considering way:

'John Christow. There are too many John Christows in this world.'

'You're wrong,' said Henrietta. 'There are very few people like John.'

'If that's so – it's a good thing! At least, that's what I think!'

He got up. 'We'd better go back again.'

CHAPTER 7

As they got into the car and Lewis shut the front door of the Harley Street house, Gerda felt the pang of exile go through her. That shut door was so final. She was barred out – this awful weekend was upon her. And there were things, quite a lot of things, that she ought to have done before leaving. Had she turned off that tap in the bathroom? And that note for the laundry – she'd put it – where had she put it? Would the children be all right with Mademoiselle? Mademoiselle was so – so – Would Terence, for instance, ever do anything that Mademoiselle told him to? French governesses never seemed to have any authority.

She got into the driving-seat, still bowed down by misery, and nervously pressed the starter. She pressed it again and again. John said: 'The car will start better, Gerda, if you switch on the engine.'

'Oh, dear, how stupid of me.' She shot a quick, alarmed glance at him. If John was going to become annoyed straight away – But to her relief he was smiling.

'That's because,' thought Gerda, with one of her flashes of acumen, 'he's so pleased to be going to the Angkatells.'

Poor John, he worked so hard! His life was so unselfish, so completely devoted to others. No wonder he looked forward to this long weekend. And, her mind harking back to the conversation at lunch, she said, as she let in the clutch rather too suddenly so that the car leapt forward from the kerb:

'You know, John, you really shouldn't make jokes about hating sick people. It's wonderful of you to make light of all you do, and *I* understand. But the children don't. Terry, in particular, has such a very literal mind.'

'There are times,' said John Christow, 'when Terry seems to me almost human – not like Zena! How long do girls go on being a mass of affectation?'

Gerda gave a little quiet sweet laugh. John, she knew, was teasing her. She stuck to her point. Gerda had an adhesive mind.

'I really think, John, that it's *good* for children to realize the unselfishness and devotion of a doctor's life.'

'Oh God!' said Christow.

Gerda was momentarily deflected. The traffic lights she was approaching had been green for a long time. They were almost sure, she thought, to change before she got to them. She began to slow down. Still green.

John Christow forgot his resolutions of keeping silent about Gerda's driving and said, 'What are you stopping for?'

'I thought the lights might change –'

She pressed her foot on the accelerator, the car moved forward a little, just beyond the lights, then, unable to pick up, the engine stalled. The lights changed.

The cross-traffic hooted angrily.

John said, but quite pleasantly:

'You really are the worst driver in the world, Gerda!'

'I always find traffic lights so worrying. One doesn't know just when they are going to change.'

John cast a quick sideways look at Gerda's anxious unhappy face.

'Everything worries Gerda,' he thought, and tried to imagine what it must feel like to live in that state. But since he was not a man of much imagination, he could not picture it at all.

'You see,' Gerda stuck to her point, 'I've always impressed on the children just what a doctor's life is – the self-sacrifice, the dedication of oneself to helping pain and suffering – the desire to serve others. It's such a noble life – and I'm so proud of the way you give your time and energy and never spare yourself –'

John Christow interrupted her.

'Hasn't it ever occurred to you that I *like* doctoring – that it's a pleasure, not a sacrifice! – Don't you realize that the damned thing's *interesting*!'

But no, he thought, Gerda would never realize a thing like that! If he told her about Mrs Crabtree and the Margaret Russell Ward she would only see him as a kind of angelic helper of the Poor with a capital P.

'Drowning in treacle,' he said under his breath.

'What?' Gerda leaned towards him.

He shook his head.

If he were to tell Gerda that he was trying to 'find a cure for cancer', she would respond – she could understand a plain sentimental statement. But she would never understand the peculiar fascination of the intricacies of Ridgeway's Disease – he doubted if he could even make her understand what Ridgeway's Disease actually was. ('Particularly,' he thought with a grin, 'as we're not really quite sure ourselves! We don't really know *why* the cortex degenerates!')

But it occurred to him suddenly that Terence, child though he was, might be interested in Ridgeway's Disease. He had liked the way that Terence had eyed him appraisingly before stating: 'I think Father does mean it.'

Terence had been out of favour the last few days for breaking the Cona coffee machine – some nonsense about trying to make ammonia. Ammonia? Funny kid, why should he want to make ammonia? Interesting in a way.

Gerda was relieved at John's silence. She could cope with driving better if she were not distracted by conversation. Besides, if John was absorbed in thought, he was not so likely to notice that jarring noise of her occasional forced changes of gear. (She never changed down if she could help it.)

There were times, Gerda knew, when she changed gear quite well (though never with confidence), but it never happened if John were in the car. Her nervous determination to do it right this time was almost disastrous, her hand fumbled, she accelerated too much or not enough, and then she pushed the gear lever quickly and clumsily so that it shrieked in protest.

'Stroke it in, Gerda, stroke it in,' Henrietta had pleaded once, years ago. Henrietta had demonstrated. 'Can't you feel the way it wants to go – it wants to slide in – keep your hand flat till you get the feeling of it – don't just push it anywhere – *feel* it.'

But Gerda had never been able to feel anything about a gear lever. If she was pushing it more or less in the proper direction it ought to go in! Cars ought to be made so that you didn't have that horrible grinding noise.

On the whole, thought Gerda, as she began the ascent of Mersham Hill, this drive wasn't going too badly. John was still absorbed in thought – and he hadn't noticed rather a bad crashing of gears in Croydon. Optimistically, as the car gained speed, she changed up into third, and immediately the car slackened. John, as it were, woke up.

'What on earth's the point of changing up just when you're coming to a steep bit?'

Gerda set her jaw. Not very much farther now. Not that she wanted to get there. No, indeed, she'd much rather drive on for hours and hours, even if John *did* lose his temper with her!

But now they were driving along Shovel Down – flaming autumn woods all round them.

'Wonderful to get out of London into this,' exclaimed John. 'Think of it, Gerda, most afternoons we're stuck in that dingy drawing-room having tea – sometimes with the light on.'

The image of the somewhat dark drawing-room of the flat rose up before Gerda's eyes with the tantalizing delight of a mirage. Oh, if only she could be sitting there now.

'The country looks lovely,' she said heroically.

Down the steep hill – no escape now. That vague hope that something, she didn't know what, might intervene to save her from the nightmare, was unrealized. They were there.

She was a little comforted as she drove in to see Henrietta sitting on a wall with Midge and a tall thin man. She felt a certain reliance on Henrietta, who would sometimes unexpectedly come to the rescue if things were getting very bad.

John was glad to see Henrietta too. It seemed to him exactly the fitting journey's end to that lovely panorama of autumn, to drop down from the hilltop and find Henrietta waiting for him.

She had on the green tweed coat and the skirt he liked her in and which he thought suited her so much better than London clothes. Her long legs were stuck out in front of her, ending in well-polished brown brogues.

They exchanged a quick smile – a brief recognition of the fact that each was glad of the other's presence. John didn't want to talk to Henrietta now. He just enjoyed feeling that she was there – knowing that without her the weekend would be barren and empty.

Lady Angkatell came out from the house and greeted them. Her conscience made her more effusive to Gerda than she would have been normally to any guest.

'But how *very* nice to see you, Gerda! It's been such a *long* time. *And* John!'

The idea was clearly that Gerda was the eagerly awaited guest, and John the mere adjunct. It failed miserably of its object, making Gerda stiff and uncomfortable.

Lucy said: 'You know Edward? Edward Angkatell?'

John nodded to Edward and said: 'No, I don't think so.'

The afternoon sun lighted up the gold of John's hair and the blue of his eyes. So might a Viking look who had just come ashore on a conquering mission. His voice, warm and resonant, charmed the ear, and the magnetism of his whole personality took charge of the scene.

That warmth and that objectiveness did no damage to Lucy. It set off, indeed, that curious elfin elusiveness of hers. It was Edward who seemed, suddenly, by contrast with the other man, bloodless – a shadowy figure, stooping a little.

Henrietta suggested to Gerda that they should go and look at the kitchen garden.

'Lucy is sure to insist on showing us the rock garden and the autumn border,' she said as she led the way. 'But I always think kitchen gardens are nice and peaceful. One can sit on the cucumber frames, or go inside a greenhouse if it's cold, and nobody bothers one and sometimes there's something to eat.'

They found, indeed, some late peas, which Henrietta ate raw, but which Gerda did not much care for. She was glad to have got away from Lucy Angkatell, whom she had found more alarming than ever.

She began to talk to Henrietta with something like animation. The questions Henrietta asked always seemed to be questions to which Gerda knew the answers. After ten minutes Gerda felt very much better and began to think that perhaps the weekend wouldn't be so bad after all.

Zena was going to dancing class now and had just had a new frock. Gerda described it at length. Also she had found a very nice new leathercraft shop. Henrietta asked whether it would be difficult to make herself a handbag. Gerda must show her.

It was really very easy, she thought, to make Gerda look happy, and what an enormous difference it made to her when she did look happy!

'She only wants to be allowed to curl up and purr,' thought Henrietta.

They sat happily on the corner of the cucumber frames where the sun, now low in the sky, gave an illusion of a summer day.

Then a silence fell. Gerda's face lost its expression of placidity. Her shoulders drooped. She sat there, the picture of misery. She jumped when Henrietta spoke.

'Why do you come,' said Henrietta, 'if you hate it so much?'

Gerda hurried into speech.

'Oh, I don't! I mean, I don't know why you should think –'

She paused, then went on:

'It is really delightful to get out of London, and Lady Angkatell is so *very* kind.'

'Lucy? She's not a bit kind.'

Gerda looked faintly shocked.

'Oh, but she *is*. She's so very nice to me always.'

'Lucy has got good manners and she can be gracious. But she is rather a cruel person. I think really because she isn't quite human – she doesn't know what it's like to feel and think like ordinary people. And you *are* hating being here, Gerda! You know you are. And why should you come if you feel like that?'

'Well, you see, John likes it –'

'Oh, John likes it all right. But you could let him come by himself?'

'He wouldn't like that. He wouldn't enjoy it without me. John is so unselfish. He thinks it is good for me to get out into the country.'

'The country is all right,' said Henrietta. 'But there's no need to throw in the Angkatells.'

'I – I don't want you to feel that I'm ungrateful.'

'My dear Gerda, why should you like us? I always have thought the Angkatells were an odious family. We all like getting together and talking an extraordinary language of our own. I don't wonder outside people want to murder us.'

Then she added:

'I expect it's about teatime. Let's go back.'

She was watching Gerda's face as the latter got up and started to walk towards the house.

'It's interesting,' thought Henrietta, one portion of whose mind was always detached, 'to see exactly what a female Christian martyr's face looked like before she went into the arena.'

As they left the walled kitchen garden, they heard shots, and Henrietta remarked: 'Sounds as though the massacre of the Angkatells has begun!'

It turned out to be Sir Henry and Edward discussing fire-arms and illustrating their discussion by firing revolvers. Henry Angkatell's hobby was firearms and he had quite a collection of them.

He had brought out several revolvers and some target cards, and he and Edward were firing at them.

'Hallo, Henrietta, want to try if you could kill a burglar?'

Henrietta took the revolver from him.

'That's right – yes, so, aim like this.'

Bang!

'Missed him,' said Sir Henry.

'You try, Gerda.'

'Oh, I don't think I –'

'Come on, Mrs Christow. It's quite simple.'

Gerda fired the revolver, flinching, and shutting her eyes. The bullet went even wider than Henrietta's had done.

'Oh, I want to do it,' said Midge, strolling up.

'It's more difficult than you'd think,' she remarked after a couple of shots. 'But it's rather fun.'

Lucy came out from the house. Behind her came a tall, sulky young man with an Adam's apple.

'Here's David,' she announced.

She took the revolver from Midge, as her husband greeted David Angkatell, reloaded it, and without a word put three holes close to the centre of the target.

'Well done, Lucy,' exclaimed Midge. 'I didn't know shooting was one of your accomplishments.'

'Lucy,' said Sir Henry gravely, 'always kills her man!'

Then he added reminiscently, 'Came in useful once. Do you remember, my dear, those thugs that set upon us that day on the Asian side of the Bosphorus? I was rolling about with two of them on top of me feeling for my throat.'

'And what did Lucy do?' asked Midge.

'Fired two shots in the mêlée. I didn't even know she had the pistol with her. Got one bad man through the leg and the other in the shoulder. Nearest escape in the world *I've* ever had. I can't think how she didn't hit me.'

Lady Angkatell smiled at him.

'I think one always has to take some risk,' she said gently. 'And one should do it quickly and not think too much about it.'

'An admirable sentiment, my dear,' said Sir Henry. 'But I have always felt slightly aggrieved that *I* was the risk you took!'

CHAPTER 8

I

After tea John said to Henrietta, 'Come for a walk,' and Lady Angkatell said that she *must* show Gerda the rock garden though of course it was quite the wrong time of year.

Walking with John, thought Henrietta, was as unlike walking with Edward as anything could be.

With Edward one seldom did more than potter. Edward, she thought, was a born potterer. Walking with John, it was all she could do to keep up, and by the time they got up to Shovel Down she said breathlessly: 'It's not a marathon, John!'

He slowed down and laughed.

'Am I walking you off your feet?'

'I can do it – but is there any need? We haven't got a train to catch. Why do you have this ferocious energy? Are you running away from yourself?'

He stopped dead. 'Why do you say that?'

Henrietta looked at him curiously.

'I didn't mean anything particular by it.'

John went on again, but walking more slowly.

'As a matter of fact,' he said, 'I'm tired. I'm very tired.'

She heard the lassitude in his voice.

'How's the Crabtree?'

'It's early days to say, but I think, Henrietta, that I've got the hang of things. If I'm right' – his footsteps began to quicken – 'a lot of our ideas will be revolutionized – we'll have to reconsider the whole question of hormone secretion –'

'You mean that there will be a cure for Ridgeway's Disease? That people won't die?'

'That, incidentally.'

What odd people doctors were, thought Henrietta. Incidentally!

'Scientifically, it opens up all sorts of possibilities!'

He drew a deep breath. 'But it's good to get down here – good to get some air into your lungs – good to see you.' He gave her one of his sudden quick smiles. 'And it will do Gerda good.'

'Gerda, of course, simply loves coming to The Hollow!'

'Of course she does. By the way, have I met Edward Angkatell before?'

'You've met him twice,' said Henrietta dryly.

'I couldn't remember. He's one of those vague, indefinite people.'

'Edward's a dear. I've always been very fond of him.'

'Well, don't let's waste time on Edward! None of these people count.'

Henrietta said in a low voice:

'Sometimes, John – I'm afraid for you!'

'Afraid for me – what do you mean?'

He turned an astonished face upon her.

'You are so oblivious – so – yes, *blind*.'

'Blind?'

'You don't know – you don't see – you're curiously insensitive! You don't know what other people are feeling and thinking.'

'I should have said just the opposite.'

'You see what you're looking *at*, yes. You're – you're like a searchlight. A powerful beam turned on to the one spot where your interest is, and behind it and each side of it, darkness!'

'Henrietta, my dear, what is all this?'

'It's *dangerous*, John. You assume that everyone likes you, that they mean well to you. People like Lucy, for instance.'

'Doesn't Lucy like me?' he said, surprised. 'I've always been extremely fond of her.'

'And so you assume that she likes you. But I'm not sure. And Gerda and Edward – oh, and Midge and Henry. How do you know what they feel towards you?'

'And Henrietta? Do I know how she feels?' He caught her hand for a moment. 'At least – I'm sure of you.'

She took her hand away.

'You can be sure of no one in this world, John.'

His face had grown grave.

'No, I won't believe that. I'm sure of you and I'm sure of myself. At least –' His face changed.

'What is it, John?'

'Do you know what I found myself saying today? Something quite ridiculous. "*I want to go home.*" That's what I said and I hadn't the least idea what I meant by it.'

Henrietta said slowly: 'You must have had some picture in your mind.'

He said sharply: 'Nothing. Nothing at all!'

II

At dinner that night, Henrietta was put next to David, and from the end of the table Lucy's delicate eyebrows telegraphed not a command – Lucy never commanded – but an appeal.

Sir Henry was doing his best with Gerda and succeeding quite well. John, his face amused, was following the leaps and bounds of Lucy's discursive mind. Midge talked in rather a stilted way to Edward, who seemed more absent-minded than usual.

David was glowering and crumbling his bread with a nervous hand.

David had come to The Hollow in a spirit of considerable unwillingness. Until now, he had never met either Sir Henry or Lady Angkatell, and disapproving of the Empire generally, he was prepared to disapprove of these relatives of his. Edward, whom he did not know, he despised as a dilettante. The remaining four guests he examined with a critical eye. Relations, he thought, were pretty awful, and one was expected to talk to people, a thing which he hated doing.

Midge and Henrietta he discounted as empty-headed. This Dr Christow was just one of these Harley Street charlatans – all manner and social success – his wife obviously did not count.

David shifted his neck in his collar and wished fervently that all these people could know how little he thought of them! They were really all quite negligible.

When he had repeated that three times to himself he felt rather better. He still glowered but he was able to leave his bread alone.

Henrietta, though responding loyally to the eyebrows, had some difficulty in making headway. David's curt rejoinders were snubbing in the extreme. In the end she had recourse to a method she had employed before with the tongue-tied young.

She made, deliberately, a dogmatic and quite unjustifiable pronouncement on a modern composer, knowing that David had much technical and musical knowledge.

To her amusement the plan worked. David drew himself up from his slouching position where he had been more or less reclining on his spine. His voice was no longer low and mumbling. He stopped crumbling his bread.

'That,' he said in loud, clear tones, fixing a cold eye on Henrietta, 'shows that you don't know the first thing about the subject!'

From then on until the end of dinner he lectured her in clear and biting accents, and Henrietta subsided into the proper meekness of one instructed.

Lucy Angkatell sent a benignant glance down the table, and Midge grinned to herself.

'So clever of you, darling,' muttered Lady Angkatell as she slipped an arm through Henrietta's on the way to the drawing-room. 'What an awful thought it is that if people had less in their heads they would know better what to do with their hands! Do you think Hearts or Bridge or Rummy or something terribly terribly simple like Animal Grab?'

'I think David would be rather insulted by Animal Grab.'

'Perhaps you are right. Bridge, then. I am sure he will feel that Bridge is rather worthless, and then he can have a nice glow of contempt for us.'

They made up two tables. Henrietta played with Gerda against John and Edward. It was not her idea of the best grouping. She had wanted to segregate Gerda from Lucy and if possible from John also – but John had shown determination. And Edward had then forestalled Midge.

The atmosphere was not, Henrietta thought, quite comfortable, but she did not quite know from whence the discomfort arose.

Anyway, if the cards gave them anything like a break, she intended that Gerda should win. Gerda was not really a bad Bridge player – away from John she was quite average – but she was a nervous player with bad judgment and with no real knowledge of the value of her hand. John was a good, if slightly over-confident player. Edward was a very good player indeed.

The evening wore on, and at Henrietta's table they were still playing the same rubber. The scores rose above the line on either side. A curious tensity had come into the play of which only one person was unaware.

To Gerda this was just a rubber of Bridge which she happened for once to be quite enjoying. She felt indeed a pleasurable excitement. Difficult decisions had been unexpectedly eased by Henrietta's over-calling her own bids and playing the hand.

Those moments when John, unable to refrain from that critical attitude which did more to undermine Gerda's self-confidence than he could possibly have imagined, exclaimed: 'Why on earth did you lead that club, Gerda?' were countered almost immediately by Henrietta's swift, 'Nonsense, John, of course she had to lead the club! It was the only possible thing to do.'

Finally, with a sigh, Henrietta drew the score towards her.

'Game and rubber, but I don't think we shall make much out of it, Gerda.'

John said: 'A lucky finesse,' in a cheerful voice.

Henrietta looked up sharply. She knew his tone. She met his eyes and her own dropped.

She got up and went to the mantelpiece, and John followed her. He said conversationally: 'You don't *always* look deliberately into people's hands, do you?'

Henrietta said calmly: 'Perhaps I was a little obvious. How despicable it is to want to win at games!'

'You wanted Gerda to win the rubber, you mean. In your desire to give pleasure to people, you don't draw the line at cheating.'

'How horribly you put things! And you are always quite right.'

'Your wishes seemed to be shared by my partner.'

So he *had* noticed, thought Henrietta. She had wondered herself, if she had been mistaken. Edward was so skilful – there was nothing you could have taken hold of. A failure, once, to call the game. A lead that had been sound and obvious – but when a less obvious lead would have assured success.

It worried Henrietta. Edward, she knew, would never play his cards in order that she, Henrietta, might win. He was far too imbued with English sportsmanship for that. No, she thought, it was just one more success for John Christow that he was unable to endure.

She felt suddenly keyed up, alert. She didn't like this party of Lucy's.

And then dramatically, unexpectedly – with the unreality of a stage entrance, Veronica Cray came through the window.

The french windows had been pushed to, not closed, for the evening was warm. Veronica pushed them wide, came through them and stood there framed against the night, smiling, a little rueful, wholly charming, waiting just that infinitesimal moment before speaking so that she might be sure of her audience.

'You must forgive me – bursting in upon you this way. I'm your neighbour, Lady Angkatell – from that ridiculous cottage Dovecotes – and the most frightful catastrophe has occurred!'

Her smile broadened – became more humorous.

'Not a match! Not a single match in the house! And Saturday evening. So stupid of me. But what could I do? I came along here to beg help from my only neighbour within miles.'

Nobody spoke for a moment, for Veronica had rather that effect. She was lovely – not quietly lovely, not even dazzlingly lovely – but so efficiently lovely that it made you gasp! The waves of pale shimmering hair, the curving mouth – the platinum foxes that swathed her shoulders and the long sweep of white velvet underneath them.

She was looking from one to the other of them, humorous, charming!

'And I smoke,' she said, 'like a chimney! And my lighter won't work! And besides there's breakfast – gas stoves –' She thrust out her hands. 'I do feel such a complete fool.'

Lucy came forward, gracious, faintly amused.

'Why, of course –' she began, but Veronica Cray interrupted. She was looking at John Christow. An expression of utter amazement, of incredulous delight, was spreading over her face. She took a step towards him, hands outstretched.

'Why, surely – *John*! It's John Christow! Now isn't that too extraordinary? I haven't seen you for years and years and years! And suddenly – to find you *here*!'

She had his hands in hers by now. She was all warmth and simple eagerness. She half-turned her head to Lady Angkatell.

'This is just the most wonderful surprise. John's an old old friend of mine. Why, John's the first man I ever loved! I was crazy about you, John.'

She was half-laughing now – a woman moved by the ridiculous remembrance of first love.

'I always thought John was just wonderful!'

Sir Henry, courteous and polished, had moved forward to her.

She must have a drink. He manoeuvred glasses. Lady Angkatell said:

'Midge, dear, ring the bell.'

When Gudgeon came, Lucy said:

'A box of matches, Gudgeon – at least, has Cook got plenty?'

'A new dozen came in today, m'lady.'

'Then bring in half a dozen, Gudgeon.'

'Oh, no, Lady Angkatell – just one!'

Veronica protested, laughing. She had her drink now and was smiling round at everyone. John Christow said:

'This is my wife, Veronica.'

'Oh, but how lovely to meet you.' Veronica beamed upon Gerda's air of bewilderment.

Gudgeon brought in the matches, stacked on a silver salver.

Lady Angkatell indicated Veronica Cray with a gesture and he brought the salver to her.

'Oh, dear Lady Angkatell, not all these!'

Lucy's gesture was negligently royal.

'It's so tiresome only having one of a thing. We can spare them quite easily.'

Sir Henry was saying pleasantly:

'And how do you like living at Dovecotes?'

'I adore it. It's wonderful here, near London, and yet one feels so beautifully isolated.'

Veronica put down her glass. She drew the platinum foxes a little closer round her. She smiled on them all.

'Thank you *so* much! You've been so kind.' The words floated between Sir Henry, Lady Angkatell, and for some reason, Edward. 'I shall now carry home the spoils. John,' she gave him an artless, friendly smile, 'you must see me safely back, because I want dreadfully to hear all you've been doing in the years and years since I've seen you. It makes me feel, of course, dreadfully *old*.'

She moved to the window, and John Christow followed her. She flung a last brilliant smile at them all.

'I'm so dreadfully sorry to have bothered you in this stupid way. Thank you *so* much, Lady Angkatell.'

She went out with John. Sir Henry stood by the window looking after them.

'Quite a fine warm night,' he said.

Lady Angkatell yawned.

'Oh, dear,' she murmured, 'we must go to bed. Henry, we must go and see one of her pictures. I'm sure, from tonight, she must give a lovely performance.'

They went upstairs. Midge, saying goodnight, asked Lucy:

'A lovely performance?'

'Didn't you think so, darling?'

'I gather, Lucy, that you think it's just possible she may have some matches in Dovecotes all the time.'

'Dozens of boxes, I expect, darling. But we mustn't be uncharitable. And it *was* a lovely performance!'

Doors were shutting all down the corridor, voices were murmuring goodnights. Sir Henry said: 'I'll leave the window for Christow.' His own door shut.

Henrietta said to Gerda: 'What fun actresses are. They make such marvellous entrances and exits!' She yawned and added: 'I'm frightfully sleepy.'

Veronica Cray moved swiftly along the narrow path through the chestnut woods.

She came out from the woods to the open space by the swimming pool. There was a small pavilion here where the Angkatells sat on days that were sunny but when there was a cold wind.

Veronica Cray stood still. She turned and faced John Christow.

Then she laughed. With her hand she gestured towards the leaf-strewn surface of the swimming pool.

'Not quite like the Mediterranean, is it, John?' she said.

He knew then what he had been waiting for – knew that in all those fifteen years of separation from Veronica she had still been with him. *The blue sea, the scent of mimosa, the hot dust* – pushed down, thrust out of sight, but never really forgotten. They all meant one thing – Veronica. He was a young man of twenty-four, desperately and agonizingly in love, and this time he was not going to run away.

CHAPTER 9

John Christow came out from the chestnut woods on to the green slope by the house. There was a moon and the house basked in the moonlight with a strange innocence in its curtained windows. He looked down at the wrist-watch he wore.

It was three o'clock. He drew a deep breath and his face was anxious. He was no longer, even remotely, a young man of twenty-four in love. He was a shrewd, practical man of just on forty, and his mind was clear and level-headed.

He'd been a fool, of course, a complete damned fool, but he didn't regret that! For he was, he now realized, completely master of himself. It was as though, for years, he had dragged a weight upon his leg – and now the weight was gone. He was free.

He was free and himself, John Christow – and he knew that to John Christow, successful Harley Street specialist, Veronica Cray meant nothing whatsoever. All that had been in the past – and because that conflict had never been resolved, because he had always suffered humiliatingly from the fear that he had, in plain language, 'run away', so Veronica's image had never completely left him. She had come to him tonight out of a dream, and he had accepted the dream, and now, thank God, he was delivered from it for ever. He was back in the present – and it was 3 am, and it was just possible that he had mucked up things rather badly.

He'd been with Veronica for three hours. She had sailed in like a frigate, and cut him out of the circle and carried him off as her prize, and he wondered now what on earth everybody had thought about it.

What, for instance, would Gerda think?

And Henrietta? (But he didn't care quite so much about Henrietta. He could, he felt, at a pinch explain to Henrietta. He could never explain to Gerda.)

And he didn't, definitely he didn't want to lose anything.

All his life he had been a man who took a justifiable number of risks. Risks with patients, risks with treatment, risks with investments. Never a fantastic risk – only the kind of risk that was just beyond the margin of safety.

If Gerda guessed – if Gerda had the least suspicion . . .

But would she have? How much did he really know about Gerda? Normally, Gerda would believe white was black if he told her so. But over a thing like this . . .

What had he looked like when he followed Veronica's tall, triumphant figure out of that window? What had he shown in his face? Had they seen a boy's dazed, lovesick face? Or had they only observed a man doing a polite duty? He didn't know. He hadn't the least idea.

But he was afraid – afraid for the ease and order and safety of his life. He'd been mad – quite mad, he thought with exasperation – and then took comfort in that very thought. Nobody would believe, surely, he could have been as mad as that?

Everybody was in bed and asleep, that was clear. The french window of the drawing-room stood half-open, left for his return. He looked up again at the innocent, sleeping house. It looked, somehow, too innocent.

Suddenly he started. He had heard, or he had imagined he heard, the faint closing of a door.

He turned his head sharply. If someone had come down to the pool, following him there. If someone had waited and followed him back that someone could have taken a higher path and so gained entrance to the house again by the side garden door, and the soft closing of the garden door would have made just the sound that he had heard.

He looked up sharply at the windows. Was that curtain moving, had it been pushed aside for someone to look out, and then allowed to fall? Henrietta's room.

Henrietta! Not Henrietta, his heart cried in a sudden panic. I can't lose Henrietta!

He wanted suddenly to fling up a handful of pebbles at her window, to cry out to her.

'Come out, my dear love. Come out to me now and walk with me up through the woods to Shovel Down and there listen – listen to everything that I now know about myself and that you must know, too, if you do not know it already.'

He wanted to say to Henrietta:

'I am starting again. A new life begins from today. The things that crippled and hindered me from living have fallen away. You were right this afternoon when you asked me if I was running away from myself. That is what I have been doing for years. Because I never knew whether it was strength or weakness that took me away from Veronica. I have been afraid of myself, afraid of life, afraid of you.'

If he were to wake Henrietta and make her come out with him now – up through the woods to where they could watch, together, the sun come up over the rim of the world.

'You're mad,' he said to himself. He shivered. It was cold now, late September after all. 'What the devil is the matter with you?' he asked himself. 'You've behaved quite insanely enough for one night. If you get away with it as it is, you're damned lucky!' What on earth would Gerda think if he stayed out all night and came home with the milk?

What, for the matter of that, would the Angkatells think?

But that did not worry him for a moment. The Angkatells took Greenwich time, as it were, from Lucy Angkatell. And to Lucy Angkatell, the unusual always appeared perfectly reasonable.

But Gerda, unfortunately, was not an Angkatell.

Gerda would have to be dealt with, and he'd better go in and deal with Gerda as soon as possible.

Supposing it had been Gerda who had followed him tonight?

No good saying people didn't do such things. As a doctor, he knew only too well what people, high-minded, sensitive, fastidious, honourable people, constantly did. They listened at doors, and opened letters and spied and snooped – not because for one moment they approved of such conduct, but because before the sheer necessity of human anguish they were rendered desperate.

Poor devils, he thought, poor suffering human devils. John Christow knew a good deal about human suffering. He had not very much pity for weakness, but he had for suffering, for it was, he knew, the strong who suffer.

If Gerda knew –

Nonsense, he said to himself, why should she? She's gone up to bed and she's fast asleep. She's no imagination, never has had.

He went in through the french windows, switched on a lamp, closed and locked the windows. Then, switching off the light, he left the room, found the switch in the hall, went quickly and lightly up the stairs. A second switch turned off the hall light. He stood for a moment by the bedroom door, his hand on the door-knob, then he turned it and went in.

The room was dark and he could hear Gerda's even breathing. She stirred as he came in and closed the door. Her voice came to him, blurred and indistinct with sleep.

'Is that you, John?'

'Yes.'

'Aren't you very late? What time is it?'

He said easily:

'I've no idea. Sorry I woke you up. I had to go in with the woman and have a drink.'

He made his voice sound bored and sleepy.

Gerda murmured: 'Oh? Goodnight, John.'

There was a rustle as she turned over in bed.

It was all right! As usual, he'd been lucky. As *usual* – just for a moment it sobered him, the thought of how often his luck had held! Time and again there had been a moment when he'd held his breath and said, 'If *this* goes wrong.' And it hadn't gone wrong! But some day, surely, his luck would change.

He undressed quickly and got into bed. Funny that kid's fortune. '*And this one is over your head and has power over you . . .*' Veronica! And she *had* had power over him all right.

'But not any more, my girl,' he thought with a kind of savage satisfaction. 'All that's over. I'm quit of you now!'

CHAPTER 10

It was ten o'clock the next morning when John came down. Breakfast was on the sideboard. Gerda had had her breakfast sent up to her in bed and had been rather perturbed since perhaps she might be 'giving trouble'.

Nonsense, John had said. People like the Angkatells who still managed to have butlers and servants might just as well give them something to do.

He felt very kindly towards Gerda this morning. All that nervous irritation that had so fretted him of late seemed to have died down and disappeared.

Sir Henry and Edward had gone out shooting, Lady Angkatell told him. She herself was busy with a gardening basket and gardening gloves. He stayed talking to her for a while until Gudgeon approached him with a letter on a salver.

'This has just come by hand, sir.'

He took it with slightly raised eyebrows.

Veronica!

He strolled into the library, tearing it open.

Please come over this morning. I must see you.
Veronica.

Imperious as ever, he thought. He'd a good mind not to go. Then he thought he might as well and get it over. He'd go at once.

He took the path opposite the library window, passed by the swimming pool which was a kind of nucleus with paths radiating from it in every direction, one up the hill to the woods proper, one from the flower walk above the house, one from the farm and the one that led on to the lane which he took now. A few yards up the lane was the cottage called Dovecotes.

Veronica was waiting for him. She spoke from the window of the pretentious half-timbered building.

'Come inside, John. It's cold this morning.'

There was a fire lit in the sitting-room, which was furnished in off-white with pale cyclamen cushions.

Looking at her this morning with an appraising eye, he saw

the differences there were from the girl he remembered, as he had not been able to see them last night.

Strictly speaking, he thought, she was more beautiful now than then. She understood her beauty better, and she cared for it and enhanced it in every way. Her hair, which had been deep golden, was now a silvery platinum colour. Her eyebrows were different, giving much more poignancy to her expression.

Hers had never been a mindless beauty. Veronica, he remembered, had qualified as one of our 'intellectual actresses'. She had a university degree and had views on Strindberg and on Shakespeare.

He was struck now with what had only been dimly apparent to him in the past – that she was a woman whose egoism was quite abnormal. Veronica was accustomed to getting her own way, and beneath the smooth beautiful contours of flesh he seemed to sense an ugly iron determination.

'I sent for you,' said Veronica, as she handed him a box of cigarettes, 'because we've got to talk. We've got to make arrangements. For our future, I mean.'

He took a cigarette and lighted it. Then he said quite pleasantly:

'But have we a future?'

She gave him a sharp glance.

'What do you mean, John? Of course we have got a future. We've wasted fifteen years. There's no need to waste any more time.'

He sat down.

'I'm sorry, Veronica. But I'm afraid you've got all this taped out wrong. I've – enjoyed meeting you again very much. But your life and mine don't touch anywhere. They are quite divergent.'

'Nonsense, John. I love you and you love me. We've always loved each other. You were incredibly obstinate in the past! But never mind that now. Our lives needn't clash. I don't mean to go back to the States. When I've finished this picture I'm working on now, I'm going to play a straight play on the London stage. I've got a wonderful play – Elderton's written it for me. It will be a terrific success.'

'I'm sure it will,' he said politely.

'And you can go on being a doctor.' Her voice was kind and condescending. 'You're quite well known, they tell me.'

'My dear girl, I'm married. I've got children.'

'I'm married myself at the moment,' said Veronica. 'But all these things are easily arranged. A good lawyer can fix up everything.' She smiled at him dazzlingly. 'I always did mean to marry you, darling. I can't think why I have this terrible passion for you, but there it is!'

'I'm sorry, Veronica, but no good lawyer is going to fix up anything. Your life and mine have nothing to do with each other.'

'Not after last night?'

'You're not a child, Veronica. You've had a couple of husbands, and by all accounts several lovers. What does last night mean actually? Nothing at all, and you know it.'

'Oh, my dear John.' She was still amused, indulgent. 'If you'd seen your face – there in that stuffy drawing-room! You might have been in San Miguel again.'

John sighed. He said:

'I *was* in San Miguel. Try to understand, Veronica. You came to me out of the past. Last night, I, too, was in the past, but today – today's different. I'm a man fifteen years older. A man you don't even know – and whom I dare say you wouldn't like much if you did know.'

'You prefer your wife and children to me?'

She was genuinely amazed.

'Odd as it may seem to you, I do.'

'Nonsense, John, you love me.'

'I'm sorry, Veronica.'

She said incredulously:

'You don't love me?'

'It's better to be quite clear about these things. You are an extraordinarily beautiful woman, Veronica, but I don't love you.'

She sat so still that she might have been a waxwork. That stillness of hers made him just a little uneasy.

When she spoke it was with such venom that he recoiled.

'Who is she?'

'She? Who do you mean?'

'That woman by the mantelpiece last night?'

Henrietta! he thought. How the devil did she get on to Henrietta? Aloud he said:

'Who are you talking about? Midge Hardcastle?'

'Midge? That's the square, dark girl, isn't it? No, I don't mean her. And I don't mean your wife. I mean that insolent devil who was leaning against the mantelpiece! It's because of *her* that you're turning me down! Oh, don't pretend to be so moral about your wife and children. It's that other woman.'

She got up and came towards him.

'Don't you understand, John, that ever since I came back to England, eighteen months ago, I've been thinking about you? Why do you imagine I took this idiotic place here? Simply because I found out that you often came down for weekends with the Angkatells!'

'So last night was all planned, Veronica?'

'You *belong* to me, John. You always have!'

'I don't belong to anyone, Veronica. Hasn't life taught you even now that you can't own other human beings body and soul? I loved you when I was a young man. I wanted you to share my life. You wouldn't do it!'

'*My* life and career were much more important than *yours*. Anyone can be a doctor!'

He lost his temper a little.

'Are you *quite* as wonderful as you think you are?'

'You mean that I haven't got to the top of the tree. I shall! *I shall!*'

John Christow looked at her with a sudden, quite dispassionate interest.

'I don't believe, you know, that you will. There's a *lack* in you, Veronica. You're all grab and snatch – no real generosity – I think that's it.'

Veronica got up. She said in a quiet voice:

'You turned me down fifteen years ago. You've turned me down again today. I'll make you sorry for this.'

John got up and went to the door.

'I'm sorry, Veronica, if I've hurt you. You're very lovely, my dear, and I once loved you very much. Can't we leave it at that?'

'Goodbye, John. We're not leaving it at that. You'll find that out all right. I think – I think I hate you more than I believed I could hate anyone.'

He shrugged his shoulders:

'I'm sorry. Goodbye.'

John walked back slowly through the wood. When he got to the swimming pool he sat down on the bench there. He had no regrets for his treatment of Veronica. Veronica, he thought dispassionately, was a nasty bit of work. She always had been a nasty bit of work, and the best thing he had ever done was to get clear of her in time. God alone knew what would have happened to him by now if he hadn't!

As it was, he had that extraordinary sensation of starting a new life, unfettered and unhampered by the past. He must have been extremely difficult to live with for the last year or two. Poor Gerda, he thought, with her unselfishness and her continual anxiety to please him. He would be kinder in future.

And perhaps now he would be able to stop trying to bully Henrietta. Not that one could really bully Henrietta – she wasn't made that way. Storms broke over her and she stood there, meditative, her eyes looking at you from very far away.

He thought: 'I shall go to Henrietta and tell her.'

He looked up sharply, disturbed by some small unexpected sound. There had been shots in the woods higher up, and there had been the usual small noises of woodlands, birds, and the faint melancholy dropping of leaves. But this was another noise – a very faint businesslike click.

And suddenly, John was acutely conscious of danger. How long had he been sitting here? Half an hour? An hour? There was someone watching him. Someone –

And that click was – of course it was –

He turned sharply, a man very quick in his reactions. But he was not quick enough. His eyes widened in surprise, but there was no time for him to make a sound.

The shot rang out and he fell, awkwardly, sprawled out by the edge of the swimming pool.

A dark stain welled up slowly on his left side and trickled slowly on to the concrete of the pool edge; and from there dripped red into the blue water.

CHAPTER 11

....

I

Hercule Poirot flicked a last speck of dust from his shoes. He had dressed carefully for his luncheon party and he was satisfied with the result.

He knew well enough the kind of clothes that were worn in the country on a Sunday in England, but he did not choose to conform to English ideas. He preferred his own standards of urban smartness. He was not an English country gentleman. He was Hercule Poirot!

He did not, he confessed it to himself, really like the country. The weekend cottage – so many of his friends had extolled it – he had allowed himself to succumb, and had purchased Resthaven, though the only thing he had liked about it was its shape, which was quite square like a box. The surrounding landscape he did not care for though it was, he knew, supposed to be a beauty spot. It was, however, too wildly asymmetrical to appeal to him. He did not care much for trees at any time – they had that untidy habit of shedding their leaves. He could endure poplars and he approved of a monkey puzzle – but this riot of beech and oak left him unmoved. Such a landscape was best enjoyed from a car on a fine afternoon. You exclaimed, '*Quel beau paysage!*' and drove back to a good hotel.

The best thing about Resthaven, he considered, was the small vegetable garden neatly laid out in rows by his Belgian gardener Victor. Meanwhile Françoise, Victor's wife, devoted herself with tenderness to the care of her employer's stomach.

Hercule Poirot passed through the gate, sighed, glanced down once more at his shining black shoes, adjusted his pale grey Homburg hat, and looked up and down the road.

He shivered slightly at the aspect of Dovecotes. Dovecotes and Resthaven had been erected by rival builders, both of whom had acquired a small piece of land. Further enterprise on their part had been swiftly curtailed by a National Trust for preserving the beauties of the countryside. The two houses remained representative of two schools of thought. Resthaven was a box with a roof, severely modern and a little dull. Dovecotes was a riot of half-timbering and Olde Worlde packed into as small a space as possible.

Hercule Poirot debated within himself as to how he should approach The Hollow. There was, he knew, a little higher up the lane, a small gate and a path. This, the unofficial way, would save a half-mile *détour* by the road. Nevertheless Hercule Poirot, a stickler for etiquette, decided to take the longer way round and approach the house correctly by the front entrance.

This was his first visit to Sir Henry and Lady Angkatell. One should not, he considered, take short-cuts uninvited, especially when one was the guest of people of social importance. He was, it must be admitted, pleased by their invitation.

'*Je suis un peu snob,*' he murmured to himself.

He had retained an agreeable impression of the Angkatells from the time in Baghdad, particularly of Lady Angkatell. '*Une originale!*' he thought to himself.

His estimation of the time required for walking to The Hollow by road was accurate. It was exactly one minute to one when he rang the front-door bell. He was glad to have arrived and felt slightly tired. He was not fond of walking.

The door was opened by the magnificent Gudgeon, of whom Poirot approved. His reception, however, was not quite as he had hoped. 'Her ladyship is in the pavilion by the swimming pool, sir. Will you come this way?'

The passion of the English for sitting out of doors irritated Hercule Poirot. Though one had to put up with this whimsy in the height of summer, surely, Poirot thought, one should be safe from it by the end of September! The day was mild, certainly, but it had, as autumn days always had, a certain dampness. How infinitely pleasanter to have been ushered into a comfortable drawing-room with, perhaps, a small fire in the grate. But no, here he was being led out through french windows across a slope of lawn, past a rockery and then through a small gate and along a narrow track between closely planted young chestnuts.

It was the habit of the Angkatells to invite guests for one o'clock, and on fine days they had cocktails and sherry in the small pavilion by the swimming pool. Lunch itself was scheduled for one-thirty, by which time the most unpunctual of guests should have managed to arrive, which permitted Lady Angkatell's excellent cook to embark on soufflés and such accurately timed delicacies without too much trepidation.

To Hercule Poirot, the plan did not commend itself.

'In a little minute,' he thought, 'I shall be almost back where I started.'

With an increasing awareness of his feet in his shoes, he followed Gudgeon's tall figure.

It was at that moment from just ahead of him that he heard a little cry. It increased, somehow, his dissatisfaction. It was incongruous, in some way unfitting. He did not classify it, nor indeed think about it. When he thought about it afterwards he was hard put to it to remember just what emotions it had seemed to convey. Dismay? Surprise? Horror? He could only say that it suggested, very definitely, the unexpected.

Gudgeon stepped out from the chestnuts. He was moving to one side, deferentially, to allow Poirot to pass and at the same time clearing his throat preparatory to murmuring, 'M. Poirot, my lady' in the proper subdued and respectful tones when his suppleness became suddenly rigid. He gasped. It was an unbutlerlike noise.

Hercule Poirot stepped out on to the open space surrounding the swimming pool, and immediately he, too, stiffened, but with annoyance.

It was too much – it was really too much! He had not suspected such cheapness of the Angkatells. The long walk by the road, the disappointment at the house – and now *this*! The misplaced sense of humour of the English!

He was annoyed and he was bored – oh, how he was bored. Death was not, to him, amusing. And here they had arranged for him, by way of a joke, a set-piece.

For what he was looking at was a highly artificial murder scene. By the side of the pool was the body, artistically arranged with an outflung arm and even some red paint dripping gently over the edge of the concrete into the pool. It was a spectacular body, that of a handsome fair-haired man. Standing over the body, revolver in hand, was a woman, a short, powerfully built, middle-aged woman with a curiously blank expression.

And there were three other actors. On the far side of the pool was a tall young woman whose hair matched the autumn leaves in its rich brown; she had a basket in her hand full of dahlia heads. A little farther off was a man, a tall, inconspicuous man in a shooting-coat, carrying a gun. And immediately on his left, with a basket of eggs in her hand, was his hostess, Lady Angkatell.

It was clear to Hercule Poirot that several different paths converged here at the swimming pool and that these people had each arrived by a different path.

It was all very mathematical and artificial.

He sighed. *Enfin*, what did they expect him to do? Was he to pretend to believe in this 'crime'? Was he to register dismay – alarm? Or was he to bow, to congratulate his hostess: 'Ah, but it is very charming, what you arrange for me here'?

Really, the whole thing was very stupid – not *spirituel* at all! Was it not Queen Victoria who had said: 'We are not amused'? He felt very inclined to say the same: 'I, Hercule Poirot, am not amused.'

Lady Angkatell had walked towards the body. He followed, conscious of Gudgeon, still breathing hard, behind him. 'He is not in the secret, that one,' Hercule Poirot thought to himself. From the other side of the pool, the other two people joined them. They were all quite close now, looking down on that spectacular sprawling figure by the pool's edge.

And suddenly, with a terrific shock, with that feeling as of blurring on a cinematograph screen before the picture comes into focus, Hercule Poirot realized that this artificially set scene had a point of reality.

For what he was looking down at was, if not a dead, at least a dying man.

It was not red paint dripping off the edge of the concrete, it was blood. This man had been shot, and shot a very short time ago.

He darted a quick glance at the woman who stood there, revolver in hand. Her face was quite blank, without feeling of any kind. She looked dazed and rather stupid.

'Curious,' he thought.

Had she, he wondered, drained herself of all emotion, all feeling, in the firing of the shot? Was she now all passion spent, nothing but an exhausted shell? It might be so, he thought.

Then he looked down on the shot man, and he started. For the dying man's eyes were open. They were intensely blue eyes and they held an expression that Poirot could not read but which he described to himself as a kind of intense awareness.

And suddenly, or so it felt to Poirot, there seemed to be in all this group of people only one person who was really alive – the man who was at the point of death.

Poirot had never received so strong an impression of vivid and intense vitality. The others were pale shadowy figures, actors in a remote drama, but this man was *real*.

John Christow opened his mouth and spoke. His voice was strong, unsurprised and urgent.

'*Henrietta –*' he said.

Then his eyelids dropped, his head jerked sideways.

Hercule Poirot knelt down, made sure, then rose to his feet, mechanically dusting the knees of his trousers.

'Yes,' he said. 'He is dead.'

II

The picture broke up, wavered, refocused itself. There were individual reactions now – trivial happenings. Poirot was conscious of himself as a kind of magnified eyes and ears – recording. Just that, *recording*.

He was aware of Lady Angkatell's hand relaxing its grip on her basket and Gudgeon springing forward, quickly taking it from her.

'Allow me, my lady.'

Mechanically, quite naturally, Lady Angkatell murmured:

'Thank you, Gudgeon.'

And then, hesitantly, she said:

'Gerda –'

The woman holding the revolver stirred for the first time. She looked round at them all. When she spoke, her voice held what seemed to be pure bewilderment.

'John's dead,' she said. 'John's *dead*.'

With a kind of swift authority, the tall young woman with the leaf-brown hair came swiftly to her.

'Give that to me, Gerda,' she said.

And dexterously, before Poirot could protest or intervene, she had taken the revolver out of Gerda Christow's hand.

Poirot took a quick step forward.

'You should not do that, Mademoiselle –'

The young woman started nervously at the sound of his voice. The revolver slipped through her fingers. She was standing by the edge of the pool and the revolver fell with a splash into the water.

Her mouth opened and she uttered an 'Oh' of consternation, turning her head to look at Poirot apologetically.

'What a fool I am,' she said. 'I'm sorry.'

Poirot did not speak for a moment. He was staring into a pair of clear hazel eyes. They met his quite steadily and he wondered if his momentary suspicion had been unjust.

He said quietly:

'Things should be handled as little as possible. Everything must be left exactly as it is for the police to see.'

There was a little stir then – very faint, just a ripple of uneasiness.

Lady Angkatell murmured distastefully: 'Of course. I suppose – yes, the police –'

In a quiet, pleasant voice, tinged with fastidious repulsion, the man in the shooting-coat said: 'I'm afraid, Lucy, it's inevitable.'

Into that moment of silence and realization there came the sound of footsteps and voices, assured, brisk footsteps and cheerful, incongruous voices.

Along the path from the house came Sir Henry Angkatell and Midge Hardcastle, talking and laughing together.

At the sight of the group round the pool, Sir Henry stopped short, and exclaimed in astonishment:

'What's the matter? What's happened?'

His wife answered: 'Gerda has –' She broke off sharply. 'I mean – John is –'

Gerda said in her flat, bewildered voice:

'John has been shot. He's dead.'

They all looked away from her, embarrassed.

Then Lady Angkatell said quickly:

'My dear, I think you'd better go and – and lie down. Perhaps we had better all go back to the house? Henry, you and M. Poirot can stay here and – and wait for the police.'

'That will be the best plan, I think,' said Sir Henry. He turned to Gudgeon. 'Will you ring up the police station, Gudgeon? Just state exactly what has occurred. When the police arrive, bring them straight out here.'

Gudgeon bent his head a little and said: 'Yes, Sir Henry.' He was looking a little white about the gills, but he was still the perfect servant.

The tall young woman said: 'Come, Gerda,' and putting her hand through the other woman's arm, she led her unresistingly away and along the path towards the house. Gerda walked as though in a dream. Gudgeon stood back a little to let them pass, and then followed carrying the basket of eggs.

Sir Henry turned sharply to his wife. 'Now, Lucy, what is all this? What happened exactly?'

Lady Angkatell stretched out vague hands, a lovely helpless gesture. Hercule Poirot felt the charm of it and the appeal.

'My dear, I hardly know. I was down by the hens. I heard a shot that seemed very near, but I didn't really think anything about it. After all,' she appealed to them all, 'one *doesn't*! And then I came up the path to the pool and there was John lying there and Gerda standing over him with the revolver. Henrietta and Edward arrived almost at the same moment – from over there.'

She nodded towards the farther side of the pool, where two paths ran into the woods.

Hercule Poirot cleared his throat.

'Who are they, this John and this Gerda? If I may know,' he added apologetically.

'Oh, of course.' Lady Angkatell turned to him in quick apology. 'One forgets – but then one doesn't exactly *introduce* people – not when somebody has just been killed. John is John Christow, Dr Christow. Gerda Christow is his wife.'

'And the lady who went with Mrs Christow to the house?'

'My cousin, Henrietta Savernake.'

There was a movement, a very faint movement from the man on Poirot's left.

'*Henrietta* Savernake,' thought Poirot, 'and he does not like that she should say it – but it is, after all, inevitable that I should know . . .'

('*Henrietta!*' the dying man had said. He had said it in a very curious way. A way that reminded Poirot of something – of some incident . . . now, what was it? No matter, it would come to him.)

Lady Angkatell was going on, determined now on fulfilling her social duties.

'And this is another cousin of ours, Edward Angkatell. And Miss Hardcastle.'

Poirot acknowledged the introductions with polite bows. Midge felt suddenly that she wanted to laugh hysterically; she controlled herself with an effort.

'And now, my dear,' said Sir Henry, 'I think that, as you suggested, you had better go back to the house. I will have a word or two here with M. Poirot.'

Lady Angkatell looked thoughtfully at them.

'I do hope,' she said, 'that Gerda *is* lying down. Was that the right thing to suggest? I really couldn't think what to say. I mean, one has no *precedent*. What *does* one say to a woman who has just killed her husband?'

She looked at them as though hoping that some authoritative answer might be given to her question.

Then she went along the path towards the house. Midge followed her. Edward brought up the rear.

Poirot was left with his host.

Sir Henry cleared his throat. He seemed a little uncertain what to say.

'Christow,' he observed at last, 'was a very able fellow – a *very* able fellow.'

Poirot's eyes rested once more on the dead man. He still had the curious impression that the dead man was more alive than the living.

He wondered what gave him that impression.

He responded politely to Sir Henry.

'Such a tragedy as this is very unfortunate,' he said.

'This sort of thing is more your line than mine,' said Sir Henry. 'I don't think I have ever been at close quarters with a murder before. I hope I've done the right thing so far?'

'The procedure has been quite correct,' said Poirot. 'You have summoned the police, and until they arrive and take charge there is nothing for us to do – except to make sure that nobody disturbs the body or tampers with the evidence.'

As he said the last word he looked down into the pool where he could see the revolver lying on the concrete bottom, slightly distorted by the blue water.

The evidence, he thought, had perhaps already been tampered with before he, Hercule Poirot, had been able to prevent it.

But no – that had been an accident.

Sir Henry murmured distastefully:

'Think we've got to stand about? A bit chilly. It would be all right, I should think, if we went inside the pavilion?'

Poirot, who had been conscious of damp feet and a disposition to shiver, acquiesced gladly. The pavilion was at the side of the pool farthest from the house, and through its open door they commanded a view of the pool and the body and the path to the house along which the police would come.

The pavilion was luxuriously furnished with comfortable settees and gay native rugs. On a painted iron table a tray was set with glasses and a decanter of sherry.

'I'd offer you a drink,' said Sir Henry, 'but I suppose I'd better not touch anything until the police come – not, I should imagine, that there's anything to interest them in here. Still, it is better to be on the safe side. Gudgeon hadn't brought out the cocktails yet, I see. He was waiting for you to arrive.'

The two sat down rather gingerly in two wicker chairs near the door so that they could watch the path from the house.

A constraint settled over them. It was an occasion on which it was difficult to make small talk.

Poirot glanced round the pavilion, noting anything that struck him as unusual. An expensive cape of platinum fox had been flung carelessly across the back of one of the chairs. He wondered whose it was. Its rather ostentatious magnificence did not harmonize with any of the people he had seen up to now. He could not, for instance, imagine it round Lady Angkatell's shoulders.

It worried him. It breathed a mixture of opulence and self-advertisement – and those characteristics were lacking in anyone he had seen so far.

'I suppose we can smoke,' said Sir Henry, offering his case to Poirot.

Before taking the cigarette, Poirot sniffed the air.

French perfume – an expensive French perfume.

Only a trace of it lingered, but it was there, and again the scent was not the scent that associated itself in his mind with any of the occupants of The Hollow.

As he leaned forward to light his cigarette at Sir Henry's lighter, Poirot's glance fell on a little pile of matchboxes – six of them – stacked on a small table near one of the settees.

It was a detail that struck him as definitely odd.

CHAPTER 12

I

'Half-past two,' said Lady Angkatell.

She was in the drawing-room, with Midge and Edward. From behind the closed door of Sir Henry's study came the murmur of voices. Hercule Poirot, Sir Henry and Inspector Grange were in there.

Lady Angkatell sighed:

'You know, Midge, I still feel one ought to do something about lunch. It seems, of course, quite heartless to sit down round the table as though nothing had happened. But after all, M. Poirot was asked to lunch – and he is probably hungry. And it can't be upsetting to *him* that poor John Christow has been killed like it is to us. And I must say that though I really do not feel like eating myself, Henry and Edward must be extremely hungry after being out shooting all the morning.'

Edward Angkatell said: 'Don't worry on my account, Lucy, dear.'

'You are always considerate, Edward. And then there is David – I noticed that he ate a great deal at dinner last night. Intellectual people always seem to need a good deal of food. Where *is* David, by the way?'

'He went up to his room,' said Midge, 'after he had heard what had happened.'

'Yes – well, that was rather tactful of him. I dare say it made him feel awkward. Of course, say what you like, a murder is an awkward thing – it upsets the servants and puts the general routine out – we were having ducks for lunch – fortunately they are quite nice eaten cold. What does one do about

Gerda, do you think? Something on a tray? A little strong soup, perhaps?'

'Really,' thought Midge, 'Lucy is inhuman!' And then with a qualm she reflected that it was perhaps because Lucy was too human that it shocked one so! Wasn't it the plain unvarnished truth that all catastrophes were hedged round with these little trivial wonderings and surmises? Lucy merely gave utterance to the thoughts which most people did not acknowledge. One did remember the servants, and worry about meals. And one did, even, feel hungry. She felt hungry herself at this very moment! Hungry, she thought, and at the same time, rather sick. A curious mixture.

And there was, undoubtedly, just plain awkward embarrassment in not knowing how to react to a quiet, commonplace woman whom one had referred to, only yesterday, as 'poor Gerda' and who was now, presumably, shortly to be standing in the dock accused of murder.

'These things happen to other people,' thought Midge. 'They can't happen to *us*.'

She looked across the room at Edward. 'They oughtn't,' she thought, 'to happen to people like Edward. People who are so very *un*violent.' She took comfort in looking at Edward. Edward, so quiet, so reasonable, so kind and calm.

Gudgeon entered, inclined himself confidentially and spoke in a suitably muted voice.

'I have placed sandwiches and some coffee in the dining-room, my lady.'

'Oh, *thank* you, Gudgeon!'

'Really,' said Lady Angkatell as Gudgeon left the room. 'Gudgeon is wonderful: I don't know what I should do without Gudgeon. He always knows the right thing to do. Some really substantial sandwiches are as good as lunch – and nothing *heartless* about them, if you know what I mean!'

'Oh, Lucy, *don't*.'

Midge suddenly felt warm tears running down her cheek. Lady Angkatell looked surprised, murmured:

'Poor darling. It's all been too much for you.'

Edward crossed to the sofa and sat down by Midge. He put his arm round her.

'Don't worry, little Midge,' he said.

Midge buried her face on his shoulder and sobbed there comfortably. She remembered how nice Edward had been to her when her rabbit had died at Ainswick one Easter holidays.

Edward said gently: 'It's been a shock. Can I get her some brandy, Lucy?'

'On the sideboard in the dining-room. I don't think –'

She broke off as Henrietta came into the room. Midge sat up. She felt Edward stiffen and sit very still.

What, thought Midge, does Henrietta feel? She felt almost reluctant to look at her cousin – but there was nothing to see. Henrietta looked, if anything, belligerent. She had come in with her chin up, her colour high, and with a certain swiftness.

'Oh, there you are, Henrietta,' cried Lady Angkatell. 'I have been wondering. The police are with Henry and M. Poirot. What have you given Gerda? Brandy? Or tea and aspirin?'

'I gave her some brandy – and a hot-water bottle.'

'Quite right,' said Lady Angkatell approvingly. 'That's what they tell you in First Aid classes – the hot-water bottle, I mean, for shock – *not* the brandy; there is a reaction nowadays against stimulants. But I think that is only a fashion. We always gave brandy for shock when I was a girl at Ainswick. Though, really, I suppose, it can't be exactly *shock* with Gerda. I don't know really *what* one would feel if one had killed one's husband – it's the sort of thing one just can't begin to imagine – but it wouldn't exactly give one a *shock*. I mean, there wouldn't be any element of *surprise*.'

Henrietta's voice, icy cold, cut into the placid atmosphere.

She said: 'Why are you all so sure that Gerda killed John?'

There was a moment's pause – and Midge felt a curious shifting in the atmosphere. There was con- fusion, strain and, finally, a kind of slow watchfulness.

Then Lady Angkatell said, her voice quite devoid of any inflection:

'It seemed – self-evident. What else do you suggest?'

'Isn't it possible that Gerda came along to the pool, that she found John lying there, and that she had just picked up the revolver when – when we came upon the scene?'

Again there was that silence. Then Lady Angkatell asked:

'Is that what Gerda says?'

'Yes.'

It was not a simple assent. It had force behind it. It came out like a revolver shot.

Lady Angkatell raised her eyebrows, then she said with apparent irrelevancy:

'There are sandwiches and coffee in the dining-room.'

She broke off with a little gasp as Gerda Christow came through the open door. She said hurriedly and apologetically:

'I – I really didn't feel I could lie down any longer. One is – one is so terribly restless.'

Lady Angkatell cried:

'You must sit down – you must sit down *at once.*'

She displaced Midge from the sofa, settled Gerda there, put a cushion at her back.

'You poor dear,' said Lady Angkatell.

She spoke with emphasis, but the words seemed quite meaningless.

Edward walked to the window and stood there looking out.

Gerda pushed back the untidy hair from her forehead. She spoke in a worried, bewildered tone.

'I – I really am only just beginning to realize it. You know I haven't been able to feel – I still can't feel – that it's *real* – that John – is *dead.*' She began to shake a little. 'Who can have killed him? Who can possibly have killed him?'

Lady Angkatell drew a deep breath – then she turned her head sharply. Sir Henry's door had opened. He came in accompanied by Inspector Grange, who was a large, heavily built man with a down-drooping, pessimistic moustache.

'This is my wife – Inspector Grange.'

Grange bowed and said:

'I was wondering, Lady Angkatell, if I could have a few words with Mrs Christow –'

He broke off as Lady Angkatell indicated the figure on the sofa.

'Mrs Christow?'

Gerda said eagerly:

'Yes, I am Mrs Christow.'

'I don't want to distress you, Mrs Christow, but I would like to ask you a few questions. You can, of course, have your solicitor present if you prefer it –'

Sir Henry put in:

'It is sometimes wiser, Gerda –'

She interrupted:

'A solicitor? Why a solicitor? Why should a solicitor know anything about John's death?'

Inspector Grange coughed. Sir Henry seemed about to speak. Henrietta put in:

'The inspector only wants to know just what happened this morning.'

Gerda turned to him. She spoke in a wondering voice:

'It seems all like a bad dream – not real. I – I haven't been able to cry or anything. One just doesn't feel anything at all.'

Grange said soothingly:

'That's the shock, Mrs Christow.'

'Yes, yes – I suppose it is. But you see it was all so *sudden*. I went out from the house and along the path to the swimming pool –'

'At what time, Mrs Christow?'

'It was just before one o'clock – about two minutes to one. I know because I looked at that clock. And when I got there – there was John, lying there – and blood on the edge of the concrete.'

'Did you hear a shot, Mrs Christow?'

'Yes, – no – I don't know. I knew Sir Henry and Mr Angkatell were out shooting. I – I just saw John –'

'Yes, Mrs Christow?'

'John – and blood – and a revolver. I picked up the revolver –'

'Why?'

'I beg your pardon?'

'Why did you pick up the revolver, Mrs Christow?'

'I – I don't know.'

'You shouldn't have touched it, you know.'

'Shouldn't I?' Gerda was vague, her face vacant. 'But I did. I held it in my hands.'

She looked down now at her hands as though she was, in fancy, seeing the revolver lying in them.

She turned sharply to the inspector. Her voice was suddenly sharp – anguished.

'Who could have killed John? Nobody could have wanted to kill him. He was – he was the best of men. So kind, so unselfish – he did everything for other people. Everybody loved him, Inspector. He was a wonderful doctor. The best and kindest of husbands. It must have been an accident – it must – it *must*!'

She flung out a hand to the room.

'Ask anyone, Inspector. Nobody could have wanted to kill John, could they?'

She appealed to them all.

Inspector Grange closed up his notebook.

'Thank you, Mrs Christow,' he said in an unemotional voice. 'That will be all for the present.'

Hercule Poirot and Inspector Grange went together through the chestnut woods to the swimming pool. The thing that had been John Christow but which was now 'the body' had been photographed and measured and written about and examined by the police surgeon, and had now been taken away to the mortuary. The swimming pool, Poirot thought, looked curiously innocent. Everything about today, he thought, had been strangely fluid. Except John Christow – he had not been fluid. Even in death he had been purposeful and objective. The swimming pool was not now pre-eminently a swimming pool, it was the place where John Christow's body had lain and where his life-blood had welled away over concrete into artificially blue water.

Artificial – for a moment Poirot grasped at the word. Yes, there had been something artificial about it all. As though –

A man in a bathing suit came up to the inspector.

'Here's the revolver, sir,' he said.

Grange took the dripping object gingerly.

'No hope of fingerprints now,' he remarked, 'but luckily it doesn't matter in this case. Mrs Christow was actually holding the revolver when you arrived, wasn't she, M. Poirot?'

'Yes.'

'Identification of the revolver is the next thing,' said Grange. 'I should imagine Sir Henry will be able to do that for us. She got it from his study, I should say.'

He cast a glance round the pool.

'Now, let's have that again to be quite clear. The path below the pool comes up from the farm and that's the way Lady Angkatell came. The other two, Mr Edward Angkatell and Miss Savernake, came down from the woods – but not together. He came by the left-hand path, and she by the right-hand one which leads out of the long flower walk above the house. But they were both standing on the far side of the pool when you arrived?'

'Yes.'

'And this path here, beside the pavilion, leads on to Podder's Lane. Right – we'll go along it.'

As they walked, Grange spoke, without excitement, just with knowledge and quiet pessimism.

'Never like these cases much,' he said. 'Had one last year – down near Ashridge. Retired military man, he was – distinguished career. Wife was the nice quiet, old-fashioned kind, sixty-five, grey hair – rather pretty hair with a wave in it. Did a lot of gardening. One day she goes up to his room, gets out his service revolver, and walks out into the garden and shoots him. Just like that! A good deal behind it, of course, that one had to dig out. Sometimes they think up some fool story about a tramp! We pretend to accept it, of course, keep things quiet whilst we're making inquiries, but we know what's what.'

'You mean,' said Poirot, 'that you have decided that Mrs Christow shot her husband.'

Grange gave him a look of surprise.

'Well, don't you think so?'

Poirot said slowly: 'It could all have happened as she said.'

Inspector Grange shrugged his shoulders.

'It *could* have – yes. But it's a thin story. And *they* all think she killed him! They know something we don't.' He looked curiously at his companion. 'You thought she'd done it all right, didn't you, when you arrived on the scene?'

Poirot half-closed his eyes. Coming along the path . . . Gudgeon stepping . . . Gerda Christow standing over her husband with the revolver in her hand and that blank look on her face. Yes, as Grange had said, he *had* thought she had done it . . . had thought, at least, that that was the impression he was meant to have.

Yes, but that was not the same thing.

A scene staged – set to deceive.

Had Gerda Christow looked like a woman who had just shot her husband? That was what Inspector Grange wanted to know.

And with a sudden shock of surprise, Hercule Poirot realized that in all his long experience of deeds of violence he had never actually come face to face with a woman who had just killed her husband. What would a woman look like in such circumstances? Triumphant, horrified, satisfied, dazed, incredulous, empty?

Any one of these things, he thought.

Inspector Grange was talking. Poirot caught the end of his speech.

'– Once you get all the facts behind the case, and you can usually get all that from the servants.'

'Mrs Christow is going back to London?'

'Yes. There's a couple of kids there. Have to let her go. Of course, we keep a sharp eye on her, but she won't know that. She thinks she's got away with it all right. Looks rather a stupid kind of woman to me . . .'

Did Gerda Christow realize, Poirot wondered, what the police thought – and what the Angkatells thought? She had looked as though she did not realize anything at all. She had looked like a woman whose reactions were slow and who was completely dazed and heartbroken by her husband's death.

They had come out into the lane.

Poirot stopped by his gate. Grange said:

'This your little place? Nice and snug. Well, goodbye for the present, M. Poirot. Thanks for your co-operation. I'll drop in some time and give you the lowdown on how we're getting on.'

His eye travelled up the lane.

'Who's your neighbour? That's not where our new celebrity hangs out, is it?'

'Miss Veronica Cray, the actress, comes there for weekends, I believe.'

'Of course. Dovecotes. I liked her in *Lady Rides on Tiger*, but she's a bit high-brow for my taste. Give me Hedy Lamarr.'

He turned away.

'Well, I must get back to the job. So long, M. Poirot.'

II

'You recognize this, Sir Henry?'

Inspector Grange laid the revolver on the desk in front of Sir Henry and looked at him expectantly.

'I can handle it?' Sir Henry's hand hesitated over the revolver as he asked the question.

Grange nodded. 'It's been in the pool. Destroyed whatever fingerprints there were on it. A pity, if I may say so, that Miss Savernake let it slip out of her hand.'

'Yes, yes – but of course it was a very tense moment for all of us. Women are apt to get flustered and – er – drop things.'

Again Inspector Grange nodded. He said:

'Miss Savernake seems a cool, capable young lady on the whole.'

The words were devoid of emphasis, yet something in them made Sir Henry look up sharply. Grange went on:

'Now, do you recognize it, sir?'

Sir Henry picked up the revolver and examined it. He noted the number and compared it with a list in a small leather-bound book. Then, closing the book with a sigh, he said:

'Yes, Inspector, this comes from my collection here.'

'When did you see it last?'

'Yesterday afternoon. We were doing some shooting in the garden with a target, and this was one of the firearms we were using.'

'Who actually fired this revolver on that occasion?'

'I think everybody had at least one shot with it.'

'Including Mrs Christow?'

'Including Mrs Christow.'

'And after you had finished shooting?'

'I put the revolver away in its usual place. Here.'

He pulled out the drawer of a big bureau. It was half-full of guns.

'You've got a big collection of firearms, Sir Henry.'

'It's been a hobby of mine for many years.'

Inspector Grange's eyes rested thoughtfully on the ex-Governor of the Hollowene Islands. A good-looking, distinguished man, the kind of man he would be quite pleased to serve under himself –

in fact, a man he would much prefer to his own present Chief Constable. Inspector Grange did not think much of the Chief Constable of Wealdshire – a fussy despot and a tuft-hunter. He brought his mind back to the job in hand.

'The revolver was not, of course, loaded when you put it away, Sir Henry?'

'Certainly not.'

'And you keep your ammunition – where?'

'Here.' Sir Henry took a key from a pigeon-hole and unlocked one of the lower drawers of the desk.

'Simple enough,' thought Grange. The Christow woman had seen where it was kept. She'd only got to come along and help herself. Jealousy, he thought, plays the dickens with women. He'd lay ten to one it *was* jealousy. The thing would come clear enough when he'd finished the routine here and got on to the Harley Street end. But you'd got to do things in their proper order.

He got up and said:

'Well, thank you, Sir Henry. I'll let you know about the inquest.'

CHAPTER 13

They had the cold ducks for supper. After the ducks there was a caramel custard which, Lady Angkatell said, showed just the right feeling on the part of Mrs Medway.

Cooking, she said, really gave great scope to delicacy of feeling.

'We are only, as she knows, moderately fond of caramel custard. There would be something very gross, just after the death of a friend, in eating one's favourite pudding. But caramel custard is so easy – slippery if you know what I mean – and then one leaves a little on one's plate.'

She sighed and said that she hoped they had done right in letting Gerda go back to London.

'But quite correct of Henry to go with her.'

For Sir Henry had insisted on driving Gerda to Harley Street.

'She will come back here for the inquest, of course,' went on Lady Angkatell, meditatively eating caramel custard. 'But naturally she wanted to break it to the children – they might see it in the papers and only a Frenchwoman in the house – one knows how excitable – a *crise de nerfs*, possibly. But Henry will deal with her, and I really think Gerda will be quite all right. She will probably send for some relations – sisters perhaps. Gerda is the sort of person who is sure to have sisters – three or four, I should think, probably living at Tunbridge Wells.'

'What extraordinary things you do say, Lucy,' said Midge.

'Well, darling, Torquay if you prefer it – no, not Torquay. They would be at least sixty-five if they were living at Torquay. Eastbourne, perhaps, or St Leonards.'

Lady Angkatell looked at the last spoonful of caramel custard, seemed to condole with it, and laid it down very gently uneaten.

David, who only liked savouries, looked down gloomily at his empty plate.

Lady Angkatell got up.

'I think we shall all want to go to bed early tonight,' she said. 'So much has happened, hasn't it? One has no idea from reading about these things in the paper how *tiring* they are. I feel, you know, as though I had walked about fifteen miles. Instead of actually having done nothing but sit down – but that is tiring, too, because one does not like to read a book or a newspaper, it looks so heartless. Though I think perhaps the leading article in *The Observer* would have been all right – but *not* the *News of the World*. Don't you agree with me, David? I like to know what the young people think, it keeps one from losing touch.'

David said in a gruff voice that he never read the *News of the World*.

'I always do,' said Lady Angkatell. 'We pretend we get it for the servants, but Gudgeon is very understanding and never takes it out until after tea. It is a most interesting paper, all about women who put their heads in gas ovens – an incredible number of them!'

'What will they do in the houses of the future which are all electric?' asked Edward Angkatell with a faint smile.

'I suppose they will just have to decide to make the best of things – so much more sensible.'

'I disagree with you, sir,' said David, 'about the houses of the future being all electric. There can be communal heating laid on from a central supply. Every working-class house should be completely labour-saving.'

Edward Angkatell said hastily that he was afraid that was a subject he was not very well up in. David's lip curled with scorn.

Gudgeon brought in coffee on a tray, moving a little slower than usual to convey a sense of mourning.

'Oh, Gudgeon,' said Lady Angkatell, 'about those eggs. I meant to write the date in pencil on them as usual. Will you ask Mrs Medway to see to it?'

'I think you will find, my lady, that everything has been attended to quite satisfactorily.' He cleared his throat. 'I have seen to things myself.'

'Oh, thank you, Gudgeon.'

As Gudgeon went out she murmured: 'Really, Gudgeon is wonderful. The servants are all being marvellous. And one does so sympathize with them having the police here – it must be dreadful for them. By the way, are there any left?'

'Police, do you mean?' asked Midge.

'Yes. Don't they usually leave one standing in the hall? Or perhaps he's watching the front door from the shrubbery outside.'

'Why should he watch the front door?'

'I don't know, I'm sure. They do in books. And then somebody else is murdered in the night.'

'Oh, Lucy, don't,' said Midge.

Lady Angkatell looked at her curiously.

'Darling, I am so sorry. Stupid of me. And of course nobody else could be murdered. Gerda's gone home – I mean – Oh, Henrietta dear, I am sorry. I didn't mean to say *that*.'

But Henrietta did not answer. She was standing by the round table staring down at the bridge score she had kept last night.

She said, rousing herself, 'Sorry, Lucy, what did you say?'

'I wondered if there were any police left over.'

'Like remnants in a sale? I don't think so. They've all gone back to the police station, to write out what we said in proper police language.'

'What are you looking at, Henrietta?'

'Nothing.'

Henrietta moved across to the mantelpiece.

'What do you think Veronica Cray is doing tonight?' she asked.

A look of dismay crossed Lady Angkatell's face.

'My dear! You don't think she might come over here again? She must have heard by now.'

'Yes,' said Henrietta thoughtfully. 'I suppose she's heard.'

'Which reminds me,' said Lady Angkatell. 'I really must telephone to the Careys. We can't have them coming to lunch tomorrow just as though nothing had happened.'

She left the room.

David, hating his relations, murmured that he wanted to look up something in the *Encyclopædia Britannica*. The library, he thought, would be a peaceful place.

Henrietta went to the french windows, opened them, and passed through. After a moment's hesitation Edward followed her.

He found her standing outside looking up at the sky. She said:

'Not so warm as last night, is it?'

In his pleasant voice, Edward said: 'No, distinctly chilly.'

She was standing looking up at the house. Her eyes were running along the windows. Then she turned and looked towards the woods. He had no clue to what was in her mind.

He made a movement towards the open window.

'Better come in. It's cold.'

She shook her head.

'I'm going for a stroll. To the swimming pool.'

'Oh, my dear.' He took a quick step towards her. 'I'll come with you.'

'No, thank you, Edward.' Her voice cut sharply through the chill of the air. 'I want to be alone with my dead.'

'Henrietta! My dear – I haven't said anything. But you do know how – how sorry I am.'

'Sorry? That John Christow is dead?'

There was still the brittle sharpness in her tone.

'I meant – sorry for you, Henrietta. I know it must have been a – a great shock.'

'Shock? Oh, but I'm very tough, Edward. I can stand shocks. Was it a shock to you? What did you feel when you saw him lying there? Glad, I suppose. You didn't like John Christow.'

Edward murmured: 'He and I – hadn't much in common.'

'How nicely you put things! In such a restrained way. But as a matter of fact you did have one thing in common. Me! You were both fond of me, weren't you? Only that didn't make a bond between you – quite the opposite.'

The moon came fitfully through a cloud and he was startled as he suddenly saw her face looking at him. Unconsciously he always saw Henrietta as a projection of the Henrietta he had known at Ainswick. She was always to him a laughing girl, with dancing eyes full of eager expectation. The woman he saw now seemed to him a stranger, with eyes that were brilliant but cold and which seemed to look at him inimically.

He said earnestly:

'Henrietta, dearest, do believe this – that I do sympathize with you – in – in your grief, your loss.'

'*Is* it grief?'

The question startled him. She seemed to be asking it, not of him, but of herself.

She said in a low voice:

'So quick – it can happen so quickly. One moment living, breathing, and the next – dead – gone – emptiness. Oh, the emptiness! And here we are, all of us, eating caramel custard and calling ourselves alive – and John, who was more alive than any of us, is dead. I say the word, you know, over and over again to myself. Dead – dead – dead – dead – *dead*. And soon it hasn't got any meaning – not any meaning at all. It's just a funny little word like the breaking off of a rotten branch. *Dead – dead – dead – dead*. It's like a tom-tom, isn't it, beating in the jungle. Dead – dead – dead – dead – dead –'

'Henrietta, stop! For God's sake, stop!'

She looked at him curiously.

'Didn't you know I'd feel like this? What did you think? That I'd sit gently crying into a nice little pocket handkerchief while you held my hand? That it would all be a great shock but that presently I'd begin to get over it? And that you'd comfort me very nicely? You *are* nice, Edward. You're very nice, but you're so – so inadequate.'

He drew back. His face stiffened. He said in a dry voice:

'Yes, I've always known that.'

She went on fiercely:

'What do you think it's been like all the evening, sitting round, with John dead and nobody caring but me and Gerda! With you glad, and David embarrassed and Midge distressed and Lucy delicately enjoying the *News of the World* come from print into real life! Can't you see how like a fantastic nightmare it all is?'

Edward said nothing. He stepped back a pace, into shadows.

Looking at him, Henrietta said:

'Tonight – nothing seems real to me, nobody *is* real – but John!'

Edward said quietly: 'I know . . . I am not very real.'

'What a brute I am, Edward. But I can't help it. I can't help resenting that John, who was so alive, is dead.'

'And that I who am half-dead, am alive.'

'I didn't mean that, Edward.'

'I think you did, Henrietta. I think, perhaps, you are right.'

But she was saying, thoughtfully, harking back to an earlier thought:

'But it is not grief. Perhaps I cannot feel grief. Perhaps I never shall. And yet – I would like to grieve for John.'

Her words seemed to him fantastic. Yet he was even more startled when she added suddenly, in an almost businesslike voice:

'I must go to the swimming pool.'

She glided away through the trees.

Walking stiffly, Edward went through the open window.

Midge looked up as Edward came through the window with unseeing eyes. His face was grey and pinched. It looked bloodless.

He did not hear the little gasp that Midge stifled immediately.

Almost mechanically he walked to a chair and sat down. Aware of something expected of him, he said:

'It's cold.'

'Are you very cold, Edward? Shall we – shall I – light a fire?'

'What?'

Midge took a box of matches from the mantelpiece. She knelt down and set a match to the fire. She looked cautiously sideways at Edward. He was quite oblivious, she thought, of everything.

She said: 'A fire is nice. It warms one.'

'How cold he looks,' she thought. 'But it can't be as cold as that outside? It's Henrietta! What has she said to him?'

'Bring your chair nearer, Edward. Come close to the fire.'

'What?'

'Oh, it was nothing. Just the fire.'

She was talking to him now loudly and slowly, as though to a deaf person.

And suddenly, so suddenly that her heart turned over with relief, Edward, the real Edward, was there again. Smiling at her gently:

'Have you been talking to me, Midge? I'm sorry. I'm afraid I was thinking – thinking of something.'

'Oh, it was nothing. Just the fire.'

The sticks were crackling and some fir-cones were burning with a bright, clean flame. Edward looked at them. He said:

'It's a nice fire.'

He stretched out his long, thin hands to the blaze, aware of relief from tension.

Midge said: 'We always had fir-cones at Ainswick.'

'I still do. A basket of them is brought every day and put by the grate.'

Edward at Ainswick. Midge half-closed her eyes, picturing it. He would sit, she thought, in the library, on the west side of the house. There was a magnolia that almost covered one window and which filled the room with a golden green light in the afternoons. Through the other window you looked out on the lawn and a tall Wellingtonia stood up like a sentinel. And to the right was the big copper beech.

Oh, Ainswick – Ainswick.

She could smell the soft air that drifted in from the magnolia which would still, in September, have some great white sweet-smelling waxy flowers on it. And the pine-cones on the fire. And a faintly musty smell from the kind of book that Edward was sure to be reading. He would be sitting in the saddle-back chair, and occasionally, perhaps, his eyes would go from the book to the fire, and he would think, just for a minute, of Henrietta.

Midge stirred and asked:

'Where is Henrietta?'

'She went to the swimming pool.'

Midge stared. 'Why?'

Her voice, abrupt and deep, roused Edward a little.

'My dear Midge, surely you knew – oh, well – guessed. She knew Christow pretty well.'

'Oh, of course one knew *that*. But I don't see why she should go mooning off to where he was shot. That's not at all like Henrietta. She's never melodramatic.'

'Do any of us know what anyone else is like? Henrietta, for instance.'

Midge frowned. She said:

'After all, Edward, you and I have known Henrietta all our lives.'

'She has changed.'

'Not really. I don't think one changes.'

'Henrietta has changed.'

Midge looked at him curiously.

'More than we have, you and I?'

'Oh, I have stood still, I know that well enough. And you –'

His eyes, suddenly focusing, looked at her where she knelt by the fender. It was as though he was looking at her from a long way away, taking in the square chin, the dark eyes, the resolute mouth. He said:

'I wish I saw you more often, Midge, my dear.'

She smiled up at him. She said:

'I know. It isn't easy, these days, to keep in touch.'

There was a sound outside and Edward got up.

'Lucy was right,' he said. 'It has been a tiring day – one's first introduction to murder. I shall go to bed. Goodnight.'

He had left the room when Henrietta came through the window.

Midge turned on her.

'What have you done to Edward?'

'Edward?' Henrietta was vague. Her forehead was puckered. She seemed to be thinking of something a long way away.

'Yes, Edward. He came in looking dreadful – so cold and grey.'

'If you care about Edward so much, Midge, why don't you do something about him?'

'Do something? What do you mean?'

'I don't know. Stand on a chair and shout! Draw attention to yourself. Don't you know that's the only hope with a man like Edward?'

'Edward will never care about anyone but you, Henrietta. He never has.'

'Then it's very unintelligent of him.' She threw a quick glance at Midge's white face. 'I've hurt you. I'm sorry. But I hate Edward tonight.'

'Hate Edward? You *can't.*'

'Oh, yes, I can! You don't know –'

'What?'

Henrietta said slowly:

'He reminds me of such a lot of things I would like to forget.'

'What things?'

'Well, Ainswick, for instance.'

'Ainswick? You want to forget Ainswick?'

Midge's tone was incredulous.

'Yes, yes, *yes*! I was happy there. I can't stand, just now, being reminded of happiness. Don't you understand? A time when one didn't know what was coming. When one said confidently, everything is going to be lovely! Some people are wise – they never expect to be happy. I did.'

She said abruptly:

'I shall never go back to Ainswick.'

Midge said slowly:

'I wonder.'

CHAPTER 14

Midge woke up abruptly on Monday morning.

For a moment she lay there bemused, her eyes going confusedly towards the door, for she half-expected Lady Angkatell to appear. What was it Lucy had said when she came drifting in that first morning?

A difficult weekend? She had been worried – had thought that something unpleasant might happen.

Yes, and something unpleasant had happened – something

that was lying now upon Midge's heart and spirits like a thick black cloud. Something that she didn't want to think about – didn't want to remember. Something, surely, that *frightened* her. Something to do with Edward.

Memory came with a rush. One ugly stark word – *Murder!*

'Oh, no,' thought Midge, 'it can't be true. It's a dream I've been having. John Christow, murdered, shot – lying there by the pool. Blood and blue water – like a jacket of a detective story. Fantastic, unreal. The sort of thing that doesn't happen to oneself. If we were at Ainswick now. It couldn't have happened at Ainswick.'

The black weight moved from her forehead. It settled in the pit of her stomach, making her feel slightly sick.

It was not a dream. It was a real happening – a *News of the World* happening – and she and Edward and Lucy and Henry and Henrietta were all mixed up with it.

Unfair – surely unfair – since it was nothing to do with them if Gerda had shot her husband.

Midge stirred uneasily.

Quiet, stupid, slightly pathetic Gerda – you couldn't associate Gerda with melodrama – with violence.

Gerda, surely, couldn't shoot *anybody*.

Again that inward uneasiness rose. No, no, one mustn't think like that. Because who else *could* have shot John? And Gerda had been standing there by his body with the revolver in her hand. The revolver she had taken from Henry's study.

Gerda had said that she had found John dead and picked up the revolver. Well, what else could she say? She'd have to say *something*, poor thing.

All very well for Henrietta to defend her – to say that Gerda's story was perfectly possible. Henrietta hadn't considered the impossible alternatives.

Henrietta had been very odd last night.

But that, of course, had been the shock of John Christow's death.

Poor Henrietta – who had cared so terribly for John.

But she would get over it in time – one got over everything. And then she would marry Edward and live at Ainswick – and Edward would be happy at last.

Henrietta had always loved Edward very dearly. It was only

the aggressive, dominant personality of John Christow that had come in the way. He had made Edward look so – so *pale* by comparison.

It struck Midge when she came down to breakfast that morning that already Edward's personality, freed from John Christow's dominance, had begun to assert itself. He seemed more sure of himself, less hesitant and retiring.

He was talking pleasntly to the glowering and unresponsive David.

'You must come more often to Ainswick, David. I'd like you to feel at home there and to get to know all about the place.'

Helping himself to marmalade, David said coldly:

'These big estates are completely farcical. They should be split up.'

'That won't happen in my time, I hope,' said Edward, smiling. 'My tenants are a contented lot.'

'They shouldn't be,' said David. 'Nobody should be contented.'

'If apes had been content with tails –' murmured Lady Angkatell from where she was standing by the sideboard looking vaguely at a dish of kidneys. 'That's a poem I learnt in the nursery, but I simply can't remember how it goes on. I must have a talk with you, David, and learn all the new ideas. As far as I can see, one must hate everybody, but at the same time give them free medical attention and a lot of extra education (poor things, all those helpless little children herded into schoolhouses every day) – and cod-liver oil forced down babies' throats whether they like it or not – such nasty-smelling stuff.'

Lucy, Midge thought, was behaving very much as usual.

And Gudgeon, when she passed him in the hall, also looked just as usual. Life at The Hollow seemed to have resumed its normal course. With the departure of Gerda, the whole business seemed like a dream.

Then there was a scrunch of wheels on the gravel outside, and Sir Henry drew up in his car. He had stayed the night at his club and driven down early.

'Well, dear,' said Lucy, 'was everything all right?'

'Yes. The secretary was there – competent sort of girl. She

took charge of things. There's a sister, it seems. The secretary telegraphed to her.'

'I knew there would be,' said Lady Angkatell. 'At Tunbridge Wells?'

'Bexhill, I think,' said Sir Henry, looking puzzled.

'I dare say' – Lucy considered Bexhill. 'Yes – quite probably.'

Gudgeon approached.

'Inspector Grange telephoned, Sir Henry. The inquest will be at eleven o'clock on Wednesday.'

Sir Henry nodded. Lady Angkatell said:

'Midge, you'd better ring up your shop.'

Midge went slowly to the telephone.

Her life had always been so entirely normal and commonplace that she felt she lacked the phraseology to explain to her employers that after four days' holiday she was unable to return to work owing to the fact that she was mixed up in a murder case.

It did not sound credible. It did not even feel credible.

And Madame Alfrege was not a very easy person to explain things to at any time.

Midge set her chin resolutely and picked up the receiver.

It was all just as unpleasant as she had imagined it would be. The raucous voice of the vitriolic little Jewess came angrily over the wires.

'What wath that, Mith Hardcathle? A death? A funeral? Do you not know very well I am short-handed? Do you think I am going to stand for these excutheth? Oh, yeth, you are having a good time, I dare thay!'

Midge interrupted, speaking sharply and distinctly.

'The poleeth? The poleeth, you thay?' It was almost a scream. 'You are mixed up with the poleeth?'

Setting her teeth, Midge continued to explain. Strange how sordid that woman at the other end made the whole thing seem. A vulgar police case. What alchemy there was in human beings!

Edward opened the door and came in, then seeing that Midge was telephoning, he was about to go out. She stopped him.

'Do stay, Edward. Please. Oh, I want you to.'

The presence of Edward in the room gave her strength – counteracted the poison.

She took her hand from where she had laid it over the mouthpiece.

'What? Yes. I am sorry, Madame. But after all, it is hardly my fault –'

The ugly raucous voice was screaming angrily.

'Who are thethe friendth of yourth? What thort of people are they to have the poleeth there and a man shot? I've a good mind not to have you back at all! I can't have the tone of my ethtablishment lowered.'

Midge made a few submissive non-committal replies. She replaced the receiver at last, with a sigh of relief. She felt sick and shaken.

'It's the place I work,' she explained. 'I had to let them know that I wouldn't be back until Thursday because of the inquest and the – the police.'

'I hope they were decent about it? What is it like, this dress shop of yours? Is the woman who runs it pleasant and sympathetic to work for?'

'I should hardly describe her as that! She's a Whitechapel Jewess with dyed hair and a voice like a corncrake.'

'But my dear Midge –'

Edward's face of consternation almost made Midge laugh. He was so concerned.

'But my dear child – you can't put up with that sort of thing. If you must have a job, you must take one where the surroundings are harmonious and where you like the people you are working with.'

Midge looked at him for a moment without answering.

How explain, she thought, to a person like Edward? What did Edward know of the labour market, of jobs?

And suddenly a tide of bitterness rose in her. Lucy, Henry, Edward – yes, even Henrietta – they were all divided from her by an impassable gulf – the gulf that separates the leisured from the working.

They had no conception of the difficulties of getting a job, and once you had got it, of keeping it! One might say, perhaps, that there was no need, actually, for her to earn her living. Lucy and Henry would gladly give her a home – they would with equal gladness have made her an allowance. Edward would also willingly have done the latter.

But something in Midge rebelled against the acceptance of ease offered her by her well-to-do relations. To come on rare occasions and sink into the well-ordered luxury of Lucy's life was delightful. She could revel in that. But some sturdy independence of spirit held her back from accepting that life as a gift. The same feeling had prevented her from starting a business on her own with money borrowed from relations and friends. She had seen too much of that.

She would borrow no money – use no influence. She had found a job for herself at four pounds a week, and if she had actually been given the job because Madame Alfrege hoped that Midge would bring her 'smart' friends to buy, Madame Alfrege was disappointed. Midge discouraged any such notion sternly on the part of her friends.

She had no particular illusions about working. She disliked the shop, she disliked Madame Alfrege, she disliked the eternal subservience to ill-tempered and impolite customers, but she doubted very much whether she could obtain any other job which she would like better since she had none of the necessary qualifications.

Edward's assumption that a wide range of choice was open to her was simply unbearably irritating this morning. What right had Edward to live in a world so divorced from reality?

They were Angkatells, all of them. And she – was only half an Angkatell! And sometimes, like this morning, she did not feel like an Angkatell at all! She was all her father's daughter.

She thought of her father with the usual pang of love and compunction, a grey-haired, middle-aged man with a tired face. A man who had struggled for years running a small family business that was bound, for all his care and efforts, to go slowly down the hill. It was not incapacity on his part – it was the march of progress.

Strangely enough, it was not to her brilliant Angkatell mother but to her quiet, tired father that Midge's devotion had always been given. Each time, when she came back from those visits to Ainswick, which were the wild delight of her life, she would answer the faint deprecating questions in her father's tired face by flinging her arms round his neck and saying: 'I'm *glad* to be home – I'm glad to be *home*.'

Her mother had died when Midge was thirteen. Sometimes Midge realized that she knew very little about her mother. She had been vague, charming, gay. Had she regretted her marriage, the marriage that had taken her outside the circle of the Angkatell clan? Midge had no idea. Her father had grown greyer and quieter after his wife's death. His struggles against the extinction of his business had grown more unavailing. He had died quietly and inconspicuously when Midge was eighteen.

Midge had stayed with various Angkatell relations, had accepted presents from the Angkatells, had had good times with the Angkatells, but she had refused to be financially dependent on their goodwill. And much as she loved them, there were times, such as these, when she felt suddenly and violently divergent from them.

She thought with rancour: 'They don't know *anything*!'

Edward, sensitive as always, was looking at her with a puzzled face. He asked gently:

'I've upset you? Why?'

Lucy drifted into the room. She was in the middle of one of her conversations.

'– you see, one doesn't really know whether she'd *prefer* the White Hart to us or not?'

Midge looked at her blankly – then at Edward.

'It's no use looking at Edward,' said Lady Angkatell. 'Edward simply wouldn't know; you, Midge, are always so practical.'

'I don't know what you are talking about, Lucy.'

Lucy looked surprised.

'The *inquest*, darling. Gerda has to come down for it. Should she stay here? Or go to the White Hart? The associations here are painful, of course – but then at the White Hart there will be people who will stare and quantities of reporters. Wednesday, you know, at eleven, or is it eleven-thirty?' A smile lit up Lady Angkatell's face. 'I have never been to an inquest! I thought my grey – and a hat, of course, like church – but *not* gloves.

'You know,' went on Lady Angkatell, crossing the room and picking up the telephone receiver and gazing down at it earnestly,

'I don't believe I've *got* any gloves except gardening gloves nowadays! And of course lots of long evening ones put away from the Government House days. Gloves are rather stupid, don't you think so?'

'The only use is to avoid fingerprints in crimes,' said Edward, smiling.

'Now, it's very interesting that you should say that, Edward – very interesting. What am I doing with this thing?' Lady Angkatell looked at the telephone receiver with faint distaste.

'Were you going to ring up someone?'

'I don't think so.' Lady Angkatell shook her head vaguely and put the receiver back on its stand very gingerly.

She looked from Edward to Midge.

'I don't think, Edward, that you ought to upset Midge. Midge minds sudden deaths more than we do.'

'My dear Lucy,' exclaimed Edward. 'I was only worrying about this place where Midge works. It sounds all wrong to me.'

'Edward thinks I ought to have a delightful sympathetic employer who would appreciate me,' said Midge dryly.

'Dear Edward,' said Lucy with complete appreciation.

She smiled at Midge and went out again.

'Seriously, Midge,' said Edward, 'I am worried.'

She interrupted him:

'The damned woman pays me four pounds a week. That's all that matters.'

She brushed past him and went out into the garden.

Sir Henry was sitting in his usual place on the low wall, but Midge turned away and walked up towards the flower walk.

Her relations were charming, but she had no use for their charm this morning.

David Angkatell was sitting on the seat at the top of the path.

There was no overdone charm about David, and Midge made straight for him and sat down by him, noting with malicious pleasure his look of dismay.

How extraordinarily difficult it was, thought David, to get away from people.

He had been driven from his bedroom by the brisk incursion of housemaids, purposeful with mops and dusters.

The library (and the *Encyclopædia Britannica*) had not been the sanctuary he had hoped optimistically it might be. Twice Lady Angkatell had drifted in and out, addressing him kindly with remarks to which there seemed no possible intelligent reply.

He had come out here to brood upon his position. The mere weekend to which he had unwillingly committed himself had now lengthened out owing to the exigencies connected with sudden and violent death.

David, who preferred the contemplation of an Academic past or the earnest discussion of a Left Wing future, had no aptitude for dealing with a violent and realistic present. As he had told Lady Angkatell, he did not read the *News of the World*. But now the *News of the World* seemed to have come to The Hollow.

Murder! David shuddered distastefully. What would his friends think? How did one, so to speak, *take* murder? What was one's attitude? Bored? Disgusted? Lightly amused?

Trying to settle these problems in his mind, he was by no means pleased to be disturbed by Midge. He looked at her uneasily as she sat beside him.

He was rather startled by the defiant stare with which she returned his look. A disagreeable girl of no intellectual value.

She said, 'How do you like your relations?'

David shrugged his shoulders. He said:

'Does one really *think* about relations?'

Midge said:

'Does one really think about anything?'

Doubtless, David thought, *she* didn't. He said almost graciously:

'I was analysing my reactions to murder.'

'It is certainly odd,' said Midge, 'to be *in* one.'

David sighed and said:

'Wearisome.' That was quite the best attitude. 'All the clichés that one thought only existed in the pages of detective fiction!'

'You must be sorry you came,' said Midge.

David sighed.

'Yes, I might have been staying with a friend of mine in London.' He added, 'He keeps a Left Wing bookshop.'

'I expect it's more comfortable here,' said Midge.

'Does one really care about being comfortable?' David asked scornfully.

'There are times,' said Midge, 'when I feel I don't care about anything else.'

'The pampered attitude to life,' said David. 'If you were a worker –'

Midge interrupted him.

'I *am* a worker. That's just why being comfortable is so attractive. Box beds, down pillows – early-morning tea softly deposited beside the bed – a porcelain bath with lashings of hot water – and delicious bath salts. The kind of easy-chair you really sink into . . .'

Midge paused in her catalogue.

'The workers,' said David, 'should have all these things.'

But he was a little doubtful about the softly deposited early-morning tea, which sounded impossibly sybaritic for an earnestly organized world.

'I couldn't agree with you more,' said Midge heartily.

CHAPTER 15

Hercule Poirot, enjoying a mid-morning cup of chocolate, was interrupted by the ringing of the telephone. He got up and lifted the receiver.

'*'Allo?*'

'M. Poirot?'

'Lady Angkatell?'

'How nice of you to know my voice! Am I disturbing you?'

'But not at all. You are, I hope, none the worse for the distressing events of yesterday?'

'No, indeed. Distressing, as you say, but one feels, I find, quite *detached*. I rang you up to know if you could possibly come over – an imposition, I know, but I am really in great distress.'

'But certainly, Lady Angkatell. Did you mean now?'

'Well, yes, I did mean now. As quickly as you can. That's very sweet of you.'

'Not at all. I will come by the woods, then?'

'Oh, of course – the shortest way. Thank you so much, dear M. Poirot.'

Pausing only to brush a few specks of dust off the lapels of his coat and to slip on a thin overcoat, Poirot crossed the lane and hurried along the path through the chestnuts. The swimming pool was deserted – the police had finished their work and gone. It looked innocent and peaceful in the soft misty autumn light.

Poirot took a quick look into the pavilion. The platinum fox cape, he noted, had been removed. But the six boxes of matches still stood upon the table by the settee. He wondered more than ever about those matches.

'It is not a place to keep matches – here in the damp. One box, for convenience, perhaps – but not six.'

He frowned down on the painted iron table. The tray of glasses had been removed. Someone had scrawled with a pencil on the table – a rough design of a nightmarish tree. It pained Hercule Poirot. It offended his tidy mind.

He clicked his tongue, shook his head, and hurried on towards the house, wondering at the reason for this urgent summons.

Lady Angkatell was waiting for him at the french windows and swept him into the empty drawing-room.

'It was nice of you to come, M. Poirot.'

She clasped his hand warmly.

'Madame, I am at your service.'

Lady Angkatell's hands floated out expressively. Her wide, beautiful eyes opened.

'You see, it's all so difficult. The inspector person is inter-viewing – no, questioning – taking a statement – what *is* the term they use? – *Gudgeon*. And really our whole life here depends on Gudgeon, and one does so sympathize with him. Because naturally it is terrible for him to be questioned by the police – even Inspector Grange, who I do feel is really nice and probably a family man – boys, I think, and he helps them with Meccano in the evenings – and a wife who has everything spotless but a little overcrowded . . .'

Hercule Poirot blinked as Lady Angkatell developed her imagi-nary sketch of Inspector Grange's home life.

'By the way his moustache droops,' went on Lady Angkatell, 'I think that a home that is too spotless might be sometimes depressing – like soap on hospital nurses' faces. Quite a *shine*! But that is more in the country where things lag behind – in London nursing homes they have lots of powder and really *vivid* lipstick. But I was saying, M. Poirot, that you really must come to lunch *properly* when all this ridiculous business is over.'

'You are very kind.'

'I do not mind the police myself,' said Lady Angkatell. 'I really find it all quite interesting. "Do let me help you in any way I can," I said to Inspector Grange. He seems rather a bewildered sort of person, but methodical.

'Motive seems so important to policemen,' she went on. 'Talking of hospital nurses just now, I believe that John Christow – a nurse with red hair and an upturned nose – quite attractive. But of course it was a long time ago and the police might not be interested. One doesn't really know how much poor Gerda had to put up with. She is the loyal type, don't you think? Or possibly she believes what is told her. I think if one has not a great deal of intelligence, it is wise to do that.'

Quite suddenly, Lady Angkatell flung open the study door and ushered Poirot in, crying brightly, 'Here is M. Poirot.' She swept round him and out, shutting the door. Inspector Grange and Gudgeon were sitting by the desk. A young man with a notebook was in a corner. Gudgeon rose respectfully to his feet.

Poirot hastened into apologies.

'I retire immediately. I assure you I had no idea that Lady Angkatell –'

'No, no, you wouldn't have.' Grange's moustache looked more pessimistic than ever this morning. 'Perhaps,' thought Poirot, fascinated by Lady Angkatell's recent sketch of Grange, 'there has been too much cleaning or perhaps a Benares brass table has been purchased so that the good inspector he really cannot have space to move.'

Angrily he dismissed these thoughts. Inspector Grange's clean but overcrowded home, his wife, his boys and their addiction to Meccano were all figments of Lady Angkatell's busy brain.

But the vividness with which they assumed concrete reality interested him. It was quite an accomplishment.

'Sit down, M. Poirot,' said Grange. 'There's something I want to ask you about, and I've nearly finished here.'

He turned his attention back to Gudgeon, who deferentially and almost under protest resumed his seat and turned an expressionless face towards his interlocutor.

'And that's all you can remember?'

'Yes, sir. Everything, sir, was very much as usual. There was no unpleasantness of any kind.'

'There's a fur cape thing – out in that summer-house by the pool. Which of the ladies *did* it belong to?'

'Are you referring, sir, to a cape of platinum fox? I noticed it yesterday when I took out the glasses to the pavilion. But it is not the property of anyone in this house, sir.'

'Whose is it, then?'

'It might possibly belong to Miss Cray, sir. Miss Veronica Cray, the motion-picture actress. She was wearing something of the kind.'

'When?'

'When she was here the night before last, sir.'

'You didn't mention her as having been a guest here?'

'She was not a guest, sir. Miss Cray lives at Dovecotes, the – er – cottage up the lane, and she came over after dinner, having run out of matches, to borrow some.'

'Did she take away six boxes?' asked Poirot.

Gudgeon turned to him.

'That is correct, sir. Her ladyship, after having inquired if we had plenty, insisted on Miss Cray's taking half a dozen boxes.'

'Which she left in the pavilion,' said Poirot.

'Yes, sir, I observed them there yesterday morning.'

'There is not much that that man does not observe,' remarked Poirot as Gudgeon departed, closing the door softly and deferentially behind him.

Inspector Grange merely remarked that servants were the devil!

'However,' he said with a little renewed cheerfulness, 'there's always the kitchenmaid. Kitchenmaids *talk* – not like these stuck-up upper servants.

'I've put a man on to make inquiries at Harley Street,' he went on. 'And I shall be there myself later in the day. We ought to get something there. Dare say, you know, that wife of Christow's had a good bit to put up with. Some of these fashionable doctors and their lady patients – well, you'd be surprised! And I gather from Lady Angkatell that there was some trouble over a hospital nurse. Of course, she was very vague about it.'

'Yes,' Poirot agreed. 'She would be vague.'

A skilfully built-up picture . . . John Christow and amorous intrigues with hospital nurses . . . the opportunities of a doctor's life . . . plenty of reasons for Gerda Christow's jealousy which had culminated at last in murder.

Yes, a skilfully suggested picture, drawing attention to a Harley Street background – away from The Hollow – away from the moment when Henrietta Savernake, stepping forward, had taken the revolver from Gerda Christow's unresisting hand . . . Away from that other moment when John Christow, dying, had said 'Henrietta'.

Suddenly opening his eyes, which had been half-closed, Hercule Poirot demanded with irresistible curiosity:

'Do your boys play with Meccano?'

'Eh, what?' Inspector Grange came back from a frowning reverie to stare at Poirot. 'Why, what on earth? As a matter of fact, they're a bit young – but I was thinking of giving Teddy a Meccano set for Christmas. What made you ask?'

Poirot shook his head.

What made Lady Angkatell dangerous, he thought, was the fact that those intuitive, wild guesses of hers might be often right. With a careless (seemingly careless?) word she built up a picture – and if part of the picture was right, wouldn't you, in spite of yourself, believe in the other half of the picture? . . .

Inspector Grange was speaking.

'There's a point I want to put to you, M. Poirot. This Miss Cray, the actress – she traipses over here borrowing matches. If she wanted to borrow matches, why didn't she come to your place, only a step or two away? Why come about half a mile?'

Hercule Poirot shrugged his shoulders.

'There might be reasons. Snob reasons, shall we say? My little cottage, it is small, unimportant. I am only a weekender, but Sir Henry and Lady Angkatell are important – they live here – they are what is called in the country. This Miss Veronica Cray, she may have wanted to get to know them – and after all, this was a way.'

Inspector Grange got up.

'Yes,' he said, 'that's perfectly possible, of course, but one doesn't want to overlook anything. Still, I've no doubt that everything's going to be plain sailing. Sir Henry has identified the gun as one of his collection. It seems they were actually practising with it the afternoon before. All Mrs Christow had to do was to go into the study and get it from where she'd seen Sir Henry put it and the ammunition away. It's all quite simple.'

'Yes,' Poirot murmured. 'It seems all quite simple.'

Just so, he thought, would a woman like Gerda Christow commit a crime. Without subterfuge or complexity – driven suddenly to violence by the bitter anguish of a narrow but deeply loving nature.

And yet surely – *surely*, she would have had *some* sense of self-preservation. Or had she acted in that blindness – that darkness of the spirit – when reason is entirely laid aside?

He recalled her blank, dazed face.

He did not know – he simply did not know.

But he felt that he ought to know.

CHAPTER 16

Gerda Christow pulled the black dress up over her head and let it fall on a chair.

Her eyes were piteous with uncertainty.

She said: 'I don't know – I really don't know. Nothing seems to matter.'

'I know, dear, I know.' Mrs Patterson was kind but firm. She knew exactly how to treat people who had had a bereavement. 'Elsie is *wonderful* in a crisis,' her family said of her.

At the present moment she was sitting in her sister Gerda's bedroom in Harley Street being wonderful. Elsie Patterson was tall and spare with an energetic manner. She was looking now at Gerda with a mixture of irritation and compassion.

Poor dear Gerda – tragic for her to lose her husband in such an awful way. And really, even now, she didn't seem to take in the – well, the *implications*, properly. Of course, Mrs Patterson reflected, Gerda always was terribly slow. And there was shock, too, to take into account.

She said in a brisk voice: 'I think I should decide on that black marocain at twelve guineas.'

One always did have to make up Gerda's mind for her.

Gerda stood motionless, her brow puckered. She said hesitantly:

'I don't really know if John liked mourning. I think I once heard him say he didn't.'

'John,' she thought. 'If only John were here to tell me what to do.'

But John would never be there again. Never – never – never . . . Mutton getting cold – congealing on the table . . . the bang of the consulting-room door, John running up two steps at a time, always in a hurry, so vital, so alive . . .

Alive.

Lying on his back by the swimming pool . . . the slow drip of blood over the edge . . . the feel of the revolver in her hand . . .

A nightmare, a bad dream, presently she would wake up and none of it would be true.

Her sister's crisp voice came cutting through her nebulous thoughts.

'You *must* have something black for the inquest. It would look most odd if you turned up in bright blue.'

Gerda said: 'That awful inquest!' and half-shut her eyes.

'Terrible for you, darling,' said Elsie Patterson quickly. 'But after it is all over you will come straight down to us and we shall take great care of you.'

The nebulous blur of Gerda Christow's thoughts hardened. She said, and her voice was frightened, almost panic-stricken:

'What am I going to do without John?'

Elsie Patterson knew the answer to that one. 'You've got your children. You've got to live for *them*.'

Zena, sobbing and crying, 'My Daddy's dead!' Throwing herself on her bed. Terry, pale, inquiring, shedding no tears.

An accident with a revolver, she had told them – poor Daddy has had an accident.

Beryl Collins (so thoughtful of her) had confiscated the morning papers so that the children should not see them. She had warned the servants too. Really, Beryl had been most kind and thoughtful.

Terence coming to his mother in the dim drawing-room, his lips pursed close together, his face almost greenish in its odd pallor.

'Why was Father shot?'

'An accident, dear. I – I can't talk about it.'

'It wasn't an accident. Why do you say what isn't true? Father was killed. It was murder. The paper says so.'

'Terry, how did you get hold of a paper? I told Miss Collins –'

He had nodded – queer repeated nods like a very old man.

'I went out and bought one, of course. I knew there must be something in them that you weren't telling us, or else why did Miss Collins hide them?'

It was never any good hiding truth from Terence. That queer, detached, scientific curiosity of his had always to be satisfied.

'*Why* was he killed, Mother?'

She had broken down then, becoming hysterical.

'Don't ask me about it – don't talk about it – I can't talk about it . . . it's all too dreadful.'

'But they'll find out, won't they? I mean, they have to find out. It's necessary.'

So reasonable, so detached. It made Gerda want to scream and laugh and cry. She thought: 'He doesn't care – he can't care – he just goes on asking questions. Why, he hasn't cried, even.'

Terence had gone away, evading his Aunt Elsie's ministrations, a lonely little boy with a stiff, pinched face. He had always felt alone. But it hadn't mattered until today.

Today, he thought, was different. If only there was someone who would answer questions reasonably and intelligently.

Tomorrow, Tuesday, he and Nicholson Minor were going to make nitroglycerine. He had been looking forward to it with a thrill. The thrill had gone. He didn't care if he never made nitroglycerine.

Terence felt almost shocked at himself. Not to care any more about scientific experiment. But when a chap's father had been murdered . . . He thought: 'My father – murdered.'

And something stirred – took root – grew . . . a slow anger.

Beryl Collins tapped on the bedroom door and came in. She was pale, composed, efficient. She said:

'Inspector Grange is here.' And as Gerda gasped and looked at her piteously, Beryl went on quickly: 'He said there was no need for him to worry you. He'll have a word with you before he goes, but it is just routine questions about Dr Christow's practice and I can tell him everything he wants to know.'

'Oh thank you, Collie.'

Beryl made a rapid exit and Gerda sighed out:

'Collie is such a help. She's so practical.'

'Yes, indeed,' said Mrs Patterson. 'An excellent secretary, I'm sure. Very plain, poor girl, isn't she? Oh, well, I always think that's just as well. Especially with an attractive man like John.'

Gerda flamed out at her:

'What do you mean, Elsie? John would never – he never – you talk as though John would have flirted or something horrid if he had had a pretty secretary. John wasn't like that at all.'

'Of course not, darling,' said Mrs Patterson. 'But after all, one knows what men are *like*!'

In the consulting-room Inspector Grange faced the cool, belligerent glance of Beryl Collins. It *was* belligerent, he noted that. Well, perhaps that was only natural.

'Plain bit of goods,' he thought. 'Nothing between her and the doctor, I shouldn't think. *She* may have been sweet on *him*, though. It works that way sometimes.'

But not this time, he came to the conclusion, when he leaned back in his chair a quarter of an hour later. Beryl Collins's answers to his questions had been models of clearness. She replied promptly, and obviously had every detail of the doctor's practice at her fingertips. He shifted his ground and began to probe gently into the relations existing between John Christow and his wife.

They had been, Beryl said, on excellent terms.

'I suppose they quarrelled every now and then like most

married couples?' The inspector sounded easy and confidential.

'I do not remember any quarrels. Mrs Christow was quite devoted to her husband – really quite slavishly so.'

There was a faint edge of contempt in her voice. Inspector Grange heard it.

'Bit of a feminist, this girl,' he thought.

Aloud he said:

'Didn't stand up for herself at all?'

'No. Everything revolved round Dr Christow.'

'Tyrannical, eh?'

Beryl considered.

'No, I wouldn't say that. But he was what I should call a very selfish man. He took it for granted that Mrs Christow would always fall in with *his* ideas.'

'Any difficulties with patients – women, I mean? You needn't think about being frank, Miss Collins. One knows doctors have their difficulties in that line.'

'Oh, that sort of thing!' Beryl's voice was scornful. 'Dr Christow was quite equal to dealing with any difficulties in *that* line. He had an excellent manner with patients.' She added, 'He was really a wonderful doctor.'

There was an almost grudging admiration in her voice.

Grange said: 'Was he tangled up with any woman? Don't be loyal, Miss Collins, it's important that we should know.'

'Yes, I can appreciate that. Not to my knowledge.'

A little too brusque, he thought. She doesn't know, but perhaps she guesses.

He said sharply, 'What about Miss Henrietta Savernake?'

Beryl's lips closed tightly.

'She was a close friend of the family's.'

'No – trouble between Dr and Mrs Christow on her account?'

'Certainly not.'

The answer was emphatic. (Over-emphatic?)

The inspector shifted his ground.

'What about Miss Veronica Cray?'

'Veronica Cray?'

There was pure astonishment in Beryl's voice.

'She was a friend of Dr Christow's, was she not?'

'I never heard of her. At least, I seem to know the *name* –'

'The motion-picture actress.'

Beryl's brow cleared.

'Of course! I wondered why the name was familiar. But I didn't even know that Dr Christow knew her.'

She seemed so positive on the point that the inspector abandoned it at once. He went on to question her about Dr Christow's manner on the preceding Saturday. And here, for the first time, the confidence of Beryl's replies wavered. She said slowly:

'His manner *wasn't* quite as usual.'

'What was the difference?'

'He seemed distrait. There was quite a long gap before he rang for his last patient – and yet normally he was always in a hurry to get through when he was going away. I thought – yes, I definitely thought he had something on his mind.'

But she could not be more definite.

Inspector Grange was not very satisfied with his investigations. He'd come nowhere near establishing motive – and motive had to be established before there was a case to go to the Public Prosecutor.

He was quite certain in his own mind that Gerda Christow had shot her husband. He suspected jealousy as the motive – but so far he had found nothing to go on. Sergeant Coombes had been working on the maids but they all told the same story. Mrs Christow worshipped the ground her husband walked on.

Whatever happened, he thought, must have happened down at The Hollow. And remembering The Hollow he felt a vague disquietude. They were an odd lot down there.

The telephone on the desk rang and Miss Collins picked up the receiver.

She said: 'It's for you, Inspector,' and passed the instrument to him.

'Hallo, Grange here. What's that?' Beryl heard the alteration in his tone and looked at him curiously. The wooden-looking face was impassive as ever. He was grunting – listening.

'Yes . . . yes, I've got that. That's absolutely certain, is it? No margin of error. Yes . . . yes . . . yes, I'll be down. I've about finished here. Yes.'

He put the receiver back and sat for a moment motionless. Beryl looked at him curiously.

He pulled himself together and asked in a voice that was quite different from the voice of his previous questions:

'You've no ideas of your own, I suppose, Miss Collins, about this matter?'

'You mean –'

'I mean no ideas as to who it was killed Dr Christow?'

She said flatly:

'I've absolutely no idea at all, Inspector.'

Grange said slowly:

'When the body was found, Mrs Christow was standing beside it with the revolver in her hand –'

He left it purposely as an unfinished sentence.

Her reaction came promptly. Not heated, cool and judicial.

'If you think Mrs Christow killed her husband, I am quite sure you are wrong. Mrs Christow is not at all a violent woman. She is very meek and submissive, and she was entirely under the doctor's thumb. It seems to me quite ridiculous that anyone could imagine for a moment that she shot him, however much appearances may be against her.'

'Then if she didn't, who did?' he asked sharply.

Beryl said slowly, 'I've no idea.'

The inspector moved to the door. Beryl asked:

'Do you want to see Mrs Christow before you go?'

'No – yes, perhaps I'd better.'

Again Beryl wondered; this was not the same man who had been questioning her before the telephone rang. What news had he got that had altered him so much?

Gerda came into the room nervously. She looked unhappy and bewildered. She said in a low, shaky voice:

'Have you found out any more about who killed John?'

'Not yet, Mrs Christow.'

'It's so impossible – so absolutely impossible.'

'But it happened, Mrs Christow.'

She nodded, looking down, screwing a handkerchief into a little ball.

He said quietly:

'Had your husband any enemies, Mrs Christow?'

'John? Oh, no. He was wonderful. Everyone adored him.'

'You can't think of anyone who had a grudge against him' – he paused – 'or against you?'

'Against me?' She seemed amazed. 'Oh, no, Inspector.'

Inspector Grange sighed.

'What about Miss Veronica Cray?'

'Veronica Cray? Oh, you mean the one who came that night to borrow matches?'

'Yes, that's the one. You knew her?'

Gerda shook her head.

'I'd never seen her before. John knew her years ago – or so she said.'

'I suppose she might have had a grudge against him that you didn't know about.'

Gerda said with dignity:

'I don't believe anybody could have had a grudge against John. He was the kindest and most unselfish – oh, and one of the noblest men.'

'H'm,' said the inspector. 'Yes. Quite so. Well, good morning, Mrs Christow. You understand about the inquest? Eleven o'clock Wednesday in Market Depleach. It will be very simple – nothing to upset you – probably be adjourned for a week so that we can make further inquiries.'

'Oh, I see. Thank you.'

She stood there staring after him. He wondered whether, even now, she had grasped the fact that she was the principal suspect.

He hailed a taxi – justifiable expense in view of the piece of information he had just been given over the telephone. Just where that piece of information was leading him, he did not know. On the face of it, it seemed completely irrelevant – crazy. It simply did not make sense. Yet in some way he could not yet see, it must make sense.

The only inference to be drawn from it was that the case was not quite the simple, straightforward one that he had hitherto assumed it to be.

CHAPTER 17

Sir Henry stared curiously at Inspector Grange.

He said slowly: 'I'm not quite sure that I understand you, Inspector.'

'It's quite simple, Sir Henry. I'm asking you to check over your collection of firearms. I presume they are catalogued and indexed?'

'Naturally. But I have already identified the revolver as part of my collection.'

'It isn't quite so simple as that, Sir Henry.' Grange paused a moment. His instincts were always against giving out any information, but his hand was being forced in this particular instance. Sir Henry was a person of importance. He would doubtless comply with the request that was being made to him, but he would also require a reason. The inspector decided that he had got to give him the reason.

He said quietly:

'Dr Christow was not shot with the revolver you identified this morning.'

Sir Henry's eyebrows rose.

'Remarkable!' he said.

Grange felt vaguely comforted. Remarkable was exactly what he felt himself. He was grateful to Sir Henry for saying so, and equally grateful for his not saying any more. It was as far as they could go at the moment. The thing was remarkable – and beyond that simply did not make sense.

Sir Henry asked:

'Have you any reason to believe that the weapon from which the fatal shot was fired comes from my collection?'

'No reason at all. But I have got to make sure, shall we say, that it doesn't.'

Sir Henry nodded his head in confirmation.

'I appreciate your point. Well, we will get to work. It will take a little time.'

He opened the desk and took out a leather-bound volume.

As he opened it he repeated:

'It will take a little time to check up –'

Grange's attention was held by something in his voice. He looked up sharply. Sir Henry's shoulders sagged a little – he seemed suddenly an older and more tired man.

Inspector Grange frowned.

He thought: 'Devil if I know what to make of these people down here.'

'Ah –'

Grange spun round. His eyes noted the time by the clock, thirty minutes – twenty minutes – since Sir Henry had said, 'It will take a little time.'

Grange said sharply:

'Yes, sir?'

'A .38 Smith and Wesson is missing. It was in a brown leather holster and was at the end of the rack in this drawer.'

'Ah!' The inspector kept his voice calm, but he was excited. 'And when, sir, to your certain knowledge, did you last see it in its proper place?'

Sir Henry reflected for a moment or two.

'That is not very easy to say, Inspector. I last had this drawer open about a week ago and I think – I am almost certain – that if the revolver had been missing then I should have noticed the gap. But I should not like to swear definitely that I *saw* it there.'

Inspector Grange nodded his head.

'Thank you, sir, I quite understand. Well, I must be getting on with things.'

He left the room, a busy, purposeful man.

Sir Henry stood motionless for a while after the inspector had gone, then he went out slowly through the french windows on to the terrace. His wife was busy with a gardening basket and gloves. She was pruning some rare shrubs with a pair of secateurs.

She waved to him brightly.

'What did the inspector want? I hope he is not going to worry the servants again. You know, Henry, they *don't* like it. They can't see it as amusing or as a novelty like we do.'

'Do we see it like that?'

His tone attracted her attention. She smiled up at him sweetly.

'How tired you look, Henry. Must you let all this worry you so much?'

'Murder *is* worrying, Lucy.'

Lady Angkatell considered a moment, absently clipping off some branches, then her face clouded over.

'Oh, dear – that is the worst of secateurs, they are so fascinating – one can't stop and one always clips off more than one means. What was it you were saying – something about murder being worrying? But really, Henry, I have never seen *why*. I mean, if one has to die, it may be cancer, or tuberculosis in one of those dreadful bright sanatoriums, or a stroke – horrid, with one's face all on one side – or else one is shot or stabbed or strangled perhaps. But the whole thing comes to the same in the end. There one is, I mean, dead! Out of it all. And all the worry over. And the relations have all the difficulties – money quarrels and whether to wear black or not – and who was to have Aunt Selina's writing-desk – things like that!'

Sir Henry sat down on the stone coping. He said:

'This is all going to be more upsetting than we thought, Lucy.'

'Well, darling, we shall have to bear it. And when it's all over we might go away somewhere. Let's not bother about present troubles but look forward to the future. I really *am* happy about that. I've been wondering whether it would be nice to go to Ainswick for Christmas – or leave it until Easter. What do you think?'

'Plenty of time to make plans for Christmas.'

'Yes, but I like to *see* things in my mind. Easter, perhaps . . . yes.' Lucy smiled happily. 'She will certainly have got over it by then.'

'Who?' Sir Henry was startled.

Lady Angkatell said calmly:

'Henrietta. I think if they were to have the wedding in October – October of next year, I mean, then we could go and stop for *that* Christmas. I've been thinking, Henry –'

'I wish you wouldn't, my dear. You think too much.'

'You know the barn? It will make a perfect studio. And Henrietta will need a studio. She has real talent, you know. Edward, I am sure, will be immensely proud of her. Two boys and a girl would be nice – or two boys and two girls.'

'Lucy – Lucy! How you run on.'

'But, darling,' Lady Angkatell opened wide, beautiful eyes. 'Edward will never marry anyone but Henrietta. He is very, *very* obstinate. Rather like my father in that way. He gets an idea in his head! So of course Henrietta *must* marry him – and she *will* now that John Christow is out of the way. He was really the greatest misfortune that could possibly have happened to her.'

'Poor devil!'

'Why? Oh, you mean because he's dead? Oh, well, everyone has to die sometime. I never worry over people dying . . .'

He looked at her curiously.

'I always thought you liked Christow, Lucy?'

'I found him amusing. And he had charm. But I never think one ought to attach too much importance to *anybody*.'

And gently, with a smiling face, Lady Angkatell clipped remorselessly at a *Viburnum Carlesii*.

CHAPTER 18

Hercule Poirot looked out of his window and saw Henrietta Savernake walking up the path to the front door. She was wearing the same green tweeds that she had worn on the day of the tragedy. There was a spaniel with her.

He hastened to the front door and opened it. She stood smiling at him.

'Can I come in and see your house? I like looking at people's houses. I'm just taking the dog for a walk.'

'But most certainly. How English it is to take the dog for a walk!'

'I know,' said Henrietta. 'I thought of that. Do you know that nice poem: "The days passed slowly one by one. I fed the ducks, reproved my wife, played Handel's *Largo* on the fife and took the dog a run."'

Again she smiled, a brilliant, insubstantial smile.

Poirot ushered her into his sitting-room. She looked round its neat and prim arrangement and nodded her head.

'Nice,' she said, 'two of everything. How you would hate my studio.'

'Why should I hate it?'

'Oh, a lot of clay sticking to things – and here and there just one thing that I happen to like and which would be ruined if there were two of them.'

'But I can understand that, Mademoiselle. You are an artist.'

'Aren't you an artist, too, M. Poirot?'

Poirot put his head on one side.

'It is a question, that. But on the whole I would say, no. I have known crimes that were artistic – they were, you understand, supreme exercises of imagination. But the solving of them – no, it is not the creative power that is needed. What is required is a passion for the truth.'

'A passion for the truth,' said Henrietta meditatively. 'Yes, I can see how dangerous that might make you. Would the truth satisfy you?'

He looked at her curiously.

'What do you mean, Miss Savernake?'

'I can understand that you would want to *know*. But would knowledge be enough? Would you have to go a step further and translate knowledge into action?'

He was interested in her approach.

'You are suggesting that if I knew the truth about Dr Christow's death – I might be satisfied to keep that knowledge to myself. Do *you* know the truth about his death?'

Henrietta shrugged her shoulders.

'The obvious answer seems to be Gerda. How cynical it is that a wife or a husband is always the first suspect.'

'But you do not agree?'

'I always like to keep an open mind.'

Poirot said quietly:

'Why did you come here, Miss Savernake?'

'I must admit that I haven't your passion for truth, M. Poirot. Taking the dog for a walk was such a nice English countryside excuse. But of course the Angkatells haven't got a dog – as you may have noticed the other day.'

'The fact had not escaped me.'

'So I borrowed the gardener's spaniel. I am not, you must understand, M. Poirot, very truthful.'

Again that brilliant brittle smile flashed out. He wondered why he should suddenly find it unendurably moving. He said quietly:

'No, but you have integrity.'

'Why on earth do you say that?'

She was startled – almost, he thought, dismayed.

'Because I believe it to be true.'

'Integrity,' Henrietta repeated thoughtfully. 'I wonder what that word really means.'

She sat very still, staring down at the carpet, then she raised her head and looked at him steadily.

'Don't you want to know why I did come?'

'You find a difficulty, perhaps, in putting it into words.'

'Yes, I think I do. The inquest, M. Poirot, is tomorrow. One has to make up one's mind just how much –'

She broke off. Getting up, she wandered across to the mantelpiece, displaced one or two of the ornaments and moved a vase of Michaelmas daisies from its position in the middle of a table to the extreme corner of the mantelpiece. She stepped back, eyeing the arrangement with her head on one side.

'How do you like that, M. Poirot?'

'Not at all, Mademoiselle.'

'I thought you wouldn't.' She laughed, moved everything quickly and deftly back to its original position. 'Well, if one wants to say a thing one has to say it! You are, somehow, the sort of person one can talk to. Here goes. Is it necessary, do you think, that the police should know that I was John Christow's mistress?'

Her voice was quite dry and unemotional. She was looking, not at him, but at the wall over his head. With one forefinger she was following the curve of the jar that held the purple flowers. He had an idea that in the touch of that finger was her emotional outlet.

Hercule Poirot said precisely and also without emotion:

'I see. You were lovers?'

'If you prefer to put it like that.'

He looked at her curiously.

'It was not how you put it, Mademoiselle.'

'No.'

'Why not?'

Henrietta shrugged her shoulders. She came and sat down by him on the sofa. She said slowly:

'One likes to describe things as – as accurately as possible.'

His interest in Henrietta Savernake grew stronger. He said: 'You had been Dr Christow's mistress – for how long?'

'About six months.'

'The police will have, I gather, no difficulty in discovering the fact?'

Henrietta considered.

'I imagine not. That is, if they are looking for something of that kind.'

'Oh, they will be looking, I can assure you of that.'

'Yes, I rather thought they would.' She paused, stretched out her fingers on her knee and looked at them, then gave him a swift, friendly glance. 'Well, M. Poirot, what does one do? Go to Inspector Grange and say – what does one say to a moustache like that? It's such a domestic, family moustache.'

Poirot's hand crawled upwards to his own proudly borne adornment.

'Whereas mine, Mademoiselle?'

'Your moustache, M. Poirot, is an artistic triumph. It has no associations with anything but itself. It is, I am sure, unique.'

'Absolutely.'

'And it is probably the reason why I am talking to you as I am. Granted that the police have to know the truth about John and myself, will it necessarily have to be made public?'

'That depends,' said Poirot. 'If the police think it had no bearing on the case, they will be quite discreet. You – are very anxious on this point?'

Henrietta nodded. She stared down at her fingers for a moment or two, then suddenly lifted her head and spoke. Her voice was no longer dry and light.

'Why should things be made worse than they are for poor Gerda? She adored John and he's dead. She's lost him. Why should she have to bear an added burden?'

'It is for her that you mind?'

'Do you think that is hypocritical? I suppose you're thinking that if I cared at all about Gerda's peace of mind, I would never have become John's mistress. But you don't understand – it was not like that. I did not break up his married life. I was only one – of a procession.'

'Ah, it was like that?'

She turned on him sharply.

'No, no, *no*! Not what you are thinking. That's what I mind most of all! The false idea that everybody will have of what John was like. That's why I'm here talking to you – because I've got a vague, foggy hope that I can make you understand. Understand, I mean, the sort of person John was. I can see so well what will happen – the headlines in the papers – A Doctor's Love Life – Gerda, myself, Veronica Cray. John wasn't like that – he wasn't, actually, a man who thought much about women. It wasn't women who mattered to him most; it was his *work*. It was in his work that his interest and excitement – yes, and his sense of adventure – really lay. If John had been taken unawares at any moment and asked to name the woman who was most in his mind, do you know who he would have said? – Mrs Crabtree.'

'Mrs Crabtree?' Poirot was surprised. 'Who, then, is this Mrs Crabtree?'

There was something between tears and laughter in Henrietta's voice as she went on:

'She's an old woman – ugly, dirty, wrinkled, quite indomitable. John thought the world of her. She's a patient in St Christopher's Hospital. She's got Ridgeway's Disease. That's a disease that's very rare, but if you get it you're bound to die – there just isn't any cure. But John was finding a cure – I can't explain technically – it was all very complicated – some question of hormone secretions. He'd been making experiments and Mrs Crabtree was his prize patient – you see, she's got *guts*, she *wants* to live – and she was fond of John. She and he were fighting on the same side. Ridgeway's Disease and Mrs Crabtree is what has been uppermost in John's mind for months – night and day – nothing else really counted. That's what being the kind of doctor John was really means – not all the Harley Street stuff and the rich, fat women, that's only a sideline. It's the intense scientific curiosity and the achievement. I – oh, I wish I could make you understand.'

Her hands flew out in a curiously despairing gesture, and Hercule Poirot thought how very lovely and sensitive those hands were.

He said:

'*You* seem to understand very well.'

'Oh, yes, I understood. John used to come and talk, do you see? Not quite to me – partly, I think, to himself. He got things clear that way. Sometimes he was almost despairing – he couldn't see how to overcome the heightened toxicity – and then he'd get an idea for varying the treatment. I can't explain to you what it was like – it was like, yes, a *battle*. You can't imagine the – the fury of it and the concentration – and yes, sometimes the agony. And sometimes the sheer tiredness . . .'

She was silent for a minute or two, her eyes dark with remembrance.

Poirot said curiously:

'You must have a certain technical knowledge yourself?'

She shook her head.

'Not really. Only enough to understand what John was talking about. I got books and read about it.'

She was silent again, her face softened, her lips half-parted. She was, he thought, remembering.

With a sigh, her mind came back to the present. She looked at him wistfully.

'If I could only make you see –'

'But you have, Mademoiselle.'

'Really?'

'Yes. One recognizes authenticity when one hears it.'

'Thank you. But it won't be so easy to explain to Inspector Grange.'

'Probably not. He will concentrate on the personal angle.'

Henrietta said vehemently:

'And that was so unimportant – so completely unimportant.'

Poirot's eyebrows rose slowly. She answered his unspoken protest.

'But it was! You see – after a while – I got between John and what he was thinking of. I affected him, as a woman. He couldn't concentrate as he wanted to concentrate – because of me. He began to be afraid that he was beginning to love me – he didn't want to love anyone. He – he made love to me because he didn't want to think about me too much. He wanted it to be light, easy, just an affair like other affairs that he had had.'

'And you –' Poirot was watching her closely. 'You were content to have it – like that.'

Henrietta got up. She said, and once more it was her dry voice:

'No, I wasn't – content. After all, one is human . . .'

Poirot waited a minute then he said:

'Then why, Mademoiselle –'

'Why?' She whirled round on him. 'I wanted John to be satisfied, I wanted *John* to have what he wanted. I wanted him to be able to go on with the thing he cared about – his work. If he didn't want to be hurt – to be vulnerable again – why – why, that was all right by me.'

Poirot rubbed his nose.

'Just now, Miss Savernake, you mentioned Veronica Cray. Was she also a friend of John Christow's?'

'Until last Saturday night, he hadn't seen her for fifteen years.'

'He knew her fifteen years ago?'

'They were engaged to be married.' Henrietta came back and sat down. 'I see I've got to make it all clearer. John loved Veronica desperately. Veronica was, and is, a bitch of the first water. She's the supreme egoist. Her terms were that John was to chuck everything he cared about and become Miss Veronica Cray's little tame husband. John broke up the whole thing – quite rightly. But he suffered like hell. His one idea was to marry someone as unlike Veronica as possible. He married Gerda, whom you might describe inelegantly as a first-class chump. That was all very nice and safe, but as anyone could have told him the day came when being married to a chump irritated him. He had various affairs – none of them important. Gerda, of course, never knew about them. But I think, myself, that for fifteen years there has been something wrong with John – something connected with Veronica. He never really got over her. And then, last Saturday, he met her again.'

After a long pause, Poirot recited dreamily:

'He went out with her that night to see her home and returned to The Hollow at 3 am.'

'How do you know?'

'A housemaid had the toothache.'

Henrietta said irrelevantly, 'Lucy has far too many servants.'

'But you yourself knew that, Mademoiselle.'

'Yes.'

'How did you know?'

Again there was an infinitesimal pause. Then Henrietta replied slowly:

'I was looking out of my window and saw him come back to the house.'

'The toothache, Mademoiselle?'

She smiled at him.

'Quite another kind of ache, M. Poirot.'

She got up and moved towards the door, and Poirot said:

'I will walk back with you, Mademoiselle.'

They crossed the lane and went through the gate into the chestnut plantation.

Henrietta said:

'We need not go past the pool. We can go up to the left and along the top path to the flower walk.'

A track led steeply uphill towards the woods. After a while they came to a broader path at right angles across the hillside above the chestnut trees. Presently they came to a bench and Henrietta sat down, Poirot beside her. The woods were above and behind them, and below were the closely planted chestnut groves. Just in front of the seat a curving path led downwards, to where just a glimmer of blue water could be seen.

Poirot watched Henrietta without speaking. Her face had relaxed, the tension had gone. It looked rounder and younger. He realized what she must have looked like as a young girl.

He said very gently at last:

'Of what are you thinking, Mademoiselle?'

'Of Ainswick.'

'What is Ainswick?'

'Ainswick? It's a place.' Almost dreamily, she described Ainswick to him. The white, graceful house, the big magnolia growing up it, the whole set in an amphitheatre of wooded hills.

'It was your home?'

'Not really. I lived in Ireland. It was where we came, all of us, for holidays. Edward and Midge and myself. It was Lucy's home actually. It belonged to her father. After his death it came to Edward.'

'Not to Sir Henry? But it is he who has the title.'

'Oh, that's a KCB,' she explained. 'Henry was only a distant cousin.'

'And after Edward Angkatell, to whom does it go, this Ainswick?'

'How odd, I've never really thought. If Edward doesn't marry –' She paused. A shadow passed over her face. Hercule Poirot wondered exactly what thought was passing through her mind.

'I suppose,' said Henrietta slowly, 'it will go to David. So that's why –'

'Why what?'

'Why Lucy asked him here . . . David and Ainswick?' She shook her head. 'They don't fit somehow.'

Poirot pointed to the path in front of them.

'It is by that path, Mademoiselle, that you went down to the swimming pool yesterday?'

She gave a quick shiver.

'No, by the one nearer the house. It was Edward who came this way.' She turned on him suddenly. 'Must we talk about it any more? I hate the swimming pool. I even hate The Hollow.'

Poirot murmured:

> *'I hate the dreadful hollow behind the little wood;*
> *Its lips in the field above are dabbled with blood-red heath,*
> *The red-ribb'd ledges drip with a silent horror of blood*
> *And Echo there, whatever is ask'd her, answers "Death."'*

Henrietta turned an astonished face on him.

'Tennyson,' said Hercule Poirot, nodding his head proudly. 'The poetry of your Lord Tennyson.'

Henrietta was repeating:

'*And Echo there, whatever is ask'd her . . .*' She went on, almost to herself, 'But of course – I see – that's what it is – Echo!'

'How do you mean, Echo?'

'This place – The Hollow itself! I almost saw it before – on Saturday when Edward and I walked up to the ridge. An echo of Ainswick. And that's what we are, we Angkatells. Echoes! We're not real – not real as John was real.' She turned to Poirot. 'I wish you had known him, M. Poirot. We're all shadows compared to John. John was really alive.'

'I knew that even when he was dying, Mademoiselle.'

'I know. One felt it . . . And John is dead, and we, the echoes, are alive . . . It's like, you know, a very bad joke.'

The youth had gone from her face again. Her lips were twisted, bitter with sudden pain.

When Poirot spoke, asking a question, she did not, for a moment, take in what he was saying.

'I am sorry. What did you say, M. Poirot?'

'I was asking whether your aunt, Lady Angkatell, liked Dr Christow?'

'Lucy? She is a cousin, by the way, not an aunt. Yes, she liked him very much.'

'And your – also a cousin? – Mr Edward Angkatell – did he like Dr Christow?'

Her voice was, he thought, a little constrained, as she replied:

'Not particularly – but then he hardly knew him.'

'And your – yet another cousin? Mr David Angkatell?'

Henrietta smiled.

'David, I think, hates all of us. He spends his time immured in the library reading the *Encyclopædia Britannica*.'

'Ah, a serious temperament.'

'I am sorry for David. He has had a difficult home life. His mother was unbalanced – an invalid. Now his only way of protecting himself is to try to feel superior to everyone. It's all right as long as it works, but now and then it breaks down and the vulnerable David peeps through.'

'Did he feel himself superior to Dr Christow?'

'He tried to – but I don't think it came off. I suspect that John Christow was just the kind of man that David would like to be. He disliked John in consequence.'

Poirot nodded his head thoughtfully.

'Yes – self-assurance, confidence, virility – all the intensive male qualities. It is interesting – very interesting.'

Henrietta did not answer.

Through the chestnuts, down by the pool, Hercule Poirot saw a man stooping, searching for something, or so it seemed.

He murmured: 'I wonder –'

'I beg your pardon?'

Poirot said: 'That is one of Inspector Grange's men. He seems to be looking for something.'

'Clues, I suppose. Don't policemen look for clues? Cigarette ash, footprints, burnt matches.'

Her voice held a kind of bitter mockery. Poirot answered seriously.

'Yes, they look for these things – and sometimes they find them. But the real clues, Miss Savernake, in a case like this, usually lie in the personal relationships of the people concerned.'

'I don't think I understand you.'

'Little things,' said Poirot, his head thrown back, his eyes half-closed. 'Not cigarette ash, or a rubber heel mark – but a gesture, a look, an unexpected action . . .'

Henrietta turned her head sharply to look at him. He felt her eyes, but he did not turn his head. She said:

'Are you thinking of – anything in particular?'

'I was thinking of how you stepped forward and took the revolver out of Mrs Christow's hand then dropped it in the pool.'

He felt the slight start she gave. But her voice was quite normal and calm.

'Gerda, M. Poirot, is rather a clumsy person. In the shock of the moment, and if the revolver had had another cartridge in it, she might have fired it and – and hurt someone.'

'But it was rather clumsy of *you*, was it not, to drop it in the pool?'

'Well, I had had a shock too.' She paused. 'What are you suggesting, M. Poirot?'

Poirot sat up, turned his head, and spoke in a brisk, matter-of-fact way.

'If there were fingerprints on that revolver, that is to say, fingerprints made *before Mrs Christow handled it*, it would be interesting to know whose they were – and that we shall never know now.'

Henrietta said quietly but steadily:

'Meaning that you think they were *mine*. You are suggesting that I shot John and then left the revolver beside him so that Gerda could come along and pick it up and be left holding the baby. That is what you are suggesting, isn't it? But surely, if I did that, you will give me credit for enough intelligence to have wiped off my own fingerprints first!'

'But surely *you* are intelligent enough to see, Mademoiselle, that if you had done so and if the revolver had had *no fingerprints on it but Mrs Christow's, that* would have been very remarkable! For you were all shooting with that revolver the day before. Gerda Christow would hardly have wiped the revolver clean of fingerprints *before* using it – why should she?'

Henrietta said slowly:

'So you think I killed John?'

'When Dr Christow was dying, he said: "*Henrietta*."'

'And you think that that was an accusation? It was not.'

'What was it then?'

Henrietta stretched out her foot and traced a pattern with the toe. She said in a low voice:

'Aren't you forgetting – what I told you not very long ago? I mean – the terms we were on?'

'Ah, yes – he was your lover – and so, as he is dying, he says: "*Henrietta*". That is very touching.'

She turned blazing eyes upon him.

'Must you sneer?'

'I am not sneering. But I do not like being lied to – and that, I think, is what you are trying to do.'

Henrietta said quietly:

'I have told you that I am not very truthful – but when John said: "*Henrietta*" he was not accusing me of having murdered him. Can't you understand that people of my kind, who *make* things, are quite incapable of taking life? I don't kill people, M. Poirot. I *couldn't* kill anyone. That's the plain stark truth. You suspect me simply because my name was murmured by a dying man who hardly knew what he was saying.'

'Dr Christow knew perfectly what he was saying. His voice was as alive and conscious as that of a doctor doing a vital operation who says sharply and urgently: "Nurse, the forceps, please."'

'But –' She seemed at a loss, taken aback. Hercule Poirot went on rapidly:

'And it is not just on account of what Dr Christow said when he was dying. I do not believe for one moment that you are capable of premeditated murder – that, no. But you might have fired that shot in a sudden moment of fierce resentment – and if so – *if* so, Mademoiselle, you have the creative imagination and ability to cover your tracks.'

Henrietta got up. She stood for a moment, pale and shaken, looking at him. She said with a sudden, rueful smile:

'And I thought you liked me.'

Hercule Poirot sighed. He said sadly:

'That is what is so unfortunate for me. I do.'

CHAPTER 19

I

When Henrietta had left him, Poirot sat on until he saw below him Inspector Grange walk past the pool with a resolute, easy stride and take the path on past the pavilion.

The inspector was walking in a purposeful way.

He must be going, therefore, either to Resthaven or to Dovecotes. Poirot wondered which.

He got up and retraced his steps along the way he had come. If Inspector Grange was coming to see him, he was interested to hear what the inspector had to say.

But when he got back to Resthaven there was no sign of a visitor. Poirot looked thoughtfully up the lane in the direction of Dovecotes. Veronica Cray had not, he knew, gone back to London.

He found his curiosity rising about Veronica Cray. The pale, shining fox furs, the heaped boxes of matches, that sudden imperfectly explained invasion on the Saturday night, and finally Henrietta Savernake's revelations about John Christow and Veronica.

It was, he thought, an interesting pattern. Yes, that was how he saw it: a pattern.

A design of intermingled emotions and the clash of personalities. A strange involved design, with dark threads of hate and desire running through it.

Had Gerda Christow shot her husband? Or was it not quite so simple as that?

He thought of his conversation with Henrietta and decided that it was not so simple.

Henrietta had jumped to the conclusion that he suspected her of the murder, but actually he had not gone nearly as far as that in his mind. No further indeed than the belief that Henrietta knew something. Knew something or was concealing something – which?

He shook his head, dissatisfied.

The scene by the pool. A set scene. A stage scene.

Staged by whom? Staged *for* whom?

The answer to the second question was, he strongly suspected, Hercule Poirot. He had thought so at the time. But he had thought then that it was an impertinence – a joke.

It was still an impertinence – but not a joke.

And the answer to the first question?

He shook his head. He did not know. He had not the least idea.

But he half-closed his eyes and conjured them up – all of them – seeing them clearly in his mind's eye. Sir Henry, upright, responsible, trusted administrator of Empire. Lady Angkatell, shadowy, elusive, unexpectedly and bewilderingly charming, with that deadly power of inconsequent suggestion. Henrietta Savernake, who had loved John Christow better than she loved herself. The gentle and negative Edward Angkatell. The dark, positive girl called Midge Hardcastle. The dazed, bewildered face of Gerda Christow clasping a revolver in her hand. The offended adolescent personality of David Angkatell.

There they all were, caught and held in the meshes of the law. Bound together for a little while in the relentless aftermath of sudden and violent death. Each of them had their own tragedy and meaning, their own story.

And somewhere in that interplay of characters and emotions lay the truth.

To Hercule Poirot there was only one thing more fascinating than the study of human beings, and that was the pursuit of truth.

He meant to know the truth of John Christow's death.

II

'But of course, Inspector,' said Veronica. 'I'm only too anxious to help you.'

'Thank you, Miss Cray.'

Veronica Cray was not, somehow, at all what the inspector had imagined.

He had been prepared for glamour, for artificiality, even possibly for heroics. He would not have been at all surprised if she had put on an act of some kind.

In fact, she was, he shrewdly suspected, putting on an act. But it was not the kind of act he had expected.

There was no overdone feminine charm – glamour was not stressed.

Instead he felt that he was sitting opposite to an exceedingly good-looking and expensively dressed woman who was also a good business woman. Veronica Cray, he thought, was no fool.

'We just want a clear statement, Miss Cray. You came over to The Hollow on Saturday evening?'

'Yes, I'd run out of matches. One forgets how important these things are in the country.'

'You went all the way to The Hollow? Why not to your next-door neighbour, M. Poirot?'

She smiled – a superb, confident camera smile.

'I didn't know who my next-door neighbour was – otherwise I should have. I just thought he was some little foreigner and I thought, you know, he might become a bore – living so near.'

'Yes,' thought Grange, 'quite plausible.' She'd worked that one out ready for the occasion.

'You got your matches,' he said. 'And you recognized an old friend in Dr Christow, I understand?'

She nodded.

'Poor John. Yes, I hadn't seen him for fifteen years.'

'Really?' There was polite disbelief in the inspector's tone.

'Really.' Her tone was firmly assertive.

'You were pleased to see him?'

'Very pleased. It's always delightful, don't you think, Inspector, to come across an old friend?'

'It can be on some occasions.'

Veronica Cray went on without waiting for further questioning:

'John saw me home. You'll want to know if he said anything that could have a bearing on the tragedy, and I've been thinking over our conversation very carefully – but really there wasn't a pointer of any kind.'

'What did you talk about, Miss Cray?'

'Old days. "Do you remember this, that and the other?"' She smiled pensively. 'We had known each other in the South of France. John had really changed very little – older, of course, and more assured. I gather he was quite well known in his profession. He didn't talk about his personal life at all. I just got the impression that his married life wasn't perhaps frightfully happy – but it was only the vaguest impression. I suppose his wife, poor thing, was one of those dim, jealous women – probably always making a fuss about his better-looking lady patients.'

'No,' said Grange. 'She doesn't really seem to have been that way.'

Veronica said quickly:

'You mean – it was all *underneath*? Yes – yes, I can see that that would be far more dangerous.'

'I see you think Mrs Christow shot him, Miss Cray?'

'I oughtn't to have said that. One mustn't comment – is that it – before a trial? I'm extremely sorry, Inspector. It was just that my maid told me she'd been found actually standing ever the body with the revolver still in her hand. You know how in these quiet country places everything gets so exaggerated and servants do pass things on.'

'Servants can be very useful sometimes, Miss Cray.'

'Yes, I suppose you get a lot of your information that way?'

Grange went on stolidly:

'It's a question, of course, of who had a motive –'

He paused. Veronica said with a faint, rueful smile:

'And a wife is always the first suspect? How cynical! But there's usually what's called "the other woman". I suppose *she* might be considered to have a motive too?'

'You think there was another woman in Dr Christow's life?'

'Well – yes, I did rather imagine there might be. One just gets an impression, you know.'

'Impressions can be very helpful sometimes,' said Grange.

'I rather imagined – from what he said – that that sculptress woman was, well, a very close friend. But I expect you know all about that already?'

'We have to look into all these things, of course.'

Inspector Grange's voice was strictly non-committal, but he saw, without appearing to see, a quick, spiteful flash of satisfaction in those large blue eyes.

He said, making the question very official:

'Dr Christow saw you home, you say. What time was it when you said goodnight to him?'

'Do you know, I really can't remember! We talked for some time, I do know that. It must have been quite late.'

'He came in?'

'Yes, I gave him a drink.'

'I see. I imagined your conversation might have taken place in the – er – pavilion by the swimming pool.'

He saw her eyelids flicker. There was hardly a moment's hesitation before she said:

'You really *are* a detective, aren't you? Yes, we sat there and smoked and talked for some time. How did you know?'

Her face bore the pleased, eager expression of a child asking to be shown a clever trick.

'You left your furs behind there, Miss Cray.' He added just without emphasis: 'And the matches.'

'Yes, of course I did.'

'Dr Christow returned to The Hollow at 3 am,' announced the inspector, again without emphasis.

'Was it really as late as that?' Veronica sounded quite amazed.

'Yes, it was, Miss Cray.'

'Of course, we had so much to talk over – not having seen each other for so many years.'

'Are you sure it was quite so long since you had seen Dr Christow?'

'I've just told you I hadn't seen him for fifteen years.'

'Are you quite sure you're not making a mistake? I've got the impression you might have been seeing quite a lot of him.'

'What on earth makes you think that?'

'Well, this note for one thing.' Inspector Grange took out a letter from his pocket, glanced down at it, cleared his throat and read:

> Please come over this morning. I must see you.
> Veronica.

'Ye-es.' She smiled. 'It *is* a little peremptory, perhaps. I'm afraid Hollywood makes one – well, rather arrogant.'

'Dr Christow came over to your house the following morning in answer to that summons. You had a quarrel. Would you care to tell me, Miss Cray, what that quarrel was about?'

The inspector had unmasked his batteries. He was quick to seize the flash of anger, the ill-tempered tightening of the lips. She snapped out:

'We didn't quarrel.'

'Oh, yes, you did, Miss Cray. Your last words were: "I think I hate you more than I believed I could hate anyone."'

She was silent now. He could feel her thinking – thinking quickly and warily. Some women might have rushed into speech. But Veronica Cray was too clever for that.

She shrugged her shoulders and said lightly:

'I see. More servants' tales. My little maid has rather a lively imagination. There are different ways of saying things, you know. I can assure you that I wasn't being melodramatic. It was really a mildly flirtatious remark. We had been sparring together.'

'The words were not intended to be taken seriously?'

'Certainly not. And I can assure you, Inspector, that it *was* fifteen years since I had last seen John Christow. You can verify that for yourself.'

She was poised again, detached, sure of herself.

Grange did not argue or pursue the subject. He got up.

'That's all for the moment, Miss Cray,' he said pleasantly.

He went out of Dovecotes and down the lane, and turned in at the gate of Resthaven.

III

Hercule Poirot stared at the inspector in the utmost surprise. He repeated incredulously:

'The revolver that Gerda Christow was holding and which was subsequently dropped into the pool was not the revolver that fired the fatal shot? But that is extraordinary.'

'Exactly, M. Poirot. Put bluntly, it just doesn't make sense.'

Poirot murmured softly:

'No, it does not make sense. But all the same, Inspector, it has got to make sense, eh?'

The inspector sighed heavily: 'That's just it, M. Poirot. We've got to find some way that it does make sense – but at the moment I can't see it. The truth is that we shan't get much further until we've found the gun that *was* used. It came from Sir Henry's collection all right – at least, there's one missing – and that means that the whole thing is still tied up with The Hollow.'

'Yes,' murmured Poirot. 'It is still tied up with The Hollow.'

'It seemed a simple, straightforward business,' went on the inspector. 'Well, it isn't so simple or so straightforward.'

'No,' said Poirot, 'it is not simple.'

'We've got to admit the possibility that the thing was a frame-up – that's to say that it was all set to implicate Gerda Christow. But if that was so, why not leave the right revolver lying by the body for her to pick up?'

'She might not have picked it up.'

'That's true, but even if she didn't, so long as nobody else's fingerprints were on the gun – that's to say if it was wiped after use – she would probably have been suspected all right. And that's what the murderer wanted, wasn't it?'

'Was it?'

Grange stared.

'Well, if you'd done a murder, you'd want to plant it good and quick on someone else, wouldn't you? That would be a murderer's normal reaction.'

'Ye-es,' said Poirot. 'But then perhaps we have here a rather unusual type of murderer. It is possible that *that* is the solution of our problem.'

'What is the solution?'

Poirot said thoughtfully:

'An unusual type of murderer.'

Inspector Grange stared at him curiously. He said:

'But then – what *was* the murderer's idea? What was he or she getting at?'

Poirot spread out his hands with a sigh.

'I have no idea – I have no idea at all. But it seems to me – dimly –'

'Yes?'

'That the murderer is someone who wanted to kill John Christow but who did not want to implicate Gerda Christow.'

'H'h! Actually, we suspected her right away.'

'Ah, yes, but it was only a matter of time before the facts about the gun came to light, and that was bound to give a new angle. In the interval the murderer has had time –' Poirot came to a full stop.

'Time to do what?'

'Ah, *mon ami*, there you have me. Again I have to say I do not know.'

Inspector Grange took a turn or two up and down the room. Then he stopped and came to a stand in front of Poirot.

'I've come to you this afternoon, M. Poirot, for two reasons. One is because I know – it's pretty well known in the Force – that you're a man of wide experience who's done some very tricky work on this type of problem. That's reason number one. But there's another reason. You were there. You were an eye-witness. You *saw* what happened.'

Poirot nodded.

'Yes, I *saw* what happened – but the eyes, Inspector Grange, are very unreliable witnesses.'

'What do you mean, M. Poirot?'

'The eyes see, sometimes, what they are *meant* to see.'

'You think that it was planned out beforehand?'

'I suspect it. It was exactly, you understand, like a stage scene. What I *saw* was clear enough. A man who had just been shot and the woman who had shot him holding in her hand the gun she had just used. That is what I *saw*, and already we know that in one particular the picture is wrong. That gun had *not* been used to shoot John Christow.'

'Hm!' The inspector pulled his drooping moustache firmly downwards. 'What you are getting at is that some of the other particulars of the picture may be wrong too?'

Poirot nodded. He said:

'There were three other people present – three people who had *apparently* just arrived on the scene. But that may not be true either. The pool is surrounded by a thick grove of young chestnuts. From the pool five paths lead away, one to the house, one up to the woods, one up to the flower walk, one down from the pool to the farm and one to the lane here.

'Of those three people, each one came along a different path, Edward Angkatell from the woods above, Lady Angkatell up from the farm, and Henrietta Savernake from the flower border above the house. Those three arrived upon the scene of the crime almost simultaneously, and a few minutes after Gerda Christow.

'But one of those three, Inspector, could have been at the pool *before* Gerda Christow arrived, could have shot John Christow, and could have retreated up or down one of the paths and then, turning round, could have arrived at the same time as the others.'

Inspector Grange said:

'Yes, it's possible.'

'And another possibility, not envisaged at the time. Someone could have come along the path from the lane, could have shot John Christow, and could have gone back the same way, unseen.'

Grange said: 'You're dead right. There are two other possible suspects besides Gerda Christow. We've got the same motive – jealousy. It's definitely a *crime passionel*. There were two other women mixed up with John Christow.'

He paused and said:

'Christow went over to see Veronica Cray that morning. They had a row. She told him that she'd make him sorry for what he'd done, and she said she hated him more than she believed she could hate anyone.'

'Interesting,' murmured Poirot.

'She's straight from Hollywood – and by what I read in the papers they do a bit of shooting each other out there sometimes. She could have come along to get her furs, which she'd left in the pavilion the night before. They could have met – the whole thing could have flared up – she fired at him – and then, hearing someone coming, she could have dodged back the way she came.'

He paused a moment and added irritably:

'And now we come to the part where it all goes haywire. That damned gun! Unless,' his eyes brightened, 'she shot him with her own gun and dropped one that she'd pinched from Sir Henry's study so as to throw suspicion on the crowd at The Hollow. She mightn't know about our being able to identify the gun used from the marks on the rifling.'

'How many people do know that, I wonder?'

'I put the point to Sir Henry. He said he thought quite a lot of people would know – on account of all the detective stories that are written. Quoted a new one, *The Clue of the Dripping Fountain*, which he said John Christow himself had been reading on Saturday and which emphasized that particular point.'

'But Veronica Cray would have had to have got the gun somehow from Sir Henry's study.'

'Yes, it would mean premeditation.' The inspector took another tug at his moustache, then he looked at Poirot. 'But you've hinted yourself at another possibility, M. Poirot. There's Miss Savernake. And here's where your eye-witness stuff, or rather I should say, ear-witness stuff, comes in again. Dr Christow said: "*Henrietta*" when he was dying. You heard him – they all heard him, though Mr Angkatell doesn't seem to have caught what he said.'

'Edward Angkatell did not hear? That is interesting.'

'But the others did. Miss Savernake herself says he tried to speak to her. Lady Angkatell says he opened his eyes, saw Miss Savernake, and said: "*Henrietta*." She doesn't, I think, attach any importance to it.'

Poirot smiled. 'No – she would not attach importance to it.'

'Now, M. Poirot, what about you? You were there – you saw – you heard. Was Dr Christow trying to tell you all that it was Henrietta who had shot him? In short, was that word an *accusation*?'

Poirot said slowly:

'I did not think so at the time.'

'But now, M. Poirot? What do you think *now*?'

Poirot sighed. Then he said slowly:

'It may have been so. I cannot say more than that. It is an impression only for which you are asking me, and when the moment is past there is a temptation to read into things a meaning which was not there at the time.'

Grange said hastily:

'Of course, this is all off the record. What M. Poirot thought isn't evidence – I know that. It's only a pointer I'm trying to get.'

'Oh, I understand you very well – and an impression from an eye-witness can be a very useful thing. But I am humiliated to have to say that my impressions are valueless. I was under the misconception, induced by the visual evidence, that Mrs Christow had just shot her husband; so that when Dr Christow opened his eyes and said "*Henrietta*" I never thought of it as being an accusation. It is tempting now, looking back, to read into that scene something that was not there.'

'I know what you mean,' said Grange. 'But it seems to me that since "*Henrietta*" was the last word Christow spoke, it must have meant one of two things. It was either an accusation of murder or else it was – well, purely emotional. She's the woman he's in love with and he's dying. Now, bearing everything in mind, which of the two did it sound like to you?'

Poirot sighed, stirred, closed his eyes, opened them again, stretched out his hands in acute vexation. He said:

'His voice was urgent – that is all I can say – *urgent*. It seemed to me neither accusing nor emotional – but urgent, yes! And of one thing I am sure. He was in full possession of his faculties. He spoke – yes, he spoke like a doctor – a doctor who has, say, a sudden surgical emergency on his hands – a patient who is bleeding to death, perhaps.' Poirot shrugged his shoulders. 'That is the best I can do for you.'

'Medical, eh?' said the inspector. 'Well, yes, that *is* a third way of looking at it. He was shot, he suspected he was dying, he wanted something done for him quickly. And if, as Lady Angkatell says, Miss Savernake was the first person he saw when his eyes opened, then he would appeal to her. It's not very satisfactory, though.'

'Nothing about this case is satisfactory,' said Poirot with some bitterness.

A murder scene, set and staged to deceive Hercule Poirot – and which *had* deceived him! No, it was not satisfactory.

Inspector Grange was looking out of the window.

'Hallo,' he said, 'here's Clark, my sergeant. Looks as though he's got something. He's been working on the servants – the friendly touch. He's a nice-looking chap, got a way with women.'

Sergeant Clark came in a little breathlessly. He was clearly pleased with himself, though subduing the fact under a respectful official manner.

'Thought I'd better come and report, sir, since I knew where you'd gone.'

He hesitated, shooting a doubtful glance at Poirot, whose exotic foreign appearance did not commend itself to his sense of official reticence.

'Out with it, my lad,' said Grange. 'Never mind M. Poirot here. He's forgotten more about this game than you'll know for many years to come.'

'Yes, sir. It's this way, sir. I got something out of the kitchen-maid –'

Grange interrupted. He turned to Poirot triumphantly.

'What did I tell you? There's always hope where there's a kitchenmaid. Heaven help us when domestic staffs are so reduced that nobody keeps a kitchenmaid any more. Kitchenmaids talk, kitchenmaids babble. They're so kept down and in their place by the cook and the upper servants that it's only human nature to talk about what they know to someone who wants to hear it. Go on, Clark.'

'This is what the girl says, sir. That on Sunday afternoon she saw Gudgeon, the butler, walking across the hall with a revolver in his hand.'

'Gudgeon?'

'Yes, sir.' Clark referred to a notebook. 'These are her own words. "I don't know what to do, but I think I ought to say what I saw that day. I saw Mr Gudgeon, he was standing in the hall with a revolver in his hand. Mr Gudgeon looked very peculiar indeed."

'I don't suppose,' said Clark, breaking off, 'that the part about looking peculiar means anything. She probably put that in out of her head. But I thought you ought to know about it at once, sir.'

Inspector Grange rose, with the satisfaction of a man who sees a task ahead of him which he is well fitted to perform.

'*Gudgeon*?' he said. 'I'll have a word with Mr Gudgeon right away.'

CHAPTER 20

Sitting once more in Sir Henry's study, Inspector Grange stared at the impassive face of the man in front of him.

So far, the honours lay with Gudgeon.

'I am very sorry, sir,' he repeated. 'I suppose I ought to have mentioned the occurrence, but it had slipped my memory.'

He looked apologetically from the inspector to Sir Henry.

'It was about 5.30 if I remember rightly, sir. I was crossing the hall to see if there were any letters for the post when I noticed a revolver lying on the hall table. I presumed it was from the master's collection, so I picked it up and brought it in here. There was a gap on the shelf by the mantelpiece where it had come from, so I replaced it where it belonged.'

'Point it out to me,' said Grange.

Gudgeon rose and went to the shelf in question, the inspector close behind him.

'It was this one, sir.' Gudgeon's finger indicated a small Mauser pistol at the end of the row.

It was a .25 – quite a small weapon. It was certainly not the gun that had killed John Christow.

Grange, with his eyes on Gudgeon's face, said:

'That's an automatic pistol, not a revolver.'

Gudgeon coughed.

'Indeed, sir? I'm afraid that I am not at all well up in firearms. I may have used the term revolver rather loosely, sir.'

'But you are quite sure that that is the gun you found in the hall and brought in here?'

'Oh, yes, sir, there can be no possible doubt about that.'

Grange stopped him as he was about to stretch out a hand.

'Don't touch it, please. I must examine it for fingerprints and to see if it is loaded.'

'I don't think it is loaded, sir. None of Sir Henry's collection is kept loaded. And, as for fingerprints, I polished it over with my handkerchief before replacing it, sir, so there will only be my fingerprints on it.'

'Why did you do that?' asked Grange sharply.

But Gudgeon's apologetic smile did not waver.

'I fancied it might be dusty, sir.'

The door opened and Lady Angkatell came in. She smiled at the inspector.

'How nice to see you, Inspector Grange! What is all this about a revolver and Gudgeon? That child in the kitchen is in floods of tears. Mrs Medway has been bullying her – but of course the girl was quite right to say what she saw if she thought she ought to do so. I always find right and wrong so bewildering myself – easy, you know, if right is unpleasant and wrong is agreeable, because then one knows where one is – but confusing when it is the other way about – and I think, don't you, Inspector, that everyone must do what they think right themselves. What have you been telling them about that pistol, Gudgeon?'

Gudgeon said with respectful emphasis:

'The pistol was in the hall, my lady, on the centre table. I have no idea where it came from. I brought it in here and put it away in its proper place. That is what I have just told the inspector and he quite understands.'

Lady Angkatell shook her head. She said gently:

'You really shouldn't have said that, Gudgeon. I'll talk to the inspector myself.'

Gudgeon made a slight movement, and Lady Angkatell said very charmingly:

'I do appreciate your motives, Gudgeon. I know how you always try to save us trouble and annoyance.' She added in gentle dismissal: 'That will be all now.'

Gudgeon hesitated, threw a fleeting glance towards Sir Henry and then at the inspector, then bowed and moved towards the door.

Grange made a motion as though to stop him, but for some

reason he was not able to define to himself, he let his arm fall again. Gudgeon went out and closed the door.

Lady Angkatell dropped into a chair and smiled at the two men. She said conversationally:

'You know, I really do think that was very charming of Gudgeon. Quite feudal, if you know what I mean. Yes, feudal is the right word.'

Grange said stiffly:

'Am I to understand, Lady Angkatell, that you yourself have some further knowledge about the matter?'

'Of course. Gudgeon didn't find it in the hall at all. He found it when he took the eggs out.'

'The eggs?' Inspector Grange stared at her.

'Out of the basket,' said Lady Angkatell.

She seemed to think that everything was now quite clear. Sir Henry said gently:

'You must tell us a little more, my dear. Inspector Grange and I are still at sea.'

'Oh.' Lady Angkatell set herself to be explicit. 'The pistol, you see, was *in* the basket, *under* the eggs.'

'What basket and what eggs, Lady Angkatell?'

'The basket I took down to the farm. The pistol was in it, and then I put the eggs in on top of the pistol and forgot all about it. And when we found poor John Christow dead by the pool, it was such a shock I let go of the basket and Gudgeon just caught it in time (because of the eggs, I mean. If I'd dropped it they would have been broken). And he brought it back to the house. And later I asked him about writing the date on the eggs – a thing I always do – otherwise one eats the fresher eggs sometimes before the older ones – and he said all that had been attended to – and now that I remember, he was rather emphatic about it. And that is what I mean by being feudal. He found the pistol and put it back in here – I suppose really because there were police in the house. Servants are always so worried by police, I find. Very nice and loyal – but also quite stupid, because of course, Inspector, it's the truth you want to hear, isn't it?'

And Lady Angkatell finished up by giving the inspector a beaming smile.

'The truth is what I mean to get,' said Grange rather grimly.

Lady Angkatell sighed.

'It all seems such a fuss, doesn't it?' she said. 'I mean, all this hounding people down. I don't suppose whoever it was who shot John Christow really meant to shoot him – not seriously, I mean. If it was Gerda, I'm sure she didn't. In fact, I'm really surprised that she didn't miss – it's the sort of thing that one would expect of Gerda. And she's really a very nice kind creature. And if you go and put her in prison and hang her, what on earth is going to happen to the children? If she did shoot John, she's probably dreadfully sorry about it now. It's bad enough for children to have a father who's been murdered – but it will make it infinitely worse for them to have their mother hanged for it. Sometimes I don't think you policemen *think* of these things.'

'We are not contemplating arresting anyone at present, Lady Angkatell.'

'Well, that's sensible at any rate. But I have thought all along, Inspector Grange, that you were a very sensible sort of man.'

Again that charming, almost dazzling smile.

Inspector Grange blinked a little. He could not help it, but he came firmly to the point at issue.

'As you said just now, Lady Angkatell, it's the truth I want to get at. You took the pistol from here – which gun was it, by the way?'

Lady Angkatell nodded her head towards the shelf by the mantelpiece. 'The second from the end. The Mauser .25.' Something in the crisp, technical way she spoke jarred on Grange. He had not, somehow, expected Lady Angkatell, whom up to now he had labelled in his own mind as 'vague' and 'just a bit batty', to describe a firearm with such technical precision.

'You took the pistol from here and put it in your basket. Why?'

'I knew you'd ask me that,' said Lady Angkatell. Her tone, unexpectedly, was almost triumphant. 'And of course there must be some reason. Don't you think so, Henry?' She turned to her husband. 'Don't you think I must have had a reason for taking a pistol out that morning?'

'I should certainly have thought so, my dear,' said Sir Henry stiffly.

'One does things,' said Lady Angkatell, gazing thoughtfully in front of her, 'and then one doesn't remember why one has done them. But I think, you know, Inspector, that there always is a reason if one can only get at it. I must have had *some* idea in my head when I put the Mauser into my egg basket.' She appealed to him. 'What do you think it can have been?'

Grange stared at her. She displayed no embarrassment – just a childlike eagerness. It beat him. He had never yet met anyone like Lucy Angkatell, and just for the moment he didn't know what to do about it.

'My wife,' said Sir Henry, 'is extremely absent-minded, Inspector.'

'So it seems, sir,' said Grange. He did not say it very nicely.

'Why *do* you think I took that pistol?' Lady Angkatell asked him confidentially.

'I have no idea, Lady Angkatell.'

'I came in here,' mused Lady Angkatell. 'I had been talking to Simmons about the pillow-cases – and I remember dimly crossing over to the fireplace – and thinking we must get a new poker – the curate, not the rector –'

Inspector Grange stared. He felt his head going round.

'And I remember picking up the Mauser – it was a nice handy little gun, I've always liked it – and dropping it into the basket – I'd just got the basket from the flower-room. But there were so many things in my head – Simmons, you know, and the bindweed in the Michaelmas daisies – and hoping Mrs Medway would make a really *rich* Nigger in his Shirt –'

'A nigger in his shirt?' Inspector Grange had to break in.

'Chocolate, you know, and eggs – and then covered with whipped cream. Just the sort of sweet a foreigner would like for lunch.'

Inspector Grange spoke fiercely and brusquely, feeling like a man who brushes away fine spiders' webs which are impairing his vision.

'Did you load the pistol?'

He had hoped to startle her – perhaps even to frighten her a little, but Lady Angkatell only considered the question with a kind of desperate thoughtfulness.

'Now did I? That's so stupid. I can't remember. But I should think I must have, don't you, Inspector? I mean, what's the good of a pistol without ammunition? I wish I could remember exactly what was in my head at the time.'

'My dear Lucy,' said Sir Henry. 'What goes on or does not go on in your head has been the despair of everyone who knows you well for years.'

She flashed him a very sweet smile.

'I *am* trying to remember, Henry dear. One does such curious things. I picked up the telephone receiver the other morning and found myself looking down at it quite bewildered. I couldn't imagine what I wanted with it.'

'Presumably you were going to ring someone up,' said the inspector coldly.

'No, funnily enough, I wasn't. I remembered afterwards – I'd been wondering why Mrs Mears, the gardener's wife, held her baby in such an odd way, and I picked up the telephone receiver to try, you know, just how one would hold a baby, and of course I realized that it had looked odd because Mrs Mears was left-handed and had its head the other way round.'

She looked triumphantly from one to the other of the two men.

'Well,' thought the inspector, 'I suppose it's possible that there are people like this.'

But he did not feel very sure about it.

The whole thing, he realized, might be a tissue of lies. The kitchenmaid, for instance, had distinctly stated that it was a revolver Gudgeon had been holding. Still, you couldn't set much store by that. The girl knew nothing of firearms. She had heard a revolver talked about in connection with the crime, and revolver or pistol would be all one to her.

Both Gudgeon and Lady Angkatell had specified the Mauser pistol – but there was nothing to prove their statement. It might actually have been the missing revolver that Gudgeon had been handling and he might have returned it, not to the study, but to Lady Angkatell herself. The servants all seemed absolutely besotted about the damned woman.

Supposing it was actually she who had shot John Christow? (But why should she? He couldn't see why.) Would they still back her up and tell lies for her? He had an uncomfortable feeling that that was just what they would do.

And now this fantastic story of hers about not being able to remember – surely she could think up something better than that. And looking so natural about it – not in the least embarrassed or apprehensive. Damn it all, she gave you the impression that she was speaking the literal truth.

He got up.

'When you remember a little more, perhaps you'll tell me, Lady Angkatell,' he said dryly.

She answered: 'Of course I will, Inspector. Things come to one quite suddenly sometimes.'

Grange went out of the study. In the hall he put a finger round the inside of a collar and drew a deep breath.

He felt all tangled up in the thistledown. What he needed was his oldest and foulest pipe, a pint of ale and a good steak and chips. Something plain and objective.

CHAPTER 21

In the study Lady Angkatell flitted about touching things here and there with a vague forefinger. Sir Henry sat back in his chair watching her. He said at last:

'Why did you take the pistol, Lucy?'

Lady Angkatell came back and sank down gracefully into a chair.

'I'm not really quite sure, Henry. I suppose I had some vague ideas of an accident.'

'Accident?'

'Yes. All those roots of trees, you know,' said Lady Angkatell vaguely, 'sticking out – so easy, just to trip over one. One might have had a few shots at the target and left one shot in the magazine – careless, of course – but then people *are* careless. I've always thought, you know, that accident would be the simplest way to do a thing of that kind. One would be dreadfully sorry, of course, and blame oneself . . .'

Her voice died away. Her husband sat very still without taking his eyes off her face. He spoke again in the same quiet, careful voice.

'Who was to have had – the accident?'

Lucy turned her head a little, looking at him in surprise.

'John Christow, of course.'

'Good God, Lucy –' He broke off.

She said earnestly:

'Oh, Henry, I've been so dreadfully worried. About Ainswick.'

'I see. It's Ainswick. You've always cared too much about Ainswick, Lucy. Sometimes I think it's the only thing you do care for.'

'Edward and David are the last – the last of the Angkatells. And David won't do, Henry. He'll never marry – because of his mother and all that. He'll get the place when Edward dies, and he won't marry, and you and I will be dead long before he's even middle-aged. He'll be the last of the Angkatells and the whole thing will die out.'

'Does it matter so much, Lucy?'

'Of course it matters! *Ainswick*!'

'You should have been a boy, Lucy.'

But he smiled a little – for he could not imagine Lucy being anything but feminine.

'It all depends on Edward's marrying – and Edward's so obstinate – that long head of his, like my father's. I hoped he'd get over Henrietta and marry some nice girl – but I see now that that's hopeless. Then I thought that Henrietta's affair with John would run the usual course. John's affairs were never, I imagine, very permanent. But I saw him looking at her the other evening. He really *cared* about her. If only John were out of the way I felt that Henrietta would marry Edward. She's not the kind of person to cherish a memory and live in the past. So, you see, it all came to that – get rid of John Christow.'

'Lucy. You didn't – What did you do, Lucy?'

Lady Angkatell got up again. She took two dead flowers out of a vase.

'Darling,' she said. 'You don't imagine for a moment, do you, that *I* shot John Christow? I did have that silly idea about an accident. But then, you know, I remembered that we'd *asked* John Christow here – it's not as though he proposed himself. One can't ask someone to be your guest and then arrange accidents. Even Arabs are most particular about hospitality. So don't worry, will you, Henry?'

She stood looking at him with a brilliant, affectionate smile. He said heavily:

'I always worry about you, Lucy.'

'There's no need, darling. And you see, everything has actually turned out all right. John has been got rid of without our doing anything about it. It reminds me,' said Lady Angkatell reminiscently, 'of that man in Bombay who was so frightfully rude to me. He was run over by a tram three days later.'

She unbolted the french windows and went out into the garden.

Sir Henry sat still, watching her tall, slender figure wander down the path. He looked old and tired, and his face was the face of a man who lives at close quarters with fear.

In the kitchen a tearful Doris Emmott was wilting under the stern reproof of Mr Gudgeon. Mrs Medway and Miss Simmons acted as a kind of Greek chorus.

'Putting yourself forward and jumping to conclusions in a way only an inexperienced girl would do.'

'That's right,' said Mrs Medway.

'If you see me with a pistol in my hand, the proper thing to do is to come to me and say: "Mr Gudgeon, will you be so kind as to give me an explanation?"'

'Or you could have come to me,' put in Mrs Medway. '*I'm* always willing to tell a young girl what doesn't know the world what she ought to think.'

'What you should *not* have done,' said Gudgeon severely, 'is to go babbling off to a policeman – and only a sergeant at that! Never get mixed up with the police more than you can help. It's painful enough having them in the house at all.'

'Inexpressibly painful,' murmured Miss Simmons.

'Such a thing never happened to *me* before.'

'We all know,' went on Gudgeon, 'what her ladyship is like. Nothing her ladyship does would ever surprise me – but the police don't know her ladyship the way we do, and it's not to be thought of that her ladyship should be worried with silly questions and suspicions just because she wanders about with firearms. It's the sort of thing she would do, but the police have the kind of mind that just sees murder and nasty things like that. Her ladyship is the kind of absent-minded lady who wouldn't hurt a fly, but there's no denying that she puts things in funny places. I shall never forget,' added Gudgeon with feeling, 'when she brought back a live lobster and put it in the card tray in the hall. Thought I was seeing things!'

'That must have been before my time,' said Simmons with curiosity.

Mrs Medway checked these revelations with a glance at the erring Doris.

'Some other time,' she said. 'Now then, Doris, we've only been speaking to you for your own good. It's *common* to be mixed up with the police, and don't you forget it. You can get on with the vegetables now, and be more careful with the runner-beans than you were last night.'

Doris sniffed.

'Yes, Mrs Medway,' she said, and shuffled over to the sink.

Mrs Medway said forebodingly:

'I don't feel as I'm going to have a light hand with my pastry. That nasty inquest tomorrow. Gives me a turn every time I think of it. A thing like that – happening to *us*.'

CHAPTER 22

The latch of the gate clicked and Poirot looked out of the window in time to see the visitor who was coming up the path to the front door. He knew at once who she was. He wondered very much what brought Veronica Cray to see him.

She brought a delicious faint scent into the room with her, a scent that Poirot recognized. She wore tweeds and brogues as Henrietta had done – but she was, he decided, very different from Henrietta.

'M. Poirot.' Her tone was delightful, a little thrilled. 'I've only just discovered who my neighbour is. And I've always wanted to know you so much.'

He took her outstretched hands, bowed over them.

'Enchanted, Madame.'

She accepted the homage smilingly, refused his offer of tea, coffee or cocktail.

'No, I've just come to talk to you. To talk seriously. I'm worried.'

'You are worried? I am sorry to hear that.'

Veronica sat down and sighed.

'It's about John Christow's death. The inquest's tomorrow. You know that?'

'Yes, yes, I know.'

'And the whole thing has really been so extraordinary –'

She broke off.

'Most people really wouldn't believe it. But you would, I think, because you know something about human nature.'

'I know a little about human nature,' admitted Poirot.

'Inspector Grange came to see me. He'd got it into his head that I'd quarrelled with John – which is true in a way though not in the way he meant. I told him that I hadn't seen John for fifteen years – and he simply didn't believe me. But it's true, M. Poirot.'

Poirot said: 'Since it is true, it can easily be proved, so why worry?'

She returned his smile in the friendliest fashion.

'The real truth is that I simply haven't dared to tell the inspector what actually happened on Saturday evening. It's so absolutely fantastic that he certainly wouldn't believe it. But I felt I must tell someone. That's why I have come to you.'

Poirot said quietly: 'I am flattered.'

That fact, he noted, she took for granted. She was a woman, he thought, who was very sure of the effect she was producing. So sure that she might, occasionally, make a mistake.

'John and I were engaged to be married fifteen years ago. He was very much in love with me – so much so that it rather alarmed me sometimes. He wanted me to give up acting – to give up having any mind or life of my own. He was so possessive and masterful that I felt I couldn't go through with it, and I broke off the engagement. I'm afraid he took that very hard.'

Poirot clicked a discreet and sympathetic tongue.

'I didn't see him again until last Saturday night. He walked home with me. I told the inspector that we talked about old times – that's true in a way. But there was far more than that.'

'Yes?'

'John went mad – quite mad. He wanted to leave his wife and

children, he wanted me to get a divorce from my husband and marry him. He said he'd never forgotten me – that the moment he saw me time stood still.'

She closed her eyes, she swallowed. Under her make-up her face was very pale.

She opened her eyes again and smiled almost timidly at Poirot.

'Can you believe that a – a feeling like that is possible?' she asked.

'I think it is possible, yes,' said Poirot.

'Never to forget – to go on waiting – planning – hoping. To determine with all one's heart and mind to get what one wants in the end. There are men like that, M. Poirot.'

'Yes – and women.'

She gave him a hard stare.

'I'm talking about men – about John Christow. Well, that's how it was. I protested at first, laughed, refused to take him seriously. Then I told him he was mad. It was quite late when he went back to the house. We'd argued and argued. He was still – just as determined.'

She swallowed again.

'That's why I sent him a note the next morning. I couldn't leave things like that. I had to make him realize that what he wanted was – impossible.'

'It *was* impossible?'

'Of course it was impossible! He came over. He wouldn't listen to what I had to say. He was just as insistent. I told him that it was no good, that I didn't love him, that I hated him . . .' She paused, breathing hard. 'I had to be brutal about it. So we parted in anger . . . And now – he's dead.'

He saw her hands creep together, saw the twisted fingers and the knuckles stand out. They were large, rather cruel hands.

The strong emotion that she was feeling communicated itself to him. It was not sorrow, not grief – no, it was anger. The anger, he thought, of a baffled egoist.

'Well, M. Poirot?' Her voice was controlled and smooth again. 'What am I to do? Tell the story, or keep it to myself? It's what happened – but it takes a bit of believing.'

Poirot looked at her, a long, considering gaze.

He did not think that Veronica Cray was telling the truth,

and yet there was an undeniable under-current of sincerity. It happened, he thought, but it did not happen like that.

And suddenly he got it. It was a true story, inverted. It was she who had been unable to forget John Christow. It was she who had been baffled and repulsed. And now, unable to bear in silence the furious anger of a tigress deprived of what she considered her legitimate prey, she had invented a version of the truth that should satisfy her wounded pride and feed a little the aching hunger for a man who had gone beyond the reach of her clutching hands. Impossible to admit that she, Veronica Cray, could not have what she wanted! So she had changed it all round.

Poirot drew a deep breath and spoke.

'If all this had any bearing on John Christow's death, you would have to speak out, but if it has not – and I cannot see why it should have – then I think you are quite justified in keeping it to yourself.'

He wondered if she was disappointed. He had a fancy that in her present mood she would like to hurl her story into the printed page of a newspaper. She had come to him – why? To try out her story? To test his reactions? Or to use him – to induce him to pass the story on?

If his mild response disappointed her, she did not show it. She got up and gave him one of those long, well-manicured hands.

'Thank you, M. Poirot. What you say seems eminently sensible. I'm so glad I came to you. I – I felt I wanted somebody to know.'

'I shall respect your confidence, Madame.'

When she had gone, he opened the windows a little. Scents affected him. He did not like Veronica's scent. It was expensive but cloying, overpowering like her personality.

He wondered, as he flapped the curtains, whether Veronica Cray had killed John Christow.

She would have been willing to kill him – he believed that. She would have enjoyed pressing the trigger – would have enjoyed seeing him stagger and fall.

But behind that vindictive anger was something cold and shrewd, something that appraised chances, a cool, calculating intelligence. However much Veronica Cray wished to kill John Christow, he doubted whether she would have taken the risk.

<h1 style="text-align:center">CHAPTER 23</h1>

The inquest was over. It had been the merest formality of an affair, and though warned of this beforehand, yet nearly everyone had a resentful sense of anti-climax.

Adjourned for a fortnight at the request of the police.

Gerda had driven down with Mrs Patterson from London in a hired Daimler. She had on a black dress and an unbecoming hat, and looked nervous and bewildered.

Preparatory to stepping back into the Daimler, she paused as Lady Angkatell came up to her.

'How are you, Gerda dear? Not sleeping too badly, I hope. I think it went off as well as we could hope for, don't you? So sorry we haven't got you with us at The Hollow, but I quite understand how distressing that would be.'

Mrs Patterson said in her bright voice, glancing reproachfully at her sister for not introducing her properly:

'This was Miss Collins's idea – to drive straight down and back. Expensive, of course, but we thought it was worth it.'

'Oh, I do so agree with you.'

Mrs Patterson lowered her voice.

'I am taking Gerda and the children straight down to Bexhill. What she needs is rest and quiet. The reporters! You've no idea! Simply swarming round Harley Street.'

A young man snapped off a camera, and Elsie Patterson pushed her sister into the car and they drove off.

The others had a momentary view of Gerda's face beneath the unbecoming hat brim. It was vacant, lost – she looked for the moment like a half-witted child.

Midge Hardcastle muttered under her breath: 'Poor devil.'

Edward said irritably:

'What did everybody see in Christow? That wretched woman looks completely heartbroken.'

'She was absolutely wrapped up in him,' said Midge.

'But why? He was a selfish sort of fellow, good company in a way, but –' He broke off. Then he asked: 'What did you think of him, Midge?'

'I?' Midge reflected. She said at last, rather surprised at her own words: 'I think I respected him.'

'Respected him? For what?'

'Well, he knew his job.'

'You're thinking of him as a doctor?'

'Yes.'

There was no time for more.

Henrietta was driving Midge back to London in her car. Edward was returning to lunch at The Hollow and going up by the afternoon train with David. He said vaguely to Midge: 'You must come out and lunch one day,' and Midge said that that would be very nice but that she couldn't take more than an hour off. Edward gave her his charming smile and said:

'Oh, it's a special occasion. I'm sure they'll understand.'

Then he moved towards Henrietta. 'I'll ring you up, Henrietta.'

'Yes, do, Edward. But I may be out a good deal.'

'Out?'

She gave him a quick, mocking smile.

'Drowning my sorrow. You don't expect me to sit at home and mope, do you?'

He said slowly: 'I don't understand you nowadays, Henrietta. You are quite different.'

Her face softened. She said unexpectedly: 'Darling Edward,' and gave his arm a quick squeeze.

Then she turned to Lucy Angkatell. 'I can come back if I want to, can't I, Lucy?'

Lady Angkatell said: 'Of course, darling. And anyway there will be the inquest again in a fortnight.'

Henrietta went to where she had parked the car in the market square. Her suitcases and Midge's were already inside.

They got in and drove off.

The car climbed the long hill and came out on the road over the ridge. Below them the brown and golden leaves shivered a little in the chill of a grey autumn day.

Midge said suddenly: 'I'm glad to get away – even from Lucy. Darling as she is, she gives me the creeps sometimes.'

Henrietta was looking intently into the small driving-mirror.

She said rather inattentively:

'Lucy has to give the coloratura touch – even to murder.'

'You know, I'd never thought about murder before.'

'Why should you? It isn't a thing one thinks about. It's a six-letter word in a crossword, or a pleasant entertainment between the covers of a book. But the real thing –'

She paused. Midge finished:

'*Is* real. That is what startles one.'

Henrietta said:

'It needn't be startling to you. *You* are outside it. Perhaps the only one of us who is.'

Midge said:

'We're all outside it now. We've got away.'

Henrietta murmured: 'Have we?'

She was looking in the driving-mirror again. Suddenly she put her foot down on the accelerator. The car responded. She glanced at the speedometer. They were doing over fifty. Presently the needle reached sixty.

Midge looked sideways at Henrietta's profile. It was not like Henrietta to drive recklessly. She liked speed, but the winding road hardly justified the pace they were going. There was a grim smile hovering round Henrietta's mouth.

She said: 'Look over your shoulder, Midge. See that car way back there?'

'Yes?'

'It's a Ventnor 10.'

'Is it?' Midge was not particularly interested.

'They're useful little cars, low petrol consumption, keep the road well, but they're not fast.'

'No?'

Curious, thought Midge, how fascinated Henrietta always was by cars and their performance.

'As I say, they're not fast – but that car, Midge, has managed to keep its distance although we've been going over sixty.'

Midge turned a startled face to her.

'Do you mean that –'

Henrietta nodded. 'The police, I believe, have special engines in very ordinary-looking cars.'

Midge said:

'You mean they're still keeping an eye on us all?'

'It seems rather obvious.'

Midge shivered.

'Henrietta, can you understand the meaning of this second gun business?'

'No, it lets Gerda out. But beyond that it just doesn't seem to add up to anything.'

'But, if it was one of Henry's guns –'

'We don't know that it was. It hasn't been found yet, remember.'

'No, that's true. It could be someone outside altogether. Do you know who I'd like to think killed John, Henrietta? That woman.'

'Veronica Cray?'

'Yes.'

Henrietta said nothing. She drove on with her eyes fixed sternly on the road ahead of her.

'Don't you think it's possible?' persisted Midge.

'*Possible*, yes,' said Henrietta slowly.

'Then you don't think –'

'It's no good thinking a thing because you *want* to think it. It's the perfect solution – letting all of us out!'

'Us? But –'

'We're in it – all of us. Even you, Midge darling – though they'd be hard put to it to find a motive for your shooting John. Of course I'd *like* it to be Veronica. Nothing would please me better than to see her giving a lovely performance, as Lucy would put it, in the dock!'

Midge shot a quick look at her.

'Tell me, Henrietta, does it all make you feel vindictive?'

'You mean' – Henrietta paused a moment – 'because I loved John?'

'Yes.'

As she spoke, Midge realized with a slight sense of shock that this was the first time the bald fact had been put into words. It had been accepted by them all, by Lucy and Henry, by Midge, by Edward even, that Henrietta loved John Christow, but nobody had ever so much as hinted at the fact in words before.

There was a pause whilst Henrietta seemed to be thinking. Then she said in a thoughtful voice:

'I can't explain to you what I feel. Perhaps I don't know myself.'

They were driving now over Albert Bridge.

Henrietta said:

'You'd better come to the studio, Midge. We'll have tea, and I'll drive you to your digs afterwards.'

Here in London the short afternoon light was already fading. They drew up at the studio door and Henrietta put her key into the door. She went in and switched on the light.

'It's chilly,' she said. 'We'd better light the gas fire. Oh, bother – I meant to get some matches on the way.'

'Won't a lighter do?'

'Mine's no good, and anyway it's difficult to light a gas fire with one. Make yourself at home. There's an old blind man stands on the corner. I usually get my matches off him. I shan't be a minute or two.'

Left alone in the studio, Midge wandered round looking at Henrietta's work. It gave her an eerie feeling to be sharing the empty studio with these creations of wood and bronze.

There was a bronze head with high cheek-bones and a tin hat, possibly a Red Army soldier, and there was an airy structure of twisted ribbon-like aluminium which intrigued her a good deal. There was a vast static frog in pinkish granite, and at the end of the studio she came to an almost life-sized wooden figure.

She was staring at it when Henrietta's key turned in the door and Henrietta herself came in slightly breathless.

Midge turned.

'What's this, Henrietta? It's rather frightening.'

'That? That's The Worshipper. It's going to the International Group.'

Midge repeated, staring at it:

'It's frightening.'

Kneeling to light the gas fire, Henrietta said over her shoulder:

'It's interesting your saying that. Why do you find it frightening?'

'I think – because it hasn't any face.'

'How right you are, Midge.'

'It's very good, Henrietta.'

Henrietta said lightly:

'It's a nice bit of pearwood.'

She rose from her knees. She tossed her big satchel bag and her furs on to the divan, and threw down a couple of boxes of matches on the table.

Midge was struck by the expression on her face – it had a sudden quite inexplicable exultation.

'Now for tea,' said Henrietta, and in her voice was the same warm jubilation that Midge had already glimpsed in her face.

It struck an almost jarring note – but Midge forgot it in a train of thought aroused by the sight of the two boxes of matches.

'You remember those matches Veronica Cray took away with her?'

'When Lucy insisted on foisting a whole half-dozen on her? Yes.'

'Did anyone ever find out whether she had matches in her cottage all the time?'

'I expect the police did. They're very thorough.'

A faintly triumphant smile was curving Henrietta's lips. Midge felt puzzled and almost repelled.

She thought: 'Can Henrietta really have cared for John? Can she? Surely not.'

And a faint desolate chill struck through her as she reflected: 'Edward will not have to wait very long . . .'

Ungenerous of her not to let that thought bring warmth. She wanted Edward to be happy, didn't she? It wasn't as though she could have Edward herself. To Edward she would be always 'little Midge'. Never more than that. Never a woman to be loved.

Edward, unfortunately, was the faithful kind. Well, the faithful kind usually got what they wanted in the end.

Edward and Henrietta at Ainswick . . . that was the proper ending to the story. Edward and Henrietta living happy ever afterwards.

She could see it all very clearly.

'Cheer up, Midge,' said Henrietta. 'You mustn't let murder get you down. Shall we go out later and have a spot of dinner together?'

But Midge said quickly that she must get back to her rooms.

She had things to do – letters to write. In fact, she'd better go as soon as she'd finished her cup of tea.

'All right. I'll drive you there.'

'I could get a taxi.'

'Nonsense. Let's use the car, as it's there.'

They went out into damp evening air. As they drove past the end of the Mews Henrietta pointed out a car drawn in to the side.

'A Ventnor 10. Our shadow. You'll see. He'll follow us.'

'How beastly it all is!'

'Do you think so? I don't really mind.'

Henrietta dropped Midge at her rooms and came back to the Mews and put her car away in the garage.

Then she let herself into the studio once more.

For some minutes she stood abstractedly drumming with her fingers on the mantelpiece. Then she sighed and murmured to herself:

'Well – to work. Better not waste time.'

She threw off her tweeds and got into her overall.

An hour and a half later she drew back and studied what she had done. There were dabs of clay on her cheek and her hair was dishevelled, but she nodded approval at the model on the stand.

It was the rough similitude of a horse. The clay had been slapped on in great irregular lumps. It was the kind of horse that would have given the colonel of a cavalry regiment apoplexy, so unlike was it to any flesh and blood horse that had ever been foaled. It would also have distressed Henrietta's Irish hunting forebears. Nevertheless it was a horse – a horse conceived in the abstract.

Henrietta wondered what Inspector Grange would think of it if he ever saw it, and her mouth widened a little in amusement as she pictured his face.

CHAPTER 24

Edward Angkatell stood hesitantly in the swirl of foot traffic in Shaftesbury Avenue. He was nerving himself to enter the establishment which bore the gold-lettered sign: 'Madame Alfrege'.

Some obscure instinct had prevented him from merely ringing up and asking Midge to come out and lunch. That fragment of telephone conversation at The Hollow had disturbed him – more, had shocked him. There had been in Midge's voice a submission, a subservience that had outraged all his feelings.

For Midge, the free, the cheerful, the outspoken, to have to adopt that attitude. To have to submit, as she clearly was submitting, to rudeness and insolence on the other end of the wire. It was all wrong – the whole thing was wrong! And then, when he had shown his concern, she had met him point-blank with the unpalatable truth that one had to keep one's job, that jobs weren't easy to get, and that the holding down of jobs entailed more unpleasantness than the mere performing of a stipulated task.

Up till then Edward had vaguely accepted the fact that a great many young women had 'jobs' nowadays. If he had thought about it at all, he had thought that on the whole they had jobs because they liked jobs – that it flattered their sense of independence and gave them an interest of their own in life.

The fact that a working day of nine to six, with an hour off for lunch, cut a girl off from most of the pleasures and relaxations of a leisured class had simply not occurred to Edward. That Midge, unless she sacrificed her lunch hour, could not drop into a picture gallery, that she could not go to an afternoon concert, drive out of town on a fine summer's day, lunch in a leisurely way at a distant restaurant, but had instead to relegate her excursions into the country to Saturday afternoons and Sundays, and to snatch her lunch in a crowded Lyons or a snack bar, was a new and unwelcome discovery. He was very fond of Midge. Little Midge – that was how he thought of her. Arriving shy and wide-eyed at Ainswick for the holidays, tongue-tied at first, then opening up into enthusiasm and affection.

Edward's tendency to live exclusively in the past, and to accept the present dubiously as something yet untested, had delayed his recognition of Midge as a wage-earning adult.

It was on that evening at The Hollow when he had come in cold and shivering from that strange, upsetting clash with Henrietta, and when Midge had knelt to build up the fire, that he had been first aware of a Midge who was not an affectionate child but a woman. It had been an upsetting vision – he had felt for a moment that he had lost something – something that was a precious part of Ainswick. And he had said impulsively, speaking out of that suddenly aroused feeling, 'I wish I saw more of you, little Midge . . .'

Standing outside in the moonlight, speaking to a Henrietta who was no longer startlingly the familiar Henrietta he had loved for so long – he had known sudden panic. And he had come in to a further disturbance of the set pattern which was his life. Little Midge was also a part of Ainswick – and this was no longer little Midge, but a courageous and sad-eyed adult whom he did not know.

Ever since then he had been troubled in his mind, and had indulged in a good deal of self-reproach for the unthinking way in which he had never bothered about Midge's happiness or comfort. The idea of her uncongenial job at Madame Alfrege's had worried him more and more, and he had determined at last to see for himself just what this dress shop of hers was like.

Edward peered suspiciously into the show window at a little black dress with a narrow gold belt, some rakish-looking, skimpy jumper suits, and an evening gown of rather tawdry coloured lace.

Edward knew nothing about women's clothes except by instinct, but had a shrewd idea that all these exhibits were somehow of a meretricious order. No, he thought, this place was not worthy of her. Someone – Lady Angkatell, perhaps – must do something about it.

Overcoming his shyness with an effort, Edward straightened his slightly stooping shoulders and walked in.

He was instantly paralysed with embarrassment. Two platinum blonde little minxes with shrill voices were examining dresses in a show-case, with a dark saleswoman in attendance. At the back of the shop a small woman with a thick nose, henna red hair and a disagreeable voice was arguing with a stout and bewildered customer over some alterations to an evening gown. From an adjacent cubicle a woman's fretful voice was raised.

'Frightful – perfectly frightful – can't you bring me anything *decent* to try?'

In response he heard the soft murmur of Midge's voice – a deferential, persuasive voice.

'This wine model is really very smart. And I think it would suit you. If you'd just slip it on –'

'I'm not going to waste my time trying on things that I can see are no good. Do take a little trouble. I've told you I don't want reds. If you'd listen to what you are told –'

The colour surged up into Edward's neck. He hoped Midge would throw the dress in the odious woman's face. Instead she murmured:

'I'll have another look. You wouldn't care for green I suppose, Madam? Or this peach?'

'Dreadful – perfectly dreadful! No, I won't see anything more. Sheer waste of time –'

But now Madame Alfrege, detaching herself from the stout customer, had come down to Edward and was looking at him inquiringly.

He pulled himself together.

'Is – could I speak – is Miss Hardcastle here?'

Madame Alfrege's eyebrows went up, but she took in the Savile Row cut of Edward's clothes, and she produced a smile whose graciousness was rather more unpleasant than her bad temper would have been.

From inside the cubicle the fretful voice rose sharply.

'Do be careful! How clumsy you are. You've torn my hair-net.'

And Midge, her voice unsteady:

'I'm very sorry, Madam.'

'Stupid clumsiness.' (The voice appeared muffled.) 'No, I'll do it myself. My belt, please.'

'Miss Hardcastle will be free in a minute,' said Madame Alfrege. Her smile was now a leer.

A sandy-haired, bad-tempered-looking woman emerged from the cubicle carrying several parcels and went out into the street.

Midge, in a severe black dress, opened the door for her. She looked pale and unhappy.

'I've come to take you out to lunch,' said Edward without preamble.

Midge gave a harried glance up at the clock.

'I don't get off until quarter-past one,' she began.

It was ten past one.

Madame Alfrege said graciously:

'You can go off now if you like, Miss Hardcastle, as your *friend* has called for you.'

Midge murmured: 'Oh thank you, Madame Alfrege,' and to Edward: 'I'll be ready in a minute,' and disappeared into the back of the shop.

Edward, who had winced under the impact of Madame Alfrege's heavy emphasis on 'friend', stood helplessly waiting.

Madame Alfrege was just about to enter into arch conversation with him when the door opened and an opulent-looking woman with a Pekinese came in, and Madame Alfrege's business instincts took her forward to the newcomer.

Midge reappeared with her coat on, and taking her by the elbow, Edward steered her out of the shop into the street.

'My God,' he said, 'is that the sort of thing you have to put up with? I heard that damned woman talking to you behind the curtain. How can you stick it, Midge? Why didn't you throw the damned frocks at her head?'

'I'd soon lose my job if I did things like that.'

'But don't you want to fling things at a woman of that kind?'

Midge drew a deep breath.

'Of course I do. And there are times, especially at the end of a hot week during the summer sales, when I am afraid that one day I shall let go and just tell everyone exactly where they get off – instead of "Yes, Madam," "No, Madam" – "I'll see if we have anything else, Madam."'

'Midge, dear little Midge, you can't put up with all this!'

Midge laughed a little shakily.

'Don't be upset, Edward. Why on earth did you have to come here? Why not ring up?'

'I wanted to see for myself. I've been worried.' He paused and then broke out, 'Why, Lucy wouldn't talk to a scullery maid the way that woman talked to you. It's all wrong that you should have to put up with insolence and rudeness. Good God, Midge, I'd like to take you right out of it all down to Ainswick. I'd like to hail a taxi, bundle you into it, and take you down to Ainswick now by the 2.15.'

Midge stopped. Her assumed nonchalance fell from her. She had had a long tiring morning with trying customers, and Madame at her most bullying. She turned on Edward with a sudden flare of resentment.

'Well, then, why don't you? There are plenty of taxis!'

He stared at her, taken aback by her sudden fury. She went on, her anger flaming up:

'Why do you have to come along and *say* these things? You don't mean them. Do you think it makes it any easier after I've had the hell of a morning to be reminded that there are places like Ainswick? Do you think I'm grateful to you for standing there and babbling about how much you'd like to take me out of it all? All very sweet and insincere. You don't really mean a word of it. Don't you know that I'd sell my soul to catch the 2.15 to Ainswick and get away from everything? I can't bear even to *think* of Ainswick, do you understand? You mean well, Edward, but you're cruel! Saying things – just *saying* things . . .'

They faced each other, seriously incommoding the lunchtime crowd in Shaftesbury Avenue. Yet they were conscious of nothing but each other. Edward was staring at her like a man suddenly aroused from sleep.

He said: 'All right then, damn it. You're coming to Ainswick by the 2.15!'

He raised his stick and hailed a passing taxi. It drew into the kerb. Edward opened the door, and Midge, slightly dazed, got in. Edward said: 'Paddington Station' to the driver and followed her in.

They sat in silence. Midge's lips were set together. Her eyes were defiant and mutinous. Edward stared straight ahead of him.

As they waited for the traffic lights in Oxford Street, Midge said disagreeably:

'I seem to have called your bluff.'

Edward said shortly:

'It wasn't bluff.'

The taxi started forward again with a jerk.

It was not until the taxi turned left in Edgware Road into Cambridge Terrace that Edward suddenly regained his normal attitude to life.

He said: 'We can't catch the 2.15,' and tapping on the glass he said to the driver: 'Go to the Berkeley.'

Midge said coldly: 'Why can't we catch the 2.15? It's only twenty-five past one now.'

Edward smiled at her.

'You haven't got any luggage, little Midge. No nightgowns or toothbrushes or country shoes. There's a 4.15, you know. We'll have some lunch now and talk things over.'

Midge sighed.

'That's so like you, Edward. To remember the practical side. Impulse doesn't carry you very far, does it? Oh, well, it was a nice dream while it lasted.'

She slipped her hand into his and gave him her old smile.

'I'm sorry I stood on the pavement and abused you like a fishwife,' she said. 'But you know, Edward, you *were* irritating.'

'Yes,' he said. 'I must have been.'

They went into the Berkeley happily side by side. They got a table by the window and Edward ordered an excellent lunch.

As they finished their chicken, Midge sighed and said: 'I ought to hurry back to the shop. My time's up.'

'You're going to take decent time over your lunch today, even if I have to go back and buy half the clothes in the shop!'

'Dear Edward, you are really rather sweet.'

They ate Crêpes Suzette, and then the waiter brought them coffee. Edward stirred his sugar in with his spoon.

He said gently:

'You really do love Ainswick, don't you?'

'Must we talk about Ainswick? I've survived not catching the 2.15 – and I quite realize that there isn't any question of the 4.15 – but don't rub it in.'

Edward smiled. 'No, I'm not proposing that we catch the 4.15. But I am suggesting that you come to Ainswick, Midge. I'm suggesting that you come there for good – that is, if you can put up with me.'

She stared at him over the rim of her coffee cup – put it down with a hand that she managed to keep steady.

'What do you really mean, Edward?'

'I'm suggesting that you should marry me, Midge. I don't suppose that I'm a very romantic proposition. I'm a dull dog, I know that, and not much good at anything. I just read books and potter around. But although I'm not a very exciting person, we've known each other a long time and I think that Ainswick itself would – well, would compensate. I think you'd be happy at Ainswick, Midge. Will you come?'

Midge swallowed once or twice, then she said:

'But I thought – Henrietta –' and stopped.

Edward said, his voice level and unemotional:

'Yes, I've asked Henrietta to marry me three times. Each time she has refused. Henrietta knows what she doesn't want.'

There was a silence, and then Edward said:

'Well, Midge dear, what about it?'

Midge looked up at him. There was a catch in her voice. She said:

'It seems so extraordinary – to be offered heaven on a plate as it were, at the Berkeley!'

His face lighted up. He laid his hand over hers for a brief moment.

'Heaven on a plate,' he said. 'So you feel like that about Ainswick. Oh, Midge, I'm glad.'

They sat there happily. Edward paid the bill and added an enormous tip. The people in the restaurant were thinning out. Midge said with an effort:

'We'll have to go. I suppose I'd better go back to Madame Alfrege. After all, she's counting on me. I can't just walk out.'

'No, I suppose you'll have to go back and resign or hand in your notice or whatever you call it. You're not to go on working there, though. I won't have it. But first I thought we'd better go to one of those shops in Bond Street where they sell rings.'

'Rings?'

'It's usual, isn't it?'

Midge laughed.

In the dimmed lighting of the jeweller's shop, Midge and Edward bent over trays of sparkling engagement rings, whilst a discreet salesman watched them benignantly.

Edward said, pushing away a velvet-covered tray:

'Not emeralds.'

Henrietta in green tweeds – Henrietta in an evening dress like Chinese jade . . .

No, not emeralds.

Midge pushed away the tiny stabbing pain at her heart.

'Choose for me,' she said to Edward.

He bent over the tray before them. He picked out a ring with a single diamond. Not a very large stone, but a stone of beautiful colour and fire.

'I'd like this.'

Midge nodded. She loved this display of Edward's unerring and fastidious taste. She slipped it on her finger as Edward and the shopman drew aside.

Edward wrote out a cheque for three hundred and forty-two pounds and came back to Midge smiling.

He said: 'Let's go and be rude to Madame Alfrege.'

CHAPTER 25

'But, darling, I *am* so delighted!'

Lady Angkatell stretched out a fragile hand to Edward and touched Midge softly with the other.

'You did quite right, Edward, to make her leave that horrid shop and bring her right down here. She'll stay here, of course, and be married from here. St George's, you know, three miles by the road, though only a mile through the woods, but then one doesn't go to a wedding through woods. And I suppose it will have to be the vicar – poor man, he has such dreadful colds in the head every autumn. The curate, now, has one of those high Anglican voices, and the whole thing would be far more impressive – and more religious, too, if you know what I mean. It is so hard to keep one's mind reverent when somebody is saying things through their noses.'

It was, Midge decided, a very Lucyish reception. It made her want to both laugh and cry.

'I'd love to be married from here, Lucy,' she said.

'Then that's settled, darling. Off-white satin, I think, and an ivory prayer-book – *not* a bouquet. Bridesmaids?'

'No. I don't want a fuss. Just a very quiet wedding.'

'I know what you mean, darling, and I think perhaps you are right. With an autumn wedding it's nearly always chrysanthemums – such an uninspiring flower, I always think. And unless one takes a lot of time to choose them carefully bridesmaids never *match* properly, and there's nearly always one terribly plain one who ruins the whole effect – but one has to have her because she's usually the bridegroom's sister. But of course –' Lady Angkatell beamed, 'Edward hasn't got any sisters.'

'That seems to be one point in my favour,' said Edward, smiling.

'But children are really the worst at weddings,' went on Lady Angkatell, happily pursuing her own train of thought. 'Everyone says: "How sweet!" but, my dear, the *anxiety*! They step on the train, or else they howl for Nannie, and quite often they're sick. I always wonder how a girl can go up the aisle in a proper frame of mind, while she's so uncertain about what is happening behind her.'

'There needn't be anything behind me,' said Midge cheerfully. 'Not even a train. I can be married in a coat and skirt.'

'Oh, no, Midge, that's so like a widow. No, off-white satin and *not* from Madame Alfrege's.'

'Certainly not from Madame Alfrege's,' said Edward.

'I shall take you to Mireille,' said Lady Angkatell.

'My dear Lucy, I can't possibly afford Mireille.'

'Nonsense, Midge. Henry and I are going to give you your trousseau. And Henry, of course, will give you away. I do hope the band of his trousers won't be too tight. It's nearly two years since he last went to a wedding. And I shall wear –'

Lady Angkatell paused and closed her eyes.

'Yes, Lucy?'

'Hydrangea blue,' announced Lady Angkatell in a rapt voice. 'I suppose, Edward, you will have one of your own friends for best man, otherwise, of course, there is David. I cannot help feeling it would be frightfully good for David. It would give him poise, you know, and he would feel we all *liked* him. That, I am sure, is very important with David. It must be disheartening, you know, to feel you are clever and intellectual and yet nobody likes you any the better for it! But of course it would be rather a risk. He would probably lose the ring, or drop it at the last minute. I expect it would worry Edward too much. But it would be nice in a way to keep it to the same people we've had here for the murder.'

Lady Angkatell uttered the last few words in the most conversational of tones.

'Lady Angkatell has been entertaining a few friends for a murder this autumn,' Midge could not help saying.

'Yes,' said Lucy meditatively. 'I suppose it *did* sound like that. A party for the shooting. You know, when you come to think of it, that's just what it has been!'

Midge gave a faint shiver and said:

'Well, at any rate, it's over now.'

'It's not exactly over – the inquest was only adjourned. And that nice Inspector Grange has got men all over the place simply crashing through the chestnut woods and startling all the pheasants, and springing up like jacks in the box in the most unlikely places.'

'What are they looking for?' asked Edward. 'The revolver that Christow was shot with?'

'I imagine that must be it. They even came to the house with a search warrant. The inspector was most apologetic about it, quite *shy*, but of course I told him we should be delighted. It was really most interesting. They looked absolutely *everywhere*. I followed them round, you know, and I suggested one or two places which even they hadn't thought of. But they didn't find anything. It was most disappointing. Poor Inspector Grange, he is growing quite thin and he pulls and pulls at that moustache of his. His wife ought to give him specially nourishing meals with all this worry he is having – but I have a vague idea that she must be one of those women who care more about having the linoleum really well polished than in cooking a tasty little meal. Which reminds me, I must go and see Mrs Medway. Funny how servants cannot bear the police. Her cheese soufflé last night was quite uneatable. Soufflés and pastry always show if one is off balance. If it weren't for Gudgeon keeping them all together I really believe half the servants would leave. Why don't you two go and have a nice walk and help the police look for the revolver?'

Hercule Poirot sat on the bench overlooking the chestnut groves above the pool. He had no sense of trespassing since Lady Angkatell had very sweetly begged him to wander where he would at any time. It was Lady Angkatell's sweetness which Hercule Poirot was considering at this moment.

From time to time he heard the cracking of twigs in the woods above or caught sight of a figure moving through the chestnut groves below him.

Presently Henrietta came along the path from the direction of the lane. She stopped for a moment when she saw Poirot, then she came and sat down by him.

'Good morning, M. Poirot. I have just been to call upon you. But you were out. You look very Olympian. Are you presiding over the hunt? The inspector seems very active. What are they looking for, the revolver?'

'Yes, Miss Savernake.'

'Will they find it, do you think?'

'I think so. Quite soon now, I should say.'

She looked at him inquiringly.

'Have you an idea, then, where it is?'

'No. But I *think* it will be found soon. It is *time* for it to be found.'

'You do say odd things, M. Poirot!'

'Odd things happen here. You have come back very soon from London, Mademoiselle.'

Her face hardened. She gave a short, bitter laugh.

'The murderer returns to the scene of the crime? That is the old superstition, isn't it? So you *do* think that I – did it! You don't believe me when I tell you that I wouldn't – that I *couldn't* kill anybody?'

Poirot did not answer at once. At last he said thoughtfully:

'It has seemed to me from the beginning that either this crime was very simple – so simple that it was difficult to believe its simplicity (and simplicity, Mademoiselle, can be strangely baffling) or else it was extremely complex. That is to say, we were contending against a mind capable of intricate and ingenious inventions, so that every time we seemed to be heading for the truth, we were actually being led on a trail that twisted away from the truth and led us to a point which – ended in nothingness. This apparent futility, this continual barrenness, is not *real* – it is artificial, it is *planned*. A very subtle and ingenious mind is plotting against us the whole time – and succeeding.'

'Well?' said Henrietta. 'What has that to do with me?'

'The mind that is plotting against us is a creative mind, Mademoiselle.'

'I see – that's where I come in?'

She was silent, her lips set together bitterly. From her jacket pocket she had taken a pencil and now she was idly drawing the outline of a fantastic tree on the white painted wood of the bench, frowning as she did so.

Poirot watched her. Something stirred in his mind – standing in Lady Angkatell's drawing-room on the afternoon of the crime, looking down at a pile of bridge-markers, standing by a painted iron table in the pavilion the next morning, and a question that he had put to Gudgeon.

He said:

'That is what you drew on your bridge-marker – a tree.'

'Yes.' Henrietta seemed suddenly aware of what she was doing. 'Ygdrasil, M. Poirot.' She laughed.

'Why do you call it Ygdrasil?'

She explained the origin of Ygdrasil.

'And so, when you "doodle" (that is the word, is it not?) it is always Ygdrasil you draw?'

'Yes. Doodling is a funny thing, isn't it?'

'Here on the seat – on the bridge-marker on Saturday evening – in the pavilion on Sunday morning . . .'

The hand that held the pencil stiffened and stopped. She said in a tone of careless amusement:

'In the pavilion?'

'Yes, on the round iron table there.'

'Oh, that must have been on – on Saturday afternoon.'

'It was not on Saturday afternoon. When Gudgeon brought the glasses out to the pavilion about twelve o'clock on Sunday morning, there was nothing drawn on the table. I asked him and he is quite definite about that.'

'Then it must have been' – she hesitated for just a moment – 'of course, on Sunday afternoon.'

But still smiling pleasantly, Hercule Poirot shook his head.

'I think not. Grange's men were at the pool all Sunday afternoon, photographing the body, getting the revolver out of the water. They did not leave until dusk. They would have seen anyone go into the pavilion.'

Henrietta said slowly:

'I remember now. I went along there quite late in the evening – after dinner.'

Poirot's voice came sharply:

'People do not "doodle" in the dark, Miss Savernake. Are you telling me that you went into the pavilion at night and stood by a table and drew a tree without being able to see what you were drawing?'

Henrietta said calmly: 'I am telling you the truth. Naturally you don't believe it. You have your own ideas. What is your idea, by the way?'

'I am suggesting that you were in the pavilion on *Sunday morning after twelve o'clock* when Gudgeon brought the glasses out. That you stood by that table watching someone, or waiting for someone, and unconsciously took out a pencil and drew Ygdrasil without being fully aware of what you were doing.'

'I was not in the pavilion on Sunday morning. I sat out on the terrace for a while, then I got the gardening basket and went up to the dahlia border and cut off heads and tied up some of the Michaelmas daisies that were untidy. Then just on one o'clock I went along to the pool. I've been through it all with Inspector Grange. I never came near the pool until one o'clock, just after John had been shot.'

'That,' said Hercule Poirot, 'is your story. But Ygdrasil, Mademoiselle, testifies against you.'

'I was in the pavilion and I shot John, that's what you mean?'

'You were there and you shot Dr Christow, or you were there and you saw who shot Dr Christow – or someone else was there who knew about Ygdrasil and deliberately drew it on the table to put suspicion on *you*.'

Henrietta got up. She turned on him with her chin lifted.

'You still think that I shot John Christow. You think that you can prove I shot him. Well, I will tell you this. You will never prove it. *Never!*'

'You think that you are cleverer than I am?'

'You will never prove it,' said Henrietta, and, turning, she walked away down the winding path that led to the swimming pool.

CHAPTER 26

Grange came in to Resthaven to drink a cup of tea with Hercule Poirot. The tea was exactly what he had had apprehensions it might be – extremely weak and China tea at that.

'These foreigners,' thought Grange, 'don't know how to make tea. You can't teach 'em.' But he did not mind much. He was in a condition of pessimism when one more thing that was unsatisfactory actually afforded him a kind of grim satisfaction.

He said: 'The adjourned inquest's the day after tomorrow and where have we got? Nowhere at all. What the hell, that gun must be *somewhere*! It's this damned country – miles of woods. It would take an army to search them properly. Talk of a needle in a haystack. It may be anywhere. The fact is, we've got to face up to it – we may *never* find that gun.'

'You will find it,' said Poirot confidently.

'Well, it won't be for want of trying!'

'You will find it, sooner or later. And I should say sooner. Another cup of tea?'

'I don't mind if I do – no, no hot water.'

'Is it not too strong?'

'Oh, no, it's not too strong.' The inspector was conscious of understatement.

Gloomily he sipped at the pale, straw-coloured beverage.

'This case is making a monkey of me, M. Poirot – a monkey of me! I can't get the hang of these people. They *seem* helpful – but everything they tell you seems to lead you away on a wild-goose chase.'

'Away?' said Poirot. A startled look came into his eyes. 'Yes, I see. *Away* . . .'

The inspector was now developing his grievance.

'Take the gun now. Christow was shot – according to the medical evidence – only a minute or two before your arrival. Lady Angkatell had that egg basket, Miss Savernake had a gardening basket full of dead flower heads, and Edward Angkatell was wearing a loose shooting-coat with large pockets stuffed with cartridges. Any one of them could have carried the revolver away with them. It wasn't hidden anywhere near the pool – my men have raked the place, so that's definitely out.'

Poirot nodded. Grange went on:

'Gerda Christow was framed – but who by? That's where every clue I follow seems to vanish into thin air.'

'Their stories of how they spent the morning are satisfactory?'

'The *stories* are all right. Miss Savernake was gardening. Lady Angkatell was collecting eggs. Edward Angkatell and Sir Henry were shooting and separated at the end of the morning – Sir Henry coming back to the house and Edward Angkatell coming down here through the woods. The young fellow was up in his bedroom reading. (Funny place to read on a nice day, but he's the indoor, bookish kind.) Miss Hardcastle took a book down to the orchard. All sounds very natural and likely, and there's no means of checking up on it. Gudgeon took a tray of glasses out to the pavilion about twelve o'clock. He can't say where any of the house party were or what they were doing. In a way, you know, there's something against almost all of them.'

'Really?'

'Of course the most obvious person is Veronica Cray. She had quarrelled with Christow, she hated his guts, she's quite *likely* to have shot him – but I can't find the least iota of proof that she *did* shoot him. No evidence as to her having had any opportunity to pinch the revolvers from Sir Henry's collection. No one who saw her going to or from the pool that day. And the missing revolver definitely isn't in her possession now.'

'Ah, you have made sure of that?'

'What do you think? The evidence would have justified a search warrant but there was no need. She was quite gracious about it. It's not anywhere in that tin-pot bungalow. After the inquest was adjourned we made a show of letting up on Miss Cray and Miss Savernake, and we've had a tail on them to see where they went and what they'd do. We've had a man on at the film studios watching Veronica – no sign of her trying to ditch the gun there.'

'And Henrietta Savernake?'

'Nothing there either. She went straight back to Chelsea and we've kept an eye on her ever since. The revolver isn't in her studio or in her possession. She was quite pleasant about the search – seemed amused. Some of her fancy stuff gave our man quite a turn. He said it beat him why people wanted to do that kind of thing – statues all lumps and swellings, bits of brass and aluminium twisted into fancy shapes, horses that you wouldn't know were horses.'

Poirot stirred a little.

'Horses, you say?'

'Well, *a* horse. If you'd call it a horse! If people want to model a horse, why don't they go and *look* at a horse!'

'A *horse*,' repeated Poirot.

Grange turned his head.

'What is there about that that interests you so, M. Poirot? I don't get it.'

'Association – a point of the psychology.'

'Word association? Horse and cart? Rocking-horse? Clothes horse. No, I don't get it. Anyway, after a day or two, Miss Savernake packs up and comes down here again. You know that?'

'Yes, I have talked with her and I have seen her walking in the woods.'

'Restless, yes. Well, she was having an affair with the doctor all right, and his saying: "*Henrietta*" as he died is pretty near to an accusation. But it's not quite near enough, M. Poirot.'

'No,' said Poirot thoughtfully, 'it is not near enough.'

Grange said heavily:

'There's something in the atmosphere here – it gets you all tangled up! It's as though they all *knew* something. Lady Angkatell now – she's never been able to put out a decent reason *why* she took out a gun with her that day. It's a crazy thing to do – sometimes I think she is crazy.'

Poirot shook his head very gently.

'No,' he said, 'she is not crazy.'

'Then there's Edward Angkatell. I thought I was getting something on *him*. Lady Angkatell said – no, hinted – that he'd been in love with Miss Savernake for years. Well, that gives him a motive. And now I find it's the *other* girl – Miss Hardcastle – that he's engaged to. So bang goes the case against *him*.'

Poirot gave a sympathetic murmur.

'Then there's the young fellow,' pursued the inspector. 'Lady Angkatell let slip something about him. His mother, it seems, died in an asylum – persecution mania – thought everybody was conspiring to kill her. Well, you can see what that might mean. If the boy had inherited that particular strain of insanity, he might have got ideas into his head about Dr Christow – might have fancied the doctor was planning to certify him. Not that Christow was that kind of doctor. Nervous affections of the alimentary canal and diseases of the super – super something. That was Christow's line. But if the boy was a bit touched, he *might* imagine Christow was here to keep him under observation. He's got an extraordinary manner, that young fellow, nervous as a cat.'

Grange sat unhappily for a moment or two.

'You see what I mean? All vague suspicions, leading *nowhere*.'

Poirot stirred again. He murmured softly:

'*Away* – not *towards. From*, not to. *Nowhere* instead of *somewhere* . . . Yes, of course, that *must* be it.'

Grange stared at him. He said:

'They're queer, all these Angkatells. I'd swear, sometimes, that they know all about it.'

Poirot said quietly:

'*They do.*'

'You mean, they know, all of them, who did it?' the inspector asked incredulously.

Poirot nodded.

'Yes, they know. I have thought so for some time. I am quite sure now.'

'I see.' The inspector's face was grim. 'And they're hiding it up between them? Well, I'll beat them yet. *I'm going to find that gun.*'

It was, Poirot reflected, quite the inspector's theme song.

Grange went on with rancour:

'I'd give anything to get even with them.'

'With –'

'All of them! Muddling me up! Suggesting things! Hinting! Helping my men – *helping* them! All gossamer and spiders' webs, nothing tangible. What I want is a good solid *fact*!'

Hercule Poirot had been staring out of the window for some moments. His eye had been attracted by an irregularity in the symmetry of his domain.

He said now:

'You want a solid fact? *Eh bien*, unless I am much mistaken, there is a solid fact in the hedge by my gate.'

They went down the garden path. Grange went down on his knees, coaxed the twigs apart till he disclosed more fully the thing that had been thrust between them. He drew a deep sigh as something black and steel was revealed.

He said: 'It's a revolver all right.'

Just for a moment his eye rested doubtfully on Poirot.

'No, no, my friend,' said Poirot. '*I* did not shoot Dr Christow and I did not put the revolver in my own hedge.'

'Of course you didn't, M. Poirot! Sorry! Well, we've got it. Looks like the one missing from Sir Henry's study. We can verify that as soon as we get the number. Then we'll see if it was the gun that shot Christow. Easy does it now.'

With infinite care and the use of a silk handkerchief he eased the gun out of the hedge.

'To give us a break, we want fingerprints. I've a feeling, you know, that our luck's changed at last.'

'Let me know.'

'Of course I will, M. Poirot. I'll ring you up.'

Poirot received two telephone calls. The first came through that same evening. The inspector was jubilant.

'That you, M. Poirot? Well, here's the dope. It's the gun all right. The gun missing from Sir Henry's collection *and* the gun that shot John Christow! That's definite. And there are a good set of prints on it. Thumb, first finger, part of middle finger. Didn't I tell you our luck had changed?'

'You have identified the fingerprints?'

'Not yet. They're certainly not Mrs Christow's. We took hers. They look more like a man's than a woman's for size. Tomorrow I'm going along to The Hollow to speak my little piece and get a sample from everyone. And then, M. Poirot, *we shall know where we are!*'

'I hope so, I am sure,' said Poirot politely.

The second telephone call came through on the following day and the voice that spoke was no longer jubilant. In tones of unmitigated gloom, Grange said:

'Want to hear the latest? Those fingerprints aren't the prints of anybody connected with the case! No, sir! They're not Edward Angkatell's, nor David's, nor Sir Henry's! They're not Gerda Christow's, nor the Savernake's, nor our Veronica's, nor her ladyship's, nor the little dark girl's! They're not even the kitchenmaid's – let alone any of the other servants'!'

Poirot made consoling noises. The sad voice of Inspector Grange went on:

'So it looks as though, after all, it *was* an outside job. Someone, that is to say, who had a down on Dr Christow and who we don't know anything about. Someone invisible and inaudible who pinched the guns from the study, and who went away after the shooting by the path to the lane. Someone who put the gun in your hedge and then vanished into thin air!'

'Would you like *my* fingerprints, my friend?'

'I don't mind if I do! It strikes me, M. Poirot, that you were on the spot, and that taking it all round you're far and away the most suspicious character in the case!'

CHAPTER 27

I

The coroner cleared his throat and looked expectantly at the foreman of the jury.

The latter looked down at the piece of paper he held in his hand. His Adam's apple wagged up and down excitedly. He read out in a careful voice:

'We find that the deceased came to his death by wilful murder by some person or persons unknown.'

Poirot nodded his head quietly in his corner by the wall. There could be no other possible verdict.

Outside the Angkatells stopped a moment to talk to Gerda and her sister. Gerda was wearing the same black clothes. Her face had the same dazed, unhappy expression. This time there was no Daimler. The train service, Elsie Patterson explained, was really very good. A fast train to Waterloo and they could easily catch the 1.20 to Bexhill.

Lady Angkatell, clasping Gerda's hand, murmured:

'You must keep in touch with us, my dear. A little lunch, perhaps, one day in London? I expect you come up to do shopping occasionally.'

'I – I don't know,' said Gerda.

Elsie Patterson said:

'We must hurry, dear, our train,' and Gerda turned away with an expression of relief.

Midge said:

'Poor Gerda. The only thing John's death has done for her is to set her free from your terrifying hospitality, Lucy.'

'How unkind you are, Midge. Nobody could say I didn't try.'

'You are much worse when you try, Lucy.'

'Well, it's very nice to think it's all over, isn't it?' said Lady Angkatell, beaming at them. 'Except, of course, for poor Inspector Grange. I do feel so sorry for him. Would it cheer him up, do you think, if we asked him back to lunch? As a *friend*, I mean.'

'I should let well alone, Lucy,' said Sir Henry.

'Perhaps you are right,' said Lady Angkatell meditatively. 'And anyway it isn't the right kind of lunch today. Partridges au Choux – and that delicious Soufflé Surprise that Mrs Medway makes so well. Not at all Inspector Grange's kind of lunch. A really good steak, a little underdone, and a good old-fashioned apple tart with no nonsense about it – or perhaps apple dumplings – that's what I should order for Inspector Grange.'

'Your instincts about food are always very sound, Lucy. I think we had better get home to those partridges. They sound delicious.'

'Well, I thought we ought to have *some* celebration. It's wonderful, isn't it, how everything always seems to turn out for the best?'

'Ye-es.'

'I know what you're thinking, Henry, but don't worry. I shall attend to it this afternoon.'

'What are you up to now, Lucy?'

Lady Angkatell smiled at him.

'It's quite all right, darling. Just tucking in a loose end.'

Sir Henry looked at her doubtfully.

When they reached The Hollow, Gudgeon came out to open the door of the car.

'Everything went off very satisfactorily, Gudgeon,' said Lady Angkatell. 'Please tell Mrs Medway and the others. I know how unpleasant it has been for you all, and I should like to tell you now how much Sir Henry and I have appreciated the loyalty you have all shown.'

'We have been deeply concerned for you, my lady,' said Gudgeon.

'Very sweet of Gudgeon,' said Lucy as she went into the drawing-room, 'but really quite wasted. I have really almost *enjoyed* it all – so different, you know, from what one is accustomed to. Don't you feel, David, that an experience like this has broadened your mind? It must be so different from Cambridge.'

'I am at Oxford,' said David coldly.

Lady Angkatell said vaguely: 'The dear Boat Race. So English, don't you think?' and went towards the telephone.

She picked up the receiver and, holding it in her hand, she went on:

'I do hope, David, that you will come and stay with us again. It's so difficult, isn't it, to get to know people when there is a murder? And quite impossible to have any really intellectual conversation.'

'Thank you,' said David. 'But when I come down I am going to Athens – to the British School.'

Lady Angkatell turned to her husband.

'Who's got the Embassy now? Oh, of course. Hope-Remmington. No, I don't think David would like them. Those girls of theirs are so terribly hearty. They play hockey and cricket and the funny game where you catch the thing in a net.'

She broke off, looking down at the telephone receiver.

'Now, what am I doing with this thing?'

'Perhaps you were going to ring someone up,' said Edward.

'I don't think so.' She replaced it. 'Do you like telephones, David?'

It was the sort of question, David reflected irritably, that she would ask; one to which there could be no intelligent answer. He replied coldly that he supposed they were useful.

'You mean,' said Lady Angkatell, 'like mincing machines? Or elastic bands? All the same, one wouldn't –'

She broke off as Gudgeon appeared in the doorway to announce lunch.

'But you like partridges,' said Lady Angkatell to David anxiously.

David admitted that he liked partridges.

'Sometimes I think Lucy really is a bit touched,' said Midge as she and Edward strolled away from the house and up towards the woods.

The partridges and the Soufflé Surprise had been excellent, and with the inquest over a weight had lifted from the atmosphere.

Edward said thoughtfully:

'I always think Lucy has a brilliant mind that expresses itself like a missing word competition. To mix metaphors – the hammer jumps from nail to nail and never fails to hit each one squarely on the head.'

'All the same,' Midge said soberly, 'Lucy frightens me sometimes.' She added, with a tiny shiver: 'This place has frightened me lately.'

'The Hollow?'

Edward turned an astonished face to her.

'It always reminds me a little of Ainswick,' he said. 'It's not, of course, the real thing –'

Midge interrupted:

'That's just it, Edward. I'm frightened of things that aren't the real thing. You don't know, you see, what's *behind* them. It's like – oh, it's like a *mask*.'

'You mustn't be fanciful, little Midge.'

It was the old tone, the indulgent tone he had used years ago. She had liked it then, but now it disturbed her. She struggled to make her meaning clear – to show him that behind what he called fancy, was some shape of dimly apprehended reality.

'I got away from it in London, but now that I'm back here it all comes over me again. I feel that everyone knows who

killed John Christow. That the only person who doesn't know
– is *me*.'

Edward said irritably:

'Must we think and talk about John Christow? He's dead. Dead
and gone.'

Midge murmured:

> '*He is dead and gone, lady,*
> *He is dead and gone.*
> *At his head a grass green turf,*
> *At his heels a stone.*'

She put her hand on Edward's arm. 'Who *did* kill him, Edward?
We thought it was Gerda – but it wasn't Gerda. Then who
was it? Tell me what *you* think? Was it someone we've never
heard of?'

He said irritably:

'All this speculation seems to me quite unprofitable. If the
police can't find out, or can't get sufficient evidence, then the
whole thing will have to be allowed to drop – and we shall be
rid of it.'

'Yes – but it's the not knowing.'

'Why should we want to know? What has John Christow to
do with us?'

With *us*, she thought, with Edward and me? Nothing! Comforting thought – she and Edward, linked, a dual entity. And yet – and
yet – John Christow, for all that he had been laid in his grave and
the words of the burial service read over him, was not buried
deep enough. *He is dead and gone, lady* – But John Christow
was not dead and gone – for all that Edward wished him to be.
John Christow was still here at The Hollow.

Edward said: 'Where are we going?'

Something in his tone surprised her. She said:

'Let's walk up on to the top of the ridge. Shall we?'

'If you like.'

For some reason he was unwilling. She wondered why. It was
usually his favourite walk. He and Henrietta used nearly always
– Her thought snapped and broke off. *He and Henrietta*! She said:
'Have you been this way yet this autumn?'

He said stiffly:

'Henrietta and I walked up here that first afternoon.' They went on in silence.

They came at last to the top and sat on the fallen tree.

Midge thought: '*He and Henrietta sat here, perhaps.*'

She turned the ring on her finger round and round. The diamond flashed coldly at her. ('*Not emeralds,*' he had said.)

She said with a slight effort:

'It will be lovely to be at Ainswick again for Christmas.'

He did not seem to hear her. He had gone far away.

She thought: 'He is thinking of Henrietta and of John Christow.'

Sitting here he had said something to Henrietta or she had said something to him. Henrietta might know what she didn't want, but he belonged to Henrietta still. He always would, Midge thought, belong to Henrietta . . .

Pain swooped down upon her. The happy bubble world in which she had lived for the last week quivered and broke.

She thought: 'I can't live like that – with Henrietta always there in his mind. I can't face it. I can't bear it.'

The wind sighed through the trees – the leaves were falling fast now – there was hardly any golden left, only brown.

She said: 'Edward!'

The urgency of her voice aroused him. He turned his head.

'Yes?'

'I'm sorry, Edward.' Her lips were trembling but she forced her voice to be quiet and self-controlled. 'I've got to tell you. It's no use. I can't marry you. It wouldn't work, Edward.'

He said: 'But, Midge – surely Ainswick –'

She interrupted:

'I can't marry you just for Ainswick, Edward. You – you must see that.'

He sighed then, a long gentle sigh. It was like an echo of the dead leaves slipping gently off the branches of the trees.

'I see what you mean,' he said. 'Yes, I suppose you are right.'

'It was dear of you to ask me, dear and sweet. But it wouldn't do, Edward. It wouldn't *work.*'

She had had a faint hope, perhaps, that he would argue with her, that he would try to persuade her, but he seemed, quite simply, to feel just as she did about it. Here, with the ghost of Henrietta close beside him, he too, apparently, saw that it couldn't work.

'No,' he said, echoing her words, 'it wouldn't work.'

She slipped the ring off her finger and held it out to him.

She would always love Edward and Edward would always love Henrietta and life was just plain unadulterated hell.

She said with a little catch in her voice:

'It's a lovely ring, Edward.'

'I wish you'd keep it, Midge. I'd like you to have it.'

She shook her head.

'I couldn't do that.'

He said with a faint, humorous twist of the lips:

'I shan't give it to anyone else, you know.'

It was all quite friendly. He didn't know – he would never know – just what she was feeling. Heaven on a plate – and the plate was broken and heaven had slipped between her fingers or had, perhaps, never been there.

II

That afternoon, Poirot received his third visitor.

He had been visited by Henrietta Savernake and Veronica Cray. This time it was Lady Angkatell. She came floating up the path with her usual appearance of insubstantiality.

He opened the door and she stood smiling at him.

'I have come to see you,' she announced.

So might a fairy confer a favour on a mere mortal.

'I am enchanted, Madame.'

He led the way into the sitting-room. She sat down on the sofa and once more she smiled.

Hercule Poirot thought: 'She is old – her hair is grey – there are lines in her face. Yet she has magic – she will always have magic . . .'

Lady Angkatell said softly:

'I want you to do something for me.'

'Yes, Lady Angkatell?'

'To begin with, I must talk to you – about John Christow.'

'About Dr Christow?'

'Yes. It seems to me that the only thing to do is to put a

full stop to the whole thing. You understand what I mean, don't you?'

'I am not sure that I do know what you mean, Lady Angkatell.'

She gave him her lovely dazzling smile again and she put one long white hand on his sleeve.

'Dear M. Poirot, you know perfectly. The police will have to hunt about for the owner of those fingerprints and they won't find him, and they'll have, in the end, to let the whole thing drop. But I'm afraid, you know, that *you* won't let it drop.'

'No, I shall not let it drop,' said Hercule Poirot.

'That is just what I thought. And that is why I came. It's the truth you want, isn't it?'

'Certainly I want the truth.'

'I see I haven't explained myself very well. I'm trying to find out just *why* you won't let things drop. It isn't because of your prestige – or because you want to hang a murderer (such an unpleasant kind of death, I've always thought – so *mediæval*). It's just, I think, that you want to *know*. You do see what I mean, don't you? If you were to know the truth – if you were to be *told* the truth, I think – I think perhaps that might satisfy you? Would it satisfy you, M. Poirot?'

'You are offering to tell me the truth, Lady Angkatell?'

She nodded.

'You yourself know the truth, then?'

Her eyes opened very wide.

'Oh, yes, I've known for a long time. I'd *like* to tell you. And then we could agree that – well, that it was all over and done with.'

She smiled at him.

'Is it a bargain, M. Poirot?'

It was quite an effort for Hercule Poirot to say:

'No, Madame, it is not a bargain.'

He wanted – he wanted, very badly, to let the whole thing drop, simply because Lady Angkatell asked him to do so.

Lady Angkatell sat very still for a moment. Then she raised her eyebrows.

'I wonder,' she said. 'I wonder if you really know what you are doing.'

CHAPTER 28

Midge, lying dry-eyed and awake in the darkness, turned restlessly on her pillows. She heard a door unlatch, a footstep in the corridor outside passing her door. It was Edward's door and Edward's step. She switched on the lamp by her bed and looked at the clock that stood by the lamp on the table. It was ten minutes to three.

Edward passing her door and going down the stairs at this hour in the morning. It was odd.

They had all gone to bed early, at half-past ten. She herself had not slept, had lain there with burning eyelids and with a dry, aching misery racking her feverishly.

She had heard the clock strike downstairs – had heard owls hoot outside her bedroom window. Had felt that depression that reaches its nadir at 2 am. Had thought to herself: 'I can't bear it – I can't bear it. Tomorrow coming – another day. Day after day to be got through.'

Banished by her own act from Ainswick – from all the loveliness and dearness of Ainswick which might have been her very own possession.

But better banishment, better loneliness, better a drab and uninteresting life, than life with Edward and Henrietta's ghost. Until that day in the wood she had not known her own capacity for bitter jealousy.

And after all, Edward had never told her that he loved her. Affection, kindliness, he had never pretended to more than that. She had accepted the limitation, and not until she had realized what it would mean to live at close quarters with an Edward whose mind and heart had Henrietta as a permanent guest, did she know that for her Edward's affection was not enough.

Edward walking past her door, down the front stairs. It was odd – very odd. Where was he going?

Uneasiness grew upon her. It was all part and parcel of the uneasiness that The Hollow gave her nowadays. What was Edward doing downstairs in the small hours of the morning? Had he gone out?

Inactivity at last became too much for her. She got up, slipped on her dressing-gown, and, taking a torch, she opened her door and came out into the passage.

It was quite dark, no light had been switched on. Midge turned to the left and came to the head of the staircase. Below all was dark too. She ran down the stairs and after a moment's hesitation switched on the light in the hall. Everything was silent. The front door was closed and locked. She tried the side door but that, too, was locked.

Edward, then, had not gone out. Where could he be?

And suddenly she raised her head and sniffed.

A whiff, a very faint whiff of gas.

The baize door to the kitchen quarters was just ajar. She went through it – a faint light was shining from the open kitchen door. The smell of gas was much stronger.

Midge ran along the passage and into the kitchen. Edward was lying on the floor with his head inside the gas oven, which was turned full on.

Midge was a quick, practical girl. Her first act was to swing open the shutters. She could not unlatch the window, and, winding a glass-cloth round her arm, she smashed it. Then, holding her breath, she stooped down and tugged and pulled Edward out of the gas oven and switched off the taps.

He was unconscious and breathing queerly, but she knew that he could not have been unconscious long. He could only just have gone under. The wind sweeping through from the window to the open door was fast dispelling the gas fumes. Midge dragged Edward to a spot near the window where the air would have full play. She sat down and gathered him into her strong young arms.

She said his name, first softly, then with increasing desperation. 'Edward, Edward, *Edward* . . .'

He stirred, groaned, opened his eyes and looked up at her. He said very faintly: 'Gas oven,' and his eyes went round to the gas stove.

'I know, darling, but why – *why*?'

He was shivering now, his hands were cold and lifeless. He said: 'Midge?' There was a kind of wondering surprise and pleasure in his voice.

She said: 'I heard you pass my door. I didn't know . . . I came down.'

He sighed, a very long sigh as though from very far away. 'Best way out,' he said. And then, inexplicably until she remembered Lucy's conversation on the night of the tragedy, '*News of the World*.'

'But, Edward, why, *why*?'

He looked up at her, and the blank, cold darkness of his stare frightened her.

'Because I know I've never been any good. Always a failure. Always ineffectual. It's men like Christow who do things. They get there and women admire them. I'm nothing – I'm not even quite alive. I inherited Ainswick and I've enough to live on – otherwise I'd have gone under. No good at a career – never much good as a writer. Henrietta didn't want me. No one wanted me. That day – at the Berkeley – I thought – but it was the same story. You couldn't care either, Midge. Even for Ainswick you couldn't put up with me. So I thought better get out altogether.'

Her words came with a rush. 'Darling, darling, you don't understand. It was because of Henrietta – because I thought you still loved Henrietta so much.'

'Henrietta?' He murmured it vaguely, as though speaking of someone infinitely remote. 'Yes, I loved her very much.'

And from even farther away she heard him murmur:

'It's so cold.'

'*Edward* – my darling.'

Her arms closed round him firmly. He smiled at her, murmuring:

'You're so warm, Midge – you're so warm.'

Yes, she thought, that was what despair was. A cold thing – a thing of infinite coldness and loneliness. She'd never understood until now that despair was a cold thing. She had thought of it as something hot and passionate, something violent, a hot-blooded desperation. But that was not so. *This* was despair – this utter outer darkness of coldness and loneliness. And the sin of despair, that priests talked of, was a cold sin, the sin of cutting oneself off from all warm and living human contacts.

Edward said again: 'You're so warm, Midge.' And suddenly

with a glad, proud confidence she thought: 'But that's what he *wants* – that's what I can give him!' They were all cold, the Angkatells. Even Henrietta had something in her of the will-o'-the-wisp, of the elusive fairy coldness in the Angkatell blood. Let Edward love Henrietta as an intangible and unpossessable dream. It was warmth, permanence, stability that was his real need. It was daily companionship and love and laughter at Ainswick.

She thought: 'What Edward needs is someone to light a fire on his hearth – and *I* am the person to do that.'

Edward looked up. He saw Midge's face bending over him, the warm colouring of the skin, the generous mouth, the steady eyes and the dark hair that lay back from her forehead like two wings.

He saw Henrietta always as a projection from the past. In the grown woman he sought and wanted only to see the seventeen-year-old girl he had first loved. But now, looking up at Midge, he had a queer sense of seeing a continuous Midge. He saw the schoolgirl with her winged hair springing back into two pigtails, he saw its dark waves framing her face now, and he saw exactly how those wings would look when the hair was not dark any longer but grey.

'Midge,' he thought, 'is *real*. The only real thing I have ever known . . .' He felt the warmth of her, and the strength – dark, positive, alive, *real*! 'Midge,' he thought, 'is the rock on which I can build my life.'

He said: 'Darling Midge, I love you so, never leave me again.'

She bent down to him and he felt the warmth of her lips on his, felt her love enveloping him, shielding him, and happiness flowered in that cold desert where he had lived alone so long.

Suddenly Midge said with a shaky laugh:

'Look, Edward, a blackbeetle has come out to look at us. Isn't he a *nice* blackbeetle? I never thought I could like a blackbeetle so much!'

She added dreamily: 'How odd life is. Here we are sitting on the floor in a kitchen that still smells of gas all amongst the blackbeetles, and feeling that it's heaven.'

He murmured dreamily: 'I could stay here for ever.'

'We'd better go and get some sleep. It's four o'clock. How on earth are we to explain that broken window to Lucy?' Fortunately,

Midge reflected, Lucy was an extraordinarily easy person to explain things to!

Taking a leaf out of Lucy's own book, Midge went into her room at six o'clock. She made a bald statement of fact.

'Edward went down and put his head in the gas oven in the night,' she said. 'Fortunately I heard him, and went down after him. I broke the window because I couldn't get it open quickly.'

Lucy, Midge had to admit, was wonderful.

She smiled sweetly with no sign of surprise.

'Dear Midge,' she said, 'you are always so practical. I'm sure you will always be the greatest comfort to Edward.'

After Midge had gone, Lady Angkatell lay thinking. Then she got up and went into her husband's room, which for once was unlocked.

'Henry.'

'My dear Lucy! It's not cockcrow yet.'

'No, but listen, Henry, this is really important. We must have electricity installed to cook by and get rid of that gas stove.'

'Why, it's quite satisfactory, isn't it?'

'Oh, yes, dear. But it's the sort of thing that gives people ideas, and everybody mightn't be as practical as dear Midge.'

She flitted elusively away. Sir Henry turned over with a grunt. Presently he awoke with a start just as he was dozing off. 'Did I dream it,' he murmured, 'or did Lucy come in and start talking about gas stoves?'

Outside in the passage, Lady Angkatell went into the bathroom and put a kettle on the gas ring. Sometimes, she knew, people liked an early cup of tea. Fired with self-approval, she returned to bed and lay back on her pillows, pleased with life and with herself.

Edward and Midge at Ainswick – the inquest over. She would go and talk to M. Poirot again. A nice little man . . .

Suddenly another idea flashed into her head. She sat upright in bed. 'I wonder now,' she speculated, 'if she has thought of *that*.'

She got out of bed and drifted along the passage to Henrietta's room, beginning her remarks as usual long before she was within earshot.

But now, every day, she felt it coming nearer – she'd have to start living again, to decide what to do, where to live. Already Elsie was showing a shade of impatience in her manner. 'Oh, Gerda, don't be so *slow!*'

It was all the same as it had been – long ago, before John came and took her away. They all thought her slow and stupid. There was nobody to say, as John had said: 'I'll look after you.'

Her head ached and Gerda thought: 'I'll make myself some tea.'

She went down to the kitchen and put the kettle on. It was nearly boiling when she heard a ring at the front door.

The maids had been given the day out. Gerda went to the door and opened it. She was astonished to see Henrietta's rakish-looking car drawn up to the kerb and Henrietta herself standing on the doorstep.

'Why, Henrietta!' she exclaimed. She fell back a step or two. 'Come in. I'm afraid my sister and the children are out but –'

Henrietta cut her short. 'Good, I'm glad. I wanted to get you alone. Listen, Gerda, *what did you do with the holster?*'

Gerda stopped. Her eyes looked suddenly vacant and uncomprehending. She said: 'Holster?'

Then she opened a door on the right of the hall.

'You'd better come in here. I'm afraid it's rather dusty. You see, we haven't had much time this morning.'

Henrietta interrupted again urgently.

She said: 'Listen, Gerda, you've got to tell me. Apart from the holster everything's all right – absolutely watertight. There's nothing to connect you with the business. I found the revolver where you'd shoved it into that thicket by the pool. I hid it in a place where you couldn't possibly have put it – and there are fingerprints on it which they'll never identify. So there's only the holster. I must know what you did with that?'

She paused, praying desperately that Gerda would react quickly.

She had no idea why she had this vital sense of urgency, but it was there. Her car had not been followed – she had made sure of that. She had started on the London road, had filled up at a garage and had mentioned that she was on her way to London. Then, a little farther on, she had swung across

'– and it suddenly came to me, dear, that you *might* have overlooked that.'

Henrietta murmured sleepily: 'For heaven's sake, Lucy, the birds aren't up yet!'

'Oh, I know, dear, it *is* rather early, but it seems to have been a very disturbed night – Edward and the gas stove and Midge and the kitchen window – and thinking of what to say to M. Poirot and everything –'

'I'm sorry, Lucy, but everything you say sounds like complete gibberish. Can't it wait?'

'It was only the holster, dear. I thought, you know, that you might not have thought about the holster.'

'Holster?' Henrietta sat up in bed. She was suddenly wide awake. 'What's this about a holster?'

'That revolver of Henry's was in a holster, you know. And the holster hasn't been found. And of course nobody may think of it – but on the other hand somebody might –'

Henrietta swung herself out of bed. She said:

'One always forgets something – that's what they say! And it's true!'

Lady Angkatell went back to her room.

She got into bed and quickly went fast asleep.

The kettle on the gas ring boiled and went on boiling.

CHAPTER 29

Gerda rolled over to the side of the bed and sat up.

Her head felt a little better now but she was still glad that she hadn't gone with the others on the picnic. It was peaceful and almost comforting to be alone in the house for a bit.

Elsie, of course, had been very kind – very kind – especially at first. To begin with, Gerda had been urged to stay in bed for breakfast, trays had been brought up to her. Everybody urged her to sit in the most comfortable armchair, to put her feet up, not to do anything at all strenuous.

They were all so sorry for her about John. She had stayed cowering gratefully in that protective dim haze. She hadn't wanted to think, or to feel, or to remember.

country until she had reached a main road leading south to the coast.

Gerda was still staring at her. The trouble with Gerda, thought Henrietta, was that she was so slow.

'If you've still got it, Gerda, you must give it to me. I'll get rid of it somehow. It's the only possible thing, you see, that can connect you now with John's death. *Have* you got it?'

There was a pause and then Gerda slowly nodded her head.

'Didn't you know it was madness to keep it?' Henrietta could hardly conceal her impatience.

'I forgot about it. It was up in my room.'

She added: 'When the police came up to Harley Street I cut it in pieces and put it in the bag with my leather work.'

Henrietta said: 'That was clever of you.'

Gerda said: 'I'm not quite so stupid as everybody thinks.' She put her hand up to her throat. She said: 'John – *John*!' Her voice broke.

Henrietta said: 'I know, my dear, I know.'

Gerda said: 'But you can't know . . . John wasn't – he wasn't –' She stood there, dumb and strangely pathetic. She raised her eyes suddenly to Henrietta's face. 'It was all a lie – everything! All the things I thought he was. I saw his face when he followed that woman out that evening. Veronica Cray. I knew he'd cared for her, of course, years ago before he married me, but I thought it was all over.'

Henrietta said gently:

'But it *was* all over.'

Gerda shook her head.

'No. She came there and pretended that she hadn't seen John for years – but I saw John's face. He went out with her. I went up to bed. I lay there trying to read – I tried to read that detective story that John was reading. And John didn't come. And at last I went out . . .'

Her eyes seemed to be turning inwards, seeing the scene.

'It was moonlight. I went along the path to the swimming pool. There was a light in the pavilion. They were *there* – John and that woman.'

Henrietta made a faint sound.

Gerda's face had changed. It had none of its usual slightly vacant amiability. It was remorseless, implacable.

'I'd trusted John. I'd believed in him – as though he were God. I thought he was the noblest man in the world. I thought he was everything that was fine and noble. And it was all a *lie*! I was left with nothing at all. I – I'd *worshipped* John!'

Henrietta was gazing at her fascinated. For here, before her eyes, was what she had guessed at and brought to life, carving it out of wood. Here was The Worshipper. Blind devotion thrown back on itself, disillusioned, dangerous.

Gerda said: 'I couldn't bear it! I had to kill him! I *had* to – you do see that, Henrietta?'

She said it quite conversationally, in an almost friendly tone.

'And I knew I must be careful because the police are very clever. But then I'm not really as stupid as people think! If you're very slow and just stare, people think you don't take things in – and sometimes, underneath, you're laughing at them! I knew I could kill John and nobody would know because I'd read in that detective story about the police being able to tell which gun a bullet has been fired from. Sir Henry had shown me how to load and fire a revolver that afternoon. I'd take *two* revolvers. I'd shoot John with one and then hide it, and let people find me holding the other, and first they'd think *I*'d shot him and then they'd find he couldn't have been killed with that revolver and so they'd say I hadn't done it after all!'

She nodded her head triumphantly.

'But I forgot about the leather thing. It was in the drawer in my bedroom. What do you call it, a holster? Surely the police won't bother about that *now*!'

'They might,' said Henrietta. 'You'd better give it to me, and I'll take it away with me. Once it's out of your hands, you're quite safe.'

She sat down. She felt suddenly unutterably weary.

Gerda said: 'You don't look well. I was just making tea.'

She went out of the room. Presently she came back with a tray. On it was a teapot, milk jug and two cups. The milk jug had slopped over because it was over-full. Gerda put the tray down and poured out a cup of tea and handed it to Henrietta.

'Oh, dear,' she said, dismayed, 'I don't believe the kettle can have been boiling.'

'It's quite all right,' said Henrietta. 'Go and get that holster, Gerda.'

Gerda hesitated and then went out of the room. Henrietta leant forward and put her arms on the table and her head down on them. She was so tired, so dreadfully tired. But now it was nearly done. Gerda would be safe, as John had wanted her to be safe.

She sat up, pushed the hair off her forehead and drew the teacup towards her. Then at a sound in the doorway she looked up. Gerda had been quite quick for once.

But it was Hercule Poirot who stood in the doorway.

'The front door was open,' he remarked as he advanced to the table, 'so I took the liberty of walking in.'

'You!' said Henrietta. 'How did you get here?'

'When you left The Hollow so suddenly, naturally I knew where you would go. I hired a very fast car and came straight here.'

'I see.' Henrietta sighed. 'You would.'

'You should not drink that tea,' said Poirot, taking the cup from her and replacing it on the tray. 'Tea that has not been made with boiling water is not good to drink.'

'Does a little thing like boiling water really matter?'

Poirot said gently: 'Everything matters.'

There was a sound behind him and Gerda came into the room. She had a workbag in her hands. Her eyes went from Poirot's face to Henrietta's.

Henrietta said quickly:

'I'm afraid, Gerda, I'm rather a suspicious character. M. Poirot seems to have been shadowing me. He thinks that I killed John – but he can't prove it.'

She spoke slowly and deliberately. So long as Gerda did not give herself away.

Gerda said vaguely: 'I'm so sorry. Will you have some tea, M. Poirot?'

'No, thank you, Madame.'

Gerda sat down behind the tray. She began to talk in her apologetic, conversational way.

'I'm so sorry that everybody is out. My sister and the children have all gone for a picnic. I didn't feel very well, so they left me behind.'

'I am sorry, Madame.'

Gerda lifted a teacup and drank.

'It is all so very worrying. Everything is so worrying. You see, John always arranged *everything* and now John is gone . . .' Her voice tailed off. 'Now John is gone.'

Her gaze, piteous, bewildered, went from one to the other.

'I don't know what to do without John. John looked after me. He took care of me. Now he is gone, everything is gone. And the children – they ask me questions and I can't answer them properly. I don't know what to say to Terry. He keeps saying: "Why was Father killed?" Some day, of course, he will find out why. Terry always has to *know*. What puzzles me is that he always asks *why*, not *who*!'

Gerda leaned back in her chair. Her lips were very blue.

She said stiffly:

'I feel – not very well – if John – John –'

Poirot came round the table to her and eased her sideways down in the chair. Her head dropped forward. He bent and lifted her eyelid. Then he straightened up.

'An easy and comparatively painless death.'

Henrietta stared at him.

'Heart? No.' Her mind leaped forward. 'Something in the tea. Something she put there herself. She chose that way out?'

Poirot shook his head gently.

'Oh, no, it was meant for *you*. It was in *your* teacup.'

'For *me?*' Henrietta's voice was incredulous. 'But I was trying to help her.'

'That did not matter. Have you not seen a dog caught in a trap – it sets its teeth into anyone who touches it. She saw only that you knew her secret and so you, too, must die.'

Henrietta said slowly:

'And you made me put the cup back on the tray – you meant – you meant *her* –'

Poirot interrupted her quietly:

'No, no, Mademoiselle. I did not *know* that there was anything in your teacup. I only knew that there *might* be. And when the cup was on the tray it was an even chance if she drank from that or the other – if you call it chance. I say myself that an end such as this is merciful. For her – and for two innocent children.'

He said gently to Henrietta: 'You are very tired, are you not?'

She nodded. She asked him: 'When did you guess?'

'I do not know exactly. The scene was set; I felt that from the first. But I did not realize for a long time that it was set *by Gerda Christow* – that her attitude was stagey because she was, actually, acting a part. I was puzzled by the simplicity and at the same time the complexity. I recognized fairly soon that it was *your* ingenuity that I was fighting against, and that you were being aided and abetted by your relations as soon as they understood what you wanted done!' He paused and added: 'Why did *you* want it done?'

'Because John asked me to! That's what he meant when he said "*Henrietta.*" It was all there in that one word. He was asking me to protect Gerda. You see, he loved Gerda. I think he loved Gerda much better than he ever knew he did. Better than Veronica Cray. Better than me. Gerda *belonged* to him, and John liked things that belonged to him. He knew that if anyone could protect Gerda from the consequences of what she'd done, I could. And he knew that I would do anything he wanted, because I loved him.'

'And you started at once,' said Poirot grimly.

'Yes, the first thing I could think of was to get the revolver away from her and drop it in the pool. That would obscure the fingerprint business. When I discovered later that he had been shot with a different gun, I went out to look for it, and naturally found it at once because I knew just the sort of place Gerda would have put it. I was only a minute or two ahead of Inspector Grange's men.'

She paused and then went on: 'I kept it with me in that satchel bag of mine until I could take it up to London. Then I hid it in the studio until I could bring it back, and put it where the police would not find it.'

'The clay horse,' murmured Poirot.

'How did you know? Yes, I put it in a sponge bag and wired the armature round it, and then slapped up the clay model round it. After all, the police couldn't very well destroy an artist's masterpiece, could they? What made you know where it was?'

'The fact that you chose to model a horse. The horse of Troy was the unconscious association in your mind. But the fingerprints – how did you manage the fingerprints?'

'An old blind man who sells matches in the street. He didn't know what it was I asked him to hold for a moment while I got some money out!'

Poirot looked at her for a moment.

'*C'est formidable!*' he murmured. 'You are one of the best antagonists, Mademoiselle, that I have ever had.'

'It's been dreadfully tiring always trying to keep one move ahead of *you!*'

'I know. I began to realize the truth as soon as I saw that the pattern was always designed not to implicate any one person but to implicate *everyone* – other than Gerda Christow. Every indication always pointed *away* from her. You deliberately planted Ygdrasil to catch my attention and bring yourself under suspicion. Lady Angkatell, who knew perfectly what you were doing, amused herself by leading poor Inspector Grange in one direction after another. David, Edward, herself.

'Yes, there is only one thing to do if you want to clear a person from suspicion who is actually guilty. You must suggest guilt elsewhere but never localize it. That is why every clue *looked* promising and then petered out and ended in nothing.'

Henrietta looked at the figure huddled pathetically in the chair. She said: 'Poor Gerda.'

'Is that what you have felt all along?'

'I think so. Gerda loved John terribly, but she didn't want to love him for what he was. She built up a pedestal for him and attributed every splendid and noble and unselfish characteristic to him. And if you cast down an idol, *there's nothing left.*' She paused and then went on: 'But John was something much finer than an idol on a pedestal. He was a real, living, vital human being. He was generous and warm and alive, and he was a great doctor – yes, a *great* doctor. And he's dead, and the world has lost a very great man. And I have lost the only man I shall ever love.'

Poirot put his hand gently on her shoulder. He said:

'But you are one of those who can live with a sword in their hearts – who can go on and smile –'

Henrietta looked up at him. Her lips twisted into a bitter smile.

'That's a little melodramatic, isn't it?'

'It is because I am a foreigner and I like to use fine words.'

Henrietta said suddenly:

'You have been very kind to me.'

'That is because I have admired you always very much.'

'M. Poirot, what are we going to do? About Gerda, I mean.'

Poirot drew the raffia workbag towards him. He turned out its contents, scraps of brown suède and other coloured leathers. There were some pieces of thick shiny brown leather. Poirot fitted them together.

'The holster. I take this. And poor Madame Christow, she was overwrought, her husband's death was too much for her. It will be brought in that she took her life whilst of unsound mind –'

Henrietta said slowly:

'And no one will ever know what really happened?'

'I think one person will know. Dr Christow's son. I think that one day he will come to me and ask me for the truth.'

'But you won't tell him,' cried Henrietta.

'Yes. I shall tell him.'

'Oh, *no*!'

'You do not understand. To you it is unbearable that anyone should be hurt. But to some minds there is something more unbearable still – not to *know*. You heard the poor woman just a little while ago say: "Terry always has to *know*." To the scientific mind, truth comes first. Truth, however bitter, can be accepted, and woven into a design for living.'

Henrietta got up.

'Do you want me here, or had I better go?'

'It would be better if you went, I think.'

She nodded. Then she said, more to herself than to him:

'Where shall I go? What shall I do – without John?'

'You are speaking like Gerda Christow. You will know where to go and what to do.'

'Shall I? I'm so tired, M. Poirot, so tired.'

He said gently:

'Go, my child. Your place is with the living. I will stay here with the dead.'

CHAPTER 30

As she drove towards London, the two phrases echoed through Henrietta's mind. 'What shall I do? Where shall I go?'

For the last few weeks she had been strung up, excited, never relaxing for a moment. She had had a task to perform – a task laid on her by John. But now that was over – she had failed – or succeeded? One could look at it either way. But however one looked at it, the task was over. And she experienced the terrible weariness of the reaction.

Her mind went back to the words she had spoken to Edward that night on the terrace – the night of John's death – the night when she had gone along to the pool and into the pavilion and had deliberately, by the light of a match, drawn Ygdrasil upon the iron table. Purposeful, planning – not yet able to sit down and mourn – mourn for her dead. 'I should like,' she had said to Edward, 'to grieve for John.'

But she had not dared to relax then – not dared to let sorrow take command over her.

But now she could grieve. Now she had all the time there was.

She said under her breath: 'John . . . John.'

Bitterness and black rebellion broke over her.

She thought: 'I wish I'd drunk that cup of tea.'

Driving the car soothed her, gave her strength for the moment. But soon she would be in London. Soon she would put the car in the garage and go along to the empty studio. Empty since John would never sit there again bullying her, being angry with her, loving her more than he wanted to love her, telling her eagerly about Ridgeway's Disease – about his triumphs and despairs, about Mrs Crabtree and St Christopher's.

And suddenly, with a lifting of the dark pall that lay over her mind, she thought:

'Of course. That's where I will go. To St Christopher's.'

Lying in her narrow hospital bed, old Mrs Crabtree peered up at her visitor out of rheumy, twinkling eyes.

She was exactly as John had described her, and Henrietta felt a sudden warmth, a lifting of the spirit. This was real –

this would last! Here, for a little space, she had found John again.

'The pore doctor. Orful, ain't it?' Mrs Crabtree was saying. There was relish in her voice as well as regret, for Mrs Crabtree loved life; and sudden deaths, particularly murders or deaths in childbed, were the richest parts of the tapestry of life. 'Getting 'imself bumped off like that! Turned my stomach right over, it did, when I 'eard. I read all about it in the papers. Sister let me 'ave all she could get 'old of. Reely nice about it, she was. There was pictures and everythink. That swimming pool and all. 'Is wife leaving the inquest, pore thing, and that Lady Angkatell what the swimming pool belonged to. Lots of pictures. Real mystery the 'ole thing, weren't it?'

Henrietta was not repelled by her ghoulish enjoyment. She liked it because she knew that John himself would have liked it. If he had to die he would much prefer old Mrs Crabtree to get a kick out of it, than to sniff and shed tears.

'All I 'ope is that they catch 'ooever done it and 'ang 'im,' continued Mrs Crabtree vindictively. 'They don't 'ave 'angings in public like they used to once – more's the pity. I've always thought I'd like to go to an 'anging. And I'd go double quick, if you understand me, to see 'ooever killed the doctor 'anged! Real wicked, 'e must 'ave been. Why, the doctor was one in a thousand. Ever so clever, 'e was! And a nice way with 'im! Got you laughing whether you wanted to or not. The things 'e used to say sometimes! I'd 'ave done anythink for the doctor, I would!'

'Yes,' said Henrietta, 'he was a very clever man. He was a great man.'

'Think the world of 'im in the 'orspital, they do! All them nurses. *And* 'is patients! Always felt you were going to get well when 'e'd been along.'

'So you are going to get well,' said Henrietta.

The little shrewd eyes clouded for a moment.

'I'm not so sure about that, ducks. I've got that mealy-mouthed young fellow with the spectacles now. Quite different to Dr Christow. Never a laugh! 'E was a one, Dr Christow was – always up to his jokes! Given me some norful times, 'e 'as, with this treatment of 'is. "I carn't stand any more of in, Doctor,"

I'd say to him, and "Yes, you can, Mrs Crabtree," 'e'd say to me. "You're tough, you are. You can take it. Going to make medical 'istory, you and I are." And he'd jolly you along like. Do anything for the doctor, I would 'ave! Expected a lot of you, 'e did, but you felt you couldn't let him down, if you know what I mean.'

'I know,' said Henrietta.

The little sharp eyes peered at her.

'Excuse me, dearie, you're not the doctor's wife by any chance?'

'No,' said Henrietta, 'I'm just a friend.'

'*I* see,' said Mrs Crabtree.

Henrietta thought that she did see.

'What made you come along if you don't mind me asking?'

'The doctor used to talk to me a lot about you – and about his new treatment. I wanted to see how you were.'

'I'm slipping back – that's what I'm doing.'

Henrietta cried:

'But you mustn't slip back! You've got to get well.'

Mrs Crabtree grinned.

'*I* don't want to peg out, don't you think it!'

'Well, fight then! Dr Christow said you were a fighter.'

'Did 'e now?' Mrs Crabtree lay still a minute, then she said slowly:

'Ooever shot 'im it's a wicked shame! There aren't many of 'is sort.'

We shall not see his like again. The words passed through Henrietta's mind. Mrs Crabtree was regarding her keenly.

'Keep your pecker up, dearie,' she said. She added: ''E 'ad a nice funeral, I 'ope.'

'He had a lovely funeral,' said Henrietta obligingly.

'Ar! I wish I could of gorn to it!'

Mrs Crabtree sighed.

'Be going to me own funeral next, I expect.'

'No,' cried Henrietta. 'You mustn't let go. You said just now that Dr Christow told you that you and he were going to make medical history. Well, you've got to carry on by yourself. The treatment's just the same. You've got to have the guts for two – you've got to make medical history by yourself – for him.'

Mrs Crabtree looked at her for a moment or two.

'Sounds a bit grand! I'll do my best, ducks. Carn't say more than that.'

Henrietta got up and took her hand.

'Goodbye. I'll come and see you again if I may.'

'Yes, do. It'll do me good to talk about the doctor a bit.' The bawdy twinkle came into her eye again. 'Proper man in every kind of way, Dr Christow.'

'Yes,' said Henrietta. 'He was.'

The old woman said:

'Don't fret, ducks – what's gorn's gorn. You can't 'ave it back.'

Mrs Crabtree and Hercule Poirot, Henrietta thought, expressed the same idea in different language.

She drove back to Chelsea, put away the car in the garage and walked slowly to the studio.

'Now,' she thought, 'it has come. The moment I have been dreading – the moment when I am alone.

'Now I can put it off no longer. Now grief is here with me.'

What had she said to Edward? 'I should like to grieve for John.'

She dropped down on a chair and pushed back the hair from her face.

Alone – empty – destitute. This awful emptiness.

The tears pricked at her eyes, flowed slowly down her cheeks.

Grief, she thought, grief for John. Oh, John – John.

Remembering, remembering – his voice, sharp with pain:

'If I were dead, the first thing you'd do, with the tears streaming down your face, would be to start modelling some damn' mourning woman or some figure of grief.'

She stirred uneasily. Why had that thought come into her head?

Grief – Grief . . . A veiled figure – its outline barely perceptible – its head cowled.

Alabaster.

She could see the lines of it – tall, elongated, its sorrow hidden, revealed only by the long, mournful lines of the drapery.

Sorrow, emerging from clear, transparent alabaster.

'If I were dead . . .'

And suddenly bitterness came over her full tide!

She thought: '*That's what I am!* John was right. I cannot love – I cannot mourn – not with the whole of me.

'It's Midge, it's people like Midge who are the salt of the earth.'

Midge and Edward at Ainswick.

That was reality – strength – warmth.

'But I,' she thought, 'am not a whole person. I belong not to myself, but to something outside me. I cannot grieve for my dead. Instead I must take my grief and make it into a figure of alabaster . . .'

Exhibit No. 58. 'Grief'. Alabaster. Miss Henrietta Savernake . . .

She said under her breath:

'John, forgive me, forgive me, for what I can't help doing.'